PROLOGUE

AUGUST 1967

It was the Summer of Love and I had just buried my husband when I first went back to see the reservoir that had flooded my childhood village.

I made the journey only a few months after Ronald and I had returned from one of our frequent long spells abroad. Spells which had suited me well for many years. Ronald, too, had suited me well. He was a decent man and a good husband, quite willing to accept that our marriage was one of convenience. I believe he saw me as an asset in his diplomatic career, though it was certainly neither my dazzling beauty nor my sparkling wit that snared him. I was, however, presentable and intelligent, in addition to being an exceptionally good dancer.

Whatever the reason, I became adept at playing the minor diplomat's wife. It seemed a small price to pay. In a way, I was Ronald's passport to career success and promotion, and – though I never told him this – he was my passport to flight and escape. I married him because I knew we would spend our lives far away from England, and I wanted to be as far away from England as possible. Now, after more than ten years abroad, it doesn't seem to matter very much. I shall be quite content to live out the rest of my days in the Belsize Park flat. Ronald, always a shrewd investor, also left me a tidy sum of money. Enough, at least, to live on for some years and to buy myself a new Triumph sports car. A red one. With a radio.

And so, singing along with 'All You Need is Love', 'Itchycoo Park' and 'See Emily Play', listening to the occasional news bulletins about Joe Orton's murder and the closing-down of the offshore pirate radio stations, I headed back to Hobb's End for the first time in over twenty years. For some reason I have never been able to explain, I enjoyed the raw, naive and whimsical new music the young people were listening to, even though I was in my early forties. It made me long to be young again: young without the complications of my own youth; young without the war; young without the heartbreak; young without the terror and the blood.

I don't think I saw another car after I left the main road outside Skipton. It was one of those perfect summer days when the air smells sweet with the perfume of cut grass and wild flowers. I fancied I could even smell the warm exhalations of the dry-stone walls. Berries shone like polished garnets on the rowan trees. Tewits soared and tumbled over the meadows and sheep bleated their pitiful calls from the far dalesides. The colours were all so vibrant – the green greener than ever, the blue of the sky cloudless and piercingly bright.

Not far beyond Grassington I lost my way. I stopped and asked two men carrying out repairs to a dry-stone wall. It was a long time since I had heard the characteristic broad speech of the Dales and at first it sounded foreign to me. Finally, I understood, thanked them and left them scratching their heads over the strange middle-aged lady with the sunglasses, the pop music and the flashy red sports car.

The old lane stopped at the edge of the woods, so I had to get out and walk the rest of the way along a crooked dirt path. Clouds of gnats whined above my head, wrens flitted

PETER ROBINSON

IN A DRY SEASON
&
A DEDICATED MAN

INSPECTOR BANKS MYSTERIES

PAN BOOKS

In a Dry Season
For Dad and Averil, Elaine and Mick, and Adam and Nicola

A Dedicated Man
For Jan

In a Dry Season first published 2000 by Macmillan
First published by Pan Books 2003
A Dedicated Man first published 1988 by Viking (Canada)
First published by Pan Books 2002

This omnibus first published 2011 by Pan Books
an imprint of Pan Macmillan, a division of Macmillan Publishers Limited
Pan Macmillan, 20 New Wharf Road, London N1 9RR
Basingstoke and Oxford
Associated companies throughout the world
www.panmacmillan.com

ISBN 978-0-330-54550-1

Copyright © Peter Robinson 2000, 1988

The right of Peter Robinson to be identified as the
author of this work has been asserted by him in accordance
with the Copyright, Designs and Patents Act 1988.

1 3 5 7 9 8 6 4 2

A CIP catalogue record for this book is available from
the British Library.

Typeset by SX Composing DTP, Rayleigh, Essex
Printed in the UK by CPI Mackays, Chatham ME5 8TD

IN A DRY SEASON

The past is a foreign country; they do things differently there.

L. P. Hartley, *The Go-Between*

through the undergrowth and blue tits hopped from branch to branch.

At last I broke out of the woods and stood at the edge of the reservoir. My heart started to pound and I had to lean against one of the trees. The bark felt rough on my palms. For a moment, skin flushed and fingers tingling, I thought I was going to faint. But it passed.

There had been trees long ago, of course, but not as many, and most of them had been to the north of the village, in Rowan Woods. When I had lived there, Hobb's End had been a village in a valley. Now I gazed upon a lake surrounded by forest.

The water's surface, utterly still, reflected the trees and the occasional shadow of a gull or a swallow flying over. To my right, I could see the small dam where the old river narrowed as it flowed into Harksmere. Confused, unsure what I was feeling, I sat on the bank and stared over the scene.

I was sitting where the old railway branch line used to run, the train I had travelled on so often during my childhood. A single track that ran to and from Harrogate, the railway had provided our only real access to the larger world beyond Hobb's End during the war. Dr Beeching had done away with it three or four years ago, of course, and already the lines were overgrown with weeds. The council had planted weeping willows on the spot where the old station had stood, where many a time I had bought tickets from Mrs Shipley and waited on the platform with rising excitement to hear the distant chugging and whistling of the old steam engine.

As I sat there remembering, time went by. I had started out late and the journey from London was a long one. Soon, darkness infused the woods around me, filling the spaces between the branches and the silences between the bird calls. A whisper of a breeze sprang up. The water caught the fading light in such a way that its slightly ruffled surface looked as if it had been sprinkled with salmon-pink powder. Slowly, even this darkened, until only a deep inky blue remained.

Then a full moon rose, scattering its bone-white light, in which I fancied I could see clear through the water to the village that used to be there, like an image preserved in water-glass. There it was, spread out below me, darkly glittering and shimmering under the barely perceptible rippling of the surface.

As I stared, I began to feel that I could reach out and touch it. It was like the world beyond the mirror in Cocteau's *Orpheus*. When you reach out and touch the glass, it turns to water and you can plunge through it into the Underworld.

What I saw there was a vision of the village as it had been when I lived there, smoke curling from chimneys over the slate and flagstone roofs, the dark mill on the hillock at the west end, the squat church tower, the High Street curving beside the narrow river. The longer I looked, the more I imagined I could see the people going about their daily business: shopping, making deliveries, gossiping. In my vision, I could even see our little shop, where I met her for the first time that blustery spring day in 1941. The day it all began.

1

Adam Kelly loved to play in the derelict houses, loved the musty smell of the old rooms, the way they creaked and groaned as he moved around inside them, the way the sunlight shone through the laths, casting striped shadows on the walls. He loved to leap the gaps between the broken stairs, heart in his mouth, and hop from rafter to rafter, kicking up plaster dust and watching the motes dance in the filtered light.

This afternoon, Adam had a whole village to play in.

He stood at the rim of the shallow valley, staring at the ruins below and anticipating the adventure to come. This was the day he had been waiting for. Maybe a once-in-a-lifetime opportunity. Anything could happen down there. The future of the universe depended on Adam today; the village was a test, one of the things he had to conquer before advancing to the Seventh Level.

The only other people in sight stood at the far end, near the old flax mill: a man in jeans and a red T-shirt and a woman all dressed in white. They were pretending to be tourists, pointing their video camera here and there, but Adam suspected they might be after the same thing he was. He had played the game often enough on his computer to know that deception was everywhere and things were never what they seemed. Heaven help us, he thought, if *they* got to it first.

He half-slid and half-ran down the dirt slope, skidding

to a halt when he reached the red, baked earth at the bottom. There were still patches of mud around; all that water, he supposed, wouldn't just evaporate over a few weeks.

Adam paused and listened. Even the birds were silent. The sun beat down and made him sweat behind his ears, at the back of his neck and in the crack of his bum. His glasses kept slipping down his nose. The dark, ruined cottages wavered in the heat like a wall behind a workman's brazier.

Anything could happen now. The Talisman was here somewhere, and it was Adam's job to find it. But where to begin? He didn't even know what it looked like, only that he would know it when he found it and that there must be clues somewhere.

He crossed the old stone bridge and walked into one of the half-demolished cottages, aware of the moist, cool darkness gathering around him like a cloak. It smelled like a bad toilet, or as if some gigantic alien creature had lain down to die in a hot, fetid swamp.

Sunlight slanted in through the space where the roof had been, lighting the far wall. The dark stones looked as slick and greasy as an oil spill. In places, the heavy stone flags that formed the floor had shifted and cracked, and thick gobbets of mud oozed up between them. Some of the slabs wobbled when Adam stood on them. He felt poised over a quicksand ready to suck him down to the earth's core if he made one wrong move.

There was nothing in this house. Time to move on.

Outside, he could still see no one. The two tourists seemed to have left now, unless they were hiding, lying in wait for him behind the ruined mill.

Adam noticed an outbuilding near the bridge, the kind of place that had perhaps once been used to store coal or keep food cold. He had heard about the old days before electric fires and fridges. It might even have been a toilet. Hard to believe, he knew, but once people had to go outside to the toilet, even in winter.

Whatever it had been, The Destructors had left it largely alone. About seven feet high, with a slanting flag-stone roof still intact, it seemed to beckon him to come and vanquish it. Here, at least, was a structure he could mount to get a clear view. If the pretend-tourists were hiding nearby, he would see them from up there.

Adam walked around the outbuilding and was pleased to see that on one side a number of stones stuck out farther than others, like steps. Carefully, he rested his weight on the first one. It was slippy, but it held fast. He started to climb. Every step seemed solid enough, and soon he was at the top.

He pulled himself on to the roof. It only slanted at a slight angle, so it was easy enough to walk on. First, he stood near the edge, cupped his hand over his eyes to shield out the harsh sun and looked in every direction.

To the west stood the flax mill, and the strangers were now nowhere in sight. The land to both the north and south was covered in woods, so it was hard to see any-thing through the dense green foliage. To the east lay the teardrop shape of Harksmere Reservoir. On The Edge, which ran along the south side of Harksmere, a couple of car windscreens flashed in the sun. Other than that, there was hardly any movement in the world at all, hardly a leaf trembling.

Satisfied he wasn't being watched, Adam struck out over the roof. It was only about four or five feet wide, but when he got to the middle he felt the faintest tremor, then, before he could dash the short distance to the other side,

the thick stone slabs gave way beneath him. For a
moment, he hung suspended in air, as if he might float
there for ever. He stuck his arms out and flapped them like
wings, but to no avail. With a scream, he plunged down
into the darkness.

He landed on his back on a cushion of mud; his left
wrist cracked against a fallen flagstone and his right arm,
stretched out to break his fall, sank up to the elbow.

As he lay there, winded, looking up at the square of
blue sky above him, he saw two of the remaining roof
slabs tilt and fall towards him. Each one was about three
feet square and six inches thick, enough to smash him to
a pulp if it hit him. But he couldn't move; he felt trapped
there, spellbound by the falling slabs.

They seemed to drift down in slow motion, like autumn
leaves on a windless day. His mind emptied of everything.
He felt no panic, no fear, just a sort of acceptance, as if he
had reached a turning point in his short life, and it was out
of his hands now. He couldn't have explained it if he'd
tried, but at that moment, lying on his cot of warm mud
watching the dark stone flags wheel down across the blue
of the sky, young as he was, he knew there was nothing
he could do to avoid whatever fate had in store for him;
whichever way it went, he could only go with it.

This must be the Seventh Level, he thought as he held
his breath, waiting for the impact, waiting to feel his bones
breaking, grinding against one another.

One slab fell to his left, embedded itself in the mud and
tilted against the wall like an old gravestone. The other fell
to his right and cracked in two against one of the floor
flags. One half tipped towards him, just grazing his upper
arm, which was sticking out of the mud, and raising a few
drops of blood.

Adam took a few deep breaths and looked up through the roof at the sky. No more slabs. So he had been spared; he was alive. He felt light-headed. There was nothing seriously damaged, he thought, as he started to move his limbs slowly. His left wrist hurt a lot, and it would probably come up in one hell of a bruise, but it didn't feel broken. His right arm was still thrust deep in the mud, and the slab chafed against his grazed elbow. He tried to wiggle his fingers under the mud to find out if he could still feel them, and they brushed against something hard.

It felt like a cluster of smooth, hard spindles, or a bundle of short rods. Curious, he pushed his arm in deeper and grasped it tightly, the way he used to hold his mother's hand in town when he was very small and frightened of all the crowds; then he leaned his weight back over to the left, gritting his teeth as the pain seared through his injured wrist, and tugged.

Inch by inch, he dragged his arm free, keeping a firm grasp on his prize. The mud made sucking, slurping sounds as he pulled. Finally, he was able to free the object he was holding. He rested it against the slab and edged back towards the far wall to study it.

The thing lay against the flagstone in the dim light, fingers hooked over the top, as if it were trying to pull itself out of the grave. It was the skeleton of a hand, the bones crusted with moist, dark earth.

•

Banks stepped back to survey his handiwork, whistling along with the habanera from *Carmen*, which was playing loudly on the stereo: Maria Callas past her best but still sounding fine.

Not bad for an amateur, he thought, dropping the

paintbrush in a bowl of turpentine, and a definite improvement over the mildewed wallpaper he had stripped from the walls of his new home yesterday.

He particularly liked the colour. The man at the do-it-yourself centre in Eastvale said it was calming, and after the year Banks had just suffered through, he needed all the calming he could get. The shade of blue he had chosen was supposed to resemble that of oriental tapestries, but once it was on the wall it reminded Banks more of the Greek island of Santorini, which he and his estranged wife Sandra had visited during their last holiday together. He hadn't bargained for that memory, but he thought he could live with it.

Pleased with himself, Banks pulled a packet of Silk Cut from his top pocket. First, he counted the contents. Only three gone since morning. Good. He was trying to restrict himself to ten a day or less, and he was doing well so far. He walked into the kitchen and put on the kettle for a cup of tea.

The telephone rang. Banks turned off the stereo and picked up the receiver.

'Dad?'

'Brian, is that you? I've been trying to get in touch with you.'

'Yeah, well . . . we've been on the road. I didn't think you'd be in. Why aren't you at work?'

'If you didn't expect me to be in, why did you call?'

Silence.

'Brian? Where are you? Is anything wrong?'

'Nothing's wrong. I'm staying at Andrew's flat.'

'Where?'

'Wimbledon. Look, Dad . . .'

'Isn't it about time your exam results were out?'

More silence. Christ, Banks thought, getting more than a few words in a row out of Brian was as tough as getting the truth out of a politician.

'Brian?'

'Yeah, well, that's why I was calling you. You know . . . I thought I'd just leave a message.'

'I see.' Banks knew what was going on now. He looked around in vain for an ashtray and ended up using the hearth. 'Go on,' he prompted.

'About the exams, like . . .'

'How bad is it? What did you get?'

'Well, that's it . . . I mean . . . you won't like it.'

'You *did* pass, didn't you?'

''Course I did.'

'Well?'

'It's just that I didn't do as well as I expected. It was really hard, Dad. Everyone says so.'

'What did you get?'

Brian almost whispered. 'A third.'

'A *third*? That's a bit of a disappointment, isn't it? I'd have thought you could have done better than that.'

'Yeah, well, it's more than you ever got.'

Banks took a deep breath. 'It doesn't matter a damn what I did or didn't get. It's you we're talking about. Your future. You'll never get a decent job with a third-class degree.'

'What if I don't want a *decent job*?'

'What do you want to be then? Another statistic? Another cliché? Another unemployed yobbo?'

'Thanks a lot, Dad. Nice to know *you* believe in me. Anyway, as a matter of fact, I'm not on the dole. We're going to try and make a go of it. Me and the band.'

'You're *what*?'

'We're going to make a go of it. Andrew knows this bloke who runs an indie label, and he's got a studio, like, and he's said we can go down and make a demo of some of my songs. You might not believe it, but people actually like us. We've got gigs coming out of our ears.'

'Have you any idea how tough it is to succeed in the music business?'

'The Spice Girls did it, and look how much talent they've got.'

'So did Tiny Tim, but that's not the point. Talent's got nothing to do with it. For every one that makes it, there's thousands who get trampled on the way.'

'We're making plenty of money.'

'Money's not everything. What about the future? What are you going to do when you've peaked at twenty-five and you don't have a penny in the bank?'

'What makes you an expert on the music business all of a sudden?'

'Is that why you got such a poor degree? Because you were too busy wasting your time rehearsing and going out on the road?'

'I was getting pretty bored with architecture anyway.'

Banks flicked his cigarette butt in the hearth. It scattered sparks against the dark stone. 'Have you talked to your mother about this?'

'Well, I sort of thought, maybe . . . you know . . . you could do that.'

That's a laugh, Banks thought. *Him* talk to Sandra? They couldn't even discuss the weather these days without it turning into an argument.

'I think you'd better ring her yourself,' he said. 'Better still, why don't you pay her a visit? She's only in Camden Town.'

'But she'll go spare!'

'Serves you right. You should have thought of that before.'

The kettle started whistling.

'Thanks a lot, Dad,' Brian said, his voice hard-edged with bitterness. 'I thought you'd understand. I thought I could depend on you. I thought you *liked* music. But you're just like the rest. Go see to your *fucking* kettle!'

'Brian—'

But Brian hung up. Hard.

The blue of the living room did nothing to soothe Banks's mood. Pretty sad, he thought, when you turn to DIY as therapy, house decoration to keep the darkness at bay. He sat for a moment staring at a brush hair stuck to the paint above the mantelpiece, then he stormed into the kitchen and turned off the kettle. He didn't even feel like a cup of tea any more.

'Money isn't everything. What about your future?' Banks couldn't believe he had said those things. Not because he thought that money *was* everything, but because that was exactly what his parents had said to him when he told them he wanted a weekend job in the supermarket to earn some extra money. It frightened him how deeply instinctive his whole response to Brian's news was, as if someone else – his own parents – had spoken the words and he was only the ventriloquist's dummy. Some people say that the older we get, the more we come to resemble our parents, and Banks was beginning to wonder if they were right. If so, it was a frightening idea.

Money isn't everything, his father had said, though in a way it *was* everything to him because he had never had any. *What about your future?* his mother had said, her way of telling him that he would be far better off staying at home studying for his exams than wasting his weekends making money he would only use to go hanging around billiard halls or bowling alleys. They wanted him to go into a nice, respectable, secure white-collar job like banking or insurance, just like his older brother Roy. With a good degree behind him, they said, he could *better himself*, which meant he could do better than they had done. He was bright, and that was what bright working-class kids were supposed to do back in the sixties.

Before Banks had a chance to think any further, the phone rang again. Hoping it was Brian ringing back to apologize, he dashed into the living room and picked up the receiver.

This time it was Chief Constable Jeremiah 'Jimmy' Riddle. Must be my lucky day, Banks thought. Not only was it *not* Brian, the new call also meant that Banks couldn't even dial 1471 to get Brian's Wimbledon phone number, which he had neglected to ask for. 1471 only worked for the last *one* call you received. He cursed and reached for his cigarettes again. At this rate he'd never stop. Bugger it. Extraordinary circumstances call for extraordinary measures. He lit up.

'Skiving off again, are you, Banks?'

'Holiday,' said Banks. 'It's official. You can check.'

'Doesn't matter. I've got a job for you to do.'

'I'll be back in the morning.'

'Now.'

Banks wondered what kind of job Jimmy Riddle would call him off his holidays for. Ever since Riddle had had to reinstate him reluctantly after dishing out a hasty suspension the previous year, Banks had been in career Siberia, his life a treadmill of reports, statistics and more reports. Everything short of going around to the schools giving road-safety talks. Not one active investigation in nine months. He was so far out of the loop he might as well have been on Pluto; even the few informers he had cultivated since arriving in Eastvale had deserted him. Surely the situation wasn't going to change this easily? There had to be more to it; Riddle never made a move without a hidden agenda.

'We've just got a report in from Harkside,' Riddle went on. 'A young lad found some bones at the bottom of Thornfield Reservoir. It's one of the ones that dried up over the summer. Used to be a village there, I gather. Anyway, there's nothing but a section station in Harkside, and all they've got is a lowly DS. I want you down there as senior investigating officer.'

'Old bones? Can't it wait?'

'Probably. But I'd rather you get started right away. Any problem with that?'

'What about Harrogate or Ripon?'

'Too busy. Don't be such an ungrateful bastard, Banks. Here's the perfect opportunity for you to drag your career out of the slump it's fallen into.'

Sure, Banks thought, and pigs can fly. He hadn't fallen into the slump, he had been *pushed*, and, knowing Jimmy Riddle, this case was only going to push him even deeper into it. 'Human bones?'

'We don't know yet. In fact, we know nothing at all so far. That's why I want you to get down there and find out.'

'Harkside?'

'No. Thornfield bloody Reservoir. You'll find the local DS already at the scene. Cabbot's the name.'

Banks stopped to think. What the hell was going on here? Riddle was clearly not doing him any favours; he must have got tired of confining Banks to the station and thought up some new and interesting way to torture him.

A skeleton in a dried-up reservoir?

A detective chief inspector would not, under normal circumstances, be dispatched to the remote borders of the county simply to examine a pile of old bones. Also, chief constables *never* assigned cases to detectives. That was a job for the superintendent or chief superintendent. In Banks's experience, CCs usually restricted their activities to waffling on the telly, opening farm shows and judging brass-band competitions. Except for bloody Jimmy Riddle, of course, Mr Hands-On himself, who would never miss an opportunity to rub salt in Banks's wounds.

However busy Harrogate and Ripon were, Banks was certain they could spare *someone* qualified to do the job. Riddle obviously thought the case would be boring and unpleasant, or both, and that it would lead to certain failure and embarrassment; otherwise, why give it to Banks? And this DS Cabbot, whoever he was, was probably as thick as pigshit or he would have been left to handle things himself. Besides, why else was a detective sergeant stuck in a section station in Harkside, of all places? Hardly the crime capital of the north.

'And, Banks.'

'Sir?'

'Don't forget your wellies.'

Banks could have sworn he heard Riddle snicker like a school bully.

He dug out a map of the Yorkshire Dales and checked the lie of the land. Thornfield was the westernmost in a chain of three linked reservoirs built along the River Rowan, which ran more or less east from its source high in the Pennines until it turned south and joined the River Wharfe near Otley. Though Thornfield was only about twenty-five miles away as the crow flies, there was no fast way, only minor unfenced roads for the most part. Banks traced a route on the map with his forefinger. He would probably be best heading south over the moors and along Langstrothdale Chase to Grassington, then east towards Pateley Bridge. Even then it would probably take an hour or more.

After a quick shower, Banks picked up his jacket and tapped his pockets by habit to make certain he had car keys and wallet, then walked out into the afternoon sunshine.

Before setting off, he stood for a moment, resting his hands on the warm stone wall and looked down at the bare rocks where Gratly waterfalls should be. A quote from a T. S. Eliot poem he had read the previous evening came to his mind: 'Thoughts of a dry brain in a dry season'. Very apt. It had been a long drought; everything was dry that summer, including Banks's thoughts.

His conversation with Brian still nagged on his mind; he wished it hadn't ended the way it had. Though Banks knew he fretted more about his daughter Tracy, who was at present travelling around France in an old van with a couple of girlfriends, that didn't mean he wasn't concerned about Brian.

Because of his job, Banks had seen so many kids go wrong, that it was beyond a joke. Drugs. Vandalism. Mugging. Burglary. Violent crime. Brian was too sensible to do anything like that, Banks had always told himself; he had been given every possible middle-class advantage. More than Banks had ever got. Which was probably why he felt more hurt than anything by his son's comments.

A couple of ramblers passed by the front of the cottage, heavy rucksacks on their backs, knotted leg muscles, shorts, sturdy hiking boots, Ordnance Survey maps hanging in little plastic holders around their necks in case it rained. Some hope. Banks said hello, remarked on the good weather and got into the Cavalier. The upholstery was so hot he almost jumped out again.

Well, he thought, fumbling for a cassette to play, Brian was old enough to make his own decisions. If he wanted to chuck everything in for a shot at fame and fortune, that was up to him, wasn't it?

At least Banks had a real job to do. Jimmy Riddle had made a mistake this time. No doubt he believed he had given Banks a filthy, dead-end job, full of opportunities for cock-ups; no doubt the dice were loaded against him; but anything was better than sitting in his office. Riddle had overlooked the one overriding characteristic Banks possessed, even at his lowest ebb: *curiosity*.

Feeling, for a moment, like a grounded pilot suddenly given permission to fly again, Banks slipped Love's *Forever Changes* in the cassette player and drove off, spraying gravel.

•

The book-signing started at half past six, but Vivian Elmsley had told her publicist, Wendi, that she liked to arrive early, get familiar with the place and have a chat with the staff.

There was already a crowd at quarter past. Still, it was only to be expected. All of a sudden, after twenty novels in as many years, Vivian Elmsley was a *success*.

Though her reputation and her sales had grown steadily over the years, her Detective Inspector Niven series, which accounted for fifteen of the twenty books, had recently made it to the small screen with a handsome lead actor, glossy production values and a big budget. The first three episodes had been shown, to great critical acclaim – especially given how bored many television critics had become with police dramas recently – and as a result Vivian had become, over the past month or so, about as familiar a face to the general public as a writer ever is.

She had been on the cover of *Night & Day*, had been interviewed by Melvyn Bragg on the 'South Bank Show' and featured prominently in *Woman's Own* magazine. After all, becoming an 'overnight success' in one's seventies was quite newsworthy. Some people even recognized her in the street.

Adrian, the event organizer, gave her a glass of red wine, while Thalia arranged the books on the low table in front of the settee. At half past six on the dot, Adrian introduced her by saying that she needed no introduction, and to a smattering of applause she picked up her copy of the latest Inspector Niven story, *Traces of Sin*, and began to read from the opening section.

About five minutes was enough, Vivian reckoned. Anything less made her look as if she couldn't wait to get away; anything more risked losing the audience's attention. The settee was so soft and deep that it seemed to enfold her as she read. She wondered how she would ever get out of it. She was hardly a spry young thing any more.

After the reading, people formed an orderly queue, and Vivian signed their books, pausing to chat briefly with everyone, asking if they wanted any specific sort of dedication and making sure she spelled their names right. It was all very well if someone said he was called 'John', but how were you to know it wasn't spelled 'Jon'? Then there were the more complex variations: 'Donna', or 'Dawna'? 'Janice', or 'Janis'?

Vivian looked down at her hand as she signed. Talon-like, she thought, almost skeletal, dotted with liver spots, skin shrivelled and wrinkled over the knuckle joints, puffs of flesh around the wedding ring she could never remove even if she wanted to.

Her hands were the first to go, she thought. The rest of her was remarkably well preserved. For a start, she had remained tall and lean. She hadn't shrunk or run to fat like so many elderly women, or generated that thick, hard, matronly carapace.

Steel-grey hair pulled back tightly and fastened at the back created a widow's peak over her strong, thin face; her deep blue eyes, networked with crow's-feet, were almost oriental in their slant, her nose was slightly hooked and her lips thin. Not a face that smiled often, people thought. And they were right, even though it had not always been so.

'A steely, unblinking gaze into the depths of evil,' one reviewer had written of her. And was it Graham Greene who had noted that there is a splinter of ice in the heart of the writer? How right he was, though it hadn't always been there.

'You used to live up north, didn't you?'

Vivian looked up, startled at the question. The man appeared to be about sixty, thin to the point of emaciation, with a long, gaunt pale face and lank fair hair. He was wearing faded jeans and the kind of gaudy, short-sleeved shirt you would expect to see at a seaside resort. As he held the book out for her to sign, she noticed that his hands were unnaturally small for a man's. Something about them disturbed her.

Vivian nodded. 'A long time ago.' Then she looked at the book. 'Who would you like me to sign this to?'

'What was the name of the place where you lived?'

'It was a long time ago.'

'Did you go by the same name then?'

'Look, I—'

'Excuse me, sir.' It was Adrian, politely asking the man to move along. He did as he was asked, cast one backward glance at Vivian, then he slapped her book down on a pile of John Harveys and left.

Vivian carried on signing. Adrian brought her another glass of wine, people told her how much they loved her books, and she soon forgot about the strange man and his prying questions.

When it was all over, Adrian and the staff suggested dinner, but Vivian was tired, another sign of her advancing years. All she wanted to do was go home to a long hot bath, a gin and tonic and Flaubert's *Sentimental Education*, but first she needed a little exercise and some air. Alone.

'I'll drive you home,' said Wendi.

Vivian laid her hand on Wendi's forearm. 'No, my dear,' she said. 'If you don't mind, I'd just like a little walk by myself first, then I'll take the tube.'

'But, really, it's no trouble. That's what I'm here for.'

'No. I'll be perfectly all right. I'm not over the hill yet.'

Wendi blushed. She had probably been told that Vivian was *prickly*. Someone always warned the publicists and media escorts. 'I'm sorry. I didn't mean to suggest anything like that. But it's my job.'

'A pretty young girl like you must have far better things to do than drive an old lady home in the London traffic. Why don't you go to the pictures with your boyfriend, go dancing, or something?'

Wendi smiled and looked at her watch. 'Well, I did tell Tim I wouldn't be able to meet him until later. Perhaps if

I phoned him now and went to queue at the half-price ticket booth, we could get some last-minute theatre tickets. But only if you're *sure*.'

'Quite sure, my dear. Good night.'

Vivian walked out into the warm autumn dusk on Bedford Street.

London. She still sometimes found herself unable to believe that she actually *lived* in London. She remembered her first visit – how vast, majestic and overwhelming the city had felt. She had gazed in awe at landmarks she had only heard of, read about or seen in pictures: Piccadilly Circus, Big Ben, St Paul's, Buckingham Palace, Trafalgar Square. Of course, that was a long time ago, but even today she felt that same magic when she recited the names or walked the famous streets.

Charing Cross Road was crowded with people leaving work late or arriving early for the theatres and cinemas, meeting friends for a drink. Before getting on the tube, Vivian crossed the road carefully, waiting for the pedestrian signal, and strolled around Leicester Square.

A small choir was singing 'Men of Harlech' just beside the Burger King. How it had all changed: the fast-food places, the shops, even the cinemas. It wasn't far from here, on the Haymarket, that she had been to her first London cinema, the Carlton. What had she seen? *For Whom the Bell Tolls*. Of course, that was it.

As she walked back to the Leicester Square tube entrance, Vivian thought again about the strange man in the bookshop. She didn't like to dwell on the past, but he had pushed her into a reminiscent mood, as had the recent newspaper photographs of the dried-up Thornfield Reservoir.

The ruins of Hobb's End were exposed to the light

of day for the first time in over forty years, and the memories of her life there had come crowding back. Vivian shuddered as she walked down the steps to the underground.

2

Banks paused for breath after his walk through the woods. From where he stood on the edge of Thornfield Reservoir, the entire elongated bowl of ruins lay open below him like a cupped hand, about a quarter of a mile wide and half a mile long. He didn't know the full story, but he knew that the site had been covered with water for many years. This was its first reappearance, like an excavated ancient settlement, or a sort of latter-day Brigadoon.

He could see tangles of tree roots sticking out of the slope on the opposite embankment. The difference in soil colours showed where the waterline had been. Beyond the high bank, Rowan Woods straggled away to the north.

The most dramatic part of the scene lay directly below: the sunken village itself. Bracketed by a ruined mill on a hillock to the west, and by a tiny packhorse bridge to the east, the whole thing resembled the skeleton of a giant's torso. The bridge formed the pelvic bone, and the mill was the skull, which had been chopped off and placed slightly to the left of the body. The river and High Street formed the slightly curving backbone, from which the various ribs of side-streets branched off.

There was no road surface, but the course of the old High Street by the river was easy enough to make out. It eventually forked at the bridge, one branch turning towards Rowan Woods, where it soon narrowed to a footpath, and the other continuing over the bridge, then out of the village along the Harksmere embankment, presumably all the way to Harkside. It struck Banks as especially odd that there should have been a fully intact bridge there, under water for all those years.

Below him, a group of people stood by the other side of the bridge, one of them in uniform. Banks scampered down the narrow path. It was a warm evening, and he was sweating by the time he got to the bottom. Before approaching the group, he took a handkerchief from his pocket and mopped his brow and the back of his neck. There was nothing he could do about the damp patches under his arms.

He wasn't overweight, or even especially unfit. He smoked, he ate lousy food and he drank too much, but he had the kind of metabolism that had always kept him lean. He didn't go in for strenuous exercise, but since Sandra left he had got into the habit of taking long solitary walks every weekend, and he swam half a mile at the Eastvale public baths once or twice a week. It was this damn hot weather that made him feel so out of shape.

The valley bottom wasn't as muddy as it looked. Most of the exposed reddish-brown earth had been caked and cracked by the heat. However, there were some marshy patches with reeds growing out of them, and he had to jump several large puddles on his way.

As he crossed the packhorse bridge, a woman walked towards him and stopped him in the middle. 'Excuse me, sir,' she said, arm extended, palm out. 'This is a crime scene. I'm afraid you can't come any further.'

Banks smiled. He knew he didn't look like a DCI. He had left his sports jacket in the car and wore a blue denim shirt open at the neck, with no tie, light tan trousers and black wellington boots.

'Why isn't it taped off, then?' he asked.

The woman looked at him and frowned. She was in her late twenties or early thirties, by the look of her, long-legged, tall and slim, probably not much more than an inch shorter than Banks's five foot nine. She was wearing blue jeans and a white blouse made of some silky material. Over the blouse she wore a herringbone jacket that followed the contours of her waist and the gentle outward curve of her hips. Her chestnut hair was parted in the middle and fell in layered, casual waves to her shoulders. Her face was oval, with a smooth, tanned complexion, full lips, and a small mole to the right of her mouth. She was wearing black-rimmed sunglasses, and when she took them off, her serious almond eyes seemed to appraise Banks as if he were a hitherto undiscovered species.

She wasn't conventionally good-looking. Hers wasn't the kind of face you'd find on the pages of a magazine, but her looks showed character and intelligence. And the red wellies set it all off nicely.

Banks smiled. 'Do I have to throw you off the bridge into the river before I can cross, like Robin Hood did to Little John?'

'I think you'll find it was the other way round, but you could try it,' she said. Then, after they had scrutinized one another for a few seconds, she squinted, frowned, and said, 'You'll be DCI Banks, then?'

She didn't appear nervous or embarrassed about mistaking him for a sightseer; there was no hint of apology or deference in her tone. He didn't know whether he liked that. 'DS Cabbot, I presume?'

'Yes, sir.' She smiled. It was no more than a twitch of one corner of her mouth and a brief flash of light behind her eyes, but it left an impression. Many people, Banks

26

mused, probably thought it was nice to be smiled at by DS Cabbot. Which made him all the more suspicious of Jimmy Riddle's motives for sending him out here.

'And these people?' Banks pointed to the man and woman talking to the uniformed policeman. The man was aiming a video camera at the outbuilding.

'Colleen Harris and James O'Grady, sir. They were scouting the location for a TV programme when they saw the boy fall through the roof. They ran to help him. Seems they also had their camera handy. I suppose it'll make a nice little item on the evening news.' She scratched the side of her nose. 'We'd run out of crime-scene tape, sir. At the section station. To be honest, I'm not sure we ever had any in the first place.' She toyed with the sunglasses as she spoke, but Banks didn't think it was out of nervousness. She had a slight West Country burr, not very pronounced, but clear enough to be noticeable.

'There's nothing we can do about the TV people now,' Banks said. 'They might even be useful. You'd better explain what happened. All I know is that a boy discovered some old bones here.'

DS Cabbot nodded. 'Adam Kelly. He's thirteen.'

'Where is he?'

'I sent him home. To Harkside. He seemed a bit shaken up, and he'd bruised his wrist and elbow. Nothing serious. Anyway, he wanted his mummy, so I got PC Cameron over there to drive him and then come back. Poor kid'll be having nightmares for months as it is.'

'What happened?'

'Adam was walking on the roof and it gave way under him. Lucky he didn't break his back, or get crushed to death.' She pointed at the outbuilding. 'The rafters that helped support the flagstones must have rotted, all those years under water. It didn't take much weight. I should think the demolition men were supposed to pull the whole place down before it was flooded, but they must have knocked off early that day.'

Banks looked around. 'It does seem as if they cut a few corners.'

'Why not? They probably thought no one would ever see the place again. Who can tell what's there when it's all under water? Anyway, the mud broke Adam's fall, his arm got stuck in it, and he pulled up a skeleton of a hand.'

'Human?'

'Don't know, sir. I mean, it *looks* human to me, but we'll need an expert to be certain. I've read that it's easy to mistake bear paws for human hands.'

'*Bear paws?* When was the last time you saw a bear around these parts?'

'Why, just last week, sir.'

Banks paused a moment, saw the glint in her eye and smiled. There was something about this woman that intrigued him. Nothing in her tone hinted at self-doubt or uncertainty about her actions. Most junior police officers, when questioned about their actions by a senior, generally either let a little of the 'Did I do the right thing, sir?' creep into their tone, or they became defensive. Susan Gay, his old DC, had been like that. But there was none of this with DS Cabbot. She simply stated things as they had occurred, decisions as she had made them, and something about the way she did it made her sound completely self-assured and self-possessed without being at all arrogant or insubordinate. Banks found her disconcerting.

'Right,' he said, 'let's go have a look.'

DS Cabbot folded up her sunglasses, slipped them in

her shoulder bag and led the way. Banks followed her to the outbuilding. She moved with a sort of loose-limbed grace, the way cats do whenever it's not feeding time.

On his way, he stopped and talked briefly to the TV people. They couldn't tell him much, except that they'd been exploring the area when they saw the lad fall through the roof. They rushed over immediately, and when they got to him they saw what he'd pulled up out of the earth. He hadn't seemed particularly grateful for their assistance, they said, or even pleased to see them, but they were relieved he wasn't seriously hurt. True to their profession, they asked Banks if he would mind giving them a comment for the tape. He declined politely, citing lack of information. As soon as he had turned away, the woman was on her mobile to the local news channel. It didn't sound like the first time she'd called, either.

The outbuilding was about six or seven feet square. Banks stood in the doorway and looked at the depression in the mud where the boy had landed, then at the two heavy slabs of stone on either side. DS Cabbot was right; Adam Kelly had been very lucky indeed. There were more slabs strewn around on the floor, too, many of them broken, some just fragments sticking up out of the mud. He could easily have landed on one and snapped his spine. Still, when you're that young, you think you're immortal. Banks and his friends certainly had, even after Phil Simpkins wrapped his rope all the way around a tree trunk, jumped off the top branch and spiralled all the way down on to the pointed metal railings.

Banks shook off the memory and concentrated on the scene before him. The sun shone on the top part of the far wall; the stone glistened, moist and slimy. There was a brackish smell about the place, Banks noticed, though there was no salt water for miles, and a smell of dead fish, which were probably a lot closer.

'See what I mean, sir?' said DS Cabbot. 'Because the roof kept the sun out, it's a lot more muddy in here than outside.' She swept some stray tresses from her cheek with a quick flick of her hand. 'Probably saved the kid's life.'

Banks's gaze alighted on the skeletal hand curled around the edge of a broken stone slab. It looked like a creature from a horror film trying to claw its way out of the grave. The bones were dark and clotted with mud, but it looked like a human hand to Banks.

'We'd better get some experts in to dig this place out,' he said. 'Then we'll need a forensic anthropologist. In the meantime, I haven't had my tea yet. Is there somewhere nearby we might be able to get a bite?'

'The Black Swan in Harkside's your best bet. Will you be wanting Adam Kelly's address?'

'Have you eaten?'

'No, but—'

'You can come with me, then, fill me in over a meal. I can have a chat with young Adam in the morning, when he's had time to collect himself. PC Cameron can hold the fort here.'

DS Cabbot glanced down at the skeletal hand.

'Come on,' Banks said. 'There's nothing more we can do here. This poor bugger's probably been dead longer than we've been alive.'

•

Vivian Elmsley felt bone-weary when she finally got home from the signing. She put her briefcase down in the hall and walked through to the living room. Most people would have been surprised at the modern chrome-and-glass decor in the home of a person as old as Vivian, but she far preferred it to all the dreadfully twee antiques, knick-knacks and restored woodwork that cluttered up most old people's houses – at least the ones she had seen. The only painting that adorned her plain white walls hung over the narrow glass mantelpiece, a framed print of a Georgia O'Keeffe flower, overwhelming in its yellowness and intimidating in its symmetry.

First, Vivian opened the windows to let in some air, then she poured a stiff gin and tonic and made her way to her favourite armchair. Supported by chrome tubes, upholstered in black leather, it leaned back at just the right angle to make reading, drinking or watching television sinfully comfortable.

Vivian glanced at the clock, all its polished brass-and-silver inner workings exposed by the glass dome. Almost nine. She would watch the news first. After that, she would have her bath and read Flaubert.

She reached for the remote control. After the best part of a lifetime's writing in longhand, with only an old walnut-cabinet wireless to provide entertainment, she had given in to technology five years ago. In one glorious shopping spree the day after she received a large advance from her new American publisher, she went out and bought herself a television, a VCR, a stereo system and the computer she now used to write her books.

She put her feet up and clicked on the remote control. The news was the usual rubbish. Politics, for the most part, a little murder, famine in Africa, a botched assassination attempt in the Middle East. She didn't know why she bothered watching it. Then, towards the end, came one of those little human-interest bites they use to fill up the time.

This one made Vivian sit up and take notice.

The camera panned a cluster of familiar ruins as the voice-over explained that the drought had brought this lost Dales village of Hobb's End to light for the first time since it had been officially flooded in 1953. She already knew that – this was the same film footage they had used when the story first made it to television about a month ago – but suddenly the angle changed, and she could see a group of people standing by the bridge, one of them a uniformed policeman.

'Today,' the voice-over went on, 'a young boy exploring the scene discovered something he hadn't bargained for.'

The narrator's tone was light, fluffy, the way so many of the cosy mysteries Vivian detested made light of the real world of murder. It was a mystery worthy of Miss Marple, he went on, a skeleton discovered, not in a cupboard, folks, but under the muddy floor of an old outbuilding. How could it have got there? Was foul play suspected?

Vivian clutched the cool chrome tubes at the sides of her armchair as she watched, gin and tonic forgotten on the glass table beside her.

The camera focused on the outbuilding, and Vivian saw the man and woman standing on the threshold. The narrator went on about the police arriving at the scene and refusing to comment at this early stage, then he brought the piece to a close by saying they'd be keeping an eye on the situation.

The programme was well into the weather by the time Vivian had recovered from the shock. Even then, she found that her hands were still gripping the chrome so tightly, even her liver spots had turned white.

She let go, let her body sag in the chair, and took a deep

breath. Then she reached for her gin and tonic, hands shaking now, and managed to take a gulp without spilling it. That helped.

When she felt a little calmer, she went into the study and dug through her filing cabinet for the manuscript she had written in the early 1970s, three years after her last visit to Thornfield Reservoir. She found the sheaf of papers and carried it back through to the living room.

It had never been intended for publication. In many ways, it had been a practice piece, one she had written when she became interested in writing after her husband's death. She had written it when she thought the old adage 'Write about what you know' meant 'Write about your own life, your own experiences.' It had taken her a few years to work out that that was not the case. She still wrote about what she knew – guilt, grief, pain, madness – only now she put it into the lives of her characters.

As she started to read, she realized she wasn't sure exactly *what* it was. A memoir? A novella? Certainly there was *some* truth in it; at least she had tried to stick to the facts, had even consulted her old diaries for accuracy. But because she had written it at a time in her life when she had been unclear about the blurred line between auto-biography and fiction, she couldn't be sure which was which. Would she see it any more clearly now? There was only one way to find out.

•

Banks had never been to Harkside before. DS Cabbot led the way in her metallic purple Astra, and he followed her along the winding one-way streets lined with limestone and gritstone Dales cottages with small, colourful gardens behind low walls. Many of the houses that opened directly on to the street had window boxes or baskets of red and gold flowers hanging outside.

They parked beside the village green, where a few scattered trees provided shade for the benches. Old people sat in the late-summer dusk as the shadows grew long, wrinkled hands resting on knobbly walking sticks, talking to other old people or just watching the world go by. At the centre of the green stood a small, obelisk-style war memorial listing the names of Harkside's dead over the two world wars.

The essentials were arrayed around the green: a KwikSave minimart, which from its oddly ornate façade looked as if it had once been a cinema, a Barclay's Bank, newsagent's, butcher's, grocer's, betting shop, Oddbins Wines, a fifteenth-century church and three pubs, one of them the Black Swan. Though Harkside had a population of only between two and three thousand, it was the largest place for some miles, and people from the more remote farms and hamlets still viewed it as the closest thing to the big city, full of sin and temptation. It was simply a large village, but most local people referred to it as 'town'.

'Where's the section station?' Banks asked.

DS Cabbot pointed down a side-street.

'The place that looks like a brick garage? The one with the flat roof?'

'That's the one. Ugliest building in town.'

'Do you live here?'

'For my sins, yes, sir.'

It was just a saying, Banks knew, but he couldn't help wondering what those sins were. Just imagining them gave him a little thrill of delight.

They walked over to the Black Swan, a whitewash-and-timber façade with gables and a sagging slate roof. It was dim inside, but still too warm, despite the open door and windows. Though a few tourists and ramblers lingered over after-dinner drinks at the rickety wooden tables, it was long past their bedtime. Banks walked to the bar with DS Cabbot, who asked the bartender if they could still get food.

'Depends what you want, love,' she said, and pointed to a list on the blackboard.

Banks sighed. The guessing game. He had played it often enough before. You walk in about ten minutes after opening time and ask for something on the menu, only to be told that it's 'off'. After about four or five alternatives, also declared 'off', you finally find something that they just might have. If you're lucky.

This time Banks went through tandoori chicken and chips, venison medallions in a red-wine sauce and chips, and fettucine alfredo and chips before striking gold: beef and Stilton pie. And chips. He hadn't been eating much beef for the past few years, but he had stopped worrying about mad-cow disease lately. If his brain was going to turn to sludge, there wasn't much he could do to stop it at this stage. Sometimes it felt like sludge already.

DS Cabbot ordered a salad sandwich, no chips.

'Diet?' Banks asked, remembering the way Susan Gay used to nibble on rabbit food most of the time.

'No, sir. I don't eat meat. And the chips are cooked in animal fat. There's not a lot of choice.'

'I see. Drink?'

'Like a fish.' She laughed. 'Actually, I'll have a pint of Swan's Down Bitter. I'd recommend it very highly. It's brewed on the premises.'

Banks took her advice and was glad that he did. He had never met a vegetarian beer aficionado before.

'I'll bring your food over when it's ready, dearies,' the woman said. Banks and DS Cabbot took their pints over to a table by the open window. It looked out on the twilit green. The scene had changed: a group of teenagers had supplanted the old men. They leaned against tree trunks smoking, drinking from cans, pushing and shoving, telling jokes, laughing, trying to look tough. Again, Banks thought of Brian. It wasn't such a bad thing, was it, neglecting his architectural studies to pursue a career in music? It didn't mean he'd end up a deadbeat. And if it was a matter of drugs, Brian had probably had enough opportunities to try them already. Banks certainly had by his age.

What really bothered him was his realization that he didn't really *know* his son very well any more. Brian had grown up over the past few years away from home, and Banks hadn't seen much of him. Truth be told, he had spent far more time and energy on Tracy. He had also had his own preoccupations and problems, both at work and at home. Maybe they were on the wane, but they certainly hadn't gone away yet.

If DS Cabbot felt uncomfortable with Banks's brooding silence, she didn't show it. He fished out his cigarettes. Still not bad; he had smoked only five so far that day, despite his row with Brian and Jimmy Riddle's phone call. Cutting out the ones he usually had in the car was a good idea. 'Do you mind?' he asked.

She shook her head.

'Sure?'

'If you're asking whether it'll make me suffer, it will, but I usually manage to control my cravings.'

'Reformed?'

'A year.'

'Sorry.'

'You needn't be. I'm not.'

Banks lit up. 'I'm thinking of stopping soon myself. I've cut down.'

'Best of luck.' DS Cabbot raised her glass, took a sip of beer and smacked her lips. 'Ah, that's good. Do you mind if I ask you something?'

'No.'

She leaned forward and touched the hair at his right temple. 'What's that?'

'What? The scar?'

'No. The blue bit. I didn't think DCIs went in for dye jobs.'

Banks felt himself blush. He touched the spot she had indicated. 'It must be paint. I was painting my living room when Jimmy Riddle phoned. I thought I'd washed it all off.'

She smiled. 'Never mind. Looks quite nice, actually.'

'Maybe I should get an earring to go with it?'

'Better not go *too* far.'

Banks gestured out of the window. 'Get much trouble?' he asked.

'The kids? Nah, not a lot. Bit of glue-sniffing, some vandalism. Mostly they're bored. It's just adolescent high spirits.'

Banks nodded. At least Brian wasn't bored and shift-less. He had a direction he passionately wanted to head in. Whether it was the right one or not was another matter. Banks tried to concentrate on the job at hand. 'I called my sergeant on the way here,' he said. 'He'll organize a SOCO team to dig out the bones tomorrow morning. A bloke called John Webb will be in charge. He's studied archaeology. Goes on digs for his holidays, so he ought to know what he's doing. I've also phoned our odontologist, Geoff Turner, and asked him to have a look at the teeth as soon as it can be arranged. You can phone around the universities in the morning, see if you can come up with a friendly forensic anthropologist. These people are pretty keen, as a rule, so I don't think that'll be a problem. In the meantime,' he said as his smoke curled and twisted out of the window, 'tell me all about Thornfield Reservoir.'

DS Cabbot leaned back in her chair and crossed her legs at the ankles, resting the beer glass against her flat stomach. She had swapped her red wellies for a pair of white sandals, and her jeans rode up to reveal tapered ankles, bare except for a thin gold chain around the left one. Banks had never seen anyone manage to look quite so comfortable in a hard pub chair. He wondered again what she could possibly have done to end up in such a God-forsaken outpost as Harkside. Was she another of Jimmy Riddle's pariahs?

'It's the most recent of the three reservoirs built along the River Rowan,' she began. 'Linwood and Harksmere were both created in the late-nineteenth century to supply Leeds with extra water. It's piped from the reservoirs to the big waterworks just outside the city, then it's purified and pumped into people's homes.'

'But Harksmere and Thornfield are in *North* Yorkshire, not West Yorkshire. West Riding, I suppose it was back then. Even so, why should they be supplying water to Leeds?'

'I don't know how it came about, but some sort of deal was struck between North Yorkshire and the Leeds City Council for the land use. That's why we're not part of the park.'

'What do you mean?'

'Rowandale. Nidderdale, too. We're not part of the Yorkshire Dales National Park, though we should be if you go by geography and natural beauty. It's because of the water. Nobody wanted to have to deal with National Parks Commission's rules and regulations, so it was easier just to exclude us.'

Like Eastvale, Banks thought. Because it was just beyond the park's border, the severe building restrictions that operated *inside* the Yorkshire Dales National Park didn't apply. Consequently, you ended up with monstrosities like the East Side Estate, with its ugly tower blocks and maisonettes, and the new council estate just completed down by Gallows View: 'Gibbet Acres', as everyone was calling it at the station.

Their meals arrived. Banks stubbed out his cigarette. 'What about Thornfield?' he asked after he had swallowed his first bite. The pie was good, tender beef and just enough Stilton to complement it. 'How long has it been there? What happened to the village?'

'Thornfield Reservoir was created in the early fifties, around the time the national parks system was established, but the village had already been empty a few years by then. Since the end of the war, I think. Used to have a population of around three or four hundred. It wasn't called Thornfield; it was called Hobb's End.'

'Why?'

'Beats me. There's no Hobb in its history, as far as anyone knows, and it wasn't the end of anything – except maybe civilization as we know it.'

'How long was the village there?'

'No idea. Since medieval times, probably. Most of them have been.'

'Why was it empty? What drove people away?'

'Nothing drove them away. It just died. Places do, like people. Did you notice that big building at the far west end?'

'Yes.'

'That was the flax mill. It was the village's raison d'être in the nineteenth century. The mill owner, Lord Clifford, also owned the land and the cottages. Very feudal.'

'You seem to be an expert, but you don't sound as if you come from these parts.'

'I don't. I read up on the area when I came here. It's got quite an interesting history. Anyway, the flax mill started to lose business – too much competition from bigger operations and from abroad – then old Lord Clifford died and his son wanted nothing to do with the place. This was just after the Second World War. Tourism wasn't such big business in the Dales back then, and you didn't get absentees buying up all the cottages for holiday rentals. When someone moved out, if nobody else wanted to move in, the cottage was usually left empty and soon fell to rack and ruin. People moved away to the cities or to the other dales. Finally, the new Lord Clifford sold the land to Leeds Corporation Waterworks. They rehoused the remaining tenants, and that was that. Over the next few years, the engineers moved in and prepared the site, then they created the reservoir.'

'Why that site in particular? There must be plenty of places to build reservoirs.'

'Not really. It's partly because the other two were nearby and it was easier for the engineers to add one to the string. That way they could control the levels better. But mostly I imagine it's to do with water tables and bedrock and such. There's a lot of limestone in the Dales, and apparently you can't build reservoirs on that sort of limestone. It's permeable. The Rowan Valley bottom's made of something else, something hard. It's all to do with faults and extrusions. I'm afraid I've forgotten most of my school geology.'

'Me, too. When did you say all this happened?'

'Between the end of the Second World War and the early fifties. I can check the exact dates back at the station.'

'Please.' Banks paused and tasted some beer. 'So our body, if indeed there is one, and if it's human, has to have been down there since before the early fifties?'

'Unless someone put it there this summer.'

'I'm no expert, but from what I've seen so far, it looks older than that.'

'It could have been moved from somewhere else. Maybe when the reservoir dried up, someone found a better hiding place for a body they already had.'

'I suppose it's possible.'

'Whatever happened, I doubt that whoever buried it there would have put on a frogman's outfit and swum down.'

'Whoever *buried* it?'

'Oh, yes, sir. I'd say it was buried, wouldn't you?'

Banks finished his pie and pushed the rest of the chips aside. 'Go on.'

'The stone slabs. Maybe the body *could* have got covered by two or three feet of earth without much help. Maybe. I mean, we don't know how much things shifted and silted down there over the last forty years or more. We also don't know yet whether the victim was wearing concrete wellies. But it beats me how a body could have got under those stone slabs on the outbuilding floor without a little human intervention, don't you think, sir?'

•

It was a blustery afternoon in April 1941, when she appeared in our shop for the first time. Even in her land girl uniform, the green V-neck pullover, biscuit-coloured blouse, green tie and brown corduroy knee breeches, she looked like a film star.

She wasn't very tall, perhaps about five foot two or three, and the drab uniform couldn't hide the kind of figure I've heard men whistle at in the street. She had a pale, heart-shaped face, perfectly proportioned nose and mouth, and the biggest, deepest, bluest eyes I had ever seen. Her blond hair cascaded from her brown felt hat, which she wore at a jaunty angle and held on with one hand as she walked in from the street.

I was immediately put in mind of Hardy's novel, *A Pair of Blue Eyes*, which I had read only a few weeks previously. Like Elfride Swancourt's, this land girl's eyes were 'a sublimation of her'. They were 'a misty and shady blue, that had no beginning or surface . . . looked *into* rather than *at*'. Those eyes also had a way of making you feel you were the only person in the world when she talked to you.

'Nasty out, isn't it? I don't suppose you've got five Woodbines for sale, have you?' she asked.

I shook my head. 'Sorry,' I said. 'We don't have any cigarettes at all.' It was one of the toughest times we'd had in the war thus far: the Luftwaffe was bombing our cities to ruins; the U-boats were sinking Atlantic convoys at an alarming rate; and the meat ration had just been dropped to only one and tenpence a week. But here she was, bold as brass, a stranger, walking into the shop and without a by-your-leave asking for cigarettes!

I was lying, of course. We did have cigarettes, but what small supply we had we kept under the counter for our registered customers. We certainly didn't go selling them to strange and beautiful land girls with eyes out of Thomas Hardy novels.

I was just on the point of telling her to try fluttering her eyelashes at one of the airmen knocking about the village – holding my tongue never having been my strongest point – when she totally disarmed me with a sequence of reactions.

First she thumped the counter with her little fist and cursed. Then, a moment later, she bit the corner of her lower lip and broke into a bright smile. 'I didn't think you would have,' she said, 'but it was worth asking. I ran out the day before yesterday and I'm absolutely gasping for a fag. Oh, well, can't be helped.'

'Are you the new land girl at Top Hill Farm?' I asked, curious now, and beginning to feel more than a little guilty about my deceit.

She smiled again. 'Word gets around quickly, doesn't it?'

'It's a small village.'

'So I see. Anyway, that's me. Gloria Stringer.' Then she held her hand out. I thought it rather an odd gesture for a woman, especially around these parts, but I took it. Her hand was soft and slightly moist, like a summer leaf after rain. Mine felt coarse and heavy wrapped around such a delicate thing. I always was an ungainly and awkward child, but never did I feel this so much as during that first meeting with Gloria. 'Gwen Shackleton,' I muttered, more than a trifle embarrassed. 'Pleased to meet you.'

Gloria rested her hand palm down on the counter, cocked one hip forward and looked around. 'Not a lot to do around here, is there?' she said.

I smiled. 'Not a lot.' I knew what she meant, of course, but it still struck me as an odd, even insensitive, thing to say. I got up at six o'clock every morning to run the shop, and on top of that I spent one night a week fire-watching – a bit of a joke around these parts until the Spinner's Inn was burned down by a stray incendiary bomb in February and two people were killed. I also helped with the local Women's Voluntary Service. Most days, after the nine o'clock news, I was exhausted and ready to fall asleep the minute my head hit the pillow.

I had heard how hard a land girl's job was, of course, but to judge by her appearance, especially those soft hands, you would swear that Gloria Stringer had never done a day's hard physical labour in her life. My first thought was an uncharitable one. Knowing farmer Kilnsey's wandering eye, I thought that, perhaps, when his wife wasn't around, he was teaching Gloria a new way of ploughing the furrow. Though I wasn't quite sure what that meant, being only sixteen at the time, I had heard more than one or two farmers use the phrase when they thought I was out of earshot.

But in this, as in most of my first impressions about Gloria, I was quite wrong. This freshness in her appearance was simply one of her many remarkable qualities. She could spend the day hay-making, threshing, pea-pulling, milking, snagging turnips, yet always appear fresh and alive, with energy to spare, as if, unlike the rest of us mere mortals, she had some sort of invisible shield around her through which the hard diurnal toil couldn't penetrate.

On first impressions, I have to confess that I did not like Gloria Stringer; she struck me as being vain, common, shallow and selfish. Not to mention beautiful, of course. That hurt, especially.

Then, wouldn't you know it, but right in the middle of our conversation, Michael Stanhope had to walk in.

Michael Stanhope was something of a character around the village, to put it mildly. A reasonably successful artist, somewhere, I'd guess, in his early fifties, he affected a rakish appearance and seemed deliberately to go out of his way to offend people.

That day, he was wearing a rumpled white linen suit over a grubby lavender shirt and a crooked yellow bow-tie. He also wore his ubiquitous broad-brimmed hat and carried a cane with a snake-head handle. As usual, he looked quite dissipated. His eyes were bloodshot, he had at least three days' stubble on his face, and he emanated a sort of general fug of stale smoke and alcohol.

A lot of people didn't like Michael Stanhope because he wasn't afraid to say what he thought and he spoke out against the war. I quite liked him, in a way, though I didn't agree with his views. Half the time he only said what he did to annoy people, like complaining that he couldn't get canvas for his paintings because the army was using it all. That wasn't true at all.

But he would have to walk in right then.

'Good morning, my cherub,' he said, as he always did, though I felt far from cherubic. 'I trust you have my usual?'

'Er, sorry, Mr Stanhope,' I stammered. 'We're all out.'

'All out? Come, come now, girl, that can't be.' He grinned and looked over at Gloria mischievously. Then he winked at her.

'I'm sorry, Mr Stanhope.'

'I'll bet if you looked in the usual place,' he said, leaning forward and rapping on the counter with his cane, 'you would find them.'

I knew when I was beaten. Mortified, blushing to the roots of my being, I reached under the counter and brought out the two packets of Piccadilly I had put aside for him, the way I always did whenever we were lucky enough to get some in.

'That'll be one and eight, please,' I said.

'Outrageous,' Mr Stanhope complained as he dug out the coins, 'the way this government is taxing us to death to make war. Don't you think so, my cherub?'

I muttered something noncommittal.

All the while Gloria had been watching our little display with growing fascination. When I glanced at her guiltily as I handed over the cigarettes to Mr Stanhope, she smiled at me and shrugged.

Mr Stanhope must have caught the gesture. He was always quick to sense any new nuance or current in the atmosphere. He fed on that sort of thing.

'Ah, I *see*,' he said, turning his gaze fully towards Gloria and admiring her figure quite openly. 'Do I take it that you were inquiring after cigarettes yourself, my dear?'

Gloria nodded. 'As a matter of fact, I was.'

'Well,' said Mr Stanhope, putting the brass snake-head of his cane to his chin as he reflected, 'I'll tell you what. As I very much approve of women smoking, perhaps we can come to some sort of arrangement. I have but one stipulation.'

'Oh,' said Gloria, crossing her arms and narrowing her eyes. 'And what might that be?'

'That you smoke in the street every now and then.'

Gloria stared at him for a moment, then she started to laugh. 'That won't be a problem,' she said. 'I can assure you.'

And he handed her one of the packets.

I was flabbergasted. There were ten cigarettes in each packet and they weren't cheap or easy to get.

Instead of protesting that she couldn't possibly accept them but thanking him for his generosity anyway, as I would have done, Gloria simply took the packet and said,

'Why, thank you very much, Mr . . .?'

He beamed at her. 'Stanhope. Michael Stanhope. At your service. And it's my pleasure. Believe me, my dear, it's a rare treat indeed to meet a woman as comely as thyself around these parts.' Then he moved a step closer and scrutinized her, quite rudely, I thought, rather like a farmer looking over a horse he was about to buy.

Gloria stood her ground.

When Mr Stanhope had finished, he turned to go, but before the door shut behind him he cast a quick glance over his shoulder at Gloria. 'You know, you really must visit my studio, my dear. See my etchings, as it were.' And with that he was gone, chuckling as he went.

In the silence that followed, Gloria and I stared at one another for a moment, then we both burst out giggling. When we had managed to control ourselves, I told her I was sorry for deceiving her over the cigarettes, but she waved the apology aside. 'You have your regulars to attend to,' she said. 'And these *are* difficult times.'

'I must apologize for Mr Stanhope, too,' I said. 'I'm afraid he can be quite rude.'

'Nonsense,' she said, with that little pixie-ish grin of hers. 'I rather liked him. And he did give me these.'

She opened the packet and offered me a cigarette. I shook my head; I didn't smoke then. She put one in the corner of her mouth and lit it with a small silver lighter she took from her uniform pocket. 'Just as well,' she said. 'I can see these will have to last me a while.'

'I can put some aside for you in future,' I said. 'I mean, I can try. Depending on how many we can get, of course.'

'Would you? Oh, yes, please! That would be wonderful. Now if I might just have a look at that copy of *Picture Goer* over there, the one with Vivien Leigh on the cover. I do so admire Vivien Leigh, don't you? She's so beautiful. Have you seen *Gone With the Wind*? I saw it in the West End before I went on my month's training. Absolutely—'

But before I could get the magazine for her or tell her that *Gone With the Wind* hadn't reached this far north yet, Matthew dashed in.

Gloria turned at the sound of the bell, eyebrows raised in curiosity. When he saw her, my brother stopped in his tracks and fell into her eyes so deeply you could hear the splash.

•

The first thing Banks did when he got back to the cottage that night was check the answering machine. Nothing. Damn it. He wanted to put things right after his miserable cock-up on the phone earlier that day, but he still had no access to Brian's number in Wimbledon. He didn't even know Andrew's last name. He could find out – after all, he was supposed to be a detective – but it would take time, and he could only do it during office hours. Sandra might know, of course, but the last thing he wanted to do was talk to her.

Banks poured himself a whisky, turned off the bright overhead light and switched on the reading lamp by his armchair. He picked up the book he had been reading over the past week, an anthology of twentieth-century poetry, but he couldn't concentrate. The blue walls distracted him, and the smell of paint in the deep silence of the countryside made him feel lonely and restless. He turned on the radio. Someone was playing the first movement of Tchaikovsky's Violin Concerto.

Banks glanced around the room. The walls did look good; they harmonized well with the ceiling, which he had painted the colour of ripe Brie. Maybe they were just a little too cold, he thought, though he needed all the air-conditioning he could get in this weather. He could always repaint them orange or red in winter, when the ice and snow came, and that would give the illusion of warmth.

He lit the last cigarette of the day and took his drink outside. The cottage stood on a narrow, unpaved laneway about fifty yards west of Gratly. Opposite Banks's front door was a sort of bulge in the low wall that ran between the lane and Gratly Beck. In the daytime, it was an ideal spot for ramblers to stop for a moment and admire the falls, but at night there was never anyone there. The lane wasn't a through road, and there was plenty of room for Banks to park his car there. Just beyond the cottage, it dwindled to a public footpath, which ran between the woods and the side of Gratly Beck.

Banks had come to see this area as his personal veranda, and he liked to stand out there or sit on the low wall dangling his legs over the edge late in the evening, when it was quiet. It helped him think, get things sorted.

Tonight, the stone was still warm; the smoke on his tongue tasted sweet as fresh-mown hay. A sheep bleated high on the daleside, where the silhouetted falls were only a shade or two blacker than the night itself. Sharp starlight pricked the satin sky, along with the lights of a distant farmhouse; a gibbous moon hung over Helmthorpe, in the valley bottom, and the square church tower, with its ancient weather-vane, stood solid against the night. This must have been what the blackout was like, Banks thought, remembering his mother's stories of getting around London during the Blitz.

As Banks sat by the dried-up waterfalls, he thought again about the odd way he had come to live in this isolated limestone cottage. It was a 'dream cottage' in more than one way: though he had never told anyone this, he had actually bought it because of a dream.

Over his last few months alone in the Eastvale semi, Banks had drifted so far from himself that he hadn't even cleaned or tidied the place since Christmas. Why bother? He spent most of his evenings out in pubs or driving the countryside alone, anyway, and his nights falling asleep half-drunk on the sofa, listening to Mozart or Bob Dylan, fish-and-chips wrappers and take-away cartons piling up in an ever-widening circle around him.

In April he seemed to reach his lowest ebb. Tracy, who had been to visit her mother in London that Easter weekend, let it slip over the telephone that there was a new man in Sandra's life, a photojournalist called Sean, and that they seemed serious. He looked *young*, Tracy said. Which was a hell of a compliment coming from a nineteen-year-old. Banks immediately began to wonder just how long this affair had been going on *before* he and Sandra separated last November. He asked Tracy, but she said she didn't know. She also seemed upset that Banks would even suggest it, so he backed off.

As a result, Banks was more full of anger and self-pity than usual that night. Whenever he thought of Sean, which was far more often than he would have liked, he wanted to kill him. He even considered phoning an old mate on the Met and asking if they couldn't put the bastard away for something. There were plenty of coppers on the Met who would jump at the chance to put someone called *Sean* away. But while he had certainly bent the rules occasionally, Banks had never yet abused his position for his own ends, and even at his lowest ebb he wasn't going to start.

His hatred was unreasonable, he knew, but when was

hatred ever reasonable? He had never even met Sean. Besides, if Sandra wanted to pick up some toy boy and take him home to her bed, it was hardly the toy boy's fault, was it? More likely hers. But reason didn't stop Banks from wanting to kill the bastard.

That night, after several whiskies too many, he had fallen asleep on the sofa as usual, with Dylan's *Blood on the Tracks* playing on the CD. Long after the music had finished, he woke from a dream peculiar only for its emotional intensity.

He was sitting alone at a pine table in a kitchen, and sunlight flooded through the open curtains, bathing everything in its warm and honeyed glow. The walls were off-white, with a strip of red tiles over the sink and counter area; matching red canisters for coffee, tea and sugar stood on the white Formica countertops, and copper-bottomed pots and pans hung from a wooden rack beside the set of kitchen knives. The clarity of detail was extraordinary; every grain and knot-hole in the wood, every nuance of light on steel or copper shone with a preternatural brightness. He could even smell the warm pine from the table and the fitted cupboards, the oil on the hinges.

That was it. Nothing happened. Just a dream of light. But the intense feeling of well-being it gave him, as warm and bright as the sunlight itself, still suffused him when he awoke, disappointed to find himself alone and hung over on the sofa in the Eastvale semi.

When Sandra decided a few weeks later that their separation was to be permanent – or at least that reconciliation wasn't imminent – they sold the semi. Sandra got the television and VCR; Banks got the stereo and the lion's share of the CD collection. That was fair; he had collected them in the first place. They split the kitchenware, and for

some obscure reason, Sandra also took the tin opener. Books and clothes were easily divided, and they sold most of the furniture. All in all, there hadn't been a hell of a lot to show for over twenty years of marriage. Even after the sale, Banks didn't care much where or how he lived, until a few weeks in a bed-and-breakfast place straight out of Bill Bryson changed his mind.

He began to seek isolation. When he first saw the cottage from the outside, he didn't think much of it. The view of the dale was terrific, as was the seclusion afforded by the woods, the beck, and the ash grove between the cottage and Gratly itself, but it was a squat, ugly little place that needed a lot of work.

A typical Dales mix of limestone, grit and flag, it had originally been a farm labourer's cottage. Carved into the gritstone doorhead was the date '1768' and the initials 'J.H.', probably the time it was built and the initials of the first owner. Banks wondered who J.H. was and what had become of him. Mrs Perkins, the present owner, had lost both her two sons and her husband, and she was finally leaving to move in with her sister in Tadcaster.

Inside, the place didn't make much more of an impression at first, either; it smelled of camphor and mould, and all the furniture and decor seemed dark and dingy. Downstairs was a living room with a stone fireplace at one end; upstairs, only two small bedrooms. The bathroom and toilet had been tacked on to the kitchen at the back, as they often were in such old houses. Plumbing was pretty primitive back in 1768.

Banks was not a believer in visions and prescience, but he would have been a fool to deny that when he walked into the kitchen that day he experienced the same feeling of well-being and of peace that he had experienced in the dream. It looked different, of course, but he *knew* it was the same place, the one in his dream.

What it all meant, he had no idea, except that he had to have the cottage.

He didn't think he would be able to afford it; properties in the Dales were fetching astronomical prices. But fortune and human eccentricity proved to be on his side for once. Mrs Perkins had no love whatsoever for the holiday-cottage trade and no particular greed for mere money. She wanted to sell to someone who would actually *live* in the cottage. As soon as she found out that Banks was looking for just such a place, and that his name was the same as her maiden name, the deal was as good as done. The only black mark against Banks was that he wasn't *born* a Yorkshireman, but she took to him anyway, convinced they were related, and she even flirted with him in that way some old ladies have.

When she let him have the place for £50,000, probably about half of what she could have got, telling him it would be enough to see her to her grave, Dimmoch, the estate agent, groaned and shook his head in disbelief. Afterwards, Banks always had the impression that Dimmoch suspected him of exerting undue pressure on Mrs Perkins.

The cottage became Banks's long-term project – his therapy, his refuge and, he hoped, his salvation. In an odd way he felt working on the cottage was like working on himself. Both needed renovating, and both had a long way to go. It was all new to him; he had never had the faintest interest in DIY or gardening before; nor had he been much inclined to self-analysis or introspection. But somehow he had lost his way over the past year, and he wanted to find a new one; he had also lost something of himself, and he wanted to know what it was. So far, he had fitted some pine cupboards in the kitchen, like the ones in his dream, installed a shower unit to replace the claw-footed Victorian bathtub, and painted the living room. It hadn't kept the depression away completely, but made it more manageable; at least he always managed to drag himself out of bed in the morning now, even if he didn't always view the day ahead with any real relish.

A night bird called out far in the distance – a broken, eerie cry, as if perhaps some predator was threatening its nest. Banks stubbed out his cigarette and went back inside. As he got ready for bed, he thought of the skeletal hand, possibly human; he thought of DS Cabbot, definitely human; he thought of Hobb's End, that lost, ruined village suddenly risen from the depths with its secrets; and somewhere in his mind, in the darkness way beyond the realms of logic and reason, he heard an echo, a click, felt something intangible connect across the years.

3

Banks watched from the edge of the woods the next morning as the SOCOs slowly lifted the skeleton from its muddy grave under the expert direction of John Webb.

First, they had to take down the wall next to which the bones were buried, then they made a trench around the area and dug down until the bones were exposed, about three feet below the surface. Next, they slipped a thin sheet of metal into the earth under the bones, and finally they got it in place, ready to lift out.

The bones came up on the metal sheet, still packed in earth, and four SOCO pallbearers carried it up the slope, where they laid it out on the grass at Banks's feet like a burnt offering. It was just eleven, and DS Cabbot still hadn't shown up. Banks had already talked to Adam Kelly, who hadn't been able to add anything to his previous statement.

Adam was still shaken, but Banks sensed a resilience in him that he had also possessed as an early adolescent. Banks, too, had loved playing in derelict houses, of which there had been plenty in postwar Peterborough. The worst he had ever come away with was a scraped knee, but a pupil from the girls' school had been killed by a falling rafter, so he knew how dangerous they could be. The council was always boarding them up. Anyway, Adam's little adventure had done no lasting harm, and it would give him stories to tell well into the school term. He would enjoy celebrity status of a kind among his pals for a while.

Banks stared at the filthy, twisted shape at his feet. It hardly *looked* human. The bones had taken on the muddy brown colour of the earth they had lain in for so long; they were also crusted with dark, grungy muck. It stuck to the ribs the way a hearty stew was supposed to do, and it clung to various joints, clogging the cavities and crevices. The skull looked full of it – mud in the mouth, the nose, the eye sockets – and some of the long bones looked like old rusted metal pipes that had been underground for years.

The sight of it made Banks feel vaguely sick. He had seen much worse without throwing up, of course – at least there were no gaping red holes, no spilled intestines, no legs cut off at the thighs, skin riding up over the raw edges like a tight skirt – but he hadn't seen much uglier.

The SOCOs had already photographed the skeleton during every stage of its excavation, and once they had finished carrying it up the hill they went back down and started their detailed search of the area, digging deeper and farther afield, leaving John Webb to give it a poke here and a scrape there. Webb also searched through the dirt for any objects that had been buried at the same time – buttons, jewellery, that sort of thing.

Banks leaned back against a tree trunk, as if on sentry duty, kept his nausea under control and watched Webb work. He was tired; he had not slept well after his late-night musings. Most of the night he had tossed and turned, waking up often from fragments of nightmares that scuttled off into dark corners when he woke, like cockroaches when you turn on the light. The morning heat made him drowsy. Giving in to the feeling for a moment, he closed his eyes and rested his head on the tree. He could feel the rough bark against his crown, and the sunlight made kaleidoscopic patterns behind his eyelids. He was at the edge of sleep when he heard a rustling behind him, then a voice.

'Morning, sir. Rough night?'

'Something like that,' said Banks, moving away from the tree trunk.

DS Cabbot stared down at the bones. 'So this is what we all come to in the end, is it?' She didn't sound particularly concerned about it; no more troubled than she seemed about turning up so late.

'Any luck?' Banks asked.

'That's what took me so long. The university year hasn't started yet and a lot of profs are still away on holiday, or busy running research projects overseas. Anyway, I've tracked down a Dr Ioan Williams, University of Leeds. He's a physical anthropologist with a fair bit of experience in forensic work. He sounded pretty excited by what we've found. Must be having a dull summer.'

'How quickly can he get to it?'

'He said if we could get the remains to the university lab as soon as possible, he'd have his assistants clean them up, then he'd manage a quick look by early evening. Only a preliminary look, mind you.'

'Good,' said Banks. 'The sooner we know what we're dealing with here, the better.'

If the skeleton had been lying there for a hundred years or more, the investigation wouldn't really be worth pursuing with any great vigour, as they would be hardly likely to catch a living criminal. On the other hand, *if* it turned out to be a murder victim, and *if* it had been buried there during or since the war, there was a chance that somebody still living might remember something. And there was also a chance that the killer was still alive.

'Want me to supervise the move?' Webb asked.

Banks nodded. 'If you would, John. Need an ambulance?'

Webb held his hand over his eyes to shield the sun as he looked up. A few of the silver hairs in his beard caught the light. 'My old Range Rover will do just fine. I'll get one of the lads to drive while I stay in the back and make sure our friend here doesn't fall to pieces.' He looked at his watch. 'With any luck, we can have it in the lab by one o'clock.'

DS Cabbot leaned back against a tree, arms folded, one leg crossed over the other. Today she was wearing a red T-shirt and white Nikes with her jeans, her sunglasses pushed up over her hairline. Pretty loose dress codes at Harkside, it seemed to Banks, but then he was one to talk. He had always hated suits and ties, right from his early days as a business student at London Polytechnic. He had spent three years there on a sandwich course – six months' college and six months' work – and the student life fast made encroachments on his dedication to the business world. Everyone at the Poly was joining up with the sixties thing back then, even though it was the early seventies; it was all caftans, bell-bottoms and Afghans, bright embroidered Indian cheese-cloth shirts, bandannas, beads, the whole caboodle. Banks had never committed himself fully to the spirit of the times, neither in philosophy nor in dress, but he had let his hair grow over his collar, and he was once sent home from work for wearing sandals and a flowered tie.

'I need to know a lot more about the village,' he said to DS Cabbot. 'Some names would be a great help. Try the Voters Register and the Land Registry.' He pointed towards the ruins of the cottage near the bridge. 'The outbuilding clearly belonged to that cottage, so I'd like to know who lived there and who the neighbours were. It seems to me that we've got three possibilities. Either we're dealing with someone who used the empty village as a dumping spot to bury a body during the time it was in disuse—'

'Between May 1946 and August 1953. I checked this morning.'

'Right. Either then, or the body was buried while the village was still occupied, before May 1946, and the victim wasn't buried too far from home. Or it was put there this summer, as you suggested earlier. It's too early for speculation, but we do need to know who lived in that cottage before the village emptied out, and if anyone from the village was reported missing.'

'Yes, sir.'

'What happened to the church? I'm assuming there was one.'

'A church and a chapel. St Bartholomew's was deconsecrated, then demolished.'

'Where are the parish records now?'

'I don't know. Never had cause to seek them out. I imagine they were moved to St Jude's in Harkside, along with all the coffins from the graveyard.'

'They might be worth a look if you draw a blank elsewhere. You never know what you can find out from old church records and parish magazines. There's the local newspaper, too. What's it called?'

'The *Harkside Chronicle*.'

'Right. Might be worth looking there too if our expert can narrow the range a bit this evening. And, DS Cabbot?'

'Sir?'

'Look, I can't keep calling you DS Cabbot. What's your first name?'

She smiled. 'Annie, sir. Annie Cabbot.'

'Right, Annie Cabbot, do you happen to know how many doctors or dentists there were in Hobb's End?'

'I shouldn't imagine there were many. Most people probably went to Harkside. Maybe there were a few more around when everyone was working in the flax mill. Very altruistic, very concerned about their workers' welfare, some of these old mill owners.'

'Very concerned they were fit to work a sixteen-hour shift without dropping dead, more like,' said Banks.

Annie laughed. 'Bolshevik.'

'I've been called worse. Try to find out, anyway. It's a long shot, but if we can find any dental records matching the remains, we'll be in luck.'

'I'll look into it, sir. Anything else?'

'Utilities, tax records. They might all have to be checked.'

'And what should I do next year?'

Banks smiled. 'I'm sure you can conscript one of your PCs to help. If we don't get a break soon, I'll see what I can do about manpower, though somehow I doubt this is a high-priority case.'

'Thank you, sir.'

'For now, let's concentrate on the identity of the victim. That's crucial.'

'Okay.'

'Just a thought, but do you happen to know if there's anyone who lived in Hobb's End still alive, maybe living in Harkside now? It doesn't seem an unreasonable assumption.'

'I'll ask Inspector Harmond. He grew up around these parts.'

'Good. I'll leave you to it and see these bones off to Leeds with John.'

'Do you want me to go down there this evening?'

'If you like. Meet me at the lab at six o'clock. Where is it?'

Annie told him.

'In the meantime,' he said, 'here's my mobile number. Give me a ring if you come up with anything.'

'Right you are, sir.' Annie just seemed to touch her sunglasses and they slid down perfectly into place on her nose. With that, she turned and strode off into the woods.

●

Banks was an odd fish, Annie thought as she drove back to Harkside. Of course, before she'd met him she'd heard a few rumours. She knew, for example, that Chief Constable Riddle hated him, that Banks was under a cloud, almost lost *in* the clouds, though she didn't know why. Someone had even hinted at fisticuffs between the two. Whatever the reason, his career was on hold and he was not a good horse to hitch one's wagon to.

Annie had no particular liking for Jimmy Riddle, either. On the one or two occasions she had met him, she had found him arrogant and condescending. Annie was one of Millie's projects – ACC Millicent Cummings, new Director of Human Resources, dedicated to bringing more women into the ranks and seeing that they were well treated – and the antagonism between Millie and Riddle, who had opposed her appointment from the start, was well known. Not that Riddle was especially *for* the ill treatment of women, but he preferred to avoid the problem altogether by keeping their presence among the ranks to an absolute minimum.

Annie had also heard that Banks's wife had left him for

someone else not too long ago. Not only that, but there were stories going around that he had a woman in Leeds, had had for some time, even before his wife left. She had heard him described as a loner, a skiver and a Bolshie bastard. He was a brilliant detective gone to seed, they said, over the hill since his wife left, past it, burned out, a shadow of his former self.

On first impressions, Annie didn't really know what to make of him. She thought she liked him. She certainly found him attractive, and he didn't look much older than his mid-thirties, despite the scattering of grey at the temples of his closely cropped black hair. As far as being burned out was concerned, he seemed tired and he seemed to carry a burden of sadness in him, but she could sense that the fire still smouldered somewhere behind his sharp blue eyes. A little diminished in power, perhaps, but still there.

On the other hand, perhaps he really *had* lost it, and he was simply going through the motions, content to shuffle papers until retirement. Perhaps the fire she sensed in him was simply embers, not fully extinguished yet, just about to cave in on themselves. Well, if Annie had learned one thing over the past couple of years, it was not to jump to conclusions about anyone: the brave man often appears weak; the wise man often seems foolish. After all, enough people thought she was weird, too, and it wouldn't be hard to argue that she had been merely going through the motions lately, either. She wondered if there were any rumours about her going around the region. If there were, she had a good guess what they would be: dyke bitch.

Annie parked on the strip of Tarmac beside the ugly brick section station and walked inside. Only four of them worked directly out of the station: Inspector Harmond,

Annie and PCs Cameron and Gould. Apart from Samantha, their civilian clerk, Annie was the only woman. That was okay with her; they seemed a pretty decent bunch of men, as men go. She certainly felt no threat from any of them. PC Cameron was married with two kids, to whom he was clearly devoted. Gould seemed to be one of those rare types who have no sexual dimension whatsoever, content to live at home with his mum, play with his model trains and add stamps to his album. She knew that in books such types often turn out to be the most dangerous of all, the serial killers and sexual deviants, but Gould was harmless. Even if he liked to wear women's underwear in private, Annie didn't care. Inspector Harmond was, well, *avuncular*. He liked to think of himself as a bit like Sergeant Blaketon out of *Heartbeat*, but he didn't even come close, in Annie's opinion.

Harkside police station might be ugly on the outside but at least inside it was a sparsely populated open-plan office area – apart from Inspector Harmond's office, partitioned off at the far end – and there was plenty of room to spread oneself around. Annie liked that. Her L-shaped desk was the messiest of all, but she knew where everything was and could put her hands on anything anyone asked her for so quickly that even Inspector Harmond had given up teasing her about it.

Annie's desk also took up a corner, part of which included a side window. It wasn't much of a view, only the cobbled alley, a gate and the back wall of the Three Feathers, but at least she was close to a source of light and air, and it was good to be able to see *something* of the outside world. Even if there was hardly any breeze these days, she loved each gentle waft of warm air through the window; it lifted her spirits. These little things mattered so much, Annie had discovered. She had had her shot at the big time, the fast track, with all its excitement, but it had ended badly for her. Now she was slowly rediscovering what mattered in life.

Harkside was generally a law-abiding sort of community, so there wasn't a lot for a detective sergeant to do. There was plenty of paperwork to keep her occupied, make her feel she'd earned her pay, but it was hardly a high-overtime posting, and there were slack periods. That also suited her fine. Sometimes it was good to do nothing. And why should she complain if enough people weren't getting robbed, killed or beaten up?

At the moment she had two domestic-violence cases and a spate of after-dark vandalism on her plate. And now the skeleton. Well, the others could wait. Inspector Harmond had increased patrols in the area most often hit by the vandals, who would probably be caught red-handed before long, and just now the wife-beaters were contrite and arranging to seek help.

Annie headed first to the coffee machine and filled her mug, the one with 'She Who Must Be Obeyed' written on it, then she walked over and knocked on Inspector Harmond's door. He asked her to come in.

'Sir?'

Harmond looked up from his desk. 'Annie. What is it, lass?'

'Got a minute?'

'Aye. Sit down.'

Annie sat. Harmond's was a plain office, with only his merit awards on the wall for decoration, and framed photos of his wife and children on the desk. In his early fifties, he seemed perfectly content to be a rural inspector for the rest of his working life. His head was too large for his gangly frame, and Annie always worried it might fall off if he tilted it too far to one side. It never had; not yet. He had a pleasant round, open face. The features were a bit coarse, and a few black hairs grew out of the end of his misshapen potato nose, but it was the kind of face you could trust. If eyes really were the windows of the soul, then Inspector Harmond had a decent soul.

'It's this skeleton thing,' she said, crossing her legs and cradling her coffee mug on her lap.

'What about it?'

'Well, that's just it, sir. We don't know anything about it just yet. DCI Banks wanted to know how many doctors and dentists lived in Hobb's End, and if anyone who used to live there lives here now.'

Harmond scratched his temple. 'I can answer your last question easily enough,' he said. 'You remember Mrs Kettering, the one whose budgie escaped that time she was having a new three-piece suite delivered?'

'How could I forget?' It had been one of Annie's first cases in Harkside.

Inspector Harmond smiled. 'She lived in Hobb's End. I don't know exactly when or for how long, but I know she lived there. She must be pushing ninety if she's a day.'

'Anyone else?'

'Not that I can think of. Not off-hand, at any rate. Leave it with me, I'll ask around. Remember where she lives?'

'Up on The Edge, isn't it? The corner house with the big garden?'

The Edge was what the locals called the fifty-foot embankment that ran along the south side of Harksmere Reservoir, the road that used to lead over the packhorse bridge to Hobb's End. Its real name was Harksmere View, and it didn't lead anywhere now. Only one row of cottages overlooked the water, separated from the rest of Harkside village by about half a mile of open countryside.

'What about doctors and dentists?' Annie asked.

'That's a bit trickier,' Harmond said. 'There must have been a few over the years, but Lord knows what's happened to them. Seeing as the village cleared out after the war, they're probably all dead now. Remember, lass, I'm not that old. I were still a lad myself when the place emptied out. As far as I remember, there wasn't any village bobby, either. Too small. Hobb's End was part of the Harkside beat.'

'How many schools were there?'

Inspector Harmond scratched his head. 'Just infants and junior, I think. Grammar school and secondary modern were here in Harkside.'

'Any idea where the old records would be?'

'Local education authority, most likely. Unless they were destroyed somehow. A lot of records got destroyed back then, after the war and all. Is there anything else?'

Annie sipped some coffee and stood up. 'Not right now, sir.'

'You'll keep me informed?'

'I will.'

'And, Annie?'

'Yes, sir?'

Harmond scratched the side of his nose. 'This DCI Banks. I've never met him myself, but I've heard a bit about him. What's he like?'

Annie paused at the door and frowned as she thought. 'Do you know, sir,' she said finally, 'I haven't got a clue.'

'Bit of an enigma, then, eh?'

'Yes,' Annie said, 'a bit of an enigma. I suppose you *could* say that.'

'Better watch yourself, then, lass,' she heard him say as she turned to leave.

•

Before I tell you what happened next, let me tell you a little about myself and my village. My name, as you already know, is Gwen Shackleton, which is short for Gwynneth, not for Gwendolyn. I know this sounds Welsh, but my family has lived in Hobb's End, Yorkshire, for at least two generations. My father, God bless his soul, died of cancer three years before the war began, and by 1940 my mother was an invalid, suffering from rheumatoid arthritis. Sometimes she was able to help out in the shop, but not often, so the brunt of the work fell to me.

Matthew helped me as much as he could, but university kept him busy most of the week and the Home Guard took up his weekends. He was twenty-one, but despite the call-up, the Ministry was encouraging him to finish the third year of his engineering degree at the University of Leeds. They believed, I suppose, that his training would come in useful in the forces.

Our little shop was a newsagent's-cum-general store about halfway along the High Street, near the butcher's and the greengrocer's, and we lived above it. We didn't sell perishable goods, just things like newspapers, sweets, cigarettes, stationery, jam and other odds and ends, tea and tinned goods – depending, of course, on what was available at the time. I was especially proud of the little lending library I had built up. Because paper was getting scarce and books were in short supply, I rented them out for tuppence a week. I kept a good selection of World's Classic editions: Anthony Trollope, Jane Austen and Charles Dickens in particular. I also stocked a number of the more sensational novels, Agatha Christie and the Mills and Boon romances, for those who liked such things – unfortunately, the majority of my customers!

Though most of the able-bodied men in the village had joined up and put on one uniform or another, the place had never seemed busier. The old flax mill was operating at full strength again and most of the married women worked there. Before the war, it had practically come to a standstill, but now the military wanted flax to make webbing for parachute harnesses and other things where a tough fibre was needed, like gun tarpaulins and fire hoses.

There was also a big RAF base about a mile or so away through Rowan Woods, and the High Street was often busy with Jeeps and lorries honking their horns and trying to pass one another in the narrow space. The airmen sometimes came to the village pubs – the Shoulder of Mutton just down the High Street, and the Duke of Wellington over the river – except when they went to Harkside, where there was much more to do. We didn't even have one cinema in Hobb's End, for example, but there were three in Harkside.

These things aside, though, it remains difficult to say exactly how much the war affected us in Hobb's End. I think that at first it impinged upon us very little. For those of us left behind, daily life went on much as normal. The first wave of evacuees came in September 1939, but when nothing happened for ages, they all started drifting home again, and we didn't get any more until the bombing started the following August.

Even with rationing, our diets didn't change as much as those of the city folks, for we had always been used to eating plenty of vegetables, and in the country there were always eggs, butter and milk. Our neighbour, Mr Halliwell, the butcher, was probably the most popular man in town, so we were occasionally able to swap any tea and sugar we might put aside for an extra piece of mutton or pork.

Apart from the feeling of waiting, the sense that normal life was suspended until all this was over, perhaps the hardest thing to get used to was the blackout. But even in that we were more fortunate than many, as Hobb's End had no street-lights to begin with, and the countryside is dark enough at the best of times. Still, that pinprick of light on the distant hillside was often the only thing to guide you home.

In the blackout, we had to tape up our windows to prevent damage from broken glass, and we also had to hang up the heavy blackout curtains. Every night, Mother used to send me outside to check that not a sliver of light showed because our local ARP man was a real stickler. I remember the whole village laughing the day we heard Mrs Darnley got a visit from him for blacking out only the front of her house, but not the back windows. 'Don't be so daft,' she told him. 'If the Germans come to bomb Hobb's End, young lad, they'll come from the east, won't they, not by Grassington way. Stands to reason.'

On moonlit nights, especially if there was a full moon, the effect could be spectacular: the hills were dusted with silver powder, the stars glittered like cut diamonds on black velvet, and the whole landscape looked like one of those black-and-white engravings or woodcuts you see in old books. But on cloudy or moonless nights, which seemed far more frequent, people bumped into trees and even cycled into the river with alarming regularity. You could use a torch if you wrapped the light with several layers of tissue paper, but batteries were scarce. All car and bicycle lights had to be hooded and masked with a variety of gadgets that let the light through only in muddied, useless slits. Needless to say, there were a lot of car accidents, too, until petrol became too scarce and nobody drove any more except on business.

Several events made the war more personal for us, such as the Spinner's Inn fire, or the Jowett boy getting killed at Dunkirk, but the day before Gloria Stringer arrived, something hit even closer to home: Matthew got his call-up papers. He was due to report for his medical in Leeds in two weeks.

•

Jimmy Riddle had once accused Banks of skiving off to Leeds to go shagging his mistress and shopping at the Classical Record Shop. He had been wrong that time, but if he had seen Banks nipping out of the Merrion Centre late that afternoon, a new recording of Herbert Howells's *Hymnus Paradisi* clutched in his sweaty palm, Riddle would have felt vindicated at least on one count. Not that Banks gave a toss. He didn't even bother to look furtive as he walked out past Morrison's on to Woodhouse Lane.

It was gone half past five. Shops were closing and office workers were heading home. Banks had driven to Leeds behind John Webb's Range Rover and stayed with him until they got the skeleton set up and secured in Dr Williams's lab, which turned out to be the first floor of a large red-brick house off the main campus. While there, he had called the forensic odontologist Geoff Turner again and persuaded him – at the cost of at least one pint – to drop by the following morning to examine the skeleton's teeth.

After that, Banks had watched the lab assistants start cleaning the bones, then he had gone out for a quick sandwich at a café on Woodhouse Lane, making a slight detour to the Classical Record Shop. He had been gone for about an hour and a half.

DS Cabbot was just parking her Astra when Banks arrived back at the lab. She didn't spot him. He watched her get out and look up at the building, checking with the sheet of paper in her hand and frowning.

He stepped up behind her. 'It's the right place.'

She turned. 'Ah, sir. I was expecting something a bit more . . . well . . . I don't know really. But not like *this*.'

'More labby?'

She smiled. 'Yes. I suppose so. Whatever that means. More hi-tech. This place looks like my old student digs.'

Banks nodded towards the building. 'The university bought up a lot of these old houses when the families and their servants couldn't afford to live there any more. You'd be surprised how many odd and eccentric departments are hidden away in them. Let's go inside.'

Banks followed her up the steps. This evening she was wearing black tights and shoes, a mid-length black skirt and matching jacket over a white blouse. She was also carrying a black leather briefcase. Much more business-like. Banks caught a brief whiff of jasmine as he walked behind her. It reminded him of the jasmine tea that Jem, his friend and neighbour in the Notting Hill bedsit, used to pour so fastidiously, as if he were performing the Japanese tea ceremony.

Banks pressed the intercom and got them buzzed in. The lab was on the first floor, up one flight of creaky, uncarpeted stairs. Their footsteps echoed from the high ceiling.

Dr Ioan Williams waited for them on the landing. He was a tall, rangy fellow with long, greasy blond hair. Wire-rimmed glasses magnified his grey eyes, and his Adam's apple looked like a gobstopper stuck halfway down his throat. Much younger than Banks had expected, Dr Williams wasn't wearing a white lab coat but was dressed casually in torn jeans and a black T-shirt advertising Guinness. His handshake was firm, and judging by the way he lingered over DS Cabbot, his mind was not one hundred per cent focused on science. Or maybe it was. Biology.

'Come in,' he said, leading the way down the corridor and opening the lab door. 'I'm afraid it isn't much to write home about.' Despite his name, Williams had no trace of a Welsh accent. He sounded pure Home Counties to Banks, or Oxbridge. Posh, at any rate, as Banks's mother would say.

The lab consisted of two rooms knocked into one. Apart from the long table at the centre, where the skeleton lay, there was nothing much to distinguish it. Bookcases lined one wall, a long lab bench another. On it lay various measuring instruments and pieces of bone with tags on them like shop-window goods.

Still, Banks thought, what more did Williams need? All he looked at was bones. No mess. No blood and guts to clean up, no need for dissecting knives, scalpels or brain knives. All he really needed were saws, chisels and a skull key. And, thank God, they didn't have to worry about the smell, though the air was certainly redolent of loam and stagnant mud.

There were a couple of posters on the walls, one of Pamela Anderson Lee in her 'Baywatch' swimsuit and another of a human skeleton. Perhaps, Banks speculated, the juxtaposition meant something to Dr Williams. A reflection on mortality? Or maybe he just liked tits and bones.

The bones on the table certainly looked different now that Williams's assistants had been to work on them. Much of the crusting remained, especially in the hard-to-get-at crevices, but the skull, ribs and long bones were easier to examine. They were still far from the sparkling white of the typical laboratory skeleton, more of a dirty yellow-brown in colour, like a bad nicotine stain, but at least the whole resembled something more like a human being. There was even a little matted red hair on the back of the skull. Banks had come across this sort of thing before, so he knew it didn't mean the victim had been a redhead; hair turns red when the original pigment fades, and even many of the 'bog men', Iron Age corpses preserved in peat bogs, had red hair.

'There are a number of odds and ends my lads found while they were cleaning up,' Williams said. 'They're over there on the bench.'

Banks looked at the collection of filthy objects. It was hard to make out what they were: pieces of corroded metal, perhaps? A ring? Shreds of old clothing?

'Can you get them cleaned up and sent over to me?' he asked.

'No problem. Now let's get down to work.'

Annie took out her notebook and crossed her legs.

'First of all,' Williams began, 'let me confirm, just for the record, that we *are* dealing with human remains, most likely Caucasian. I'll check a few things under the microscope tomorrow, do some more work on the skull dimensions, for the sake of scientific accuracy, but you can take my word on it at the moment.'

'What about DNA analysis?' Banks asked.

Williams grunted. 'People seem to think DNA analysis is some sort of miracle answer. It's not. Right now, I can tell you a hell of a lot more about what you want to know than any DNA could. Believe me, I've had plenty of experience in this field. May I continue?'

'Please do. But get a DNA analysis done, anyway. It might be useful for determining identity, or identifying any living descendants.'

Williams nodded. 'Very well.'

'And what about radiocarbon dating?'

'Really, Chief Inspector, shouldn't you leave the science to the scientists? There's too big a margin for error in radiocarbon dating. It's mostly useful for archaeological finds, and I think you'll find our friend here is a little more recent than that. Now, if there's nothing else . . .?' He turned back to the skeleton. 'The height of the subject was easy enough to determine in this case by simple measurement once we got the bones arranged in their original positions. A metre and a half – between a hundred and fifty-four and a hundred and fifty-five centimetres.'

'What's that in feet and inches?' Banks asked.

'Five foot two.' Dr Williams looked over and smiled at DS Cabbot. 'But I can't be sure about the eyes of blue.'

Annie gave him a chilly smile. Banks noticed her roll her eyes and tug her skirt lower over her knees when Williams had turned away.

'Also,' Williams went on, 'you are dealing with the remains of a young woman.' He paused for dramatic effect.

Annie shot him a quick glance, then looked down at her notebook again.

'Go on,' Banks said. 'We're listening.'

'In general,' Williams explained, 'a male skeleton is larger, the bone surfaces rougher, but the main differences are in the skull and the pelvic area. The male skull is thicker.'

'Well, what do you know?' Annie muttered without looking up.

Williams laughed. 'Anyway, in this case, the pelvis is intact, and that's the easiest way for the trained eye to tell.' Williams reached over and put his hand between the skeleton's legs. 'The female pelvis is wider and lower than the male's, to facilitate child-bearing.' Banks watched as Williams ran his hand over the bone. 'This pubic curve is definitely female, and here, the sciatic notch.' He touched it with his forefinger. 'Also unmistakably female. Much wider than a male's.' He hooked his finger in the sciatic notch, then looked at DS Cabbot again as he caressed the skeleton's pelvic area. Annie kept her head down.

Williams turned back to Banks. 'The symphyseal area here, as you can see, is rectangular. In males it's triangular. I could go on, but I think you get the point.'

'Definitely female,' Banks said.

'Yes. And there's one more thing.' He picked up a small magnifying glass from the lab bench and handed it to Banks. 'Look at this.' Williams pointed to where the two pelvic bones joined at the front of the body. Banks leaned over, holding the glass. On the bone surface he could just about make out a small groove, or pit, maybe about half an inch long.

'That's the dorsal margin of the pubis's articular surface,' Williams said, 'and what you're looking at is a parturition scar. It's caused by the stresses that attached ligaments put on the bone.'

'So she'd given birth to at least one child?'

Williams smiled. 'Ah, you're familiar with the technical terms?'

'Some of them. Go on.'

Annie raised her eyebrows at Banks, then got back to

her notes before Williams could nail her with his leering gaze.

'Well,' Williams went on, 'there's only a single pit on either side of the pubis, which would strongly suggest that she only gave birth once in her life. Usually, the more times a woman has given birth, the more apparent the parturition scars are.'

'How old was she when she died?'

'I'd have to do more comprehensive tests to be certain of that. With X-rays of the ossification centres – the centres that basically *produce* the calcium and other minerals that make up bone – we can make a reasonably accurate determination. We can also do a spectrographic analysis of bone particles. But all that takes time, not to mention money. I imagine you'd like a rough estimate as quickly as possible?'

'Yes,' said Banks. 'What do you have to go on at the moment?'

'Well, there's epiphyseal union, for a start. Let me explain.' He looked over towards Annie like a professor beginning his lecture. She ignored him. He seemed unperturbed. Maybe this sort of ogling was just a habit with him, Banks guessed, and he didn't even notice he was doing it. 'Here,' Dr Williams went on, 'at the very ends of the long bones in both the arms and the legs, the epiphyses have all firmly united with the shafts, which doesn't usually happen until the age of twenty or twenty-one. But look here.' He pointed towards the collar-bone. 'The epiphysis at the sternal end of the clavicle, which doesn't unite until the late twenties, has *not* united yet.'

'So what age *are* we looking at? Roughly?'

Williams scratched his chin. 'I'd say about twenty-two to twenty-eight. If you take in the skull sutures, too, you can see here that the sagittal suture shows some signs of endocranial closure, but the occipital and the lambdoid sutures are still wide open. That would also suggest somewhere in the twenties.'

'How accurate is this?'

'It wouldn't be very far off. I mean, this is definitely not the skeleton of a forty-year-old or a fourteen-year-old. You can also take into account that she was in pretty good general physical shape. There is no indication of any old healed fractures, nor of any skeletal anomalies or deformities.'

Banks looked at the bones, trying to imagine the young woman who had once inhabited them, the living flesh surrounding them. He failed. 'Any idea how long she's been down there?'

'Oh dear. I was wondering when you'd get around to asking that,' Williams folded his arms and placed his forefinger over his lips. 'It's very difficult. Very difficult indeed to be at all accurate about something like that. To the untrained eye, a skeleton that has been buried for ten years might look indistinguishable from one that has been buried, say, a thousand years.'

'But you don't think this one has been buried a thousand years?'

'Oh, no. I said to the *untrained* eye. No, there are certain indications that we're dealing with recent remains here, as opposed to archaeological.'

'These being?'

'What do you notice most about the bones?'

'The colour,' said Banks.

'Right. And what does that tell you?'

Banks wasn't too sure about the usefulness of the Socratic method at a time like this, but he had found from experience that it is usually a good idea to humour scientists. 'That they're stained or decayed.'

'Good. Good. Actually, the discoloration is an indication that they have taken on some of the colour of the surrounding earth. Then there's this. Have you noticed?' He pointed to several places on the bone surfaces where the exterior seemed to be flaking off like old paint.

'I thought that was just the crusting,' Banks said.

'No. Actually, the bone surface is crumbling, or flaking. Now if you take all this into account, along with the complete absence of any soft or ligamentous tissue, then I'd estimate it's been down there for a few decades. Certainly more than ten years, and, as we already know, it's unlikely she was buried after 1953. I'd go back about ten years from there.'

'1943?'

'Hold on. This is a very rough guess. The rate of skeletal decay is wildly unpredictable. Obviously, your odontologist will be able to tell you a bit more, narrow things down, perhaps.'

'Is there anything else you can do to get a little closer to the year of death?'

'I'll do my best, of course, but it could take some time. There are a number of tests I can carry out on the bones, tests we use in cases of relatively recent remains as opposed to archaeological finds. There's carbonate testing, I can do an ultraviolet fluorescence test, histologic determination and Uhlenhut reaction. But even they're not totally accurate. Not within the kind of time frame you're asking for. They might tell you, at a pinch, that the bones are either under or over fifty years old, but you seem to want year, month, date and time. The best you can realistically hope for is between thirty and fifty or fifty and a hundred. I don't want to appear to be telling you your job, but probably your best chance of finding out who she was and when she was killed is by checking old missing-persons files.'

'I appreciate that,' said Banks.

'Anyway, I'll need more information about soil, mineral content, bacterial content, temperature fluctuations and various other factors. Buried under an outbuilding floor, then flooded under a reservoir, you say?'

'That's right.'

'I'll visit the site first thing in the morning and take some samples, then I'll get working on the tests.' He looked at Annie. 'Perhaps DS Cabbot here would be willing to escort me there?'

'Sorry,' said Annie. 'Far too busy.'

His eyes lingered on her. 'Pity.'

'Visiting the site's no problem,' Banks said. 'I'll arrange for a car and make sure the SOCOs are expecting you. Look, we're already a bit suspicious from the way and the place the body was buried. I know you don't have a lot to go on, but can you tell us anything at all about cause of death?'

'I think I can help you a little with that, though it's not really my area of expertise, and you should definitely get your Home Office pathologist to confirm this.'

'Of course. We'll ask Dr Glendenning to have a look as soon as he can. I doubt that it'll be top of his list, though. What have you found to be going on with?'

'See those markings on the bones there?' Dr Williams pointed to several of the ribs and the pelvic area. As Banks looked more closely, he noticed a number of triangular notches. They weren't easy to spot because of the flaking and crusting, but once he saw them he knew he'd seen them before on bones.

'Stab wounds,' he muttered.

'Exactly.'

'Cause of death?' Banks leaned over and peered.

'I'd say so. See those little curls of bone there, like wood shavings?'

'Yes.'

'They're still attached to the bone, and that only happens with living bone. Also, there's no sign of healing, is there? If she'd remained alive after these injuries, the bones would have healed to some extent, starting about ten days after the injury. So, technically, she could have been stabbed anywhere from one to ten days *before* she died of something else. But, as I said, it's unlikely. Especially since the position of some of these wounds indicates the blade would most certainly have pierced vital organs. In fact, I'd conclude that she was stabbed quite viciously, more than once, almost certainly causing death. But please don't quote me on that.'

Banks looked at Annie Cabbot. 'Murder, then,' she said.

'Well, I'd hardly imagine the poor woman did it herself,' Williams agreed. 'Yes, unless I'm very much mistaken, it looks like you've definitely got yourselves a murder victim here.'

4

Annie drove up Long Hill the following morning to interview Mrs Ruby Kettering. It was another scorcher, she noted, rolling her window down. Devil-may-care this morning, she had decided not to bother wearing tights. They were damned uncomfortable in the heat. You'd certainly never catch men wearing anything quite so ridiculous.

Long Hill began at the village green and linked Harkside to the edge of Harksmere Reservoir. Close to the centre of the village, it was the busiest shopping street, with a jumbled mix of shops and pubs and most of the public buildings, including the borough council offices, the library, the Women's Institute and the Mechanics Institute. It was early for tourists, but the shops were open and the locals were doing the rounds, shopping bags hooked over their arms, standing gossiping in little knots along the pavement. The road was narrow and double yellow lines ran along each side. Towards the end, the buildings dwindled and finally gave way to half a mile of open countryside before the T-junction with The Edge.

Annie parked on the grass verge opposite the junction. From there, she could see the ruins of Hobb's End in the distance. Several tiny figures stood clustered around the outbuilding where the skeleton had been discovered, and Annie realized it must be the SOCO team still searching the area. She wondered if Dr Williams the skeleton-groper was there, too.

Annie crossed the road and opened the gate. Mrs Kettering was squatting in the garden spraying her dahlias. She looked up. Annie introduced herself.

'I know who you are,' the old lady said, placing her hands on her thighs and pushing herself to her feet. 'I remember you. You're that nice policewoman who found my Joey.'

Annie accepted the compliment with a brief nod. She hadn't actually *found* Joey herself. The budgie had been innocently standing on the village green, accepting the crumbs an old man was scattering, blissfully unaware that it was being watched by a gang of sparrows up in one of the trees *and* by a ginger tom lurking behind a bush not more than ten yards away. One of the local kids had noticed, though, and remembering the poster offering a five-pound reward for a missing budgie, he had carefully scooped up Joey and carried him to the police station. Annie had simply delivered Joey back safely into Mrs Kettering's hands. One of the many exciting jobs she had done since arriving in Harkside. It was, however, through this incident that Annie had received her first on-the-job injury. Joey pecked the base of her thumb and drew blood, but Inspector Harmond wouldn't accept her injury compensation claim.

Mrs Kettering was wearing a red baseball cap, a loose yellow smock and baggy white shorts down to her knees. Below them, her legs were pale as lard, mottled red and marbled with varicose veins. On her feet she wore a pair of black plimsolls without laces. Though a little stooped, she looked sturdy enough for her age.

'Oh dear,' she said, wiping the streaks of sweat and soil from her brow with her forearm. 'I hope you haven't come to arrest me. Has someone reported me?'

'Reported you? What for?' Annie asked.

Mrs Kettering glanced guiltily at the hose coiled near the front door. 'I *know* there's supposed to be a water shortage, but I can't just let my garden die. A garden needs a lot of watering when the weather's like this. I don't own a car, so I don't waste any on washing one, and I thought, well, if I used just a little . . .?'

Annie smiled. She hadn't washed her car in weeks, either, but that was nothing to do with the water shortage. 'Don't worry, Mrs Kettering,' she said with a wink, 'I won't report you to Yorkshire Water.'

Mrs Kettering sighed and put a gnarled, veiny hand to her heart. 'Oh, thank you, dear,' she said. 'Do you know, I don't think I could stand going to gaol at my age. I've heard that the food in there is absolutely terrible. And with my stomach . . . Anyway, please call me Ruby. What *can* I do for you?'

'It's about Hobb's End.'

'Hobb's End?'

'Yes. I understand you used to live there.'

Mrs Kettering nodded. 'Seven years Reg and me lived there. From 1933 to 1940. It was our first home together, just after we got married.'

'You didn't stay there till the end of the war?'

'Oh, no. My Reg went off to fight – he was in the navy – and I went to work at a munitions factory near Sheffield. I lived with my sister in Mexborough during the war. When Reg came back in 1945, we stayed on there for a while, then he got a job on a farm just outside Harkside, so we moved here. We always did like the country. Listen, dear, would you like a cold drink? Lemonade, perhaps?'

'Thank you.'

'I'm afraid there's not much shelter from the sun,' Mrs Kettering said, 'but we can sit over there.'

She pointed to the side of the garden that abutted Long Hill. A short path led to a flagstone patio where two red-and-green-striped deck-chairs sat, half in the sun and half out of it. Various creeping plants coiled around the trellises fixed to the wall, which provided a little shade.

'That'll be just fine,' Annie said, walking over and taking off her sunglasses.

Mrs Kettering disappeared inside the house. Annie settled herself into one of the deck-chairs, stretched out her legs and luxuriated. She could feel the heat on her bare shins, warm and sensuous as a lover's caress. The sensation took her back to the beach at St Ives, where she had grown up and spent many a summer's day with her father, whose job it had been to rent out deck-chairs to the holidaymakers. The memory of those summers took her back to Rob, too: his days off, when they used to go for walks along the cliff tops, sail around the headland in his small boat and make love in secluded coves as the sunset colours emblazoned the horizon and waves crashed on the beach. How romantic it had all been, and how long ago it seemed.

Annie inhaled the sweet scent of the flowers. Bees droned around her, gathering pollen. She opened her eyes again and saw gulls circling over Harksmere.

'Here we are, dear,' said Mrs Kettering, coming back out with a tray. First she offered a tall glass to Annie, then she took the other for herself, set the tray aside and sat down. The deck-chairs faced each other at an angle, so it was easy to talk without straining one's neck.

'Hobb's End,' Mrs Kettering said. 'That takes me back. I can't say I've really given the place much thought in years, though I can see it from the bottom of the garden now, of course. What do you want to know?'

'As much as you can tell me,' Annie said. Then she told Mrs Kettering about the skeleton.

'Yes, I saw something about that on the news. I'd been wondering who all the people were, coming and going.' Mrs Kettering thought for a moment. Annie watched her and sipped lemonade. A robin alighted on the lawn for a few seconds, cocked an eye at them, shat on the grass and took off again.

'A young woman, about five foot two, with a baby?' Mrs Kettering repeated, brow knotted in concentration. 'Well, there was the McSorley lass, but that was when we arrived. I mean, she'd have been well over thirty by the time we left, and she had three children by then. No, dear, I can't honestly say anyone comes to mind. The far cottage, you say, the one by the fairy bridge?'

'Fairy bridge?'

'That's what we used to call it. Because it was so small, only fairies could cross over it.'

'I see. That's right. Under the outbuilding.'

Mrs Kettering pulled a face. 'Reg and me lived at the far end, just down from the mill. Still, I must have passed the place a hundred times or more. Sorry, love, it's a blank. I certainly don't remember any young woman living there.'

'Never mind,' said Annie. 'What can you tell me about the village itself?'

'Well, however close to Harkside it was, it had its own distinct identity, I can tell you that for a start. Harksiders looked down on the Hobb's End people because it was a mill village. Thought they were a cut above us.' She shrugged. 'Still, I suppose everyone's got to have someone to look down on, don't they?'

'Do you remember any doctors and dentists who used to practise there?'

'Oh, yes. Dr Granville was the village dentist. Terrible man. He drank. And if I remember correctly there were two doctors. Ours was Dr Nuttall. Very gentle touch.'

'Do you know what happened to his practice? I'm assuming he's dead now?'

'Oh, long since, I should imagine. And Granville was probably pushing sixty when the war started, too. You'll be after medical and dental records, I suppose?'

'Yes.'

'I doubt you'll have much luck there, love, not after all this time.'

'Probably not. What other sorts of people lived in the village?'

'All sorts, really. Let me see. We had shopkeepers, milkmen, publicans – we had three village pubs – farm labourers, dry-stone wallers, van drivers, travelling sales-men of one sort or another, a number of retired people, colonels and the like. Teachers, of course. We even had our very own famous artist. Well, not exactly Constable or Turner, you understand, and he's not very fashionable these days. Come with me a minute.'

She struggled out of her deck-chair and Annie followed her into the house. It was hot inside and Annie felt the sweat trickle down the tendons at the backs of her ears. It itched. She was glad she wasn't wearing tights.

Because of the sudden contrast between bright sunlight and dim interior, she couldn't make out the furnishings at first, except that they seemed old-fashioned: a rocking chair, a grandfather clock, a glass-fronted china cabinet full of crystalware. The room into which Mrs Kettering led her smelled of lemon-scented furniture polish.

They came to a halt in front of the dark wood mantel-piece, and Mrs Kettering pointed to the large watercolour that hung over it. 'That's one of his,' she said. 'He gave it me as a going-away present. Don't ask me why, but he took a bit of a shine to me. Maybe because I wasn't a bad-looking lass in my time. Bit of a rogue, Michael Stanhope, if truth be told. Most artists are. But a fine painter. You can see for yourself.'

Annie's eyes had adjusted to the light, and she was able to take in Stanhope's painting. She had a passion for art, inherited from her father. She smiled to herself at Mrs Kettering's remark. 'Bit of a rogue.' Yes, she supposed that fitted her father, too. Annie also painted as a hobby, so she was intrigued to look upon the work of Hobb's End's neglected genius.

'Is that Hobb's End before the war?'

'Yes,' said Mrs Kettering. 'Just after war broke out, actually. It was painted from the fairy bridge, looking towards the mill.'

Annie stood back and examined the work carefully. The first thing she noticed was Stanhope's peculiar use of colour. The season was autumn, and he seemed to take the hues and tones hidden deep in stone, fields, hillsides and water and force them out into the open, creating such a pattern of purples, blues, browns and greens as you never saw in a real Yorkshire village. But it made perfect sense to the eye. Nothing seemed to be its true colour, yet everything seemed right somehow. It was uncanny, almost surreal in its effect.

Next, she noticed the subtly distorted perspective, probably a result of cubist influences. The mill was there, perched on the rise in the top left corner, and though it looked as if it *should* dominate the scene, somehow, by some trick of perspective over size, it didn't. It was just there. The church, just to the right of the river, managed much more prominence through its dark and subtly menacing square tower and the rooks or ravens that seemed to be circling it.

The rest of the composition appeared simple and realistic enough: a village high-street scene whose people reminded her of Brueghel's. There was a lot of detail; an art teacher might even describe the work as *too* busy.

The villagers were doing the normal things – shopping, gossiping, pushing prams. Someone was painting a front door; a man straddled a roof repairing a chimney, shirt-sleeves rolled up; a tall girl stood arranging newspapers in a rack outside the newsagent's shop; a butcher's boy was cycling down the High Street beside the river with his basket full of brown-paper packages, blood-streaked apron flapping in the wind.

The rows of houses on each side differed in size and design. Some were semis or terraces, front doors opening directly on to the pavement, while some of the larger, detached houses stood back behind low stone walls enclosing well-kept gardens. Here and there, on the High Street side, a row of shops broke up the line of houses. There was also a pub, the Shoulder of Mutton, and its sign looked crooked, as if it were swinging in the wind.

Normal life. But there was something sinister about it. Partly it was the facial expressions. Annie could detect the smug, supercilious smiles of moral rectitude or the malicious grins of sadism on the faces of so many people. And Stanhope had included so much detail that the effect had to be deliberate. How he must have hated them.

If you looked long enough, you could almost believe that the man on the roof was about to drop a flagstone on some passer-by, and that the butcher's boy was wielding a cleaver ready to chop off someone's head.

The only characters who looked in any way attractive were the children. The River Rowan was neither very wide nor very deep where it ran through the village. Children were playing in the shallows, splashing one another, paddling, the girls with their skirts gathered around their thighs, boys in short trousers. Some of them looked angelic; all of them looked innocent.

The more Annie looked, the more she recognized that there was something religious, ecstatic, in the children's aspects, and the link with the water also brought to mind baptism. It was a sort of religious symbolism reminiscent of Stanley Spencer, though not quite so blatant. Over it all, the church brooded with its sense of menace and evil. The mill was nothing but a husk.

Annie looked away. When she turned back, the scene appeared more normal, and she noticed the strange colours the most again. It was a powerful work. Why had she not heard of Stanhope before?

In the bottom right, just above the artist's signature, stood the outbuilding where the skeleton had been found, next to a small, semi-detached cottage. Beside the door, a wooden sign announced the name: BRIDGE COTTAGE.

'What do you think?' Mrs Kettering asked.

'Have you noticed the way everyone looks? As if—'

'As if they were all either hypocrites or sadists? Yes, I have. That's Stanhope's vision. I must say I didn't see Hobb's End like that at all. We had our share of unpleasant characters, of course, but I'd hardly say they dominated the place. Michael Stanhope was, in some ways, a very disturbed individual. Would you like to go back out to the garden?'

Annie looked at the painting once more, seeing nothing that she had missed, then she followed Mrs Kettering outside.

The sunlight came as a shock. Annie shielded her eyes until she got to the chair and sat down again. There was still an inch or so of lemonade in the bottom of her glass. She drank it down in one. Warm and sweet. For some reason, the painting had unsettled her in the same way some of her father's more disturbed works did; she wanted to know more about it, more about Michael Stanhope's vision of Hobb's End.

'How old was Stanhope at that time?'

'He'd be in his late forties when I knew him.'

'What became of him?'

'I think he stayed in the village until the bitter end, and then I heard he moved to a small studio in London. But he didn't do much after that. Didn't *achieve* much, I should say. I saw his name in the papers once or twice, but I think he was like a fish out of water when he left Hobb's End. I don't think he managed to find a foothold in the big city art world. I heard he was in and out of mental institutions during the fifties, and the last I saw was his obituary in 1968. He died of lung cancer. The poor man always seemed to have a cigarette hanging out of the corner of his mouth. It made him squeeze his eyes almost shut against the drifting smoke when he painted. I was convinced that must have affected his perspective.'

'Probably,' said Annie. 'What happened to his paintings?'

'I wouldn't know, dear. All over the place, I suppose. Private collectors. Small galleries.'

Annie sat quietly for a moment, taking it all in. 'Bridge Cottage,' she said, 'where we found the skeleton. It looked neglected in the painting.'

'I noticed that, too,' said Mrs Kettering, 'and it made me remember something. Now, I can't be certain of this, not after so much time, but I think an old lady lived there. Bit of a recluse.'

'An *old* lady, you said?'

'Yes, I think so. Though I can't tell you anything about her. I just remembered, looking at the painting, that some of the children thought she was a witch. She had a long, hooked nose. She used to scare them away. I think it was her, anyway. I'm sorry I can't be of much help.'

Annie leaned forward and touched Mrs Kettering's arm. 'You *have* been helpful. Believe me.'

'Is there anything else you want to know?'

Annie stood up. 'Not that I can think of. Not right now.'

'Please call again if you do think of anything. It's so nice to have a visitor.'

Annie smiled. 'I will. Thank you.'

Back in her car, Annie sat drumming on the steering wheel and watching the gulls' reflections on the water's surface. She had learned that the place was called Bridge Cottage and an old woman may have been living there in the autumn of 1939. Of course, she still had no idea *how long* the body had lain under the outbuilding floor, so she didn't know whether this new information helped or not.

Perhaps more important, though, she had got her first real *feel* for Hobb's End from the Stanhope painting, and that might come in useful farther down the road. Annie had always thought it important to develop a feel for a case, though she had never expounded her philosophy to any of her male colleagues. Why was it that *feminine intuition* sounded as insulting to her as *hysterical* and *time of the month*?

She turned round and headed back down towards the station, a long day on the telephone looming ahead of her.

•

When Matthew met Gloria that first time, I could feel their immediate attraction like that eerie electric sensation you get before a storm, when you feel jumpy and ill at ease for no apparent reason. It scared me; I don't know why.

Something about Gloria changed when a man entered the room. It was as if she were suddenly *on*, the way I feel when the curtain goes up on one of our amateur dramatic productions and the real audience is there to watch us at last. I don't mean to indicate that there was anything deliberate about this, just that a change came over her and she moved and spoke in a subtly different way when there was a man around. I even noticed it with Michael Stanhope. He must have sensed something, too, or he wouldn't have given her those cigarettes.

But with Matthew it was the real thing. From that first April meeting, events progressed quickly between them. That very afternoon, Matthew showed her around the village, what little there was to see. A few days later they went to the pictures in Harkside and then to the Mayday dance at the Mechanics Institute there. I was helping out behind the refreshments counter, and I could see the way they danced so close together, the way they looked at one another.

I wasn't at all surprised when Matthew announced that he had invited Gloria to tea one Sunday. It was the eleventh of May, and Mother was in one of her states, so the preparation all fell to me. I'm sure I could have got away with a plate of sandwiches, but I was a good cook and, more important, I was good at making the best of what little was available, and I suppose I wanted to show off my skills.

All day we had been hearing disturbing rumours of a terrible air raid on London. Some people claimed that the House of Commons and Westminster Abbey had been completely destroyed and that thousands had been killed. I had already learned to take these things with a pinch of salt. After all, one of the first casualties of war is truth, to paraphrase Hiram Johnson.

I was listening to 'The Brains Trust' after putting the rabbit stew on to simmer. Joad and Huxley were arguing about why you can tickle other people but not yourself, when Gloria popped her head round the door, Matthew right behind her. They were a bit early and Mother was still titivating herself in her bedroom.

Gloria's golden hair, parted on the left, tumbled in long wreaths of sausage curls over her shoulders. She wore very little makeup, just a dab of face powder and a trace of lipstick. She was wearing a blue blouse with padded shoulders and puffed sleeves tucked into a simple black skirt with silver buttons down the side. I must admit that I was surprised at her restraint; I would have expected something far more garish from her. Even so, I felt dowdy in my plain old pinafore dress.

'Look what Gloria's brought for us,' Matthew said, holding out a pint of milk and half a dozen eggs. I took them and thanked her. As soon as Mother saw the eggs, I knew, her eyes would light up. She would put them in water-glass, the way she always did. Suspended in the clear jelly, they would last for months. Seeing them like that always made me uneasy; they looked sinister floating there in the transparent space, like wombs forever on the verge of giving birth, but never quite managing it, trapped there instead, frozen for ever in stillborn becoming.

Sinister or not, though, the water-glass meant we always

had fresh eggs as well as the powdered stuff, which was only good for scrambling.

'Hello, Gwen,' Gloria said, 'I should have known you'd be a "Brains Trust" fan. Tell me, who's your favourite? Joad or Campbell? Surely not Huxley?'

'Joad.'

'Why?'

'He's the most intelligent, the best-read, the most eloquent.'

'Hmm. Probably,' said Gloria, sitting down on the sofa, carefully arranging her skirt as she crossed her legs. Matthew sat next to her looking like the proud new owner of . . . well, of *something*. 'I like Campbell myself,' she said. 'I think he's far more entertaining.'

'I wouldn't have thought you even listened to something like that,' I said, regretting my rudeness almost as soon as the words were out of my mouth. After all, this was the woman my beloved brother clearly adored.

Gloria just shrugged. 'I've heard it once or twice.' Then her eyes lit up in that way they had. 'But you're right. If I had a wireless, I'd listen to nothing but music all day long.'

'You don't have a wireless?' I couldn't believe it. We might have been short of food, but surely everyone had a wireless?

'Mr Kilnsey won't have one in the house. He's rather a strict sort of Methodist, you know. Thinks they're the devil's loudspeaker.'

I put my hand to my mouth and giggled, then blushed. 'Oh dear. I am sorry.'

'It *is* rather funny, isn't it? Anyway, I don't mind that much. All I do is work and sleep there. It's sad for Mrs Kilnsey, though. I don't think she'd mind a bit of music now and then to cheer her up, but, of course, if the wireless is the devil's loudspeaker, then music is his voice at its most seductive.'

'Oh, good heavens,' said Matthew, shaking his head.

Gloria nudged him. 'It's true! He really talks like that.'

'I must go see to the food,' I said.

First I put the kettle on to make us all some tea, then I peeled a few potatoes and prepared the carrots and parsnips. If I say so myself, it was a good meal I put together that Sunday. Matthew had caught the rabbit in Rowan Woods on one of his weekend Home Guard exercises, and there was plenty of meat on it to feed the four of us. We also had some onions from the garden, and some rhubarb for a pie. Talk about *Dig for Victory*!

The kettle boiled. I made tea and carried it through, along with a plate of biscuits. With rationing, you had to be sparing, and the tea was a lot weaker than we were used to. With sugar rationed at only a pound a fortnight, and most of that in the rhubarb pie, the three of us had all stopped taking it. I didn't know about Gloria, so I offered her some.

'I gave it up,' she said. 'Actually, I've got a far better use for *my* sugar ration.'

'Oh?' I said.

'Yes.' She shook her curls. 'If you mix it with warm water, you can use it as a setting lotion.'

That was something I had never thought about, my rather fine and mousy hair being short, in the pageboy style, at the time. 'It must make your head feel terribly sticky,' I said.

She laughed. 'Well, sometimes it's hard to get my hat off, I can tell you. But that can be quite a blessing in the wind we get up at the farm some days.'

At that moment, Mother made her grand entrance. She walked slowly because of her arthritis and her stick tapped against the bare floorboards, so you could hear her coming long before you saw her. She was wearing one of her old flower-patterned frocks and had taken the trouble to curl her hair, though I doubt she had used sugar and warm water. Mother never wore makeup. She was a small, rather frail-looking figure, a little stooped, with a round, ruddy, pleasant face. It was a kind face, and she was a kind woman. Like me, though, she had a sharp way with words some-times. Whatever the arthritis had done to the rest of her body, it hadn't progressed as far as her tongue. I expected fireworks when she met Gloria for the first time, but then I had been wrong about a lot of things lately.

'What a lovely blouse, my dear,' Mother said after the introductions. 'Did you make it yourself?'

I almost choked.

'Yes,' said Gloria. 'I managed to scrounge a bit of para-chute silk, then I dyed it. I'm glad you like it. I can make one for you, if you like. I've got a bit more put away up at the farm.'

Mother put her hand to her chest. 'Good heavens, my dear, you don't want to waste your time making fancy clothes for an old crippled woman like me. No, what I've got will do to see me out.' Typical Mother that, the world-weary tone, as if we might well 'see her out' in the next few minutes.

'The Brains Trust' ended and a special about Jerome Kern came on. Gloria liked that better, all the songs she had heard in her beloved Hollywood musicals. She hummed along with 'A Fine Romance', 'You Couldn't Be Cuter' and 'The Way You Look Tonight'.

You could have knocked me over with a feather when Mother and Gloria got talking about how they both loved Fred Astaire and Ginger Rogers in *Swing Time*. It was time to serve tea and I was feeling really sick by then.

Jerome Kern finished and we turned the wireless off

while we ate. 'So, my dear,' said Mother when the stew was served, 'tell us all about yourself.'

'There's not much to tell, really,' Gloria said.

'Oh, come, come. Where are you from?'

'London.'

'Oh, you poor girl. What about your parents?'

'They were both killed in the bombing.'

'Oh dear, I'm so sorry.'

'A lot of people have died.'

'When was this?'

'Last year. September. I'm all alone now.'

'Nonsense, my dear,' said Mother. 'You've got us.'

I almost choked on my rabbit. 'It's not as if we're adopting her or anything, Mother,' I managed.

'Don't be so rude, Gwen. It's wartime, in case you hadn't noticed. People have to pull together.'

'Anyway,' Matthew said, 'Gloria's away from all that now, aren't you, darling?'

She looked at him with those big beautiful eyes of hers, adoration just dripping out of them like treacle. 'Yes,' she said. 'I am. And no matter what happens, I'm never going back.'

'Is there no one left?'

'No one. I was out visiting a friend a few streets away when the air raid came. We had no warning. My friends had an Anderson shelter in their back garden, so we went down there. I wasn't even worried. I thought my family would go to the underground or the church on the corner like we always did in air raids, but they didn't make it in time. Our house went up and the ones on either side along with it. My grandparents lived next door, so they were killed, too.'

We were all silent for a few moments, digesting the matter-of-fact horror of what Gloria had just told us.

Somehow it made us and our little rationing problems seem insignificant.

'What made you decide on a God-forsaken place like Hobb's End?' Mother asked.

'It wasn't my choice. That's where they sent me, the Land Army. I did my training at Askham Bryan, which isn't far away. Mr Kilnsey needs a lot of help since his boy joined up, and he's not getting any younger. I was just glad to get away to the countryside. I just couldn't stand the idea of working in a dirty, smelly munitions factory.'

'Still,' said Mother, 'farming's not an easy life.'

Gloria laughed. 'You can say that again. It's dirty and smelly, too. But I can cope. I've never minded hard work. Actually, I quite enjoy it.' She shot me a sidelong glance. 'This stew is delicious, Gwen. I really mean it. It's the tastiest meal I've had in a long time. Thank you very much.'

I felt absurdly pleased and struggled to stop myself from blushing, but you can't do it, like you can't tickle yourself. I blushed. 'My pleasure,' I said.

After the rhubarb pie, which Gloria once again was kind enough to remark upon, Matthew made more tea and we put the wireless on again for 'The Happidrome'.

I just caught the end of a news bulletin which confirmed that Westminster Abbey, the British Museum and the Houses of Parliament had been bombed, but only damaged, not destroyed. Still, you never knew whether to believe newsreaders or not, even though they had to say their names before each bulletin now, so we'd know the Germans hadn't taken over the BBC. After all, the Germans could listen to the broadcasts, too, and we didn't want them to think we were badly hurt or demoralized in any way. We had enough with Lord Haw-Haw doing that for us. Just the previous week he had actually said something about the Germans bombing the flax mill in Hobb's End, which nearly gave our ARP man apoplexy.

Over a cup of tea, Matthew and Gloria lit cigarettes. I knew Mother didn't approve of women smoking, but she said nothing. Then Matthew cleared his throat and said, 'Mother, I invited Gloria here tonight for a specific reason, because, well, we have something to tell you.'

Mother raised her eyebrows; my heart started to thump against my rib-cage.

'We want to get married.'

I gaped at Matthew: tall, dashing, handsome, that charming lock of dark brown hair always slipping over his eye, the dimples at each side of his mouth when he smiled, the clear eyes and strong chin. And then I looked at Gloria, saw her radiance.

Somehow, it was all so inevitable.

At that moment, I hated her.

'Ah,' said Mother, after a calming sip of tea. 'You do, do you?'

'Yes.'

'And you, young lady?'

'Very much,' said Gloria, leaning over and taking Matthew's hand. 'I know it's not been long that we've known one another, but it's wartime and—'

Mother waved her down. 'Yes, yes, my dear, I know all about that. Have you thought, though, that Matthew might be going far away soon?'

'We've thought about that, Mother,' he said. 'Even though I passed the medical, I'll still have my military training to do after the degree, and there's a good chance I'll be able to come home every weekend until after Christmas, probably, at least.'

'And the rest of the week?'

'I'll be working at the farm, as usual,' Gloria said, 'and Matt will be at university in Leeds until July, then he'll go wherever they send him for training. I know it's not perfect. We'd love nothing more than to be together *all* the time.' They held hands and she gazed at him. 'But we know that's not realistic. Not yet, anyway.'

I couldn't believe it; she called him *Matt*. How could she? He had always been Matthew to Mother and me.

'What about your studies?' Mother asked him.

'I'll be working just as hard as usual.'

'Hmph. A lot of couples are waiting to marry,' she said. 'Until times are less uncertain.'

'But a lot of people are getting married, too,' Matthew argued, 'making the best of the time they have. Yes, we know life is very uncertain now. But if anything happens to me in the forces, I'll die a far happier man for having been married to Gloria. Even if it was only for a day.'

'Don't talk like that, Matthew,' Mother said, putting her hand to her chest again. Then she glanced at me. 'What do you think about all this, Gwen?'

I swallowed. 'Me? Well, I suppose if it's what they really want to do, then there's nothing we can say to stop them.'

'Good old Gwen,' said Matthew. 'I knew I could depend on you.'

'Where will you live?' Mother demanded. 'Have you thought about that? It's not that we wouldn't have you, but there's not enough room here, you know, even if you *wanted* to live with Gwen and me. We don't even have enough room to take in evacuees. And you certainly can't both live at the farm.'

'Yes,' said Matthew, 'we've thought about that, too. That's why we want to get married as soon as possible.'

Mother frowned. 'Oh?'

'We're going to live in Bridge Cottage.'

'What? That run-down hovel by the fairy bridge?'

'Yes. It'll be big enough for us. And it'll be ours. Well, we'll only be renting it, but you know what I mean. As you know, it's been used for housing evacuees since old Miss Croft died. Anyway, I've talked to Lord Clifford's agent in Leeds, and he says that the people there now are moving out next week. It's a woman and her two children, evacuees from Birmingham. Apparently they're homesick and they're going home. I know it'll need a lot of fixing up, but I'm good with my hands. And it's only five shillings a week.'

'What about children? Have you thought about that, too?'

'I'm not having a baby, Mrs Shackleton, if that's what you mean,' said Gloria.

'Of course not, my dear. That's not what I meant at all. I wouldn't suggest such a thing. But if you *do* have a baby after you're married, the child's father will most likely be away and you'll have a lot on your hands.'

That sad look came over Gloria's face the way it did sometimes, a dark cloud blocking the sun. 'We haven't planned to have children,' she said. 'Not yet, anyway. I wouldn't want to bring a child into the world the way things are now, not after what I've been through.' Then the cloud passed and she smiled again. 'After the war, though, we'll see. Things will be different then.'

Mother was silent for a moment, then she grimaced as if in pain, which she probably was, and said, 'You've thought of everything, haven't you?'

Matthew beamed. 'Everything, Mother. We want to start having the banns called next Sunday. Please say you'll give us your blessing. Please!'

Mother held her cup out and I poured more tea. Her

hand was shaking and the cup rattled on the saucer. She looked at Gloria again. 'And you're an orphan, my dear? You have no living relatives?'

'None. But you *did* say I've got you, didn't you?'

Mother smiled. Only a little one. That's all she allowed herself those days. Little ones. 'I did, didn't I?'

'Oh, please, Mrs Shackleton, *please* give us your permission.'

'It doesn't look as if I've got much choice, does it? Go on, then, you have my blessing.' Then she sighed and looked at me. 'I suppose we'll have to start saving our coupons up, won't we, Gwen, love?'

•

Some mornings, especially when the weather was good, Vivian Elmsley liked to walk up Rosslyn Hill to the High Street, take a table outside one of the cafés and linger over her morning coffee. She walked slowly, finding her breath came with more difficulty these days.

One or two people on the street recognized her from her television and magazine-cover appearances, as usual, but the people of Hampstead took celebrity in their stride, especially the literary kind, so no one pestered her for autographs or 'simply had to' tell her how good or how bad her latest book was.

She found an empty table easily enough, bought her coffee and unfolded the *Times*. Her routine varied. Some days she found herself thinking about the book she was working on as she walked, hardly noticing the people in the street, unaware even of what season it was. On those days, she would sit down with her notebook and scribble a few ideas as she sipped. Today, though, the book was much farther from her mind than she would have liked.

Instead, she opened her newspaper. The brief item she was looking for appeared in a column on one of the inside pages usually reserved for news items from the provinces:

FOUL PLAY SUSPECTED IN
RESERVOIR SKELETON CASE

In a surprise statement given yesterday evening to local reporters, North Yorkshire Police indicated that the skeletal remains found under Thornfield Reservoir were those of a female murder victim. Detective Chief Inspector Alan Banks, in charge of the case, said that while police have not yet discovered the victim's identity, they do know that the body is that of a woman in her early twenties. All indications are that she was stabbed to death. How long the body has lain there, DCI Banks added, is much more difficult to determine, but preliminary information indicates that they are dealing with a twentieth-century crime. Thornfield Reservoir was constructed on the site of a village called Hobb's End, whose remains have now come into view for the first time since 1953. The skeleton was found buried under an outbuilding by a thirteen-year-old boy, Adam Kelly, while he was playing in the area. Anyone with information is asked to get in touch immediately with the North Yorkshire Police.

So they knew that much already. Her hand trembling slightly, Vivian put the newspaper down and sucked some of the frothy milk from the top of her coffee. She wouldn't be able to concentrate on the rest of the news now, or attempt the crossword. That little item had quite spoiled her day.

It was funny, she thought, how time played tricks. Over the years she had managed to distance herself from the past: the years with Ronald in Africa, Hong Kong, South America and Malaysia; her early struggles as a writer after his death; the rejections and humiliations; the flush of first publication; the slow rise to success; the television series. Before Ronald, she had thought her life completely blighted by fate. What she discovered instead, over the years, was that while it had been in some ways diminished, it had also been far more fulfilling than she could ever have dreamed. Time might not heal everything, but some things just die, dry up and flake off.

Of course, after Ronald's death, she had never been involved with another man. (One might say she hadn't even been involved with Ronald in *that* way.) But there is always a price to pay, and that was a relatively small one, far less than the nightmares and the deep, gnawing guilt that, while it fuelled her imaginative flights of fancy, crippled her in just about every other way and brought on black moods and sleepless nights she sometimes feared would never end.

Now this. She watched the innocent pedestrians passing to and fro on the pavement: a young woman in a smart grey business suit talking into her mobile telephone; a young fair-haired couple carrying rucksacks, Scandinavian tourists by the look of them, holding hands; a man with a grey beard, wearing a paint-smeared smock; two girls with green and orange hair and rings through their noses. Vivian sighed. The streets of Hampstead. 'All human life is here', as the old *News of the World* used to proclaim about itself. Well, perhaps not *all* – not in Hampstead, at least – but certainly the more privileged classes.

Were they all so innocent? Perhaps not. No doubt there

walked among the crowds of Hampstead a murderer or two.

Vivian gave a little shudder. She remembered how she had felt there was someone following her on and off over the past couple of weeks. She had put it down to an overactive imagination. After all, she made her living from writing about crime, and the same morbid imagination that made her so good at that also sparked off occasional panic attacks and fits of depression. They were two sides of the same coin; she profited from her fears, but she had to live with them, too. So perhaps she *had* been imagining it all. Who would want to follow her anyway? The police? Surely not. If they wanted to talk to her, they would approach her directly.

Vivian glanced back at her newspaper, folded open at the Hobb's End item, and sighed. Well, it shouldn't take them long now, should it? And then what would become of her hard-earned peace?

•

Banks started with Brian's university administration office, and ten minutes later, after a few white lies about the importance of the information he was requesting, he had managed to convince the assistant to break her 'strict code of privacy'. On the pad in front of him was the London telephone number of one Andrew Jones.

He paused before dialling, unsure of what he was going to say to Brian if he did get through. The only thing he knew was that they had to get beyond the argument, get to some position where they could talk like reasonable human beings. Still, both he and Brian had always been quick to forgive. Whenever they had disagreements in the past, one or the other would make a conciliatory move within minutes, and it was all over. Sandra was the one who kept things on a slow simmer; sometimes it took her a week of cool distance and moody silences before she let you know exactly *why* she was upset with you in the first place.

Whether Banks could manage reconciliation this time without slipping into the irate-father role, he wasn't sure. Besides, he had damn good reason to be irate. Brian had cocked up three years of higher education – which hadn't been easy on Banks and Sandra financially – and then he had bottled out of telling anyone for weeks, practically disappearing off the face of the earth.

As it turned out, Banks needn't have worried. When he dialled the number, no one picked the phone up, and there was no answering machine.

Next he phoned Annie, who seemed excited about a painting of Hobb's End done by an artist called Michael Stanhope. Banks couldn't share her enthusiasm, though he was glad to find out she had discovered the name of the cottage by the outbuilding.

Waiting for John Webb to call with an inventory of the material recovered at the crime scene, he examined the contents of his 'in' tray. Designs for new uniforms had been approved at a conference of the Association of Chief Police Officers. Fascinating stuff. Had they nothing better to do? What the hell did the top brass think the police force was, a bloody fashion statement? Soon they'd have PCs and WPCs flouncing down the catwalks in see-through uniforms with feather boas.

Under that was a copy of the latest report from Ms Millicent Cummings, Assistant Chief Constable, or Director of the Department of Human Resources, as her real title went. North Yorkshire had been under fire lately

for its excessive number of sexual-harassment claims –
accusations of bullying, sexual assault, discrimination and
bizarre initiation ceremonies – and Millie had been
brought in as the new broom. On a broomstick, too, so the
lads had it. Banks liked Millie, though; she was a bright,
fair woman with a tough job to do. As far as he was
concerned, the more thugs and yobs kicked off the force,
the better all round.

Banks turned to a report on tightening up alcohol sales.
It included an incident report about a ten-year-old kid who
got pissed on alco-pop and rode his bicycle through a
shoe-shop window. Minor cuts and bruises. Lucky bugger.
Which was more than could be said for the poor sales clerk
who just happened to be bending over a prospective
customer's feet with a shoehorn at the time. Instant
haemorrhoid surgery.

Banks signed off on the reports and memos – including
one that informed him CID was having its name changed
to Crime Management – then he worked for a while on an
article he was writing on policing in the nineties. One of
the advantages of his new computer and his desk-bound
existence was that he had written two of these over the
past couple of months, and he found he enjoyed the process. He had also given a few talks and lectures and
discovered he was good at that, too. There had been times
when he had thought it might not be a bad idea to try for
some sort of police-related teaching career, but the cards
were stacked against him in the form of his education – or
lack of it. Banks didn't have a university degree, as Brian
had so cruelly reminded him the other day. He had come
out of the Poly with a Higher National Diploma in Business
Studies. It was supposed to be the equivalent of a pass
degree, but only the *equivalent*. And that had been almost

a quarter of a century ago. As far as he knew, such diplomas probably didn't even exist any more. A prospective employer would take one look at it and burst out laughing. The thought made Banks flush with shame and anger.

At least Brian had got a third-class honours, which beat a mere pass, or equivalent. Christ, it sounded like a poker game. Was he in competition with his son all of a sudden?

Luckily, the phone rang before he could frame an answer. It was John Webb.

'I've just picked up the stuff we dug up with the Hobb's End skeleton,' he said. 'Dr Williams's lads have given it a good clean.'

'What did you find? Not much after all this time, I imagine.'

'Actually, you'd be amazed at some of the things that *do* survive. It's all very unpredictable. I found a few buttons and some metal clips that look as if they might have come from a brassière or a suspender belt. I also found some small leather shoes which look as though they might have belonged to the corpse.'

'So you're saying she was buried in her clothes?'

'Looks like it.'

'Anything else?'

'Yes, some other material, black and heavy. Definitely not clothing.'

'Any ideas?'

'Some sort of curtains, perhaps?'

'Did you find a wedding ring, or anything that looked as if it might have been one?' he asked.

'I think so. I wasn't sure at first because of the corrosion, but that's what it looks like all right.'

'I don't suppose there's a name and date engraved on the inside, is there?'

Webb laughed. 'Even if there was, I wouldn't be able to read it after this long.'

'Thought not. Any sign of the murder weapon? Most likely some sort of knife.'

'Nothing like that.'

'Handbag or a purse? Anything with identification.'

'Sorry, no. Just what I've told you. And a locket, no inscription and nothing inside. Nothing that survived the years underground, anyway. If there *was* a photo or something like that, it probably disintegrated.'

'Okay, thanks a lot, John.'

'No problem. I'll have it sent over to you later today.'

Banks walked over to the window. The heat was still getting to him; he felt sleepy and woolly-headed, as if he'd had a couple of drinks, which he hadn't. The cobbled market square was chock-a-block with tourists, coaches from Leeds, Wigan and Scunthorpe, cars parked in every available nook and cranny, a riot of primary colours. All summer the tourist hordes had been coming to the Dales. Pubs, hotels, shops and B and Bs had all done record business. Of course, it hadn't rained in two months, and even before that there had been nothing much more than minor showers since April.

Though the health fascists had finally succeeded in banning smoking from every police station in the country, Banks lit a cigarette. He had been quietly ignoring the no-smoking order for a while now. In the larger open-plan stations, you couldn't get around it, of course; you simply had to go outside. But here, in the old Tudor-fronted warren, he had his own office. With the door closed and the window open, who would know? What did he care, anyway? What were they going to do, put him in detention?

Watching a couple of pretty young tourists dressed in T-shirts and shorts sitting eating ice lollies on the raised parapet of the market cross, Banks started to drift into pleasurable fantasies involving Annie Cabbot and her red wellies. He had been fantasizing a lot lately, and he didn't know whether it was a healthy sign or not.

Officially, of course, fellow police officers did not sleep together. Especially DCIs and sergeants. That was a real no-no. From one perspective it could be called sexual harass-ment, and from the other, sleeping your way to the top.

In reality, it happened all the time. All over the country, coppers were shagging one another like rabbits, fucking away like minks, regardless of rank. Murder scenes in par-ticular got them going: sex and death, the old aphrodisiac combination.

Dream on, he told himself, snapping out of the fantasy. The truth was that Annie Cabbot wouldn't have him, and he wouldn't try it anyway. Any facility at chatting up women he might have had as a teenager had deserted him now. How do you start that sort of thing all over again? He was too old to go out on dates and worry about whether a goodnight kiss would be welcome. Or a night-cap. Or an invitation to stay the night. Or who should take care of the condoms. The whole idea made him feel nervous and awkward. He wouldn't know where to begin.

He had had only one sexual encounter since Sandra left, and that had been a complete disaster. In his cups at Susan Gay's farewell party in the Queen's Arms, Banks had picked up a woman called Karen something-or-other. Or perhaps Karen had picked *him* up. Either way, the beer was boosting his confidence, and Karen was tipsy and definitely frisky. Instant lust. Without much preamble, they went back to his place where, after only the briefest of hesitations, they got into a clinch and fell on to the sofa, clothes flying everywhere. Despite the booze, everything worked just fine.

Somehow, later, they must have crawled up into the bed, because Banks awoke around four in the morning with a pounding headache, a naked woman wrapped around him and a burning desire to be alone. He had used Karen – as perhaps she had used him – and now all he wanted to do was discard her. Instead, he lay awake beside her thinking gloomy thoughts until she stirred in the early dawn and said she had to go home. He didn't object, didn't show any tenderness on parting, and he never saw her again.

The telephone dragged him out of his depressing memory and back to his desk. It was Geoff Turner, the forensic odontologist. This reminded Banks that he had a dentist's appointment looming, and he had hated the dentist's since his school days. Maybe he would have an excuse to cancel if this case went anywhere.

'Alan?'

'Geoff. You're fast. Any news?'

'Nothing dramatic. Too soon for that. But I was keen to make a start. I've always been fascinated by skeletal remains.'

Banks thought of Dr Williams caressing the skeleton's pelvic region. 'Pervert.'

Turner laughed. 'Scientifically, I mean.'

'Go on.'

'I'm calling from the lab. What I wanted to do first of all was confirm Dr Williams's estimate of her age at the time of death. He's right. The third molars are up – that's wisdom teeth to you laymen – but the apexes haven't quite closed yet, nor have the medial sides of the incisal sutures. The third molars don't usually come up until your early twenties, so there's our first clue. Then the apexes are usually closed by the age of twenty-five and medials by thirty. Which makes her mid-twenties, give or take a year or two.'

'Thanks, Geoff. Any idea how long she's been down there?'

'Hold your horses. I told you I've only managed a quick look so far. What few fillings there are seem to indicate fairly recent dental work, if that's of any interest to you. And by recent, I mean twentieth-century.'

'Any closer? A rough guess?'

'By the look of the material and techniques, probably not later than the fifties, if that's any help.'

'Are you sure it's not more recent? Like nineties?'

'No way. You might not believe it when you're sitting in the chair, but dentistry's come a hell of a long way in the past thirty years or so, and this mouth shows no signs of that. No modern techniques or materials. And there are several missing teeth.'

'Could that have happened after death?'

'You mean could the killer have pulled her teeth out?'

'Could he?'

'Possible, but unlikely. They look like pretty clean extractions to me.'

'She can't have been buried between 1953 and this summer, if that's any help.'

'Then I'd say definitely before 1953.'

'Are you sure it couldn't just be someone who neglected her teeth?'

'It's not a matter of neglect, Alan, though I'll get back to that in a moment. It's materials and procedures.'

'Go on.'

'There's not much more to tell, really. Just a couple of vague ideas.'

'Where would we be in our business without vague ideas?'

Turner laughed. 'You shouldn't say that to a scientist. It's heresy. Anyway, I can't be certain until the X-rays, but we're not talking top-quality dental work here and we're also not talking regular visits. If I had to guess, I'd say this lass only went to the dentist's when she had a problem.'

'What do you mean?' asked Banks, who was beginning to feel even more empathy with the victim. He felt exactly the same way about dentists.

'The fillings might have lasted a few years longer, had she lived, but in one case the decay wasn't quite eradicated. That sort of thing. A bit sloppy. Also, as I said, there are signs of neglect, which may indicate we're dealing with someone from a poor background, someone who couldn't afford the best treatment. Quite often, you know, girls had all their teeth pulled out in their twenties and wore dentures for the rest of their lives.'

'Right. Thanks, Geoff.' Banks had always thought that the idea of *paying* for so much pain was the quintessence of masochism.

'Another possibility is wartime.'

'Really? Why do you say that?'

'Think about it. Most of the good young dentists and doctors were in the forces, and there were only old dodderers left. Poor equipment. Repairs were hard to get done. Military got priority over everything.'

'Right. I didn't think of that.'

'And there's another thing.'

'There is?'

'We didn't get the National Health Service until 1948. Before that you had to pay for dental work. Naturally, the working class had the hardest time of it.'

'Didn't they always,' said Banks, remembering his father coming home silent and exhausted after long shifts at the steel factory and his mother falling asleep in the evenings after spending her day cleaning other people's houses. 'So possibly wartime, possibly poor?'

'Right.'

'Thanks again. I owe you, Geoff.'

'It'll be my pleasure to collect. Of course, if you could track down her actual dentist, if there are still records . . .'

'We're trying,' said Banks. 'But it happened a long time ago. How long is a dentist likely to hang on to old records, even if he is still alive?'

'True enough. Best of luck, Alan. Talk to you later.'

Banks put down the receiver and leaned back in his chair to think about what he had just heard. Both Ioan Williams and Geoff Turner agreed that the skeleton had not been put there after Thornfield Reservoir dried up earlier in the summer, and Dr Williams had estimated the late thirties at the earliest. So the skeleton wasn't a hundred years old or more; it was more like fifty or sixty. Which meant that if the victim had been between twenty-two and twenty-eight when she was killed, she would probably have been between seventy and eighty had she lived. Not only might she still have been alive, then, but so might her killer, and so might a witness, or at least someone who *remembered* her.

This was quickly turning into a real case. What had been dug up from Thornfield Reservoir was no longer just a collection of filthy old bones; in Banks's mind, the woman was slowly assuming flesh. He had no idea what she had really looked like, but in his mind's eye he could already see a sort of amalgam of the wartime film stars in the fashions of the period: Greer Garson, Deanna Durbin, Merle Oberon. What he needed to know next was her name; that would make her even more real to him.

He looked at his watch. Just turned four. If he set off now, he could be in Harkside in an hour or so. Plenty of time to compare notes with Annie.

5

As weddings go, Matthew and Gloria's was a relatively small affair. A few family members came from as far away as Eastvale and Richmond, some of them distant uncles, aunts and cousins I hadn't seen for years. Gloria had no family, of course, so the rest of the guests were made up of people from the village. Mr and Mrs Kilnsey from the farm were there, though Mr Kilnsey looked terrified for his mortal soul to find himself in the Church of England, that hotbed of idolatry.

Gloria had also insisted on inviting Michael Stanhope, as they had become quite close friends, and he looked almost as uncomfortable as Mr Kilnsey to find himself in such hallowed surroundings. He was sober, though, and at least he had made the effort to shave, comb his hair and wear a decent, if rather frayed and shiny, suit. He also remembered to remove his hat during the service.

I must say Gloria looked radiantly beautiful. With her angelic face and earthly figure, she had a natural advantage to start with. Wizard that she was at making things, she had decided it was more expedient to buy her wedding dress. She had found one on sale at Foster's in Harkside for two pounds ten shillings. It was a simple white affair, neither voluminous nor trailing half a mile of material, both elegant and tasteful. She did, however, make her own veil out of lace, which wasn't rationed. Whether she had set them with sugar and water or not, I don't know, but her glistening blond sausage curls tumbled to her shoulders in an even more dazzling array than usual.

Gloria had bought her wedding dress almost as soon as Mother gave her blessing, so she was all right, but wouldn't you know it, clothes rationing came into force the Sunday before the wedding. Luckily, we had all got used to mending and making do by then. Matthew dug out his only suit and we had it cleaned and pressed. It would have cost him almost an entire half-year's clothes ration to get newly kitted out. Mother put on her best flowered frock, adding a belt here and a little lace there, just to make it look new, and she bought a new hat for the occasion, hats being one of the few items of clothing, along with lace and ribbon, *not* rationed.

Cynthia Garmen and I were bridesmaids and we wore matching taffeta dresses made out of some old curtains. Just for an extra-special touch, I cut up some lace to trim our knickers. I don't know about Cynthia – she certainly never said anything – but the things made my thighs itch through the entire service.

It was the seventh of June, 1941, and a lovely day, with clouds like trails of spilled milk spelling out Arabic characters in the sky.

The ceremony went smoothly. The Reverend Graham conducted the service with his usual oratorical skill and gravity. Barry Naylor, Matthew's best man, didn't forget the ring, and they all got their lines right. Nobody fainted, though it was exceedingly hot in the church. Mother shed a few tears. There was no confetti, of course, there being a paper shortage, and there was something else different that nagged away at the back of my mind, but I didn't remember what it was until much later that night.

We stood outside for photographs. Film was expensive and hard to obtain, but we weren't going to let Matthew's wedding day go by without some sort of visual record, and one of his friends from the Home Guard, Jack Cheswick, fancied himself as a bit of an amateur photographer. Mr Truewell, the chemist, was obliging, and the film cost us only twenty Passing Cloud cigarettes. Luckily for us, the pictures turned out all right, though the album got lost in one of the many moves that came later.

We held the reception in the church hall. Of course, I had done most of the catering myself, though I was able to leave the last-minute assembly to my helpers, Sue and Olive. We had to apply in Leeds for an allocation of rations, and Sue, who had got married herself just a couple of months earlier, had warned me it was advisable to double your estimate of the number of guests. Consequently, I said we were expecting a hundred people. Even so, we only got two ounces of tea, which we had to eke out with some of our own ration to make it even drinkable.

Luckily, our first American food on lend-lease had just arrived in the shop, so we had Spam for sandwiches, and tinned sausage meat, which was wonderful for making sausage rolls because you could also use the fat left in the tin to make the pastry. There wasn't much to drink, but we did manage to get a keg of watery beer from the Shoulder of Mutton and there was some sweet sherry we had been keeping in our cupboard. Mr Stanhope supplied a bottle of gin and some wine. The wedding cake was the biggest disappointment. Icing had been banned nearly a year earlier, so we had to make do with a cardboard-and-crêpe fake. Still, it looked nice in the photographs.

The highlight of the reception was the band. Matthew's friend, Richard Bright, played trumpet with the Victor Pearson Dance Band, so we got at least half the band to come and play for their supper.

Gloria and Matthew led off the dancing, of course, and a lump came to my throat as I watched them. After that, it was a free-for-all. The music was all right if you liked that sort of thing, but I found it all either too noisy and frenetic or too mushy and sentimental.

I talked to Michael Stanhope for a while and he remarked on how beautiful he thought Gloria looked and what a lucky man Matthew was. For once, he didn't say anything nasty about the war. Betty Warden, who had managed to wangle an invitation somehow, sat with her nose in the air most of the night, disapproving of everything and everyone, but I must say that when she danced with William Goodall, she seemed like a different person. So did he, for that matter. Almost human, both of them.

Alice Hill was cheerful and talkative as ever, and I rather think she developed a fancy for Eric Poole that very night. They certainly danced closely together often enough.

Gloria came up to me at one point – she had changed now into a long flared skirt and pink blouse – with a little sweat beaded on her brow and upper lip from dancing too energetically. Her eyes were shining. I think she'd had a drink or two.

She rested her soft, delicate hand on my arm. 'This is the happiest day of my life, Gwen,' she said. 'Do you know, just six months ago I thought I would never laugh or dance again. But thanks to you, your mother and, of course, dear Matt . . . Thank you, Gwen, thank you so much.' Then she leaned forward quickly and clasped me to her bosom, giving me a little peck on the cheek. It was awkward, and with her being so small, I had to bend. I could smell the gin on her breath. I'm sure I blushed, but she didn't remark on it.

'I haven't seen you dancing,' she said.

I shook my head. 'I don't. I mean, I can't.'

'I'll teach you,' she said. 'Not right now, of course . . . but I'll teach you. Will you let me?'

I nodded stupidly. 'Yes. If you want.'

'It's the *least* I can do.'

Then she excused herself and went to talk to Mother and Cynthia, smiling on everyone she passed with those Hardy-heroine eyes of hers.

I did my bit, moving from table to table, being polite to my distant relations, removing Uncle Gerald's hand from my knee without drawing attention to the fact that it was there.

The local people started to drift home around sunset to make sure they had all got their blackout curtains in place. Our relations were staying with friends in Harkside, so they began to leave, too, before it got too dark to see their way across the fields.

Matthew and Gloria went to Bridge Cottage for their first night together as man and wife. Whether this was their first *time* together, I have no idea. It may be hard to believe now, when everyone seems to be very sophisticated about sex, but I knew very little of such things back then. I had no idea, for example, what men and women actually *did* when they made babies.

The next day they were going to Scarborough for a three-day honeymoon. Matthew had already booked a room at a guest-house in St Mary's, near the castle. After that, it was back to university for Matthew – with his finals coming up soon – and back to Top Hill Farm for Gloria, though she would live at Bridge Cottage and walk or cycle to and from work.

Mother was talking to Sue and Olive at the door when I finally excused myself through tiredness and set off home alone. It had been a long, hard day.

Though it was late, a deep purple-and-vermilion glow

still lit the sky in the west, behind the dark mill. The streets were quiet, though I could still hear music coming from the church hall behind me. Back home, I made sure the blackout curtains were drawn tightly, then, weary to the bone, I went to bed.

It was only when I was on the very edge of sleep and heard the thrumming and droning of the bombers taking off from Rowan Woods RAF Base that I remembered what had bothered me so much outside the church after the wedding.

Not only had there been no confetti, there had been no wedding bells, either. All the church bells had been silent since 1940 and were only supposed to ring if there was an invasion. The thing was, I hadn't even noticed at first because I had got so used to the silence.

I thought that was very sad, and I cried myself to sleep that night.

•

Annie paused with the dusty file folder in her hands when she heard footsteps on the stairs. She hoped it would be PC Gould bringing her a cup of tea, so she was surprised when she saw, instead, DCI Banks.

'Inspector Harmond told me you were down here,' Banks said.

Annie turned her nose up and gestured around at the musty-smelling, ill-lit basement room. 'Welcome to Central Records,' she said. 'You can see how often we dip into our history around here.'

'Don't worry. One day it'll all be on the computer.'

'When I'm long since dead and buried.'

Banks smiled as he ducked under an overhead pipe and walked over to join her. 'Anything yet?'

'Quite a lot, as a matter of fact. I've been on the phone most of the day, and I was just checking some missing-persons files.'

'And?'

'It's a bit of a confusing period for that sort of thing. Just after the war. There were so many changes, so many people coming and going. Anyway, most of the ones who went missing seemed to turn up eventually, either dead or alive, or in the colonies. There are a couple of young women who fit the general description still unaccounted for. I'll follow up on them.'

'Fancy a pint? The Black Swan?'

Annie smiled. 'You took the words right out of my mouth.'

What a relief. If she had been hoping for a cup of tea, the prospect of a pint of Swan's Down was even more appealing. She had been in the stifling basement for the best part of the afternoon, and her mouth was full of dust, her contact lenses beginning to dry out. And it *was* gone five on a Friday afternoon.

Comfortably ensconced on a padded bench just a few minutes later, legs stretched out and crossed at the ankles, pint already half finished, Annie smacked her lips. If she were a cat, she would have been purring.

'I checked the Voters Register first,' she said, 'but the clerk in the council office told me it was frozen at the start of the war. The last person they've got listed for Bridge Cottage is a Miss Violet Croft. I had a bit more luck with the Land Registry. Violet Croft rented the cottage from the Clifford estate, and the manager kept impeccable records. She lived there between the fourteenth of September, 1919, and the third of July, 1940, so she must be the old lady Ruby Kettering remembered, the one the village kids thought was a witch. The cottage remained empty until June 1941, when a Mr and Mrs Shackleton took up residence there. It might have been requisitioned for the billeting of evacuees or military personnel in the interim period, but there was no record of that, and there's no way of finding out.'

'I doubt that many places stayed empty for long during the war,' said Banks. 'Maybe some soldiers got billeted there, killed a local tart in a drunken orgy and then decided to cover their tracks?'

'It's possible.' Annie gave a slight shiver.

'We're talking about wartime,' Banks went on. 'Army camps and air force bases sprang up overnight, like mushrooms. Evacuees came and went. It was easy to disappear, change identity, slip through the cracks.'

'But people had identity cards and ration books. The council clerk told me. He said there was a National Registry at the beginning of the war, and everyone got identity cards.'

'I imagine those sort of things were open to a fiddle easily enough. Who knows, maybe we're dealing with a Nazi spy done in by the secret service?'

Annie laughed. 'Mata Hari?'

'Maybe. Anyway, what happened to Miss Violet Croft?'

Annie flipped over a page in her notebook. 'I dropped by Saint Jude's next and found the young curate very helpful. They've got all the old parish registry records and magazines from Saint Bart's stored in the vestry there. Boxes of them. Violet Croft, spinster of the parish, died in July 1940 of pneumonia. She was seventy-seven.'

'That lets her out. What about the Shackletons?'

'Much more interesting. They were married at Saint Bart's on the seventh of June, 1941. The husband's name was Matthew Stephen Shackleton, the wife's maiden name Gloria Kathleen Stringer. The witnesses were Gwynneth Shackleton and Cynthia Garmen.'

'Were they Hobb's End residents?'

'Matthew Shackleton was. His parents lived at 38 High Street. They ran the newsagent's shop. The bride's listed as being from London, parents deceased.'

'Big place,' Banks muttered. 'How old was she?'

'Nineteen. Born the seventeenth of September, 1921.'

'Interesting. That would put her within Dr Williams's age range by the end of the war.'

'Exactly.'

'Any mention of children?'

'No. I looked through the registry of baptisms, but there's nothing there. Was he certain about that, do you think?'

'He seemed to be. You saw the pitting for yourself.'

'I wouldn't know a parturition scar from a hole in the ground. It *could* have been a post-mortem injury, couldn't it? I mean, these things are often far from accurate.'

'It could have been. We'll check with Dr Glendenning after he's done the post-mortem. Do you know what? I'm beginning to get a vision of St Catherine's House looming large in your future.'

Annie groaned. Checking birth, marriage and death certificates was one of the most boring jobs a detective could get. The only positive aspect was that you got to go to London, but even that was offset by the department's lack of willingness to grant expenses for an overnight stay. No time to check out the shops.

'Any luck with the education authorities?' Banks asked.

'No. They said they lost the Hobb's End records, or misplaced them. Same with the doctors and the dentist.

The ones who practised in Hobb's End are all dead, and
their practices went with them. Records, too, I imagine. I
think we can say goodbye to that line of inquiry.'

'Pity. What does your instinct tell you, Annie?'

Annie pointed her thumb towards her chest. '*Moi?*'

'Yes, you. I want your feelings on the case so far.'

Annie was surprised. No senior officer had ever asked
for her *feelings* before, for her *feminine intuition*. Banks
was certainly different. 'Well, sir,' she said, 'for a start, I
don't think it's a stranger killing.'

'Why not?'

'You asked for my feelings, not logic.'

'Okay.'

'It *looks* domestic. Like that bloke who killed his wife
and sailed off to Canada.'

'Dr Crippen?'

'That's the one. I saw Donald Pleasence play him on
telly. Creepy.'

'Crippen buried his wife under the cellar.'

'Cellar. Outbuilding. Same difference.'

'All right, I take your point. Conclusion?'

'Victim: Gloria Shackleton.'

'Killer?'

'Husband, or someone else who knew her.'

'Motive?'

'God knows. Jealousy, sex, money. Pick one. Does it
matter?'

'Did you ask Mrs Kettering if she kept in touch with
anyone else who lived in Hobb's End?'

'Sorry, sir. It slipped my mind.'

'Ask her. Maybe we can track down some people who
actually *knew* the Shackletons. Who knows where the old

residents live now? We might even get a weekend in Paris or New York out of this.'

Annie noticed Banks avert his eyes. Was he flirting? 'That would be nice,' she said, sounding as neutral as possible. 'Anyway, for what it's worth, I think it's more the kind of thing someone who lived there, or near there, would do. It was a good hiding place. I don't think anyone could have foreseen the reservoir, or the drought. Not that it would matter, really. I mean, if Adam Kelly hadn't been playing truant and larking about on that roof, we'd never have found out. You can't anticipate an accident of fate like that.'

'*Blackout curtains*.' Banks slapped his palm on the table.

'Come again, sir?'

'Blackout curtains. It's something John Webb told me. He said they found some heavy black material with the body. I didn't make the connection at the time, but it makes sense now. The body was wrapped in blackout curtains, Annie. And Geoff Turner mentioned wartime dental work. When did the blackout end?'

'At dawn, I suppose.'

Banks smiled. 'Idiot. I mean when was it no longer required?'

'I don't know.'

'We can find out easily enough, I suppose. Either the blackout material was left over – which I'd guess was unlikely, because from what I remember my mother telling me, *nothing* was left over during the war – or it was no longer needed for its original purpose, which might help narrow down the time of the murder even more. But I certainly think we're dealing with a wartime crime, and Gloria Shackleton fits the bill as victim.'

'Brilliant, Holmes.'

'Elementary. Anyway, before we go any further, let's find out all we can about her. What was her maiden name again?'

'Stringer, sir. Gloria Stringer.'

'Right. We already know she's about the right age, and we know she lived in Bridge Cottage during the war. She hasn't shown up as missing?'

'Not in any records I've seen. And hers was the first name I looked for.'

'Okay. If you can find no trace of her existence in the local records after, say, 1946, then we could narrow things down a bit.' Banks looked at his watch. 'How about something to eat? I'm getting hungry. I don't want to eat here again. Are there any decent restaurants in Harkside?'

Annie paused for a moment, thinking of every restaurant where she had found nothing she could eat but a salad, or meat and two veg without the meat, then she gave in to the little surge of devil-may-care excitement that tingled through her and said, 'Well, sir, there's always my place.'

•

After the honeymoon, Gloria continued to report for work at the farm every day at eight o'clock and she wasn't home until five or later. On weekends, she was at Bridge Cottage, looking fresh and beautiful, ready for Matthew's arrival. Matthew passed his engineering degree, graduating with first-class honours, as I knew he would, and started his military training at Catterick, which wasn't too far away.

Gloria had managed, I discovered one evening, to barter her needlework skills for an extra half-day off work at the farm, which gave her the full weekend. Her local area supervisor would be none the wiser, so long as the Kilnseys didn't tell. And while Gloria kept them in mended clothes they were hardly likely to do that.

Most days I was busy with the shop. In my spare time I was involved in the Harkside Amateur Players' production of a new J. B. Priestley play, *When We Are Married*, so I spent a lot of time in rehearsal.

Despite all this, we managed to get to the pictures in Harkside together a few times. Gloria just loved films and sometimes she didn't even have time to change out of her uniform before pedalling at breakneck speed to meet me outside the Lyceum or the Lyric. She always managed some little eccentricity in her appearance, like wearing a bright pink ribbon or a yellow blouse instead of the regulation green.

That summer, for the first time, we had double summer-time, which meant it stayed light much later. In autumn and winter, though, it was always dark when we had to go home. Though it was only a mile or so from Harkside to Hobb's End across the fields, there was no marked path or road, and on a cloudy, moonless night you could wander for hours in the pitch-darkness and miss the place entirely. Unless there was a bright moon, we had to walk the long way home: all the way up Long Hill and then along The Edge, careful not to fall into Harksmere Reservoir.

Because it was much bigger, Harkside was eerier than Hobb's End in the blackout. For a start, they had street lamps, which we didn't, and though they weren't lit, of course, each one of them now had a white stripe painted up its length to help you see your way in the dark, the same way there were stripes of white paint along the kerbsides. People had also put the little dabs of luminous paint on their doorbells, which glowed like fireflies all along the streets.

Sometimes we accepted a lift with some of the RAF boys

from Rowan Woods, and we even became quite friendly with a couple of Canadian airmen attached to the RAF: Mark, from Toronto, and Stephen, from Winnipeg. Mark was the handsomest one, and I could have listened to his soft, smooth accent all night long. I could tell he liked Gloria by the way he looked at her. He even contrived to touch her in small ways, like taking her hand to help her step into the Jeep, and touching the spot between her shoulders if he opened a door for her and ushered her through. Gloria seemed amused by it all.

Stephen had a high, squeaky voice, ears that stuck out and hair that seemed glued on like handfuls of straw, but he was nice enough. Sometimes we let them take us to the pictures and they were both very well behaved.

For Gloria's twentieth birthday, in September, I took her to Brunton's Café on Long Hill, where we gorged ourselves on grilled sausage with mashed potatoes, braised butter-beans, followed by jam roll and custard. Matthew couldn't be with us because it was a weekday, but Gloria showed me the locket he had already given her as a birthday present. It was beautiful: dark gold with their names entwined on the heart and a photograph, cut out from one of the wedding pictures, of the two of them inside. After tea, holding our tummies, we went to the Lyceum to see *Ziegfeld Girl*, starring Jimmy Stewart and Lana Turner. It was so memorable that the next day I couldn't remember a single melody.

It was Gloria's choice, of course. Unfortunately, our tastes couldn't have been more different. Gloria liked empty-headed Hollywood musicals and romantic comedies with beautiful stars and handsome leading men, whereas I preferred something with a bit of meat on its bones, an adaptation of the classics, say. More often than not, I preferred to stay at home and listen to dramas on the Home

Service, where I very much enjoyed Mrs Gaskell's *Cranford* and Thackeray's *Vanity Fair*, among others.

Anyway, it was Gloria's birthday. She also liked the Lyceum best because of the red plush seats and the way the organ came rising up slowly and majestically through its trap-door, with the famous Teddy Marston, usually playing 'The White Cliffs of Dover', 'Shine On Victory Moon', or some such patriotic tune. Gloria would have tears in her eyes when she listened to that sort of thing. Then the lights dimmed and the heavy red velvet curtains parted slowly.

Sometimes Alice, Cynthia and Betty came to the pictures with us, even Michael Stanhope on occasion. While he often delighted us with his wicked critical commentary on the way home, he disappointed me in leaning more towards Gloria's sort of film than towards something with a bit more substance. After all, he *was* supposed to be a serious artist.

I often wondered what he and Gloria found to talk about when they went drinking together in the Shoulder of Mutton. I was too young to go with them, of course, not that they ever invited me. Anyway, I suppose they must have had long, intricate conversations about the deeper meaning of Hollywood musicals.

Matthew and Gloria tried to furnish Bridge Cottage as best they could. This was before the Government banned most furniture production, but even then the good stuff was either expensive or unavailable. You had to scrounge for the simplest of things, like curtain rods and coat hooks. They went to auctions some weekends, bought an old sideboard or a wardrobe here, a dresser there, and bit by bit they managed to furnish the house in a tasteful if not terribly elegant way. They made a home out of Bridge Cottage.

Gloria's pride and joy was the radiogram they bought from the Coopers after their son, John, was killed when the

Prince of Wales was sunk just before Christmas. It had been John's pride and joy, and his mum and dad couldn't bear to keep it around the house after he was gone.

Gloria honoured her promise to give me dancing lessons and I spent an hour or so over at Bridge Cottage each weekend while Matthew read the newspaper after dinner. It felt strange having her put her arms around me. Her body felt soft and I could smell her perfume, *Evening in Paris*. She was a good teacher, but with her being so much shorter it was awkward at first, having her lead me. I soon got used to it. I was a good pupil, too. Over the next couple of weeks I learned the waltz, the quickstep and the foxtrot. I actually tried out my skills at a Bonfire Night dance in the Harkside Mechanics Institute. We might not have been able to have bonfires during the war, but we still managed to celebrate Guy Fawkes Night. Anyway, I did very well at dancing, and that worked wonders for my confidence.

By Christmas, Matthew had almost finished his training, and there was talk of a posting. I asked him if he was going to be a commissioned officer and he said he didn't think so. He had been for an interview and was upset at the way the board asked him about what his parents did for a living and how often he rode with the local hunt. He said there wasn't much hope of a shopkeeper's son getting a commission.

It was also that Christmas, at a party Gloria and Matthew held, when I got my first real inkling of Gloria's problems with men.

•

Annie's place turned out to be a squat, narrow terrace cottage at the centre of a labyrinth. Banks left his car parked by the green and walked through so many twisting narrow streets and ginnels, by backyards where washing hung out on lines in the evening sun, where children played and dogs barked behind sturdy gates, that he was lost within seconds.

'Why do I keep thinking I should have left a piece of thread attached to the Black Swan?' he said as he followed her down a snicket narrow enough to pass through only in single file.

Annie cast a glance over her shoulder and smiled. 'Like Theseus, you mean? I hope you don't think I'm the Minotaur just because I live at the centre of all this?'

Banks's mythology was a bit rusty, but he remembered being impressed by an ancient vase he had seen on a school trip to the British Museum. It depicted Ariadne outside the Labyrinth holding one end of the thread and Theseus at its centre killing the Minotaur.

He had even seen what was left of the Labyrinth at the Palace of Knossos on Crete, where a pedantic guide inflicted with a serious case of synonymitis had explained it all to Sandra and him as they tried to hold back their giggles. 'And this is King Minos's throne, his regal seat, his chair of office . . . And they carried her body to the hill, the rise, the tor, the mountain.' He remembered the olive trees with their silver-green oily leaves and the orange trees lining the road from Heraklion.

But now wasn't the time to be thinking about Sandra.

He was about to say that he thought of Annie more as Ariadne, seeing as she was probably the only one who could get him out of there, but he bit his tongue. Considering what transpired between Theseus and Ariadne on Naxos, it didn't seem like a very good idea.

He followed Annie deeper into the labyrinth.

Her keys were jingling in her hand now. 'Almost there,' she said, glancing back at him, then she opened a high wooden gate in a stone wall, led him through a small flagged yard and in the back door.

'Where do you park?' Banks asked.

Annie dropped her keys on the kitchen table and laughed. 'A long way away. Look, it's tiny, there's not much of a view and very little light. But guess what? It's cheap, and it's mine. Well, it will be when I've paid off the mortgage. You must have been a DS once?'

'A DC, too.' Banks remembered the early days, scraping and saving to make ends meet, especially when Tracy and Brian were little and Sandra had to take extended periods off work. There were no maternity benefits back then. Not for dental receptionists, anyway. Even now, as a DCI, it was difficult making payments on the cottage. He also had to furnish the place by driving around to local auctions and car-boot sales. There would be no Greek holiday this year. 'At least you get overtime,' he said. 'You probably make more than me.'

'In Harkside? You must be joking.' Annie led him through to the living room. It was small but cosy, and she had decorated much of it in whites, lemons and creams because of the lack of outside light. As a result, the room seemed airy and cheerful. There was just enough space for a small white three-piece suite, the settee of which would probably seat two very thin people, a TV, mini-stereo and a small bookcase under the window. Several miniature watercolours hung on the walls. Local scenes, mostly. Banks recognized Semerwater, Aysgarth Falls and Rich-mond Castle. There was also one oil portrait of a young woman with flowing pre-Raphaelite hair and laughing eyes.

'Who painted these?' he asked.

'I did. Most of them.'

'They're very good.'

Annie seemed embarrassed. 'I don't think so. Not really. I mean, they're competent, but . . .' She put her hand to her head and swept back her hair. 'Anyway, look, I feel really grubby after being down in that basement. I'm going up for a quick shower first, then I'll start dinner. It won't take long. Make yourself at home. Open the window if you're too warm. There's plenty of beer in the fridge. Help yourself.' Then she turned and left the room. Banks heard stairs creak as she walked up.

This woman was an enigma, he thought. She had a DCI, her boss, as a guest in her house, yet nothing in her behaviour towards him indicated a deferential relationship. She was the same always, with everyone, not adapting herself to the various roles people play in life. He imagined she would even be the same with Jimmy Riddle. Not that she'd invite that bastard into her home, Banks hoped. He heard the shower start. Though it was small, the cottage wasn't particularly old – not like his own – and it had an upstairs bathroom and toilet. Even so, he guessed Annie must have had the shower installed herself, because it certainly wouldn't have come with the original building.

First, he did what he always did when left alone in a new room; he nosed around. He couldn't help it. Curiosity was part of his nature. He didn't open drawers or read private mail, not unless he thought he was dealing with a criminal, but he liked to look at books, choice of music and the general lie of the land.

Annie's living room was fairly Spartan. It wasn't that she didn't own books or CDs, but that she didn't have many of either. He got the impression that she might have had to pare down her existence at one time and everything that remained was important to her. There seemed to be no chaff. Unlike his own collection, where the mistakes piled up alongside the hidden gems. Discs he never listened to shared shelf space with some that were almost worn out.

First, he crouched down and checked the CD titles in the cabinet under the stereo. It was an odd collection: Gregorian chants, Don Cherry's *Eternal Now* and several 'ambient' pieces by Brian Eno. There was also an extensive blues collection, from Mississippi John Hurt to John Mayall. Next to these stood a few pop and folk titles: Emmylou Harris's *The Wrecking Ball*, Kate and Anna McGarrigle, some k. d. lang.

The books mainly centred around Eastern philosophy; it was a real sixties treasure trove, considering that Annie was a nineties woman. Banks remembered some of the titles. He had come across them first in Jem's room, in the Notting Hill days, and he had even borrowed and read some of them: Baba Ram Dass's *Be Here Now*; Gurdjieff's *Meetings With Remarkable Men*; Ouspensky, Carlos Castaneda, Thomas Merton, Alan Watts, and old blue-covered Pelican paperbacks about yoga, Zen and meditation.

Seeing them again took him right back to the dim, candle-lit room with the melting-butter walls and the jasmine joss sticks, to the first time he smoked hash, with Arlo Guthrie's 'Alice's Restaurant' on the stereo; earnest, all-night arguments about Marx and Marcuse, changing the system, love and revolution, with Banks, more often than not, playing the straight man, the devil's advocate. Gentle, sweet-natured Jem, his gaunt face always in shadows, dark hair spilling over his narrow shoulders, his soft, husky voice and his unwillingness to kill even the mice that sometimes walked across the room right in front of them as they talked. His record collection: *Rainbow Bridge*, *Bitches Brew*, *Live Dead*, *Joy of a Toy*.

Strange days. Old days.

Back then, Banks had spent half his time studying industrial psychology and cost accounting and the other half listening to Miles Davis, Jimi Hendrix, Roland Kirk and The Soft Machine. One way led to security and what his parents wanted; the other led to uncertainty and God only knew what else. Poverty and drug addiction, as like as not. Hard to believe now that there had been a time when it was all balanced on a razor's edge, when he could have gone either way.

Then Jem died and Banks joined the police, a third option he hadn't considered before, even in his wildest dreams.

The shower stopped, and a few seconds later Banks heard the roar of a hair-dryer. Shaking off the memories that seemed to cling to his mind like cobwebs, he wandered into the kitchen. Like the living room, it was decorated in light colours, white tiles for the most part, with chocolate brown around the work area, just for contrast. In addition to the small oven, fridge, sink and countertops, there was a dining table. It could probably seat about four comfortably, he guessed.

Banks opened the fridge and took out a bottle of Black Sheep. He found an opener in one of the drawers and a pint glass in one of the cupboards. Carefully, he poured out the beer so it had just enough head on it, then he took a sip and went back into the living room. The hair-dryer stopped, and he could hear Annie walking around upstairs. He took *Eternal Now* from its jewel case and put it in the CD player. He had heard of Don Cherry, a jazz trumpeter who used to play with Ornette Coleman, but didn't actually know his work.

The music started with strummed chords on oddly

tuned stringed instruments, then a deep, echoey flute-like instrument entered. Banks turned down the volume, picked up the CD liner notes and sat down to read while he waited for Annie, abandoning himself to the weird combinations of wooden saxophones, Indian harmoniums and Polynesian gamelans.

Before the first track had finished, Annie breezed into the room exuding freshly scrubbed warmth.

'I never took you for a Don Cherry fan,' she said, a wicked grin on her face.

'Life is full of surprises. I like it.'

'I thought you were an opera buff.'

'Been asking around?'

'Just station gossip. I'll start dinner now, if you want.'

Banks smiled. 'Fine with me.'

She disappeared into the kitchen. 'You can keep me company,' she called out over her shoulder.

Banks put the CD case back on the shelf and carried his beer through. He sat down at the kitchen table. Annie was bending over pulling vegetables out of the fridge. The jeans looked good on her.

'Pasta okay?' she asked, half turning her head.

'Great. It's a long time since I've had any home cooking. Mostly these days it's been either pub grub or something quick and easy from Marks and Sparks.'

'Ah, the lonely eater's friends.'

Banks laughed. It was funny, and rather sad, he had often noticed, how you saw so many young, single men and women wandering around the Marks food section just after five on a weeknight, reaching for the prawn vindaloo, then changing their minds, going instead for the single portion of chicken Kiev and the carton of mixed vegetables. He supposed it might be a good place to pick up a girl.

Annie filled a large pan with water, added a little salt and oil, then set it on the gas ring. She didn't waste a gesture as she washed and chopped mushrooms, shallots, garlic and courgettes. There was a certain economic grace to her movements that Banks found quite hypnotic; she seemed to possess a natural, centred quality that put him at ease.

She went to the kitchen cupboard, took down a bottle of red wine and uncorked it.

'Want some?'

Banks held up his beer. 'I'll finish this first.'

Annie poured herself a generous glass. Soon the oil was hot in the frying pan and she was dropping the vegetables in a handful at a time. When they were done, she added a cup or two of tinned tomatoes and a handful of herbs. Banks decided to make cooking his next project, after he had fixed up the cottage. Something else to keep depression at bay. He liked food, so it made sense to learn how to cook it properly now that he was alone.

About the time Banks finished his beer, Annie announced that dinner was ready and delivered two steaming plates to the table. Don Cherry finished, and she put on Emmylou Harris, whose voice seemed to catch on sharp notches inside her throat before it came out, singing about loneliness, loss, pain. All things Banks could relate to. He ground pepper and grated Parmesan on to the pasta and tucked in. After a couple of bites, he complimented Annie.

'See,' she said. 'It's not all salads and tofu. You learn to be more inventive in the kitchen when you're a vegetarian.'

'I can tell.'

'Wine?'

'Please.'

Annie brought over the bottle of Sainsbury's Bulgarian Merlot, refilled her glass and poured one for Banks. 'Plenty more where that came from,' she said. 'You know, I'd really like to find out more about this Hobb's End artist, Michael Stanhope.'

'Why? Because you think he's connected to the case?'

'Well, he might be, mightn't he? He *was* living in Hobb's End during the war. Maybe he knew the Shackleton woman. There may be other paintings. They might tell us something.'

'They might,' Banks agreed. 'Though I'm not sure how far art could be trusted as evidence, even if he painted the murder itself.'

Annie smiled. 'Not technically, perhaps. But artists often distort reality to reveal the truth about it.'

'Do you believe that?'

Annie's eyes, the colour of milk chocolate, shone in the failing light. 'Yes,' she said. 'I do. Not about my own work. As I said, I'm technically competent, but I lack whatever it is that makes a great artist. Vision. Passion. Intensity. Insanity. I don't know. Probably what most people call genius. But the true artist's reality is every bit as valid as any other. Perhaps more so in some ways because an artist struggles to see more deeply, to illuminate.'

'A lot of art is far from illuminating.'

'Yes, but that's often because the subject, the truth he's trying to get at, is so elusive that only symbols or vague images will do to approach it. Don't get me wrong. I'm not saying that artists are always trying to get some sort of deep message across. They're not preachers. What I'm saying is that Stanhope obviously perceived something odd about Hobb's End, something that went below the surface, beyond the superficial ideas of village life. He saw something *evil* there and maybe something redemptive in the children.'

'Isn't that a bit far-fetched? Maybe it was just because there was a war coming?'

'I'm not trying to make out he was a visionary. Just that he saw something a lot of other people would either not see or would gloss over. He really *looked* and maybe he saw something that might be useful to us. Damn!'

'What?'

'Oh, I just spilled some pasta sauce on my T-shirt, that's all.' She grinned and rubbed at the red mark over her breast. That only made it worse. 'I always was a messy eater.'

'I won't tell anyone.'

'Thanks. Where was I?'

'The artist's vision.'

'Right. It's got nothing to do with personality. In life, Stanhope might well have been a mean, lecherous, drunken slob. Believe me, I've known a lot of artists, and many of them have been exactly that. Talk about groups living up to their stereotypes.'

Banks sipped some wine. Emmylou Harris was singing about wearing something pretty and white. Banks thought he could detect Neil Young's high-pitched warble in the background. 'You seem to know a lot about the subject,' he said. 'Any particular reason?'

Annie fell silent for a moment, looking down at her empty plate, moving the fork around in her hand. Finally, she said in a quiet voice, 'My father's an artist.'

'Is he well known?'

'Not really. In some circles, perhaps.' She looked up and smiled crookedly. 'He'll never go down in history as one of the greats, if that's what you mean.'

'He's still living, I assume?'

'Ray? Oh, yes. He's just turned fifty-two. He was only twenty when I was born.'

'Does he have what it takes to be a great artist?'

'To some extent. But you have to remember, there's a big, big gap between someone like my dad and Van Gogh or Picasso. It's all relative.'

'What about your mother?'

Again, Annie was silent a few moments. 'She died,' she said at last. 'When I was six. I don't really remember her very well. I wish I could, but I can't.'

'That's sad. I'm sorry.'

'More wine?'

'Please.'

Annie poured.

'That oil portrait in the living room, is it your mother?'

Annie nodded.

'Your father painted it?'

'Yes.'

'It's very good. She was a beautiful woman. You look a lot like her.'

It was almost dark outside now. Annie hadn't put on any lights, so Banks couldn't see her expression.

'Where did you grow up?' he asked.

'St Ives.'

'Nice place.'

'You know it?'

'I've been there on holiday a couple of times. Years ago, when I worked on the Met. It's a bit far from here.'

'I don't get down as often as I should. Maybe you remember it was a magnet for hippies in the sixties? It became something of an artists' colony.'

'I remember.'

'My father lived there even before that. Over the years he's done all kinds of odd jobs to support his art. He might have even rented you a deck-chair on the beach. Now he paints local landscapes and sells them to tourists. Does some glass engraving too. He's quite successful at it.'

'So he makes a decent living?'

'Yes. He doesn't have to rent out the deck-chairs any more.'

'He brought you up alone?'

Annie pushed her hair back. 'Well, not really. I mean, yes, in the sense that my mother was dead, but we lived in a sort of artists' colony on an old farm just outside town, so there were always lots of other people around. My extended family, you might call them. Ray's been living with Jasmine for nearly twenty years now.'

'It sounds like a strange set-up.'

'Only to someone who hasn't experienced it. It seemed pefectly normal to me. It was the other kids who seemed strange. The ones with mothers and fathers.'

'Did you get teased a lot at school?'

'Tormented. Some of the locals were very intolerant. Thought we were having orgies every night, doing drugs, worshipping the devil, the usual stuff. Actually, though there always seemed to be some pot around, they couldn't have been further from the truth. There were a few wild ones – that kind of free, experimental way of life always attracts a few unstable types – but on the whole it was a pretty good environment to grow up in. Plus I got a great education in the arts – and not from school.'

'What made you join the police?'

'The village bobby took my virginity.'

'*Seriously.*'

Annie laughed and poured more wine. 'It's true. He did.

His name was Rob. He came up to see us once, looking for someone who'd passed through, one of the occasional undesirables. He was good-looking. I was seventeen. He noticed me. It seemed a suitable act of rebellion.'

'Against your par— your father?'

'Against all of them. Oh, don't get me wrong, I didn't hate them or anything. It was just that I'd had enough of that lifestyle by then. There were too many people around all the time, nowhere to escape to. Too much talk and not enough done. You could never get any privacy. That's why I value it so much now. And how many times can a grown person listen to "White Rabbit"?'

Banks laughed. 'I feel the same way about "Nessun Dorma".'

'Anyway, Rob seemed solid, dependable, more sure of himself and what he believed in.'

'Was he?'

'Yes. We went out until I went to university in Exeter. Then he turned up there a year or so later as a DC. He introduced me to some of his friends and we sort of started going out again. I suppose they found me a bit weird. After all, I didn't throw out the baby with the bathwater. I still had a lot of my father's values, and I was into yoga and meditation even back then, when nobody else was. I didn't really fit in anywhere. I don't know why, but being a detective sounded exciting. *Different.* When you get right down to it, most jobs are so bloody boring. I'd thought of becoming a teacher, but I changed my mind and joined the force. It was a bit impulsive, I'll admit.'

Banks wanted to ask her why she was in a dead-end place like Harkside, but he sensed that this wasn't the moment. At least he could ask a leading question and see if she was willing to be led. 'How has it worked out?'

'It's tough for a woman. But things are what you make them. I'm a feminist, but I'm the sort who just likes to get on with it rather than whine about what's wrong with the system. Maybe that comes from my dad. He goes his own way. Anyway, you know all about what it's like, about how *unexciting* it is most of the time. And how bloody boring it can be.'

'True enough. What happened to Rob?'

'He got killed during an armed drugs bust three years later. Poor sod. His gun jammed.'

'I'm sorry.'

Annie put her hand to her forehead, then fanned it in front of her face. 'Ooh, I'm hot. Listen to me go on. I haven't talked to anyone like this in ages.'

'I wouldn't mind a cigarette. Would you like to stand outside with me? Cool down a bit, if it's possible?'

'Okay.'

They went out into the backyard. It was a warm night, though there were signs of a breeze beginning to stir. Annie stood beside him. He could smell her scent. He lit up, inhaled and blew out a plume of dark smoke.

'It was like drawing teeth,' he said, 'getting you to talk about your personal life.'

'I'm not used to it. I'm like you in a lot of ways.'

'What do you mean?'

'Well, how much have you told me about your past?'

'What do you want to know?'

'That's not what I mean. You just wouldn't think of telling people about yourself, of letting someone in, would you? It's not in your nature. You're a loner, like me. I don't just mean now, because you're . . .'

'Because my wife left me?'

'Right. Not just because you're *physically* alone or

because you're living alone. I mean in your nature, deep inside. Even when you *were* married. I think you've got a lonely, isolated nature. It colours the way you see the world, the detachment you feel. I'm not explaining it very well, am I? I think I'm the same. I can be alone in a crowded room. I'll bet you can be, too.'

Banks thought about what Annie had said as he smoked. It was what Sandra had said when they had their final argument, what he had refused to admit was the truth. There was something in him that always stood apart, that she couldn't reach and he wouldn't offer. It wasn't just the Job and its demands, but something deeper: a central core of loneliness. He had been like that even as a child. An observer. Always on the outside, even when he played with others. As Annie said, it was a part of his nature, and he didn't think he could change it if he tried.

'Maybe you're right,' he said. 'Funny thing, though. I always thought I was a simple family man.'

'And now?'

'And now I'm not so sure I ever was.'

A cat miaowed in a nearby yard. Down the street, a door opened and closed and someone turned a television on. Emmylou drifted through the open kitchen window singing about losing this sweet old world. Banks dropped his cigarette and trod on the red ember. Suddenly a chill gust of wind rustled the distant trees and passed through the yard. Annie shivered. Banks put his arm around her and moved her gently towards him. She let her head rest on his shoulder.

'Oh dear,' she said. 'I don't know if this is a good idea.'

'Why?'

Annie paused. Banks could feel her warm shoulder under the thin T-shirt, the ridge of her bra strap.

'Well, we've both probably had too much to drink.'

'If it's the rank thing that's bothering you—'

'No. No. It's not that. I don't give a damn about that, to be honest. As I said, the Job's not my be-all and end-all. I still have a bit of the bohemian left in me. No, it's just that . . . I've had some bad experiences with men. I've been . . . I mean I haven't been . . . Oh, shit, why is this so difficult?' She rubbed her forehead. Banks kept silent. Annie sighed deeply. 'I've been celibate,' she said. 'By choice. For nearly two years now.'

'I don't want to pressure you,' Banks said.

'Don't worry. I wouldn't let you. I make my own choices.'

'I'll never find my way out of this labyrinth alone.'

'I'd lead you,' Annie said, facing him and smiling. 'If I really wanted you to go. But somehow I doubt whether you're in a fit state to drive. It's probably my duty to arrest you. Crime intervention.' She paused and frowned, then rested her hand lightly on his chest. His heart beat more loudly. Surely she could hear it, feel it? 'There are a lot of reasons for not taking this any further, you know,' she went on. 'I've heard you're a bad lot.'

'Not true.'

'A womanizer.'

'Not true.'

They looked at one another for a few moments. Annie bit her lip, shivered again and said, 'Oh, hell.'

Banks wished he hadn't just smoked a cigarette. He leaned forward and kissed her. Her lips yielded and her body moulded itself to his. Then he forgot all about cigarettes.

6

Matthew and Gloria decided to have their party on Christmas Eve, but first we all went ice-skating on Harksmere Reservoir. Already there were lots of people around and fires burned in braziers set up along the edges of the ice. It was dark and there was something hypnotic about the mix of ice and fire in the twilight – to me there was, at any rate – so I was skating in a sort of trance. If I shut my eyes I could see the flames dancing behind my eyelids and feel flashes of warmth as I sped by the bank.

People started drifting back to Bridge Cottage at about seven o'clock, then the other guests started to arrive, including more airmen from the base, some with their girlfriends. Alice's Eric was away in North Africa by then, but Betty's William hadn't passed his medical, which didn't surprise me at all, so they would only let him in the Home Guard.

Michael Stanhope came dressed in his usual artistic 'costume', including hat and cane, but he did bring two bottles of gin and some wine, which made him most welcome indeed. He must have had a cellarful of drink. Alcohol wasn't always easy to come by then, most of the distilleries having shut down, and it was very expensive if you could get it. I could picture Michael Stanhope, knowing a war was coming, hoarding his private stock away, bottle by bottle. I hoped he wouldn't run out.

Matthew and Gloria had decorated the tiny front room as

best they could, with balloons, concertina streamers and fairy lights over the mantelpiece. The whole place had a warm, cosy feel with the blackout curtains up, especially when you thought of the icicles and the frozen puddles outside. There was also plenty of mistletoe and a fake Christmas tree dressed in lights and tinsel.

The only cigarettes we had in stock were Pasha, and Gloria said they tasted like sweepings from the factory floor, which they probably were. The Canadians had some Players, though, so the room soon seemed to fill with smoke. Mark and Stephen had also contributed a bottle of Canadian Club whisky.

Unfortunately for Gloria, John Cooper's musical taste hadn't extended much farther than opera, so the record collection she'd picked up along with the radiogram was of little use to her. So far, she didn't have many records of her own, so we listened to the radio. Luckily, there was a Victor Sylvester concert on that night, and soon people were dancing close together in the cramped space.

Matthew had hardly let Gloria out of his sight for a moment all day, but as the tiny cottage grew more crowded and noisy, it was harder for them to stay together.

Couples danced or chatted. Cynthia and Johnny Marsden hogged the sofa and kissed one another. Once, I even saw him trying to put his hand up her dress, but she stopped him. Gloria drank too much Canadian Club and then switched to gin. She wasn't loud or falling down or anything, but there was a sort of glaze to her eyes and a slight wobble in her step. It all got more pronounced as the evening wore on, as did the way she held her cigarette slightly askew as she swayed in time to the music.

I got distracted by an RAF radio operator, who first dragged me under the mistletoe and gave me a kiss that tasted of tinned sardines, then proceeded to explain the intricacies of radiolocation to me. I should have told him I was a German spy. Hadn't he seen those 'Walls Have Ears' posters everywhere?

It must have been close to ten o'clock by then, and the party was still going strong. I suppose quite a few people were already drunk. I had only been drinking ginger ale – well, I *did* have just a drop of Canadian Club – but I was feeling light-headed because of all the gaiety. When you had a party in wartime, especially at some important time like Christmas, the fun was just a little louder, a little gaudier and a little more desperate than at peacetime parties.

Michael Stanhope was holding forth to a young corporal about how artists had a duty to shun propaganda in their search for truth. 'If governments listened to the artists,' he said, 'there would be no wars.' The corporal would probably have moved on ages ago had Mr Stanhope not been topping up his gin every few minutes.

Matthew, I noticed, was leaning against the wall deep in conversation with two men in army uniforms, no doubt trying to find out what military life was really like once the training was over.

I realized I hadn't seen Gloria for a while and wondered if she was sick or something. She *had* been drinking quite a lot. I needed to go to the toilet anyway, so as gently and politely as I could, I disengaged myself from the radio-location lecture. It was cold and dark outside, so I put my coat over my shoulders, picked up the torch with its tissue-filtered light and headed out into the backyard.

Bridge Cottage had two outbuildings; one was the toilet and the other was used for storage. I could hear the radio-gram playing 'In the Dark' from inside the house as I made my way down the flags to the toilet.

Suddenly, I heard sounds nearby. I paused, then I heard them again, a grunt and a muffled little voice calling out. I couldn't tell where it was coming from at first, then I realized it was behind the outbuilding. Puzzled, I tiptoed over and pointed my torch at the wall.

What I saw made my skin tingle. Even in the poor tissue-weakened light, I could see it was Gloria pinned to the wall by Mark, the Canadian airman. Her back was against the large 'V' sign someone had chalked there during the summer *Victory* campaign. Her dress was bunched around her waist, and the pale white flesh of her bare thighs above the stocking-tops stood out in the darkness. I remember thinking she must be freezing cold. Mark was crushed forward into her, one hand over her mouth, the other fumbling at his waist.

Gloria was calling out in a muffled voice, 'No, please, no!' over and over again, trying to struggle against him, and he was calling her filthy names. When he saw my light, he swore at me and took off around the front of the house.

Gloria leaned back against the wall, gasping and sobbing, not looking at me, her hair and clothes in disarray. Then she straightened her dress, leaned forward with her hands on her knees and was sick right on to the garden. It was warm and made the ice crack. I could see the chalk dust from the 'V' on the back of her dress.

I didn't know what to do. I knew nothing about these things back then and I wasn't even sure what sort of scene I had witnessed – except that there was something very wrong about it.

All I knew was that Gloria looked hurt, upset and in pain. So I did what came naturally; I opened my arms and she fell into them. Then I held her close and stroked her hair and told her not to worry, that everything would be all right.

•

The birds struck up the dawn chorus first, then the milk-man's float rattled by, and soon Banks was listening to the myriad strange sounds of an unfamiliar street through the half-open window of Annie's bedroom. A baby cried for feeding; someone slammed a door; a dog started barking; a letter-box snapped shut; a motorcycle revved up. Everything sounded all the more foreign since Banks had got used to the silence of his new cottage.

Annie lay beside him breathing softly; she would be silent for a while, then let out a soft exhalation part-way between a sniff and a sigh. There was enough light through the thin curtains for Banks to see her. She lay on her side, curled away from him, hands clasped in front, where he couldn't see them. The single white sheet had slipped down far enough for him to see the curve of her waist, follow it up to her shoulders and hair. She had a small mole about halfway. Gently, Banks touched it. Annie stirred a little but still she didn't wake.

Banks lay on his back and closed his eyes. His only fear last night, what almost held him back until that intimate moment in the backyard, when his arm moved of its own volition, was that he would feel the same way he did when he slept with Karen. He should have known better; he should have known this was different. He *did* know. But the fear was still there.

Their lovemaking had been a little tentative at first, but that was only to be expected. It never happened in real life the way it did in movies, with both lovers exploding together in a climax of Wagnerian proportions as fire-works burst, orchestras crescendoed and trains rushed into tunnels. That was pure Monty Python. In real lovemaking, especially with people new to one another's bodies, there are disappointments, mistakes, hesitancies. If you can laugh at these, as Banks and Annie had, then you are halfway there. If you find yourself looking forward to the hours of practice it will take to learn to please one another more, as Banks did, then you are more than halfway.

Afterwards, skin warm and damp and tangy with sweat, she had rested in the crook of his arm and he knew then that he wouldn't wake with a burning desire to be alone.

Just for the briefest of moments he gave in to a wave of paranoia and wondered if this was a trap Riddle had set for him. A new approach. Give him enough rope to hang himself. Were there hidden cameras in the bedroom walls? Was Annie Riddle's secret mistress? Were the two of them plotting Banks's final downfall? The thoughts scudded across his mind like cloud shadows over the daleside. Then, as quick as it came, the paranoia was gone. Jimmy Riddle obviously didn't know who DS Cabbot was, or what she looked like. He clearly didn't even know her first name, otherwise he wouldn't have sent Banks within twenty miles of her.

Banks opened his eyes and looked at the Tibetan mandala on the wall, a circle of fire full of brightly coloured, intricately entwined symbols and mythological figures, some fearful, armed, some clearly benevolent. Jem had had a similar poster on his wall, too, Banks remembered. He had said that it was a map of stages you go through to reach a state of wholeness. According to Jung, Jem also said, people who were beginning to get themselves together would see mandalas in their dreams, without knowing anything at all about Tantric Buddhism.

That kind of thinking had been one of Banks's big problems with the whole sixties thing; he thought it was the mark of a brain softened by too much marijuana or LSD. In their long arguments about changing the system, Jem had always taken the view that you can't change the system from within; if you're in it, you become part of it; you become absorbed and corrupted by it. You end up with a *stake* in it. Maybe that was what had happened to Banks, but even back then he had never felt fully able to join in, especially with phoney let's-all-love-one-another togetherness. Annie was right; he was a loner. He had always kept his distance, even from Jem. Maybe if he hadn't, Jem might not have died.

Annie stirred and Banks ran his hand slowly all the way from her hip to her shoulder.

'Mmm . . .' she murmured. 'Good morning.'

'Good morning.'

'I see you're awake.'

'Have been for hours.'

'You poor man. You should have got up, made some tea.'

'I'm not complaining.' Banks hooked his arm over her side and rested his palm on her stomach, easing her closer. He kissed the soft flesh between her shoulder and neck, then slid his hand up to cup her small breast. Last night he had discovered that she had a tiny red rose tattoo just above her left breast, and he found it incredibly sexy. He had never slept with a tattooed lady before. Annie sighed and pushed herself further back towards him; curved bodies moulding to one another, skin touching every-where it could touch.

Banks forgot about Jem now. He touched Annie's shoulder gently to turn her towards him.

'No,' she whispered. 'Like this is just fine.'
And it was.

•

'The other night,' said Gloria the next time I saw her alone.
'At the Christmas party. I want to thank you. If you hadn't
come along, I don't know what would have happened. I
just don't want you to think it was something it wasn't.'

'I don't know what I think it was,' I said. I felt embarrassed, her talking to me like this. Cold, too. We were in the
High Street and the icy wind whistled through my old coat
as if it were full of holes. Which it probably was. I pulled the
collar up over my throat and felt my bare hands freezing
around the handles of the shopping bag. Foolishly, I had
forgotten my mittens.

'I was just going to the toilet,' she said, 'and he followed
me out there. Mark did. I know I'd had a bit too much to
drink. I didn't mean to, but I suppose I might have given
him some encouragement. He called me a tease, said I'd
been leading him on all night. Things just got a bit out of
hand, that's all.'

'What do you mean?' I started shifting from foot to foot,
hoping the movement would keep me warm. Gloria didn't
seem to feel the cold at all. Still, the land girls were provided
with warm khaki overcoats.

'Earlier in the evening,' she went on. 'He got me under
the mistletoe. Everyone was doing it. I didn't think anything
of it but . . . Gwen?' She chewed on her lower lip.

'What?'

'Oh, I don't know. Men. Sometimes, it's just . . . I don't
know what it is, you try to be nice to them, but they get the
wrong idea.'

'Wrong idea?'

'Yes. I was only being friendly. Like I am with everyone. I didn't do anything to make him believe I was *that* kind of girl. Men sometimes get the wrong impression about me. I don't know why. It seems like they just can't stop themselves. They're so strong. And believe it or not, sometimes it's easier just to give in.'

'Is that what you were doing? Giving in?'

'No. I was struggling. I was trying to call for Matt, for anyone, to help me but Mark had his hand over my mouth. Maybe before, I would have given in. I don't know. But now I've got Matt. I love him, Gwen, I didn't want to cause a fuss, get Matt upset, start trouble. I hate violence. I don't know what would have happened if you hadn't come along. I didn't have much fight left in me. Do you know what I mean?'

'I think so,' I said. I had given up on ever getting warm now. Luckily, I was so numb I couldn't feel the cold any more.

'Can we just forget about it?' Gloria pleaded.

I nodded. 'That's probably for the best.'

She gave me a hug. 'Good. And we're still friends, Gwen?'

'Of course.'

•

After Banks had gone, Annie did her usual twenty minutes of meditation, followed by a few yoga exercises and a shower. As she dried herself, her skin tingled and she realized how good she felt. Last night had been worth the risk. And this morning. That celibacy business wasn't all it was cracked up to be anyway.

They definitely needed more practice. Banks was a little reticent, a bit conservative. That was only to be expected, Annie thought, after twenty or more years of marriage to the same woman. She thought back to her lovemaking with Rob, and how natural they had become. Even when they had been apart for a year or two, they had picked up the rhythm again without any trouble when they got together in Exeter.

How could so many people have read Banks wrong? she wondered. Gossip distorts the truth, certainly, but to such an extent? Perhaps he was the empty canvas people used to project their fantasies on to. Whatever he was, she hoped he wasn't the kind who felt a moral obligation to fall in love just because he slept with a woman. When it came right down to it, she hadn't a clue *what* she wanted from the relationship, if indeed there was to be a relationship. She wanted to see more of him, yes; she wanted to sleep with him again, yes; but beyond that, she didn't know. Still, maybe it would be nice if he did fall a little bit in love with her. Just a little bit.

Most of all, she hoped to hell that he wouldn't regret what they had done for *her* sake, wouldn't feel that he had taken advantage of her vulnerability or her tipsiness, or any of that male rubbish. As for the career business, surely he couldn't imagine she had only slept with him because he was her boss or because she was after advancement? Annie laughed as she pulled on her jeans. Sleeping with DCI Banks was hardly likely to advance anyone's career these days. Probably quite the opposite.

For the moment, another beautiful summer's day beckoned, and it was a great luxury not to have to make any more serious choices than whether to go and do her washing or drive to Harrogate and go shopping. She liked Harrogate town centre; it was compact and manageable. The cottage needed a tidy-up, true. But that could wait. Annie didn't mind a little mess; as usual, there were far more interesting things to do than housework. She could put the washing in before she went; there wasn't much.

Before going anywhere, though, she picked up the phone and dialled a number she knew by heart.

It rang six times before a man's voice answered.

'Ray?'

'Annie? Is that you?'

'Yes.'

'How are you doing, my love? What's happening? Having fun?'

'You certainly sound as if you are.'

'We're having a bit of a party for Julie.'

Annie could hear laughter and music in the background. Some retro sixties rock like the Grateful Dead or the Jefferson Airplane. 'But it's only ten o'clock in the morning,' she said.

'Is it? Oh, well, you know how it goes, love. Carpe diem and all that.'

'Dad, when are you going to grow up? For crying out loud, you're fifty-two years old. Haven't you realized yet that we're in the nineties, not the sixties?'

'Uh-oh. I can tell you're angry at me. You only call me Dad when you're angry at me. What have I done now?'

Annie laughed. 'Nothing,' she said. 'Really. You're incorrigible. I give up. But one day the police will come and bust the lot of you, mark my words. It'll be bloody embarrassing for me. How am I supposed to explain that to my boss? My father, the dope-smoking old hippie?'

'Police? They're not interested in a couple of teeny-weeny joints, are they? At least they shouldn't be. Ought to have better things to do. And a bit less of the "old", thank you very much. Anyway, how is my little WPC Plod? Getting any, lately?'

'Dad! Let's lay off that subject, shall we, please? I thought we'd agreed that my sex life is my own business.'

'Oh, you have been! You are! I can tell by your tone. Well, that's wonderful news, love. What's his name? Is he a copper?'

'*Dad!*' Annie felt herself blushing.

'All right. Sorry. Just showing a bit of fatherly concern, that's all.'

'Much appreciated, I'm sure.' Annie sighed. Really, it was like talking to a child. 'Anyway, I'm fine,' she said. 'What's Julie got to celebrate? Something I should know about?'

'Didn't I tell you? She's finally got a publisher for that novel of hers. After all these years.'

'No, you didn't. That's great news. Tell her I'm really happy for her. How about Ian and Jo?'

'They're away in America.'

'Nice. And Jasmine?'

'Jasmine's fine.' Annie heard a voice in the background. 'She sends her love,' her father said. 'Anyway, wonderful as it is to talk to you, it's not like you to phone before discount time. Especially since you moved to Yorkshire. Anything I can help you with? Like me to beat up a couple of suspects for you? Fake a confession or two?'

Annie fitted the receiver snugly between her ear and shoulder and curled her legs under her on the settee. 'No. But as a matter of fact,' she said, 'there is something you might be able to help me with.'

'Ask away.'

'Michael Stanhope.'

'Stanhope . . . Stanhope . . . Sounds familiar. Wait a minute . . . Yes, I remember. The artist. Michael Stanhope. What about him?'

'What do you know about him?'

'Not much, really. Let me see. He didn't live up to his early promise. Died in the sixties sometime, I think. Last few years pretty unproductive. Why do you want to know?'

'I saw a painting of his in connection with a case I'm working on.'

'And you think it might be a clue?'

'I don't know. It just made me want to know more about him.'

'What was it? The painting.'

Annie described it to him. 'Yes, that'd be Stanhope. He had a reputation for Brueghelesque village scenes. Touch of Lowry thrown in for good measure. That was his problem, you know: too derivative and never developed a uniform style of his own. All over the map. A bit Stanley Spencerish, too. *Haute* symbolism. Very much out of vogue today. Anyway, what could Michael Stanhope possibly have to do with a case you're working on?'

'Maybe nothing. Like I said, he just grabbed my curiosity. Do you know where I can find out more about him? Is there a book?'

'I don't think so. He wasn't that important. Most of his stuff will be in private collections, maybe spread around the galleries, too. Why don't you try Leeds? They've got a half-decent collection there, if you can stand the Atkinson bloody Grimshaws. I'd say they're bound to have a few Stanhopes, what with him being local and all.'

'Good idea,' Annie said, kicking herself for not thinking of it first. 'I'll do that. And, Ray?'

'Yes?'

'Take care of yourself.'

'I will. Promise, love. Come see us soon. Bye.'

'Bye.'

Annie looked at her watch. Not long after ten. She could be in Leeds in an hour, do her shopping there, instead of in Harrogate, have lunch and spend a bit of time in the art gallery. She picked up her car keys and her shoulder bag from the sideboard and set off through the labyrinth to her car, which was still parked outside the section station. She wondered if Inspector Harmond would make anything of that. Not unless he also knew that Banks's car had remained parked by the village green all night. Besides, she didn't care.

•

And friends we remained. We saw the New Year in together, linked arms and sang 'Auld Lang Syne'. Hong Kong had fallen to the Japanese on Christmas Day and the fighting in North Africa and in Russia went on as bitterly as ever. As the winter weather continued through January, British troops withdrew down the Malayan Peninsula to Singapore.

Though I often thought about what I had witnessed, I didn't begin to understand what had gone on against the outbuilding wall that Christmas night until much later, and even then I had no way of knowing how culpable Gloria had been. What had Mark been trying to do to her? To me, at the time, Gloria had seemed to be resisting, struggling, but when I discovered the act of sex for myself not so very much later, I found it could often be misleading that way; one often seemed to be struggling and resisting, especially during the wildest moments. Looking back now, I'd call it attempted rape, but memory, over time, has a way of altering its content.

So I did the best I could to put the whole episode out of my mind. I certainly agreed that Gloria was right not to involve Matthew. That would only have started a fight and upset everyone. His going away soon would have made it worse, too; he would be worried enough to leave her behind as it was.

Sometimes, though, at night in bed as I listened to the bombers drone over Rowan Woods, I would remember the scene, with Gloria's bare white thighs above the stocking-tops, and those strange muffled sounds she was making that seemed lost somewhere between pain and acquiescence, and I would feel a strange fluttering excitement inside me, as if I were on the verge of some great discovery that never quite came.

On the fifteenth of January, 1942, Sergeant Matthew Shackleton shipped out. He didn't know where he was headed, but we all assumed he would be going to North Africa to fight with the Eighth Army.

Imagine our surprise when Gloria got a letter from Matthew in Cape Town, *South* Africa, three weeks later. Of course, they could hardly sail through the Mediterranean, but even so, Cape Town seemed a long way round to go to North Africa. Then we got another letter from Colombo, in Ceylon, then Calcutta, India. What a fool I was! I could have kicked myself for not guessing earlier. They didn't need bridges and roads in the desert, of course, but they needed them in the jungles of the Far East.

•

The drive to Leeds took less time than Annie had expected. She parked north of the city centre and walked down New Briggate to The Headrow. The place was busy, pavements jammed with shoppers, all wearing thin, loose clothing to alleviate the blistering heat, which seemed even more oppressive in the city than it did out Harkside way. A juggler performed for children in Dortmund Square. The sun dazzled Annie, reflecting on shop windows, making it hard to see what was inside. Annie put on her sunglasses and set off through the crowds towards Cookridge Street. A little research after her chat with Ray had revealed that Leeds City Art Gallery had in its collection several works by Michael Stanhope, and Annie wanted to see them.

Once inside, she picked up a guidebook at the reception area. The Stanhopes were on the second floor. Four of them. She started up the broad stone staircase.

Annie had never liked art galleries, with their rarefied atmosphere, uniformed custodians and stifling aura of hush. No doubt this dislike was largely due to her father's influence. Though he loved the great artists, he despised the barren way their works were put on display. He thought great art ought to be exhibited on a constant rotation in pubs, offices, trattorias, cafés, churches and bingo parlours.

He approved of the Henry Moores standing out in open weather on the Yorkshire Moors; he also approved of David Hockney's faxes, photocollages and opera-set designs. Annie had grown up in an atmosphere of irreverence towards the established art world, with its stuffy galleries, plummy accents and inflated prices. Because of this, she always felt self-conscious in galleries, as if she were an interloper. Maybe she was being paranoid, but she always thought the guards were watching *her*, from one room to the next, just waiting for her to reach out and touch something and set off all the alarms.

When she found the Stanhopes, she was at first disappointed. Two of them were rather dull landscapes, not of Hobb's End, but other Dales scenes. The third, a little more interesting, showed a distant view of Hobb's

End in its hollow, smoke drifting from chimneys, the bright vermilions and purples of sunset splashed across the sky. A fine effect, but it told Annie nothing she didn't know.

The fourth painting, though, was a revelation.

Titled *Reclining Nude*, according to the catalogue, the painting reminded Annie of Goya's *Naked Maja*, which she had seen with Ray when it came briefly to the National Gallery in 1990. No matter what his opinions about galleries were, Ray certainly never missed the opportunity to view a great work.

The woman reclined on a bed in much the same pose as Goya's original, propped on a pillow, hands behind her head, looking directly at the painter with some sort of highly charged erotic challenge in her expression, bed-sheets ruffled beneath her. Also, like the *Maja*'s, her round breasts were widely spaced and her legs bent a little, awkwardly placed as her lower half twisted slightly towards the viewer. Her waist was thin, her hips in perfect proportion, and a little triangle of hair showed between her clasped legs, connected to the navel by a barely perceptible line of fair down.

There were differences, though. Stanhope's model had golden-blond hair rather than black, her nose was shorter, her large eyes a striking blue, her lips fuller and redder. Even so, the resemblance was too close to be accident, especially the frank eroticism of her expression and the hint of pleasures recently enjoyed, conveyed by the rumpled sheets. Stanhope had obviously been strongly affected by Goya's original, and when he had encountered the same sort of sensual power in a model, he had remembered this and painted it.

But there was more to Stanhope's vision. As Annie

remembered, the background of the *Naked Maja* was dark and impenetrable; it seemed as if the bed were floating in space, the only important thing in the universe.

Stanhope hadn't given his model a realistic background either, but if you looked very closely, you could see images of tanks, aeroplanes, armies on the march, explosions and swastikas. In other words, he had painted the war into the background. It was subtle; the images didn't jump right out at you and dominate the work, but they were there, and when you looked closely, you couldn't ignore them: eroticism and weapons of mass destruction. Make of it what you would.

Annie glanced at the note on the wall beside the painting, then she stepped back with a gasp that made one of the custodians look up from his newspaper.

'Everything all right, miss?' he called out.

Annie put her hand over her heart. 'What? Yes. Oh, yes. Sorry.'

He eyed her suspiciously and went back to his paper.

Annie looked again. It wasn't mentioned in the catalogue, but there it was, plain as day, below *Reclining Nude*. A subtitle: *Gloria, Autumn 1944*.

7

On Monday morning, Banks looked again at the postcard reproduction of *Reclining Nude: Gloria, Autumn 1944* that lay on his desk. It was an uncanny and disconcerting experience to see an artist's impression of the flesh that had probably once clothed the filth-covered bones they found last week, and to feel aroused by looking at it. Banks felt an exciting flush of adolescent guilt, the same as he had on looking at his first pictures of naked women in *Swank* or *Mayfair*.

Annie had picked up several copies of the postcard at the art gallery and, thrilled by her discovery, phoned him late on Saturday afternoon. They met for dinner at Cockett's Hotel, in Hawes, with every intention of going their separate ways later, both having agreed that they shouldn't rush things, that they needed their time alone. After the second bottle of wine, though, instead of leaving, they took a room and woke to Sunday-morning church bells. After a leisurely breakfast, they left, agreeing to restrict their trysts to weekends.

At home, Banks had tried to reach Brian all weekend, without any luck. He knew he should call Sandra and find out what she had to say about it all, but he didn't want to. Maybe it was something to do with sleeping with Annie, or maybe not, but he didn't think he could handle talking to Sandra. He spent the rest of Sunday reading the papers and doing odd jobs around the cottage.

He walked over to stand by the open window. The gold hands against the blue face of the church clock stood at a quarter to eleven. Horns blared out in the street and the smell of fresh bread from the bakery mingled with the exhaust fumes. An irate van driver swore at a tourist. The tourist swore back and scurried off into the crowd. Another coach pulled up in the cobbled market square and disgorged its load of old ladies. From Worthing, Banks noticed, by the sign painted on the side. *Worthing.* Why couldn't the old biddies stay down there, maybe roll up their skirts and go for a paddle, stop and smell the seaweed? Why did everyone have to come to the bloody Dales? When it came right down to it, he blamed James Herriot. If they hadn't done that damn series on television, the place would be empty.

Banks lit a proscribed cigarette and wondered, not for the first time this past year, why he bothered with the job. There had been plenty of occasions when he felt like packing it all in. At first he hadn't done so because he simply couldn't be bothered. As long as people left him alone, it didn't really matter. He knew he wasn't working up to par, even on desk duties, but he didn't give a damn. It was easy enough to show up and push paper around without enthusiasm, or to play computer games. The truth was that he hurt so much after Sandra left that everything else seemed meaningless.

Then, when he bought the cottage and started pulling himself together, or at least managing to distance himself a bit from the pain, he seriously considered a career change, but he couldn't think of anything else he was qualified for, or even wanted to do. He was too young to retire, and he had no desire whatsoever to go into security work or a private detective agency. Lack of formal education had closed most other paths to him.

So he stuck with it. Now, though, partly because of this dirty, pointless, dead-end case – or so Jimmy Riddle must have seen it – Banks was finally getting back to some sense of why he had joined in the first place. When something becomes routine, mechanical, when you're just going through the motions, you have to dig down and find out what it was that you loved about it in the first place. What drew you to it? Or what obsessed you about it? Then you have to act on that, and to hell with all the rest.

Banks had cast his memory back and thought about those questions a lot over the past few months. It wasn't simply a matter of why he walked into the recruiting centre that day, asked for information and then followed up on it a week later. He had done that partly because of his disenchantment with the bohemian scene after Jem's death, partly because he hated business studies, and partly to piss off his parents. He and Sandra knew they were serious about one another by then, too; they wanted to get married, start a family, and he would need a steady job.

With Banks, it wasn't some abstract notion of justice, or being on the side of 'good' and putting the 'bad' guys away. He wasn't naive enough to see the police as good, for a start, or even all criminals as bad. Some people were driven to crime through desperation of one kind or another; some were so damaged inside that they were unable to make a choice. When it came right down to it, Banks believed that most violent criminals were bullies, and ever since he was a kid he had detested bullies. At school, he had always stuck up for the weaker kids against the bullies, even though he wasn't especially big or tough. He got frequent black eyes and bloody noses for his trouble.

In some way, it all came together with Mick Slack, fifth-form bully, two years older and six inches taller than Banks. One day, in the schoolyard, for no reason, Slack started pushing and shoving a kid called Graham Marshall. Marshall was in Banks's class and was always a bright, quiet, shy kid, the sort the others taunted by calling him a poof and a pansy, but mostly left alone. When Banks stepped in, Slack pushed *him* instead, and a skirmish followed. More by speed and stealth, Banks managed to wind Slack and knock him to the Tarmac before the teacher came out and stopped it. Slack swore vengeance, but he never got the chance. He was killed two days later on his way to play for the school rugby team, when his motorbike ran smack into a brick wall.

The strangest thing was, though, that about six months later, Graham Marshall disappeared and was never seen again. Police detectives came and questioned everyone in his class, asking if they had seen any strangers hanging around the school, or if Graham had told them about anyone suspicious, anyone who was bothering him. Nobody had. Banks felt especially impotent at being so useless to the police, and he remembered that feeling years later when he was on the other side of the interview table watching witnesses flounder as they tried to remember details.

The theory was that Graham had been abducted by a child molester and his body buried in some forest miles away. That made three deaths Banks had been exposed to as an adolescent, including Phil Simpkins, who had swung on to the sharp iron railings, but it was the ultimate mystery of Graham Marshall's disappearance that haunted him most of all, until Jem's death some years later, and in a way it was his curiosity and unaccountable feelings of guilt over it that were behind his decision to join the police years later.

All the petty duties and details of a policeman's job aside, Banks's obsession was with bringing down as many bullies as possible. When the victims were dead, of course, he couldn't defend them, but he could damn well find out what had happened to them and bring the bullies to justice. It wasn't foolproof; it didn't always work; but it was all he had. That was what he had to get back to, or he might as well pack it all in and join Group 7 or some other private security outfit.

He went back to his desk and sat down. As he looked at Gloria's pose again – beautiful, erotic, sensual, playful, but also challenging, mocking, as if she knew some sort of secret about the artist, or shared one with him – he felt that in this case he was needed as much as ever. He was convinced that Gloria Shackleton was the victim they had found buried at Hobb's End, and he wanted to know what she was like, what had happened to her and why no one had reported her missing. Did people just think she had vanished into space, been abducted by aliens or something? The bully who had killed her might well be dead, but that didn't matter a damn to Banks. *He needed to know*.

Dr Glendenning's call cut into his thoughts.

'Ah, Banks,' he said. 'Glad I caught you in. You're very lucky I happened to be in Leeds, you know. Otherwise you could have whistled for your post-mortem. There are plenty of fresh cadavers craving my expert attention.'

'I'm sure there are. My apologies. I promise to do better in the future.'

'I should hope so.'

'What have you got?'

'Nothing much to add to what Dr Williams told you, I'm afraid.'

'She was stabbed, then?'

'Oh, yes. And viciously, too.'

'How many times?'

'Fourteen or fifteen, as far as I can tell. I wouldn't swear to that, of course, given the condition of the skeleton and the time that has elapsed since death.'

'Is that what killed her?'

'What do you think I am, laddie? A miracle worker? It's not possible to say what killed her, though the knife wounds would have done the trick. Judging from the angles and positions of the nicks, the blade would almost certainly have pierced several vital organs.'

'Did you find evidence of any other injury?'

'Patience, laddie. That's what I'm getting to, if you'll slow down and give me the chance. It's all that caffeine, you know. Too much coffee. Try a nice herbal tea, for a change.'

'I'll do that. Tomorrow. But tell me now.'

'I found possible, and I stress *possible*, signs of manual strangulation.'

'Strangulation?'

'That's what I said. And stop echoing me. If I needed a bloody parrot I'd buy one. I'm going by the hyoid bones in the throat. Now, these are very fragile bones, almost always broken during manual strangulation, but I say it's only *possible* because the damage could have occurred over time, due to other causes. The weight of all that earth and water, for example. I must say, though, the skeleton was in remarkable condition considering where it's been for so long.'

'Would that make it more probable than possible?'

'What's the difference?'

'"When you have eliminated the impossible, whatever

remains, however *improbable*, must be the truth." Sir Arthur Conan Doyle.'

Glendenning sighed theatrically. 'And to think that fellow was a doctor. All right, shall we say it's certainly not impossible, and even quite *likely*, that the poor woman was strangled. Is that clear enough for you?'

'Before she was stabbed.'

'How would I know that? Honestly, Banks, you either have an overinflated opinion of the medical profession or you're being just plain bloody-minded. Knowing you, I'd bet on the latter. But let us, just for once, be reasonable about this, shall we, and apply a little logic?'

'By all means. My, my, you're grumpy this morning, aren't you, Doc?'

'Aye. It's what happens when my own doctor tells me to lay off the coffee. And I've told you before not to call me Doc. It's disrespectful. Now, listen. The way this poor woman was stabbed stopped just short of chopping her into little pieces. It would seem very unlikely to me – not *impossible*, but very improbable, if you like – that her killer felt any need to strangle her *after* he had done this. The degree of rage involved would probably have left him quite exhausted, for a start, not to mention the anger vented, the almost postcoital relaxation some killers feel after perpetrating extremely violent acts. So I'd say the strangulation came first and then, for whatever reason, the stabbing. That kind of thing is statistically more common, too.'

'So why the stabbing? To make sure she was dead?'

'I doubt it. Though it's true she may have still been alive after the strangulation, may just have lost conscious-ness. As I said, we're dealing with anger, with rage, here. That's the only explanation. In the vernacular, whoever did it got carried away with killing. Literally saw red. Either that or he knew exactly what he was doing and he enjoyed himself.'

'He?'

'Again, statistically more likely. Though I wouldn't rule out a strong woman. But you know as well as I do, Banks, that these sorts of things are usually lust-related. Either that or they stem from very strong passions, such as jealousy, revenge, obsession, greed and the like. I suppose it could have been a wronged wife or a woman spurned, a lesbian relationship gone wrong. But statistically speaking, it's men who do these things. I hesitate to do your job for you, but I don't think you're dealing with a run-of-the-mill sort of crime. It doesn't look like a murder committed during a robbery, or to cover up a secret. Of course, murderers can be damnably clever sometimes and disguise one sort of crime to look like another. Fault of all these detective novels, if you ask me.'

'Right,' said Banks, scrawling away on the pad he'd pulled in front of him. That was the trouble with computers; it was bloody awkward to write on them when you were speaking on the telephone. 'What about the parturition marks?'

'That's exactly what they are, in my opinion.'

'So there's no chance that they were also caused by the knife, or by time?'

'Well, there's always a *chance* that something else could have caused them, some animal, friction from a small stone or pebble, or suchlike, though given where she was found I say we can pretty much exclude the chance of scavenger activity. After so long, though, it's impossible to be a hundred per cent sure about anything. But judging by the distinctive position and appearance, I'd say they're

parturition marks. The woman had a baby, Banks. There's
no saying *when*, of course.'

'Okay,' said Banks. 'Thanks very much, Doc.'

Glendenning snorted and hung up.

•

All through February and March 1942, day after day, I followed the news reports. They were censored and incomplete, of course, but I read about the estimated sixty thousand
British taken prisoner in Singapore, and about the fighting
near the Sittang River, from where Matthew wrote Gloria
another letter, telling her how things were pretty dull and
safe really, and not to worry. Clearly, it's not only governments that lie during wartime.

Then, on the eighth of March, we heard about the fall of
Rangoon. Our morale at home was pretty low, too. In
April, the Germans gave up all pretence of bombing military
and industrial targets and started bombing cities of great
architectural beauty, such as Bath, Norwich and York,
which was getting very close to home.

I remembered when Leeds, only about thirty miles away,
had its worst raid of the war, about a month before Gloria
arrived. Matthew and I took the train in the next day to see
what it looked like. The City Museum, right at the corner
of Park Row and Bond Street, had taken a direct hit and all
the stuffed lions and tigers we had thrilled over on childhood
visits hung in the overhead tram wires like creatures thrown
from an out-of-control carousel. I wanted to go and see the
damage in York, but Mrs Shipley, our stationmaster, told
me York Station had been bombed, so no trains were
allowed in. At least she was able to assure me that they
hadn't destroyed the Minster.

It was a miserable spring, though we had the sunniest

April in forty years. There were the usual random shortages. Items simply disappeared from the shelves for weeks on end. One week you couldn't get fish for love or money; the next it was poultry. In February, soap was rationed to sixteen ounces every four weeks; the civilian petrol ration was cut out completely in March, which meant no more motoring for pleasure. We still managed to retain a small petrol ration, though, because we needed the van to make pick-ups from wholesalers.

I followed the news far more closely than I had before, scouring all the newspapers, from *The Times* and the *News Chronicle* to the *Daily Mirror*, the minute they came in on the first train, cutting out articles and pasting them into a scrapbook, spending hours tracing meandering rivers and crooked coastlines in the atlas. Even so, I never managed to get a true picture of what life was like for Matthew out there. I could imagine it from my reading of Rudyard Kipling and Somerset Maugham, but that was the best I could do.

I wrote to him every day, which was probably more often than Gloria did. She was never much of a letter writer. Matthew didn't write back that often, but when he did he would always assure us he was well. Mostly, he complained about the monsoons and the humid jungle heat, the insects and the dreadful terrain. He never said anything directly about fighting and killing, so for a long time we didn't even know if he had been in battle. Once, though, he wrote that boredom seemed the greatest enemy: 'Long stretches of boredom relieved only by the occasional brief skirmish' was the way he put it. Somehow, I had the idea that these 'brief skirmishes' were a good deal more dangerous and terrifying than the boredom.

As time passed, we got used to Matthew's absence and enjoyed what we could of him through his letters. Gloria would read bits from his to her (no doubt missing out all the embarrassing lovey-dovey stuff) and I would read from his to me. Sometimes, I sensed, she was jealous because he wrote to me more about ideas and books and philosophy and to her mostly about day-to-day things like food and mosquitoes and blisters.

That September, *Pride and Prejudice*, with Laurence Olivier and Greer Garson, finally came to the Lyceum. Gloria had just had a tooth extracted by old Granville after suffering toothache for several days. I told her I thought it was a crime the prices he charged for such poor work, but she countered that Brenchley, in Harkside, a notorious butcher, was even more expensive. As usual, Granville did more damage than good and poor Gloria had been bleeding from the torn gum for over a day. She was just beginning to feel a little better and I managed to persuade her to come to the pictures with me. As it turned out, she actually admitted to enjoying the film. That shouldn't have surprised me. It wasn't exactly the sharp-witted, ironic Jane Austen I knew from the books; it was far more romantic. Still, it made a nice change from all the silly comedies and musicals she had been dragging me to see lately.

Double summertime made it easy for us to see our way across the fields that night. It was a beautiful autumn evening tinged with smoky green and golden light, the kind of evening when I used to go out and enjoy the stubble-burning just after dark before the war, when you could smell the acrid, sweet smoke drifting in the air over the fields and see the little fires stretched out for miles along the horizon. Sadly, there was no stubble-burning in the war; we didn't want the Germans to know where our empty fields were.

This evening was almost as beautiful, even without the smoke and the little fires. I could see the purple heather darkening on the distant moor-tops to the west, hear the night birds call, smell clean, hay-scented air and feel the dry grass swish against my bare legs as I walked.

Despite the ravages of war and Matthew's being far away, I felt as deeply content as I had ever been at that moment. Yet as we came down towards the fairy bridge in the gathering darkness, I felt that chilling shudder of apprehension, as if a goose had stepped over my grave, as Mother would have said. Gloria, arm linked in mine, was chatting on and on about how handsome Laurence Olivier was, and she obviously didn't notice, so I let it go by.

As the weeks passed, I tried to dismiss the feeling, but it had a way of creeping back. There was plenty to rejoice about, I told myself: Matthew continued to write regularly and assured us he was doing well; the Red Army seemed to be making gains at Stalingrad; and the tide had turned in North Africa.

But after the victory at E1 Alamein that November, when I lay on my bed and listened to the church bells ring for the first time in years, all I could do was cry because Matthew had had no bells at his wedding.

●

'First off,' Annie told Banks over the phone later that day, 'I can find no official record of Gloria Shackleton at all after the wedding notice in 1941. There's no missing-persons report in our files and no death notice anywhere. The *Harkside Chronicle*, by the way, suspended publication between 1942 and 1946 because of paper shortages, so that's no use as a source. There's always the *Yorkshire Post*, of course, if they took any interest in the Harkside area. Anyway, it looks as if she disappeared from the face of the earth.'

'Did you check with immigration?' Banks asked.

'Yes. Nothing.'

'Okay. Go on.'

'Well, I was able to dig up a bit more about her life at Hobb's End, most of it pieced together from the parish magazine. She's first mentioned in the May 1941 issue, welcomed to the parish as a member of the Women's Land Army, assigned to work at a place called Top Hill Farm, just outside the village.'

'Top Hill Farm? Did you find out who owned the place?'

'I did. It was a Mr Frederick Kilnsey and his wife, Edith. They had one son called Joseph, who was called up. That's why they got Gloria. Apparently, it wasn't a very big farm, just a few cows, poultry, sheep and a couple of acres of land. Anyway, Joseph didn't come back. Killed at El Alamein. By then, Gloria was living at Bridge Cottage.'

'Still working for the Kilnseys?'

'Yes. I suppose it was a mutually convenient arrangement. They needed her, especially with Joseph dead, and she could live at Bridge Cottage and stay close to what family she had in Hobb's End.'

'All this from the parish magazine?'

'Well, I'm embroidering just a little. But it's remarkably informative, don't you think? I mean, it's easy enough to joke about how petty the news items they publish are at the time – you know, like "Farmer Jones loses sheep in winter storm" – but when you're looking back into something like this, it's a real treasure trove. Unfortunately, they also stopped publication early in 1942. Paper shortage again.'

'Pity. Go on.'

'That's about it, really. Gloria married the Shackletons' eldest child, Matthew. He was twenty-one and she was nineteen. He had a younger sister called Gwynneth. I assume she was the same one who witnessed the marriage.'

'What became of her?'

'She was still around in the last issue, March 1942, as far as I know. Wrote a little piece on growing your own onions, in fact.'

'How fascinating. What about Matthew?'

'The last time he was mentioned he was shipping overseas.'

'Where?'

'Didn't say. Secret, I suppose.'

'Any idea where any of these people moved when they cleared out of Hobb's End?'

'No. But I did ring Ruby Kettering. She knows two people still living who lived in Hobb's End during the war. There's Betty Goodall, who lives in Edinburgh, and Alice Poole in Scarborough. She thinks they'd be thrilled to talk to us.'

'Okay. Look, I've decided to send DS Hatchley to St Catherine's House tomorrow. Which do you fancy: Edinburgh or Scarborough?'

'Doesn't matter to me. Anything's better than checking birth, death and marriage records.'

'I'll toss for it. Heads or tails?'

'How can I trust you over the telephone?'

'Trust me. Heads or tails?'

'This is crazy. Heads.'

Annie paused a moment and heard a sound like a coin clinking on a metal desk. She smiled to herself. Insane. Banks came back on. 'It was heads. Your choice.'

'I told you, it doesn't really matter. I'll take Scarborough, though, if you insist. I like the seaside there, and it's not as far to drive.'

'Okay. If I get an early enough start I can be up to Edinburgh and back by early evening. Plenty of time for us to compare notes. I'd like to get something on tonight's news, first.'

'Like what?'

'I want to put Gloria's name out there, see if anything comes back. I know we might be jumping the gun, but you never know. We've got no idea what happened to the Shackletons, and Gloria may have had family in London who are still alive. They might know what happened to her. Or, if we're wrong about it all, she might drop by the station herself and let us know she's still alive.'

Annie laughed. 'Right.'

'Anyway, I'll try local television. That way I can get them to show the postcard.'

'What? Nudity on the local news?'

'They can crop it.'

'Let me know what time you'll be on.'

'Why?'

'So I can set my VCR. Bye.'

•

'So Jimmy Riddle thinks he's dropped you in the shit with this one, then?' said DS Hatchley after swallowing his first bite of toasted tea-cake.

'To put it succinctly, yes,' said Banks. 'I think he was also pretty sure this case wouldn't involve race relations or any of his rich and influential friends from the Lodge.'

'Oh, I don't know about that,' Hatchley said. 'I'd imagine quite a few of them have got skeletons in their cupboards.'

'Ouch.'

They were sitting in the Golden Grill, just across the

street from Eastvale Divisional HQ. Outside, Market Street was packed with tourists, jackets or cardigans slung over their shoulders, cameras round their necks. Like sheep up on the unfenced moorland roads, they strayed all over the narrow street. The local delivery vans had to inch through, horns blaring.

Most of the tables were already taken, but they had managed to find one near the back. Once the two of them had sat down and given their orders to the bustling waitress, Banks told Hatchley about the skeleton. By the time he had finished, their order arrived.

Banks knew his sergeant had a reputation as an idle sod and a thug. His appearance didn't help. Hatchley was big, slow-moving and bulky, like a rugby prop forward gone to seed, with straw hair, pink complexion, freckles and a piggy nose. His suits were shiny, ties egg-stained, and he usually looked as if he had just been dragged through a hedge backwards. But it had always been Banks's experience that once Hatchley got his teeth into something, he was a stubborn and dogged copper, and damned difficult to shake off. The problem lay in getting him motivated in the first place.

'Anyway, we think we know who the victim was, but we want to cover all possibilities. What I'd like you to do is take PC Bridges and go down to London tomorrow. Here's a list of information I'd like.' Banks passed over a sheet of paper.

Hatchley glanced at it, then looked up. 'Can't I take WPC Sexton instead?'

Banks grinned. 'Ellie Sexton? And you a married man. I'm ashamed of you, Jim.'

Hatchley winked. 'Spoilsport.'

Banks looked at his watch. 'Before you go, could you

put out a nationwide request for information on similar crimes in the same time period? This is a bit tricky because it's an old crime and they'll drag their feet. But there's a chance someone might have something unsolved with a similar MO on the books. I'll put someone on checking our local records, too.'

'You think this was part of a series?'

'I don't know, Jim, but what Dr Glendenning told me about the manner of death made me think I shouldn't overlook that possibility. I've also asked the SOCOs to broaden their search to include the general Hobb's End area. Given what I've just heard from Dr Glendenning about the way she died, I wouldn't like to think we're sitting on another 25 Cromwell Street without knowing it.'

'I'm sure the press would have a field day with that,' said Hatchley. 'They could call it the Hobb's End House of Horrors. Nice ring to it.'

'Let's hope it doesn't come to that.'

'Aye.' Hatchley paused and finished his tea-cake. 'This DS Cabbot you're working with down Harkside,' said Hatchley. 'I don't think I've come across him yet. What's he like?'

'*She*'s pretty new around here,' Banks said. 'But she seems to be working out okay.'

'She?' Hatchley raised his eyebrows. 'Bit of all right, then?'

'Depends on your type. Anyway, you seem to be showing a dangerous interest in these things for a man with a wife and child of his own. How are Carol and April, by the way?'

'They're fine.'

'Over the teething?'

'A long time ago, that were. But thanks for asking, sir.'

Banks finished his tea-cake. 'Look, Jim,' he said, 'if I've been a bit distant this past while, you know, haven't shown much interest in you and your family, it's just that . . . well, I've had a lot of problems. There's been a few changes. A lot to get used to.'

'Aye.'

Bloody hell, Banks thought. *Aye.* The word with a thousand meanings. He struggled on. 'Anyway, if you thought I ignored you or cut you out in any way, I apologize.'

Hatchley paused for a moment, eyes everywhere but on Banks. Finally, he clasped his ham-like hands on the red-and-white-checked tablecloth, still avoiding eye contact. 'Let's just forget about it, shall we, sir. Water under the bridge. We've all had our crosses to bear these past few months, maybe you more than most of us. Talking of crosses, I suppose you've heard they're changing our name to Crime Management?'

Banks nodded. 'Yes.'

Hatchley mimicked picking up a telephone. 'Good morning, Crime Management here, madam. How can we help you? Not enough crime in your neighbourhood. Dear, dear. Well, yes, I'm certain there's some to spare on the East Side Estate. Yes, I'll look into it right away and see if I can get some sent over by this afternoon. Bye-bye, madam.'

Banks laughed.

'I mean, *really*,' Hatchley went on. 'If this goes on they'll be calling you a Senior Crime Consultant next.'

The door opened and WPC Sexton walked over to them. Hatchley nudged Banks and pointed. 'Here she is. The belle of Eastvale Divisional.'

'Fuck off, Sarge,' she said, then turned to Banks. 'Sir, we just got an urgent message from a DS Cabbot in

Harkside. She wants you to get down there as soon as you can. She said a lad named Adam Kelly has something he wants to tell you.'

•

The telegram, in its unmistakable orange cover, came to the shop, for some reason. I remember the date; it was Palm Sunday, the eighteenth of April, 1943, and Mother and I had just got back from church. Gloria was working that day, so, heart thumping and heavy, I had to leave Mother to her tears and run up to Top Hill Farm. Though it was a chilly afternoon, the sweat was pouring off me by the time I got there.

I found Gloria collecting eggs in the chicken shack. She had one in her palm and she held it out to show me. 'It's so warm,' she said. 'Freshly laid. But what are you doing here, Gwen? You look out of breath. Your eyes. Have you been crying?'

Panting, I handed over the telegram to her. She read it, her face turned ashen and she sagged back against the flimsy wooden wall. A nail squealed in the wood and the chickens squawked. The sheet of paper fluttered from her tiny hand to the dirt floor. She didn't cry right there and then, but a soft moan came from her mouth. 'Oh, no,' she said. 'No.' Almost as if she had been expecting it. Then her whole body started to tremble. I wanted to go to her, but somehow I knew that I mustn't. Not just yet, not until she had let the first pangs of grief shake her and rip through her alone.

She closed her hand by her side and the egg broke. Bright yellow yolk stained her dainty fingers, and long strings of viscous glair trailed down towards the straw-covered earth.

•

The Kellys' house stood in the middle of a terrace block on the B-road east of Harkside. There was an infants' school across the road, and next to that a Pay and Display car park to encourage tourists not to clog the village centre. Beyond the car park, a meadow full of buttercups and clover descended eastwards to the West Yorkshire border and the banks of Linwood Reservoir.

Mrs Kelly answered the door and asked them in. Banks could sense the tension immediately. The aftermath of a scolding; it was a familiar childhood sensation of his, and the scoldings were usually dished out by his mother. Though it was never openly admitted, Banks knew his father believed that household discipline was a woman's job. Only if Banks cheeked her or tried to resist did his father step in and sort things out with his belt.

'He won't say owt,' Mrs Kelly said. She was a plain, harried-looking woman in her early thirties, old before her time, with limp, tired hair and a drawn face. 'I challenged him on it when he came home for his lunch, and he ran off up to his room. He wouldn't go back to school and he won't come down.'

'Challenged him on what, Mrs Kelly?' Banks asked.

'What he stole.'

'Stole?'

'Yes. I found it when I were cleaning his room. From that . . . that there skeleton. I left it where I found it. I didn't want to touch it. Anyone would think I haven't brought him up right. It's not easy when you're on your own.'

'Calm down, Mrs Kelly,' Annie said, stepping forward and resting her hand on her arm. 'Nobody's blaming you for anything. Or Adam. We just want to get to the bottom of it, that's all.'

The room was hot and a woman on television was explaining how to make the perfect soufflé. Because it was late afternoon and they were facing east, there was very little light. Banks was already beginning to feel claustrophobic.

'May I go up and talk to him?' he asked.

'You'll get nowt out of him. Clammed up, he has.'

'May I try?'

'Suit yourself. Left at the top of the stairs.'

Banks glanced at Annie, who tried to settle Mrs Kelly in an armchair, then he made his way up the narrow carpeted stairway. He knocked first on Adam's door and, getting no response, opened it a short way and stuck his head round. 'Adam?' he said. 'It's Mr Banks. Remember me?'

Adam lay on his side on the single bed. He turned slowly, wiped his forearm across his eyes and said, 'You've not come to arrest me, have you? I don't want to go to gaol.'

'Nobody's going to take you to gaol, Adam.'

'I didn't mean nothing, honest I didn't.'

'Why don't you just calm down and tell me what happened. We'll get it sorted. Can I come in?'

Adam sat up on the bed. He was a fair-haired kid with thick glasses, freckles and sticking-out ears, the kind who is often teased at school and develops an active fantasy life to escape. The kind Banks used to defend from bullies, perhaps. His eyes were red with crying. 'Suppose so,' he said.

Banks went inside the small bedroom. There were no chairs, so he sat on the edge of the bed, at the bottom. Posters of muscular sword-and-sorcery heroes wielding enormous broadswords hung on the walls. A small computer sat on a desk, and a pile of old comic books stood by the bedside. That was about all there was room for. Banks left the door open.

'Why don't you tell me about it?' he asked.

'I thought it were magic,' Adam said. 'The Talisman. That's why I went there.'

'Went where?'

'Hobb's End. It's a magic place. It were destroyed in a battle between good and evil, but there's still magic buried there. I thought it would make me invisible.'

'He reads too many of them comic books,' a voice said accusingly. Banks turned to see Mrs Kelly standing in the doorway. Annie came up beside her. 'Head in the clouds, he has,' Adam's mother went on. 'Dungeons and dragons, Conan the Barbarian. *Myst. Riven.* Stephen King and Clive Barker. Well, he's gone too far this time.'

Banks turned. 'Mrs Kelly,' he said, 'will you let me talk to Adam alone for a few minutes?'

She stood in the doorway, arms folded, then made a sound of disgust and walked off.

'Sorry,' Annie mouthed to Banks, following her.

Banks turned. 'Right, Adam,' he said. 'So you're a magician, are you?'

Adam looked at him suspiciously. 'I know a bit about it.'

'Would you tell me what happened at Hobb's End that day, when you fell?'

'I've already told you.'

'The whole story.'

Adam chewed his lower lip.

'You found something, didn't you?'

Adam nodded.

'Will you show it to me?'

The boy paused, then reached under his pillow and

pulled out a small round object. He hesitated, then passed it to Banks. It was a metal button, by the look of it. Corroded, still encrusted with dirt, but clearly a button of some sort.

'Where did you find this, Adam?'

'It fell into my hand, honest.'

Banks turned away to hide his smile. If he had a penny for every time he'd heard that from an accused thief, he'd be a rich man by now. 'All right,' he said. 'What were you doing when it fell into your hand?'

'Pulling the hand out.'

'It was in the skeleton's hand?'

'Must've been, mustn't it?'

'As if the victim had been holding it in her palm?'

'You what?'

'Never mind. Why didn't you tell us about it sooner?'

'I thought it were what I'd gone there for. The Talisman. It's not easy to get. You have to pass through the veil to the Seventh Level. There's sacrifice and fear to overcome.'

Banks hadn't a clue what the boy was talking about. In Adam's imagination, it seemed, the old button had taken on some magical quality because of how it had been delivered to him. Not that it mattered that much. The point was that Adam had taken the button from Gloria Shackleton's hand.

'You did well,' Banks said. 'But you should have passed this on to me the first time I came to see you. It's not what you were looking for.'

Adam seemed disappointed. 'It's not?'

'No. It's not a talisman, it's just an old button.'

'Is it important?'

'I don't know yet. It might be.'

'Who was it? Do you know? The skeleton?'

'A young woman.'

Adam paused to take it in. 'Was she pretty?'

'I think she was.'

'Has she been there a long time?'

'Since the war.'

'Did the Germans kill her?'

'We don't think so. We don't know who killed her.' He held out the button on his palm. 'This might help us find out. You might help us.'

'But whoever did it will be dead by now, won't he?'

'Probably,' said Banks.

'My granddad died in the war.'

'I'm sorry to hear it, Adam.' Banks stood up. 'You can come down now, if you want. Nobody's going to do you any harm.'

'But my mum—'

'She was just upset, that's all.' Banks paused in the doorway. 'When I was a lad your age, I once stole a ring from Woolworth's. It was only a plastic ring, not worth much, but I got caught.' Banks could remember it as if it were yesterday: the smell of smoke on the department-store detectives' breath; their overbearing size as they stood over him in the cramped triangular office tucked away under the escalator; the rough way they handled him and his fear that they were going to beat him up or molest him in some way, and that everyone would think he deserved it because he was a thief. All for a plastic ring. Not even that, really. Just to show off.

'What happened?' Adam asked.

'They made me tell them my name and address and my mother had to go down and see them about it. She stopped my pocket money and wouldn't let me go out to play for a month.' They had searched him roughly, pulling everything from his pockets: string, penknife, cricket cards, pencil stub, a gobstopper, bus fare home, and his cigarettes. That was why his mother had stopped his pocket money: because the Woolworth's store detectives told her about the cigarettes. Which they no doubt smoked themselves. He always thought that was unfair, that the cigarettes had nothing to do with it. Punish him for stealing the ring, yes, but leave him his cigarettes. Of course, over the subsequent years, he had come across many more examples of life's basic unfairness, not a few of them perpetrated by himself. He had to admit that there were occasions when he had arrested someone for a driving offence, found a few grams of coke or hash in his pocket and added that to the charge sheet.

'Anyway,' he went on, 'it took me a long time to work out why she was so upset over something so unimportant as a plastic ring.'

'Why?'

'Because she was ashamed. It humiliated her to have to go down there and listen to these men tell her that her son was a thief. To have them talk down to her as if it were her fault and have to thank them for not calling the police. It didn't matter that I hadn't done anything serious. She was ashamed that a son of hers would do such a thing. And worried it might be a sign of what I'd turn into.'

'But you're a copper, not a thief.'

Banks smiled. 'Yes, I'm a copper. So come on downstairs and we'll see if we can make your mother a bit more forgiving than mine was.'

Adam hesitated, but at last he jumped up from the bed. Banks moved aside and let him go down the narrow staircase first.

Adam's mother was in the kitchen making tea, and Annie was leaning against the counter talking to her.

'Oh, so you've decided to join us, have you, you little devil?' said Mrs Kelly.

'Sorry, Mum.'

She ruffled his hair. 'Get on with you. Just don't do owt like that again.'

'Can I have a Coke?'

'In the fridge.'

Adam turned to the fridge and Banks winked at him. Adam blushed and grinned.

8

Vivian Elmsley sat down with her gin and tonic to watch the news that evening. The drinks were becoming more frequent, she had noticed, since her memories had started disturbing her. Though it was the only chink in her iron discipline, and she only allowed herself to indulge at the end of the day, it was a worrying sign nonetheless.

Watching the news had become a sort of grim duty now, a morbid fascination. Tonight, what she saw shook her to the core.

Towards the end of the broadcast, after the major world news and government scandals had been dealt with, the scene shifted to a familiar sight. A young blonde woman held the microphone. She stood in Hobb's End, where crime-scene searchers in their white boiler suits and wellies were still digging up the ruins.

'Today,' the reporter began, 'in a further bizarre twist to a story we have been covering in the north of England, police investigating some skeletal remains found by a local schoolboy are almost certain they have established the identity of the victim. Just over an hour ago, Detective Chief Inspector Alan Banks, who is heading the investigation, talked with our northern office.'

The scene shifted to a studio background, and the camera settled on a lean, dark-haired man with intense blue eyes.

'Can you tell us how this discovery was made?' the reporter asked.

'Yes.' Banks looked straight into the camera as he spoke, she noticed, not letting his eyes flick left or right the way so many amateurs did when they appeared on television. He had clearly done it before. 'When we discovered the identity of the people living in the cottage during the Second World War,' he began, 'we found that one of them, a woman called Gloria Shackleton, hasn't shown up on any postwar records so far.'

'And that made you suspicious?'

The detective smiled. 'Naturally. Of course, there could be a number of reasons for this, and we're still looking into other possibilities, but one thing we are forced to consider is that she doesn't show up because she was dead.'

'How long have the woman's remains been buried?'

'It's hard to be accurate, but we're estimating between the early to mid-forties.'

'That's a long time ago, isn't it?'

'It is.'

'Don't trails go cold, clues go stale?'

'Indeed they do. But I'm very pleased with the progress we've made so far, and I'm confident we can take this investigation forward. The remains were discovered only last Wednesday, and within less than a week we are reasonably certain we have established the identity of the victim. I'd say that's pretty good going for this sort of case.'

'And the next step?'

'The identity of the murderer.'

'Even though he or she may be dead?'

'Until we know that one way or the other, we're still dealing with an open case of murder. As they say in America, there's no statute of limitations on murder.'

'Is there any way the public can help?'

'Yes, there is.' Banks shifted in his chair. The next moment, the screen was filled with the head and shoulders of a woman. Surely it couldn't be? But even though it wasn't a photographic likeness, there was no mistaking who it was: *Gloria*.

Vivian gasped and clutched her chest.

Gloria.

After all these years.

It looked like part of a painting. Judging from the odd angle of the head, Vivian guessed that Gloria had been lying down as she posed. Michael Stanhope? It looked like his style. In the background, Banks's voice went on, 'If anyone recognizes this woman, who we think lived in London between 1921 and 1941 and in Hobb's End after that, if there is any living relative who knows something about her, would they please get in touch with the North Yorkshire Police.' He gave out a phone number. 'There's still a great deal we need to know,' he went on, 'and as the events occurred so long ago, that makes it all the more difficult for us.'

Vivian tuned out. All she could see was Gloria's face: Stanhope's vision of Gloria's face, with that cunning blend of naivety and wantonness, that come-hither smile and its promise of secret delights. It both was and *wasn't* Gloria.

Then she thought, with a tremor of fear: if they had already discovered Gloria, how long would it take them to discover *her*?

•

'It only said he's *missing*,' Gloria insisted over two months later, at the height of the summer of 1943. We were standing by one of Mr Kilnsey's dry-stone walls drinking

Tizer and looking out over the gold-green hills to the northwest. She thrust the most recent Ministry letter towards me and pointed at the words. 'See. "Missing during severe fighting east of the Irrawaddy River in Burma." Wherever that is. When Mr Kilnsey's son was killed at El Alamein it said he was definitely dead, not just missing.'

What had kept us going the most since we heard the news of Matthew's disappearance was our attempt to get as much information as we possibly could about what had happened to him. First we had written letters, then we had even telephoned the Ministry. But they wouldn't commit themselves. *Missing* was all they would tell us, and nobody seemed to know anything about the exact circumstances of his disappearance or where he might be if he was still alive. If they did, they weren't saying.

The most we could get out of the man on the telephone was that the area in which Matthew had disappeared was now in the hands of the Japanese, so there was no question of going in to search for bodies. Yes, he admitted, an unspecified number of casualties had been confirmed, but Matthew was not among them. While it was still likely he might have been killed, the man concluded, there was also a chance he had been taken prisoner. It was impossible to get anything further out of him. Since the telephone call, Gloria had been brooding over what to do next.

'I think we should go there,' she said, crumpling the letter into a ball.

'Where? *Burma*?'

'No, silly. London. We should go down there and buttonhole someone. Get some answers.'

'But they won't talk to us,' I protested. 'Besides, I don't think they're in London any more. All the government people have moved out to the country somewhere.'

'There has to be *somebody* there,' Gloria argued. 'It stands to reason. Even if it's just a skeleton staff. A government can't just pack up and leave everything behind. Especially the War Office. Besides, this is London I'm talking about. It's still the capital of England, you know. If there are answers to be found, you can bet we'll find them there.'

There was no arguing with Gloria's passionate rhetoric. 'I don't know,' I said. 'I wouldn't have the faintest idea where to start.'

'Whitehall,' she said, nodding. 'That's where we start. Whitehall.'

She sounded so certain that I didn't know what to reply.

For the rest of that month I tried to talk Gloria out of the London trip, but she was adamant. Once she got like that, I knew there could be no stopping her getting her own way. Even Cynthia and Alice and Michael Stanhope said it would be a waste of time. Mr Stanhope had no time at all for government bureaucrats and assured us they would tell us nothing.

Gloria insisted that if I didn't want to come with her, that was fine, she would go by herself. I didn't have the courage to tell her that I had never been to London, not even in peacetime, and the whole prospect scared me stiff. London seemed about as remote to me as the moon.

It was finally arranged for September. Gloria decided it would be best if we went and returned by night train. That way she would only have to rearrange her one and a half days off for midweek rather than ask Mr Kilnsey for more time when things were busy. To her surprise, Mr Kilnsey said she could take longer if she wished. Since he had lost Joseph at E1 Alamein, he had become a more compassionate and sympathetic man, and he understood her grief. We still decided to stick to the original plan because I didn't want to leave Mother alone for any longer.

Cynthia Garmen said she would look after Mother and the shop while we were gone. She said Norma Prentice owed her a day's work at the NAAFI in exchange for babysitting the previous week, so it should be no problem. Mother offered to buy the train tickets and gave Gloria some of her clothes coupons to use down there if we had time to visit the big shops. Though she accepted them gratefully, for once clothes were the last thing on Gloria's mind.

•

It was about ten o'clock when the road crested the hill and Banks could see Edinburgh spread out in the distance in all its hazy glory: the stepped rows of tenements; the dark Gothic spire of the Sir Walter Scott Monument, like some alien space rocket; the hump of Arthur's Seat; the castle on its crag; the glimmer of sea beyond.

Apart from one or two brief police-related visits, it was years since Banks had spent any time there, he realized as he coasted down the hill, Van Morrison's 'Tupelo Honey' on the stereo. When he was a student, he used to drive up to see friends quite often for weekends and holidays. At one time he had a girlfriend, a raven-haired young beauty called Alison, who lived down on St Stephen Street. But as is the nature of such long-distance relationships, 'out of sight, out of mind' beats 'absence makes the heart grow fonder' any day of the week, and during one visit she simply turned up at the pub with someone else. Easy come, easy go. By then he had his eye on another woman, called Jo, anyway.

Banks tried to recollect if he had ever taken Jem up to Edinburgh with him, but for the life of him he couldn't remember even seeing Jem outside his room, though he must have gone out to buy food, records and dope, as well as to sign on the dole. Banks had never even seen him out in the hallway. He saw people come and go from time to time, strangers, sometimes at weird hours of the night, but Jem never mentioned any other friends.

Banks's Edinburgh days were all pre-*Trainspotting* and the place didn't look quite so romantic when he came down off the hill into the built-up streets of dark stone, the roundabouts and traffic lights, shopping centres and zebra crossings. He got through Dalkeith easily enough, but shortly afterwards he made one simple mistake and found himself heading towards Glasgow on a dual carriageway for about three miles before he found an exit.

Elizabeth Goodall lived just off Dalkeith Road, not far from the city centre. She had given him precise directions on the telephone the previous evening, and after only a couple more wrong turns, he found the narrow street of tall tenements.

Mrs Goodall lived on the ground floor. She answered Banks's ring promptly and led him into a high-ceilinged living room which smelled of lavender and peppermint. All the windows were shut fast, and not the slightest breeze stirred the warm, perfumed air. Only a little daylight managed to steal through. The wallpaper was patterned with sprigs of rosemary and thyme. Parsley and sage, too, for all Banks could tell. Mrs Goodall bade him sit in a sturdy damask armchair. Like all the other chairs in the room, its arms and back were covered by white lace antimacassars.

'So you found your way all right?' she asked.

'Yes,' Banks lied. 'Nothing to it.'

'I don't drive a motor-car myself,' she said, with a trace of her old Yorkshire accent. 'I have to rely on buses and

trains if I want to go anywhere, which is rare these days.'
She rubbed her small, wrinkled hands together. 'Well,
then, you're here. Tea?'

'Please.'

She disappeared into the kitchen. Banks surveyed the
room. It was a nondescript sort of place: clean and tidy,
but not much character. A few framed photographs stood
on the sideboard, but none of them showed Hobb's End.
One glass-fronted cabinet held a few knick-knacks, including trophies, silverware and crystal. That would be
tempting to burglars, Banks thought: old woman in a
ground-floor flat with a nice haul of silverware just there
for the taking. He hadn't noticed any signs of a security
system.

Mrs Goodall walked back into the room slowly, carrying a China tea-set on a silver tray. She set it down on a
doily on the low table in front of the sofa, then sat down,
knees together, and smoothed her skirt.

She was a short, stout woman, dressed in a grey tweed
skirt, white blouse and a navy-blue cardigan, despite the
heat. Her recently permed hair was almost white, and its
waves looked frozen, razor-sharp to the touch, Margaret
Thatcher style. Her forehead was high, and her glaucous,
watery eyes pink-rimmed. She had a prissy slit of a mouth
that seemed painted on with red lipstick.

'We'll just let it mash a few minutes, shall we?' she
said. 'Then we'll pour.'

'Fine,' said Banks, banishing the image of the two of
them holding the thin teapot handle and pouring.

'Now,' she said, hands clasped on her lap, 'let us begin.
You mentioned Hobb's End on the telephone, but that was
all you saw fit to tell me. What do you wish to know?'

Banks leaned forward and rested his forearms on his

thighs. A number of general questions came to mind, but he needed something more specific, something to take her memory right back, if possible. 'Do you remember Gloria Shackleton?' he asked. 'She lived in Bridge Cottage during the war.'

Mrs Goodall looked as if she had just swallowed a mouthful of vinegar. 'Of course I remember her,' she said. 'Dreadful girl.'

'Oh? In what way?'

'Not to put too fine a point on it, Chief Inspector, the girl was a brazen hussy. It was perfectly obvious. The flirtatious manner, the tilt of her head, the lascivious smile. I knew it the first moment I set eyes on her.'

'Where was that?'

'Where? Why, in church, of course. My father was the verger at St Bartholomew's. Though how such a . . . a painted strumpet would dare to show herself like that in the sight of the Lord is beyond me.'

'So you first met her in church?'

'I didn't say I *met* her, just that I *saw* her there first. She was still called Gloria Stringer then.'

'Was she religious?'

'No true Christian woman would go about flaunting herself the way she did.'

'Why did she go to church, then?'

'Because the Shackletons went, of course. She had her feet firmly under their kitchen table.'

'She was from London originally, wasn't she?'

'So she said.'

'Did she ever say anything about her background, about her family?'

'Not to me, though I vaguely remember someone told me her parents were killed in the Blitz.'

'She'd come to Hobb's End with the Women's Land Army, hadn't she?'

'Yes. A *land girl*. Tea?'

'Please.'

Mrs Goodall sat up, back erect, and poured. The tea-cups – with matching saucers – were tiny, fragile bone-china things with pink roses painted inside and out, a gold rim and a handle he couldn't possibly get a finger through. Not a drop stained the white lace doily. 'Milk? Sugar?'

'Just as it comes, thanks very much.'

She frowned, as if she didn't approve of that. Anything other than milk and two sugars was probably unpatriotic in her book. 'Of course,' she went on. 'One hoped that over time she would make attempts to fit in, to alter her manner and appearance according to the standards of village society, but—'

'She made no attempt?'

'She did not. None at all.'

'Did you know her well?'

'Chief Inspector, does she sound like the kind of person whose company I would cultivate?'

'It was a small village. You must have been about the same age.'

'I was one year older.'

'Even so.'

'Alice – that's Alice Pool – used to spend quite a bit of time with her. Against my advice, I might add. But then Alice always was a bit too free and easy.'

'Did you have any dealings with Gloria at all?'

Mrs Goodall paused, as if to bring to mind an unpleasant memory. Then she nodded. 'Indeed I did. It fell to me to advise her that her behaviour was unacceptable, as was the way she looked.'

'Looked?'

'Yes. The sort of clothes she wore, the way she sashayed about, the way she wore her hair, like some sort of cheap American film star. It was not ladylike. Not in the least. As if that weren't bad enough, *she smoked in the street.*'

'You say it *fell* to you? On what authority? Was there strong general feeling against her?'

'In my capacity as a member of the Church of England.'

'I see. Was everyone else in Hobb's End ladylike?'

She pursed her lips again and let him know with a quick dagger glance that she hadn't missed the insolence in his tone. 'I'm not saying that there weren't lower elements in the village, Chief Inspector. Don't get me wrong. Of course, there were. As there are in every village society. But even the lowly of birth can aspire to at least a certain level of good manners and decent behaviour. Wouldn't you agree?'

'How did Gloria react when you rebuked her?'

Mrs Goodall flushed at the memory. 'She laughed. I pointed out that it might do her much good, morally and socially, were she to become active in the Women's Institute and the Missionary Society.'

'What was her response to this?'

'She called me an interfering busybody and indicated that there was only one missionary position she was interested in, and it was *not* the Church's. Can you believe it? And she used such language as I would not expect from the mouth of the lowest mill girl. Despite her put-on speech, I think she showed her true colours then.'

'How did she speak?'

'Oh, she had her airs and graces. She spoke like someone on the wireless. Not the way they do these days, of course, but as they did back then, when people spoke properly on the wireless. But you could tell it was put on. She had clearly been practising the arts of imitation and deception.'

'She married Matthew Shackleton, didn't she?'

Mrs Goodall sucked in her breath with an audible hiss. 'Yes. I was at their wedding. And I must say that, although Matthew was only a shopkeeper's son, he married well beneath himself when he married the Stringer girl. Matthew was an exceptional boy. I expected far better of him than that.'

'Do you know anything about their relationship?'

'It wasn't long after they were married he was sent abroad. He went missing in action, poor Matthew. Missing, presumed dead.'

Banks frowned. 'When was this?'

'When he went missing?'

'Yes.'

'Sometime in 1943. He was in the Far East. Captured by the Japanese.' She gave a little shudder.

'What happened to him?'

'I have no idea. I presume he was dead.'

'You lost touch?'

She fiddled with her wedding ring. 'Yes. My husband, William, was engaged in top-secret work for the home front, and he was assigned to Scotland early in 1944. I accompanied him. My parents came to live with us, and we didn't have anything more to do with Hobb's End. I still keep in touch with Ruby Kettering and Alice Poole, but they are my only connections. It was all so long ago. We women don't dwell on the war the way the men do, with their legions and their regimental reunions.'

'Do you know if Gloria had affairs with anyone other than Matthew?'

Mrs Goodall sniffed. 'Almost certainly.'

'Who with?'

She paused a moment, as if to let him know that she shouldn't be telling him this, then she uttered just one word. 'Soldiers.'

'What soldiers?'

'This was wartime, Chief Inspector. Contrary to what you might imagine, not every man in the armed forces was over fighting the Hun or the Nip. Unfortunately. There were soldiers everywhere. Not all of them British, either.'

'What soldiers were these?'

For the first time in their conversation, Mrs Goodall let a small smile slip. It endeared her to Banks tremendously. 'Oversexed,' she said, 'overpaid and over here.'

'Americans?'

'Yes. The RAF handed Rowan Woods over to the American Air Force.'

'Did you see much of these Americans?'

'Oh, yes. They often used to come and drink in the village pubs, or attend our occasional dances at the church hall. Some even came to the Sunday services. They had their own on the base, of course, but St Bartholomew's was a beautiful old church. Such a pity it had to be knocked down.'

'Did Gloria have American boyfriends, then?'

'Several. And I needn't tell you about the opportunities for immorality and indiscretion that a wide area of wooded land like Rowan Woods has to offer, need I?'

Banks wondered if she would take a positive answer as an indication of personal experience. He decided not to risk it. 'Was there anyone in particular?' he asked.

'I have no first-hand knowledge. I kept my distance from them. According to Cynthia Garmen, she had more than one. Not that Cynthia was one to talk. No better than she ought to be, that one.'

'Why?'

'She married one of them, didn't she? Went off to live in Pennsylvania or some such place.'

'So there was no one serious for Gloria?'

'Oh, I've no doubt her liaisons were every bit as serious as a woman such as Gloria Shackleton was capable of. A *married* woman.'

'But you said she thought her husband was dead.'

'Missing, *presumed* dead. It's not quite the same. Besides, that's no excuse.' Mrs Goodall remained silent for a few moments, then said, 'May I ask *you* a question, Chief Inspector?'

'Go ahead.'

'Why are you asking me about the Shackleton girl after all these years?'

'Don't you watch the news?'

'I prefer to read historical biography.'

'Newspapers?'

'On occasion. But only the obituaries. What are you hinting at, Chief Inspector? Am I missing something?'

Banks told her about the reservoir drying up and the discovery of the body they believed to be Gloria's. Mrs Goodall paled and clutched at the silver crucifix around her neck. 'I don't like to speak ill of the dead,' she muttered. 'You should have told me sooner.'

'Would that have changed what you said?'

She paused a moment, then sighed and said, 'Probably not. I have always considered telling the truth to be an important virtue. All I can tell you, though, is that Gloria Shackleton was alive and well when William and I left Hobb's End in May 1944.'

'Thank you,' said Banks. 'That helps us narrow things down a bit. Do you know if she had any enemies?'

'Not what you'd call enemies. Nobody who would do what you have just described. Many people, like myself, disapproved of her. But that's quite a different thing. One would hardly murder a person for not joining the Women's Institute. Might I make a suggestion?'

'Please.'

'Given Gloria's wayward nature, don't you think you should be looking at this as a *crime passionnel*?'

'Perhaps.' Banks shifted in his chair and crossed his legs the other way. Mrs Goodall poured more tea. It was lukewarm. 'What about Michael Stanhope?' he asked.

She raised her eyebrows. 'There's another one.'

'Another what?'

'Debauched, perverted. I could go on. Birds of a feather, him and Gloria Shackleton. Have you *seen* any of his so-called paintings?'

Banks nodded. 'One of them seems to be a nude of Gloria. I wonder if you knew anything about that?'

'I can hardly say it surprises me, but no. Believe me, if such a painting exists, it was *not* public knowledge in Hobb's End. At least not while I was there.'

'Do you think Gloria might have had an affair with Michael Stanhope?'

'I can't say. Given that the two of them shared similar natures and views, I wouldn't rule it out. They did spend a lot of time together. *Drinking*. As I recollect, though, even Gloria's tastes weren't quite so exotic as to extend as far as a tortured, drunken, depraved artist.'

'Did Gloria and Matthew have any children?'

'Not that I ever knew of.'

'And you would have known?'

'I think so. It's hard to hide such things in a small village. Why do you ask?'

'There were certain indications in the post-mortem, that's all.' Banks scratched the tiny scar beside his right eye. 'But nobody seems to know anything about it.'

'She could have had a child after we left in 1944.'

'It's possible. Or perhaps she gave birth *before* she arrived in Hobb's End and married Matthew Shackleton. After all, she was nineteen when she came to the village. Perhaps she abandoned the baby and its father in London.'

'But . . . but that means . . .'

'Means what, Mrs Goodall?'

'Well, I never assumed that Matthew was her first conquest, not a woman like her. But a child . . .? Surely that would indicate she was already married, and that her marriage to Matthew was bigamous?'

'Just one more sin to add to her list,' said Banks. 'But it wasn't necessarily so. I imagine even back then, in the good old days, the odd child was born on the wrong side of the blanket.'

Mrs Goodall's lips tightened to a single red line for a moment, then she said, 'I don't appreciate your sarcasm, Chief Inspector, or your coarseness. Things *were* better back then. Simpler. Clearer. Ordered. And the wartime spirit brought people together. People of all classes. Say what you will.'

'I'm sorry, Mrs Goodall. I don't mean to be sarcastic, really, but I'm trying to get to the bottom of a particularly nasty murder here, one that I probably have hardly any chance of solving because it was committed so long ago. I believe the victim deserves my best efforts, no matter what you may think of her.'

'Of course she does. I stand corrected. Gloria Shackleton could not possibly have deserved what you say happened to her. But I'm sorry, I don't think I can help you any further.'

'Did you know Matthew's sister, Gwynneth?'

'Gwen? Oh, yes. Gwen was always rather the quiet one, head buried in a book. I imagined her becoming a teacher or something like that. Perhaps even a university professor. But she worked in the shop throughout the war, besides taking care of her mother and doing fire-watching at night. She was no shirker, wasn't Gwen.'

'Do you know what became of her? Is she still alive?'

'I'm afraid we lost touch when William and I went to Scotland. We weren't especially close, though she was a regular church-goer and wrote for the parish magazine.'

'Were she and Gloria close?'

'Well, they had to be, to some extent, being family. But they were different as chalk and cheese. There was some talk about Gloria leading Gwen astray. They were always off to dances together in Harkside, or to the pictures. Gwen had generally avoided social intercourse until Gloria arrived on the scene, preferring her own company, or that of books. Gwen was always a rather impressionable girl. Though she took Gloria under her wing at first, so to speak, it was soon quite clear who exactly was under whose wing.'

'What was their age difference?'

'Gwen was two or three years younger, perhaps. Believe me, though, it makes a vast difference at that age.'

'What did she look like?'

'Gwen? She was rather a plain girl, apart from her eyes. Remarkable eyes, almost oriental the way they slanted. And she was tall. Tall and awkward. A gangly sort of girl.'

'What about Matthew?'

'A dashing, handsome fellow. Very mature. Gifted with wisdom beyond his years.' Again, she allowed a little smile to flit across her hard-set features. 'If I hadn't met my William and the Stringer girl hadn't arrived on the scene, well . . . who knows? Anyway, she got her hands on him, and that was that.'

Banks let the silence stretch. He could hear a clock ticking in the background.

'If you'll excuse me, Chief Inspector,' she said after a few moments, 'I'm extremely tired. All those memories.'

Banks stood up. 'Yes, of course. I'm sorry for taking up so much of your time.'

'Not at all. It seems you've come a long way for nothing, or very little.'

Banks shrugged. 'Part of the job. Besides, you've been a great help.'

'If there's anything else I can help you with, please don't hesitate to telephone.'

'Thank you.' Banks looked at his watch. Going on for one. Time for a spot of lunch before the long drive home.

•

We took the night train from Leeds, where the platform was crowded with young soldiers. The train clanked and steamed into the station only an hour late, and we felt ourselves jostled and pushed along by the crowd like corks in a fast-flowing river. I was terrified that we were going to fall between the carriages and be run over by the huge iron wheels, but we clung on to each other for dear life amid all the shoving and heaving and hissing steam, and we finally managed to get ourselves more or less pushed on to seats in a cramped compartment that soon grew even more cramped.

Another hour passed before the engine groaned and shuddered out of the station.

I had loved train journeys ever since I was a little girl, loved the gentle rocking motion, the hypnotic clickety-click of the wheels on the lines and the way the landscape drifts by like images from a dream.

Not that time.

A lot of trains had been damaged and most of the railway workshops were being used for munitions production. As a result, many of the engines in use would have been good for nothing but scrap iron if it hadn't been for the war. The motion was jerky and we never really got going fast enough for a rhythmic clickety-click. Everyone was crushed far too closely together to make sleep possible. At least for me. I couldn't even read. The blinds were drawn tight and the whole compartment was lit by one ghostly blue pinpoint of light, so dim you could hardly make out the features of the person sitting opposite you. There wasn't even a restaurant car.

We talked for a while with two young soldiers, who offered us Woodbine after Woodbine. I think that was when I started to smoke, out of sheer boredom. Even when the first few puffs made me feel sick and dizzy, I persevered. It was something to do.

The soldiers sympathized and wished us luck when Gloria told them about Matthew. Then people started to fall silent, each drifting into his own world. For me it was a matter of gritting my teeth and enduring the long journey, the constant, unexplained delays, the jerking stops and starts.

Gloria managed to doze off after a while and her head slid slowly sideways until she was resting her cheek on my shoulder and I could feel her warm breath against my throat. I still couldn't sleep. I was left with nothing but my own gloomy thoughts and rasping snores from the soldiers. We stopped in the middle of nowhere for nearly two hours at one point. No explanation.

Because of the double summertime, it didn't get light as early as it used to, but even so we weren't more than six or seven hours into the journey before we were able to open the blinds on muted early morning sunlight slanting across the fields. People had put odd objects like old mangles and broken cars on some of the empty meadows to make obstacles for any enemy planes that might try to land there.

One field was scattered with country signposts stuck in the ground at strange angles. The signposts had been taken down at the start of the war, along with all the station nameplates, to confuse the enemy in case of invasion, but I was still surprised to see where some of them had ended up.

All in all, the journey took ten hours, and the last hour or two seemed to take us through the endless London suburbs. It was here that I caught my first sight of street after street of bombed-out terraces, shattered lamp-posts, powdered plaster, twisted girders and jagged walls. Rosebay willowherb and Oxford ragwort grew from the rubble, pushing between the cracks in the bombed masonry and brickwork.

Packs of children roved through the streets, playing among the derelict houses. One ingenious group had rigged up a rope from a lamp-post that seemed to be leaning at a precarious angle, like the Tower of Pisa, and they were proceeding to take it in turns to swing back and forth, playing at Tarzan the Ape Man.

Some houses were only half-destroyed, split open like a cross-section. You could see wallpaper, framed paintings and photographs on the walls, a bed half hanging over the jagged remains of the floor. Here and there, people had moved damaged items of furniture into the street: a doorless wardrobe, a cracked sideboard and a pram with buckled wheels. I felt like a voyeur at a disaster site, which is what I was, I suppose, but I couldn't stop looking. I'm not sure that I had any real grasp of the full extent of the war's devastation until then, despite seeing Leeds after that air raid.

It seemed that on every area of spare ground not taken up by allotments, a barrage balloon station had been set up to deter low-flying enemy planes. The fat silver balloons glinted in the sun and looked like whales trying to fly. In some of the green areas, rows of anti-aircraft guns pointed at the sky like steel arrows.

Of course, there were also plenty of buildings left standing and some of these were surrounded by sandbags, often to a height of about ten feet or more. I also noticed a lot of posters, on just about every available hoarding; they told us to grow our own food, save coal, buy war bonds, walk when we can and Lord knows what else.

I was so lost in the sights that I hardly noticed the time pass until King's Cross. It was after ten o'clock in the morning when we arrived at the station and I was starving. Gloria wanted to head straight for Whitehall, but I persuaded her to stop and we found a Lyons, where we managed to get a rasher of bacon and an egg.

After breakfast, we walked back into the street and I was at last able to take in where I was. My first sensation was of being a very small, tiny, insignificant little creature lost in an immense and sprawling city. People pressed in on me from all directions; tall buildings towered over me.

The whole place had a shabby, worn and slightly defeated air about it. Everybody looked pinched and pale, the kind of look you get after years of rationing, bombing and uncertainty. Even so, for a Yorkshire country girl, it might

as well have been another planet. I had never been anywhere bigger than Leeds before and I'm sure London would
have overwhelmed me even in peacetime.

It had started to drizzle, though the air was still warm, and
the damp sandbags gave off a musky smell. There were so
many people rushing about, most of them in uniform, that I
began to feel quite panicky and dizzy. I clutched at Gloria's
arm as she led me purposefully towards a bus stop. Often
people smiled or said hello as we passed. I saw my first
wounded soldiers, sad-looking men with bandaged heads,
missing limbs, eye patches, some on crutches or with their
arms in slings. All of them lucky ones; they were still alive.

Gloria was in her element. After only a few moments of
disorientation at first, something seemed to click, as if the
city actually made sense to her, which it certainly didn't to
me. She seemed to have only the slightest doubt over which
bus to catch, and a quick word with the clippie, who was
trying to look like Joan Crawford, soon set her right on that.
We went upstairs, where you could smoke, and then we
were off.

It was a whirlwind journey and more than once I feared
the bus would tip over turning a corner. In the east, I fancied
I could see the immense dome of St Paul's in the grey light
through the dirty, rain-streaked window. I was overwhelmed by the size of the buildings all around me. White
and grey stone darkened by rain; curving Georgian or
Edwardian façades five or six storeys high, with pediments,
gargoyles and pointed gables. Huge Ionic columns. Surely,
I thought, this must be a city built by giants.

At one point my heart jumped into my throat. I saw
broken glass and rubble on the pavement and, strewn among
it all, human body parts: a head, a leg, a torso. But when I
looked more closely, I could see no blood, and the limbs all

had a hard, unnatural look about them. I realized that a bomb must have hit a dress shop and blown all the mannequins into the street.

We passed Trafalgar Square, where Nelson's Column stood, much taller in reality than it had been even in my imagination. You could hardly see poor Lord Nelson up at the top. The base of the column was covered with hoardings asking us to buy National War Savings Bonds. Across the square, near the Insurance Office and the Canadian Pacific Building, was a huge billboard advertising Famel cough mixture.

There were a lot of soldiers milling about. I didn't recognize all the caps and uniforms, in just about every colour you could imagine, from black to bright blue and cherry-red. I also saw my first-ever Negro from that bus in Trafalgar Square. I knew they existed, of course – I had read about them – but I had never actually seen a black man before. I remember being rather disappointed that, apart from being black, he didn't look all that much different from anyone else.

Gloria nudged me gently and we got off on a broad street flanked with even more tall buildings.

And that was when our search began in earnest. I felt like a small child dragged along by its mother as Gloria took me from building to building. We asked policemen, knocked on doors, asked soldiers, strangers in the street, knocked on even more doors.

Finally, wet and weary and ready to give up, I rejoiced when Gloria found some sort of minor clerk who took pity on us. I don't honestly think he knew anything about Matthew or what had happened to him, but he did seem to know a little more about the war in the Far East than anyone else would admit to. And he seemed to take a shine to Gloria.

He was a tidy little man in a pinstripe suit, with grey hair parted at the centre and a neat, trim moustache. He glanced at his watch, pursed his lips and frowned before suggesting he might spare us ten minutes if we cared to accompany him to the tea house on the corner. He had a rather high-pitched, squeaky voice and spoke with a posh, educated accent. At that point I would have cheerfully murdered for a cup of tea. We dragged ourselves inside, bought tea at the counter, and Gloria started to pump the poor fellow for information before we had even had our first sip.

'What are the chances that Matthew might still be alive?' she asked.

This clearly wasn't the sort of question the man, who told us his name was Arthur Winchester, was trained to answer. He hemmed and hawed a bit, then measured his words as carefully as the sugar cubes in the bowl were rationed. 'I'm afraid I can't really answer that question,' he said. 'As I told you, I have no knowledge of the individual case to which you refer, merely a little general knowledge of the situation in the East.'

'All right,' Gloria went on, undaunted, 'tell me about what happened at Irridaddy, or whatever it is. That's if it's not classified.'

Arthur Winchester sniffed and granted us a little smile. 'Irrawaddy. It happened six months ago, so it's hardly classified,' he said. Then he paused, sipped some more tea and rubbed the bristly bottom of his moustache with the back of his hand. I glanced towards the window and saw the rain slanting down, distorting the shapes of the people passing by on Victoria Street.

'Burma,' he went on, 'as you probably know, stands between India and China, and it would be of inestimable value if our forces could reopen the Burma Road and clear the way to China, which could then be used as a direct base for operations against Japan. This, as I say, is general knowledge.'

'Not to me it isn't.' Gloria lit a Craven A. 'Go on,' she prompted, blowing out a long plume of smoke.

Arthur Winchester cleared his throat. 'To put things simply, since Burma fell, we have been trying to get it back. One of the offensives with this end in mind was the Chindit Operation, launched in February. They began east of the Irrawaddy, a river in central Burma. While they were there, the Japanese launched a major offensive on the Arakan Front and the British had to withdraw. Are you following me?'

We both nodded.

'Good.' Arthur Winchester finished his tea. 'Well, the Chindits were trapped behind the enemy lines, cut off, and they began to filter back in some disarray.' He looked at Gloria. 'This, no doubt, is why no one has been able to give you any specific information about your husband. He's an engineer, you said?'

'Yes.'

'Hmm.'

'What happened next?'

'Next? Oh, well the Chindits had suffered severe hard-ships. Most severe. Not long after, they were ordered to leave Burma.'

'But we're still trying to get Burma back?'

'Oh, yes. It's of great strategic importance.'

'So there's still a chance?'

'A chance of what?'

'That someone might find Matthew. When the British win back Burma.'

Arthur Winchester glanced out of the window. 'I wouldn't get your hopes up, my dear. A long time might pass before that happens.'

'Were the losses heavy?' I asked.

Arthur Winchester gazed at me for a moment, but he wasn't seeing me. 'What? Oh, yes. Rather worse than we had hoped for.'

'How do you know all this?' Gloria asked.

Arthur Winchester inclined his head modestly. 'I don't know very much, I'm afraid. But before the war, before this government work, I was a history teacher. The Far East has always interested me.'

'So you don't really have anything to tell us?' Gloria said.

'Well, any excuse to take tea with a pretty lady will do for me, if you don't mind my saying so.'

Gloria got to her feet in a fury and was about to storm out of the place, leaving even me behind, when Arthur Winchester blushed and grabbed hold of her sleeve meekly. 'I say, my dear, I'm sorry. Poor taste. I really didn't mean to offend you. A compliment, that's all. I meant no hint of any sort of prurient suggestion.'

If Gloria didn't know what *prurient* meant, she never let on. She merely sat down again, slowly, a hard, suspicious look in her eyes, and said, 'Can you tell us anything at all, Mr Winchester?'

'All I can tell you, my dear,' he went on gravely, 'is that during the retreat, many of the wounded had to be left behind enemy lines. They simply couldn't be transported. They were left with a little money and a weapon, of course, but what became of them, I can't say.'

Gloria had turned pale. I found myself twisting the fabric of my dress in my fist over my lap until my knuckles turned white. 'Are you saying this is what happened to Matthew?' she asked, her voice no louder than a whisper.

'I'm saying it may be what happened, if he is simply being described as missing, presumed dead.'

'And what if that was the case?'

Arthur Winchester paused and brushed an imaginary piece of lint from his lapel. 'Well,' he said, 'the Japanese don't like taking wounded prisoners. It would depend how badly wounded he was, of course, whether he could work, that sort of thing.'

'So you're saying they might have simply murdered him as he lay there wounded and defenceless?'

'I'm saying it's possible. Or . . .'

'Or what?'

He looked away. 'As I said, the wounded were left behind with a weapon.'

It took a second or two for what he was getting at to sink in. I think it was me who responded first. 'You mean Matthew might have committed suicide?'

'If capture was inevitable, and if he was badly hurt, then I'd say, yes, it's a possibility.' His tone brightened a little. 'But this is all pure conjecture, you understand. I know nothing at all of the circumstances. Maybe he was simply captured by the enemy, and he's going to while away the rest of the war in the relative safety of a prison camp. I mean, you've seen how well we take care of our Germans and Italians here, haven't you?'

It was true. The Italians in Yorkshire even worked on the farms at planting and harvest times. Gloria and I had talked to them on occasion and they seemed cheerful enough, for prisoners of war. They liked to sing opera while they worked, and some of them had beautiful voices.

'But you said the Japanese don't like taking prisoners.'

'It's true they despise the weak and the defeated. But if they capture fit men, they can put them to work on railways and bridges and suchlike. They're not fools. You *did* say

217

your husband was an engineer, so he could be useful to them.'

'*If* he cooperated.'

'Yes. The main problem is that we don't know a lot about the Japanese, and our lines of communication are very poor, almost to the point of not existing at all. Even the Red Cross has great difficulties getting its parcels delivered and getting information out of them. The Japanese are notoriously difficult to deal with.'

'So he may be a prisoner of war and nobody has bothered to let anyone know? Is that what you're telling us?'

'That is a distinct possibility. Yes. There are probably hundreds, if not thousands, of others in that same position, too.'

'But you said you're a teacher. You know about the Japanese, don't you?'

Arthur Winchester laughed nervously. 'I know a little about their geography and history, but the Japanese have always been very insular. Comes from living on an island, perhaps.'

'We live on an island, too,' I reminded him.

'Yes, well, I mean insular more in that they've screened themselves off from the rest of the world, actively resisted contact with the West. We knew practically nothing at all about them until the turn of the century – their customs, beliefs – and even now we don't know a lot.'

'What *do* you know? What *can* you tell us?' Gloria asked.

He paused again. 'Well,' he said. 'I don't want to upset you, but you asked me to be honest with you. I'd say it's best to hope he's dead. It's best that way.' He paused. 'Look. It's wartime. Things are very different. You have to let go of the past. Your husband is probably dead. Or, if he isn't, he might as well be. Nothing will be the same when it's done.

All over the city people are living as if there's no tomorrow. How long are you staying in London?'

Gloria looked at him suspiciously. 'Until tonight. Why?'

'I know a place. Very nice. Very discreet. Perhaps I could—'

Gloria got to her feet so fast she bumped the table with her thighs and the remains of her tea spilled on to Arthur Winchester's lap. But he didn't stop around to mop it up. Instead, he bolted for the door saying, 'Good Lord, is that the time? I must dash.'

And with that, he was out of the door before Gloria could even pick up something to throw at him. She glared after him for a moment, then touched up her curls and sat down again. The serving girl frowned at us, then turned away. I thought we were lucky not to get thrown out.

We dawdled over our tea, Gloria calming down, smoking another cigarette and gazing out through the steamed-up window at the phantoms drifting by outside. In the café, soldiers came and went with their girls. I could smell the rain on their uniforms.

'What did he mean, it's best that way?' Gloria asked.

'I don't know,' I said. 'I suppose he meant to say that the Japanese don't treat their prisoners as well as we do.'

'What do they do? Torture them? Beat them? Starve them?'

'I don't know, Gloria,' I said, putting my hand over hers. 'I just don't know. All I can say is that it sounded to me as if he was saying Matthew would be better off dead.'

9

Annie parked in one of the hilly streets around St Mary's, at the back of the castle, and went looking for Alice Poole's cottage. The sky was bright blue, with only a few wisps of white cloud borne on the sea breeze. Pity she had to work. She could have brought her bucket and spade. As a child she had spent hours amusing herself on the beach. Some of her only memories of her mother took place on the beach at St Ives: building sandcastles together, burying one another in the sand so that only a head showed, or maybe a head and feet, running into the big waves and getting knocked over. In Annie's memory, her mother was a bright, mercurial figure, mischievous, devil-may-care, always laughing. Though her father, on the surface, was easygoing, bright, funny and caring, there was a darkness in his art that Annie felt excluded her; she didn't know where it came from or how he reconciled it with the rest of his life. Did he suffer terribly in private and simply put on a public face, even for his own daughter? She hardly knew him at all.

She found the cottage easily enough, according to directions she had received over the telephone. It was in a high, quiet part of town, away from the pubs and shopping centres crowded with holidaymakers from Leeds and Bradford. From the garden she could see a wedge of the North Sea far below, beyond Marine Drive, steely grey-blue today, dotted with small boats. Flocks of gulls gathered, squealing, above a shoal of fish.

The woman who answered the door was tall, with thin, wispy hair like candyfloss. She was wearing a long, loose purple dress with gold embroidery around the neck, hem and sleeves, and gold earrings of linked hoops that dangled almost as far as her shoulders. It reminded Annie of the sort of thing hippies used to wear. A pair of black horn-rimmed glasses hung on a chain around her neck.

'Come in, love.' She led the way into a bright, cluttered room. Dust motes spun in the rays of sunlight that lanced through the panes of the mullioned window. 'Can I offer you anything?' she asked, having settled Annie in an armchair so soft and deep she wondered how she'd ever get out of it. 'Only, I usually have elevenses around this time. Coffee and a Kit Kat. Instant coffee, mind you.'

Annie smiled. 'That'll be fine; thanks, Mrs Poole.'

'Alice. Call me Alice. And why don't you have a look through this while I see to things in the kitchen. Your call got me thinking about the old days and I realized I hadn't had it out in years.'

She handed Annie a thick leatherbound photograph album and headed for the kitchen. Most of the deckle-edged black-and-white photographs were family groups, what Annie took to be Alice and her parents, aunts, brothers and sisters, but several were village scenes: women stopping to chat in the street, baskets over their arms, scarves knotted on their heads; children fishing from the riverbanks. There were also a couple of pictures of the church, which was smaller and prettier than she had imagined from Stanhope's painting, with a squat, square tower, and of the dark, brooding flax mill, like a skull perched on its promontory.

Alice Poole came back holding a mug of coffee in each

hand and a Kit Kat, still in its wrapper, between her teeth. When she had freed her hands, she took the chocolate bar from her mouth and put it on a small coffee table beside her chair. 'A little indulgence of mine,' she said. 'Would you like one? I should have asked.'

'No,' said Annie. 'No, that's fine.' She accepted her coffee. It was milky and sweet, just the way she liked it.

'What do you think of the photos?'

'Very interesting.'

'You've come about poor Gloria, then?'

'You've heard?'

'Oh, yes. Your boss was on telly last night. I don't see very well, but there's nothing wrong with my ears. I don't watch a lot of television, but not much local news slips by me. Especially something like that. How horrible. Have you got any suspects yet?'

'Not really,' said Annie. 'We're still trying to find out as much as we can about Gloria. It's very difficult, what with it all being so long ago.'

'You don't say. I was seventy-five last birthday. Can you believe it?'

'Quite honestly, Mrs – sorry, Alice – I can't.' She really did seem remarkably spry for a woman of that age. Apart from a few liver spots on her hands and wrinkles on her face, the only real indication of the ravages of age was her sparse and lifeless hair, which Annie was now coming to believe had probably fallen victim to chemotherapy and not yet grown back properly.

'Look,' Alice pointed out, 'this is Gloria.' She turned to a photograph of four girls standing in front of a Jeep and pointed to the petite blonde with the long curls, the narrow waist and the provocative smile. Without a doubt it was the same girl from Stanhope's painting. Underneath,

in tiny white letters, was written 'July 1944'. 'This one's
Gwen, her sister-in-law.' Gwen was the tallest of them all.
She wasn't smiling and had half turned away from the
camera, as if shy about her looks. 'And this one here is
Cynthia Garmen. The Four Musketeers, we were. Oh, that
one's me.' Alice had been a svelte blonde, by the look of
her. Also in the photograph, standing in the Jeep behind
the girls, were four young men in uniform.

'Who are they?' Annie asked.

'Americans. That one's Charlie, and that's Brad. We
saw quite a lot of them. I don't remember the names of the
other two. They just happened to be there.'

'I'd like to make a copy of that photo, if you don't mind.
We'll send it back to you.'

'Not at all.' Alice detached the photograph from its
corners. 'Please take care of it, though.'

'I promise.' Annie slipped it in her briefcase. 'You knew
Gloria well?' she went on.

'Quite well. She married Matthew Shackleton, as you
probably know, and while he was away at war, Gloria and
Gwen, Matthew's sister, became inseparable. But quite
often the gang of us would do something together. Anyway, I wouldn't say we were the best of friends, but I did
know her. And I liked her.'

'What was she like?'

'Gloria?' Alice unwrapped her Kit Kat and took a bite.
When she had swallowed it, she said, 'Well, I'd say she
was a good sort. Cheerful. Fun to be with. Kind. Generous.
She'd give you the shirt off her back. Or make one for you.'

'Pardon?'

'Magic fingers. Gloria was such an expert sewer you
could give her rags and she'd turn out a ball gown. Well,
I might be exaggerating a little, but I'm sure you get my

point. It was a skill in much demand back then, I can tell you. There wasn't a heck of a lot in the shops, and your clothing coupons didn't go very far.'

'She worked at Top Hill Farm, didn't she?'

'Yes. For Kilnsey. The lecherous old sod.'

'Do you think there was anything funny going on up there between him and Gloria?'

Alice laughed. 'Kilnsey and Gloria? In his wildest fantasies, maybe. Nellie, his wife, would have had his guts for garters if he'd so much as looked twice at another woman. And Gloria . . . well, she might have been generous in some ways, but she wasn't *that* generous. Old Kilnsey? No. You're barking up the wrong tree there, love. He was one of them serious religious types that always look like perverts to me. Probably need more religion than the rest of us just to keep their unnatural urges down.'

Annie made a note of the name. In her experience, that repressed type was more likely to lose control and kill than most. 'What kind of things did you do together?'

'The usual. Gloria was impulsive. She'd suggest a spur-of-the-moment picnic on Harksmere bank. Or a film at the Lyceum in Harkside. It's been converted to the KwikSave last time I saw it, but back then it was a popular place for lads and lasses to meet. Or walking in the fields at night during the blackout. And swimming.' She lowered her voice and leaned forward. 'Believe it or not, dearie, we once went swimming without costumes in Harksmere after dark. What a time we had of it! That was Gloria's idea, too. Spontaneous. She didn't like everything all planned out for her, but she always liked to have something to do or to look forward to doing.'

'Did she tell you anything about her past?'

'She never spoke much about that at all. From what

little I could gather, it must have been very painful for her, so I just thought if she doesn't want to talk about it, then that's all right with me. All she said was that she lost her family in the Blitz. She did sometimes seem very distracted. She had deep, quiet, sad moods that would just come on her out of nowhere, in the middle of a picnic, at a dance, whatever. But not often.'

'How did she fit into village life?'

'Well,' said Alice, 'I suppose that depends on your point of view. At first she wasn't around very much. Land girls worked very long hours. After she'd married Matthew and moved to Bridge Cottage we saw a bit more of her.'

'Did she have any enemies? Anyone who had reason to dislike her?'

'Quite a few people disapproved of her. Jealous, if you ask me. Gloria didn't care what people thought of her. She went in the pubs by herself, and she smoked in the street. I know that's nothing now, love, the street's the only place you *can* smoke in some places, but back then it was . . . well, to some people it meant you were nigh on being a prostitute. People had some funny ideas back then.' She shook her head slowly. 'They call them the good old days, but I'm not so sure. There was a lot of hypocrisy and intolerance. Snobbery, too. And Gloria was far too cheeky and flighty for some people.'

'Anyone in particular?'

'Betty Goodall could never take to her. Betty always was a bit of a snob, and a bit too High Church, too, if you ask me, but she's a good soul underneath it all, don't get me wrong. She has a good heart. She was always just a bit too quick with her moral judgments. I think she fancied Matthew Shackleton for herself, and I think it rather put her nose out of joint, Matthew marrying Gloria. Like I said,

Gloria was free and easy in her nature, besides being a real "stunna", as they say in the papers these days. I think a lot of women were just plain jealous of her.'

Annie smiled. From this description of Alice's, she could imagine what a time Banks would be having up in Edinburgh. 'Betty Goodall wasn't in the photograph,' she remarked.

'No. Betty and William had gone by then. He was some sort of dogsbody with the Home Guard, and they kept sending him from council to council. Not fit for real war work, apparently, and no one could quite figure out what to do with him.'

'Do you know if Gloria actually *did* anything to merit such disapproval, or was it simply because of her nature, her personality?'

'Oh dear. You want me to tell tales out of school?'

Annie laughed. 'Not if you don't want to. But it *is* a long time ago, and it might help us find her killer.'

'Oh, I know, love. I know.' Alice waved her hand. 'Just let me get my cigarettes. I usually have one after my elevenses, one after lunch and one after tea. And perhaps one with a nightcap before bed. But never more than five a day.' She got up and brought her purse over, fiddled for a packet of Dunhill and lit one with a slim gold lighter. 'Now then, dearie, where was I?'

'I wanted to know if Gloria had affairs, slept around.'

'Certainly no more than a lot of others did then, ones you'd generally consider "nice" girls. But people made a lot of assumptions about Gloria just because she was a free-thinking woman and spoke her mind. She definitely was a bit of a flirt, there's no denying that. But that doesn't mean anything, does it? It's just a bit of fun.'

'Depends on who you flirt with.'

'I suppose so. Anyway, I may have been naive, but I think there was more smoke than fire. Most of the time.'

'What did you think of Matthew?'

'Not very much, to tell you the truth. There was always something just a bit too smarmy and cocky about him for my taste. Oh, he was nice enough on the outside, handsome and charming, and one had to feel sorry for what happened to him later.'

'What happened?'

'Killed by the Japanese. Over in Burma. Anyway, Matthew was a big talker. I also heard he got more than one lass in the family way before Gloria came on the scene, while he was a student in Leeds. So he was no saint, wasn't Matthew Shackleton, though to hear some speak you'd think butter wouldn't melt in his mouth. Some folk said she only married him because he was a bright, handsome lad with a great future ahead of him – which seems to me like a very good reason to marry someone. I'm sure he made her all kinds of promises about how wonderful their future would be. He filled her head full of dreams of all the things he would build and all the far-off exotic lands they'd visit and all that rubbish. Underneath it all, Gloria was a romantic. I think she fell in love with this new world Matthew painted for her. All the bridges and cathedrals he was going to build, and her by his side. She was impatient for it all.'

'How did Gloria take his death?'

'She was heartbroken. Devastated. I was worried about her and I mentioned it to Gwen once or twice. Gwen said she'd be okay in a while, but then Gwen didn't look too good herself, either. Very close, they were, her and Matthew. Anyway, when Gloria started to go out again, she was more devil-may-care, you know, the way some people get when they feel they've nothing left to lose. A lot of people were like that then.' She paused and took another drag on her cigarette, then fiddled with the chain around her neck.

'So Gloria started going out again, to dances and things?'

'Yes, a few months later.'

'When did she form her relationship with Michael Stanhope, the artist?'

'Oh, he'd always been around. He was at their wedding. Gloria spent a lot of time with him. Used to drink with him in the Shoulder of Mutton. That's another reason those religious types disapproved of her.'

'Did you know Stanhope?'

'Just to say hello to. *Michael Stanhope*. I haven't thought of him in years. He was an eccentric. Always wearing that floppy hat of his. And the cane. Very affected. There was no mistaking that he was an *Artist*, if you know what I mean. I can't say I had much time for him, myself, but I think he was harmless enough. Anyway, he wouldn't have had anything to do with Gloria. It was all just a show.'

'What do you mean?'

'He was a homosexual, dearie. Queer as a three-pound note, as we used to say. Anyway, as you probably know, it was illegal back then.'

'I see. Would it surprise you to know that a painting of Gloria by Michael Stanhope *did* show up?' Annie asked.

'It did?'

'Yes. A nude. It's in Leeds Art Gallery.'

Alice put her hand to her mouth and laughed. 'Well, bless my soul. Is it really? A nude? Of Gloria? Still, I can't say it really surprises me. Gloria was never really shy about her body. I told you about the swimming party, didn't I? I'm not much of a one for art galleries, but I must go see it next time I'm in Leeds.'

'What *was* their relationship?'

'I think they genuinely liked one another. They were friends. Both of them were outsiders, free-thinkers. On some strange level, they *understood* one another. And I think she genuinely *liked* him and respected him as a painter. Not that she was an intellectual or anything, but she responded to his work. It touched her in some way.'

Annie could understand that. Over the years, her father had had many female friends who genuinely admired his art. No doubt he had also slept with some of them, but then Ray certainly wasn't homosexual, and it didn't mean the women hadn't respected him as a painter, too. 'Was she involved with anyone in particular after her husband's death?' she asked.

'She had a bit of a fling with a Yank from Rowan Woods called Billy Joe something or other. I never did like him. Wouldn't trust him and those bedroom eyes of his as far as I could throw him. She got a bit of a reputation for hanging around with American airmen, disappearing into the woods late at night, that sort of thing.' Alice winked. 'Not that she was the only one.'

'Do you think there was anything in it?'

'I'd be surprised if there wasn't. I think she was lonely. And she was also lovely. We met a lot of them, Betty, Cynthia, Gloria, Gwen and me. We'd go to dances, mostly at the base or in Harkside. There were a few in Hobb's End, at the church, but they were rather tame affairs. Betty Goodall tended to take charge, and I'm sure you can imagine there wasn't much fun to be had. Betty was a keen dancer – oh, did she *love* to dance! – but it was all waltzes and foxtrots, old-fashioned stuff. No jitterbugging. She was good, though. Her and Billy went in for ballroom dancing in a serious way after the war. Won trophies and all. Where was I?'

'Dances. Americans.'

'Oh, yes. Well, let's face it, most of the local lads were at war, except those unfit for service or in reserved occupations. And they just hung out in the Shoulder of Mutton and complained all the time. The Americans were different. They talked differently, spoke about places we'd only dreamed of or seen at the pictures. They were exotic. Exciting. They also had all sorts of things we hadn't been able to get because of rationing. You know – nylons, cig-arettes and that stuff. We were friendly with PX, which was the nickname of the chap who ran their stores, sort of quartermaster, I suppose, and he used to get us all sorts of stuff. Gloria in particular. She was definitely his favourite. But she was everyone's favourite. Gloria was like a beauti-ful, exotic butterfly; she attracted every man who met her. There was something special about her. She sparkled and glowed. She radiated *it*.'

'This PX, what was his real name?'

'Sorry, love, I can't remember. Come to think of it, I don't know if I ever knew. We always just called him PX.'

'Was there anyone else in particular?'

'After Billy Joe, she developed a real soft spot for Brad, but after what happened to Matthew, she didn't want anything serious.'

'What about this Brad? What did he want?'

'He was a nice lad. No doubt about it, he was head over heels.'

'Do you remember his second name?'

'Sorry, love.'

'That's all right,' said Annie. 'How long did they go out together?'

'There you've got me. The best part of 1944, I think. At least they were still seeing each other when I left at Christmas.'

'Christmas 1944?'

'Yes.' She beamed. 'Best Christmas of my life. My Eric got wounded in the Battle of the Bulge, silly bugger. Nothing serious, but it got him an early discharge and he was home for Christmas. The doctor recommended a bit of sea air, so we came here, fell in love with the place and ended up staying. We left Hobb's End on Boxing Day 1944.'

'Where's Eric now?'

'Oh, he's out and about. Likes to go for his constitutional along the prom every morning, then he stops by the pub and plays dominoes with his mates.'

'Did Gloria ever mention anything about having a baby?'

Alice looked puzzled. 'No, not to me. And I never saw any evidence of children. I'm not even sure she liked them. Wait a minute, though . . .'

'What?'

'It was something I noticed when I was crossing the fairy bridge once. Something odd. A bloke turned up – a bloke in a soldier's uniform – with a little lad in tow, couldn't have been more than about six or seven, holding his hand. I'd never seen them before. They went in to see Gloria, talked for a while, then they left. I heard voices raised.'

'When was this?'

'Sorry, love, I can't remember. It was after Matthew had gone, though. I do know that.'

'And that's all that happened?'

'Yes.'

'Did you hear what was said?'

'No.'

'Who was he, do you know?'

'Sorry, dearie, I've no idea.'

'Did you ever ask Gloria about him?'

'Yes. She went all quiet on me. She did that sometimes. All she would say was that it was relations from down south. I thought maybe it was her brother and nephew or something. You don't think . . . .?'

'I don't know,' said Annie. 'Did they ever come back, the man and the child?'

'Not that I ever heard of.'

'And what happened to Gwen and Gloria after you'd left?'

'I don't know. I sent Gloria a postcard, must have been March or April of 1945, telling her that Eric was better now and we were going to stay in Scarborough, and that she should come and visit us.'

'What happened?'

'Nothing. She never replied.'

'Didn't you think that odd?'

'Yes, I did, but there wasn't much I could do about it. Life goes on. I wrote again a few months later and still got no reply. After that, I gave up. You lose touch with a lot of people over the course of your life, I've found. It was the same with Gwen. I wouldn't say we were really *close* – she was a bit too quiet and bookish for that – but we did have some good times together. After we moved here, though, I never saw or heard of her again.'

'Did you ever go back to Hobb's End?'

'No reason to. After the war, it was like a new life –

except for the same old rationing. You just got on with it and tried not to dwell on the past. I'm sorry I never saw Gloria again – she was a breath of fresh air – but, as I said, when you get to my age you realize people lose touch all the time.'

Annie had found that true enough, even in her own short life. Schoolfriends, university colleagues, lovers, work partners, there were so many people she had completely lost touch with. They could be dead for all she knew. Like Rob.

She let the silence stretch for a few moments, then shifted in her armchair. 'Well, Alice,' she said, 'I think that's all for now. I'll make sure I get the photograph back to you within a couple of days. If I think of anything else, I'll get in touch with you.' She managed to get herself out of the deep, comfortable chair by pushing her hands down hard on the arms.

'Please do.' Alice got to her feet. 'It's been a great pleasure to me, though I can't see as it's done you much good, me rabbiting on like this about the past.'

'You've been very helpful.'

'Well, it's nice of you to say so, dearie. I must admit, I've enjoyed having a good chin-wag. It's been years since I thought about all that stuff. Hobb's End. Gloria. Gwen. Matthew. The war. I hope you find out who did this to her. Even if he's dead, I'd like to know he died as slow and painful a death as he deserved.'

•

We left the café saddened and dazed, with hours to kill before our train home. To tell the truth, I don't think either of us at that time had much hope that Matthew was still alive. I asked Gloria if she would take me to where she used to live, but she refused. That would have been simply too much for her to bear, she said, and I felt cruel for asking.

It stopped raining and the sun was trying to pierce its way through the ragged clouds. We walked through St James's Park, past the barrage-balloon station and the anti-aircraft guns, towards Oxford Street. Though our hearts weren't in it, we did some shopping. At least it took our minds off Matthew for a short while. On Charing Cross Road, I bought Graham Greene's new 'entertainment', *The Ministry of Fear*, as well as the last two issues of *Penguin New Writing*, the latest *Horizon* and some second-hand World's Classics copies of Trollope and Dickens for the lending library.

Gloria bought a black-red-and-white-checked Dorville dress at John Lewis's. It cost her three pounds fifteen shillings and eleven coupons. She persuaded me into buying a Utility design by Norman Hartnell in a shop nearby for only three pounds and nine coupons.

After fish and chips at a British Restaurant, we went to the Carlton in the Haymarket to see Gary Cooper and Ingrid Bergman in *For Whom the Bell Tolls*. It was one of the first films I ever saw in Technicolor, colour films not having made a real impact in Harkside by then. I hadn't read the Hemingway novel, so I couldn't judge how faithful the film version was.

It was getting dark when we walked out into the Haymarket, and Gloria suggested we catch the underground back to King's Cross.

It is hard to describe the London blackout, especially on a broad, busy street like the Haymarket. As it is never fully silent anywhere, so it is never fully dark, either. You can see the sharp edges and cornices of the buildings etched against the night sky in varying shades of darkness. If the half-moon slips out from behind the clouds, everything shimmers in its pale light for a few moments and then disappears again.

What I noticed most of all was the noise, the way blind people develop a more acute sense of hearing. Distant shouts and whistles, engines, laughter and singing from a public house, perhaps a dog howling in the distance or a cat miaowing down a ginnel – all these sounds seem to carry farther and echo longer in the darkness of the blackout. They all sound more sinister, too.

'Unnatural' is the word that comes to mind. But what could be more natural than darkness? Perhaps it is a matter of context. In the city, especially such a sprawling, busy city as London, darkness is unnatural.

In Piccadilly Circus, I could just make out the statue of Eros buttressed by sandbags. There was music coming from somewhere, too, a tune I later learned was Duke Ellington's 'Take the "A" Train'. There were soldiers all over the place, many of them drunk, and on more than one occasion men approached us and grabbed us or offered us money for sexual favours.

At one point, I heard some sounds down an alley and could just make out the silhouette of a man grunting as he thrust himself towards a woman, her back against a wall. It made me think of that icy Christmas of 1941, when I had seen Gloria and the Canadian airman, Mark, in exactly the same position.

The underground platforms, where people came to shelter during the air raids, were crowded, and I fancied I could smell sweat, unwashed clothes and urine mixed in with the sooty smell the trains made. Everything was grimy and run-down. The train soon came and we had to stand all the way. No one stood up to offer us seats.

I was glad our train for home left on time, and though I knew I would dream about the trip for weeks to come, I can't say I was sorry when, after a boring and uneventful journey of some seven hours, we caught the morning train from Leeds to Harrogate, thence to hook up with our little branch line back to Hobb's End.

•

It was after seven o'clock by the time Banks and Annie met up that evening. On his way back from Edinburgh, Banks got stuck in the mid-afternoon traffic around Newcastle, then he had to call in at the station to see if there had been any developments during his absence.

He had found about twenty telephone messages waiting for him in response to Monday evening's television news appearance. He spent an hour or so returning calls, but all he found out was that someone thought the Shackletons had moved to Leeds after VE day, and someone else remembered drinking with Matthew Shackleton in Hobb's End near the end of the war. Most people, though, simply wanted to relive wartime memories and had no useful information whatsoever.

There was also a message from John Webb, who said he had cleaned up the button Adam Kelly had taken from the skeleton. It was made of brass, probably, about half an inch in diameter, and had a raised pattern on the front, possibly reminiscent of wings. The expert who had examined it suggested it might be some sort of bird. Clearly, he added, given the time period under consideration, the armed forces came to mind, perhaps the RAF.

When Banks had finished at the station, he phoned Annie and asked if she would mind coming up to Gratly, as he had been on the road most of the day. She said she didn't mind at all. Then he went home, took a long shower and tidied the place up. It didn't take long. Next he tried phoning Brian in Wimbledon again. Still no luck. What the hell was he supposed to do? It was nearly a week since their argument. He could go down there, he supposed, but not until the case was over. Anyway, he decided to try again the next day.

He thought of cooking something for Annie, then decided against it. Learning to cook might be his next project after fixing up the cottage, but he still had a long way to go. Besides, there was nothing in the fridge except a couple of cans of lager, half a tomato and a piece of mouldy Cheddar. He would take her out to the Dog and Gun in Helmthorpe for dinner and hope to God there was something vegetarian on the menu.

When Annie arrived, she first showed him the photograph of Gloria and her friends with the American airmen. Then, after a lightning tour of the house, which she described as 'very bijou', she agreed it was a perfect evening for a stroll. They left their cars parked in Banks's gravel laneway and headed for Helmthorpe in the hazy evening light, sharing the information each had learned that day as they walked.

Sheep grazed on the lynchets that descended towards the dried-up beck. Some of them had even managed to get through the gate at the back of the churchyard, where they grazed among the lichen-dappled tombstones.

'Have time for a walk on the prom in Scarborough?' Banks asked.

'Of course. Had to eat, didn't I? I can tell you, though, there's not much choice for a vegetarian in Scarborough. I ended up buying some chips – cooked in vegetable oil, or so the woman said – and sat on a bench by the harbour to eat them, watching a man painting his fishing boat. He tried to chat me up.'

'Oh?'

'He didn't get very far. I'm used to being chatted up by fishermen. It takes more than heroic tales of landing haddock or halibut to get into *my* knickers, I can tell you.'

Banks laughed. 'St Ives?'

'Right. Heard it all before. Got the T-shirt. Anyway, after that I went for a quick look at Anne Brontë's grave, then I came back to the station to write up the interview.'

'Do you like Anne Brontë's books?'

'I haven't read any. It's just the sort of thing you do, isn't it, when you're nearby. Go and see where famous people are buried. I saw *The Tenant of Wildfell Hall* on TV. It's all right if you like that sort of thing.'

'What sort of thing?'

'Governesses, bodices, tight corsets, all that repressed Victorian sexuality.'

'And you don't?'

Annie cocked her head. 'I didn't say that.'

It was early September now, and the nights were drawing in fast. When they got to the High Street, the sun was already low in the west, a red ball glowing like an ember through the gathering haze, and the shadows were lengthening. Sounds of laughter and music came from the open pub doors. Tourists, tired after the day out and a big meal, were getting in their cars and driving back to their cities.

Annie and Banks walked through the crowded bar and managed to find a table in the beer garden out back. Between the trees, the dying sunlight streaked the river shallows blood-orange and crimson. Annie sat down while Banks went to buy a couple of pints and order their food. Luckily, Annie said she wasn't very hungry and a cheese-and-pickle sandwich would do her fine. He was just in time; they were about to stop serving.

'It's nice out here,' Annie said when he came back with the drinks. 'Thanks.'

'Cheers.' Banks took a sip. Though there were a few other people sitting outside, conversations seemed hushed. 'So who have we got now, then?' he asked. 'Now we've discovered that Matthew was killed before Gloria was?'

Annie leaned back, stretched out her long legs and set them on the third white plastic chair at the table. 'What about the boyfriend?' she suggested. 'The American.'

'Brad? As her killer? Why?'

'Why not? Or one of his pals. She could have stirred them up, set them against one another. I get the impression that Gloria was the kind of woman who exerted an enormous power over men. Brad could have been hoping for more than he got. Alice said she thought he was more keen on Gloria than she was on him. Maybe she tried to shake him loose and he wouldn't go. Rowan Woods wasn't far away. It would have been easy for him to sneak in and out the back way, I should think.'

'We definitely need to find out more about the Americans in Hobb's End,' said Banks.

'How do we go about that?'

'You can start with the American Embassy. They might be able to point you in the right direction.'

'I notice the subtle pronoun usage there: "you". I don't suppose you're planning on spending a day on the phone?'

Banks laughed. 'Rank has its privileges. Besides, you're so good at it.'

Annie pulled a face and flicked some beer at him.

'If it makes you feel any better,' he added, 'I'll be trying to get more information on Matthew Shackleton from our own military authorities.'

PETER ROBINSON

Their food arrived, and they both ate in silence for a while. The river looked like an oil slick now. There were no clouds, but the air had turned more humid during the day, and the setting sun turned the western sky scarlet and purple. Clusters of small buzzing insects, gnats or midges, hovered over the still, shallow water.

'What about Michael Stanhope?' Banks suggested.

'What possible motive could he have? They were friends.'

'Inordinate desire? Drink? They can push a person beyond the normal limits, and it's likely Stanhope was a bit beyond them anyway to start with. If he was powerfully attracted to Gloria, if she wouldn't have anything to do with him sexually, then painting her in the nude might have inflamed him beyond all reason. Let's admit it, a man like Stanhope can't have been *entirely* dispassionate all the time he had a naked Gloria Shackleton in his studio.'

Annie raised her eyebrows. 'Can't he? Perhaps you mean *you* couldn't be. You'd be surprised how dispassionate an artist can be. Anyway, Alice Poole said she was sure they weren't lovers, and I believe her. The impression I get is that a lot of villagers – like the one you talked to – projected negative feelings on to Gloria. I think she was basically a decent woman and a devoted wife, but her good looks and her free and easy attitude gave her no end of problems, especially with men. Eventually someone went over the top.'

'You sound as if you know what you're talking about.'

Annie turned away and stared at the dark river. It had only been a teasing, offhand remark, but Banks felt as if he had trespassed on some private reserve, set her hackles up. They still had to be careful with one another, he realized. A couple of nights of passionate abandon and a

240

sense of having something in common as mutual outsiders weren't enough to map the route through the emotional minefields that lay between them. *Tread carefully*, he warned himself.

After a pause, Annie went on, 'I think Gloria was one of the few people in Hobb's End who understood Michael Stanhope, who took him seriously. Besides, Alice also said he was gay.'

'She couldn't know that for certain. Or he could have been bisexual.'

'I think you're pushing it a bit, that's all.'

'You're probably right. Anyway, there's one obvious flaw with the Stanhope theory.'

'There is?'

Banks shoved his empty plate aside. 'Where do you think Gloria was killed?' he asked.

'In, or very close to, Bridge Cottage. I thought we'd already agreed on that because of where she was buried. By the way' – Annie consulted her notebook – 'I forgot to tell you before, but the blackout ended officially on the seventeenth of September, 1944. Not that it matters now we know Gloria was still alive that Christmas.'

'Every little bit helps.'

'Anyway, what's your point?'

'Most of the time Gloria visited Stanhope at his studio. That would certainly have been the case if he was painting her that autumn. If anything happened between them, it would be more likely to have happened there, that's all. That's where she was naked in front of him. If he killed her, I don't think he would have risked carrying the body all the way back to Bridge Cottage. He would have found some other way of disposing of her, somewhere closer.'

'Unless they were having an affair, as you suggest. In which case he might well have visited her at her own home.'

'Would she risk that, with Gwen so close by?'

'Possibly. Gloria certainly sounds unconventional and unpredictable, from everything I've heard. Just going to his studio must have been scandalous enough, given his reputation in the village.'

'Good point. Elizabeth Goodall certainly seemed to think their relationship was a scandal. Another drink?'

'Better not,' Annie said, placing her hand over her glass. 'One's my limit when I'm driving.'

Banks paused a moment, his voice lost somewhere deep in his chest. 'You don't *have* to drive home,' he said finally, sure he was croaking.

Annie smiled and put her hand on his arm. Her touch set his pulse going faster. 'No, but I think I should, with it being a weeknight and all. I've got a busy day tomorrow. Besides, we agreed, didn't we?'

'Can't blame a bloke for trying. Mind if I have one?'

She laughed. 'Course not.'

Banks went inside. He hadn't expected Annie to rise to his offer, but he was disappointed that she hadn't. He knew they had agreed to stick to weekends, but surely there was room for a little spontaneity now and then? He wondered if he would ever be able to figure out this relationship business. It was easy when you were married; at least you didn't usually have to make appointments to see one another. On the other hand, he and Sandra hadn't seen all that much of each other, and they had been married over twenty years. Perhaps, if they had made more time for one another, they would still be together.

The dinner crowd had thinned out, leaving the lounge

half empty, mostly locals playing dominoes and darts in the public bar. A group of kids sat in one corner, and one of them put 'Concrete and Clay' on the jukebox. Christ Almighty, thought Banks. *Unit 4 + 2*. It had been recorded before they were born.

He bought himself another pint and went back outside. Annie wasn't much more than a silhouette now – and a beautiful one to his eyes, with her graceful neck and strong profile – staring at the river in that peculiarly relaxed and centred way she had.

He sat down and broke the spell. Annie stirred languidly. She still had half her drink left, which she swirled in her glass a few times before sipping.

'What about her family?' Banks asked.

'Family? Whose family?'

'Gloria Shackleton's.'

'Her family was killed in the Blitz.'

'All of them?'

'That's what she told Alice.'

'What about this mysterious stranger and the child who turned up looking for her? You said she told Alice that it was relations.'

'I know.' Annie shook her head slowly. 'That's what I don't understand. It does seem odd, doesn't it?'

'If she ran off and left a husband or boyfriend stuck with her kid, that might be someone else with reason to be angry with her. He could have tracked her down and killed her.'

'Yes, but maybe whoever it was didn't feel *stuck* with the kid. Maybe he loved the boy. Besides, men do that sort of thing all the time and women don't kill them for it.'

Banks wasn't going to jump at that one. 'The point is,' he said, 'did *this* particular man feel strongly enough to track down the wife or girlfriend who bore his child and deserted him? They did argue, according to what Alice Poole told you.'

'Gloria was still alive after he left.'

'He could have stewed for a while, gone back weeks, months later.'

'Possibly,' Annie admitted. 'I'd also like to know what happened to the sister-in-law, Gwynneth. Even with your appeals on the telly, no one's come forward with any useful leads.'

'Maybe she's dead?'

'Maybe she is.'

'Do you see her as a suspect?'

Annie frowned. 'She looked like a tall, strong woman in the photograph. Something could have happened between them.'

'Maybe DS Hatchley came up with something in London. We'll find out tomorrow. It's been a long day.'

A night bird called across the river in the silence. Then someone put an Oasis song on the jukebox. 'The kind of crime it was ought to be telling us something,' Annie said after a slight pause.

'What does it tell you that we haven't considered already?'

'Well, it was obviously violent, passionate. *Somebody* felt strongly enough about Gloria Shackleton to stab her so many times. *After* strangling her first.'

'You've said it yourself: Gloria was the kind of woman men felt passionately about, the sort to spark off strong feelings. But there are probably a lot of things we don't know about what happened.'

'Sorry, I don't follow.'

'It's an old crime scene, Annie. All we've got is bones

and a few odds and ends of corroded jewellery. We don't know whether she was raped or sexually interfered with in any way first. Or after. For all we know, this might be a sex crime, pure and simple.'

'The SOCOs haven't found any other victims buried in the area.'

'Not yet. Besides, sex crimes don't always mean multiple victims.'

'Usually they do. You can't tell me that someone raped and murdered Gloria Shackleton the way he did and never did it again before or after.'

'That's the point,' said Banks. 'Think about it. The body was buried in the outbuilding of Gloria and Matthew's cottage. The fact that we haven't found any other bodies in the vicinity doesn't mean there aren't any anywhere else. It *doesn't* mean that whoever did it didn't kill *elsewhere*, in exactly the same way.'

'A serial killer, then? A stranger to the area?'

'It's possible. DS Hatchley's already put out a request for information on crimes with similar MOs. It'll take time, though, and that's if anyone even bothers following it up. People can be pretty lazy, especially when what they want isn't on the computer. Let's face it, we're not exactly high on anyone's priority list with this one. Still, some curious or industrious PC might poke about and discover something. I'll have Jim send out a reminder.'

Annie paused. 'You realize we might never know who killed her, don't you?'

Banks finished his drink and nodded. 'If that's what it comes down to, we make out a final report based on all the evidence we've collected and point at the most likely solution.'

'How do you think you'll feel about that?'

'What do you mean?'

'It's become important to you, hasn't it? Oh, I'm not saying I don't care. I do. But for you it's something else. It goes deeper. You have a sort of compulsion.'

Banks lit a cigarette. As he did so, he realized how often he hid behind the smoke of his cigarettes. 'Somebody has to give a damn.'

'That sounds melodramatic. Besides, is it really as simple as that?'

'Nothing ever is, really, is it?'

'Meaning?'

Banks paused and tried to frame his nebulous thoughts. 'Gloria Shackleton. I know what she looked like. I've got some idea of her character and her ambitions, who her friends were, the things she liked to do to amuse and entertain herself.' He tapped the side of his head. 'She's real enough for me in there, where it counts. Somebody took all that away from her. Somebody strangled her, then stabbed her fifteen or sixteen times, wrapped her body in blackout curtains and buried it in an outbuilding.'

'But it happened years ago. The war's been over for ages now. Murders happen all the time. What's so different about this one?'

Banks shook his head. 'I don't know. Nothing, really. Partly, it's the war itself. I'm older than you. I grew up in its shadow, and it cast a long one for a long time after it was over. I was born with a ration book and a National Identity Card.' He laughed. 'It's funny, you know, the way people resist being named and counted these days, but I was proud of that card when I was a kid. It actually *gave* me an identity, told me who I was. Maybe I was already in training for my warrant card. Anyway, there were ruins all over the place in my hometown. I used to play in them

just like Adam Kelly. And my dad had a collection of
mementoes I used to sneak up to the attic and play with
when he was out – an SS dagger, a Nazi armband. There
were pictures I used to look at, photographs of the col-
laborators hanging from the balustrades in Brussels. It was
another age, before my time, but in a way it wasn't; it
was much closer than that. We used to play at being
commandos. We even used to dig tunnels and pretend to
escape from prison camps. I bought every book about
fighter and bomber planes I could get my hands on. My
childhood and early adolescence were saturated with the
war. Somehow the idea of a vicious murder like this one
being committed while all that carnage was going on in the
world makes it seem even more of a travesty, if you see
what I mean.'

'I think so. What else bothers you?'

'That's the simple part. As far as we can tell, nobody
reported Gloria missing; there was no hue and cry. It looks
as if nobody cared. I had a friend once . . . one day I'll tell
you about him. Anyway, nobody cared then. Somebody
has to. I seem to be good at it, overburdened with compassion, a natural.' Banks smiled. 'Am I still making sense?'

Annie brushed his sleeve with her fingers. 'I care, too,'
she said. 'Maybe not for the same reasons or in the same
way, but I do.'

Banks looked into her eyes. He could tell she meant
what she was saying. He nodded. 'I know you do. Home?'

Annie stood up.

They walked out into the street, much quieter now
night had fallen. The fish-and-chip shop was still serving,
and two of the kids who had been in the pub were leaning
against the wall eating from newspaper. A whiff of vinegar
drifted by.

At the top of the ginnel that ran past the churchyard was a swing gate, and after that the narrow, flagged footpath curved around the steep banks of Gratly Beck about half a mile up the daleside to the village itself. Luckily, there was a moon, for there was no other illumination on the path. Sheep scampered out of the way and bleated. Again Banks thought of the blackout. His mother had told him a story of a friend of hers who made her way home from work at the munitions factory by touching 176 railings along the canalside before her left turn, then five lamp-posts down the street. It must have been in the early days, Banks thought, before Lord Beaverbrook ordered the collection of all railings for the war effort. His mother had also told him about the enormous mountain of pots and pans on the cricket pitch that were supposed to be turned into aircraft.

Once through the narrow stile at the other end, Banks and Annie turned left past the new houses. The pavement was broader there, and Annie slipped her arm through his. The small act of intimacy felt good. They crossed the stone bridge, walked along the lane and stood at Banks's front door.

'Coffee?' Banks asked.

Annie smiled. 'No, but I'll have a cold drink if you've got one. Non-alcoholic.'

He left her in the front room rummaging through his compact-disc collection while he went to the fridge. It was eerie how the kitchen always gave him that feeling of peace and belonging, even at night when the sun wasn't shining. He wondered if he would ever be able to tell Annie about it without feeling like an idiot.

He took out a carton of orange juice and poured them each a glass. An old Etta James CD started playing in the living room. Funky and fiery. He hadn't played it in years. Annie walked in, clearly pleased with her find.

'You've got a hell of a CD collection,' she said. 'It's a wonder you can ever decide what to play.'

'It *is* a problem sometimes. Depends on the mood.' He handed her the glass and they went through to the living room.

Soon Etta was belting out 'Jump Into My Fire' and 'Shakey Ground'.

'Sure you won't have a nightcap?' Banks asked when Annie had finished her orange juice.

'No. I told you, I've got to drive back. I don't want to get stopped by an overzealous country copper.'

'It's a pity,' said Banks. 'I was hoping you might change your mind.' His mouth felt dry.

'Come to Mama' was playing now, and the music's rhythmic, slow-moving sensuality was getting to him. He had to keep telling himself that Annie was a detective sergeant, someone he was working with on a case, and he shouldn't even be thinking like this. But the problem was that Annie Cabbot didn't seem like any detective sergeant he had ever come across before. And she was the first woman, apart from his daughter Tracy, to visit his new home.

'Well,' said Annie, smiling. 'I didn't say I had to go just yet, did I? You don't have to get me drunk to get me into bed, you know.' Then she stood up, crossed her arms in front of her and pulled her T-shirt slowly up over her head. She stood holding it in her hand, head tilted to one side, then smiled, held her hand out and said, 'Come to Mama.'

•

There are giant redwood trees in California, they say, that can grow another layer around the dead and blackened wood if they ever burn in a forest fire. Matthew's disappearance burned out my core like that and while, over time, I did grow another skin over it, a harder skin, there was part of me inside that was always black and dead. There still is, though over the years the new skin has grown so thick that most people take it for the real thing. I suppose, in a way, it is real, but it is not the *original*.

Of course, life went on. It always does. In time, we laughed and smiled again, stood on the fairy bridge and discussed the Italian campaign, lamented the shortages and complained about Lord Woolton Pie and the National Wholemeal Loaf.

Gloria threw herself into her work at the farm, making it clear that she was indispensable because the government was putting even more pressure on women to work in the aircraft and munitions factories, the idea of which terrified her. Rumour had it that there were spies from the Labour Exchange all over the place just looking for idle women. If there were, they left me alone, too, as I had enough work on my hands looking after an invalid mother and running the shop, as well as fire-watching and helping with the WVS, taking out pies and snacks to the field workers in the area.

In October, Gloria had her hair done like Veronica Lake, with a side parting, curling inwards over her shoulders. I had the new, short liberty cut because it was easy to manage and my hair just wouldn't do the things Gloria's did, even if I put sugar water on it.

That month also, *Gone With the Wind* finally came to Harkside, and Gloria and Mr Stanhope practically dragged me to see it. As it turned out, I enjoyed the film, and found it was made even more poignant by the death of Leslie

Howard, whose aeroplane had been shot down by Nazi fighters in June. Mr Stanhope, battered hat on his head, tapping with his snake-head-handled cane as we walked back, was enthusiastic about the use of colour and Gloria, needless to say, was potty about Clark Gable.

Autumn mists came to our shallow valley, often making it impossible for the aeroplanes to land or take off for days. In September we heard that the Rowan Woods Aerodrome had been closed and the RAF had gone somewhere else. It was hard to get a clear answer to any questions in those days, but one of the ground crew told me that the two-engined bombers they had been flying were old and were being phased out of operation. The runways at Rowan Woods had to be converted to be able to handle four-engined bombers. He didn't know whether his squadron would be back or not; things were so uncertain, people coming and going at a moment's notice.

Whatever the reason, the RAF moved out and a crew of labourers, mostly Irish, came in. Over the next couple of months, they brought in tons of cement, gravel and Tarmac to bring the runways up to standard. They also put up more Nissen huts.

Of course, the character of village life changed a little during this period: we had a few fights between the Irish and the soldiers at the Shoulder of Mutton, and we got used to the whiff of tar that would drift through the woods when the wind was blowing the right way.

Early in December the labourers finished their work and shortly before Christmas, Rowan Woods became the new home to the United States Eighth Air Force's 448th Bomber Group.

Just like that.

The Yanks had arrived.

•

Alone after Annie had left, Banks couldn't sleep, despite the lovemaking and the long day's drive. He lay in the dark for a while, his mind racing, images of the old days in Edinburgh, of Alison and Jo, keeping him awake. And Jem. And Annie. And Sandra. And Brian. The first night Banks had spent in the cottage, a bat flew in the open window and it took him half an hour to coax it out again. That was how his mind felt now, like a misshapen black rag flapping about wildly inside him. He felt an over-whelming sense of anxiety, not about anything specific, to such an extent that he began to sweat and his heart beat fast.

He put on his jeans and went downstairs to pour himself a small whisky. Ever since he had become worried about his drinking in the dark months after Sandra's departure, he had got into the habit of totting up his daily intake, as he did with cigarettes. A pint at lunchtime in Edinburgh, two pints with Annie at the Dog and Gun, and now one finger of Laphroaig close to midnight. Not bad. He had only smoked seven cigarettes, too, and he was especially proud of that.

He took the drink out to the wall and sat with his legs dangling over the dried-up falls. It was a warm night, but a slight breeze rustled through the leaves and cooled the sweat on his forehead a little. A small animal rustled through the undergrowth, probably a squirrel or a rabbit. Banks looked into the dark woods and remembered Robert Frost's words, which he had read recently in his anthology. 'And miles to go before I sleep.' It was the repetition of that line that made it so memorable, he thought, that sent that tingle up your spine. He didn't profess to understand it – at least he couldn't have stood up in class and described what it was *about* – but he got something from it.

He remembered what he had said to Annie earlier about *caring* and how he couldn't tell her it was partly because of Jem. Banks had found Jem's body himself on the bare dusty floor of the bedsit, the needle still in his arm, which was oddly discoloured here and there where the mice had nibbled.

He was sick, the same way he had been when Phil Simpkins spiralled slowly and inevitably down on to the spiked railings. But people had cared about Phil's accident; they even had a minute's silence in assembly and a morning off school for the funeral. Nobody had cared about Jem, though, the way no one seemed to have cared about Gloria's disappearance.

Over the years, Banks became inured to seeing corpses, like any other detective who investigates a fair number of murders. He developed a protective shell; he could crack jokes at the scene with someone's entrails spilling over his feet or brain matter sticking to the soles of his shoes. But no matter how hard his carapace, Banks had always felt *something*, no matter how low on the food chain the victim was. He always felt some connection with what had once been a living person.

After Jem's death, Banks had felt driven to find out more about him: who he was, where he came from, why no one seemed to care. He realized how little he knew, even though Jem had been his first and closest friend in a new and overpowering city. He was so innocent, he hadn't even suspected that Jem was a heroin addict. They had smoked hash and grass together on occasion, but that was all.

The police themselves hadn't been impressive, hardly

an advertisement for recruitment. They interviewed Banks, who described the man he had seen entering Jem's flat the previous evening, but they didn't seem interested. One of them, DC Carter, Banks remembered, played the concerned-parent role, feigning sadness at Jem's death, lecturing Banks on the drug subculture, while the other, DS Fallon, pockmarked face, a cynical smile on his thin, cruel lips, rifled through Banks's drawers and cupboards, looking for drugs.

Later, Banks found out that three junkies had died in Notting Hill that week because a shipment of unusually pure heroin hadn't been adequately cut. No arrests were made.

Disenchanted with both business and sixties navel-gazing, Banks joined the police force to change the system from within, despite Jem's advice, and when he found he couldn't do that, he settled for the adrenalin buzz of the investigation, the chase, the revelation, the strange bond with the murder victim, who couldn't speak for herself. And this bond was true no less in the case of Gloria Shackleton's cracked and filthy bones than it was with a corpse so fresh you could still see the flush on its cheek.

Finally, tired with remembering, Banks put out his cigarette, finished the whisky and went back inside. His bed still smelled of Annie, and he was grateful for that much, at least, as he tossed and turned and tried to get to sleep.

•

Ever since she had seen Gloria's image and heard her name on television, Vivian Elmsley had been expecting the police to come knocking at her door. It wasn't as if she had taken any great steps to cover her tracks. She had never consciously sought to hide her past and her identity, although she had certainly glossed over it. Perhaps, also, the life she had lived hinted at a certain amount of conscious escape. At every stage, she had had to reinvent herself: the selfless carer; the diplomat's wife; the ever so slightly 'with-it' young widow with the red sports car; the struggling writer; the public figure with the splinter of ice in her heart. Would that be the last? Which was the real one? She didn't know. She didn't even know if there *was* a real one.

Though the worry and fear gnawed away at her since the TV broadcast, Vivian tried to live a normal life: wandering up to Hampstead in the morning; reading the newspaper; sitting down in her study for the day, whether she wrote anything worth keeping or not; talking to her agent and publisher; answering correspondence. All the while waiting for that knock on the door, wondering what she would say, how she could convince them she knew nothing; or thinking that perhaps she should just tell them what she knew and let the chips fall where they would. Would it really make a difference, after all this time?

Yes, she decided; it would.

When it came, though, the shock came in a form she hadn't in the least expected.

That Tuesday night, the phone rang just as she was dropping off. When she picked up the receiver, all she heard was silence, or as much silence as you ever get on a telephone line.

'Who is it?' she asked, gripping the receiver more tightly. 'Please speak up.'

More silence.

She was just about to hang up when she heard what she thought was a sharp intake of breath. Then a voice she didn't recognize whispered, 'Gwen? Gwen Shackleton?'

'My name's Vivian Elmsley. There must be some mistake.'

'There's no mistake. I know who you are. Do you know who I am?'

'I don't know what you're talking about.'

'You will. Soon.'

Then the caller hung up.

10

Christmas 1943. It was a gloomy, chill and moonless night when the 448th held their first dance at Rowan Woods. Gloria, Cynthia, Alice and I walked there together along the narrow lane through the woods, our breaths misting in the air. We wore court shoes and carried our dance shoes because they were far too precious and flimsy to walk in. Luckily, the ground wasn't too muddy, because none of us would have been caught dead wearing wellies to a dance, even if we had to walk through Rowan Woods in a storm.

'How many of them do you think there are?' Cynthia asked.

'I don't know,' said Gloria. 'It's a big aerodrome, though. Probably hundreds. Thousands, even.'

Alice did a little dance. 'Ooh, just think of it, all those Yanks with money to throw away. They get paid much more than our boys, you know. Ellen Bairstow told me. She went out with a GI when she was working at that factory near Liverpool, and she'd never seen so much money.'

'Don't you try to tell yourself they won't want *something* in return, Alice Poole,' said Gloria. 'And don't you forget your poor Eric away fighting for his country.'

We were all a bit quiet after that. I don't know about the others, but I couldn't help thinking of Matthew. A fox or a badger suddenly flashed across the path and scared us, but the adrenalin at least broke the silence. We were still excited, and we giggled like silly schoolgirls the rest of the way.

Most villagers had already seen the newcomers around, and I had even served some of them in the shop, where they had looked puzzled at our meagre offerings and confused by the unfamiliar brand names. Some people disapproved of their arrival – especially Betty Goodall – thinking it would lower moral standards, but most of us quickly accepted them as part of the general scenery. I even helped the local WVS set up a Welcome Club for them in Harkside. Thus far, in my limited experience, Americans had always been friendly and polite, though I can't say I really warmed to the way they called me 'ma'am'. It made me feel so old.

They were certainly far more casual and confident in their manner than our lads, and they had much smarter uniforms. They even wore shoes rather than the great clodhopping boots the Ministry saw fit to issue to our poor armed forces. Of course, our view of Americans was still almost entirely formed by the glamour of Hollywood films, magazines and popular songs. To some, they were all cowboys and gangsters; to others, the men were handsome heroes and the women beautiful and rather vulgar molls.

That evening as we trudged through the forest, we had little real idea of what to expect. We had all fussed about what to wear for days, and we had taken special care with our appearance – even me, who was generally not overly concerned about such superficial matters. Under the overcoats we wore to keep out the chill, we all had on our best dresses. Gloria, of course, looked gorgeous in her black velvet V-neck dress with the puff sleeves and wide, padded shoulders. She had added a red felt rose at the neckline on the left side. I was a little more serviceable in the Utility dress I had bought in London.

One big problem was that we had all run out of fashion stockings and either we didn't have enough coupons to get new ones or we couldn't find any in the shops. When Gloria dropped by to meet me after I closed up shop, the first thing she told me to do was stand on a chair.

'Why?' I asked.

'Go on. You'll see.'

I could have said no, but I was curious, so I stood. The next thing I knew, Gloria was lifting up my skirt and applying some sort of cold greasy stuff to my legs.

I squirmed. 'What *is* that?'

'Shut up and keep still. It's Miner's Liquid Make-Up Foundation. Cost me two and sevenpence halfpenny, it did.'

I kept still. When the stuff she had slathered on my legs finally dried, Gloria had me stand on the chair again and she carefully drew a seam all the way down the backs of my legs with a special sort of pencil. It tickled and again she had to tell me to keep still.

'There.' She bit down on the corner of her lip and stepped back to admire her handiwork. I stood on the stool feeling like an idiot, holding my skirt up around my thighs. 'That'll do,' she pronounced at last. 'Me next.'

As I 'did' her, rubbing the foundation on her soft, pale skin, she started to laugh. 'Marvellous stuff, this,' she said. 'I was at my wits' end the summer before last, before Matthew . . . well, anyway, I was so desperate I tried a mixture of gravy powder and water.'

'What happened?'

'Bloody flies! Chased me all the way from here to Harkside, and the damn things even buzzed around my legs *inside* the hall. I felt like a piece of meat in a butcher's window.' She paused. 'Ooh, Gwen, do you remember what that looked like? All those lovely cuts of meat in the butcher's window?'

'Don't,' I said. 'You'll only make us miserable.'

We met the others by the fairy bridge. Cynthia Garmen was going for the Dorothy Lamour look. She had a black pageboy hairdo and wore a lot of makeup. She even had mascara on her eyes, which looked *really* strange, as women tended not to use a lot of eye makeup back then. It wasn't good-quality mascara. When she got hot from dancing later in the evening, it started to melt, and she looked as if she had been crying. She said she had bought it on the black market in Leeds, so she could hardly go back and complain.

Alice was in her Marlene Dietrich period: plucked eyebrows pencilled in a high arch, wavy blond hair parted in the centre, hanging down to her shoulders. She was wearing a Princess-style burgundy dress with long, tight sleeves and buttons all down the front. It came in at the waist to show how thin she was: almost as thin as Marlene Dietrich.

The dance was held in the mess. We could hear the music before we even got there. It was the song I remembered hearing in Piccadilly Circus a few months ago: 'Take the "A" Train'. We stood outside the door touching up our hair, checking our appearance one last time in our compact mirrors. Then we took off our coats – not wanting to walk in wearing bulky winter overcoats – stuffed our court shoes in the pockets and put on our dance shoes. Ready at last, we made our grand entrance.

The music didn't stop, though I swear it faltered for a moment the way records do sometimes when they become warped. It was a sextet, playing on a makeshift stage at the far end from the bar, and they all wore American air force uniforms. I suppose the odds are that when you gather so many disparate people together, you're bound to end up with enough musicians for a band.

Already the place was crowded with airmen and local girls, mostly from Harkside. The dance floor was busy and a knot of people stood laughing and drinking by the bar. Others sat at the rickety tables smoking and chatting. I had expected the large Nissen hut to be cold, but there was a peculiar-looking squat thing giving out heat in one corner, which I later discovered was called a 'pot-bellied stove' (a very apt description, I thought). Apparently, the air force had brought it all the way from America, having heard English winters were cold and wet, and so were the summers.

They hardly needed it tonight, though, as the press of bodies and the motion of dancing exuded all the heat we needed. The men had already covered the walls with photographs taken from magazines: landscapes of vast, snow-capped mountain ranges; long flat plains and prairie wheatfields; deserts dotted with huge, twisted cacti; and city streets that looked like scenes from Hollywood films. Little bits of America brought over to make them feel less far away from home. A Christmas tree stood in one corner, covered with tinsel and fairy lights, and paper trimmings hung around the ceiling.

'Take your coats, ladies?'

'Why, thank you,' said Gloria.

It was Gloria who had turned the heads, of course. Even with Dorothy Lamour and Marlene Dietrich for competition, she still stood way ahead of the field.

We handed our coats to the young airman, who was tall, slim and dark in complexion. He spoke with a lazy drawl and moved with agile, unhurried grace. He had brown eyes, short black hair and the whitest teeth I had ever seen.

'Over here.' He led us to the far wall, beside the bar, where everyone's coats hung. 'They'll be safe here, now don't you ladies worry.' When he turned his back, Gloria looked at me and raised an eyebrow in approval.

We followed him and held on to our handbags. It was always awkward not knowing what to do with your handbag when you danced. Usually, you left it under the table, but Cynthia once had hers stolen at a dance in Harkside.

'And now, ma'am,' he said, turning straightaway to Gloria, 'if I may have the pleasure of the first dance?'

Gloria inclined her head slightly, passed her handbag to me, took his hand and went off. It didn't take long before someone snapped up Cynthia, too, and I was holding three handbags. But, if I say so myself, a rather handsome young navigator from Hackensack, New Jersey, called Bernard – which he pronounced with the emphasis on the second syllable – asked me to dance even before his friend asked Alice. I passed the three handbags to her and left her standing there gawping in a way that Marlene Dietrich never gawped.

'First, you have to answer a question for me,' I said, before I let him lead, just to show I could be quite brave when I wanted to, though I was secretly scared to death of all these brash and handsome young men all around me.

Bernard scratched his head. 'What's that, ma'am?'

'What's an "A" train?'

'Huh?'

'The music that was playing when we came in. "Take the 'A' Train." What's an "A" train? I've always wondered. Is it better than a "B" train, for example?'

He grinned. 'Well, no, ma'am. I mean, it's just a subway train.'

'Subway? You mean the underground?'

'Yes, ma'am. In New York City. The "A" train's the subway that's the fastest way to Harlem.'

'Ah,' I said, the light finally dawning. 'Well, I never. Okay, then, let's dance.'

After 'Kalamazoo', 'Stardust' and 'April in Paris', we gathered at the bar and the tall airman who had taken our coats bought us all bourbon, which we took to the table. His name was Billy Joe Farrell. He hailed from Tennessee and worked on the ground crew. He introduced us to his friend, Edgar Konig, whom everyone called PX because on American bases PX meant the quartermaster's stores, which was exactly what he ran.

PX was a gangly young Iowan with a baby face and his fair hair shaved almost to his skull. He was tall, with Nordic cheekbones, pouting lips and the longest eyelashes over his cornflower-blue eyes. He was also very shy, far too shy to dance with any of us. He never quite made full eye contact with anyone. He was the sort of person who is always around but never really gets noticed, and I think the reason he was so generous to us all was simply that it made him feel needed.

When I look back on that evening now, over twenty-five years ago, especially considering all that has happened since, it seemed to go round in a whirl of dancing and talking and drinking, and it finished before it really began. I still remember the strange accents and the unfamiliar place names and phrases we heard; the young faces; the surprisingly soft feel of a uniform under my palm; the biting, yet sweet, taste of bourbon; the kisses; whispered plans to meet again.

As the four of us walked tipsily back through the woods, arms linked with our gallant escorts, little did we know how, before long, we'd be using words like 'lousy', 'bum' and 'creep' in our daily conversation, not to mention chewing gum and smoking Luckies. As we walked we sang 'Shenandoah' and after goodnight kisses agreed to meet them again in Harkside the following week.

•

It was the first time Banks had been to the Queen's Arms for lunch in some months. He had been trying to avoid boozing too much during the day, partly because it was sometimes hard to stop, and partly because it seemed too much a part of his old life.

It wasn't so much that he used to go there with Sandra frequently – though they often dropped in for a quick jar if they'd been in town together to see a film or a play – just that the Queen's Arms brought back memories of the days when his life and work were in harmony: the days before Jimmy Riddle; the days when he had enjoyed long brain-storming sessions with Gristhorpe, Hatchley, Phil Richmond and Susan Gay over a steak-and-kidney pud and a pint of Theakston's bitter; the days when Sandra had been happy with their marriage and with her work at the gallery.

Or so he had believed.

Like many things he had believed, it had all been an illusion, only true because he had been gullible enough to *believe* in it. In reality, it had all been as flimsy and fleeting as an optical illusion; it depended entirely on your point of view. In calendar time, perhaps, those days weren't so long ago, but in his memory they sometimes seemed as if they had been dreamed by another person in another century.

Even before he bought the cottage, in those days when he had been out on the booze in Eastvale nearly every night, he had avoided the Queen's Arms. Instead, he had sought out modern, anonymous pubs tucked away on the estates, places where the regulars enjoyed their quiz trivia nights and their karaoke and paid no attention to the sad figure in the corner who bumped against the table a little harder each time he went for a piss.

He got into a fight only once, with a paunchy loud-mouth who thought Banks was eyeballing his girlfriend, a pasty-faced scrubber with bad hair. It didn't matter that Banks didn't think she was worth fighting over, her boy-friend was ready to rock and roll. Luckily, Banks was never so pissed that he forgot the rules of bar-room brawling: get in first and get in nasty. While the boyfriend was still building up steam verbally, Banks punched him in the stomach and brought up his knee to connect with his nose. Blood, snot and vomit spattered his trousers. Everyone went quiet, and no one tried to stop him leaving.

Banks had always had a violent streak; he knew that even when he used to talk about love and peace with Jem. That was one reason he could never fully give himself to the sixties scene in the first place, only hang around the fringes. The music was fine, the pot was okay, the girls were willing, but the turn-the-other-cheek philosophy sucked.

Today, he felt like indulging himself at the Queen's Arms. Cyril, the landlord, welcomed him back like a long-lost friend, not remarking on his absence, and Glenys, Cyril's wife, gave him her usual shy smile. He bought a pint and ordered a Yorkie filled with roast beef and onion gravy. The pub was busy with its usual lunchtime mix of tourists, local office workers and shopkeepers on their lunch breaks, but Banks managed to snag a small copper-topped table in the far corner, between the fireplace and the diamond-shaped amber and green window-panes.

He had brought with him the folder DS Hatchley had just dropped on his desk: information gleaned from the central registry of births, marriages and deaths. With any luck, it would answer a number of his questions. Already that morning, he had phoned army records and asked about Matthew Shackleton's service history. They said they would verify his identity and call him back. He knew from experience that the military didn't like people snooping into their affairs, even the police, but he didn't expect much trouble with this one; after all, Matthew Shackleton was long dead.

Hatchley's notes confirmed that Gloria was born on September 17, 1921, as she had correctly noted on the St Bartholomew's register. Instead of simply giving 'London' as her place of birth, the official record listed London Hospital, Mile End. Christ, Banks thought, that was in the thick of the East End, all right, and a real villains' thoroughfare these days. It would certainly have made her a Cockney, an accent she had worked hard to lose, if Elizabeth Goodall was to be believed.

Her father was Jack Stringer, whose illegible signature appeared in the 'Signature, Residence and Description of Informant' column along with the Mile End address. Her mother's name was Patricia McPhee. The father's rank or profession was listed as 'dock worker'. There was no column on the form to record the mother's.

Next, Hatchley had checked to see if Gloria's parents had, indeed, been killed in the Blitz, and had pulled death certificates for the two of them, dated September 15, 1940, listing the same Mile End address and 'injuries sustained during bombing' as the cause of death.

A series of black-and-white images passed through Banks's mind: vast stretches of rubble and craters; acrid smoke drifting through the night air; children's screams, flames licking soot-blackened walls, the screeching of the bombs before the shattering explosions; houses only half-destroyed, so you could see inside the rooms – the pathetic sticks of furniture, framed photographs askew on the walls, peeling wallpaper; families huddled together under blankets in underground stations, a few valued possessions with them.

The images came mostly from films and documentaries he had seen on the Blitz. His parents had actually lived through it, moving to Peterborough from Hammersmith only after the war. They never spoke about it much, as most people who had been through it didn't, but his mother had told him a comical story or two about the war days.

Some of the images of the war's devastation came from Banks's own experience, when he was a child, even that long after the war. As he had told Annie, wastelands of rubble and half-destroyed buildings remained in some areas for years. He remembered visiting London as a child and being surprised when his father told him that the acres of flattened streets in the East End were there because of the war.

Hatchley had been unable to find a death certificate for Gloria Kathleen Shackleton, but he did find one for Matthew, and the information on it caused Banks almost to choke on his beer.

According to the death certificate, Matthew Shackleton died at Leeds General Infirmary on 15 March, 1950, by his own hand. Cause of death was given as a 'self-inflicted gunshot wound'. At the time, he was thirty-one years of age, of no occupation, living at an address in Bramley, Leeds. The informant of his death was listed as Gwynneth Vivian Shackleton, of the same address. Banks checked again, but Hatchley had made no mistake.

He lit a cigarette and thought for a moment. Matthew

Shackleton was supposed to have died in Burma, but obviously he hadn't. Of the three survivors of the old Hobb's End days that Banks and Annie had talked to over the past few days, one had left the village in 1940, before Gloria's arrival there, the second had gone in May 1944, and the third at Christmas 1944. Neither Elizabeth Goodall nor Alice Poole had mentioned Matthew Shackleton's returning, so he must have come back after they had left.

Which made him a definite suspect in his wife's murder. Again.

What had he come home to?

And why had he killed himself five years later?

Banks flipped the sheet and carried on reading. A marriage certificate existed for Gwynneth Vivian Shackleton and Ronald Maurice Bingham. They were married at Christ Church, Hampstead, on 21 August, 1954. The groom's profession was listed as 'Civil Servant'. Ronald died of liver cancer at home on 18 July, 1967.

There was no death certificate for Gwynneth.

Hatchley had dug even deeper, and he had also discovered that there *was* a record of a child being born to Gloria Kathleen Stringer at her parents' home address in Mile End, London, on 5 November, 1937, shortly after her sixteenth birthday.

5 November. Guy Fawkes Night.

Banks imagined Gloria struggling to give birth as Catherine-wheels spun and jumping jacks and bangers exploded outside in the street, as volcanoes erupted dark red fire, changing to green, then white, and rockets burst into showers of bright colours in the darkness beyond the bedroom windows. Did she look out on the scene from her pain? Did the noise and colours take her mind off what she was going through?

The boy was christened Francis Paul Henderson, taking his father's surname. George Henderson, like Jack Stringer, was listed as 'dock worker'.

There was no trace of a wedding certificate.

So Gloria had given birth over three years before she turned up in Hobb's End. What had become of the child and its father? Had she turned over the boy's care completely to George Henderson? It looked that way. She had certainly indicated to none of her new friends that she had a son. Was George Henderson the man with the boy who had turned up at Bridge Cottage during the war? The one Gloria had argued with?

Glenys brought over Banks's Yorkie. He tucked into the huge stuffed Yorkshire pudding and washed each mouthful down with a sip of Theakston's.

According to Hatchley's final search, George Henderson had died of a heart attack just five months ago. There was no death or marriage certificate for his son Francis. That made three of them unaccounted for by death certificates. Gloria, in all likelihood, had been buried under the outbuilding, but that still left Gwynneth Shackleton and Francis Henderson. Why hadn't they come forward? One possibility was that they might both be dead, though Gwynneth would be in her early seventies and Francis only pushing sixty, hardly old in this day and age. Another possibility was that neither of them knew what was going on, which was too much of a coincidence for Banks to swallow. There again, maybe they had something to hide. But what?

Francis wouldn't be able to tell Banks much. Everything that happened in Hobb's End happened before he turned eight, so he was hardly a suspect in the murder of Gloria Shackleton. He would have been about sixteen when the village was flooded to make Thornfield Reservoir, and Banks doubted that the event would have meant anything to him.

Nonetheless, it would be interesting to know what had become of him. If nothing else, Francis Henderson's DNA could help determine beyond a shadow of a doubt whether the skeleton really was Gloria Shackleton's.

There was another issue, too: someone had to lay Gloria's body to rest, bury her properly, in a churchyard, this time. Two people who had been intimately involved with her were possibly still alive: her sister-in-law, Gwynneth Bingham, and her son, Francis Henderson. They should be the ones to do it, to bury their dead.

Banks sighed, put the files back in his briefcase and walked through the crowds across Market Street. He found a message waiting at the front desk from army personnel, informing him that Matthew Shackleton had been listed as 'Missing presumed dead' in 1943, and that was all they had on him. Curiouser and curiouser. Back in his office, Banks picked up the phone and called Detective Inspector Ken Blackstone at Millgarth Station, in Leeds.

'Alan,' said Blackstone. 'Long time no see.'

There was a coolness and distance in his voice. They hadn't been in touch often over the past year or so, and Banks realized he had probably alienated Ken along with just about everyone else who had tried to be his friend during the dark days. Ken had left a number of messages on his answering machine suggesting they get together and talk, but Banks had responded to none of them. He didn't feel like explaining how he just hadn't been able to handle people offering help and encouragement, feeling sorry for him, how he was managing to feel quite sorry enough for himself, thank you very much, and how he had preferred to seek anonymity among the crowds instead. 'You know how it is,' he said.

'Sure. So what can I do for you? Don't tell me this is just a social call.'

'Not exactly.'

'I thought not.' There was a slight pause, then Blackstone's tone softened a little. 'Any new developments between you and Sandra?'

'Nothing. Except I've heard she's seeing someone.'

'I'm sorry, Alan.'

'These things happen.'

'Tell me about it. I've been there.'

'Then you should understand.'

'I do. Want to get rat-arsed and talk about it sometime?'

Banks laughed. 'It'll be a pleasure.'

'Good. So, what can I do for you?'

'Well, if this little idea works out, we might have that piss-up quicker than you think. I'm looking for the details of a suicide. Leeds. Bramley. Gunshot wound. Name's Matthew Shackleton. Died the fifteenth of March, 1950. The local cop shop should have some sort of record, especially as there was a firearm involved.'

'Is there an explanation in here somewhere?'

'Long story, Ken. By the way, have you ever heard anything on the grapevine about a DS called Cabbot? Annie Cabbot?'

'Can't say as I have. But then I've not exactly been around the grapevine much for the past while. Why do you want to know? All right, I know, don't bother, another long story, right? Look, about this suicide. It could take a while.'

'You mean you're talking minutes instead of seconds?'

Blackstone laughed. 'Hours instead of minutes, more

like. I'll get DC Collins to make some phone calls – if I can drag him away from his paper. I'll call you back later.'

Banks heard a grunt and the rustle of a newspaper in the background. 'Thanks, Ken,' he said. 'Appreciate it.'

'You'd better. You owe me a curry.'

'You're on.'

'And, Alan . . .?'

'Yes.'

'I know some of what you've been going through, but don't be a stranger.'

'I know, I know. I told you; you're on. Curry and piss-up and talk about girls. Just like a couple of teenagers. Soon as you get the info.'

Blackstone chuckled. 'Okay. Talk to you later.'

•

Billy Joe and Gloria soon became a couple. Billy Joe was seen going alone to Bridge Cottage, and that got the village tongues wagging. Especially when PX was seen coming and going there the next day. He, too, seemed to have taken a shy sort of shine to Gloria, happy to be her slave and get for her whatever her heart desired. I suggested Gloria tell them to use the back door, where they couldn't be seen from High Street, but she just laughed and shrugged it off.

There was no real mystery to the visits. Gloria told me she wanted sex and she had chosen Billy Joe to supply it. She said he was good at it. I still didn't understand what *it* was all about. When I asked her if I had to be in love before I let men take liberties with me, she lapsed into one of her mysterious silences, then said, 'There's love, Gwen, and then there's sex. They don't have to be the same. Especially not these days. Not while there's a war on. Just try not to get them mixed up.' Then she smiled. 'But it's always nice to be a little bit in love.' After this, I was more confused than ever, but I let the subject drop.

Gloria also needed her Luckies, nylons, lipstick, rouge and scented soap. She drank too much, so she needed a source for whisky, too, and she also took to chewing gum, which she insisted on chewing in church, just to annoy Betty Goodall. And PX, of course, would get her all these things at the flutter of an eyelash. Whether she ever granted him any favours in exchange, I can't say for certain, but I doubt it. Whatever she was, Gloria was never a whore, and I couldn't imagine PX actually being *with* a woman in that way. He looked even younger and seemed even shyer and more awkward than me. There was some health reason that prevented him from serving in a more active branch of the forces – after all, he looked young and strong enough for combat – but he never told anyone exactly what it was.

PX did little favours for us all – for me, Cynthia, Alice, even Mother – especially when it came to nylons and makeup. One thing I soon started to wonder about was why the American forces, undoubtedly male as they were for the most part, had storage rooms full of women's underwear and cosmetics. It was either intended to endear them to the local women, or they had certain private proclivities that they managed to hide from the rest of the world.

Anyway, lucky for us, PX seemed willing and able to get hold of just about anything we needed. If we bemoaned the lack of decent meat, for example, he would mysteriously produce bacon, and on occasion, even a piece of beef. Once he even, miracle of miracles, came up with some oranges! I hadn't seen an orange in years.

I don't think his empire was limited to the contents of the Rowan Woods PX, either. Sometimes, when he got a weekend pass, he would disappear for the entire time. He never said where he went or why, but I suspected he had a few dealings with the Leeds black market. I think I rather liked him, even though he seemed so young, and I *might* have gone out with him if he had asked me. But he never did, and I was too shy to ask him. We were only together in a group. Besides, I know he preferred Gloria.

Billy Joe had other uses, too. He was essentially an aeroplane mechanic, but he could also fix anything on wheels. That came in useful when our little Morris van gave up the ghost. Billy Joe came down in the evening, with PX and a couple of others tagging along, fixed it in a jiffy, then the whole gang of us picked up Gloria and went to the Shoulder of Mutton for a drink. A curious incident occurred that night that coloured my view of Billy Joe for some time to come.

They were the only Americans in the pub and we were the only women. In addition to getting us plenty of suspicious and disapproving glances, even from people I had known for years and served in the shop, this also drew a few loud and pointed comments. Most of the men there were either too old to go to war or were excused because of health reasons. Some were in reserved occupations.

'Just think about it, Bert,' said one local as we bought our first drinks. 'Our lads are over there fighting the Nazis, and them damn Yanks are over here sniffing around our women like tomcats on heat.'

We ignored them, took a table in a quiet corner and kept to ourselves.

The next time we were ready for drinks, Billy Joe went to the bar. He was drinking pints of watery beer, and I had told him to hold on to his glass because there was a shortage. A lot of locals took their own, and some even used jam jars, but if you got one early in the evening you had to hold on to it for the night. As he was on his way back, one of the local strapping farm lads who hadn't been called up – something to do with an allergy to tinned food, I think – called out after him: 'Hey, Yank. Tha's ta'en me glass.'

Billy Joe tried to ignore him, but the man, Seth his name was, had drunk enough to make him feel brave. He lumbered over from the bar and stood right behind Billy Joe, back at the table. The place went quiet.

'I said that's *my* glass tha's got tha beer in, Yank.'

Billy Joe put the tray down on the table, glanced at the pint glass and shrugged. 'Same one I've had all evening, sir,' he said in that lazy Southern drawl.

'"Same one I've had all evening, sir."' Seth tried to mock him, but it didn't come out right. 'Well it's mine, sithee.'

Billy Joe picked up his glass of beer, turned to face Seth slowly and shook his head. 'I don't think so, sir.'

Seth thrust his chin forward. 'Well, I bloody do. Gimme it back.'

'You sure, sir?'

'Aye, Yank.'

Billy Joe nodded in that slow way of his, then he poured the beer all over Seth's feet and held out the glass to him. 'You can take the glass,' he said. 'But the beer was mine. I paid for it. And, by the way, sir, ah am not a Yankee.'

Even Seth's friends had started to laugh by now. It was that sort of fulcrum moment, when so much hangs in the balance, just the lightest touch the wrong way sends it all tumbling down. I could feel my heart beating hard and fast.

Seth made the wrong move. He stepped back and raised his fist. But he was slow. Billy Joe might have had that exaggerated sort of lazy grace, but his speed amazed me. Before anyone knew what had happened, there was the sound of breaking glass and Seth was on his knees, screaming, hands over his face, blood gushing out between his fingers.

'Ah am not a Yankee, sir,' Billy Joe repeated, then turned his back and sat down. The mood had soured, nobody wanted anything more to drink, and we all left shortly afterwards.

•

Vivian Elmsley got up at about one o'clock, turned on the bedside light and took a sleeping pill. She didn't like them, didn't like the way they made her feel woolly-minded the next morning, but this was getting ridiculous. They said old people didn't need as much sleep, but lying tossing and turning all night imagining someone scratching at the window or tapping at the door was exhausting. It was probably the wind, she told herself as she turned off the light and settled back on the pillows.

But there was no wind.

Slowly, the chemical Morpheus insinuated its way into her system. She felt sluggish, her blood heavy as lead, pushing her down into the mattress. Soon she hovered on the threshold between sleep and waking, where thoughts take on the aspect of dreams, and an image you conjure up consciously is suddenly snatched away for unconscious improvisations, like variations on a musical theme.

At first, she pictured Gloria's tilted head as she had appeared on the TV screen, the detail from Stanhope's painting, looking like a cartoon-Gloria.

Then the cartoon-Gloria started talking about a night in Rio de Janeiro when Vivian had had too much to drink and – the only time – succumbed to sexual advances at a cocktail party in a big hotel, remembered a whispered room number, waited until Ronald was fast asleep and slipped out into the corridor.

The cartoon-Gloria's monologue was cut with images of the night, which flicked past jerkily like the series of cards in an old 'What the Butler Saw' machine.

Vivian had always wondered what it would be like. They only did it once. Her lover was a gentle and sensitive woman from the French Embassy, conscious it was Vivian's first time, but ultimately frustrated at her lack of ability to respond. It wasn't for want of trying, Vivian thought. She couldn't lose herself in sex with a man, so she had hoped she could abandon herself to the caresses of another woman, enjoy the bliss that writers wrote about and people risked everything for.

But she couldn't. It wouldn't happen.

Finally, she put on her robe and hurried out, humiliated, back to her own room. Ronald was still snoring away. She lay on her own bed and stared at the dark ceiling, tears welling in her eyes, a dull ache in her loins.

As the cartoon-Gloria retold the story of Vivian's failed attempt at sex and infidelity, it was as if the TV camera started to move away from her, and the rest of Gloria came into view, showing more of her figure, and before long Vivian realized that Gloria wasn't wearing a red dress; she was covered in blood which oozed from cuts deep into the gristle of her flesh.

Yet she was still talking.

Talking about something that happened years after her death.

Vivian tried to stop it but she felt as if she were being held down by the weight of her own blood, an anchor hooked deep into the darkness and the horror. Too heavy.

She struggled to wake, and as she did, the telephone

rang. Her bonds were suddenly cut, and she shot up, gasping for air as if she had been drowning.

Without thinking, she picked up the receiver. A lifeline.

After a short pause, the monotone voice whispered, 'Gwen. Gwen Shackleton.'

'Go away,' she mumbled, her tongue thick and furred.

The voice laughed. 'Soon, Gwen,' the man said. 'Soon.'

11

Banks and Annie drove out to the estate from Millgarth police headquarters. When Annie asked Banks why he always wanted to do the driving himself, he didn't really know the answer. Being driven was one of the perks of his rank that he had never really capitalized on. Partly, he would always rather use his own car than sign one out because he didn't want to have to put up with other coppers' cigarette butts in the ashtrays, chocolate wrappers, used tissues and God knows what else all over the floor, not to mention the lingering germs and odours. Mostly, though, he needed to be in control, with *his* feet on the pedals, *his* hands on the steering wheel.

He also liked to control the music. It had always angered Sandra, the way he put on whatever CD *he* wanted to listen to, or turned on the television to a programme *he* wanted to watch. She claimed he was selfish. He said he always knew what he wanted to listen to or watch and she didn't; besides, why should he listen to music, or watch films he didn't like? Another stand-off.

Banks parked in front of a strip of shops set back from the main road near Bramley Town End, and he and Annie strolled down the hill towards the street where Gwen and Matthew Shackleton had lived. Both were dressed casually; neither looked like a police officer. Sometimes, feelings against all forms of authority ran high on these estates. People spotted strangers quickly enough as it was, and they were naturally suspicious of anyone in a suit. Which was hardly surprising: on an estate like this, if you saw someone you knew wearing a suit, you assumed he had a court appearance coming up; and if you saw a stranger wearing one, it was either the cops or the social.

Banks had grown up on a similar estate in Peterborough. More modern than this one, but basically the same mix of grim and grimy terrace houses alongside the newer red-brick maisonettes and tower blocks, all covered in graffiti. When he was a kid, the street was cobbled, and they would have bonfires there every Guy Fawkes Night. The whole estate would come out and share their fireworks and food. Potatoes baked in foil at the edges of the fire, and people passed around trays of homemade parkin and treacle toffee. Neighbours would seize the opportunity to chuck their old furniture on the fire – a practice Banks's mother said she thought was showing off. If Mrs Green at number 16 threw her battered armchair on the bonfire, it was tantamount to telling everyone she could afford a new one.

Eventually, the council Tarmacked the street and put an end to the celebrations. Afterwards, they had to have their bonfire on a large field half a mile away; strangers from other estates started muscling in, looking for trouble, and the older people began to stay at home and lock their doors.

'How are we going to approach this?' Annie asked.

'We'll play it by ear. I just want to get a look at the lie of the land.'

It was another hot day; people sat out on their doorsteps or had dragged striped deck-chairs on to postage-stamp lawns, where the grass was parched pale brown for lack of rain. Banks couldn't help but be aware of the suspicious eyes following their progress. From one garden, a couple of semi-naked teenage boys whistled at Annie and flexed the tattoos on their arms. Banks looked at her and saw her stick her hand behind her back and give them two fingers. They laughed.

They passed two girls, neither of whom looked older than fifteen. Each was pushing a pram with one hand and holding a cigarette with the other. One of them had short pink-and-white-dyed hair, green nail varnish, black lipstick and a nose-stud; the other had jet-black hair, a large butterfly tattoo on her shoulder, and a red dot in the centre of her forehead. Both wore high-heeled sandals, tight shorts and midriff-revealing tops; the one with the red dot also had a ring in her navel.

'Get *her*,' one of them sneered as Banks and Annie walked by. 'Little Miss Hoity-Toity.'

'I'm beginning to think this wasn't such a good idea, after all,' Annie said, when the girls had passed.

'Why not? What's wrong?'

'Easy for you to ask. Nobody's insulted *you* yet.'

'They're only jealous.'

'What of? My good looks?'

'No. Your designer jeans. Ah, here it is.'

The address turned out to be on one of the narrower side-streets. Most of the doors had scratched and weathered paintwork, and the whole street looked run-down. All the windows of the old Shackleton house were open, and loud music blasted from inside.

Next door, two men with huge beer bellies sat smoking and drinking Carlsberg Special Brew. An enormous woman sat on a tiny chair at an angle to them, hips and thighs flowing over the edge. She looked as if she might be their mother. Both men were stripped to the waist, skin white as lard despite the sun; the woman wore a bikini top and garish pink shorts. All three of them followed Banks and Annie with their narrowed piggy eyes, but nobody said anything.

Banks knocked on the door. A dog growled inside the house. The people next door laughed. Finally, the door jerked open and a young skinhead in a red T-shirt and torn jeans stuck his head out, holding the barking dog by its studded collar. It looked like a Rottweiler to Banks.

Banks swallowed and stepped back a couple of paces. He wasn't normally scared of dogs, but this one had wicked-looking teeth. Maybe Annie was right. What could they find out anyway, nearly fifty years after the fact?

'Who the fuck are you? What do you want?' the skinhead asked. The cords stood out on his neck. He couldn't have been older than eighteen or nineteen. Banks thought he could hear a baby crying somewhere beyond the music in the depths of the house.

'Your mum and dad in?' Banks asked.

He laughed. 'I should think so,' he said. 'They never go anywhere. Trouble is, you'll have a bloody long journey. They live in Nottingham.'

'So *you* live here?'

''Course I fucking do. Look, I haven't got all day.' The dog was still straining at its collar, drool dripping from its jowls, but it had turned quieter now and seemed to be settling down, just growling rather than barking and snapping.

'I'd like some information,' said Banks.

'About what?'

'Look, can we come in?'

'You must be fucking joking, mate. One step over this threshold and Gazza here'll have you singing soprano in the church choir before you know it.'

Banks looked at Gazza. He could believe it. He considered his options. Call Animal Control? The RSPCA? 'Fine,' he said. 'Then maybe you can tell us what we want to know out here?'

'Depends.'

'It's the house I'm interested in.'

The kid looked Annie up and down, then looked back at Banks. 'House-hunting are you, then? I'd've thought you two would be after something a bit more up-market than this fucking slum.'

'Not exactly house-hunting, no.'

'Who is it, Kev?' came a woman's voice from inside.

Kev turned round and yelled back. 'Mind yer own fucking business, yer stupid cunt! Or you'll be sucking yer meals through a straw for a week.'

Banks sensed Annie stiffen beside him. He touched her gently on the forearm. The trio next door howled with laughter. The kid stuck his head farther round the door, so they could see him, and grinned at them, pleased with himself. He gave them the thumbs-up sign.

'How long have you lived here?' Banks asked.

'Two years. What's it to you?'

'I'm interested in something that happened here fifty years ago. A suicide.'

'Suicide? Fifty years ago? What, fucking haunted, is it?' He stuck his head round the door again to talk to the people next door. 'Hear that, lads? This is a fucking haunted house, this is. Maybe we could start charging an entry fee like those fucking stately homes.'

They all laughed. Including Banks.

The kid seemed so thrilled with his audience response that he repeated the comment. He then let go of the dog, which glanced uninterestedly at Banks and Annie and slunk off deeper into the house, no doubt towards a bowl of food. Maybe it wasn't a Rottweiler after all. Banks was about as good on dogs as he was on wild flowers, constellations and trees. Most of nature, come to think of it. But he would get better now he had the cottage by the edge of the woods. He had already learned to identify some of the birds – nuthatches, dunnocks and blue tits – and he had often heard a woodpecker knocking away at an ash trunk.

'Do you know who lived here before you?' he asked.

'Haven't a clue, mate. But you can ask the wrinklies over the road. They've been here since the fucking ice age.' He pointed to the middle terrace house directly opposite. Mirror image. Banks could already see a figure peeking from behind moth-eaten curtains.

'Thanks,' he said. Annie followed him across the street.

'I smell pork,' said one of the doorstep trio as they went. The others laughed. Someone made a hawking sound and spat loudly.

After Banks and Annie had held their warrant cards up to the letter-box for inspection, the deadbolt and the chain came off and a hunched man, probably somewhere in his early seventies, opened the door. He had a hollow chest, deep-set eyes, a thin, lined face and sparse black-and-grey hair larded back with lashings of Brylcreem. That glint of self-pitying malice peculiar to those who have been knocked on their arses too many times by life had not been entirely extinguished from his rheumy eyes; a few watts of indignant outrage, at least, remained.

Making sure he'd locked up behind him, he led them into the house. The windows were all shut tight and most of the curtains were closed. The living room had the atmosphere of a hot and stuffy funeral parlour; it smelled of cigarette smoke and dirty socks.

IN A DRY SEASON

'What's it all about, then?' The old man flopped down on a sagging brown corduroy settee.

'The past,' said Banks.

A woman walked through from the kitchen. About the same age as the man, she seemed a little better preserved. She certainly had a bit more flesh on her bones.

The old man reached for his cigarettes and lighter balanced on the threadbare arm of the settee, and he coughed when he lit up. What the future holds in store for us smokers if we don't stop, Banks thought glumly, deciding against joining him just at the moment.

'Police, Elsie,' the man said.

'Come to do something about those hooligans?' she asked.

'No,' said the man, a puzzled frown creasing his brow. 'They say it's about the past.'

'Aye, well, there's plenty of that about for everyone,' she said. 'Like a cuppa?'

'Please,' said Banks. Annie nodded.

'Sit yerselves down then. I'm Mrs Patterson, by the way. You can call me Elsie. And this is my Stanley.'

Stanley leaned forward and offered his hand. 'Call me Stan,' he said, with a wink. Elsie went to make the tea. 'I see you met that lot over the street?' Stan said with a jerk of his head.

'We did,' said Banks.

'He threatened to beat his wife,' Annie said. 'Have you ever seen any evidence of that, Mr Patterson? Any cuts or bruises?'

'Nay, lass,' said Stan. 'He's all wind and piss, is yon Kev. Colleen'd kill him like as not if he ever laid a finger on her. And she's not his wife, neither. Not that it seems to matter these days. It's not even his kid.' He took a drag on his cigarette, which Banks noticed was untipped, and launched into a coughing fit. When he recovered, his face was red and his chest was heaving. 'Sorry,' he said, thumping his chest. 'All them years grafting in that filthy factory. Ought to bloody sue, I did.'

'How long have you lived here?' Banks asked.

'For ever. Or so it seems,' Stan said. 'It were always a rough estate, even back then, but it weren't really such a bad place when we first moved in. Lucky to get it, we were.' He smoked and coughed again.

Elsie came back with the tea. A cold drink would probably have made more sense, Banks thought, but you take what you're offered.

'Stan was just saying you've lived here a long time,' Banks said to her.

She poured the tea into heavy white mugs. 'Since we got married,' she said. 'Well, we lived with Stan's mum and dad in Pontefract for a few months, didn't we, love, but this was our first home together.' She sat beside her husband.

'And our last, way things turned out,' Stan said.

'Well, whose fault were that?'

'Weren't mine, woman.'

'You knew I wanted to move to that new Raynville Estate when they built it, didn't you?'

'Aye,' said Stan. 'When were that? In 1963? And where is it now? They've had to knock the bloody place down now, things got so bad.'

'There were other places we could have moved. Poplars. Wythers.'

'*Wythers!* Wythers is worse than this.'

'What year was it?' Banks butted in. 'When you first came to live here?'

The Pattersons glared at one another for a moment, then Elsie stirred her tea. She sat up straight, knees pressed together, hands around the mug on her lap. In the distance, Banks could hear the music from the skinhead's house: tortured guitars, heavy bass, a testosterone-pumped voice snarling lust and hatred. Christ, he hoped Brian's band was better than that.

'In 1949,' Elsie said. 'October 1949. I remember because I were three months gone with Derek at the time. He was our first. Remember, Stan,' she said, 'you'd just got that job at Blakey's Castings?'

'Aye,' said Stan, turning to Banks. 'I were just twenty years old, and Elsie here were eighteen.'

Banks hadn't even been born then. The war had been over four years and the country was going through a lot of changes, setting up the Welfare State in the wake of the Beveridge Report, setting up the whole system that had given Banks far more opportunities and chances of self-improvement than previous generations had. And to his parents' dismay, he had become a copper instead of a business executive or managing director, the sort of position his father had always looked up to. Now, though, having felt very much like a business executive this past year, he was pleased to discover that he still thought he had made the right choice.

Banks tried to imagine the Pattersons as a young couple with hope in their hearts and a promising future before them crossing the threshold of their first home together. The image came in black and white, with a factory chimney in the background.

'Do you remember anything about your neighbours across the street?' Annie asked. 'Directly opposite, where Kev and his family live now.'

Elsie spoke first. 'Weren't that where those, you know, those . . . what's-their-names . . . lived, Stanley? A bit stuck up. There were some trouble.'

'A suicide,' Banks prompted her.

'Aye. That's right. Don't you remember, Stanley? Shot himself. That tall skinny young fellow, used to walk with a stick, never said a word to anyone. What were his name?'

'Matthew Shackleton.'

'That's right. We had police all over the place. They even came over and talked to us. By gum, that takes me back a bit. Matthew Shackleton. Don't you remember, Stanley?'

'Aye,' said Stan hesitantly. 'I think so.' He lit another cigarette and coughed. Then he glanced at his watch. Opening time.

'Did you know the Shackletons?' Banks asked.

'Not really,' Elsie said. 'Acted like they'd gone down in the world, fallen on hard times, like. From the country somewhere, though I found out she were nowt better than a shopkeeper's daughter. Not that there's owt wrong with that, mind you. I'm no snob. I tried to be friendly, you know, like you do, seeing as we were the newcomers and all that. But nobody bothered with them. The time or two I did talk to her, she didn't say owt about where they came from, except to mention that things had been different back in the village, like. Well, la-di-da, I thought.'

Well, Banks thought, from Hobb's End to this Leeds council estate would have been quite a frightening journey into purgatory for Gwen and Matthew, unless they were in a purgatory of their own making already.

'How many of them lived there?'

'Just the two,' Elsie said. 'I remember her saying her

mother used to live with them and all, but she died a year or so before we moved here.'

'Aye,' Stan chirped in. 'I remember them now. Just the two of them, weren't there? Him and his wife. Tall, gangly lass, herself.'

'Nay,' said Elsie, 'she were never his wife. He weren't right in his head.'

'Who were she, then?'

'I don't know, but she weren't his wife.'

'How do you know?' Banks asked Elsie.

'They didn't act like man and wife. I could tell.'

'Don't be so bloody daft, woman,' Stan said. Then he looked at Banks and rolled his eyes. 'She were his wife. Take it from me.'

'What was her name?' Banks asked.

'It's on the tip of my tongue,' Elsie said.

'Blodwyn,' said Stan. 'Summat Welsh, any road.'

'No, it weren't. Gwynneth, that were it. Gwynneth Shackleton.'

'What did she look like?'

'Ordinary, really, apart from them beautiful eyes of hers,' said Elsie. 'Like Stanley said, she were a bit taller than your average lass, and a bit clumsy, you know, the way some big people are. She were nearly as tall as Matthew.'

'How old, would you say?'

'She can't have been that old, but she had a hard-done-by look about her. I don't know how to say it, really. Old before her time. Tired, like.'

'Must've been from looking after her husband. He were an invalid. Battle fatigue. War wound.'

'He weren't her husband.'

Stan turned to face her. 'Did you ever see her stepping out with a young man?'

'Come to think on it, no, I don't recall as I did.'

'There you are then. Goes to show.'

'Show what?'

'You'd've thought if she weren't married she'd have had a boyfriend or two, girl like that, wouldn't you? I'll grant you she were no oil painting, but she were well enough shaped where it counts, and she were bonny enough.'

'Did they ever have many visitors?' Banks asked.

'Not as I noticed,' Elsie answered. 'But I'm not one of your nose-at-the-window types, you know.'

'How about an attractive young woman with blond hair?' Annie said, turning to Stanley. 'Might have looked like this.' She handed him the copy of Alice Poole's photograph and pointed to Gloria.

'No,' said Stan. 'Never seen anyone looked like her. And I think I'd remember.' He winked at Annie. 'I'm not that old, tha knows. But the other one's Gwynneth all right.' He pointed to the woman Alice had identified as Gwen Shackleton. 'I can't recall as they ever had *any* visitors, come to think on it.'

'Aye, you're right there, Stanley,' she said. 'They kept to themselves.'

'What happened after the suicide?' Banks asked.

'She went away.'

'Do you know where?'

'No. She never even said goodbye. One day she were there, the next she were gone. I'll tell you what, though.'

'What?' asked Banks.

A wicked smile twisted her features. 'I know who she is.'

'What do you mean?'

'Her. That Gwynneth Shackleton. That's not her name

290

now, of course, but it's her, right enough. Done right well for herself, she has.'

'Who is she?'

'I've seen her on telly, seen her picture in *Woman's Own*.'

'Yer barmy, woman,' Stan piped up.

'I'm telling you, Stanley: it's her. Those eyes. The height. The voice. I don't forget things like that. I'm surprised you can't see it for yourself.'

Banks was trying hard to remain patient and beginning to think he was fighting a losing battle. 'Mrs Patterson. Elsie,' he said finally. 'Do you think you could tell me *who* you think Gwen Shackleton is?'

'It's that woman writes those books, isn't it? Always being interviewed on telly. And she did that documentary about that little church in London, you know, like Alan Bennett did on Westminster Abbey. Used to live just down the road, did Alan Bennett. His dad were a butcher. Any road, you could see it were her, how tall she were. And those eyes.'

'What books?' Banks asked.

'Them detective books. Always on telly. With that good-looking what's-'is-name playing the inspector. Good they are, too. I've had her books out of the library. I must go through ten books a week. It's her, I'm telling you.'

'She's thinking of that Vivian Elmsley woman,' sighed Stan. 'Swore the first time she saw her interviewed by that bloke who talks through his nose.'

'Melvyn Bragg.'

'Aye, him. Swore blind it were Gwen Shackleton.'

'You don't agree?' Annie asked.

'Nay, I don't know, lass. I'm not good at faces, not the way our Elsie is. She's always telling me someone's baby

looks like his mum or dad but I'm buggered if I can see it.
They all look like Winston Churchill to me. Or Edward G.
Robinson. There *is* a resemblance, but . . .' He shook his
head. 'It's so long ago. People change. And things like that
don't happen to people like us, do they, people from
places like this? Someone across the street gets famous and
writes books that get done on telly and all? I mean, life's
not like that, is it? Not here. Not for the likes of us.'

'What about Alan Bennett?' Elsie argued. 'And she
were well read. You could tell that about her.'

In the brief silence that followed, Banks heard more
music and laughter from across the street.

'You hear what it's like?' Stan said. 'Never a moment's
peace. Day and night, night and day, bloody racket. We
keep our windows shut and curtains closed. You never
know what's going to happen next. We had a murder last
week. Bloke down the street playing cards with some
bloody gyppos. Vinnie and Derek, our lads, they worry
about us. They'd like us to go live in sheltered housing.
We might just do it and all. Right now, I'd settle for three
squares a day and a bit of peace and quiet.'

'Back to this woman,' said Banks, turning to Elsie.
'Gwen Shackleton.'

'Aye?'

'How long did she stay on the estate after the suicide?'

'Oh, not long. I'd say as long as it took to get him buried
and get everything sorted out with the authorities.'

'Were the police suspicious about what happened?'

'Police are always suspicious, aren't they?' said Stan.
'It's their job.' He laughed and coughed. 'Nay, lad, you
ought to know that.'

Banks smiled. 'Was Gwen in the house at the time of
the suicide?' he asked.

Elsie paused and lowered her head. 'That's what they asked us back then,' she said. 'I've thought and thought about it to this day, and I still don't know. I *thought* I saw her get back from the shops – that was where she'd been, shopping up Town Street – *before* I heard the bang.' She frowned. 'But, you see, I were so close to having our Derek, and I weren't always seeing things right. I could have been wrong.'

'Did you tell the police this?'

'Yes. But nowt came of it. Or they'd have put her in gaol, wouldn't they?'

Now Banks *definitely* wanted to have a look at the Matthew Shackleton file. 'We might as well be off,' he said to Annie, then turned to Stan and Elsie. 'Thanks very much. You've been a great help.'

'Tell me summat,' said Stan. 'I know getting information out of you lot's like prising a penny from a Scotsman's arse, but I'm curious. This Gwen, were she his wife?'

Banks smiled. 'His sister. We think.'

Elsie nudged her husband hard in the ribs. He started coughing. 'See, Stanley. I told yer so, yer great lummox.'

Banks insisted they could find their own way out, and soon he and Annie walked gratefully in the fresh air. The people across the street were still enjoying their party, joined now by Kev and his dog, which was running wild across the tiny lawns, scratching on doors and ripping up what weeds had survived summer so far. Another woman, whom Banks assumed to be Colleen, was also there, holding her baby. She was a skinny girl, about seventeen, smiling, no bruises, but with a hard, defeated look about her.

As Banks and Annie neared the end of the street, an empty beer can skittered across the Tarmac behind them.

'What do you think about this Vivian Elmsley business?' Annie asked.

'I don't know. I'm surprised that neither Elizabeth nor Alice mentioned it.'

'Maybe they didn't know? Alice said she's got very poor eyesight, and Elizabeth Goodall didn't even know why you were visiting her, she pays so little attention to current affairs.'

'True,' said Banks. 'And Ruby Kettering left Hobb's End in 1940, when Gwen was only about fifteen. Definitely worth looking into.'

'So,' said Annie back in the car. 'What next?'

'The local nick. I want to see Matthew Shackleton's file.'

'I thought so. And then?'

'Back to Millgarth.'

'Have we time for a drink and a bite to eat later?'

'Sorry. I've got a date.'

She thumped him playfully. 'Seriously?'

'Seriously. With a detective inspector. A *male* detective inspector called Ken Blackstone. You met him briefly. He gave us the address.'

'I remember him. The snappy dresser. Cute.' If Annie was disappointed, she didn't show it. Banks explained his tenuous friendship with Ken and how he was in a mood for building bridges. Things seemed to be coming together for him – the cottage, an active investigation, Annie – and he realized that he had been neglecting his friends for too long.

'I see,' Annie said. 'A boys' night out, then?'

'I suppose so.'

She laughed. 'I wouldn't mind being a fly on the wall at *that* one.'

•

Billy Joe was confined to base for a few weeks. They said his punishment would have been far more severe had not all the witnesses, even Seth's friends, attested that he didn't start the fight. Seth was fine, too. At first, I thought Billy Joe had broken the glass in his face, but it had simply fallen off the edge of the table when he had tried to put it back there before preparing to defend himself. All Billy Joe had done was punch Seth in the nose, and everyone agreed it was well deserved.

Gloria never said as much, but I think the incident put her off Billy Joe. She hated violence. Some girls like being fought over. I'll never forget the primal blood lust in Cynthia Garmen's eyes when two soldiers fought over her favours at one of the Harkside dances. She didn't care who was hitting whom as long as someone was getting hit and blood was flowing. But Gloria wasn't like that. Violence upset her.

It was while Billy Joe was confined to base that we first met Brad and Charlie.

We were walking out of the Lyceum. It was a miserable February night in 1944, not snowing, but freezing cold, with icicles hanging from the cinema's eaves. We hadn't been out for a few days and Gloria was getting depressed with the cold and the hard working conditions at the farm. She needed cheering up.

We had been to see Bette Davis and Paul Henreid in *Now, Voyager*, and we were both humming the theme song as we put our coats back on in the foyer before going out into the bitter cold evening.

Before Gloria could dig out her own cigarettes, a young man in a fleece-lined leather jacket walked over, put two cigarettes in his mouth, lit them, then handed one to her. It was the same thing they had done in the film. We doubled over laughing.

'Brad,' said the young man. 'Brad Szikorski. And this is my pal Charlie Markleson.'

Gloria did a little mock curtsy. 'Charmed to meet you, I'm sure.'

'We're with the Four Hundred Forty-Eighth? Over at Rowan Woods?' Though they were statements, they sounded like questions. I had noticed this before with both Americans and Canadians. 'I don't mean to be forward,' said Brad, 'but would you ladies care to honour us by joining us for a drink?'

We exchanged glances. I could tell Gloria wanted to go. Brad was tall and handsome, with a twinkle in his eye and a little Clark Gable moustache. I looked at Charlie, who was probably destined to be my companion for the evening, and I had to admit I quite liked what I saw. About the same age as Brad, he had intelligent eyes, if a little puppy-dog, and a rather pale, thin face. His nose was too big, and it had a bump in the middle, but then mine was nothing to write home about, either. He also seemed reserved and serious. All in all, he'd do. At least for a drink.

We walked across to the Black Swan. The village green was deserted and the ice crackled under our feet. Icicles hung from the branches and twigs of the chestnut trees and frost covered the bark. If it hadn't been so cold, I could have imagined they were blossoms in May. Behind us, the illuminated sign over the Lyceum went off. Even in the blackout, cinemas, shops and a few other establishments were allowed a small measure of light, unless the air-raid siren went off. Ahead, St Jude's was partially lit, and close by stood the Black Swan, with its familiar timber-and-whitewash façade and sagging roof. We could hear the sounds of talking and laughter from inside, but heavy blackout curtains covered the mullioned windows.

The pub was crowded and we were lucky to get a table. Brad went to the bar for drinks while we took our coats off. A meagre fire burned in the hearth, but with all the warm bodies in there, it was enough. Also, in the Black Swan, Brad and Charlie weren't the only Americans; it seemed to be a popular place among the Rowan Woods crowd, and there were even some GIs from the army base near Otley. They were loud and they used hand gestures a lot; they also seemed to push and shove one another a lot, in a friendly way, as children do.

Brad came back bearing a tray of six drinks. We wondered who was going to join us. Gloria and I were both drinking gin, and when Brad and Charlie picked up their beer glasses, then poured the small measures of whisky into them, our unspoken question was answered. Nobody. Just another American peculiarity.

We toasted one another and drank, then Brad did the thing with the cigarettes again, and Charlie did it for me.

'What do you do?' Gloria asked.

'I'm a pilot,' said Brad, 'and Charlie here's my navigator.'

'A pilot! How exciting. Where are you from?'

'California.'

Gloria clapped her hands together. 'Hollywood!'

'Well, not exactly. A little place called Pasadena. You probably haven't heard of it.'

'But you must *know* Hollywood?'

Brad smiled, revealing straight white teeth. They must have wonderful dentists over in America, I thought, and people must have enough money to be able to afford them. 'As a matter of fact, yeah, I do,' he said. 'I did a little stunt flying there in the movies before I came over here.'

'You mean you've actually been in pictures?'

'Well, you can't really see it's me, but, I mean, yeah, I

guess so.' He named a couple of titles; we hadn't heard of either of them. 'That's what I want to do when all this is over,' he went on. 'Get back there and get in the movie business. My father's in oil and he wants me to join him. I know there's plenty of money there, but that's not what I want. I want a shot at being a stunt man.'

If Gloria was disappointed that Brad didn't want to be an oil millionaire or a movie star, she didn't show it. As they chatted away excitedly about films and Hollywood, Charlie and I started our own hesitant conversation.

The beer and whisky must have melted a little of his reserve, because he opened by asking me what I did. He regarded me seriously as I told him, his expression unchanging, nodding his head every now and then. Then he told me his father was a professor at Harvard, that he had completed his university degree in English just before the war, and when he went back he wanted to go to Harvard, too, to study law. He liked flying, he said, but he didn't see it as a career.

The more we talked, the more we found we had in common – Jane Austen and Thomas Hardy, for example, and the poetry of T. S. Eliot. And Robert Frost and Edward Thomas. He hadn't heard of many of our younger poets, so I offered to lend him some issues of *Penguin New Writing*, with poems by MacNeice, Auden and Day Lewis, and he said he would lend me Tate and Bishop's *American Harvest* anthology, if I took special care with it. I told him that I would no more damage a book than I would a living human being and that made him smile for the first time.

'Have you got a husband?' I overheard Brad ask Gloria. 'I mean, I don't mean to . . . you know . . .'

'It's all right. I did have. But he's dead. Killed in Burma. At least I hope to God he was.'

I turned from Charlie. It was true that we had tried to convince ourselves of Matthew's death, but there was still a lingering hope, at least in my mind, and I thought that was a terrible thing to say. I told her so.

She turned on me, eyes flashing. 'Well, you should know better than anyone that I'm right, Gwen. You're the one who reads the newspapers and listens to the news, aren't you?'

'Yes.'

'Look, I'm really sorry,' Brad cut in, but Gloria ignored him, kept staring at me.

'So you must know what they're saying about the Japanese, about the way they treat their prisoners?' she went on.

I had to admit that I had read one or two rather grim stories alleging that the Japanese beat and starved prisoners to death, and according to Anthony Eden, torture and decapitation were favourite pastimes in their POW camps. The *Daily Mail* called them 'monkey men', claimed that they were 'sub-human' and should be outlawed after they had been beaten back to their 'savage land'. I didn't know what to believe. If the stories were true, then I should probably agree with Gloria and hope to God Matthew was dead.

'I've got friends fighting in the Pacific,' said Charlie. 'I hear it's pretty rough out there. A lot of these stories are true.'

'Well, he's dead, anyway,' said Gloria. 'So nothing can hurt him now. Look, this is too depressing. Can we have another round of drinkies, please?'

Brad and Charlie drove us home in their Jeep. Charlie seemed a little embarrassed when Brad and Gloria started kissing passionately by the fairy bridge, but he managed to

pluck up the courage to put his arm around me. We kissed
dutifully and arranged to meet again soon to swap books.
Brad told Charlie to drive on, that he'd walk back to the base
alone later, and he followed Gloria into Bridge Cottage.

•

The Indian restaurant Ken Blackstone had chosen was a
hole-in-the-wall on Burley Road with red tablecloths and
a bead curtain in front of the kitchen. Every time the
waiter walked through, the beads rattled. Sitar music
droned from speakers high on the walls, and the aromas
of cumin and coriander filled the air.

'Did you find what you were looking for in those
incident reports?' Blackstone asked as they shared pop-
padams, samosas and pakoras.

'I wasn't after anything in particular,' Banks said. 'Elsie
Patterson was unsure as to whether she saw Gwen
Shackleton enter the house with her shopping before or
after she heard the shot. She even thought the shot might
have been a car backfiring. And she was the only witness.
Nobody else saw Gwen or Matthew that day. The other
neighbours were at work, the local kids at school.'

'What did Gwen Shackleton say in her statement?'

Banks swallowed a mouthful of samosa. So far, the
food was excellent, as Ken had promised; it was neither
too greasy nor needlessly hot, the way many Indian
restaurants made it, mistaking chili peppers and cayenne
for creative spicing. Banks thought he might like to try his
hand at Indian cooking, have Annie over for a vegetarian
curry. 'She just said she found Matthew dead in the
armchair when she got home from shopping.'

'Was there any real doubt? Was she ever a suspect?'

'I didn't get that impression. Matthew Shackleton had a

history of mental illness since the war. He was also an alcoholic. Functioning, more or less, but an alcoholic. According to the report, he had tried to kill himself once before, head in the gas oven that time. A neighbour smelled gas and saved him. The hospital suggested a period of psychiatric observation, which they carried out, then they sent him home again.'

'Why didn't he use the gun that time?'

'No idea.'

'But it was just a matter of time?'

'Seems that way.'

'You disagree?'

'No. Though I suppose there's always the possibility that he was helped on his way, that he had become an intolerable burden to his sister. Remember, Gwen had been taking care of both her mother *and* her brother. It's not much of a life for a young woman, is it? Anyway, if Elsie Patterson really did see Gwen Shackleton go into the house before the shot was fired, it's possible Gwen might have stood by and let him get on with it.'

'Still a crime.'

'Yes, but it happened over forty years ago, Ken. And we'd never prove it.'

'Not unless Gwen Shackleton confessed.'

'Why should she do that?'

'Years of accumulated guilt? The need to get it off her chest before her final confrontation with the Almighty? I don't know. Who knows why people confess? They do, though.'

Their main courses arrived: aloo gobi, rogan josh, and king prawns, with pilau rice, lime chutney and chapattis. They ordered more lager.

Banks looked at Blackstone. *Cute*, Annie had said. Cute

was the last thing that came to Banks's mind. Elegant, yes; donnish, even. But cute? No matter where Blackstone was – student hang-out, backstreet pub, five-star restaurant, cop shop – he was aways immaculately dressed in his Burton's best pinstripe or herringbone, monogrammed silk handkerchief poised over the edge of his top pocket, folds so aesthetic and delicate they might have been set by a Japanese flower arranger. Crisp white shirt, neat Windsor knot in his subdued tie. Thinning sandy hair curled around his ears and his wire-rimmed glasses balanced on the bridge of his straight nose.

'What about forensics?' Blackstone asked.

'Single shot in the mouth. Splattered his brains over the wall like blancmange. No evidence of a struggle. Empty whisky bottle by the chair. The angle of the wound was also consistent with the suicide theory.'

'Note?'

'Yes. The genuine article, according to forensics.'

'So what's bothering you?'

Banks ate some curry and washed it down before answering. Already a pleasant glow was spreading from his mouth and stomach throughout the rest of his body. The curry was just hot enough to produce a mild sweat, but not to burn his taste buds off. 'Nothing, really. Outside of normal curiosity, I'm not really interested in whether Gwen Shackleton helped her brother commit suicide or not. But I would like to know if he murdered Gloria Shackleton.'

'Perhaps he couldn't live with the guilt?'

'My first thought.'

'But now?'

'Oh, it's still the most likely explanation. The only person who can tell us is Gwen Shackleton.'

'What happened to her? Is she still alive?'

'That's another interesting thing. Elsie Patterson swears she's Vivian Elmsley.'

Blackstone whistled and raised his thin, arched eyebrows. 'The writer?'

'That's the one.'

'What do you think?'

'I don't know. It's possible, I suppose. The Pattersons said they could tell Gwen was well read, and everyone who remembers her said she always had her head stuck in a book. Annie's going to ask around, but there's only one way to find out for certain, isn't there? We'll have to talk to her. Like Gloria's son, if he's still alive, she certainly hasn't been in touch with us, and we've had calls out all over the country for information. It's hard to imagine that many people don't know the story.'

'Which may mean that, if it is her, she has a reason for not wanting to be found?'

'Exactly. A guilty secret.'

'Wasn't that the title of one of her books?'

Banks laughed. 'Was it? I can't say as I've read any.'

'I have,' said Blackstone. 'Seen them on telly, too. She's actually a very talented writer. Hasn't a clue about how we really operate, of course, but then none of them do.'

'It'd make for some pretty boring books if they did.'

'True enough.'

Blackstone ordered a couple more pints of lager. He looked at his watch. 'How about heading into town after this one?' he asked.

'Okay.'

'How are the kids?'

'Fine, I suppose. Well, at least Tracy is.'

'Brian?'

'Silly bugger's just cocked up his finals and come out with a third.'

Blackstone, who had a degree in art history, frowned. 'Any particular reason? You don't blame yourself, do you? The break-up? Stress?'

Banks shook his head. 'No, not really. I think he just sort of lost interest in the subject and found something he felt more passionate about.'

'The music?'

'Uh-huh. He's in a band. They're trying to make a go of it.'

'Good for him,' said Blackstone. 'I would have thought you'd approve.'

'That's the bloody problem, Ken, I do. Only when he first told me I said some things I regret. Now I can't get in touch with him to explain. They're out on the road somewhere.'

'Keep trying. That's about all you can do.'

'I sounded just like my own parents. It brought back a lot of stuff, things I hadn't really thought much about in years, like why I made some of the choices I did.'

'Any answers?'

Banks smiled. 'On a postcard, please.'

'Any great change in your circumstances tends to make you introspective. It's one of the stages you go through.'

'Been reading those self-help books again, Ken?'

Blackstone smiled. 'Fruits of experience, mate. This DS you were asking me about on the phone, the one who was with you at Millgarth. What's her name again?'

'Annie. Annie Cabbot.'

'Good-looking woman?'

'I suppose so.'

'You involved with her?'

Banks paused. If he told Ken Blackstone the truth, that would be *one* person too many who knew about them. But why keep it a secret? Why lie? Ken was a mate. He nodded briefly.

'Is it serious?'

'For crying out loud, Ken, I've only known her a week.'

Blackstone held his hand up. 'Okay, okay. Is she the first one since Sandra?'

'Yes. Well, apart from a mistake one night. Yes. Why?'

'Just be careful, that's all.'

'Come again?'

Blackstone leaned back in his chair. 'You're still vulnerable, that's what I'm talking about. It takes a long time to get over a relationship as long-lasting and as deep as yours and Sandra's.'

'I'm not sure how deep it went, Ken. I'm beginning to think I believed what I wanted to believe, missed the signposts to the real world.'

'Whatever. All I'm saying is that when someone goes through what you're going through, he either ends up angry at women for a long time or he misses what he had. Or both. If he's angry, then he probably just shags them and leaves them. But if he misses the relationship, then he looks for another one to replace it, and his judgment is not necessarily in the best of nick. If he's both, then he gets into another relationship and fucks it up royally all round and wonders why everyone ends up in tears.'

Banks pushed his chair back and stood up. 'Well, thanks for the amateur psychology, Ken, but if I'd wanted Claire fucking Rayner—'

Blackstone grabbed on to Banks's sleeve. 'Alan. Sit down. Please. I'm not suggesting you do anything except be aware of the pitfalls.' He smiled. 'Besides, you're bloody-minded enough to do what you want in any situation, I know that. All I'm saying is think about what you want and why you want it. Be aware of what's going on. That's all the wisdom I have to offer. You've always struck me as a bit of a romantic underneath it all.'

Banks hesitated, still half ready to leave and half ready to punch Blackstone. 'What do you mean?'

'The kind of detective who cares just a bit too much about every victim. The kind of bloke who falls a little bit in love with every woman he sleeps with.'

Banks glanced at Blackstone through narrowed eyes. 'I haven't slept with that many women,' he said. 'And as for—'

'Sit down, Alan. Please.'

Banks paused for a moment. When he felt the anger sluice away, he sat.

'What does she feel about it all?'

Banks reached for a cigarette. He felt uncomfortable, as if he were in the dentist's chair and Blackstone were probing a particularly sensitive nerve. He had never been good at talking about his feelings, even with Jenny Fuller, who *was* a psychologist. It was something he had in common with most of his male friends, and it gave him a special solidarity with Yorkshiremen. He should have remembered that Ken Blackstone was a bit artsy, read Freud and that sort of thing. 'I don't know,' he said. 'I haven't asked her. We haven't really talked about it.'

Blackstone paused. Banks lit his cigarette. On a night like this one was shaping up to be, he might go over his allowance. 'Alan,' Blackstone went on, 'ten months ago you thought you had a stable marriage of more than twenty years' standing, house, kids, the full Monty. Then, all of a sudden, the carpet's pulled out from under you and you find you've got nothing of the kind. The emotional fall-out from that sort of upset doesn't go away overnight, mate, I can tell you. And believe me, I speak from experience. It takes years to get it out of your system. Enjoy yourself. Just don't make it more than it is. You're not ready to deal with that yet. Don't confuse sex and love.' He slapped the table. 'Shit, now I *am* starting to sound like Claire Rayner. I didn't really want to get into this.'

'Why did you start it, then?'

Blackstone laughed. 'God knows. Because I've been there, maybe? Bit of personal therapy? Like anything, it's probably more about me than you. Maybe I'm just jealous. Maybe I wouldn't mind sleeping with an attractive young DS myself. Lord knows, it's been a bloody long time. Ignore me.'

Banks finished his pint and put the glass down slowly. 'Look, I take your point, Ken, really I do, but to be honest, it's the first time I've felt comfortable with a woman since Sandra left. Not comfortable, so much, that's not the right word. Annie's not a woman you necessarily feel comfortable with. She's a little weird. Bit of a free spirit. Very private. Hell, though, it's the first time I've really felt free enough to jump into something and say damn the consequences.'

Blackstone laughed and shook his head slowly. 'Sounds like you've got it bad.' He looked at his watch. 'What say we hit the fleshpots of Leeds and get irredeemably pissed?'

Banks smiled. 'Most sensible thing you've said all night. Let's do it.'

'And I've got a fine malt tucked away at home for afters.'

'Even better. Lead on.'

•

Winter finally gave way to a slow spring, with its snowdrops in Rowan Woods, then the bluebells, crocuses and daffodils. Brad and Charlie became our regular 'beaux' and we saw far less of Billy Joe, who became very sulky after he found he had lost Gloria to a pilot.

The Americans always seemed more casual about rank, unlike the English. I suppose it is because our class system instilled it in us from birth, while Americans were all created equal, or so they say. It must be nice for them; it would probably be confusing for *us*. But it's one thing for officers and enlisted men to eat, drink and billet together and quite another for a second lieutenant to steal a mere sergeant's girl.

I was worried that Billy Joe would start a fight, given his violent streak, but he soon found another girl and even started talking to us again when we met at dances and in pubs. He pestered Gloria on occasion to go back with him, or at least just to sleep with him again, but she was able to keep him at bay, even when she'd been drinking.

PX, of course, remained absolutely essential, so we made sure we still cultivated him. As none of us had actually gone out with him, anyway, we had no reason to think our new relationship with Brad and Charlie would have any effect on the friendship, and it didn't seem to.

I won't say that my affair with Charlie was a grand passion, but we became less awkward with the physical side of things as time went on, and he did become the first man I ever slept with. He was gentle, patient and sensitive, which was exactly what I needed, and I came to look forward to those times we spent in bed together at Bridge Cottage, courtesy of Gloria.

Our relationship remained more of an intellectual one;

we passed books back and forth with abandon: Forster, Proust, Dostoevsky. Charlie wasn't dull and dry, though; he loved to dance and was a great Humphrey Bogart fan. He took me to see *Casablanca* and *The Maltese Falcon*, even though he had seen them both before. He was also far more passionate about classical music than I was, and we sometimes went to concerts. Once, I remember, we went all the way to Huddersfield to see Benjamin Britten conduct his own *Hymn to St Cecilia*.

In all the excitement we were probably guilty of neglecting the people who had been good to us in the worst days after Matthew's disappearance, especially Michael Stanhope. We redeemed ourselves with him a little when he had an exhibition in Leeds. Charlie and I made a weekend of it and went to stay at the Metropole Hotel.

Charlie, who knew a lot more about painting than I did, praised the exhibition to the skies and I think Mr Stanhope was rather taken with him. Even Gloria went to see Mr Stanhope at his studio that summer and autumn far more often than she had before.

I tried not to dwell on the dangers inherent in Charlie's job, and for his part, he never seemed to want to talk about them. The war receded into the distance during those hours we spent together reading or making love, though it was difficult to ignore the rest of the time. The Americans were carrying out precision daylight bombing raids over Germany, often without fighter cover, and their casualties were appalling. Instead of listening to the drone of the planes taking off after dark, I now heard them in the mornings. The Flying Fortresses were much louder than the RAF planes that had been there before. They would warm up the engines at about five o'clock, which was the time I usually awoke anyway, and I would lie there stealing an extra few minutes of warmth and imagine Charlie checking his maps and preparing himself for another raid.

Charlie told me that up around twenty thousand feet they were flying at temperatures of between minus 30 and minus 50 degrees Fahrenheit. I couldn't imagine anything that cold. He had to wear long woollen underwear and electrically heated flying suits under his fleece-lined leather jacket. I had to laugh when he said it would take him half an hour to get undressed and into bed with me.

And so life went on. Books. Bed. Pictures. Dances. Concerts. Talk. Double summertime began on the second of April that year, giving us the long spring evenings to go for walks to pick wild flowers in Rowan Woods or idle down by the river. In May, when it was warmer, we would often sit on the banks of Harksmere and read Coleridge and Wordsworth out loud to one another. We had picnics of Spam and potted-shrimp sandwiches on the terraces just off The Edge.

Mother liked Charlie, I could tell, though she didn't say much. She never did. Matthew's disappearance had taken most of the wind out of her sails. But Charlie brought her Lifesavers and Hershey bars, and she thanked him and ate them all.

After the excitement of the Normandy landing, we soon got back to reality: the summer of the doodlebugs. We only experienced one V-1 rocket in Hobb's End, one which had badly lost its way.

I was standing on the fairy bridge chatting with Cynthia Garmen. It was a typical July day: muggy, with dark, leaden clouds and the threat of storm. We were talking about the Japanese defeat at Imphal, wishing Matthew could have been there to experience it, when we heard the awful sound in the sky, like a motorcycle without a silencer. All of a sudden it spluttered to a stop. Then there was a dreadful silence. We could see it by then, a dark, pointed shape beginning the silent arc of its descent.

Fortunately, it fell in one of the fields between Hobb's End and Harkside without exploding, and by the time we had rushed down to see what was going on, the local ARP people already had the area cordoned off and were waiting for the UXB team to arrive.

The advance continued, and slowly things began to improve. The blackout was replaced by the 'dim-out' in September, but most of us left the curtains up anyway and didn't get round to taking them down until the following year. If by autumn, then, we were feeling flush with the possibility of victory, we had little idea of the grim winter to come.

•

By ten o'clock that night Annie was feeling so restless that even a large glass of wine didn't help settle her down.

She knew what part of the problem was: Banks. When he told her he was going out boozing with a mate instead of going to dinner with her, she *did* feel pissed off with him. She felt disappointed that he would rather go drinking with someone else than be with her, especially at such an early and delicate stage in their relationship. True, it was she who had suggested they limit their time together to weekends, but it was also she who had broken the rule the other night. Why couldn't he do the same tonight?

But at least she hadn't wasted *her* time that evening.

The long trail that had started on Wednesday, over the telephone, was beginning to bear fruit.

At first, she had come to the conclusion that it was easier finding a fully dressed woman in the *Sunday Sport* than getting information out of the American Embassy. People were polite – insufferably so – but she was shunted from one minion to another for the best part of an hour and came out with nothing but an earache and a growing distaste for condescending and suspicious American men who called her 'ma'am'.

By the end of the day, she had managed to discover that the personnel at Rowan Woods in late 1943 would have been members of the United States Eighth Air Force, and it was very unlikely that there would be any local records of who they were. One of the more helpful employees suggested that she try contacting the USAFE base in Ramstein and gave her the number.

When she got back from the Leeds council estate, even though it was early evening, she phoned Ramstein, where she discovered that all air force personnel records were kept at the National Personnel Records Center in St Louis, Missouri. She checked the time difference and found that St Louis was six hours behind Harkside. Which meant it would be afternoon there.

After a little more shunting around and a few abrupt requests to 'please hold', she was put through to a woman called Mattie, who just 'adored' her accent. They chatted about the differences in weather – it was raining hard in St Louis – and about other things for a short while, then Annie plucked up the courage to ask for what she wanted.

Expecting some sort of military smoke screen, she was pleasantly surprised when Mattie told her that there was no problem; the records were generally available to the public, and she would see what she could do. When Annie mentioned the initials 'PX', Mattie laughed and said that was the man who looked after the store. She also warned Annie that some of their records had been burned in a fire a few years ago, but if she still had Rowan Woods, she'd set the fax to send it out during the night. Annie should get it the next morning. Annie thanked her profusely and went home feeling absurdly pleased with herself.

But it didn't last.

Sometimes when she felt irritable and restless like this, she would go for a drive, and that was exactly what she did. Without making a conscious decision, she took the road west out of Harkside, and when she reached the turn-off for Thornfield Reservoir, she turned right.

By then she had realized that Banks wasn't the problem; *she* was. She was pissed off at herself for letting him get to her. She was behaving like some sort of silly love-struck schoolgirl. Vulnerable. Hurt. Let's face it, Annie, she told herself, life has been pretty simple, pretty much regimented for some time now. No real highs; no real lows. Only herself to think of. Manageable, but diminished.

She had been hiding from life in a remote corner of Yorkshire, protecting her emotions from the harsh world she had experienced 'out there'. Sometimes when you open yourself up to that life again, it can be confusing and painful, like when you open your eyes to bright light. Your emotions are tender and raw, more than usually sensitive to all its nuances, its little hurts and humiliations. So that was what was happening. Well, at least she knew that much. So much for cool, Annie, so much for detachment.

A misshapen harvest moon hung low in the western sky, bloated and flattened into a red sausage shape by the gathering haze. Otherwise the road was unlit, surrounded on both sides by tall dark trees. Her headlights caught dozens of rabbits.

She pulled into the car park and turned off the engine. Silence. As she got out and stood in the warm night air, she started to feel at peace. Her problems seemed to slip away; one way or another, she knew they would sort themselves out.

Annie loved being alone deep in the countryside at night, where you might hear only the very distant progress of a car, the rustles of small animals, see only the dark shapes of the trees and hills, perhaps a few pinpricks of light from farmhouses on distant hillsides. She loved the sea at night even more – the relentless rhythm of the waves, the hiss and suck, and the way the reflected moonlight sways and bends with the water's swell and catches the crests of the waves. But the sea was fifty miles away. She would have to make do with the woods for now. The appeal was still to the deep, primitive part of her.

She took the narrow footpath towards Hobb's End, walking carefully because of the gnarled tree roots that crossed it in places and the stones that thrust up out of the dirt. Hardly any moonlight penetrated the tree cover, but here and there she caught a slat or two of reddish-silver light between branches. She could smell the loamy, earthy smell of trees and shrubs. The slightest breeze butterfly-kissed the upper leaves.

When Annie reached the slope, she paused and looked down on the ruins of Hobb's End. It was easy to make out the dark, skeletal shape, the spine and ribs, but somehow tonight, with the slight curve of the High Street and the dry river-bed, the ruins looked more like the decayed stubs of teeth in a sneering mouth.

Annie skipped down the slope and walked towards the fairy bridge. From there, she looked along the river and saw the blood-red moonlight reflected in the few little puddles of water that remained on its muddy bed. She walked on past the outbuilding where Gloria's skeleton had been found, and the ruins of Bridge Cottage next to it. The ground around had all been dug up and was now taped off for safety. The SOCOs from headquarters had brought their own crime-scene tape. She headed down what was once the High Street.

As she went, Annie tried to visualize the scene from Michael Stanhope's painting: children laughing and splashing in the river shallows; knots of local women gossiping outside a shop; the butcher's boy in his blood-stained apron riding like the wind; the tall young woman arranging newspapers in a rack. *Gwynneth Shackleton.* That was who it was. Why hadn't she realized it before? Somehow, the revelation that Stanhope had also painted Gwen Shackleton into his scene thrilled her.

She looked at the ruins to her right and saw where once was a detached cottage with a little garden, once a row of terrace houses opening directly on to the pavement. This was where the ginnel led off to the tanner's yard; here was the Shackletons' newsagent's shop, here the butcher's, and a little farther down stood the Shoulder of Mutton, where the sign had swayed and creaked in the wind.

So real did it all seem as she walked towards the flax mill that she began to fancy she could even hear long-silent voices whispering secrets. She passed the street that led to the old church and stood at the western end of the village, on that stretch of empty ground where the houses ended and the land rose towards the mill.

As she stood and breathed in the air deeply, she realized how much she wanted to know what had happened here, every bit as much as Banks did. Without her wishing for it, or asking for it, Hobb's End and its history had imposed themselves on her, thrust themselves into her consciousness and become part of her life. It had happened at the same time that Banks had become part of her life, too. She knew that, whatever became of them, the two events would be united in her mind for ever.

When she had challenged him on *his* obsession with it the other night, she hadn't even attempted to explain hers. It wasn't because of the war, but because she identified with Gloria. This was a woman who had struggled and dared to be a little different in a time that didn't tolerate such behaviour. She had lost her parents, then had either abandoned or been cast out by the father of her child, had come to a remote place, taken on a hard job and fallen in love. Then she had lost her husband in the war, or so she must have believed. If Gloria had been still alive when Matthew came back, then she would have had to face a stranger, most likely. Whatever else happened, someone strangled her, stabbed her nearly twenty times and buried her under an outbuilding. And nobody had tried to find out what happened to her.

Suddenly, Annie noticed a movement and saw a figure scuttle across the fairy bridge towards the car parks. Her blood froze. At that moment, she became a little girl frightened of the dark, and she could believe that witches, demons and hobgoblins haunted Hobb's End. She was the whole length of the village away, so what she saw was nothing more than a fleeting silhouette.

Finding her voice, she called out. No answer came. The figure disappeared up the slope into the woods. Annie set off in pursuit. With every stride, the policewoman in her started to overcome the scared, superstitious girl.

Just when she had got back up the slope and was heading for the woods, she heard a car start ahead of her. There were two small car parks, separated by a high hedge, and whoever this was must have been parked in the other one, or Annie would have seen the car earlier.

She put on an extra burst of speed but could only get to the road in time to see the tail-lights disappearing. Even in the moonlight, all she could tell was that the car was dark in colour. She stood there leaning forward, hands resting on her knees, getting her breath back and wondering who the hell could be in such a hurry to escape discovery.

12

'He asked me to marry him,' Gloria repeated.

'I still don't believe you,' I said.

'Well, you can ask him yourself. It's true.'

It was early in the new year, 1945, and I had dropped by
Bridge Cottage one evening to see how Gloria was coping.
She had had a terrible cold over Christmas – had even
missed Alice Poole's farewell party – and the doctor said she
had almost caught pneumonia. Though she was weak and
pale and had lost some weight, she seemed to be on the
mend.

'You should have seen my nose when he asked me. It was
red-raw.'

I laughed. It was good to laugh at something. Christmas
that year had been a miserable affair not only because it was
the coldest one I could remember, but because the advance
that had seemed to be going so well earlier had bogged
down in the Ardennes. It was all right for Alice. Her Eric
had been wounded there and shipped home. But how long
was this bloody war going to drag on? Couldn't everyone
see we had all had enough? Sometimes I felt that I had never
even known life during peacetime.

'What did you say?' I asked.

'I told him I'd think about it, but he'd have to wait until
the war was over, until we could find out for certain about
Matt.'

'Do you love him?'

'In a way. Not . . . Oh, I mean I don't really think I could ever love anyone like I loved Matt, but Brad and I get on well enough, in *and* out of bed. I like his company. And he's good to me. When the war's over, he wants to take me back to Hollywood with him.'

'It'll be a new lease of life, I suppose.'

'Yes.'

'And I'll have someone I can visit out there.'

'You will.'

'But?'

'What do you mean?'

'I still sense a "but". You only told him you'd think about it.'

'Oh, I don't know, Gwen. You know I can't even consider getting married again until the war's over, for a start. But I will think about it. Oh, look what PX brought me when I was ill. Isn't he sweet?'

It was a box of chocolates. A bloody *box* of chocolates! I hadn't even seen a single chocolate in years. Gloria held out the box. 'Please, take one. Take them all, in fact. They'll only make me fat.'

'What about me?' I asked, picking out the caramel.

'You could do with a bit of meat on your bones.'

I threw the screwed-up wrapper at her. 'Cheeky.'

'Well, you could. What about Charlie?'

'Oh, he's still depressed about Glenn Miller disappearing.'

'That's not what I mean, and you know it. Has he asked you yet?'

I'm sure I blushed. 'No,' I said. 'We haven't talked about marriage.'

'Books, that's all you two ever talk about.'

'It's not.'

She smiled. 'I'm teasing, Gwen. I'm glad you're happy. Honest, I am.'

'We still haven't talked about marriage.'

'Well, there's no hurry, I suppose. But you could do a lot worse. A lawyer! He'll be rich, just you wait and see.'

'Money isn't everything.'

'It certainly helps. Anyway, you can go to America, too, and be a rich lawyer's wife. We can see each other all the time. Have lunch together.'

'Gloria, Boston is miles away from Los Angeles.'

'Is it? Well, at least we'll be in the same country.'

And so we chatted on about love and marriage and what the future might offer us. Gloria soon recovered her health, and the round of dances, films and pub nights started all over again. February brought the prospect of victory closer and I actually began to believe that we were entering the last spring of the war.

Everything changed one grey afternoon in March, when a tall, gaunt stranger walked down the High Street towards me, struggling against the wind.

•

Banks really must have had a night on the tiles, Annie thought, pursing her lips and tapping her pen against the side of her thigh. It was after nine, and he wasn't in his office yet. Was he still in Leeds? Had he and his friend picked up some women?

She fought back the acid-burn of jealousy that curdled in her stomach. Jealousy and suspicion had ruined relationships for her before. Just before Rob got killed she had suspected he was seeing someone else and had consequently treated him badly. She thought she had conquered her feelings by now, thought she had learned detachment, but perhaps she had only put her insecurity in mothballs, along with everything else, since she had transferred to North Yorkshire. It was a frightening thought. Until she had met Banks, she had imagined she was in control, doing just fine.

Annie remembered she was supposed to check on the Gwen Shackleton/Vivian Elmsley link. First, she phoned Ruby Kettering, who said – as expected – that it was so long ago she couldn't even remember what Gwen looked or sounded like. Besides, Gwen would have only been fifteen then. Elizabeth Goodall told Annie that she had no idea who Vivian Elmsley was, and Alice Poole said that with her poor eyesight she couldn't be relied upon to tell Queen Elizabeth from Prince Charles.

Next, Annie phoned Millgarth and asked to speak to DI Blackstone. He told her Banks was on his way back to Eastvale. She could have sworn he was suppressing laughter as he said it. They had probably been talking about her; images of Banks telling all the steamy details to his pal after a few pints made her face burn and her throat constrict. All of a sudden, her pleasure in wanting to tell him about her success with USAFE evaporated.

Men, Annie thought. Never anything but bloody big kids when you got right down to it. And that was the most charitable view.

The fax machine hummed into action. Annie hurried over to see if it was the information from Mattie in St Louis. It was: a personnel breakdown of the 448th Bomber Group at Rowan Woods AAF base between 19 December, 1943, and 17 May, 1945, when they had left. There were a lot of names. Too many.

As she glanced over the list, Annie thought again about the Hobb's End incident last night. It had rattled her more than she realized at first, and she had had a difficult time getting to sleep. She didn't know why it should have affected her that way, apart from the misshapen red moon, the eerie atmosphere and the way the ruins had seduced her into believing in ghosts and goblins and things that go bump in the night. But ghosts and goblins don't run away and drive off in cars. Now, in the light of day, what bothered her most of all was *why* someone should hide from her in the first place, and then why take off like a bat out of hell when she gave chase?

There might be a simple explanation, of course. Whoever it was might have been more afraid of her than she was of him: a mischievous kid, perhaps. Given everything else they had discovered since Adam Kelly found the Hobb's End skeleton, however, Annie felt inclined to be more suspicious.

The answer still eluded her. There was nothing left at the site; the SOCOs had been over it thoroughly. Perhaps someone might *think* there was something there, though. Even so, how could anything buried there incriminate anyone living now? From what Annie had seen briefly of the figure last night, whoever it was hadn't been old enough to have murdered Gloria Shackleton over fifty years ago. People in their seventies or eighties don't usually move that fast.

So it remained a mystery. She wanted to talk to Banks about it, but he'd been off behaving like a silly kid getting pissed with his mates and telling tales about her sexual appetite and his ability to satisfy it. She hoped he had a hangover the size of China.

•

Debussy's chamber music for harp and wind instruments got Banks back to Gratly safe and sane via the slow back roads. He thought of stopping in at Harkside on his way to see how Annie was doing, but decided against it. He didn't want her to see him until he had at least managed a change of clothes. The ones he was wearing still stank of smoke and stale beer.

His head ached, despite the Paracetamol he had downed at Ken's flat that morning, and his mouth tasted like the bottom of a birdcage. When he had awoken and looked around Ken's living room, he had groaned at the detritus of a wild and foolish night. an empty bottle of Glenmorangie on the coffee table, alongside an empty bottle of claret and an overflowing ashtray. He didn't think the whisky bottle had been full when they got into it, but even a fifteen-year-old would have had more sense than to mix beer, wine and whisky that way.

Still, he had enjoyed what he remembered of their rambling talk about women, marriage, divorce, sex and loneliness. And there was wonderful music. Ken was an aficionado of female jazz singers – a vinyl-freak, too – and the LP sleeves scattered over the floor attested to this: Ella Fitzgerald, June Christy, Dinah Washington, Helen Forrest, Anita O'Day, Keely Smith, Peggy Lee.

The last thing Banks remembered was drifting off to late-period Billie Holiday singing 'Ill Wind', her smoked-honey voice beautifully mingling with Ben Webster's tenor sax. Then came oblivion.

He groaned and rubbed his stubbly face. All the hangover clichés ran through his mind, one after another: *You're getting too old for this sort of thing*; *Time you grew up*; and *I'll never touch another drop as long as I live*. It was a familiar litany of guilt and self-disgust. Last night would have to remain a one-off, a brief lapse, a necessary sacrifice to friendship.

As Banks emptied his pockets before dropping his jeans in the laundry basket – noticing how full it was getting – he found a slip of paper. On it was the name 'Maria' followed by a Leeds telephone number.

He racked his brains but he couldn't remember which one of the two girls they'd talked to in the Adelphi was Maria. Was it the petite blonde or the slender redhead with the freckles and the wide gap between her front teeth? He thought the blonde had been more interested in Ken, and he vaguely remembered them talking about the Pre-Raphaelites. If Maria was the redhead, she had a sort of Pre-Raphaelite look about her. Maybe that was how the subject had come up. No good. He couldn't remember. It had been that kind of night. He screwed up the slip of paper, aimed it at the waste-bin, then stopped, straightened it out and put it in the top drawer of his bedside table. You never know.

After a shave, a shower and a change of clothes, Banks drove to Eastvale and arrived at his office just after ten o'clock. He hardly had time to turn on his computer when his door opened and in strode Chief Constable Jeremiah 'Jimmy' Riddle himself, making one of his rare forays to Eastvale. Banks muttered a silent curse. Just what he needed, in his fragile state.

Banks looked up. 'Sir?'

'Banks, you look bloody awful,' said Riddle. 'What have you been doing, man? Drinking yourself silly?'

'Touch of flu, sir.'

'Flu, my arse. Anyway, that's your problem, you want to go on poisoning your liver.'

'What can I do for you, sir?'

'It's that skeleton case I gave you. Been all over the news lately. Attracting a lot of publicity. I hope you're on top of things?'

'Definitely, sir.'

'Good. I want you to bring me up-to-date. I've got to go to London today to tape an interview for "Panorama". They're putting together a special segment on the investigation of old cases, how DNA makes a difference, that sort of thing.' He brushed some imaginary fluff from the front of his uniform and glanced at his watch. 'I need an angle. And you'd better make it quick. My train leaves in an hour and a half.'

Well, be thankful for small mercies, Banks told himself. 'Where do you want me to begin, sir?' he asked.

'At the bloody beginning, man; where do you think?'

Banks told him what he and Annie had discovered so far from the SOCOs, from talking to Elizabeth Goodall and Alice Poole and from the visit to Leeds. When he had finished, Riddle ran his hand over his shiny bald scalp and said, 'It's not much to go on, is it? Memory of a couple of old biddies?'

'We're not likely to get much better,' said Banks. 'Not at this point. Too much time's gone by. I suppose you could make a point about how unreliable people's memories become over the years.'

Riddle nodded and made a note.

'Anyway, there's a lot we're still waiting on. We've got a report on Dr Williams's physical examination of the bones, but we're still waiting for the results of further tests both from him and our forensic odontologist. These things take time.'

'And cost money. It'd better be worth it, Banks. Don't think I'm not keeping my eye on the bottom line on this one.'

'We also found a button, possibly military, close to the body. She may have been holding it when she was killed. There's still a lot we don't know yet.'

Riddle rubbed his chin. 'Still,' he said, 'there's a good angle in what you've already told me. Nude paintings. Village scandals. Women playing around with Yanks. Yes. That's good stuff. That'll play. And give me a copy of the forensic anthropologist's report to read on my way. I want to sound as if I know what I'm talking about.'

You've been trying to do that for years without much success, Banks wanted to say, but he held his tongue and phoned the input clerk for a photocopy. Riddle could pick it up on his way out, seeing as he was in such a hurry. 'You mentioned DNA, sir,' he said. 'You might mention that we think her son is still alive and it would be a great help if he could get in touch with us. That way we could verify the identity of the remains once and for all.'

Riddle stood up. 'If I've got time, Banks. If I've got time.' He paused with his hand on the doorknob and half-turned. 'By the way,' he said. 'DS Cabbot. How's she working out?'

She. So he did know. 'Fine,' said Banks. 'She's a good detective. Wasted in a place like Harkside.'

A malicious smile flitted across Riddle's face. 'Ah, yes. Pity, really. I understand there was some trouble in her previous posting. Nice-looking girl, though, by all accounts?'

'Trouble, sir?'

'You should know all about that, Banks. Insubordination, failure to respect senior ranks.'

'I respect the rank, sir,' said Banks. 'But not always the person who fills it.'

Riddle stiffened. 'Well, I hope you're enjoying yourself

– for your sake, Banks – because this is about as good as it's going to get for you around here.'

With that he walked out and slammed the door.

Banks thought about what he had just heard. So Jimmy Riddle knew who Annie Cabbot was and had assigned him to work with her anyway. Why? Riddle already thought Banks was a rampant cocksman, making trysts with exotic Asians in Leeds during police time and basically shagging everything in a skirt. Riddle had also mentioned some trouble. What could all that be about?

Most of all, though, why would Riddle think that working with Annie Cabbot would be hell on earth for Banks? Because, if one thing was certain, hell on earth was all Riddle had in store for him.

On his way to the coffee machine, Banks bumped into DS Hatchley and asked him to find out what he could about Francis Henderson, Gloria's illegitimate child. It was probably a pointless exercise, but it was a loose end that nagged him.

Banks was still getting the hang of the station's new voicemail system, and was more often than not likely to forget about it or delete everything waiting for him, but that morning he got Annie's message loud and clear. The ice in her tone was enough to freeze his eardrum. There was also a message from a Major Gargrave, in military personnel. Banks phoned him first, building up the courage to call Annie later.

'It's about that query you made the other day,' said Major Gargrave. 'Matthew Shackleton.'

'Yes?'

'Well, it's all a bit embarrassing really.'

'He came back, didn't he? We found a death certificate dated 1950. I was going to ask you about it.'

'Yes, well, these things happen sometimes, you know. When my assistant was returning the file, he found some papers wedged down between two folders. It was because of the irregularity of it all, you see.'

'And a filing error.'

'Yes.'

'When did he return?' Banks asked.

'It was his sister who reported his return, actually. March 1945. Place called Hobb's End. Does that make any sense?'

'Yes,' said Banks. 'Go on.'

'I'm afraid there's not much more to tell, really. Sergeant Shackleton simply discharged himself from a London hospital and went home. The hospital said he'd been liberated from a Japanese POW camp in the Philippines and shipped home in pretty bad shape. No identification.'

'And that's all?'

'Yes. It would seem so. Very odd.'

'Okay,' said Banks, 'thanks very much for calling, Major.'

'No problem.'

After he hung up, Banks opened the window and let the sunshine in. He thought of lighting a cigarette but realized he didn't really feel like one. Too many last night. His throat and lungs still felt raw. There was something that didn't make sense in what the major had just told him; it was on the tip of his consciousness, but he couldn't quite force it out. Too many dead brain cells in the way.

Back at his desk, Banks steeled himself and picked up the phone. He was as ready as he would ever be for Annie now. She answered on the third ring.

'You're back, then,' was all she said.

'Yes.'

'Have a good time?'

'Pretty good, thanks.'

'Good. I'm glad.'

'I'd rather forget this morning, though.'

'You probably deserved it.'

'Probably.'

'I've got the info on the Rowan Woods personnel.'

'Wonderful.'

'It's a long list, though. It'll take a bit of whittling down. There was more than one person working in the PX, for a start.'

Banks sensed that her tone was softening a little. Should he tell her he had missed her last night? Or ask her what was wrong? Better hold off awhile. He ventured a tentative, 'Is there anything else?'

Annie told him about what happened at Hobb's End.

'What were you doing out there?' he asked.

'What does it matter? Maybe I just wanted to see what it looks like in the dark.'

'And?'

'It looks spooky.'

'It was probably just a kid.'

'I thought about that. It didn't look like a kid. And it drove away.'

'I've known ten-year-olds do that. Still, I take your point. There's not much we can do about it now, though, is there?'

'I just thought I'd let you know. For the record. It was interesting, that's all.'

'Sounds like it. Anything else?'

Annie told him about drawing a blank on trying to confirm Vivian Elmsley's identity through Ruby, Betty and Alice.

'We'd better track her down, anyway,' Banks said.

'I've already done that.'

'Now I'm *really* impressed.'

'So you should be. While you've been recovering from your self-inflicted damage, I've been on the phone.' Was there a hint of forgiveness there, perhaps? Depended how he played it: he needed to strike the right balance of remorse and praise, guilt and compliments.

'And?'

'Well, in her case it was easy. She's in the London telephone directory.'

'You didn't phone her, did you?'

'*Please*. Give me some credit. I'm not that gormless. But I've got her address. What do you want to do about it?'

'We should talk to her as soon as possible. If she really is the one we're looking for, she's holding something back. She might also know the names we want. There was another thing nagging at me a few minutes ago and I've just realized what it was.'

'Apart from the hangover?'

'Yes.'

'All right. What was it?'

Banks explained to her about the call from Major Gargrave. 'It's to do with the gun,' he said.

'What gun?'

'The one Matthew Shackleton's supposed to have shot himself with.'

'What about it? Handguns must have been common enough just after the war. You'd just had hundreds of thousands of *men* running around armed to the teeth killing one another, remember?'

'Yes, but why would Matthew have a gun?'

'I don't – wait a minute, I think I *do* see what you mean.'

'If he was a released POW, he'd hardly have his service revolver. I should imagine the Japanese confiscated the weapons off the people they captured, wouldn't you?'

'Unless his liberators gave him one?'

'I suppose that's remotely possible. Especially if they were Americans. Americans feel naked without guns.'

'But you don't think so?'

'I think it's highly unlikely,' said Banks. 'Why should they? And why would he still have it when he went back to Hobb's End from hospital? Anyway, it's a minor point, probably doesn't mean a thing.'

'If he did have a gun, though, why didn't he use that on Gloria instead of strangling her and stabbing her?'

'*If* it was Matthew who killed her.'

'Have you considered Gwen as a serious suspect?' Annie asked.

'Certainly. According to everything we've heard, she was very close to her brother. If Gloria was hurting him, running around with other men, Gwen might just have fought back on his behalf. At the very least she should be able to tell us more about Matthew's relationship with Gloria after he came back, assuming Gloria was still alive at the time. Fancy a trip to London tomorrow?'

'Who's driving?'

'We'll take the train. It's faster, and the London traffic's murder. If my memory serves me well, there's a train leaves York around a quarter to nine that'll have us at King's Cross by twenty to eleven. Can you manage that?'

'No problem. In the meantime I'll see if I can get any more information on the airmen.'

After Annie hung up, Banks walked over to the window

and looked out over the square, with its ancient market cross and square-towered church, grey-gold in the sunlight. He thought about Vivian Elmsley. Could she really be Gwen Shackleton? It seemed a preposterous idea, but stranger things had happened. He decided it wouldn't be a bad idea to have a go at one or two of Vivian Elmsley's books before he set off to interview her. Her writing might give him some insight into her character.

He tried dialling Brian's Wimbledon number again. Still nothing. Ken Blackstone was right, though; all he could do for the moment was keep on trying. If he was going to London tomorrow, he hoped he might be able to see Brian, have a talk, get things sorted. He didn't want Brian to keep on thinking his father was disappointed in him for what he was doing, the way Banks's own father always made clear his dismay at Banks's choice of career, even now, every time they met.

Banks went back to his desk. For about the third time since the case began, he spread out the objects found with Gloria Shackleton's body before him. Not much for the remnants of a life, or the detritus of a death: a locket whose original heart shape had been squashed and bent; a corroded wedding ring; clips from a brassière or suspenders; a pair of tiny, deformed leather shoes, which reminded him of the ones he had seen at the Brontë parsonage once; a few scraps of blackout cloth; and the button from Adam Kelly, greenish-blue with verdigris. Superintendent Gristhorpe might be able to tell him a bit about the button, he thought. Gristhorpe was a bit of an expert on military history, especially the Second World War.

Banks grabbed his jacket and was just about to leave the office when his phone rang.

'Hello, Alan.'

A woman's voice.

'Yes?'

'It's me. Jenny. Jenny Fuller. Don't you recognize my voice?'

'Jenny. It's been a long time. Where are you?'

'Home. Just got back yesterday. Look—'

'A bit early, aren't you?'

'It's a long story.'

'I'm glad you called. I need some advice.'

'If it's personal, I'm the last person to ask, believe me.'

'Professional?'

'I might be able to manage that. The reason I was phoning is, I know I shouldn't bother you at work and all, but I'm in town and I wondered if you've got time for lunch?'

Banks had intended to drive out to Lyndgarth to see Gristhorpe, who was taking his annual holidays at home, but that could wait until after. 'Queen's Arms, half-twelve?'

'Wonderful. I'll see you there.'

Banks smiled as he put down the receiver. He hadn't seen Jenny Fuller in almost a year, not since she'd decided to take a leave of absence from the University of York to teach in California. That was around the time he and Sandra had split up. He had received a couple of postcards asking how he was doing, but that was all.

Jenny was one of the two women his colleagues expected him to sleep with after Sandra left. Perhaps he would have slept with her if she had been around. But timing is everything. Jenny was spending most of her time in California these days, and there was a man at the bottom of that. The other friend, Pamela Jeffries, feeling restless and hemmed in, had taken off to play in an orchestra in Australia, of all places, and he hadn't seen her for months. Again, he got the occasional postcard from such exotic locales as Sydney, Melbourne, Adelaide and Perth. It made him want to travel more, too.

Now he and Jenny were having lunch in about an hour's time. Just enough time, in fact, to prepare his questions on Matthew Shackleton and nip over to Waterstone's for a couple of Vivian Elmsley's novels.

•

For some reason I was standing out in the street to check the window display (which was pretty meagre) when I glanced to my left and saw him coming across the fairy bridge. I had just heard the train arrive, so I assumed that he had come from the station. The wind howled around the chimneys, and clouds as black as a Nazi's heart besmirched the sky like grease stains. There was nobody else about. That was why I noticed him. That, and the fact that he was wearing only an over-large, baggy brown suit and carrying no luggage.

He was tall but stooped, as if suffering some affliction of the spine, and he walked with a sturdy stick. He moved slowly, almost like a figure in a dream, as if he knew where he was going, but felt no hurry to get there. His frame was thin to the point of emaciation. As he came closer, I realized that he wasn't as old as I had first thought, though his lank, lifeless hair was tinged here and there with grey, or white.

The wind tugged at my hair and clothes and chilled me to the marrow, but something about him compelled me to stand and watch, as if in a trance. When he got within a few feet of the shop, I saw his eyes. Deep, hollow, haunted eyes, turned completely inward, as if he was subjecting himself to a most intense and unflinching scrutiny.

He saw me, though, and he stopped.

I don't know when the truth dawned on me; it could have been seconds; it could have been minutes. But I started to shake like a leaf and it had nothing to do with the cold. I ran to him and threw my arms around him but his body felt stiff and unyielding as a tree. I caressed his cheek with my palm, noticing the puckered white scar that curved up from the side of his mouth in an ugly parody of a grin. Tears were pouring down my cheeks.

'Matthew!' I cried. 'Oh my God. Matthew!' And I took his arm and led him inside to Mother.

•

Banks walked into the Queen's Arms a couple of minutes before twelve-thirty carrying two of Vivian Elmsley's paperback mysteries in his Waterstone's bag. He bought a pint and sat down at a table near the empty fireplace. Jenny was always late, he remembered, opening the bag and looking at the books.

One was a suspense novel called *Guilty Secrets* – certainly an interesting title from Banks's point of view – which bore review quotes from the *Sunday Times*, *Scotland on Sunday*, the *Yorkshire Post* and the *Manchester Evening News*, all to the general effect that it was an 'amazing' and 'disturbing' achievement by one our best mystery writers, a true equal of P. D. James and Ruth Rendell.

The other was called *The Shadow of Death* and featured her regular series character, Detective Inspector Niven. In this one, he was called on to investigate the murder of an up-market Shepherd's Bush restaurateur. Banks didn't even know that such a creature existed. As far as he could remember, there weren't any up-market restaurants in

Shepherd's Bush. Still, it was a long time since he'd been there, so he gave her the benefit of the doubt. Anyway, the novel was praised for its 'compassionate realism in the portrayal of ordinary people' and its 'believable depictions of policemen's lives and police procedures'. Banks smiled. He'd see about that. On the cover was a picture of the handsome, craggy-faced young actor who, so the blurb informed Banks, played DI Niven in the television series. And got paid far more than a real copper did.

He was on page ten when Jenny dashed in, out of breath, tousled red hair flaming around her face as she looked this way and that. When she saw him she waved, patted her chest and hurried over. She bent and gave him a quick peck on the cheek. 'Sorry I'm late. My God, you look awful.'

Banks smiled and raised his glass. 'Hair of the dog.'

Jenny picked up the paperback he had set down on the table and turned up her nose. 'I didn't think this sort of thing was up your alley.'

'Work.'

'Aha.' She raised her eyebrows. The California tan looked good on her, Banks thought. The sun hadn't burned her, the way it did with most redheads, only darkened the natural creams and reds of her complexion and brought out her freckles, especially across her nose. Her figure looked as good as ever in tight black jeans and a loose jade silk top.

'So,' Banks said, when Jenny had settled herself down and deposited her oversized shoulder bag on the floor beside her. 'Can I get you a drink?'

'Campari and soda, please.'

'Food?'

'Scampi and chips. I've been craving scampi and chips for about a month now.'

'Scampi and chips it is.' Banks made his way to the bar, got them each a drink and ordered the food. There were a few more exotic dishes finding their way on to the menu these days, like fajitas and Thai noodles, but Banks finally settled for plaice and chips. It wasn't that he had anything against exotic food, but from experience he didn't trust the pub version of it. Besides, he could still taste the curry he had eaten in Leeds last night.

He carried the drinks back and found Jenny poring over *The Shadow of Death*, one hand holding her hair back from her eyes. When he approached she flashed him a quick smile and closed the book. 'I think I saw this on TV over there,' she said, touching the cover. 'On PBS. They interviewed her afterwards. Vivian Elmsley. She's very popular in the States, you know. Quite a striking woman.'

Banks told her briefly about the case so far, including the possibility of Vivian Elmsley's having a role in the affair. By the time he had finished, their food arrived.

'Is it as good as you remembered?' he asked after she had taken a couple of bites.

'Nothing ever is,' Jenny said. He noticed a new sadness and weariness in her eyes. 'It's good, though.'

'What happened over there?'

'What do you mean?' She glanced at him, then looked away quickly. Too quickly. He saw fear in her eyes.

He thought of the very first time he had met her in Gristhorpe's office, shortly after he had first arrived in Eastvale, how he had been struck by her sharp intelligence and her quick sense of humour, as well as her natural beauty, the flaming red hair, full lips and green eyes with their attractive laugh lines.

Jenny Fuller had been thirty-one then; she was nearly thirty-eight now. The lines had etched themselves a little

PETER ROBINSON

deeper, and they weren't so easy to associate with laughter any more. His first impression had been that she was a knockout. He felt exactly the same today. They had come close to an affair, but Banks had backed off, unwilling to commit himself to infidelity. He had been different then, more confident, more certain of what his life was all about and where it was going. Life had been simpler for him then, or perhaps he had approached it on more absolute terms. It had *seemed* simple, at least: he loved Sandra and believed she loved him; therefore, he didn't want to do anything to jeopardize that, no matter how tempting. They had just moved up from London, where Banks felt he was quickly burning out, to a less hectic region, partly to save their marriage. And it had worked, up to a point. Seven years.

Against all odds, Banks and Jenny had remained friends. Jenny had become friends with Sandra, too, though Banks got the impression they had drifted apart over the past two or three years.

'Come on, Jenny,' he said. 'This sudden return wasn't on the agenda. I thought you'd become a California beach bunny for good.'

'*Beach bunny?*' Jenny laughed. 'I guess I just didn't quite make the grade, did I?'

'What do you mean?'

She sighed, looked away, tried to form some words, sighed again, then laughed. There were tears in her eyes. She seemed a lot more twitchy than he remembered, always moving her hands. 'It's all washed up, Alan. That's what I've been meaning to say.'

'What's all washed up?'

'All of it. The job. Randy. My life.' She cocked her head. 'I never did have much luck with men, did I? I should have listened to you years ago.'

338

There was no arguing with that. Banks remembered one or two of Jenny's disasters that he had been around to mop up after.

Jenny pushed her plate aside, scampi and chips unfinished, and took a long swig of Campari and soda. Her glass was almost empty; Banks still had the best part of his pint left. He didn't want any more. 'Another?' he asked.

'Am I becoming an alcoholic, too? No, don't answer that. I'll get it myself.' Before he could stop her, she stood up and headed for the ladies' loo.

Banks finished his plaice and chips and looked at the back cover of *The Shadow of Death* on the table beside him. 'A masterpiece.' 'Top-rate work.' 'A must read.' The critics obviously loved Vivian Elmsley. Or were the brief quotes cunningly edited from less flattering sentences? 'Whereas Dostoevsky wrote *a masterpiece*, Vivian Elmsley can be said to have written only a pot-boiler of the lowest kind.' Or 'Had this book shown even the slightest sign of literary talent or creative imagination, I would not have hesitated to declare it a *must read* and a piece of *top-rate work*, but as it possesses neither of these qualities, I have to say it's a dud.'

When Jenny came back, she had repaired what little damage the tears had caused to her makeup. She had also picked up another Campari and soda.

'You know,' she said, 'I've been imagining sitting here and talking this over with you like this all the way over on the plane. Picturing how it would be, just you and me here in the Queen's Arms, like old times. I don't know why I found it so difficult. I think I might still be jet-lagged.'

'Take it easy,' said Banks. 'Just tell me what you want to, at your own pace.'

She smiled and patted his arm. 'Thanks. You're sweet.' She snatched a cigarette from his packet and lit up.

'You don't smoke,' Banks said.

'I do now.' Jenny blew out a long plume. 'I've just about had it up to here with those nico-Nazis out there. You can't smoke anywhere. And to think California was a real hotbed of protest and innovation in the sixties. It's like a fucking kindergarten run by fascists now.'

He hadn't heard Jenny swear before. Something else new. Smoking, drinking, swearing. He noticed that she wasn't inhaling, and she stubbed the cigarette out halfway through. 'As I'm sure you've gathered already,' she went on, 'Randy, my main man, my paramour, my significant other, my reason for staying out there as long as I did, is no longer a part of my life. The little shit.'

'What happened?'

'Graduate students. Or, to put it more bluntly, blonde twenty-something bimbos with their brains between their legs.'

'I'm sorry, Jenny.'

She waved her hand. 'I should have seen it coming. Anyone else would have. Anyway, soon as I found out about what he was up to, there wasn't much to keep me there. After I confronted him with the evidence, my dear Randy made damn sure I wasn't going to be offered another year's visiting lectureship.'

'What are you going to do?'

'Well, thank God they're not all like that. I'll be going back to my old lecturing job at York. Start next month. If that doesn't work out, I'll hang up my sign next door to the cop shop and go into private practice. I'm quite the expert on deviants and criminal psychology, should you happen to have such a creature as a serial killer lurking in the general vicinity. I've even been on training courses with the FBI profilers.'

IN A DRY SEASON

'I've heard that's all a load of bollocks,' said Banks. 'But I'm impressed. Sorry we don't have anything at the moment.'

'I know – don't call us . . . Story of my life.'

'I don't think you'll have any problem staying in work, Jenny, but if there's ever anything I can do . . .'

'Thanks. You're a pal.' She patted his hand.

'I do want to ask your advice on something.'

'Go ahead. I'm finished blubbering and moaning. And I didn't even ask about you. I haven't seen you since Sandra left. How are *you* doing?'

'I'm doing fine, thanks.'

'Seeing anyone?'

Banks paused a moment. 'Sort of.'

'Serious?'

'What kind of a question is that?'

'So it *is* serious. How about Sandra?'

'Do you mean is *she* seeing anyone? Yes, she is.'

'Oh.'

'It's okay. I'm fine, Jenny.'

'If you say so. What was it you wanted to ask me?'

'It's about Matthew Shackleton. Gwen's – possibly Vivian Elmsley's – brother. Apparently he was captured by the Japanese and spent a few years in one of their prison camps. By all accounts, he was pretty disturbed when he came home. Ended up committing suicide five years after the war. Thing is, all I can come up with in terms of psychiatric diagnoses are such vague terms as "shell shock".'

'I thought that went out with the First World War?'

'Apparently not, they just changed the name to "battle fatigue" or "combat fatigue". I was wondering what sort of diagnosis you'd come up with today.'

'That's a good one, Alan.' Jenny pointed her thumb at her chest. 'You want me, a *psychologist,* to come up with a *psychiatric* diagnosis of a dead man's mental problems? I like that, I really do. That takes the biscuit.'

Banks grinned. 'Oh, don't be such a nitpicker, Jenny.'

'This had better be between you and me.'

'Cross my heart.'

Jenny toyed with her beer mat, ripping off little pieces of damp cardboard. 'Well,' she said, 'I'm only guessing, you understand, but if your man had indeed been a prisoner of war under such terrible conditions, then he was probably suffering from some kind of post-traumatic stress disorder.'

Banks took his notebook from his inside pocket and jotted a few words down.

'Don't you dare quote me on this,' Jenny warned him. 'I told you, it's strictly between you and me.'

'Don't worry, you won't be called upon to testify in court. I realize this is pure speculation. Anyway, it all happened a long time ago. This condition would have been caused by his experiences in the war and the camp, right?'

'Right. Basically, PTSDs are caused by some event or series of events well beyond the normal range of human experience. Maybe we should redefine exactly what that means these days, given the state of the so-called normal world, but it generally refers to extreme experiences. Things that go way beyond marital breakdowns, broken love affairs, simple bereavement, chronic illness or bankruptcy. The things most of us suffer from on a daily basis.'

'That bad?'

Jenny nodded. 'Things like rape, assault, kidnapping, military combat, floods, earthquakes, fires, car crashes, bombing, torture, death camps. The list of divine and human atrocities goes on and on, but I'm sure you get the picture.'

'I get the picture. What are the symptoms?'

'Many and varied. Recurrent nightmares about the event are common. As is feeling that the event is recurring – things like flashbacks and hallucinations. Anything that reminds the person of the event is painful, too, such as an anniversary. Also things that were part of it. If a man was kept in a small cage for a long period, for example, then he would be likely to experience suffocating claustrophobia whenever those conditions were approximated. Maybe in a lift, for example.'

'What about amnesia?'

'Yes, there's psychological memory loss sometimes. Believe me, most of the people who suffer from this would find the memory loss preferable to the persistent nightmares. But the problem is that strong feelings of detachment, estrangement and separation come with it. You can't even enjoy your lack of recollection of the horror. People who suffer from PTSDs often find it difficult to feel or accept love, they become alienated from society, from their families and loved ones, and they have an extremely diminished sense of the future. Add to that insomnia, difficulty in concentrating, hypervigilance, depressive or panic disorders.'

'Sounds like me.'

'Much worse. Suicide is also not uncommon. He's a suspect, I assume?'

'Yes. That was another thing I wanted to ask you. Might he be likely to become violent?'

'That's a difficult one to answer. Anyone can become violent given the right stimulus. He would certainly be prone to irritability and outbursts of anger, but I'm not sure they'd necessarily lead him to murder.'

'I was thinking he might have killed his wife because he found out she'd been having an affair.'

'I suppose it's possible he got a bee in his bonnet about it,' Jenny said.

'But you don't think so?'

'I didn't say that. Let me just say I hold reservations. Don't forget the constraints you've got me working under.'

'I won't. Tell me about your reservations.'

'The outbursts of anger in PTSD are usually fairly irrational. By linking them to his wife's behaviour, you're making it all far more logical, do you see? Cause and effect.'

'Yes.'

'And the other thing is that if he did feel detached and was unable to love, then where does the hate come in? Or the jealousy?'

'So could he or couldn't he?'

'Oh, no, you're not trapping me like that. Of course he *could* have committed murder. People do all the time, often for no reason whatsoever. Yes, he could have heard about his wife having it off with some other bloke and as a result he could have, quite reasonably, come to hate her and to want rid of her. Or he could have just done it in an outburst of irrational rage, for no apparent reason.'

'Whoever did it probably strangled the woman, at least until she was unconscious, then stabbed her about fifteen or sixteen times.'

'Such rage. I don't know, Alan. From what you've told me about this man, and from what I know of PTSD, I'd say that most of his pain and anger would have been directed inward, not out at the world. While I wouldn't rule it out, I'd maybe hedge on the side of saying it's unlikely he would have killed that way for that reason. But it's hard to say anything about someone you've never met, never had the chance to talk to. Also, it's often too easy to pick on the mentally disturbed person as the most likely murderer. Most mentally ill people wouldn't harm a fly. I'm not saying all of them – there are some really sick puppies out there who manage to keep it well hidden – but most of the obvious ones are harmless. Sad and pathetic, perhaps, sometimes even a little scary, but rarely dangerous.'

'Thanks. You've given me a lot to think about.'

'Well, I'm just glad I can still be of some use to somebody.'

They both sat in silence, nursing what was left of their drinks. Banks thought about Matthew Shackleton's suffering and about what Jenny had said about his possible alienation, his estrangement from the world of normal human affairs. Maybe that could have made a killer out of him and maybe not. If you couldn't feel love for someone, why would you feel hate? When Banks first found out about Sandra and Sean, he had hated them both because he still loved Sandra. If he hadn't cared, he wouldn't have felt so passionate. Now, the feelings were receding into the distance. He wasn't sure if he loved Sandra any more. At least he was trying to make a life without her, reinventing and discovering himself. If she came and asked him to take her back tomorrow, he honestly didn't know what he would do.

'I fell apart, you know,' Jenny said suddenly, startling him out of his train of thought.

'You did what?'

She played with her hair. A number of expressions

battled for pride of place on her face. A sort of crooked grin won out. 'I had a breakdown. After all that with Randy. I suddenly found myself alone out there, completely cut off from everything and everyone I'd grown up with, alone in a foreign country. It's one of the scariest feelings I've ever had. I mean, they speak sort of the same language and all, but that only makes things worse, like a parody of all you've known. I'm not making myself clear . . . I felt like I was on another planet, a hostile one, and I couldn't get home. I fell to pieces.' She laughed. 'Do you know the song?'

'I've heard it,' said Banks, who tried to avoid country and western music the way he did a dose of clap.

'Well, I've done it.' She shook her head slowly. 'I even went to see a shrink.'

'Do any good?'

'Some. One of the things I realized was that I wanted to go home. I mean, that wasn't part of being ill. The desire was real and perfectly reasonable. It wasn't just Randy or not having the contract renewed, I could have got a teaching job somewhere else if I'd wanted. But I *missed* this place too much. Can you believe it? I actually missed overcooked scampi and chips. And, bloody hell, wouldn't you know it if I didn't miss winter too. It gets you down, all that sun, day in, day out, only the occasional flood, fire or earthquake for variety. Pretty soon you begin to feel like you're living in some kind of suspended animation, like everything's on hold. Or maybe you're not really living at all, you're in limbo. You keep telling yourself one day the snow's going to come, but it never does. Anyway, as soon as I realized what I really wanted to do, I gave myself the best therapy I could think of. I chucked my tranquillizers down the toilet and took the next flight home. Well,

almost the next flight. I had a few things to do first –
including, I'm almost ashamed to admit, a little act of
girlish revenge on poor, dear Randy.'

'What did you do?'

Jenny paused for a moment, then licked her lips and
flashed him a wicked grin. 'I planted one of those little
voice-activated tape recorders in his office and taped one
of his trysts. Then I retrieved the machine and sent the
tape to the dean.'

'In his *office*?'

'Yes. Over the desk. Don't be such a prude, Alan. It
happens all the time over there. What are offices for? Oh,
you should have heard them: "Give it to me, big boy. Fuck
me. Go on. Oh, yeah. Stick that big hard cock in me. Go
deep. Fuck me harder."'

Her voice had risen, and one or two tourist families
looked at her uncomfortably. 'Oops, sorry,' she said,
putting her hand over her mouth. 'Wash your mouth out,
Jenny Fuller. Anyway, there was no mistaking whose
voices they were.'

'What happened?'

'I don't know. I left before the shit hit the fan. So if I get
murdered, you know where to start looking. I should
imagine he got suspended. Maybe fired. Of course, it was
hardly evidence you could use at a tribunal, but they can
get quite stroppy about things like that over there. Fucking
your students is almost as bad as being caught smoking in
a restaurant.' She tossed back the rest of her drink and
looked at her watch. 'Look, I'm sorry, I'll have to go. The
university's been very good to me so far, but they won't
continue to be unless I get my courses prepared. It's great
seeing you again.'

She picked up her bag, paused and rested it on her lap.

Then she looked Banks in the eye, reached out and touched his hand softly and said, 'Why don't you give me a ring? We could . . . you know, have dinner or something together, if that's okay?'

Banks swallowed. 'I will. That would be great. And you've got to come out and see the cottage.'

'I'd love to.' She patted his hand, blew him a kiss and then she was gone in a whirl of red, jade and black, leaving a faint trace of Miss Dior behind in the smoky air. Banks looked down at his hand. It still tingled where she had touched him. Now that he had found the courage and desire to start a relationship with Annie, Jenny was a complication he didn't need. But she was a friend; he couldn't turn his back. And there was no reason at all why Annie should object to his having dinner with her. Even so, he felt more confused than he had half an hour earlier as he picked up his books and left the pub.

13

It took some time, but after I had run and fetched Gloria from the farm, I was finally able to piece together what had happened. Matthew himself wouldn't say a word. He looked at us as if he remembered knowing us once, as if some sort of deep homing instinct had brought him here, but our fussing didn't make much sense to him.

Gloria and Mother comforted him while I went down to the telephone and began the long round of calls. The Ministry was about as much help as usual, the Red Cross a little more forthcoming, but it was ultimately a doctor in one of the big London hospitals (for it was clear Matthew was ill and had probably discharged himself from hospital) who told me the most.

At first, he didn't know whom I was talking about, because they didn't know the name of the man who had walked out of the hospital yesterday. When I described Matthew, however, he was certain we were talking about the same person.

Matthew had been found, along with several other British and Indian soldiers, at a Japanese POW camp near Luzon, in the Philippines. All his identification was missing, and all anyone could tell about him, from the scraps of his uniform that remained, was that he was British. He hadn't spoken to any of the other prisoners and none of them had been captured in the same place or at the same time as he had. Consequently, nobody knew where he had come from or who he was.

When I asked the doctor why Matthew wouldn't speak and why he also refused, when offered pen and paper, to write anything down, he paused, then said, 'He's probably suffering from some form of combat fatigue. That's why he won't communicate. There may be other problems, but I'm afraid I can't be any more specific than that.'

'Is that why he refuses to talk?'

He paused again, longer this time, then went on slowly, 'I'm sorry to say, but when we gave him a thorough physical examination, one of the things we found was that his tongue had been cut out.'

I could think of nothing to say. I stood there, head spinning, clinging to the telephone as if it were all that was holding me to the earth.

'Miss Shackleton? Miss Shackleton? Are you there?'

'Yes . . . I'm sorry . . . Please go on.'

'I'm the one who should be sorry. It must have sounded so abrupt and callous to you. I didn't know how else to tell you. If you only knew . . . some of the lads we've got in here. Well . . . I apologize.'

'That's all right, Doctor. So Matthew is physically incapable of talking?'

'Yes.'

'But he could write if he wanted?'

'There's no reason why not. There's some damage to the fingers of his left hand, as if they have been broken and badly reset, but his right hand is fine, and as far as I can tell, he seems to be right-handed. Am I correct?'

'Yes, Matthew's right-handed.'

'All I can assume then is that he simply chooses not to communicate.'

'What should we do?'

'What do you mean?'

'Well, he ran away, didn't he? Should we send him back?'

'I can't see much point in doing that,' said the doctor. 'And, quite frankly, we need all the beds we can get. No, physically, there's nothing more we can do for him. There's some deformity of the spine, probably due to being forced into a cramped environment, like a box or a cage, for long periods of time. A pronounced limp in the left leg, caused by an improperly set fracture. He was also shot in the arm and the abdomen. The wounds are healed now, though by the looks of the scars the surgery was of a poor quality.'

I swallowed, trying not to think of all the suffering poor Matthew must have gone through. 'And mentally?'

'As I said, we don't really know what's wrong. He refuses to communicate. It's a good sign that he came home, though. He knew his way and he negotiated the journey with what little money he took.'

'Took?'

'Ah, yes. Please don't worry about it. We hadn't supplied him with any clothes or money. He took another patient's suit before he left.'

'Will there—'

'Don't worry. The other patient is most understanding. He knows something of what your brother has been through. Please don't worry about it any further.'

'But the money?'

'There wasn't much. Enough for his train fare and perhaps a bite to eat.'

'He doesn't look as if he's eaten in months. Is there any treatment? Will he get better?'

'It's impossible to say. There are treatments.'

'What sort of treatments?'

'Narcosynthesis is the most common.'

'And that is?'

'A drug-induced re-enactment of the traumatic episode, or episodes. It's used to assist the ego to accept what happened.'

'But if you don't know what the traumatic episode was . . .?'

'There are ways of getting at that. But I don't want to get your hopes up. The problem is, of course, that Matthew can't express himself vocally, and that could mean a severe limitation in the value of narcosynthesis.'

'What do you suggest?'

'I suggest you tell me where you live and I'll do my best to put you in touch with a doctor who knows about these things.'

I told him where I lived and where it was.

'It may mean visits to Leeds,' he said.

'That will be no problem.'

'I promise I'll get working on it. In the meantime, just take good care of him. I don't think I need to tell you that he has suffered appallingly.'

'No. Thank you, Doctor.' I put down the receiver and went back upstairs.

Matthew was sitting staring towards the window, though not through it, and Mother and Gloria seemed at their wits' end.

'I've tried to talk to him, Gwen,' Gloria said, voice quivering. 'I don't think he even knows me. I don't think he even knows where he is.'

I told her some of what the doctor had said. 'He came back here, didn't he?' I said, to comfort her. 'He made his way here by himself. It was the only place he knew to come. Home. Don't worry, he'll be fine now he's back with the people who love him.'

Gloria nodded, but she didn't seem convinced. I couldn't blame her; I wasn't convinced, either.

•

It was a long time since Banks had driven up the rutted driveway in front of Detective Superintendent Gristhorpe's squat stone house on the daleside above Lyndgarth.

As expected, he found Gristhorpe out back working on his dry-stone wall. Walling was a hobby the superintendent had taken up years ago. It was the ideal pointless activity; his wall went nowhere and fenced nothing in. He said he found it relaxing, like some form of meditation. You could just empty your mind and get in harmony with the natural world. So he said. Maybe the super and Annie would have a lot in common.

Gristhorpe was wearing a baggy pair of brown corduroy trousers held up by frayed red braces, and a checked shirt that might once have had a white background. He was holding a triangular lump of limestone in his hand and squinting at the wall. When Banks approached, he turned. His pockmarked face was redder than usual after the sun and exertion. He was also sweating, and his unruly mop of thatched hair lay plastered to his skull. Was it a trick of the light, Banks wondered, or was Gristhorpe suddenly looking old?

'Alan,' he said. It wasn't a greeting, or a question. Just a statement. Hard to tell anything much from the flat tone.

'Sir.'

Gristhorpe pointed towards the wall. 'They say a good waller doesn't put a stone aside once he's picked it up,' he said, then looked at the rock in his hand. 'I wish I could figure out where to put this bugger.' He paused for a moment, then he tossed the stone back on the pile, slapped his hands on his trousers to get rid of the dust and walked over. 'You'll have a glass of something?'

'Anything cold.'

'Coke, then. I've got some in the fridge. We'll sit out here.' Gristhorpe pointed to two fold-up chairs in the shade by the back wall of the old farmhouse.

Banks sat down. He thought he could see some tiny figures making their way along the limestone escarpment that ran along the top of Fremlington Hill.

Gristhorpe came out with two glasses of Coke, handed one to Banks and sat down beside him. At first, neither of them spoke.

Finally, Gristhorpe broke the silence. 'I hear Jimmy Riddle's given you a real case to work on.'

'Sort of. I'm sure he thinks of it as more of a dead end.'

Gristhorpe raised his bushy eyebrows. 'Is it?'

'I don't think so.' Banks told Gristhorpe what he and Annie Cabbot had discovered so far and handed him the button Adam Kelly had taken from the skeleton's hand. 'It's impossible to say,' he went on, 'but it *might* have been in the victim's hand. It was certainly buried with her, and it didn't walk there. She could have ripped it from her attacker's uniform when she was being strangled.'

Gristhorpe examined the button and took a sip of Coke. 'It looks like an American Army Air Force button,' he said. 'I could be wrong – it's so old and corroded it's hard to tell – but that design looks like the American eagle. It's not what the husband would have been wearing, even if he had been in uniform. Not from what you've told me. And it's very unlikely that he would have been in uniform if he had been liberated from a Japanese POW camp and repatriated.'

'So you think it's American?'

Gristhorpe weighed the metal in his palm. 'I wouldn't swear to it in court,' he said. 'The American armed forces were very casual dressers compared to our lot. Most of the time they wore "Ike jackets" with hidden front buttons, but this could have come from the collar. Usually it was worn on the right side. Officers wore them left or right, with the branch of service below. GIs not assigned to any specific service wore the eagle on both sides.'

'If she was being strangled,' said Banks, 'then it's quite likely she reached out to try to scratch her attacker's face and grab at his collar. Gloria and her friends went around with a group of American airmen from Rowan Woods.'

Gristhorpe handed back the button. 'It sounds like a reasonable theory to me.'

'There's another thing that puzzles me. Matthew Shackleton committed suicide in 1950. Shot himself. I'm wondering where he got the gun.'

'Anyone can get a gun if he wants one badly enough. Even today.'

'He was in no state to go out and buy one on the black market, even if he knew where to look.'

'So you're assuming he already had it?'

'Yes, but he wouldn't have had one in the prison camp, would he?'

'He could have got it from someone on his way home. Long journey, lots of opportunities.'

'I suppose so. All we know is that he went missing presumed dead in Burma in 1943, turned up at Hobb's End again in March 1945, then committed suicide in Leeds in 1950. It's a long gap.'

'What kind of gun was it?'

'A Colt forty-five automatic.'

'Really?'

'Yes. Why?'

'That was the gun the American military issued their
servicemen. It raises interesting possibilities, doesn't it?
American button in the wife's hand. American gun in the
husband's mouth.'

Banks nodded. Though what the possibilities were, he
hadn't a clue. The two events were separated by five
years, more or less, and happened in different places. He
sipped some more Coke.

'How's Sandra?' Gristhorpe asked.

'Fine, as far as I know.'

'I'm sorry about what happened, Alan.'

'Me, too.'

Gristhorpe gazed at a point in space somewhere above
Fremlington Edge. 'This Annie Cabbot,' he said. 'What's
she like?'

Banks felt himself blush. 'She's good,' he said.

'Too good for a God-forsaken outpost like Harksmere?'

'I think so.'

'Then what's she doing there?'

'I don't know.' Banks glanced sideways at Gristhorpe.
'Maybe she pissed somebody off, like I did.'

Gristhorpe narrowed his eyes. 'Alan,' he said, 'I don't
approve of what you did last year, taking off like that
without so much as a by-your-leave. You dropped me right
in it. I can see why you did it. I might even have done it
myself in your place. But I can't condone it. And while it
pulled your chestnuts out of the fire in one sense, it's
probably dropped them in it in another way.'

'What do you mean?'

'Jimmy Riddle already hated you. He also hates being
proved wrong, especially *after* he's done his crowing to
the press. Your maverick actions helped solve the case,

but now he hates you even more. I can't do anything for you. You must be aware your grasp at Eastvale is pretty tenuous, to say the least.'

Banks stood up. 'I'm not asking for any favours.'

'Sit down, Alan. Hear me out.'

Banks sat and fumbled for a cigarette. 'I'd probably have looked for a transfer before now,' he said, 'but I've had a few other things on my mind.'

'Aye, I know. And I know you'd not ask for any favours, either. That's not your way. I might have a bit of good news for you, though, if you can promise to keep it to yourself.'

'Good news. That makes a change.'

'Between you and me and the stone wall, Jimmy Riddle might not be around much longer.'

Banks could hardly believe his ears. '*What*? Riddle's retiring? At his age?'

'A little bird tells me that the crooked finger of politics beckons. As you know, he can't enter into that as a copper, so you tell me what the logical solution is.'

'Politics?'

'Aye. His local Conservative member is practically gaga. Not that anyone would notice something like that much in the House. High-echelon rumour has it that Riddle has already had several interviews with the selection committee and they're pleased with him. Like I said, Alan, this is just between you and me.'

'Of course.'

'There's no guarantee he'll go. Or get elected, for that matter. Though the Conservative seat around here is so secure they could put Saddam Hussein up and he'd probably win it. Even if Riddle does go, he'll leave a bad smell around and swear it's yours. So I'm not saying there's no damage done. For a start, a lot depends on whether we get a CC who can tell the smell of shit from perfume.'

Banks began to feel a sort of warm glow deep inside. An interesting case. Annie Cabbot. Now this. Maybe there was a God, after all. Maybe his dry season really was coming to an end.

'Do you know,' he said, 'it might even be worth voting Conservative, just to make sure the bastard wins his seat.'

•

Charlie was killed on the nineteenth of March during a big raid over Berlin. Their Flying Fortress got badly shot up by a Messerschmitt. Brad managed to fly the burning aeroplane back across the Channel and land in an airfield in Sussex, only to find Charlie and two other members of his crew dead. Brad himself escaped with cuts and bruises and after a couple of days' observation in hospital, he returned to Rowan Woods.

Coming right after Matthew's return, this news was almost impossible for me to bear. Poor, gentle Charlie, with his poetry and his puppy-dog eyes. Gone.

When Brad got back from Sussex, he came over to the shop with a bottle of bourbon and told me the news in person. Though he had only known Charlie a couple of years, during that time they had become close friends. He tried to explain the kind of bond that is forged between pilot and navigator. I could tell he was devastated by what happened. He blamed himself and felt guilty about his own survival.

Gloria was busy taking care of Matthew and she had told Brad she couldn't see him again, that it would only upset her and would do them no good. Brad was angry and upset about her rejection, but there was nothing he could do except come to me and pour his heart out.

We sat in the small room above the shop after Mother had gone to bed, drank bourbon and smoked Luckies. We had the Home Service on the wireless and Vivien Leigh was reading poetry by Christina Rossetti and Elizabeth Barrett Browning. Neither of us said very much; there was nothing, really, *to* say. Charlie was gone, and there was an end to it. Poetry filled our periods of silence.

Not far down the High Street, Gloria – who adored Vivien Leigh, I remembered from our very first meeting – was devoting her time to caring for a man who couldn't speak, wouldn't communicate and probably didn't even know who she was. She was spoon-feeding him, bathing him, for all I knew, with no end in sight. That was what our lives had been reduced to by the war: the essence of misery and hopelessness.

The bottle lay empty; my head spun; the room reeked of cigarette smoke. "'How do I love thee? Let me count the ways,'" read Vivien Leigh. How Charlie hated such maudlin poetry. I let my head rest on Brad's shoulder and cried.

•

Banks went home early on Thursday evening. He didn't need to be in his office to prepare a list of questions for Vivian Elmsley, and he was far more comfortable at the pine table in his kitchen, a mug of strong tea beside him, Arvo Pärt's *Stabat Mater* on the stereo, and the early evening light, gold as autumn leaves, flooding through the window behind him.

When he had made a list of the essential things he

wanted to know, he went through to the living room and tried Brian's number yet again.

On the fifth ring, someone answered.

'Yeah?'

'Brian?'

'Andy. Who's calling?'

'His father.'

Pause. 'Just a sec.'

Banks heard muffled voices, then a few moments later, Brian came on the phone. 'Dad?'

'Where've you been? I've been trying to get in touch with you all week.'

'Playing holiday resorts in South Wales. We were doing some gigs with the Dancing Pigs. Look, Dad, I told you, we've got gigs coming out of our ears. We're busy. You weren't interested.'

Banks paused. He didn't want to blow it this time, but he was damned if he was going to grovel to his own son. 'That's not the point,' he said. 'I don't think it's out of line for a father to express some concern at his son's sudden change of plans, do you?'

'You know I'm into the band. You've always known I've loved music. Dad, it was *you* who bought me that guitar for my sixteenth birthday. Don't you remember?'

'Of course I do. All I'm saying is that you have to give it a little time to sink in. It's a shock, that's all. We were all expecting you to come out with a good degree and start working at a good firm somewhere. Music's a great hobby but a risky living.'

'So you keep saying. We're doing all right. Anyway, did you always do what your parents wanted you to?'

Low blow, Banks thought. *Almost never* would have been the truth, but he wasn't ready to admit to that. 'Not always,' he said. 'Look, I'm not saying you aren't old enough to make your own decisions. Just think about it, that's all.'

'I *have* thought about it. This is what I want to do.'

'Have you spoken to your mother?'

Banks swore he could almost hear the guilt in Brian's pause. 'She's always out when I call,' he said at last.

Bollocks, Banks thought. 'Well, keep trying.'

'I still think it would come better from you.'

'Brian, if it's your decision, you can take responsibility for it. Believe me, it *won't* come any better from me.'

'Yeah, yeah. Fine. All right. I'll try her again.'

'You do that. Anyway, the main reason I'm calling is that I'll be down in your neck of the woods tomorrow, so I wondered if we could get together and talk about things. Let me buy you a pint.'

'I don't know, Dad. We're really busy right now.'

'You can't be busy *all* the time.'

'There's rehearsals, you know . . .'

'Half an hour?'

Another pause followed. Banks heard Brian say something to Andrew, but he couldn't catch what it was. Then Brian came back on again. 'Look,' he said, 'tomorrow and Saturday we're playing at a pub in Bethnal Green. If you want to come and listen, we can have that pint during the break.'

Banks got the name of the pub and the time and said he'd do his best.

'It's all right,' said Brian. 'I'll understand if something else comes up and you can't make it. Wouldn't be the first time. One of the joys of being a copper's son.'

'I'll be there,' said Banks. 'Goodbye.'

It was almost dark by now. He took his cigarettes and

small whisky and went outside to sit on the wall. A few remaining streaks of crimson and purple shot the sky to the west and the waning moon shone like polished bone over the valley. The promise of a storm had dissipated and the air was clear and dry again.

Well, Banks thought, at least he had talked to Brian and would get to see him soon. He looked forward to hearing the band. He had heard Brian practising his guitar when he lived at home, of course, and had been impressed by the way he had picked it up so easily. Unlike Banks.

Way back in the Beatles days, when every kid tried to learn guitar, he had managed about three badly fingered chords before packing it in. He envied Brian his talent, perhaps in the same way he envied him his freedom. There had been a time when Banks had also contemplated the bohemian life. What he would actually have *done*, he didn't know; after all, he had no facility for music or writing or painting. He could have been a hanger-on, perhaps, a roadie, or just a real cool guy. It didn't seem to matter back then. But Jem's death soured the dream for him and he ended up joining the police. He was living with Sandra, too, by then, wildly in love and thinking seriously, for the first time in his life, of a real future together with someone. Kids. Mortgage. The lot. Besides, deep down, he knew he needed a career with some sort of disciplined structure, or God knew what would happen to him. He didn't really fancy the armed forces, and with images of the never-to-be-found Graham Marshall in his mind, that left the police. Mysteries to solve; bullies to send down.

Maybe he should have followed his original impulse and dropped out, he thought, looking back and considering all that had happened lately. But no. He wasn't going to fall into that trap. It would be far too easy. He had chosen the life and the job he had wanted – had two great kids and a slightly shop-soiled career to show for it – and he couldn't imagine himself doing anything else.

Nobody had ever promised him it was going to be a breeze. The dark moods, depressions that settled upon him like a flock of crows, would disappear eventually; the sense of futility, the feeling that the dark pit of his despair actually *had* no bottom would also dissipate over time. As Brian had said when Banks had first told him about the separation from Sandra, he just had to *hang in* there, hang in there and make the best of what he had: the cottage, Annie, a challenging case.

An agitated curlew screeched and shrieked way up the daleside. Some animal threatening its nest, perhaps. Banks heard his phone ring again. Quickly, he stubbed out the cigarette and went back inside.

'Sorry to disturb you at this time of night, sir,' said DS Hatchley, 'but I know you're off to London in the morning.'

'What is it?' Banks looked at his watch. Half past nine. 'It's not like you to be working so late, Jim.'

'I'm not. I mean, I wasn't. I was just over at the Queen's Arms with a couple of mates from the rugby club, so I thought I'd pop in the station, like, and see if I'd got any answers to my inquiries.'

'And?'

'Francis Henderson. Like I said, I know you're off down there tomorrow, so that's why I'm calling. I've got an address.'

'He lives in London?'

'Dulwich.' Hatchley read the address. 'What's interesting, why it came back so quick, is he's got form.'

Banks's ears pricked up. 'Go on.'

'According to Criminal Intelligence, Francis Henderson started working for one of the East End gangs in the sixties. Not the Krays, exactly, but that sort of thing. Mostly he dug up information for them, found people they were after, watched people they wanted watched. He developed a drug habit and started dealing to support it in the seventies. They say he's been retired and clean for years now, at least as far as they know.'

'Sure it's *our* Francis Henderson?'

'Yes, sir.'

'Okay. Thanks a lot for calling, Jim. Get yourself home now.'

'Don't worry, I will.'

'And give another push on that nationwide tomorrow if you can find time.'

'Will do. *Bon voyage.*'

14

Annie was waiting on the platform at York Station looking very businesslike in a navy mid-length skirt and silver-buttoned blazer over a white blouse. She had tied her hair back so tightly it made a V on her forehead and arched her dark eyebrows. For once, though, Banks didn't feel underdressed. He wore a lightweight cotton summer suit and, with it, a red and grey tie, top shirt button undone.

'Good Lord,' she said, smiling, 'I feel like we're sneaking away for a dirty weekend.'

Banks laughed. 'If you play your cards right . . .'

The station smelled of diesel oil and ancient soot from the days of steam. Gouts of compressed air rushed out from under the trains with a deafening hiss, and pigeons flapped around the high ceiling. Announcements about late arrivals and departures echoed from the public address system.

The London train pulled out of the station only eleven minutes after the advertised departure time. Banks and Annie chatted for a while, lulled by the rattling and rocking rhythm, and Banks ascertained that whatever had been bothering Annie on the phone yesterday was no longer a problem. He had been forgiven.

Annie started reading the *Guardian* she had bought at the station news-stand and Banks went back to *Guilty Secrets*. In bed the previous evening, he had given up on *The Shadow of Death* when the erstwhile DI Niven arrested his first suspect, saying, 'You have the right to remain silent. If you don't have a lawyer, one will be provided for you.' So much for the realistic depiction of police procedures. Allowing that it was one of her early DI Niven books and feeling that she deserved a second chance, he started *Guilty Secrets*, her most recent non-series book, and had trouble putting it down to get to sleep.

The basic plot device was the kind of thing everyone has seen a dozen times on television. A man on holiday in a foreign country becomes involved in an altercation with another man in a crowded bar. He tries to calm the situation and eventually leaves, but the man pursues him outside and attacks him. Someone else, a stranger, comes to his aid, and together they get carried away and beat the attacker to death. They hide the body, then go their separate ways, and nothing more is heard of the incident.

Back in England, the first man becomes very successful in business and is poised at the edge of what promises to be an equally successful career in politics. Until the inevitable blackmailer turns up. What does he do? Pay up or kill again?

Despite the thinness of the plot, *Guilty Secrets* turned out to be a fascinating exploration of conscience and character. Because of the situation he finds himself in, the central character is forced to re-examine his entire life in relation to the crime he got away with, while at the same time agonizing over what to do to secure his future.

To complicate matters, killing does not come easy to this man; he is human, with a firm, if understated, belief in Christianity. At one point he considers letting it all come out so that he can pay the consequences he feels he should have paid years ago. But he also likes his life the way it is. Not without a streak of self-interest, he is ambitious, enjoys power and feels he can do the country some genuine good if he gets in the right position. He also has others to consider: family and employees who rely or depend on him for their livelihoods.

Chapter after chapter, with merciless compassion, Vivian Elmsley strips the man to his soul, lays bare his moral and spiritual dilemmas and tightens the net around him. In his time, Banks had arrested a number of men who had killed to protect their ill-gotten fame or fortune, or both, but rarely had he come across a character as complex as the one Vivian Elmsley had created here. Perhaps he just hadn't looked deeply enough into them. A police interview room was not the best place to get to know someone, and Banks had been far more concerned with obtaining a confession than with striking up a relationship. That was where real life and fiction parted ways, he thought; one is messy and incomplete, the other ordered and finished.

Banks finished the book just before Peterborough. Annie had closed her eyes by then and was either napping or meditating. He gazed out of the window at the uninspiring landscape of his childhood: a brick factory, a red-brick school, stretches of waste ground littered with weeds and rubbish. Even the spire of the beautiful Norman cathedral behind the shopping centre failed to inspire him. The train squealed to a halt.

Of course, it hadn't been so uninspiring back then; his imagination had imbued every miserable inch of the place with magical significance. The waste grounds were battlefields where the local lads re-enacted the great battles of two world wars, using tree branches or sticks of wood for rifles, bayoneting opponents with great relish. Even when Banks was playing alone or fishing in the River Nene, it was easy enough for him to believe he was an Arthurian knight on a quest. Adam Kelly had been doing the same thing in Hobb's End when the world of his imagination had suddenly become real.

As the train left Peterborough Station, Banks thought of his parents, not more than a mile away. He looked at his watch. About now, he guessed, his mother would be drinking milky instant coffee and reading her latest women's magazine, and his father would be having his morning nap, snoring gently, feet up on the green velour pouffe, newspaper spread over his lap. Unchanging routine. It had been the same since his father was made redundant from his job as a steelworker in 1982, and his mother grew too old and tired to clean other people's houses any more. Banks thought of the disappointment and bitterness that had twisted their lives, problems that he had certainly contributed to, as well as Margaret Thatcher. But their disappointments had been visited on him, too, in turn. No matter how well he did, it was never good enough.

Even though Banks had 'bettered' himself – he had a secure job with a steady source of income and good opportunities for advancement – his parents didn't approve of his joining the police. His father never tired of pointing out the traditional opposition between the working classes and the police force. When the riot police on overtime taunted striking miners by waving rolls of five-pound notes at them in the '84 strike, he accused Banks of being 'the enemy' and tried to persuade him to resign. It didn't matter that Banks was working the drugs squad on the Met at the time and had nothing to do with the troubles up north. As far as his father was concerned, the police were merely Maggie's bully-boys, the enforcers of unpopular government policies, oppressors of the working man.

Banks's mother, for her part, took a more domestic view and relayed tales of police divorces she heard about over the grapevine. Being a policeman wasn't a good career choice for a family man, she never ceased to tell him. Never mind that it was over twenty years later when he and Sandra split up – most of that time relatively successful as modern marriages go – his mother took great satisfaction that she had finally been vindicated.

And there lay the main problem, Banks thought as he watched the city disappear behind him. He had never been able to do anything right. When bad things happened to other kids, parents usually took their side, but when bad things happened to Banks, it was his own fault. It had always been that way, ever since he started getting cuts and bruises in schoolyard fights, always him who must have started it, whether he did or not. As far as his parents were concerned, Banks thought, if he got killed on the job, *that* would probably be his own fault too. When it came to blame, they offered no quarter for family.

Still, he thought, in a way that was what made him good at his job. When he had been junior in rank, he had never blamed his bosses when things went wrong, and now he was DCI, he took the responsibility for his team, whether it consisted of Hatchley and Susan Gay or just Annie Cabbot. If the team failed, it was *his* failure. A burden, yes, but also a strength.

King's Cross was the usual madness. Banks and Annie negotiated their way through the crowds and the maze of tiled, echoing tunnels to the Northern Line and managed to cram into the first Edgware-bound train that came along.

A few minutes later, they came out of Belsize Park tube station, walked up Rosslyn Hill and turned into the side-street where Vivian Elmsley lived. Banks knew the area vaguely from his years in London, though after Notting Hill, he and Sandra had mostly lived south of the river, in Kennington. Keats used to live near here, Banks remembered; it was in one of these streets that the poor sod fell in love with his next-door neighbour, Fanny Brawne.

A woman's voice answered the intercom.

There was a long pause after Banks had stated his rank and his business, then a more resigned voice said, 'You'd better come up.' The lock buzzed and Banks pushed open the front door.

They walked up three flights of thickly carpeted stairs to the second-floor landing. That this was a well-maintained building was clear from the fresh lemon scent, the gleaming woodwork and freshly painted walls, decorated here and there with a still-life print or a seascape. Probably cost an arm and a leg, but then Vivian Elmsley could no doubt afford an arm and a leg.

The woman who opened the door was tall and slim, standing ramrod-straight, her grey hair fastened in a bun. She had high cheekbones, a straight, slightly hooked nose and a small, thin mouth. Crow's-feet spread around her remarkable deep blue eyes, slanted at an almost oriental angle. Banks could see what Elsie Patterson meant: if you were at all observant, there was no mistaking those eyes. She was dressed like a jogger, in baggy black exercise trousers and a white sweatshirt. Still, he supposed, it didn't matter what you wore if all you had to do was sit around and write all day. Some people have all the luck.

She looked tired. Bags puffed under her eyes, and broken blood vessels criss-crossed the whites. She also looked strained and edgy, as if she were running on reserves.

The flat was Spartan and modern in its furnishings, chrome and glass giving the small living room a generous sense of space. A framed print of one of Georgia O'Keeffe's huge yellow flowers hung on the wall over the mantelpiece.

'Please, sit down.' She gestured Banks and Annie towards two matching chrome-and-black-leather chairs, then sat down herself, clasping her hands on her lap. They looked older than her face, skeletal and liver-spotted. They were also unusually large for a woman's hands.

'I must admit, I'm quite used to talking to the police,' she said, 'but usually I'm the one questioning them. How can I help you?'

Banks remembered the police procedure in *The Shadow of Death* and bit his tongue. Maybe she hadn't known any police officers when she wrote that book. 'First of all,' he asked, 'are you Gwynneth Shackleton?'

'I was, though most people called me Gwen. Vivian is my middle name. Elmsley is a pseudonym. Actually, it's my mother's maiden name. It's all perfectly legal.'

'I'm sure it is. You grew up in Hobb's End?'

'Yes.'

'Did you kill Gloria Shackleton?'

Her hand went to her chest. 'Kill Gloria? Me? What a suggestion. I most certainly did not.'

'Could Matthew, your brother, have killed her?'

'No. Matthew loved her. She looked after him. He *needed* her. I'm afraid this is all rather overwhelming, Chief Inspector.'

'No doubt.' Banks glanced at Annie, who remained expressionless, notebook on her lap. 'May I ask why you haven't come forward in response to our requests for information?' he asked.

Vivian Elmsley paused before answering, as if composing her thoughts carefully, the way she might revise a page of manuscript. 'Chief Inspector,' she said, 'I admit that I have been following developments both in the newspapers and on television, but I honestly don't believe I can tell you anything of any value. I have also found it all very distressing. That's why I haven't come forward.'

'Oh, come off it,' said Banks. 'Not only did you live in Hobb's End throughout the war, and not only did you know the victim well, you were also her sister-in-law. You can't expect me to believe that you know nothing at all about what happened to her.'

'Believe what you will.'

'Were the two of you close?'

'I wouldn't say we were close, no.'

'Did you like her?'

'I can't honestly say I knew her very well.'

'You were about the same age. You must have had things in common besides your brother.'

'She was older than I. It does make a difference when you're young. I wouldn't say we had much in common. I was always a bookish sort of girl, whereas Gloria was the more flamboyant type. As with many extroverts, she was also a secretive person, very difficult to get to know.'

'Did you see a lot of her?'

'Quite a bit. We were in and out of one another's houses. Bridge Cottage wasn't far from the shop.'

'Yet you claim you didn't know her well?'

'I didn't. You probably have cousins or in-laws you hardly know at all, Chief Inspector.'

'Didn't you ever do things together?'

'Like what?'

'I don't know. Girl things.'

Annie shot him a glance that he felt even before he noticed it out of the corner of his eye. The hell with it, he thought, they *were* girls back then. He had been a boy once, too; he did boy things, and he didn't object to anyone saying so.

Vivian pursed her lips, then shrugged. 'Girl things? I suppose we did. The same sorts of things other people did during the war. We went to the pictures, to dances.'

'Dances with American airmen?'

'Sometimes, yes.'

'Was there anyone in particular?'

'I suppose we were quite friendly with several of them over the last year of the war.'

'Do you remember their names?'

'I think so. Why?'

'What about Brad? Ring a bell?'

'Brad? Yes, I think he was one of them.'

'What was his second name?'

'Szikorski. Brad Szikorski.'

Banks checked the list of Rowan Woods personnel he had brought with him. *Bradford J. Szikorski, Jr.* That had to be the one.

'And PX? Billy Joe?'

'Edgar Konig and Billy Joe Farrell.'

They were on the list, too.

'What about Charlie?'

Vivian Elmsley turned pale; a muscle by the side of her jaw began to twitch. 'Markleson,' she whispered. 'Charlie Markleson.'

Banks checked the sheet. 'Charles Christopher Markleson? That the one?'

'*Charlie.* He was always called *Charlie.*'

'Whatever.'

'How did you find out their names? I haven't heard them in so long.'

'It doesn't matter how we found out. We also discovered that Gloria was having an affair with Brad Szikorski. Was she still seeing him when Matthew came back? Is that what happened?'

'Not that I knew of. I don't know what you're getting at. You've been misinformed, Chief Inspector. Gloria was married to Matthew, whether he was there or not. Yes, we went to the pictures with those boys on occasion, perhaps to dances, but that's all there was to it. There was no question of romantic involvement.'

'Are you sure?'

'Of course I am.'

'How did Gloria behave during her husband's absence?'

'What do you mean?'

'When she thought he was dead. Obviously things would be different then, wouldn't they? It wasn't as if she were waiting for him any more. As far as she was concerned, she would never see him again. After a reasonable period of mourning, she could enter back into the spirit of the times, couldn't she? Surely an attractive woman like her must have had boyfriends?'

Vivian paused again. 'Gloria had a very gregarious side to her nature. She liked parties, group excursions, that sort of thing. She liked to keep things superficial. At a distance. Besides, we never gave Matthew up for dead completely. You must understand that, Chief Inspector; we never gave up hope. There was always *hope*, hope that he would return. And it proved well founded.'

'You haven't answered my question. Did Gloria have a

romantic affair with Brad Szikorski, or with anyone else?'

She looked away. 'Not that I knew about.'

'So she lived like a nun, even though she believed her husband was dead?'

'I didn't say that. I didn't spy on her. Whatever she got up to behind locked doors was none of my business.'

'So she *did* get up to something?'

'I told you: I didn't spy on her. You're twisting my words.'

'How did Brad take it when Matthew came back alive?'

'How should I know? Why would it matter to him?'

'It might have. If he fell in love with Gloria, and if she rejected him in favour of her husband. He might have been angry.'

'Are you suggesting that *Brad* killed Gloria?' Vivian sniffed. 'You're really clutching at straws now.'

Banks leaned forward. 'Somebody did, Ms Elmsley, and the most immediate suspects that come to mind are Matthew, one of the Americans, Michael Stanhope, or you.'

'Ridiculous. It must have been a stranger. We've got plenty of them in the village, you know.'

'What about Michael Stanhope?'

'It's been years since I've heard *his* name. They were friends. That's all.'

'Would it surprise you to hear that Gloria posed nude for a painting by Stanhope in 1944?'

'Yes, it would. Very much. I know that Gloria wasn't as fastidious about her body as some would have wished her to be, but I never saw any evidence of anything like that.'

'Next time you're in Leeds,' Banks said, 'drop by the art gallery and have a look. You're sure she never told you?'

'I would have remembered.'

'Was Gloria having an affair with Michael Stanhope?'

'I shouldn't think so. He was too old for her.'

'And homosexual?'

'I wouldn't know about that. As I said, I was very young. It certainly wasn't something people went around boasting about back then.'

'Did she ever tell you about her family in London? About her son Francis?'

'She did mention him to me once, yes. But she said she'd cut off all relations with him and his father.'

'Even so, they could have come to drag her back. Maybe they fought and he killed her?'

Vivian shook her head. 'I'm sure I would have known.'

'Was Matthew ever violent towards her?'

'Never. Matthew had always been a gentle person, and even his war experiences didn't change that.' Her voice had taken on a strained, wavering quality.

Banks paused and softened his tone. 'There is one thing that really puzzles me,' he said, 'and that's what you *did* think had happened to Gloria? Surely you can't have thought she had simply disappeared from the face of the earth?'

'It wasn't a mystery at the time. Not really. She left. That's what I had always thought until you found the remains. You *are* certain it's Gloria, aren't you?'

Banks felt a twinge of doubt, but he tried not to let it show. They still had no definite proof of the skeleton's identity. For that, they would need Francis Henderson so they could run DNA checks. 'We're sure,' he said. 'Why would she leave?'

'Because she couldn't stand it any more, taking care of Matthew, the way he was. After all, it wouldn't have been the first time she'd done that. She had clearly broken off all contact with whatever life she had had in London before coming to Hobb's End. I don't think Gloria was particularly strong when it came to emotional fortitude.'

True enough, Banks thought. If a person has bid one life goodbye, then it probably wouldn't be too difficult to do it again. But Gloria Shackleton hadn't bid Hobb's End goodbye, he reminded himself; she had been killed and buried there.

'When did she disappear?' he asked.

'Shortly after VE day. A week or so.'

'You must see how the discovery casts suspicion on your brother, most of all. Gloria was buried in an out-building adjoining Bridge Cottage. Matthew was living with her there at the time.'

'But he was never violent. I had never known him be violent. Never.'

'War can change a man.'

'Even so.'

'Did he go out much?'

'What do you mean?'

'After his return. Did he go out much? Was Gloria often alone in the house?'

'He went to the pub of an evening. The Shoulder of Mutton. Yes, she was alone there sometimes.'

'Did Gloria ever say anything to you about leaving?'

'She hinted at it once or twice, but I didn't take her seriously.'

'Why not?'

'Her manner. It was as if she was joking. You know, "Some day my prince will come. I'm going to leave all this behind and run off to untold wealth and riches." Gloria was a dreamer, Chief Inspector. I, on the other hand, have always been a realist.'

'I suppose that's debatable,' Banks said. 'Given what you do for a living.'

'Perhaps my dreams are very realistic.'

'Perhaps. Even though she hinted, you didn't believe Gloria would actually go?'

'No.'

'What were the circumstances surrounding her departure?' Banks asked. 'Did you see her go?'

'No. It happened on one of the days when I accompanied Matthew to his doctor in Leeds. When we got back that evening, she was gone.'

'*You* accompanied him? Why not Gloria? She was still his wife.'

'And he was still *my* brother. Anyway, she asked me to, on occasion. It was the only respite she got. She looked after him the rest of the time. I thought it only fair she got some time to herself once in a while.'

'Did she take anything with her when she left?'

'A few clothes, personal items. She didn't have much.'

'But she took her clothes?'

'Yes. A few.'

'That's interesting. What did she carry them in?'

'An old cardboard suitcase. The same one she arrived with.'

'Did she leave a note?'

'Not that I saw. If Matthew found one, he never indicated it to me.'

'Would he have?'

'Possibly not. He wasn't very communicative. In his condition, it's impossible to predict what he would have done.'

'Murder?'

'*No*. Not Matthew. I've already told you, he had a gentle

nature. Even his dreadful war experiences and his illness didn't change that about him, though they changed everything else.'

'But Gloria's belongings were definitely missing?'

'Yes.'

'And you and Matthew were in Leeds during the time she made her exit?'

'Yes.'

'So she never even said goodbye?'

'Sometimes it's easier that way.'

'So it is.' Banks remembered that Sandra, once she had made her mind up, had given him little time for protracted goodbyes. He paused for a moment. 'Ms Elmsley,' he asked, 'knowing what you know now, why do you think her clothes and suitcase were missing? Where do you think they got to?'

'I have no idea. I'm only telling you what I witnessed at the time, what I thought must have happened. Perhaps someone stole them? Perhaps she interrupted a burglar and he killed her?'

'Were they particularly fine clothes? Minks, a few diamond necklaces perhaps? A tiara or two?'

'Don't be absurd.'

'It's not me who's being absurd. You see, it's not often people get murdered for their clothes, especially if they're ordinary clothes.'

'Perhaps they were taken for some other reason.'

'Like what?'

'To make it *look* as if she had gone away.'

'Ah. Now *that* would be clever, wouldn't it? Who do you think would feel the need to risk taking time burying her body under the outbuilding floor?'

'I don't know.'

'Not a casual burglar, I don't think.'

'As I suggested, perhaps someone wanted to make it appear as if she had gone away.'

'But who would want to do that? And, perhaps more important: why?'

'To avoid suspicion.'

'Exactly. Which brings us back very close to home, doesn't it? Why try to avoid suspicion unless you have some reason to believe suspicion will fall on you?'

'Your rhetoric is too much for me, Chief Inspector.'

'But you write detective novels. I've read one of them. Don't play the fool with me. You know exactly what I'm talking about.'

'I'm very flattered that you have read my books, Chief Inspector, but I'm afraid you attribute to me a far more logical mind than I actually possess.'

Banks sighed. 'If someone took great pains to make it look as if Gloria had run away, I'd say that someone wasn't likely to be a stranger just passing through, or a burglar. It had to be someone who felt suspicion was likely to fall on him or her: Matthew, Brad Szikorski or *you*.'

'Well, it wasn't me. And I told you, Matthew never raised a finger to her.'

'Which leaves Brad Szikorski.'

'Perhaps. Though I doubt it. It doesn't matter, anyway.'

'Why not?'

She allowed him a thin smile. 'Because Brad Szikorski was killed in a flying stunt in the desert outside Los Angeles in 1952. Ironic, isn't it? During the war, Brad flew on bombing raids over Europe and survived, only to be killed in a stunt for a war film seven or eight years later.'

'What about Charles Markleson?'

'*Charlie*. He would have had no reason at all to harm Gloria. Besides, he was killed in the war.'

'Edgar Konig? Billy Joe Farrell?'

'I don't know what happened to them, Chief Inspector. It's all so long ago. I only know about Brad because it was in the newspapers at the time. I suppose you'll have to ask them yourself, won't you? That is, if you can find them.'

'Oh, I'll find them, if they're still alive. Had either of them reason to kill Gloria?'

'Not that I know of. They were simply part of a group we went around with. Though Billy Joe, I remember, did have a violent temper, and PX was rather smitten with Gloria.'

'Did she go out with him?'

'Not to my knowledge. You couldn't . . . he wasn't . . . I mean, he just seemed so *young* and so shy.'

'Did you notice any blood in Bridge Cottage after Gloria's disappearance?'

'No. Obviously, if I had done, I would have been suspicious and called the police. But then I can't say I was actually *looking* for blood.'

'Not one little spot? Nothing that might, in retrospect, have been blood?'

'Nothing. Anyway, what makes you think she was killed in Bridge Cottage?'

'It's a logical assumption.'

'She could have been killed outside, in the backyard, or even in the outbuilding where you found her remains.'

'Possibly,' Banks allowed. 'Even so, whoever did it was very thorough. What happened next?'

'Nothing. We just carried on. Actually, we only stayed on in the village a few weeks longer, then we got a council house in Leeds.'

'I know. I've seen it.'

'I can't imagine why you'd want to do that.'

'So you're saying you have absolutely no idea what happened to Gloria?'

'None at all. As I said, I simply thought she couldn't face life with Matthew any more – in his condition – so she ran off and started up elsewhere.'

'Did you think she might have run off with Brad Szikorski, arranged to meet him over in America or something? After all, the Four Hundred and Forty-Eighth Bomber Group moved out around the same time, didn't they?'

'I suppose it crossed my mind. It was always possible that she had ended up in America.'

'Did it not surprise you that she never got in touch?'

'It did. But there was nothing I could do about it if she wanted to disappear, sever all ties. As I said, she'd done it before.'

'Did you ever try to find her?'

'No.'

'Did anyone?'

'Not that I know of.'

'What about Matthew?'

'What about him?'

'Did you kill him?'

'I did not. He committed suicide.'

'Why?'

'It wasn't related to Gloria's disappearance. He was ill, confused, depressed, in pain. I did my best for him, but it was ultimately no use.'

'He shot himself, didn't he?'

'Yes.'

'With a Colt forty-five automatic.'

'Was it? I'm afraid I know nothing about guns.'

'Where did he get the gun?'

'The gun? I'm sorry, I don't follow.'

'Simple question, Ms Elmsley. Where did Matthew get the gun he shot himself with?'

'He always had it.'

'Always? Since when?'

'I don't know. Since he came back from the war, I suppose. I can't remember when I first saw it.'

'From the Japanese POW camp?'

'Yes.'

Banks got to his feet, shaking his head.

'What's wrong, Chief Inspector?' Vivian asked, hand plucking at the turkey flap at the base of her throat.

'Everything,' said Banks. 'None of it makes any sense. Think over what you've just told us, will you? You're telling us you believed that Gloria simply upped sticks and left without leaving a note, taking her clothes and a few personal belongings with her in a cardboard suitcase. If you're telling the truth, then whoever killed Gloria must have packed the suitcase and either taken it away with him or buried it somewhere to make it look as if she had run off. Then, five years later, your brother Matthew shot himself with an *American* service revolver he just happened to bring back from a Japanese POW camp. You write detective novels. Ask yourself if your Inspector Niven would believe it. Ask yourself if your readers would believe it.' He reached in his pocket. 'Here's my card. I want you to think seriously about our little talk. We'll be back. Soon. Don't bother yourself, we'll see ourselves out.'

Once they were out in the hot street again, Annie turned to Banks, whistled and said, 'What was all that about?'

'All what?'

'She was lying. Couldn't you tell?'

'Of course she was.' Banks looked at his watch. 'Want to grab a bite to eat?'

'Yes. I'm starving.'

They found a small café and sat outside. Annie had a Greek salad, and Banks went for the prosciutto, provolone and sliced red-onion sandwich.

'But why was she lying?' Annie asked when they had sat down with their food. 'I don't get it.'

Banks swatted a fly away from his sandwich. 'She's protecting herself. Or someone else.'

'After seeing her,' Annie said, 'I'd say she was probably big and strong enough to kill and bury Gloria. Fifty years ago, anyway. Did you notice her hands?'

'Yes. And Gloria Shackleton was petite.'

'So what do we do now?'

'Nothing,' said Banks. 'We'll leave her to stew overnight and then have another go at her tomorrow. I get the impression she has a lot on her conscience. There was a definite struggle going on inside her. If I'm right, she's near the end of her tether on this. It's amazing how guilt has a way of gnawing away at you through the small hours. She wants to tell the truth, but she still has a few things to weigh up, to settle with herself; she doesn't quite know how to go about it yet. It's like that character in her book.'

'The one you were reading on the train?'

'*Guilty Secrets*, yes.'

'And what did he do?'

Banks smiled and put his finger to his lips. 'That would be telling. I wouldn't want to spoil the ending for you.'

Annie thumped his arm. 'Bastard. And in the mean-time?'

'Vivian Elmsley's not going to do a runner. She's too old and too tired to run. She also has nowhere to go. First, we'll go see if we can find Francis Henderson.'

'And then?'

'If it's okay with you, I'd like to head out to Bethnal Green and see my son. His band's playing there. We've got a few things to talk over.'

'Of course. I understand. Maybe I'll go to the pictures. What about later?'

'Remember that naughty weekend you mentioned?'

Annie nodded.

'I don't know if you're still interested, but there's this discreet little hotel out Bloomsbury way. And it *is* Friday. Even CID get to work regular hours sometimes. We'll let Vivian Elmsley sleep on it. If she can.'

Annie blushed. 'But I didn't bring my toothbrush.'

Banks laughed. 'I'll buy you one.'

'Last of the big spenders.' She turned to him, the corner of her mouth twitching in a smile. 'I didn't bring my nightie, either.'

'Don't worry,' said Banks. 'You won't need your nightie.'

15

Over the next couple of weeks, as I continued to mourn Charlie, I noticed no improvement in Matthew's condition. He remained at Bridge Cottage with Gloria. I don't really think it mattered to him at that point *where* he was, if indeed he even *knew*, as long as his basic creature comforts were taken care of. There wasn't a day went by when I didn't spend time sitting with him, talking to him, though he never responded and hardly even acknowledged that he heard; he just stared off into space with that intense inward gaze of his, as if looking on horrors and agonies we could never even imagine in our wildest nightmares.

The London doctor was as good as his word and we soon got Matthew fixed up with Dr Jennings, a psychiatrist attached to the staff of the University of Leeds. He had his office in one of those big old houses in the streets behind the campus, houses where large families with servants used to live before the First War. Once a week, either I or Gloria would take him to his appointment, spend an hour or so looking around the shops, then collect him and take him home. Dr Jennings admitted to me privately on the third visit that he was having little success with straightforward methods and that he was considering narcosynthesis, despite the problems.

Matthew wasn't any trouble; he just wasn't there. He did, however, get into the habit of going to the Shoulder of Mutton every night and sitting alone in a corner drinking until closing time. Friends and neighbours who knew him would approach at first and ask how he was doing, but soon even those who remembered him most fondly left him alone. Once in a while he would have an angry outburst and smash a glass or kick a chair. But these were infrequent and soon passed over.

Gloria gave me a key, so I was able to pop in and out of Bridge Cottage whenever I could. She took as much time off from the farm as possible, of course, but she needed the income, and I don't think she could have borne the pain and the heartbreak of being with him twenty-four hours a day.

It was hard to believe that the war was almost over after all this time, even though you could smell victory in the air. The Americans had crossed the Rhine, and so had Monty's men. The Russians had Berlin surrounded. In April and May we started hearing the first rumours about concentration camps and human atrocities on a scale that had only been hinted at in the reports about Lublin the previous year. All the newspapers seemed at a loss as to how to describe what the liberating armies had found at places such as Belsen and Buchenwald. In addition to reading about Japanese cannibalism and the appalling tortures inflicted on prisoners like Matthew, I also read about the German camps where hundreds of thousands of people, or so we thought at the time, were shot, starved, beaten or made the subject of medical experiments.

Along with all our personal losses, such as Charlie, and Matthew's ruined health, it was impossible to take it all in. I don't think we even tried. We had suffered five years of fear and hardship and we were damned if we were going to be cheated out of the big party when it was all over.

●

Banks walked into the cavernous Victorian pub, all smoked and etched glass, brass fittings and mirrors. Somehow, it had survived the Blitz, as much of east London hadn't. Years of cigarette smoke had turned the high ceiling and the walls brown.

It wasn't far from Mile End, where Gloria Shackleton had been born. She may have even been here, Banks fancied, though he doubted it. People tended to stick very close to home, hardly venturing more than a street or two away except on emergencies or special occasions.

He and Annie had just been to Dulwich to see Francis Henderson, only to find him out. A neighbour told them she thought he had most likely gone on holiday, as he had cancelled his newspapers and milk. Banks slipped his card with a note through the letter-box and left it at that. What more could he do? As far as he was concerned, Francis Henderson wasn't guilty of any crime – or if he was, it was nothing to do with the Gloria Shackleton case. He wanted to meet Francis, mostly out of curiosity, to see what he was like and find out what he knew, if anything, but he could hardly justify the expense of a manhunt. The DNA would be helpful, but not essential.

It was half past five, and the band was due to start at six to draw in the after-work crowd. Not that anyone Banks could see in the audience looked as if they had been at work, unless they were all students or bicycle couriers. Brian stood on the low wooden stage along with the others, setting their equipment up. Maybe they were making money, but they clearly couldn't afford a crew of roadies yet. The mountain of speakers made Banks a little nervous. He loved music, and he knew that rock sometimes benefited from being played loud, but he feared deafness perhaps even more than blindness. Back in his

Notting Hill days, he had been to see just about all the major bands live – The Who, Led Zeppelin, Pink Floyd, Jimi Hendrix, The Doors – and more than once he had woken up the next day with ringing ears.

Brian waved him over. He looked a little nervous, but that was only to be expected; after all, he was with his mates and here was his old man coming to a gig. They would no doubt tease him about that. He introduced Banks to Andy, the keyboard player, Jamisse, the bassist, who was from Mozambique, and the percussionist, Ali. Banks didn't know if Brian had told them he was a detective. Probably not, he guessed. There might be a bit of pot around, and Brian wouldn't want to alienate himself from his friends.

'I've just got to tune up,' said Brian, 'then I'll come over. Okay?'

'Fine. Pint?'

'Sure.'

Banks bought a couple of pints at the bar and found an empty table about halfway down the room. Occasionally, feedback screeched from the amps, Ali hit a snare drum or Jamisse plucked at a bass string. It was a quarter to six when Brian, apparently satisfied with the sound, detached himself from the others and came over. Banks hadn't realized until now how much his son had changed. Brian wore threadbare jeans, trainers and a plain red T-shirt. His dark hair was long and straight, and he had a three or four days' growth around his chin. He was tall, maybe a couple of inches more than Banks's five foot nine and, being skinny, he looked even taller.

He sat down and scratched his cheek, avoiding Banks's eyes. Banks didn't want to launch right into the midst of things. The last thing he wanted was another row. 'I'm looking forward to this,' he said, nodding towards the stage. 'I haven't heard you play since you used to practise at home.'

Brian looked surprised. 'That was a long time ago, Dad. I hope I've got better since then.'

'Me, too.' Banks smiled. 'Cheers.' They clinked glasses, then Banks lit a cigarette.

'Still got that filthy habit, then?' said Brian.

Banks nodded. ''Fraid so. I've cut down a lot, though. What kind of music do you play?'

'You'll have to wait and hear it for yourself. I can't describe it.'

'Blues?'

'Not straight blues, no. That was the band I was with a couple of years ago. We broke up. Ego problems. Lead singer thought he was Robert Plant.'

'*Robert Plant*? I wouldn't have thought you'd have heard of him.'

'Why wouldn't I have? You were always playing "Stairway to Heaven" when you weren't playing bloody operas. The long version.' He smiled.

'I don't remember doing that,' Banks complained. 'Anyway, who writes the songs?'

'All of us, really. I do most of the lyrics, Jamisse does most of the music. Andy can read music, so he arranges and stuff. We do some cover versions, too.'

'Anything an old fogy like me would recognize?'

Brian grinned. 'You might be surprised. Got to go now. Will you be around after?'

'How long's the set?'

'Forty-five minutes, give or take.'

Banks looked at his watch. Six. Plenty of time. He was a short walk from the Central Line and it wouldn't take him more than an hour to get to Leicester Square. 'I don't have to leave until about eight,' he said.

'Great.'

Brian walked back up to the stage where the others looked ready to begin. The pub was filling up quickly now, and Banks was joined at his table by a young couple. The girl had jet-black hair, pale makeup and a stud in her upper lip. Was she a Goth? he wondered. But her boyfriend looked like a beatnik with his beret and goatee, and Brian's band didn't play Goth music.

Matching the fashions with the music used to be easy: parkas and motor-scooters with The Who and The Kinks; Brylcreem, leather and motorbikes with Eddie Cochran and Elvis; mop-tops and black polo-necks with The Beatles. And later, tie-dye and long hair with Pink Floyd and The Nice; skinheads, braces and bovver-boots with The Specials; torn clothes and spiky hair with The Sex Pistols and The Clash. These days, though, all the fashions seemed to coexist. Banks had seen kids with tie-dye *and* skinhead haircuts, leather jackets *and* long hair. He was definitely overdressed in his suit, even though he had put his tie in his pocket long ago, but he hadn't brought a change of clothes. Maybe he was just getting old.

The next thing he knew, the band had started. Brian was right; they played a blend of music difficult to pin down. There was blues underlying it, definitely, variations on the twelve-bar structure with a jazzy spring. Andy's ghostly keyboards floated around it all, and Brian's guitar cut through the rhythms clear as a bell. When he soloed, which he did very well, his sound reminded Banks of a cross between early Jerry Garcia and Eric Clapton. Not that he was as technically accomplished as either, but the echoes were present in his tone and phrasing, and he got the same sweet, tortured sounds out of his guitar. In each number, he did something a little different. The rhythm section was great; they kept the beat, of course, but both Jamisse and Ali were creative musicians who played off one another and liked to spring surprises. There was an improvisational, jazzy element to the music, but it was accessible, *popular*. For a few songs they were joined by a soprano saxophone player. Banks thought his tone was a bit too harsh and his style too staccato, but bringing the instrument in was a good idea, if only they could find a better player.

They paused between songs and Brian leaned into the microphone. 'This one's for an old geezer I know sitting in the audience,' he said, looking directly at Banks. The girl with the stud in her lip frowned at him and he felt himself blush. After all, he was the only old geezer in the place.

It took a few moments for Banks to recognize what the song was, so drastically had the group altered its rhythm and tempo, and so different was Brian's plaintive, reedy voice from the original, but what emerged from Banks's initial confusion was a cover version of one of his favourite Dylan songs, 'Love Minus Zero/No Limit'. This time it swung and swayed with interlaced Afro rhythms and a hint of reggae. Andy's organ imbued the whole piece, and Brian's guitar solo was subdued and lyrical, spinning little riffs and curlicues off the melody line.

Dylan's cryptic lyrics didn't really mesh with Brian's own songs, mostly straightforward numbers about teenage angst, lust, alienation and the evils of society, but they resonated in Banks the same way they did the first time he heard them on the radio at home all those years ago.

Before the song was over, Banks got a lump in his throat and he felt his eyes prick with tears. He lit another cigarette, his fourth of the day. He wasn't feeling emotional only because his son was up there on a stage, giving something back, but the song also brought back memories of Jem.

After Jem's death, no one came to the bedsit to claim his belongings. The landlord, whose musical taste ran more towards skiffle than sixties rock, let Banks take the small box of LPs. Being more into Harold Robbins than Baba Ram Dass, he also let Banks take the books.

Banks and Jem had listened to *Bringing It All Back Home* a lot, and the first time he took it out to play in Jem's memory he found a letter stuffed inside the sleeve. It was addressed to Jeremy Hylton at an address in Cambridge-shire. At first, he wasn't going to read it, respecting Jem's privacy, but as it usually did, his curiosity got the better of him. According to the postmark, the letter was dated five years earlier. He had known Jem was older than him, but not by how much. The letter was very short.

Dear Jeremy,

I'm writing to your parents' address because I know you're going home for Whitsuntide, and I won't be here when you get back. I'm sorry, I've been trying to tell you that it just isn't working between us, but you won't listen to me. I know this is the coward's way out, and I know it's hurtful to you, but I don't want the baby, and it's my body, my lifelong burden. I have made arrangements with a good doctor, so you needn't worry about me. I've got the money, too, so I don't need anything from you. After that I'm going a long way away, so don't even try to look for me. I'm sorry, Jeremy, really I am, but things were going badly between us before the pregnancy, you must know that. I don't know how you could think that having a baby would bring us closer together. I'm sorry.

Clara

Banks remembered being puzzled and upset by what he read. Jem had never mentioned anyone named Clara, nor had he ever mentioned where his family lived or what they did. He looked at the address again: Croft Wynde. It sounded posh. He hadn't a clue what Jem's background was; his accent was neutral, really, and he never spoke about the world he had grown up in. He was clearly educated, well read, and he introduced Banks to a whole world of writing, from Kerouac and Ginsberg to Hesse and Sartre, but he never said anything about having been to university. Still, everyone was reading that kind of stuff then; you didn't need a university course to read On the *Road* or *Howl*.

When Banks had finished thinking about what he'd just read in the letter, he made a note of the address. He decided to drive out to see Jem's parents. The least he could do was offer his condolences. His time in London had been lonely, and would have been a lot more so if not for the shared conversations, music and warmth of Jem's tiny bedsit.

The song finished and the audience's applause brought Banks out of his reverie.

'That was weird,' the kid next to him said.

The black-haired girl nodded and gave Banks a mystified glance. 'I don't think they wrote it themselves.'

Banks smiled at her. 'Bob Dylan,' he said.

'Oh, yeah. Right. I knew that.'

After that, the band launched into one of Brian's songs, an upbeat rocker about race relations. Then the first set was over. The band acknowledged the applause, then Brian came over. Banks bought them both another pint. The couple at the table asked Banks if he would please save their seats, then they wandered off to talk with some friends across the room.

'That was great,' Banks said. 'I didn't know you liked Dylan.'

'I don't, really. I prefer The Wallflowers. It used to drive me crazy when I was a kid and you played him all the time. That whiny voice of his and the bloody awful harmonica. It's just a nice structure, that song, easy to deconstruct.'

Banks felt disappointed, but he didn't let it show. 'I liked the ones you wrote, too,' he said.

Brian glanced away. 'Thanks.'

There was no point putting it off any longer, Banks thought, taking a deep breath. Soon the band would be starting again, and he didn't know when he would get another chance to talk to his son. 'Look,' he said, 'about what we said on the phone the other day. I'm disappointed, of course I am, but it's your life. If you think you can really make a go of this, I'm certainly not going to stand in your way.'

Brian met Banks's gaze, and Banks thought he could see relief in his son's eyes. So his approval *did* matter, after all. He felt curiously light-headed.

'You mean it?'

Banks nodded.

'It was just so boring, Dad. You're right. I screwed it up, and I'm sorry if I caused you any grief. But it was only partly because of the band. I didn't do enough work last year because I was bored by the whole subject. I was lucky to get a third.'

Banks had felt exactly the same way about his business-studies course – bored – so he could hardly get on his moral high horse. Well, he could, but he managed to put a rein on his parents' voices this time. 'Have you told your mother yet?'

Brian looked away and shook his head.

'You'll have to tell her, you know.'

'I left a message on her machine. She's always out.'

'She has to work. Why don't you go over and pay her a visit? She's not far away.'

Brian said nothing for a while. He swirled the beer in his glass, pushed back his hair. The place was noisy and crowded around them. Banks managed to focus and cut out the laughter and shouted conversations. Just the two of them on a floodlit island, the rest of the world a buzz in the distance.

'Brian? Is there something wrong?'

'Nah, not really.'

'Come on.'

Brian sipped some beer and shrugged. 'It's nothing. It's just Sean, that's all.'

Banks felt a tingling at the back of his neck. 'What about him?'

'He's a creep. He treats me like a kid. Whenever I go over there he can't wait to get rid of me. He can't keep his hands off of Mum, either. Dad, why can't you two get back together? Why can't things be the way they were?' He looked at Banks, brow furrowed, tears of anger and pain in his eyes. Not the cool, accomplished young man any more but, for a moment, the scared little kid who has lost his parents and his only safe, reliable haven in the world.

Banks swallowed and reached for another cigarette. 'It's not that easy,' he said. 'Do you think I didn't want to?'

'*Didn't?*'

'A lot's changed.'

'You mean you've got a new girlfriend?'

If it were possible to inflect the word with more venom

than Brian did, Banks couldn't imagine how. 'That's not the point,' he said. 'Your mother has made it quite clear, over and over again, that she doesn't want to get back together. I've tried. I did have hopes at first, but . . . What more can I do?'

'Try harder.'

Banks shook his head. 'I don't know,' he said. 'It takes two to do that, and I'm getting no encouragement whatsoever from her quarter. I've sort of given up on it. I'm sorry about Sean. Sorry you don't get along.'

'He's a plonker.'

'Yeah, well . . . Look, when you get a bit of free time, why don't you come up to Gratly? You can help me work on the cottage. You haven't even seen it yet. We can go for long walks together. Remember the way we used to? Semerwater? Langstrothdale? Hardraw Force?'

'I don't know,' said Brian, pushing his hair back. 'We're gonna be really busy the next while.'

'Whenever. I'm not asking you to put a date to it. It's an open invitation. Okay?'

Brian looked up from his beer and smiled that slightly crooked smile that always reminded Banks so much of his own father. 'Okay,' he said. 'I'd like that. It's a deal. Soon as we get a few days' break I'll be knocking on your door.'

A bass note and drum roll cut through the buzz of conversation as if to echo what Brian had said. He looked up. 'Gotta go, Dad,' he said. 'Be around later?'

'I don't think so,' said Banks. 'I've got work to do. I'll stick around for part of the set, but I might be gone before you're through. It's been great seeing you. And don't be a stranger. Remember my offer. There's a bed there for you whenever you want, for as long as you want.'

'Thanks, Dad. What's it they say? "Home's the place

where they have to take you in." Wish I knew where mine was. Take care.'

Banks stuck out his hand and Brian shook it. Then, feeling guilty, he checked his watch. Time to hear a few more songs before slinking off to keep his date with Annie.

•

One day Gloria came to me and asked if I would mind closing the shop for an hour or so and walking with her. She looked pale and hadn't taken her usual pains with her appearance.

It was the beginning of May, I remember, and it was all over but the shouting. Hitler was dead, the Russians had Berlin, and all the German troops in Italy had surrendered. It could only be days from the end now.

I closed the shop, as she asked, and we walked into Rowan Woods, leaving the road behind and wandering in the filtered green light of the new leaves. The woodland flowers were all in bloom, clusters of bluebells here and there, wild roses, violets and primroses. Birds were singing and the air was pungent with the smell of wild garlic. Now and then, I could hear a cuckoo call in the distance.

'I don't know what to do with him, Gwen,' she said, wringing her hands as we walked, close to tears. 'Nothing I do to try to reach him does any good.'

'I know,' I said. 'We just have to be patient. Let the doctor do his job. Time will heal him.' Even as I spoke them, I felt the triteness and inadequacy of my words.

'It's all right for you. He's not your husband.'

'Gloria! He's my brother.'

She put her hand on my arm. 'Oh, I'm sorry, Gwen, that's not the way I meant it. I'm just too distraught. But it's not the same. He's taken to sleeping on the Chesterfield now when he gets in from the pub.'

'You don't . . . I mean, he doesn't . . .?'

'Not since he came back. It's not fair, Gwen. I know I'm being selfish, but this isn't the man I married. I'm living with a stranger. It's getting unbearable.'

'Are you going to leave him?'

'I don't know what to do. I don't think I can. Brad is still pestering me to run off back to America with him as soon as his new orders come in. He says he might have to go out to the Pacific first – the war's not over there yet – but he says he'll send for me. Just imagine it, Gwen: Hollywood! A new life in the sunshine under the palm trees in a faraway magical land. A young, healthy, handsome, vigorous man who dotes on me. Endless possibilities of riches and wealth. I could even become a movie star. Ordinary people like you and me can do that over there, you know.'

'But?'

She turned away, eyes downcast. 'A dream. That's all. I can't go. Silly, isn't it? A few years ago I did exactly that. Walked away from a life I didn't want and ended up here.'

'But you'd lost your whole family then. You had nothing to stay for. Anyone can understand your doing that.'

'Haven't I lost Matt now?'

'It's not the same.'

'You're right; it's not. Anyway, I'd walked away even before I lost them.'

'What do you mean?'

She paused and touched my arm again lightly. 'There are things you don't know about me, Gwen. I haven't been a good person. I've done terrible things. I've been selfish. I've hurt people terribly. But I want you to know one thing. This is important.'

'What?'

'Matt is the only man I have ever truly loved.'

'Not Brad?'

'Not Brad, not . . . Never mind.'

'What were you going to say?'

Gloria paused and looked away from me. 'I told you, I've done terrible things. If I tell you, you must promise never to tell anyone else.'

'I promise.'

She looked at me with those blue eyes of hers. I was shocked that I hadn't noticed the tragedy in them before. 'I won't ask you to forgive me,' she said. 'You might not be able to do that. But at least hear me out.'

I nodded. She leaned back against a tree.

'When I was sixteen,' she began, 'I had a baby. I didn't love the father, not really. Oh, I suppose I was infatuated. George was a few years older than me, good-looking, popular with all the girls. I was advanced for my age and flattered by his attentions. We . . . well, you know all about it. We only did it once, but I didn't know anything about . . . you know . . . then, and I got pregnant. Our families wanted us to get married. George would have done it like a shot – he said he loved me – but . . . I *knew*, I *knew* deep down that it would be the worst mistake of my life. I knew if I married George I would be unhappy. He loved me then, but how long would it last? He drank, like they all did down on the docks, and I really believed it was just a matter of time before he would start beating me, looking upon me as his slave. I'd seen it in my own home. My own father. I hated him. That was why I wanted so desperately to escape. I used to listen to the wireless for hours trying to learn to speak the way I thought real people spoke. If my dad caught me, he'd either laugh at me or beat me, depending on how much he'd had to drink. So I left them all.'

'Where did you go?'

'To a friend's house. Not far away. I didn't know anyone from outside the East End, except for my Uncle Jack in Southend, and he'd have just sent me right back home.'

'And you were with this friend when your parents were killed?'

'Yes. I was heartbroken about Joe, my little brother, but my father can rot in hell as far as I was concerned. And my mother . . . she was harmless, I suppose, but she did nothing to stop him. In a way she was better off dead. She didn't have much of a life. I don't remember ever seeing her smile.'

'But what about the baby?'

Again, Gloria paused, as if struggling for words. 'I hated being pregnant. I was sick all the time. After I had Francis I got very depressed and I didn't . . . I didn't feel what they said a normal mother should. I'm ashamed to say it, but I didn't like holding him. I felt revolted that such a thing could have come out of me. I hated my own baby, Gwen. That's why I could never be a real mother to him or to anyone else.'

She sobbed and fell forward into my arms. I held her and comforted her as best I could. I didn't understand; I had no idea that a mother could *not* love her child; I knew nothing about postnatal depression in those days. I'm not sure that anybody did. My heart felt hot and too big for my chest. Sniffling, dabbing her handkerchief to her eyes, Gloria went on, 'Francis is alive. George's sister Ivy can't have any children of her own. They live on the canal. Her husband John's a lock-keeper. I know he's teetotal and I've met Ivy once or twice. They're decent people, not like the others. They'd got away and bettered themselves. They said they would take care of Francis. I knew he would be better off with them.'

'What did George say?'

'He already knew that whatever there had been between us was over – though it never stopped him trying – but he couldn't understand it when I didn't object to giving up Francis to Ivy and John. George is a simple man. Traditional. He believes in family. He believes a mother should love her baby. Simple as that. Of course, he agreed. He could hardly bring up Francis on his own. He said I would still be the boy's mother no matter what happened, that a boy needed a real mother to love. When I agreed without any fuss and said I didn't mind if they kept him for ever, George refused to believe me. That's what he always did when I had one of my "funny turns", as he called them. Refused to believe me. He wasn't a bad man, Gwen, that's not what I'm saying. It's me who's bad. I think he loved his son more than I did. He wanted to be a father as much as he could. But he got called up, of course, like all the rest. Anyway, he always thought I would change my mind. He's stubborn, the way some men are. He's already been up to see me once with Francis. He said he still loves me, urged me to go back. I told him I was married and we had an argument. He went off. But he'll be back, Gwen. He won't give up that easily.'

'Are you afraid of him?'

'I don't know. Maybe. A little. He's got a temper, like his own father. Especially when he's been drinking.'

I didn't know what to say.

'Say you don't hate me, Gwen, please! I couldn't bear it if you hated me. You're my only real friend.'

'Of course I don't hate you. I just don't understand, that's all.'

'I don't know if I do, either, but don't you see that's exactly why I *can't* leave, no matter what life is like with Matt? Because of what I did before. Oh, I have plenty of excuses: I was too young; it was a mistake; I wasn't in love; I thought I was cut out for better things. But that's just what they are: excuses. When it came right down to it, I was selfish; I was a coward. I'm not going to be a coward again. This is my punishment, Gwen. Don't you see? Matt is my penance.'

'I think so,' I said.

She smiled through her tears. 'Good old Gwen. I'll bet there aren't many in Hobb's End would give me that much credit, don't you think? I've heard their tongues wagging already.' She imitated the local accent. '"She'll be off," they say. "Off with one of them Yanks before he's been back ten minutes, you just mark my words." Well, I won't, Gwen. Let them talk. But I *won't.*'

'Are you and Brad still . . .?'

'Sometimes. Don't be angry. I tried to stop seeing him when Matt first got back, I really did, but when I found out that he couldn't . . . I mean . . . Brad brings me comfort from time to time and as long as Matt doesn't know . . . To be honest, though, he's more trouble than he's worth right now. I just can't keep him off the subject of running away together. It's all getting to be too much of a strain. I told him if he didn't stop pushing me I'd run off and leave the whole lot of you behind, him included.'

I can't say that I approved of Gloria's seeing Brad after Matthew had returned, but I said nothing. I only felt that way because I was being protective towards Matthew; I wasn't a moral busybody like Betty Goodall. These were extraordinary times and Gloria was an extraordinary woman.

She laughed. 'You know, I don't know what I'd do without PX. It's funny, isn't it, but in times like this, when things are so grim, it's the little things that give you a moment's cheer. A piece of beef, a new shade of lipstick, a little whisky, a packet of cigarettes. New stockings. He's a gem.'

'What about Billy Joe? Have you had any more trouble from him?'

'No, not really. I saw him the other day. I got the impression he was secretly pleased that Matt had come back and spoiled things for me and Brad. He had that look in his eye, too, as if he thought he had a chance of getting me in bed again. I don't think he gives a damn about what it's all doing to *me*.'

'Well, he wouldn't, would he? I can't say I ever did really trust him. He's got a nasty, violent streak, you know.'

'Billy Joe? Oh, I can handle him. He's nothing but a big child, really.' She leaned back against the tree. 'But you're right, he can be violent. I don't like that in a man.' She paused, averting her eyes. 'Look, Gwen, I don't know if I should be telling you this, but I have to talk to someone. I've been having a few problems with Michael.'

'Michael? Good Lord. You don't mean he's—'

'Don't be a fool, Gwen. The man's only interested in boys. The younger, the better. No. Well, I suppose I'll have to tell you now, but you mustn't say a word to anyone. Promise?'

'What a day for secrets. All right, I promise.'

'Last summer and autumn, you might have noticed I spent quite a bit of time at his studio.'

'Yes.'

'Guess what?'

'He was painting you?'

'Oh. You guessed!'

'Well, it wasn't difficult. I mean, he is an artist. But that's wonderful, Gloria. Can I see it? Is it finished?'

'Yes. And it's very good.'

'So what's wrong?'

'It's a nude.'

I swallowed. 'You posed in the *nude* for Michael Stanhope?'

She laughed. 'Why not? There certainly wasn't much chance of him trying to put his hands on me, was there? Anyway, the point is, I went over to see him yesterday and begged him not to exhibit it, or even to sell it privately, as long as Matthew is alive. I know he just seems to sit there like a zombie between going to the pub and drinking himself to sleep, but I just don't know how it would affect him. Or if it would. The thing is, I don't want to take the chance. You know what this village is like. Matthew's health is hanging by a thread already. Who knows if seeing a nude painting of his wife, done while he was suffering in a Japanese POW camp, won't send him right over the edge?'

'That sounds reasonable,' I told her. 'What did Michael Stanhope have to say?'

'Oh, he agreed in the end. But he's not happy about it. Thinks it's one of the best things he's done, blah-blah-blah, opens up a new direction for him. Says his career needs a boost and this could give it one. He also argued that Matthew wouldn't be any the wiser and that even if he *did* see it he wouldn't recognize who it was. He's probably right. I'm being silly.'

'But he did agree?'

'He complained a lot, but, yes, he agreed in the end. He likes to play the miserable cynic, but he's pretty decent, deep down. He's got a good heart.'

And there she finished. We walked back to Hobb's End enjoying the sound of the breeze through the leaves and the songs of the birds in the high branches.

I didn't see Gloria again until a couple of days later, on

the afternoon of the seventh of May, and by then everyone knew Germany had surrendered. The war was over and everywhere people started putting up flags and closing up shop.

The last party had begun.

•

'Enjoy the film?' Banks asked, when he met Annie outside the Leicester Square Odeon at nine o'clock. She had been to see the latest megamillion special-effects extravaganza by one of those highly touted directors who used to make television adverts.

'Not much,' said Annie. 'I suppose it had its good points.'

'What?'

'*The End*, for one.'

Banks laughed. Leicester Square was crowded with tourists, as usual. Street kids, buskers, jugglers, clowns and sword swallowers were all working hard to prise a quid or two out of the punters' pockets, while the pickpockets took an easier route. The Hare Krishnas were back in force, too. Banks hadn't seen them in years.

'How were things with your son?' Annie asked.

'We mended a bridge or two.'

'And the band?'

'Pretty good, though I suppose I'm biased. We'll go see them if they ever play up north, and you can make your own mind up.'

'It's a date.'

Banks took Annie to a small bistro-style restaurant he knew just off Shaftesbury Avenue. The place was busy, but they managed to get a table for two after a short wait at the bar.

'I'm starving,' said Annie as she squeezed herself into the chair between the table and the wall, twisting around and setting her packages down behind her. 'But I can see that eating with you is going to become a serious problem.'

'What do you mean?'

'This kind of place hardly caters to the vegetarian eater,' she whispered. 'Just look at the menu.'

Banks looked. She was right: lamb, beef, chicken, fish, seafood, but little in the way of interesting vegetarian dishes, other than salads. Still, as far as Banks was concerned, 'interesting vegetarian dish' was up there with 'corporate ethics' as far as oxymorons went.

'Sorry,' he said. 'Do you want to try somewhere else?'

She put her hand on his arm. 'No, it doesn't matter. Next time, though, it's *my* choice.'

'Visions of tofu and seaweed are already dancing before my eyes.'

'Idiot. It doesn't have to be like that. Indian restaurants do great vegetarian dishes. So do Italian ones. You didn't complain about the meal I made last week, did you?'

'It was delicate timing. I didn't want to offend you just before I made a pass.'

Annie laughed. 'Well, there's something to be said for honesty, I suppose.'

'I wasn't being honest. I was being facetious. It was a great meal. Dessert wasn't bad, either.'

'There you go again.'

'Anyway, you're right. Next time, it's your choice. Okay?'

'Deal.'

'How about some wine?'

They chose a relatively inexpensive claret – relatively

being the key word – and Banks went for the roast leg of lamb with rosemary, while Annie, pulling a martyred expression, settled for a large green salad and some bread and cheese. The waiter, who must have been imported from France along with the decor and food style, grunted with disapproval and disappeared.

Their food arrived quicker than Banks expected, and they paused until the waiter had gone. The lamb was tender and succulent, still pink in the middle; Annie turned her nose up at it and said her salad was okay. There was a tape of romantic dinner music playing in the background, and beyond the bustling waiters, the hum of conversation, clinking of cutlery and glassware, Banks could hear strains of the *andante cantabile* from Tchaikovsky's String Quartet Number 1.

After his talk with Brian, he felt as if a burden had been lifted from his mind. There were still problems – Sean, for one – but Brian would just have to learn to live with the way things were. Banks had to admit that this Sean sounded like a real prick. Not for the first time, he speculated about going over there and kicking the shit out of him. Really mature way to deal with the problem, he told himself. A lot of good that would do everyone concerned. The important thing at the moment was that he and his son were talking again. And from what he had heard, the kid had talent; he might make it in the business yet. Banks tried to imagine being father to a famous rock star. When he was old and grey, would Brian buy him a mansion and a Mercedes?

The candlelight brought out the slight wine flush on Annie's cheeks and filled her dark eyes with mysterious shadows and reflections. She was still wearing the same business suit she had worn that morning, but she had loosened her hair so that it tumbled over her shoulders in sexy waves. It would probably just brush against the tattoo over her breast.

'What are you thinking about?' she asked, looking up and pushing some stray hair back behind one ear.

Perhaps this was the moment, Banks thought, emboldened by his buoyant mood, to take the plunge anyway. 'Annie, can I ask you a personal question?'

She arched her eyebrows and Banks sensed a part of her scurry back into the shadows. Too late now. 'Of course,' she said. 'But I can't promise to answer it '

'Fair enough. What are you doing at Harkside?'

'What do you mean?'

'You know what I mean. It's a nowhere posting. It's the kind of place they send naughty boys and girls. You're bright. You're keen. You've got a future ahead of you if you want it, but you'll not get the job experience you need at Harkside.'

'I think that's rather insulting to Inspector Harmond and the others up there, don't you?'

'Oh, come on, Annie. You know as well as I do that's where they want to be. It's their choice. And it's not an insult that they choose the easy life.'

'Well, maybe it's what I've chosen, too.'

'Is it?'

'I didn't promise to answer your question.' Her mouth took on a sulky cast Banks hadn't seen before, the corners of her lips downturned; her fingers drummed on the tablecloth.

'No, you didn't,' Banks said, leaning towards her. 'But let me tell you something. Jimmy Riddle hates my guts. He isn't in the business of putting me in the way of anything I might find even remotely pleasant. Now, given that he knows who you are, and given that what's happened between us since could never in a million years fulfil his idea of the circle of hell he thinks he's cast me into, I find myself wondering why.'

'Or waiting for the punch line?'

'What?'

'Isn't that what you're saying? You think something's wrong. You think there's some sort of a plot to get you. You think I'm part of it.'

'That's not what I said,' said Banks, who realized guiltily that the thought had crossed his mind.

Annie turned her head away. Her profile looked stern.

'Annie,' he said, after a few moments' silence, 'I'm not saying I haven't been suspicious. But, believe me, the only reason I'm asking you now is because I've come to . . . Because I'm afraid you're being used, too.'

She glanced at him, not moving her head, eyes narrowed. 'How?'

'I don't know. What else can I say? Riddle had to have some reason for putting us together, something he thought would be unpleasant for me. I hope you agree that it hasn't turned out at all that way. Do you blame me for wondering what's going on?'

Her expression softened a little. She tilted her head. 'Perhaps this is it?' she suggested. 'What he expected.'

'In what way?'

'That we'd get together somehow, break the rules and get caught. That way he could be rid of both of us.'

'No, that's not enough. It's too easy. What we're doing isn't . . . I mean, it's only the same kind of thing he thought I was doing before. He has a far more sadistic mind than that. And to be honest, I don't think he's as clever as that, either. What is it the spies call it, a "honey trap"? Jimmy

Riddle feels no need to give me honey, only arsenic.'

'Jimmy Riddle didn't *give* you anything.'

'Okay. Sorry, you know what I mean.'

Annie shook her head slowly and the shadows danced through her hair. Dessert came, but she left it untouched for a while, then she seemed to come to some kind of decision. She picked up her spoon, tasted a mouthful, then looked at Banks. 'All right,' she said. 'I'll tell you, but only if you'll tell me something, too.'

•

Yorkshire weather has a very ironic sense of occasion. On the eighth of May, 1945, it poured down all morning, despite the fact that this was VE Day. By early afternoon, the rain was tapering off and we were left with clouds and light showers. I closed the shop at lunchtime and Gloria came down from the farm. That afternoon, leaving Mother and Matthew together, the two of us bicycled into Harkside and went to see a matinée of *Phantom of the Opera* at the Lyric.

All over Harkside we heard excited talk of parties and dances; people on the streets were hanging streamers and putting out flags. All the church bells were ringing. We bumped into some people we knew on the village green and they suggested we come back that evening to the celebration dance at the Mechanics Institute, to be followed by a street party. The Americans from Rowan Woods would be there, they assured us. We said we would try to come as soon as we had done some celebrating in Hobb's End first.

After tea, the sun lanced through the raggedy black clouds, sending shafts of light into Rowan Woods. Soon, all the clouds had gone and it was as beautiful a warm May evening as you could ever ask for, the grass green and moist from the rain.

Gloria gave me a pair of stockings she had got from PX, and helped me with my makeup. First, we spent an hour or so at the Hobb's End street party. People had brought little tables and put them together in a row all along High Street. It was a dull affair, though, as there were so few people left in the village, and the whole thing felt more like a wake than a celebration.

Mother sat at one of the tables with her friend, Joyce Maddingley, and she told us to behave ourselves when we slipped away to Harkside with Cynthia Garmen. Matthew refused to come out of the cottage at all; he wouldn't budge. Mother said not to worry, she would look in on him from time to time and make sure he was comfortable.

The three of us set off, taking the long way round on the roads so we wouldn't get our ankles and court shoes wet in the grass.

Harkside was much wilder than Hobb's End. Most of the soldiers and airmen from the nearby bases had come, so there were men in uniform all over the place. From the minute we got to the village green, we were swept into a mad whirl. It didn't take Gloria long to meet up with Brad. Billy Joe was there with his new girlfriend, and PX was tagging along, too. I felt a sudden pang of missing Charlie, then I tried to enter into the spirit of victory.

First we went to the dance. There was a big band playing Glenn Miller, Duke Ellington and Benny Goodman tunes, and people kept throwing coloured streamers across the dance floor.

Out in the streets, between songs, we could hear fireworks and people whooping with joy. At one point, when I was dancing a waltz with Billy Joe and trying to explain how Matthew took up so much of our time, I noticed Gloria and Brad slip outside. It was over an hour before I saw them again, and Gloria had retouched her makeup. She couldn't hide the ladder in one of her stockings, though. I resolved to say nothing. Since our talk a few days ago, I had thought a lot about Gloria and what she was sacrificing to care for Matthew, and I decided that she deserved her little pleasures, as long as she remained discreet about them.

The band was still playing when we piled out into the street. There was a huge bonfire on the village green and people were singing, dancing and setting off fireworks all around it, just like Guy Fawkes Night. The air was full of the acrid smell of smoke and the sky full of exploding colours. Someone had made up an effigy of Hitler and they were heaving it on top of the fire. Everyone was drunk. I don't know where Cynthia got to. I was with a group of people, and I could see Gloria and Brad through the flames having an argument. At least they looked as if they were shouting at one another, but I couldn't hear for all the singing and explosions.

At one point we went to someone's house and drank some whisky. It was a wild party. People were packed in like sardines and I felt hands all over my body as I pushed my way through the crowd to go to the toilet. The house was full of smoke and it stung my eyes. Gloria was dancing, but I couldn't see Brad. Someone fell down the stairs. At one point, I'm sure I saw a Negro dancing on the piano. PX was drunk, eyes closed almost to slits, and I saw him try to kiss a woman. She pushed him away and his face turned red. Then he stormed off. Cynthia reappeared with a sailor in tow. I don't know where she'd managed to find him, as we were at least fifty miles from the coast. It was almost one o'clock and we were back out on the street again when I told Cynthia and Gloria it was time for us to go.

The three of us were a little drunk. It was the emotion

and excitement as much as the alcohol, I think. We didn't even bother trying to cadge a lift but danced and laughed our way home instead. Hobb's End was quiet as a tomb.

Bridge Cottage was dark. I went in with Gloria to make sure everything was all right and we heard Matthew snoring on the Chesterfield as soon as we opened the door. Gloria put her finger to her lips and gestured me towards the kitchen. With the door shut, she poured us both another whisky, which was probably the last thing we needed. When she put her handbag down on the countertop, it slipped off and fell on the floor. I bent over to pick it up for her and noticed how heavy it was. Curious, I opened the clasp and nearly fainted when I saw a gun. Gloria turned with the bottle and glasses in time to see me.

'You weren't supposed to see that,' she said.

'But, Gloria, where did you get it?'

'From one of the Americans at the party. He was so drunk he won't miss it.'

'Not Brad?'

'No, not Brad. Nobody we know.'

'But whoever he was, he'll get into serious trouble.'

'I don't think so. Anyway, I don't care. It serves him right for being so careless, doesn't it? He was trying to put his hand up my skirt at the time.'

'What do you want a gun for?'

She shrugged. 'War souvenir.'

'Gloria!'

'All right!' She was whispering as loudly as she could, so as not to wake Matthew. 'Maybe I just feel a bit more comfortable knowing it's there, that's all.'

'But Matthew's harmless. He wouldn't hurt you.'

She looked at me as if I were the biggest fool she had ever met. 'Who said anything about Matthew?' she said, not even bothering to whisper, then she took the gun from me and put it in one of the kitchen cupboards behind the meagre supplies of tea and cocoa. 'Now will you have that drink?'

•

Vivian Elmsley was having a difficult time. Close to midnight she was sitting in her sparse living room, her third gin and tonic in her hand and some dreadful rubbish on television. Sleep refused to come. Her mysterious caller hadn't rung again, but she still regarded the telephone as an object of terror, ever on the verge of destroying what little peace of mind she had left. She wondered if she should have told the police about him. But what could they do? It was all so vague.

She had known the police would find out who she was and come for her eventually – she had known that the minute she knew Gloria's body had been dug up – but she hadn't been prepared for the effect that their visit would have on her. They knew she was lying; that was obvious. Chief Inspector Banks wasn't a fool; he knew that nobody who had been as close to the people involved as Vivian had could know so little as she had professed. And she wasn't a good liar.

Why *hadn't* she told them the truth? Fear for her own well-being? Partly. She didn't want to go to gaol. Not at her age. But would they really prosecute her after so long, no matter what the law books said? When they heard her full story, would they really go ahead and put her through the pain and humiliation of a trial and a gaol sentence? Were there not such things as mitigating circumstances?

She didn't know what they would do, and that was the problem. When it comes right down to it, we fear the unknown more than anything else.

On the other hand, if she didn't tell them, then they would never find out the truth about what happened that night. Nobody else knew. Living or dead. If she was careful, Vivian could take her secret to the grave with her.

Only one thing was certain: the police would be back; she had seen it in the chief inspector's eyes. Tonight she had to make her decision.

•

'You're right about one thing,' Annie began. 'I'm in Harkside because I was a naughty girl.'

'What happened?'

'Depends on your point of view. They called it an initiation rite. I called it attempted gang rape. Look, I'm not going to tell you where it was or who was involved. All I'm saying is it happened in a big city, and it wasn't in Yorkshire. Okay?'

'Okay. Go on.'

'This is hard.' Annie spooned down some more chocolate mousse. 'Harder than I ever thought.'

'You don't have to.'

She held up her hand. 'No. I've come this far.' The waiter drifted by and they both ordered coffee. He didn't give any indication that he had heard, but the coffee arrived in a matter of moments. Annie pushed aside her dessert bowl; it was empty. She played with the spoon.

'It was when I made DS,' she said. 'Nearly two years ago now. I'd done my stint in uniform there, and I wasn't sure where they were going to send me next. But I didn't care. I was happy just to be back in CID again after . . . well, you know what I mean.'

'Patrols? Shifts?'

'Exactly. Anyway, there was a celebration at the local

coppers' pub. The "private" room upstairs. I suppose I was dead chuffed with myself. I'd always wanted to be one of the boys. Naturally, we closed the place. It got down to just four of us left. One of them suggested we go back to his place and drink some more and we all agreed that was a good idea.'

She was speaking very quietly so that no one would hear. There wasn't much chance of that. The restaurant was packed now, full of laughter and loud voices. Banks had to strain to hear her, and somehow that made what he heard so much more affecting, that it was delivered in not much more than a whisper. He sipped some black coffee. Through the occasional hush in the background noise, he could hear the lush, romantic strains of Liszt's 'Liebestraum'.

'We were already three sheets to the wind,' Annie went on, 'and I was the only female. I didn't know the others well. Things were getting pretty wild. I suppose I should have known what was coming by the way the conversation was going in the taxi. You know. Flirting. Sexual innuendoes. Casual touches. That sort of thing. Call me naive. The other three kept making veiled references to initiation ceremonies, and there was a lot of nudging and winking going on, but I'd been drinking, too, and I didn't really think much of it until we'd been at the flat for a while and drunk some more. One of them grabbed my arm and suggested we go in the bedroom, said he could tell I'd been wanting it all night. I laughed and brushed him off. I thought he was joking. He got angry. Things got out of hand. The other two grabbed me and held me down over the back of the settee while he pulled up my skirt, tore off my underwear and raped me.'

Banks noticed that Annie was gripping the spoon

handle tightly in her fist. Her knuckles were white. She took a deep breath and went on. 'When he'd finished, they started rearranging positions, and I knew what was coming. It was like there were no individuals in the room any more; they were all caught up in this blind male lust and I was the object of it. It overwhelmed everything, conscience . . . decency. It's hard to describe. I was terrified, but I'd sobered up pretty damn quickly over the last few minutes. Soon as I got my chance, I slipped free from their grip, kicked the one who'd raped me hard as I could in the balls and caught another on the jaw with my elbow. I'd done some martial-arts training. I don't know, maybe if I hadn't been drinking, my reflexes would've been quicker, my coordination a bit more accurate. Anyway, I managed to put two of them out of action long enough to make it to the door. The third one caught me, and by then the one I'd hit with my elbow was up again. They were sweating, red in the face, and mad as hell. One of them punched me in the stomach and the other hit me hard in the chest. I went down. I think I was sick. I thought that was it again, that they were going to do what they'd intended, but they'd lost their bottle. It had all got too real for them. Suddenly they were individuals again, each looking out for number one, and they knew what they'd done. It was time to close ranks. They called me a lesbian bitch, told me to get out and if I knew what was good for me I wouldn't say a word. I left.'

'Did you report it? For crying out loud, Annie, you'd been *raped*.'

She laughed harshly. 'Isn't that so easy for a man to say? To sit in judgment over what a person in that position should or shouldn't do? To be *oh so* understanding about it?' She shook her head. 'You know what I did? I walked the city most of the night in a complete daze. People must have thought I was crazy. I wasn't drunk any more, I was plain cold sober, but I was drained, numb, I couldn't feel anything. I remember trying to feel some sort of emotion, thinking I ought to feel anger or pain. I was really angry at myself for not feeling angry. I know it sounds impossible, but that's the only way I can describe it. There was nothing. Just a deep cold numbness. When I finally found myself back at my flat, I had a long hot bath. Hours I must have lain there, just listening to the radio. News. Weather. Normal life. That was soothing somehow. And do you know what? I understand every one of those rape victims who never comes forward to report the crime.'

Banks could see tears glistening at the corners of her eyes, but as she noticed him looking, she seemed to draw them back in.

'What happened?' he asked.

'By morning I'd got a bit of nerve back. First thing, I went to see the chief super to tell him what they did. Know what?'

'What?'

'Two of the others had got there before me and queered the pitch. Pre-emptive strike. They told the super there'd been a spot of bother at a party last night, just an initiation rite that got a bit out of hand, nothing serious, like, but that I'd probably be coming to complain, making up all sorts of wild allegations. According to them I'd got totally rat-arsed and gone way over the top, telling them I'd take them all on and then backing down when it came to it.'

'And he believed them?'

'Their word against mine. Besides, they were all mates. People around the station already thought I was a bit weird. Some of them even used to call me the "Hippie

Cop" behind my back, or so they thought. You know, I did yoga and meditation and I didn't eat meat and watch sport on the telly and talk about sex all the time. That's enough to make you seem weird, for a start. I also had a reputation around the place for not being very interested in men, just because I didn't find any of the blokes I worked with particularly attractive. I'm sure they all thought I was gay. That hits a certain kind of male the wrong way. He thinks all a lesbian needs is a big hard cock in her and she'll soon come to her senses. And, of course, he's just the bloke to give it to her. As it happened, I did have a boyfriend at the time, nothing serious, but I kept my private life separate from the Job.'

'Did you tell the chief super what really happened?'

'Yes. Every detail.'

'What was his reaction?'

'He looked very embarrassed.'

'Didn't he initiate some sort of inquiry?'

'Like I said, their word against mine. And apart from a pair of torn knickers, I'd pretty much destroyed the evidence, hadn't I?'

'Even so . . . these days . . .'

'What about these days?'

'Annie, there are procedures to guard against these things.'

'Procedures? Hah. Tell that to the chief super. He also told me, by the way, that no one wants that sort of internal investigation going on. It hurts everyone, and it especially hurts the force. He said the officers involved would be disciplined for their excessive high spirits, but it would be best for all concerned if it went no further than his office. He told me to put the good of the force as a whole above my own selfish concerns.'

'You agreed to that?'

'What choice had I?'

'He should have been kicked off the force.'

'I'm glad you agree.'

'So all that happened was they got a slap on the wrist and you got shipped off to the middle of nowhere?'

'Not quite. Not immediately.' Annie looked down into her coffee cup. 'There were complications.'

'What complications?'

She wrapped a strand of hair around her forefinger and stared down into her cup for a few more seconds before looking up at Banks. 'Remember, I told you I kicked one of them in the balls?'

'Yes? What about it?'

'Something went wrong. They had to operate. He lost them. Both of them. The devil of it was that he was the youngest of the three and the most junior in rank. Just a DS himself and only married a year. Planning a family.'

'Jesus. I can imagine you were a popular woman around the station after that.'

'Exactly. For a while I thought of leaving the force altogether. But I'm stubborn. The chief super suggested it might be better for all concerned if I transferred somewhere else. He said he'd look into some possibilities, and they came up with Harkside. Millicent Cummings was immediately sympathetic, of course, and I think our ACC used to work with Chief Constable Riddle.'

'So Riddle knows all about what happened?'

'He knew my chief super's side of the story, yes.'

'Which means that to him you're a troublemaker? A ball-busting lesbian bitch?'

Annie mustered a crooked smile. 'Well, I've been called worse, but thanks for the compliment.'

'No wonder he put us together. Never was much of a judge of character, though, wasn't Jimmy Riddle. I'm surprised he got as far as he did. I'm sorry about what happened to you, Annie. Sorrier than I can say.'

'All water under the bridge.'

'I'm also amazed you would even consider getting involved with me, a DCI. I would have thought that what happened would have been enough to put you off your fellow coppers for life, especially senior CID ranks.'

'Oh, come on, Alan. You do yourself a disservice. Do you really think I'm that stupid? That's insulting to both of us. I've never, not for one moment, seen any similarity whatsoever between you and the men who assaulted me. I didn't even know you were a DCI when I first saw you, and I fancied you right away. The thing is, I thought I'd faced up to it and got on with my life.'

'Haven't you? You seem to be doing all right to me.'

'I've been in hiding. I shut myself away. I thought I was over it and that I'd simply chosen a quieter life. The celibate life of reflection and contemplation. There's a laugh. I thought that was my choice, but it was really a result of what happened, of not facing up. But I'd already practised meditation and yoga, had done for years, and I came from a small seaside town, so it seemed only natural to dig in my heels at Harkside.'

'You aren't happy there?'

'What's happiness? Something you measure in relation to unhappiness? I get by. I have my nice safe little life at the centre of the labyrinth, as you so astutely pointed out. I have few possessions. I go to work, I do my job, and then I come home. No social life, no friends. I certainly didn't dwell on what had happened to me. I didn't have recurring nightmares about it. I suppose I was lucky that way. And

I felt no guilt about what happened to that young DS. That might sound harsh, but I've probed myself deeply enough to know it's the case. He was egged on by his superiors, true, caught up in the spirit of drunken revelry. I suppose some people might excuse him by saying he was too weak to resist or he simply lost his rag, temporary insanity. But I was the one he raped. And I was the one who saw his face while he was doing it. He *deserved* all he got. The only real shame is that I didn't get the chance to do it to the other two as well.' She paused. 'But let's face it, I haven't even done any serious detective work in Harkside. I know I'm good at the job – I'm quick, I'm bright and I'm hard-working – but until this case came along it's all been break-ins, vandalism, the occasional runaway kid.'

'And now?'

She shrugged. 'Now I don't know. You're the first person I've told since it happened.'

'You didn't tell your father?'

'Ray? No. He'd be sympathetic, but he wouldn't understand. He didn't want me to join the police to start with.'

'A hippie artist? I shouldn't think he did.'

'He'd probably have led a protest march to New Scotland Yard.' She paused and played with her hair again. 'Now it's your turn. Remember, you promised to tell me something, too.'

'Did I?'

'Uh-huh.'

'What do you want to know?'

'Did you really punch Jimmy Riddle?'

Banks stubbed out his cigarette and slipped his credit card on the little tray the waiter had left. It was snatched up almost immediately. The theatres had come out now and people were queuing at the restaurant door.

'Yes,' he said. 'I did.'

She laughed. 'Bloody hell. I wish I'd been there.'

The waiter finished with the card in no time flat. Banks signed the receipt, Annie gathered her packages and they walked out into the busy West End evening. The streets were packed with people standing drinking outside the pubs. Four men blocked the pavement, all talking and laughing at once into a mobile phone. Banks and Annie skirted them. Across the street, Banks saw a drunken woman in a tartan schoolgirl mini, black thigh stockings and fuck-me shoes try to carry on an argument with her 'boyfriend' and walk at the same time. She failed, teetered at the edge of the pavement and went sprawling in the gutter, cursing all the way. Sirens blared in the distant city night.

'Don't laugh at this,' said Annie, 'but that time . . . you know, in the backyard, when you put your arm around me?'

'Yes.'

'Well, I was sort of expecting something might happen, and I didn't know if I was ready for it yet. I was going to tell you I was a lesbian. Just to let you down lightly, to make you think it wasn't anything personal, you know, that it wasn't that I didn't fancy you or anything, but that I just didn't go for men. I'd got it all worked out.'

'Why didn't you?'

'When the time came, I didn't want to. Believe me, I was probably just as surprised as you were about what happened. Just as scared. I know I invited you to my house and fed you drinks, but I really wasn't planning to seduce you.'

'I didn't think you were.'

'I was going to offer you the couch.'

'And I would have accepted gracefully.'

'But when it came to it, I wanted you. I was terrified. It was the first time since the night I've just told you about. But I wanted to do it as well. I suppose I wanted to overcome my fear. Sometimes it's the only way.'

They walked along Charing Cross Road, past all the closed bookshops, and crossed Oxford Street. As they turned on to Great Russell Street, Annie slipped her arm through Banks's. It was only the second time they had had any little intimate physical contact in public, and it felt good: the warmth, the gentle pressure. Annie leaned her head a little so it rested on his shoulder; her hair tickled his cheek.

Neither of them had been to the hotel yet; Banks had simply phoned earlier to book a room and said they would be arriving late. It was only a small place. He had stayed there twice before while on police business in London – both times alone – and had been impressed by the general cleanliness and level of service, not to mention the reasonable rates.

They passed the dark mass of the British Museum, set back behind its railings and courtyard, then crossed Russell Square. Conversation and laughter carried on the night air from a pub round the corner. A couple walked by, arms wrapped around one another.

'Here we are,' said Banks. 'Did you buy a toothbrush?'

'Yup.' Annie held up one of her bags. 'And a new pair of jeans, new shoes, a skirt and blouse, undies.'

'You really did go shopping, didn't you?'

'Hey. It's not often I get to the big city. I bought a nightie, too.'

'I thought I said you wouldn't need one.'

She laughed and moved closer. 'Oh, don't worry. It's

only a *little* nightie. I promise you'll like it.' And they walked up the stone steps to the hotel.

•

I couldn't stop thinking about the gun. Usually, the way the scene ran in my mind was that Gloria shot Matthew first and then herself. The images were so vivid I could even see the blood gush from their wounds. Finally, I determined I had to do something.

As I said, I had a key to Bridge Cottage. It wasn't that Matthew locked himself in, but he sometimes wouldn't bother getting up to answer the door. Most of the time he was in a sort of comatose state from alcohol anyway. When he wasn't at the pub he was sipping whisky at home. Whisky that Gloria got from PX.

So the next time it was Gloria's turn to take Matthew to see Dr Jennings in Leeds, I let myself in. Even if someone saw me, it wouldn't seem at all strange because I was in and out of Bridge Cottage all the time and everyone in the village knew about Matthew's condition.

I found the gun in the same place Gloria had left it: behind the cocoa and tea in the kitchen cupboard. I put it in the shopping bag I had brought with me, put the cupboard back in order and left. I didn't know how long it would take her to miss it, but the best I could hope for was that by the time she did she wouldn't feel the need for it any more and would realize what a favour I had done her.

We can be such fools for love, can't we?

16

It was about eleven o'clock on Saturday morning when Banks and Annie arrived back at Vivian Elmsley's building. Before Banks could even press the buzzer, the door opened and Vivian almost bumped into them.

'Going somewhere, Ms Elmsley?' asked Banks.

'You?' She put her hand to her heart. 'I didn't think . . . so soon . . . I was just . . . you'd better come in.'

They followed her upstairs to the flat. She was carrying a large buff envelope, which she dropped on the hall table as she entered the room. Banks glanced at it, saw his name and the Eastvale station address on it.

She turned to face them as they entered her living room. 'I suppose I should thank you for coming back,' she said. 'You've saved me the postage.'

'What were you sending me?' Banks asked. 'A confession?'

'Of sorts. Yes. I suppose you could call it that.'

'So you *were* lying yesterday?'

'Fiction's my trade. Sometimes I can't help it.'

'You should know the difference.'

'Between what?'

'Fiction and reality.'

'I've learned to leave that to the most arrogant among us. They're the only ones who seem to think they know everything.' She turned, walked back to the hall and picked up the envelope. 'Anyway,' she went on, handing it to Banks, 'I'm sorry for being flippant. I've found this whole thing extremely difficult. I tend to hide behind language when I'm frightened. I'd like you to grant me the favour of taking this away with you and reading it. I had a copy made this morning. If you're worried about my fleeing from justice, please don't. I'm not going to run anywhere, I promise you.'

'Why the change of heart?'

'Conscience, would you believe? I thought I could live with it, but I can't. The telephone calls didn't help, either. In the early hours of the morning, I arrived at the end of a long struggle, and I decided to tell the truth. What you do with it once you know is up to you. I'd just rather do things this way than answer a lot of questions at the moment. I think it will help you understand. Of course, you'll have questions eventually. I have to be in Leeds next week to do some book signings, so you'll soon have the opportunity. Will you allow me this much, at least?'

It was an unusual request, and if Banks were to go by the book, he wouldn't let a murder suspect hand him a written 'confession', then go away and leave her to her own devices. But it was time for a judgment call. This had been an unusual case right from the start, and he believed that Vivian Elmsley wasn't going anywhere. She was in the public eye, and he didn't think she had anywhere to run, even if she wanted to. The other possibility was suicide. It was a risk, to be certain, but he decided to take it. If Vivian Elmsley wanted to kill herself rather than suffer through a criminal trial that cost the taxpayers thousands and drew the media like blood draws leeches, who was Banks to judge her? If Jimmy Riddle found out about it, of course, Banks's career wouldn't be worth a toss, but since when had he let thoughts of Jimmy Riddle get in his way?

'You mentioned telephone calls,' he said. 'What do you mean?'

'Anonymous calls. Sometimes he says things, others he just hangs up.'

'What kind of things does he say?'

'Nothing, really. He just sounds vaguely threatening. And he calls me Gwen Shackleton.'

'Have you any idea who it might be?'

'No. It wouldn't be too difficult for anyone to find out my real name, and my number's in the directory. But why?'

'What about the accent? Is it American?'

'No. But it's hard to say exactly what it is. The voice sounds muffled, as if he's speaking through a handkerchief or something.'

Banks thought for a moment. 'We can't really do anything about it. I wouldn't worry too much, though. In most cases people who make threatening phone calls don't confront their victims. That's why they use the phone in the first place. They're afraid of personal contact.'

Vivian shook her head. 'I don't know. He didn't sound like one of those heavy breathers or nutcases. It seemed more . . . personal.'

'Perhaps your line of work attracts one or two crackpot fans?' Banks suggested. 'Someone who thinks he's giving you an idea for a story, or helping you know what it's like to experience fear. I honestly wouldn't worry too much, but you should get in touch with your local police station as soon as possible. They'll be able to help. Do you have any contacts there?'

'Yes. There's Detective Superintendent Davidson. He helps me with my research.'

'Even better. Talk to him.' Banks held up the envelope. 'We'll do as you ask,' he said, 'but how do we know this is the truth and not just more fiction?'

'You don't. Actually, it's a bit of both, but the parts you'll be interested in are true. You'll just have to take my word for it, won't you?'

•

The day it happened began like any ordinary day; if any day could be deemed ordinary in those extraordinary times. I opened the shop, took in the ration coupons, apologized for shortages, made lunch and tea for Mother and settled down to an evening's reading and the wireless. The Americans were having a farewell party up at the base that night, as they had heard they would be moving out in a matter of days. We had been invited, but neither Gloria nor I had felt like going. Somehow, that part of our lives seemed over. Charlie was dead and Gloria had made it clear to Brad, after their last fling on VE Day, that she was sticking with Matthew and it would be best if they didn't see each other any more.

I'd like to say I felt some sort of premonition of disaster, some sense of foreboding, but I didn't. I was distracted and found it hard to concentrate on Trollope's *The Last Chronicle of Barset*, but I had a lot on my mind: Charlie's death, Matthew's illness, Gloria's problems, Mother.

I wouldn't normally have gone to Bridge Cottage so late in the evening except that Cynthia Garmen had dropped off some parachute silk on her way to Harkside. I hadn't seen Gloria for two or three days and I thought she might appreciate a small gift; she had been very drawn and depressed since VE Day and hadn't been taking care of herself at all. I can't say that I heard any small voice telling me to go; nor can I recollect any great feeling of apprehension, any involuntary shudder or burning of the ears. I couldn't concentrate on my book, and Gloria was on my mind; it was as simple as that.

This is where my diary stops, but however much I have tried over the years to expunge the events from my memory, I haven't been able to succeed.

It was just after ten o'clock and Mother had gone to bed. Distracted, I put my book aside and fingered the silky material. I thought the prospect of a new dress to make might cheer Gloria up. I was also feeling guilty over stealing the gun, I suppose, and I wanted to know whether she had noticed it missing yet. If she had, she certainly hadn't said anything.

I assumed Matthew would still be at the Shoulder of Mutton, so I thought I would call in there first and persuade him to walk home with me. Even though he didn't communicate, I believed that he knew who I was and knew that I loved him. I also think he felt comfortable being with me. As it turned out, he had been asked to leave a little earlier because he had had one of his little tantrums and broken a glass.

I walked down the dark, deserted High Street to Bridge Cottage. Over the river I could hear music and laughter from the Duke of Wellington, where, it seemed, the VE Day celebrations were still going on over a week after the day itself. Moonlight silvered the flowing water and made it look like some sort of sleek, slinking animal.

There was light showing between the curtains in Bridge Cottage. New curtains, I noticed, now we didn't have to worry about the blackout, or even the dim-out, any more. I knocked at the door but no one answered. I knocked again.

I didn't think Gloria would be out; she rarely went out

in the evenings except to the pictures with me. She certainly wouldn't go out and leave the lights on. Besides, Matthew should be there. Where else would he have gone after being ejected from the Shoulder of Mutton?

I knocked again.

Still nothing.

I put my key in the lock, turned it and entered, calling out Gloria's name.

There was no one in the living room but I noticed a strong smell of whisky. I called out Gloria's name again, then thought I heard a movement in the kitchen. Puzzled, I walked over and when I got to the doorway I saw her.

Gloria lay on the flagstone floor, legs and arms splayed at awkward angles like a rag doll a sulking child has tossed aside. One of her little fists was curled tight, as if she were about to hit someone, except for the little finger, which stuck out.

There wasn't a lot of blood; I remember being surprised at how little blood there was. She was wearing her royal-blue dress with the white lace collar, and the stains on the material looked like rust. They were all over the place: breast, stomach, ribs, loins. Everywhere the royal-blue dress was stained with blood, yet very little of it had flowed to the floor.

Not far from her body lay a broken whisky bottle, the source of the smell I had noticed earlier. Bourbon. An unopened carton of Lucky Strikes sat on the countertop. Above it, the cupboard was open and tea and cocoa had spilled all over the counter and the floor nearby, along with knives and forks from the cutlery drawer.

Beside her, holding a bloody kitchen knife, Matthew knelt in a small pool of blood. I went over to him, took the knife gently out of his hand and led him through to his armchair. He accompanied me as meekly as a weary, defeated soldier goes with his captors and flopped back in the chair like a man who hasn't slept for months.

'Matthew, what happened?' I asked him. 'What have you done? You've got to tell me. Why did you do it?'

I gave him pencil and paper, but he just drew in on himself and I could tell I would get nothing out of him. I put my hands on his shoulders and shook him lightly, but he seemed to shrink away, blood-stained thumb in his mouth. I noticed more blood on the cuffs of his white shirt.

I don't know how long I tried to get him to communicate something, but in the end I gave up and went back to the kitchen. I wasn't thinking clearly. I suppose if I assumed anything at all, it was that someone must have told him there was nasty gossip going around about what his wife got up to while he was out. I already knew that he had had a tantrum in the Shoulder of Mutton and I guessed that one way or the other, it had set off the explosion that had been building in him the way pressure builds in a boiler; now Gloria was dead and Matthew was empty of his rage.

As I stared down at poor Gloria's body, still half unable to believe what had happened, I knew I had to do something. If anyone found out about this, Matthew might be hanged, or, more likely, found insane and put in the lunatic asylum for the rest of his days. However difficult his life was right now, I knew he wouldn't be able to bear that; it would be purgatory for him. Or worse. I would have to care for him from now on.

As for Gloria, my heart wept for her; I had come to love her almost as much as I loved Matthew. But she was dead. There was nothing I could do for her. She had no other family; I was the only one who knew her story; it didn't matter now what happened to her. Or so I told myself.

I still had some vestiges of religion in me back then, though most of it had disappeared during the war, especially after Matthew's death and resurrection, which seemed to me a very cruel parody of Easter, but I didn't particularly give any thoughts to Gloria's immortal soul, a proper burial or things like that. The church didn't come into it. I didn't think of what I was doing in terms of right or wrong; nor did I really consider that I would be breaking the law. All I could think about was what to do to protect Matthew from all the prying policemen and doctors who would torment him if word of this got out.

Did I think of Matthew as a murderer? I don't think I did, though there was undoubted evidence of this at my feet. In a strange way, I also saw Gloria as my partner in wanting to protect Matthew from further cruelty and suffering. She wouldn't want him to go to gaol, I told myself; she wouldn't want him put away in a lunatic asylum. She had sacrificed so much to protect him. His comfort and ease were all she had lived for after his return; he was her penance, after all, and that was why she would never leave him; that was why she was dead. *Gloria wanted me to do this.*

I offer no more excuses. The blackout cloth was still rolled up below the windows in the living room, where it had been left after I helped Gloria take it down a couple of months ago. I carried it into the kitchen and gently rolled Gloria on to it, then I wrapped it around her as tightly as a shroud. Before I had finished I bent over, kissed her gently on the forehead and said, 'Goodbye, sweet Gloria. Goodbye, my love.' She was still warm.

Where could I hide her? The only place I could think of was the old outbuilding they never used. In the light of a small oil lamp I started to dig the hole. I wanted to make it deeper, but I couldn't manage more than about three or four feet before exhaustion overcame me. I went back to the house, where Matthew hadn't moved, and managed to find the energy to drag out the roll of blackout cloth and drop it in the hole. There was no one around. The cottage next door was empty and there was neither a light nor a sound out back. Only the black night sky with its uncaring stars.

With tears running down my cheeks, I shovelled back the earth. Some heavy stone slabs stood propped against the wall and I levered them down on top of the makeshift grave. It was the best I could do.

That left only the inside of the house. First, I swept up the broken glass, the spilled tea-leaves and cocoa powder, and put the tins back in the cupboard. As I said, there was very little blood and I managed to scrub that off the floor easily enough. There might have been minute traces left but nobody would be able to tell what they were. If things went according to plan, nobody would even look.

I say 'plan' now, but it was just something I had come up with while burying Gloria. I had to explain where she had gone.

After I had managed to lead Matthew upstairs and wash and undress him, I put him to bed. I packed his bloody shirt and trousers in a small suitcase and added as many of Gloria's favourite clothes as I could fit in. Then I went and picked up her personal odds and ends and put them in the suitcase too.

After checking the kitchen carefully to make sure that I had collected everything of importance and cleaned up to the best of my ability, I wrote a note on the same paper I had got out for Matthew earlier. Gloria's childlike handwriting and style were easy to imitate. After that, carrying the suitcase, I took the back way to the shop. I didn't want to leave Matthew, God knows, but what else could I do? Things had to appear more or less normal. He didn't seem aware of what was happening and I had no idea how he would face the next day, whether he would remember what he had done, feel remorse or guilt. Would he even notice she was gone?

Early the next day I went to Bridge Cottage, found Matthew still in bed, 'found' the note and proceeded to tell everyone we knew, including Mother, that Gloria had run away during the night because she couldn't bear her life with Matthew any more. She said she loved him, and she always would, but she couldn't be responsible for her actions if she stayed. Then I showed them the note, which said exactly that. She ended by saying that we shouldn't go looking for her because we would never be able to find her.

There was no reason to call in the police. Everyone believed the note without question. Hadn't Gloria already told me she had heard people predicting that she would run off with a Yank at the first opportunity? Of course, she hadn't gone off with a Yank, and Brad, for one, would know that, but I would cross that bridge when I came to it.

I gave up Bridge Cottage, sold the contents, including the radiogram and the records Gloria loved so much, and brought Matthew back to live with us above the shop.

One evening when Mother was at Joyce Maddingley's, I took Matthew's blood-stained clothes and Gloria's dresses and burned them in the grate. I cried as I watched all those beautiful dresses catch fire. The black-red-and-white-checked Dorville dress she had bought in London; the black velvet V-neck dress with the puff sleeves, wide, padded shoulders and red felt rose that she had worn to our first dance with the Americans at Rowan Woods; her fine underwear. I watched it all flare and twist, then collapse into ashes. I disposed of her trinkets in Leeds the next time I went there on shop business. I just stood on Leeds Bridge at the bottom of Briggate and dropped them one by one into the River Aire.

As I had expected, it was Brad who gave me the most trouble. On his last day at Rowan Woods, he came to the shop and pestered me with questions. He just couldn't believe that Gloria had simply left. If she wanted to go, he argued, then why didn't she go with him? He had asked her often enough. I told him I thought she wanted to escape from everyone; she needed a completely new start. He said she could have had that in California. Again, I argued that living with him in Los Angeles would always have felt tainted to her because of the circumstances in which it came about. No matter what, she would still have been Matthew's wife.

It hurt him deeply, which I hated to do, but he had to accept what I said in the end. After all, she had told him she didn't want to see him any more after VE Day. Absolutely no one suspected anything like the truth. The 448th Bomber Group moved out of Rowan Woods and I heard nothing more from Brad. It was all over.

Michael Stanhope expressed sorrow that such a beautiful spirit had left the community. He said something about Hobb's End having glimmered briefly, then turned dark again. He was free to sell the nude now, not that I ever saw or heard anything of it again. Perhaps it wasn't as good as he thought it was.

As for Matthew, he never really showed any sign that anything was different. He was a little more withdrawn, perhaps, but he went on with the same drinking and staring into space as before. I had to stop the visits to Dr Jennings, of course. Who knew what narcosynthesis might draw out of Matthew, should it work? Though the doctor protested, I think he was quite relieved. Doctors don't like failures and Dr Jennings had been getting nowhere with Matthew.

Soon, we were hearing rumours that the village was to be sold as a reservoir site, and when I looked around, it didn't surprise me.

Hobb's End had turned into a ghost village.

I hadn't noticed it happening because of other matters, but hardly anyone lived there any more. Those who had come back from the war had had a taste of more interesting locales or had been trained for jobs they could only get in the cities. Even the women, who had perhaps gained the most in terms of employment, were heading off for factory jobs in Leeds and Bradford. The mill closed. Buildings fell into disrepair. Old people died. Finally, there was nobody left.

A strange incident occurred before we left for Leeds, though Gloria had, in a way, predicted it. One day, a man in a brown demob suit came into the shop with a little boy of about eight or nine and asked to see Gloria. I knew immediately who they were, though I didn't want to admit it to them.

'Are you a relative?' I asked him.

'No,' he said. 'Nothing like that. Just an old friend, that's all. I was passing this way, so I thought I'd look her up.' He sounded rather sad, and I noticed he had a Cockney accent, just as Gloria did when she let her guard slip. And, of course, nobody just *passes* Hobb's End way.

I asked him more questions, to show interest and politeness, but I could get nothing more out of him. Most of all, I wanted him to be satisfied by my explanation of Gloria's disappearance; I certainly didn't want him to come back and pester Matthew and me.

I needn't have worried. When he left, he just said, 'If you do see her again, tell her George called, will you?' He looked down at the boy. 'Tell her George and little Frankie dropped by and send their love.'

I assured him I would. The little boy had said nothing at all, but I felt him staring at me the whole time, as if he were etching my features on to the tissue of his memory. On impulse, I gave him a quarter ounce of gumdrops, quite a rarity, as sweets were still rationed. He thanked me solemnly and then they left.

The following week, Matthew, Mother and I moved to Leeds and Hobb's End ceased to exist. Our life in Leeds was not without incident, but that's another story.

•

'If we go to the CPS with Vivian Elmsley's story,' Banks said to Annie, 'they'll laugh us out of the office.'

It was Sunday morning, and they were both lounging about Banks's cottage rereading Vivian Elmsley's manuscript and drinking coffee. It had been against Annie's better judgment to take up Banks's suggestion of spending the weekend together. What she had meant to do after getting in her car at York was drive straight home and spend the rest of the weekend in blissful, idle solitude. But next Friday, she was taking two weeks' holiday and was planning to go down to stay with her father at the colony. Best enjoy some time together now, she thought. She would have plenty of time for long, lonely coast walks when she got to St Ives.

So, on Sunday morning, she was lying back in Banks's front room, barefoot, wearing shorts, her feet dangling over the arm of the settee, reading about Gwen Shackleton's war.

'Why would they laugh?' she said. 'It's a confession of sorts, isn't it? She does admit to interfering with the body. That makes her an accessory.'

'I very much doubt that any judge would admit the manuscript as evidence. All she has to do is say it's fiction. The Crown knows that. It's a load of bollocks, Annie. Just as well the woman writes fiction and doesn't have to solve *real* crimes.'

'But she uses real names.'

'Doesn't matter. Any decent lawyer would make mincemeat of it as a confession to aiding and abetting. Look at what we've got. We've got a woman in her seventies who presented us with a manuscript she wrote nearly thirty years ago hinting that she covered up a murder she thinks her brother committed over twenty years before that in a village that no longer exists. Add to that she makes her living writing detective fiction.' He ran his hand across his head. 'Believe me, the CPS have enough of a backlog already. They can't even keep up with today's crimes, let alone put staff on prosecuting yesterday's on evidence so flimsy a puff of wind would blow it away.'

'So that's it? We go no further? She goes scot-free?'

'Do you *want* to see her in prison?'

'Not particularly. I'm just playing devil's advocate. To be honest, it looks as if the poor woman's suffered enough to me. What a blighted life.'

'I don't know. She's had a fair amount of success.'

'Sometimes that doesn't mean as much as those who don't have it seem to think it does.'

'Well,' Banks went on, 'we always knew the case might end nowhere. Matthew Shackleton is dead. I think Vivian Elmsley wanted to get what she did off her chest. She *wanted* us to know. Not for our sake, so we could solve the mystery, but for hers, so she wouldn't have to bear the burden alone any more. The discovery of Gloria Shackleton's skeleton was a tremendous catalyst for her. It pushed her towards some sort of catharsis, and when we found out who she was it was just a matter of time. I would imagine now it seems less important to her to protect Matthew's memory than it did all those years ago. He's in no position to hang or spend his days in a psychiatric institution.'

'She still committed a crime, though.'

'Yes, but she's not the killer.'

'Unless she's lying in the story.'

'I don't think so. She did what she did to protect her brother, who had already suffered terribly in the war. And she kept the secret to protect herself and Matthew's name. If she'd called the police at the time, it's almost certain he would have been convicted of Gloria's murder. Unless . . .'

'Unless what?'

'Unless he didn't do it. There are a number of things in Gwen's version that bother me. Look at the scenario. Gwen walks into the cottage and sees Matthew bent over Gloria's body, a kitchen knife in his hand. So far so good?'

Annie nodded.

'She also notices that Gloria's fist is clenched and the little finger appears to be broken. Right?'

'Right.'

'And Gloria's body is still warm.'

'Yes.'

'Which means that the clenched fist wasn't caused by rigor mortis; it was caused by a cadaveric spasm. What if the killer, the *real* killer, had been trying to take something out of Gloria's hand when he was disturbed by Matthew coming home, chucked out of the pub early

for causing a ruckus? Something that might have incrim-
inated him.'

'The button?'

'It makes sense, doesn't it?'

'It's certainly possible.'

Banks shook his head. 'But they'd still probably have
arrested Matthew, depending on the copper in charge.
Remember, most of the bright young detectives were at
war. The crazy husband would have looked the most
obvious suspect, and the button, even if they had found it,
could have been explained away. From Vivian's point of
view, if Matthew had even a scrap of sanity left before all
hell broke loose, he wouldn't have had any by the time it
was over. So she committed a crime. And a serious one at
that. But not only would the CPS throw it out; if it ever got
as far as a jury, *they* would chuck it out too. Think of the
sympathy angle. Any decent barrister – and I'll bet you
Vivian Elmsley can afford a more-than-decent barrister –
would have the whole courtroom in tears.'

'So what do we do next?'

'We could hand the report to Jimmy Riddle and get on
with our lives.'

'Or?'

'Or look into those one or two little inconsistencies I
mentioned. For a start, I'm not convinced that—'

The doorbell rang.

Banks went to answer it. Curious, Annie let the
manuscript drop on her lap. 'Maybe it's that hard-working
DS Hatchley of yours?'

'On a Sunday morning? That'd be stretching credibility
too far.'

Banks opened the door. Annie heard a woman's voice,
then Banks stepped back slowly and in she walked.

Blonde hair, black eyebrows, attractive, good figure, nicely dressed in a pastel skirt and a white blouse.

She noticed Annie out of the corner of her eye and turned. For a moment, she seemed speechless, a slight flush suffusing her pale complexion, then she moved forward and said, 'Hello, I don't think we've been introduced.'

Feeling foolish, Annie took the manuscript off her stomach and stood up. 'Annie Cabbot,' she said. 'DS Cabbot.' She felt acutely aware of her bare legs and feet.

'Sandra Banks,' said the other. 'Pleased to meet you.'

Banks closed the door and stood behind them looking uncomfortable. 'DS Cabbot and I were just discussing the Thornfield Reservoir case,' he said. 'Maybe you've read about it?'

Sandra looked down at Annie's bare feet, then gave Banks a withering glance. 'Yes, of course,' she said. 'And on a Sunday morning, too. Such devotion to duty.' She started moving back towards the door.

Annie felt herself blush to her roots.

'Anyway,' Banks gibbered on, 'it's really nice to see you. Would you like some coffee or something?'

Sandra shook her head. 'No, I don't think so. I just came up to Eastvale to see to some things at the community centre. I'm staying with Harriet and David. While I was in the area, I thought I'd drop by to get some papers signed and talk to you about our son, but it'll do some other time. No hurry. Don't let me interrupt your brainstorming session.'

As she spoke she grasped the handle and opened the door. 'Nice meeting you, DS Cabbot,' she said over her shoulder, and with that she was gone.

Annie stood facing Banks in silence for a few moments,

aware only of her fast and loud heartbeat and burning skin. 'I didn't know what to say,' she said. 'I felt foolish, embarrassed.'

'Why should you?' said Banks. 'I've already told you, Sandra and I have been separated for almost a year.'

But you still love her, Annie thought. Where did that come from? She pushed the thought away. 'Yes, I know. It was just a shock, meeting her like that.'

Banks gave a nervous laugh. 'You can say that again. Look, let's have some more coffee and go sit outside, okay? Put Vivian Elmsley and her problems on the back burner for a while. It's a beautiful day, shame to waste it staying indoors. Maybe this afternoon we can go for a long walk? Fremlington Edge?'

'Okay.' Annie followed him outside, still feeling dazed. She sat on a striped deck-chair, feeling the warmth of the canvas against the backs of her bare thighs, the feeling that always reminded her of summers in St Ives. Banks was reading the *Sunday Times* book section, trying to pretend everything was just fine, but she knew he was rattled, too. Perhaps even more than she was. After all, he had been married to the woman for more than twenty years.

Annie stared into the distance at a straggling line of ramblers walking up Witch Fell, whose massive shape, like a truncated witch's hat, took up most of the western skyline. Crows wheeled over the heights.

'Are you okay?' Banks asked, looking up from his paper.

'Fine,' she said, mustering a smile. 'Fine.'

But she wasn't. She told herself she should have known how fleeting happiness was; how foolish it is to expect it at all, and what a mistake it is to allow oneself to get too

close to anyone. Closeness like that stirs up all the old
demons – the jealousy, the insecurity; all the things she
thought she had mastered. The only possible outcome is
pain. A shadow had blotted out her sun, just the way
Witch Fell obscured the sky; a snake had crawled into her
Eden. What, she wondered, would be the cost?

17

Vivian's manuscript haunted Banks long after he had read it. There were so many inconsistencies, so many branches in the road to Gloria's murder. On Wednesday, when they still hadn't found Gloria's son, he started thinking about the trip George and Francis Henderson had made to try to find Gloria after the war. Gwen had denied her, in a way, and that set Banks thinking about his visit to Jem's parents.

As vividly as if it were yesterday, he remembered the late May afternoon when he drove his ailing VW beetle to Cambridgeshire in search of Jem's parents. He didn't even know why he was making the journey, and more than once he thought of turning back. What could he say? What right had he to intrude on their grief? After all, he had hardly known Jem, knew nothing about his life. On the other hand, they had been friends, and now his friend was dead. The least he could do was offer his condolences and tell them they had a son they should be proud of, no matter how ignominious his death.

Besides, he was curious to see what sort of background Jem came from.

It was a fine day and Banks drove with his window down through the North London suburbs and into open countryside, the wind blowing through his hair, which at that time was well over his collar. He turned off the main road just south of Cambridge. A number of images of the drive came back: Tim Buckley on the radio singing 'Dolphins' just outside Saffron Walden; a whitewashed pub wall; a herd of cows blocking the road as they were moved, udders swinging, from field to field by a slow farmer, unconcerned about the minor traffic jam he was causing; the air smelling of warm straw and manure.

Banks stopped in the village newsagent's and asked for directions to the Hylton house. The shopkeeper looked suspicious, as if she thought he was out to rob the place, but she told him. The house – mansion, rather – stood at the end of an unpaved drive about half a mile from the village centre It was originally Tudor, by the look of it, but was crusted with so many centuries of additions, like barnacles on the bottom of a boat – a conservatory here, a garage there, a dormer window – that it seemed on the verge of buckling under its own weight.

Banks sat in his car and stared for a moment, hardly able to take in that *this* was where Jem came from. He stubbed out his cigarette. The area was quiet, except for a few birds singing and the sound of someone talking on a radio deep inside the house. Surely they must have heard him arrive? Especially with the odd hiccuping sounds his beetle was making those days.

Banks got out of the car and looked around. Beyond a neatly trimmed croquet-size lawn the land dipped away, revealing a patchwork landscape of green and brown fields under a canopy of blue sky as far as the eye could see. A few small copses and a church steeple were all that broke the monotony. This was the *old* England, the place of order, of the labourer at work in the fields and the lord at ease in his manor. It was a far cry from Peterborough and Notting Hill. Banks had visited the countryside before, of course, but he had never been to a house so opulent, had never *known* anyone who came from such a house. The old class insecurities began to surface, and if he had been wearing one, he would probably have knocked on the door cap in hand. He felt self-conscious of his accent even before he opened his mouth.

A sweet-smelling honeysuckle bush stood beside the old oak door, and Banks could hear the bees droning around the blossoms. He banged the heavy knocker against the wood. The sound echoed through the countryside and sent a nearby flock of starlings flapping off into the sky.

It seemed for ever before Banks became aware of someone approaching the door, a creak of a floorboard perhaps, or swish of a skirt. When it opened a crack, he found himself looking at a dark-haired woman with high cheekbones and sunken brown eyes. She seemed old to him back then, when he had hardly turned twenty, but he realized that she was probably only in her early forties, about the same age he was now.

She raised an eyebrow. 'Yes? What is it?'

'Mrs Hylton?'

'I'm Mrs Hylton. What can I do for you?'

'I've come about Jem.'

She frowned. 'Who?'

'Jem. Sorry: Jeremy. Your son.'

A man appeared behind her, and she opened the door all the way. He had white hair, a red face, and watery pale blue eyes. 'What is it, darling?' he asked, putting his hand on the woman's shoulder and frowning at Banks. 'Who is he? What does he want?'

She turned to her husband with a puzzled expression on her face. 'Someone come about Jeremy.'

Banks introduced himself. 'I lived across the hall from

Jeremy in Notting Hill,' he said. 'We were friends. I just wanted to come and say I'm sorry about what happened.'

'I don't understand,' said the man. 'Our son died a long time ago. It's a bit late to be coming round with condolences, don't you think?'

'Jem? *Jeremy* Hylton? I am at the right house, aren't I?'

'Oh, yes,' said the woman. 'But the thing is, our Jeremy died *five years* ago.'

'But . . . but it was only about a month ago. I mean, I knew him. I *found* him. We *are* speaking about the same person, aren't we? Did Jeremy have a brother, perhaps?'

'We had only one son,' the man said. 'And he died five years ago. Now, if you don't mind, I think my wife has been disturbed enough, don't you? Good day.'

He started to close the door.

Banks made one last-ditch attempt. He stuck his foot in the door and said, 'Please, you don't understand. Jem died last month. I don't mean to upset you, but—'

Mr Hylton opened the door a fraction and Banks slipped his foot out. 'If you don't go away and get off our property immediately, I'm going to call the police,' he said. 'Is that clear?' And this time he slammed the door shut before Banks could move.

For a few moments, Banks stared at the weathered oak, his mind spinning. He saw a curtain move and assumed they were watching, ready to phone the police, so he got in his beetle, turned and drove away.

At the end of the drive, an elderly man wearing a cloth cap waved him down. Banks stopped, and the man leaned down to the open window. He had about five days' growth on his cheeks, and his breath smelled of beer. 'What you been bothering them there for, then?' he asked.

'I wasn't bothering them,' Banks said. 'I just came to

offer them my condolences on their son's death.'

The man scratched his cheek. 'And what did they say?'

Banks told him, all the time glancing in his mirror to see if the Hyltons had followed him down the drive.

'Well,' the man said, 'see, as far as they're concerned, their Jeremy died the day he dropped out of university and went off to London to be one of them drug-smoking hippies.' He scrutinized Banks for a moment, as if trying to make up his mind where *he* fitted in the scheme of things. 'I noticed they had the police round a while back and wondered what it were all about. Jeremy's *really* dead now, then?'

'Yes,' said Banks after another quick glance in the mirror.

'Drugs, were it?'

'Looks that way.'

'I'm sorry to hear it. I've known him since he were a babe in arms. Nice young lad he were till he went bad. He were going to be a doctor, like his dad. At Cambridge he was you know. I don't know what went wrong.' He pointed with his thumb back at the house. 'They never recovered. Don't talk to anyone. Don't have any visitors.' He shook his head slowly. 'Poor little Jeremy. They never even gave him a funeral service.' Then he wandered away along the road shaking his head and muttering to himself.

Banks was left alone at the intersection of the drive and the road, with only the birdsong and his own gloomy thoughts of estrangement and denial for company. He had a pretty good idea of what went wrong for Jem, having read Clara's letter, but it seemed that nobody wanted to know.

Horns blaring on Market Street broke into his reminiscences.

Now he had another denial on his mind. Jem's parents had convinced themselves their son had died five years before he really did, just because he had disappointed their expectations. Gwen Shackleton told George and Francis Henderson that Gloria had run away when she was well aware that Gloria was actually dead and buried out back. Somehow, the two denials seemed like curious mirror images to Banks.

A knock at the door interrupted this train of thought. Sergeant Hatchley walked in. 'Coffee break?'

Banks looked up and dragged himself back from a long distance. 'What? Oh, yes.'

'You all right, sir? You look a bit pale.'

'Fine. Just thinking, that's all.'

'Can be painful, thinking. That's why I try to avoid it.'

They walked across Market Street to the Golden Grill for toasted tea-cakes and coffee. Rain had finally come to the Dales, and the place was almost empty. Doris, the proprietor, claimed they were only the fourth and fifth customers to pass through her door that day.

'Does that put us in line for summat special, like?' Hatchley asked. 'Maybe a free cuppa?'

She slapped his arm and laughed. 'Get away with you.'

'Worth a try,' said Hatchley to Banks. 'Never ask, never get. I used to know a bloke years back who claimed he asked every girl he met if she'd go to bed with him. Said he only got slapped in the face nine times out of ten.'

Banks laughed, then he asked, 'Have you heard anything on that nationwide inquiry you put out yet?'

'Something came in this morning, as a matter of fact,' said Hatchley. 'That's what I wanted to talk to you about. Lass called Brenda Hamilton. Bit of a tart, by all accounts. Not a prossie by trade, but she wasn't averse to opening her legs for anyone who looked like he had a bob or two to spare. Anyway, she was found dead in a barn.'

'MO?'

'Strangled and stabbed. In that order.'

'It certainly *sounds* promising.'

Hatchley shook his head. 'Don't get your hopes up. There's a couple of problems.'

'What problems?'

'Location and time frame. It happened near Hadleigh, Suffolk, in August 1952. I only mentioned it because it was the same MO.'

Banks chewed on his tea-cake and thought it over. 'Any suspects?'

'Naturally, the farmer who owned the barn came in for a close look, but he had a watertight alibi. I'd have sent for more details, but . . . well, it's not likely to be connected with our business, is it?'

Banks shrugged. 'Wouldn't do any harm to ask a few more questions.'

'Maybe not. But that's seven years after Gloria Shackleton was killed. It's a long gap for the kind of killer we're looking at. It also happened in another part of the country.'

'There could be reasons for that.'

'And I doubt there'd be any American Air Force personnel around by then, would there? I mean the war was long over. Most of them went off to the Pacific after VE Day and the rest buggered off home as soon as they could.'

'You're probably right, Jim, but let's be thorough. Get on to East Anglia and ask them for more details. I'll ask DS Cabbot to contact the USAFE people again and see if she can find out anything.'

'Will do.'

Back in his office, Banks put off phoning Annie at Harkside, smoking a cigarette instead and staring out of the window. A warm slow rain fell on the market square, darkening the cobbles and the ancient market cross. It wasn't bringing much relief; the air was still sticky and humid. But slowly the clouds were gathering, the humidity increasing. One day soon it would break and the heavens would open. There were only a couple of cars parked in the square, and the few people in evidence ambled around under umbrellas looking gloomily at the shops. Radio Three was playing a programme of British light music, and Banks recognized the signature theme of 'Children's Favourites'.

The reason he was avoiding talking to Annie was that Sunday had gone badly after Sandra's visit. Both Banks and Annie had been on edge, conversation awkward, and she had eventually left just after lunch, forgoing the afternoon walk, claiming she had things to see to back in Harkside. They hadn't spoken to each other since.

At the time, Banks had not been sorry to see her go. He was more upset than he had let on by Sandra's visit, and it annoyed him that he felt that way. After all, *she* had a new boyfriend. *Sean.* Why did she have to turn up just then, when everything was going so well? What gave her the right to burst in and act so shocked that *he* was seeing someone, knocking everyone's feelings out of kilter? How would she like it if he just dropped in on her and Sean, without even phoning first? And he *had* wanted to talk to her, especially after his little heart-to-heart with Brian. Now God only knew when he would get the chance again.

He also realized that Sandra had been upset by what she saw, too. The withering coolness and sarcastic tone were her way of reacting to her own discomfort. He still had feelings for her. You can't just lose your feelings that quickly for someone you loved for so long. Love lost or rejected may first turn to hate, but only over time does it become indifference.

Finally, he plucked up the courage and picked up the phone. 'How's it going?' he asked.

'Fine.'

'You sound distracted.'

'No, I'm not. Just a bit busy. Really. It's fine.'

Banks took a deep breath. 'Look, if it's about Sunday, I'm sorry. I had no idea Sandra was going to turn up. I also didn't think it would have so much of an effect on you.'

'Well, you don't always know about these things till they happen, do you? As I said, I'm fine. Except I've got a lot on my plate right now. What's on your mind?'

'Okay, if that's how you want to play it. Get on to your military contacts again and see if you can find out anything about US Air Force presence in Suffolk in 1952.'

'What about it?'

'Find out if there were any bases left, for a start. And if there were, which was the nearest one to Hadleigh. If there was one, I'd also like a list of personnel.'

'Right.'

'Can you do it today?'

'I'll try. Tomorrow at the latest.'

'Annie?'

'What?'

'Can't we get together and talk about things?'

'There's nothing to talk about. Really. Look, you know I'm off home on holiday in a couple of days. I've got a lot to do before I go. Maybe when I get back. Okay? In the meantime, I'll get that information to you as soon as I can. Goodbye.'

Feeling more depressed than ever after that pointless conversation, Banks glanced at the pile of paper beside the computer on his desk: SOCO search results, post-mortem, forensic odontology. None of it contradicted what they had previously estimated; nor did any of it tell him anything more.

What would have happened if Gwen had done as she should and reported finding Gloria's body? A good copper might have asked around and not simply tried to pin the murder on Matthew. And maybe not. Too late for asking questions now; they were all dead except Vivian. Poor Gloria. She saw Matthew as her *penance*. Somehow that told Banks more about her than anything else.

And what if Vivian's ending was the real lie? The ultimate irony. What if Gwen herself had committed the murder?

•

Vivian Elmsley put her book down as the train pulled out of Wakefield Westgate on Thursday. It would only be a few more minutes to Leeds now, and built up the whole way: a typical Northern industrial landscape of shabby red-brick housing estates, low-rise office buildings, sparkling new shopping centres, factory yards full of stacked pallets wrapped in polythene, kids fishing in the canal, stripped to the waist. The only untypical thing was the sticky sunlight that seemed to encase everything like sugar water.

The publisher's rep was supposed to meet Vivian at the station and accompany her to the Metropole Hotel, where she would be staying until Sunday. She had book signings in Bradford, York and Harrogate, as well as in Leeds, but it made no sense to move everything lock, stock and barrel from one hotel to another every day. The cities were close enough together. The rep would drive her around.

Not that Vivian needed any help to find the hotel; the Metropole wasn't more than a couple of hundred yards from City Square, and she knew exactly where it was. She had stayed there with Charlie the time they went to Michael Stanhope's exhibition in 1944. What an evening they had made of it. After the show, they went to a classical concert and then to the 21 Club, where they had danced until late. That was why she had asked to stay there again this trip. For memory's sake.

She was nervous. It wasn't anything to do with this evening's reading at Armley Library, or the Radio Leeds interview tomorrow afternoon, but with meeting Chief Inspector Banks and his female sidekick again. She knew they would want to interview her after studying the manuscript; there was no doubt she was guilty of something. But what could she do? She was too old and too tired to run. She was also too old to go to gaol. The only way now was to face up to whatever charges might be brought and hope her lawyer would do a good job.

No one, she supposed, could stop the press finding out the details eventually, and there was no doubt that they would go to town on the scandal. She wasn't sure she could face public humiliation. Perhaps, if they didn't arrest her, she would leave the country again, the way she had done so many times with Ronald. Why not? She could work anywhere, and she had enough money to buy a little place somewhere warm: Bermuda, perhaps, or the British Virgin Islands.

Once again Vivian cast her mind back to the events of fifty years ago. Was there something she had missed? Had she got it all wrong? Had she been so ready to suspect

Matthew that she had overlooked the possibility of anyone else being guilty? Banks's questions about Michael Stanhope and about PX, Billy Joe, Charlie and Brad had shocked and surprised her at first. Now she was beginning to wonder. Could one of them have done it? Not Charlie, certainly – he was dead by then – but what about Brad? He and Gloria had been arguing a lot towards the end; she had even seen them arguing through the flames at the VE Day party. Perhaps the night she died he had gone to put his case forward one last time, and when she turned him down he went berserk? Vivian tried to remember whether Brad had been the kind to go berserk or not, but all she could conclude was that we all are, given the right circumstances.

Then there was PX. He had certainly lavished a lot of gifts on Gloria in that shy way of his. Perhaps he had hoped for something in return? Something she hadn't wanted to give? And while Billy Joe seemed to have moved on to other women quite happily, Vivian remembered his bitterness at being ditched for a pilot, the smouldering class resentment that came out as gibes and taunts.

People said they didn't have a class system in America, but Billy Joe had definitely been working-class, like the farm labourers in Yorkshire; Charlie was from a well-established Ivy League background; and Brad had come from new West Coast oil money. Vivian didn't think the Americans lacked class distinction so much as they lacked the tradition of inherited aristocratic titles and wealth – which was probably why they all went gaga over British royalty.

The train was nearing Leeds City Station now, wheels squealing as it negotiated the increasingly complicated system of signals and points. It had been a much faster and easier journey than the one Vivian had made to London and back with Gloria. She remembered the pinprick of blue light, the soldiers snoring, her first look at the desolation of war in the pale dawn light. She had slept most of the way back to Leeds, a six- or seven-hour journey then, and after she got back to Hobb's End, London had grown more and more distant and magical in her imagination until it might easily have been Mars or ancient Rome.

Looking back, she began to wonder if perhaps it was *all* just a story. As the years race inexorably on, and as all the people we know and love die, does the past turn into fiction, an act of the imagination populated by ghosts, scenes and images suspended for ever in water-glass?

Wearily, Vivian stood up and reached for her overnight bag. There was something else she had steeled herself to do while she was in Leeds, and she had set aside Friday afternoon, after the interview, for it. Before that, though, she would make time to call at the art gallery and see Michael Stanhope's painting.

•

When the phone rang on Thursday morning, Banks snatched the receiver from its cradle so hard he fumbled it and dropped it on the desk before getting a good grip.

'Alan, what's going on? You almost deafened me.'

'Oh, sorry.'

'It's Jenny.'

'I know. I recognized your voice. How are you?'

'Well, don't sound so excited to hear from me.'

'I'm sorry, Jenny, really. It's just that I'm expecting an important call.'

'Your girlfriend?'

'The case I'm working on.'

'That one you told me about? The war thing?'

'It's the only one I've got. Jimmy Riddle's made sure my cases have been thin on the ground lately.'

'Well, I won't take up much of your time. It just struck me that I was rather . . . well, emotional . . . on our last meeting. I want to apologize for dumping all over you, as they say in California.'

'What are friends for?'

'Anyway,' Jenny went on, 'by way of an apology, I'd like to invite you to dinner. If you think you can tolerate my cooking, that is?'

'It's bound to be better than mine.'

She laughed a little too quickly and a little too nervously. 'Don't count on it. I thought we could, you know, just talk about things over a meal and a bottle of wine. A lot's happened to both of us this past year.'

'When?'

'How about tomorrow, sevenish?'

'Sounds fine.'

'Are you sure it won't cause any problems?'

'Why should it?'

'I don't know . . . I just . . .' Then her voice brightened. 'That's great. I'll see you tomorrow about seven, then?'

'You're on. I'll pick up some wine.'

After he hung up, Banks sat back and thought about the invitation. Dinner with Jenny. At her place. That would be interesting. Then he thought about Annie, and that cast a shadow over him. She had basically cut him dead on the phone yesterday. After such quick and surprising intimacy, her coldness came as a shock. It was a long time since he had been given the cold shoulder by a girlfriend he had known for only a few days, and the whole thing brought back shades of adolescent gloom. Time to break out the sad songs again. Cry along with Leonard Cohen and learn how to get the best out of your suffering.

But he *was* anxious to hear from Annie about the East Anglia connection. She had said today at the latest, after all. He toyed with the idea of phoning her, but in the end decided against it. Whatever their personal problems, he knew she was a good enough copper to let him know the minute she got the information he'd asked for. Shortly before eleven, she did.

'I'm sorry for the delay,' she said. 'What with time differences and faulty fax machines, well, I'm sure you know . . .'

'That's all right. Just tell me what you've discovered.' Banks had already come to one or two conclusions of his own since his last talk with Annie, and he felt the tingling tremor of excitement that usually came as the pieces started to fall together; it was a feeling he hadn't experienced in quite a while.

'First off,' Annie said, 'there definitely *was* an American air base near Hadleigh in 1952.'

'What were they doing there?'

'Well, the US armed forces cleared out of England after the war, but a lot of them stayed on in Europe, especially Berlin and Vienna. The war hadn't solved the Russian problem. Anyway, the Americans came back to operate from British air bases in 1948, during the Berlin blockade and airlift. The first thing they did was deploy long-range B-29 bombers from four air bases in East Anglia. All this is from my contact in Ramstein. Apparently, there were so many bases by 1951 that they had to change their organizational structure to deal with them.'

'Any familiar names?'

'Just one. Guess who ran the PX?'

'Edgar Konig.'

'The very same. You don't sound so surprised.'

'Not really. What did you find out about him?'

'He left Rowan Woods in May 1945, with the rest of the Four Hundred and Forty-Eighth, and spent some time in Europe, then he returned to America. He was assigned to the base near Hadleigh in summer 1952.'

'He stayed in the air force all that time?'

'Seems that way. I suppose he had a pretty good job. Lots of perks. Tell me, why doesn't it surprise you? Why not one of the other Americans?'

'The whisky and the Luckies.'

'What?'

'In Vivian Elmsley's manuscript. She said there was a bottle of whisky smashed on the floor and an *unopened* carton of Lucky Strikes on the kitchen counter. It's hardly concrete evidence of anything, but I don't think a carton of Luckies would have stayed unopened for very long in wartime, do you?'

'Brad could have brought them.'

'Possible. But it was PX who had easiest access to the stores, PX who always supplied the goodies. The manuscript also mentioned a farewell party at Rowan Woods that night. PX must have got drunk and finally plucked up courage. He'd sneaked out of the base and brought the presents that night. One last-ditch attempt to buy what he yearned for. Gloria resisted and . . . Matthew only came in afterwards, the poor sod. Any idea where PX was between 1945 and 1952?'

'No. I can ask Mattie to check if it's important. You're thinking there might have been others?'

'Possibly. Do we know *anything* more about him?'

'No. Mattie said she'd try to find out what she can –

such as when and why he was discharged and if he's still alive, but she doesn't hold out a lot of hope. It's not their official position to give out such information, but Mattie's a mystery fan and it seems I've piqued her curiosity. She's become quite an ally.'

'Good. See what you can do. Let's see if we can link him to any other murders. How old will he be now if he's still alive?'

'According to Mattie's information, he'd be about seventy-five.'

'A possibility, then.'

'Could be. I'll talk to you later.'

When Annie had hung up, Banks felt restless. Sometimes waiting was the most difficult part; that was when he smoked too much and paced up and down, bad habits from his Met days he hadn't quite got rid of. There were a couple of things he could do in the meantime. First, he dialled Jenny Fuller's number.

'Alan,' she said. 'Don't tell me you want to cancel?'

'No, no. It's nothing like that. Actually, I need you to do a little favour for me.'

'Of course. If I can.'

'Didn't you say at lunch the other day that you trained with the FBI profilers?'

'At Quantico. Yes. And you said you thought profiling was a load of bollocks.'

'Forget that for now. Do you have any contacts there? Anyone close enough to ask a personal favour?'

Jenny paused a moment. 'Well, there is *one* fellow, yes. Why do you ask?'

Banks filled her in on the new developments, then said, 'This Edgar Konig, I'd like you to ask your friend to check his record. If he's the sort of man I think he is, the odds are that he'll have one. DS Cabbot's working with the military authorities, but any information they can supply us with is limited.'

'I'm sure Bill will be happy to oblige, if he can,' said Jenny. 'Just let me get a pencil, then you can tell me what you want to know.'

When Banks had finished giving Jenny the details, he asked DS Hatchley to call East Anglia and find out if a US airman called Edgar Konig had ever been questioned or suspected in connection with the Brenda Hamilton murder. After that, he sat back and told himself there was no rush. Nobody was running anywhere. Even if Konig did turn out to be the killer, even if he was still alive, there was no way he could know the North Yorkshire Police were on to him after all this time.

18

On Friday, the rep dropped Vivian back at her hotel a little later than she had expected. There had been a delay at the radio station when the sound technician discovered, halfway through the interview, that Vivian's microphone was faulty. She had to do the whole thing again. It was after four o'clock when she got out of the car, and the sky looked heavy and dark, the air crackling with pre-storm tension. In the distance, she could hear hesitant rumbles of thunder and see faint lightning flashes. Even the Metropole's façade, lovingly restored to its original orange terracotta, looked as black as it had when she had stayed there with Charlie all those years ago.

She would have liked nothing better than to rest in her room for an hour or so, perhaps take a long bath, but it would be fully dark before long. She supposed she could put off her trip and go another time. Tomorrow would be taken up with signings in York and Harrogate, but she could always catch a later train and make the visit on Sunday morning. No. She would not procrastinate. There was also something ironically appealing to the writer in her about visiting the place during a storm.

She called the concierge and asked him to arrange for a taxi, then she put on her raincoat and waterproof boots. The car was waiting downstairs, and she ducked in the back with her umbrella and gave the driver directions. The rain had started spotting now, making huge dark blobs on the pavement. The driver, a young Pakistani, tried to practise his English by making conversation about the weather, but he soon gave up and settled in to concentrate on his driving.

Woodhouse Road was busy with people leaving work early for the weekend, and the worsening weather made it a matter of stop and start. Beyond the city limits, though, things eased up.

As Vivian gazed out of the rain-streaked window, hypnotized by the slapping of the windscreen wipers, she thought about her visit to Leeds City Art Gallery yesterday. Seeing the nude painting of Gloria had evoked such a complex response in her that she still hadn't been able to sort out all the strands.

She had never seen Gloria naked before, had never accompanied her and Alice and the others on their skinny-dipping expeditions, out of shyness and out of shame at her body, so to see the smooth skin and the alluring curves as interpreted by Michael Stanhope's expert eye and hand came as a revelation.

What disturbed Vivian most of all was the pang of desire the painting engendered in her. She had thought herself long past such feelings, if she had ever, indeed, experienced them at all. True, she had loved Gloria, but she had never admitted to herself, had never even realized, that she might have loved her in *that* way. Now, as she remembered the innocent physical intimacies they had shared – painting one another's legs; the dancing lessons, when she had felt Gloria's body close to hers and breathed her perfume; the little kiss on her cheek after the wedding – she wasn't sure how innocent it had all been. The feelings, the urges, had been there, but Vivian had been ignorant of such things and had suppressed them. In the art gallery, she had felt like a pervert looking at pornography; not because there was anything pornographic about Stanhope's painting, but because of her own thoughts and feelings attached to it.

She thought of that moment when she had kissed Gloria's still-warm forehead before covering her with the blackout cloth. *'Goodbye, sweet Gloria. Goodbye, my love.'*

'Pardon me?' said the driver, turning his head.

'What? Oh, nothing. Nothing.'

Vivian shrank into her seat. Beyond Otley there was very little traffic. The roads were narrow, and they got stuck behind a lorry doing only about thirty for a while. It was after five o'clock when the driver pulled up in the car park near Thornfield Reservoir. The rain was coming down hard now, pattering against the leaves. At least, Vivian thought, in this weather she could be sure of having the place to herself. She told the driver she would only be about fifteen minutes and asked him to wait. He picked up a newspaper from the seat beside him.

A second car pulled up in the other car park, behind the high hedge, but Vivian was already walking through the woods, and she failed to notice it. The path was treacherous, as if the parched earth had been yearning for the chance to suck up every drop of rain that fell, and Vivian had to be really careful not to slip as she made her way slowly down the embankment, poking her umbrella in the ground ahead and using it as a sort of brake. God only knew how she would get back up again.

The ruined village lay spread out before her under the dark sky. Rain lashed the crumbled stones and every few seconds a flash of lightning lit the scene like a Stanhope painting.

Vivian paused to get her breath by the fairy bridge,

unfurled her umbrella, then walked forward and stood at the humped centre. She rested her free hand on the wet stone, hardly able to believe that this was the same bridge where she had stood and chatted with Gloria, Matthew, Alice, Cynthia, Betty and the others all those years ago. The last time she had been there, it had been under water.

The rain was already finding the old river's channel by the High Street, and a small stream had formed, heading towards Harksmere. Thunder hammered across the sky, and Vivian shuddered as she moved towards Bridge Cottage. There was nothing left of the place except the foundations, a dark stone outline two or three feet high, but she remembered where every room and cupboard had been, especially the kitchen at the back, where she had found Gloria's body.

The area around and inside the cottage had been dug up and was still surrounded by police signs warning that it might be dangerous. They had been looking for more bodies, Vivian supposed. Well, they would, wouldn't they? Inspector Niven would have done exactly the same thing.

Now she was standing there in the driving rain, which dripped off her umbrella and ran down inside her boots, she was beginning to wonder why she had come. There was nothing here for her now. At least when Hobb's End was under water she could imagine it, as she had done, as a place preserved in water-glass. Now it was nothing but a heap of rubble.

She ambled through the mud up what had been the High Street, past the Shoulder of Mutton, where Billy Joe had his fight with Seth, and where Matthew spent his evenings after his return from Luzon; past Halliwell the butcher's, where she had swapped Capstans for suet and pleaded for an extra piece of scrag-end; and past the newsagent's shop, where she had lived with Mother and sold her bits and pieces, built up her private lending library, met Gloria for the first time that blustery April day she came by in her new land-girl uniform asking for cigarettes.

It was no good; there was nothing of the place left but memories, and her memories were mostly painful. She hadn't known what to expect, had in mind only a simple sort of pilgrimage, an acknowledgment of some sort. Well, she had done that. Time to head back to the hotel for a hot bath and a change of clothes, or she would catch her death.

Lost in her thoughts, she hadn't noticed the gaunt, stringy-haired man who had followed her taxi all the way from Leeds. When she passed Bridge Cottage on her way back and turned towards the fairy bridge, he stepped from behind the outbuilding and held out a gun, then he moved forward quickly, grabbed her round the throat, and she felt the hard metal pushing at the side of her neck. Her umbrella went flying and landed upside down on High Street like a large black teacup.

Then his hand appeared in front of her, holding a dog-eared photograph creased with age. It took her a few moments to realize that it was Gloria. Her hair was darker and straighter, and it looked as if it had been taken perhaps a year or two before she had come to Hobb's End. Rain spattered the photograph and the hand that held it. Such a small hand. *Gloria's hand*, she thought, remembering that first meeting, when she had shaken hands and Vivian had felt heavy and awkward holding that tiny, moist leaf.

What was he doing with hands like Gloria's?

●

By six o'clock on Friday evening, Banks was starting to get nervous about his dinner date with Jenny. The thunder and lightning and driving rain that buffeted his tiny cottage didn't help. He had already showered and shaved, agonizing over whether to put on any aftershave and finally deciding against it, not wanting to smell like a tart's window-box. Now he was surveying his wardrobe, what little there was of it, trying to decide which version of casual he should put on tonight. It was a decision made a lot easier by the overflowing laundry basket: the Marks & Sparks chinos and the light blue denim shirt.

Almost ready at last, Banks stood in front of the mirror and ran his hand over his closely cropped hair. Nothing to write home about, he thought, but it was the best he could do with what nature had given him. He wasn't a vain man, but today he seemed to take longer than a woman getting ready to go out. He remembered how he had always had to wait for Sandra, no matter how much time he gave her. It had got so bad that when they had to be somewhere for seven-thirty, he told her seven o'clock, just to get an edge.

He thought of Annie. Did he owe her fidelity, or were all bets off after the way she had cut him? He didn't know. At the very least, he owed her an explanation of the case, given all the hard work she had put in. Late that afternoon, Bill Gilchrist of the FBI had sent him, at Jenny's request, a six-page fax on Edgar 'PX' Konig, and Banks had been gob-smacked by its contents. DS Hatchley had also determined that Konig *had* been questioned in connection with the Brenda Hamilton murder. He wasn't a serious suspect, but the two had been friendly. Rationing was in force until 1954, so PX still had his uses among the locals as late as 1952.

Annie wasn't at the section station when he phoned

her. He had tried her at home, too, but either she had already left for St Ives, or she wasn't answering her phone. Next he dialled her mobile number but still got no answer. Maybe she didn't want to talk to him.

Banks went downstairs and lit a cigarette. Miles Davis's *Bitches Brew* was playing on the stereo, bringing back more memories of Jem.

During one of those periods when the Met had brought in a new broom, and corruption charges were flying right, left and centre, Banks again saw the man he had first seen walking up the stairs on the night of Jem's death. A dealer. His name was Malcolm, and he had been brought in to give evidence against a certain DS Fallon, who was charged with extorting heroin from importers he busted instead of arresting them. Fallon then set up his own distribution network, which included Malcolm. In Banks's eyes, that made Malcolm partly responsible for Jem's death, and when he saw DS Fallon, he recognized immediately the pockmarked face and cynical smile of the cop who had rifled his bedsit after he'd reported Jem's death. No wonder no charges had ever been laid.

Fallon was arrested and sentenced. He hadn't been more than eighteen months in Wormwood Scrubs before a lifer who recognized him stabbed him through the ear with a filed-down length of metal. *Karma*. After five years or more it was hardly instant, but it was karma nonetheless. Jem would have liked that sense of symmetry.

Banks stubbed out his cigarette and was just heading into the bathroom to brush his teeth when the telephone rang. The sound startled him. He hoped it wasn't Jenny phoning to cancel. With Annie going all cold on him, he had been entertaining some pleasant fantasies about the forthcoming dinner. As soon as he heard the voice, though, he realized there could be much worse things in the world than Jenny phoning to cancel dinner.

'Why is it, Banks,' growled Chief Constable Riddle, 'that you manage to make a pig's arse out of everything you do?'

'Sir?'

'You heard me.'

'Sir, it's after six on a Fri—'

'I don't give a monkey's toss what bloody time it is, or what day it is. I give you a perfectly simple case to work on. Nothing too urgent. Nothing too exacting. Out of the goodness of my heart. And what happens? All my good intentions blow up in our faces, that's what happens.'

'Sir, I don't know what you're talking about.'

'You might not, but the rest of the bloody country does. Don't you watch the news?'

'No, sir. I've been getting ready to go out.'

'Then you'd better cancel. I'm sure she'll forgive you. Not that I care about your sex life. Do you know where I'm calling from?'

'No, sir.'

'I'm calling from Thornfield Reservoir. Listen carefully and you'll hear the rain. And the thunder. Let me fill you in. Shortly over an hour ago, a woman was taken hostage. She had taken a taxi out here and told the driver to wait while she went to look at something. When he thought he'd waited long enough, he went to look for her and saw her standing with a man who appeared to be holding a gun to her head. The man fired a shot in the air and shouted his demand, and the taxi driver ran back to his car and phoned the police. The woman's name is Vivian Elmsley. Ring any bells?'

Banks's heart lurched. 'Vivian Elmsley? Yes, she's—'

PETER ROBINSON

'I know damn well who she is, Banks. What I don't
know is why some maniac is holding a gun to her head and
demanding to talk to the detective in charge of the Gloria
Shackleton investigation. Because that's what he demanded
the taxi driver report. Can you fill me in on that?'

'No, sir.'

'"No, sir." Is that all you can say?'

Banks fought back the urge to say, 'Yes, sir.' Instead he
asked, 'What's his name?'

'He hasn't said. We, however, have gone into full
bloody Hollywood production mode out here, with a big
enough budget to bankrupt us well into the millennium.
Are you still listening to me, Banks?'

'Yes, sir.'

'A hostage negotiator has spoken with him briefly from
a distance, and all he says is that he wants to see justice
done. He won't say any more until we get you to the scene.
There's an Armed Response Unit here already, and they're
getting itchy fingers. Apparently one of their marksmen
said he can get a clear shot.'

'For crying out loud—'

'Get yourself down here, man. Now! And this time you
really will need your wellies. It's pissing down cats and
dogs.'

When Riddle hung up, Banks reached for his raincoat
and shot out the door. He had a damn good idea who
Vivian Elmsley's captor might be, and why he was holding
her. Behind him, Miles's mournful trumpet echoed in the
empty cottage.

•

Annie had managed to get away from the station early,
before the shit hit the fan, and by six o'clock she was

approaching Blackburn on the M65, shuttling from lane to lane to pass the convoys of enormous lorries that seemed to cluster together at regular intervals. It was Friday rush hour, the sky dark with storm clouds that gushed torrential rain over the whole of the North. Lightning forked and flickered over the humped Pennines, and thunder rumbled and crashed like a mad percussionist in the distance. Annie counted the gaps between the lightning and thunder, wondering if that really *did* tell you how far away the storm was.

What was the gap between her and Banks now? Could it be counted, like that between the thunder and the lightning? She knew she was being a coward, running away, but a little time and distance would give her a clearer perspective and a chance to sort out her feelings.

It was all getting to be too much: first, there was the annoyance she had felt when he went out boozing with his mate in Leeds instead of going to dinner with her; then the time in London he had gone to Bethnal Green to meet his son and made it clear she wasn't welcome; and then the last straw, Sandra's appearance at the cottage on Sunday morning. She had made Annie feel about an inch high. And Banks still loved her, that was obvious enough to anyone.

It wasn't Banks's fault; it wasn't because of him she was running, but because of herself. If every little thing like that was going to rub up against her raw nerve ends, then where would she find any peace? She couldn't blame Banks for making time for friends and family, but nor could she allow herself to be drawn so deeply into his life, tangled up in his past. All she wanted was a simple, no-strings relationship, but there were already too many complications.

If she stayed with him, she would have to meet his son eventually and audition for the Dad's-new-girlfriend test. There was a daughter, too, and she would probably be even harder to win over. She would no doubt also meet the redoubtable Sandra again. Even though no one needed a co-respondent in divorce cases these days, Annie was beginning to feel like one. And there would be the divorce, something else they'd have to go through.

She didn't think she could face all the emotional detritus of someone else's life impinging on her own. She had enough to deal with as it was. No, she should cut her losses and get out now; it was time to go back home, regroup, recuperate, then return to her labyrinth, her meditation and yoga. With any luck, in a couple of weeks Banks would have let her go from his thoughts and found someone else.

Annie had the electronic gizmo in the car stereo set so that no matter what programme she was listening to, the nearest local station would cut in with its weather and travel updates. She hadn't a clue how this worked – some sort of electronic signal, she assumed – but sometimes the interruption continued beyond the traffic and weather into the local news bulletin. Just as she was overtaking a convoy of lorries churning up so much water she could hardly see, the weather cut in, and she also caught the beginning of a news bulletin about a hostage situation at Thornfield Reservoir.

Unfortunately, the same gizmo that caused the bulletins to cut in also cut them off at the most inappropriate times, and this happened halfway through the item. All she had discovered was that the detective writer Vivian Elmsley was being held by an armed man at Thornfield Reservoir.

Annie turned off the tape and jabbed at the search

buttons, sending the LCD lights into a digital frenzy. She got country and western, a gardening programme and a classical concert, but the scanner couldn't find the damn newsbreak. She swore and thumped the wheel, swerving dangerously, then tried again, searching manually this time. When she finally did get the right frequency, all she heard were the final words, '. . . bizarre twist in the affair, it seems the hostage-taker has asked to talk to the detective in charge of the so-called Hobb's End skeleton case, believed to be Detective Chief Inspector Banks of the Eastvale CID. We'll give you more details as they come in.'

Well, Annie thought on the outskirts of Blackburn, there was nothing else for it; she would have to go back. She negotiated her way carefully across the lanes of traffic, took the next exit, crossed the overpass, then followed the signs heading east. In this weather, it would take her about an hour, she calculated, and these were no conditions for impatient driving. She hoped she wouldn't be too late to find out what the hell was going on.

•

Banks arrived at Thornfield car park, put on his wellington boots and hurried through the short stretch of woods to the scene. Riddle hadn't been far wrong when he compared it to a Hollywood production. It probably cost as much as *Waterworld*. Though the patrol cars, Armed Response Vehicles and Technical Support Unit vans couldn't drive right to the rim of the reservoir because of the trees, some of them had forced their way through as far as they could, and long, thick wires and cables trailed the rest of the way. The local media people were there, too. The entire bowl of Hobb's End was floodlit, and the occasional lightning flash gave everything a split-second blue cast. At the centre of it all, two small, pathetic figures were cruelly illuminated just beyond the fairy bridge.

Riddle stood by the phalanx of TV cameras and microphones clustered well behind the police tape. Banks ignored him and went straight over to the hostage negotiator. He looked young. Banks guessed he had a psychology degree and this was his first real-life situation. Officially, the local superintendent was in charge of the scene, but as a rule the negotiator called the shots. Banks couldn't see any police sharpshooters, but he knew they were around somewhere.

'I'm DCI Banks,' he said.

'Sergeant Whitkirk,' said the negotiator.

Banks nodded towards the two figures. 'Let me go and talk to him.'

'You're not going down there,' Whitkirk said. 'That's against the rules. Do your talking on this.' He held a loud-hailer out. Banks didn't take it. Instead, he lit a cigarette and gazed out over the eerie scene, a set from a horror film, perhaps the same film that began with the skeletal hand scratching at the edge of a tombstone. He turned to Sergeant Whitkirk. 'How old are you, sonny?'

'What's that got—'

'You're clearly not old enough to realize that not all wisdom comes out of books. What's it called, this rule book of yours? *The Handy Pocket Guide to Hostage Negotiation*?'

'Now, you listen to me—'

'No. *You* listen to *me*.' Banks pointed to the two figures. 'I don't know how many scenes like this you've handled successfully, but I do know this situation. I know what it's all about, and I think I've got a hell of a lot better chance than you or anyone else of making sure no one gets hurt.'

Whitkirk thrust his chin out. There was an angry red spot in the cleft. 'You can't guarantee that. Leave it to the professionals. He's obviously a fucking madman.'

'He's not a fucking madman. What do you professionals intend to do? Shoot him?'

Whitkirk snorted. 'We could've done that an hour ago, if that's what we wanted. We're containing the situation.'

'Bully for you.'

'How do you know he's not a madman?'

Banks sighed. 'Because I know who he is and what he wants.'

'How can you know that? He hasn't communicated any demands yet.'

'Except to talk to me.'

'That's right. And our first rule is that we don't comply.'

'He hasn't done anything yet, has he?'

'No.'

'Why not, do you think?'

'How would I know? All I know is he's a fucking nutter and he's unpredictable. We can't give in to him, and you can't just go walking into the situation. Look at it this way. He asked for you. Maybe you're the one he really wants to kill.'

'I'll take my chances.'

'No, you won't. I'm in charge of the scene here and you're not going in.'

'What do we do, then?'

'We play for time.'

Banks felt like laughing, but he held it back. 'And in time, what's your plan?'

'First we do all we can to turn an imprecise situation into a precise one.'

'Oh, stop quoting the fucking textbook at me,' Banks said. 'How long have you been here already? An hour? Hour and a half? Have you turned your imprecise situation into a precise one yet?'

'We've established communication.'

Banks looked down at the loud-hailer. 'Yes. Great communicators, those.'

Whitkirk glared at him. 'We offered to send down a phone but he refused.'

'Look,' said Banks, 'he's asked for me. We might not know what he wants, but he must have something to tell me, and you and I both know there's only one way to find out. I think I can talk him out of doing any harm. Can't you give me a bit of leeway?'

Whitkirk chewed on his lip for a moment. 'Securing the scene's my responsibility,' he said.

'Let me go in.' Banks pointed over to the chief constable. 'Believe me, there's a bloke over there will give you a medal if I get shot.'

Whitkirk managed a thin smile. 'One condition,' he said.

'What is it?'

'You wear a bullet-proof vest.'

'All right.'

Whitkirk sent someone to pick up the vest from the Armed Response Vehicle, then he told the hostage taker over his loud-hailer what he was planning.

'Send him in,' the man shouted back.

Whitkirk stood aside and Banks, kitted out with his bulletproof vest, trod his cigarette in the mud and set off down the side of the reservoir. He heard Whitkirk whisper, 'Good luck', as he went. About halfway down, he slipped and went the rest of the distance on his backside. Not very dignified. Though it probably did more harm to his pride than to his clothing, it also reminded him that he had put on his best trousers for dinner with Jenny, a dinner he was very unlikely to be having now, especially as he had forgotten his mobile in all the excitement and hadn't been able to phone her and cancel.

When he got to the bottom of the embankment, he heard a curse behind him and turned to see Annie Cabbot come sliding down after him, also on her bum, feet in the air. At the bottom, she got to her feet and flashed him a grin. 'Sorry. It was the only way I could give them the slip.'

'I take it you don't have a bullet-proof vest?'

'No.'

'I could be gallant and give you mine, but we're a little too close to the scene now. Just stay back, behind me. We don't want to scare him.'

They approached the fairy bridge. Banks told the man who he was. He indicated that it was okay and told the two of them to stop at the far side. They faced one another over the bridge. Vivian Elmsley looked frightened but otherwise unhurt as far as Banks could see. The gun looked like a .32 automatic.

'This is DS Cabbot,' Banks said. 'She's been working on the case with me. Is it okay for her to be here?'

The man looked at Annie and nodded. 'I know who she is,' he said. 'I saw her on television the day you found the skeleton, then down here that night a week or so ago.'

'So it was you,' Annie said. 'What were you doing? Surely you weren't looking for anything after all this time?'

'Perhaps I was. Not the sort of thing you mean. But perhaps I was looking for something. I've been here a lot at night. Thinking.'

'Why did you run?'

'I recognized you from the television. You walked right past me and didn't even see me. But I saw you. I couldn't risk being caught, having to explain myself, before I'd finished what I had to do.'

Banks decided it was time to take charge. He held his hands up and gestured for Annie to do the same. Rain dripped down the back of his neck. 'We're not armed, Francis,' he said. 'We don't want to hurt you. We just want to talk. Let Ms Elmsley go.'

'So you know who I am?'

'Francis Henderson.'

'Clever. But my name's Stringer now. Frank Stringer.' He licked his lips. So he had adopted his mother's maiden name. Strange. That told Banks something about the situation they were dealing with. Frank looked twitchy, and Banks wondered if he had been drinking or if he was on drugs again. If it's hard to make an imprecise situation precise, he thought, then it's a bloody sight harder to make a hallucinatory situation real.

'Anyway,' Frank went on, 'I'm not ready to let anyone go yet. I want to hear it all first. I want to hear her confess to you, then I'll decide whether to kill her or not. It makes no odds to me.'

'Okay, Frank. What do you want to hear?'

'She killed my mother. I want to hear her say so, and I want to know why.'

'She didn't kill anyone, Frank.'

'What are you talking about? You're lying. You're trying to protect her.'

His grip tightened on Vivian. Banks caught her sudden intake of breath and saw the gun barrel pushed into the flesh under her ear.

'Listen to me, Frank,' he said. 'It's important you listen

to me. You asked for me to come here. You want the truth, don't you?'

'I already know the truth. I want to hear it from your mouth. I want to hear her confess in front of you. I want to hear what she did to my mother.'

'It didn't happen the way you think it did, Frank. It didn't happen the way any of us thought it did. We were all wrong.'

'My mother was murdered.'

'Yes, she was murdered.'

'And this . . . this bitch here lied to my father and me when we went and asked about her.'

'No,' said Banks. 'She didn't lie. She thought she was telling you the truth.' He noticed the look of confusion in Vivian's eyes.

'All those years,' Frank went on, as if he hadn't heard. 'Do you know he worshipped her, my father? Even though she left us. He said she was a dreamer, a free spirit, a beautiful butterfly who just had to spread her wings and fly away. But I hated her for leaving us. For depriving us of all that beauty. Why couldn't she share it with us? Why couldn't *we* be part of her dreams? We were never good enough for her. I hated her and I loved her. All my life dominated and blighted by a mother I never even knew. What do you think Mr Freud would make of that? Don't you think that's funny?'

Banks looked away. He didn't want to tell Frank the truth, that his mother had turned her back on him at birth. All those years, George had fed him on illusions. Gloria certainly had been wrong about the father of her child; he hadn't turned out so bad after all. 'No,' he said. 'I don't think it's funny at all, Frank.'

'My father used to tell me how she always wanted to be

one of those Hollywood actresses. Used to spend hours in front of the mirror practising her makeup and the way they talked. Even before I was born it was no-go for them. She was too young, he said. Made just one mistake, that's all. *Me.* It was enough.'

'She *was* very young, Frank. When she got pregnant, she was frightened. She didn't know what to do.'

'So she had to run away and leave us?'

'For some people it seems like the only solution. She obviously wanted the child, *you*, to live. She didn't have an abortion. She must have told your father where she was going? Did she keep in touch?'

He sniffed. 'A postcard every now and then, telling him she was doing fine and not to worry. When my dad came home on leave once, he took me up to Hobb's End to see her. It was the only time I . . . the only time I really remember seeing her, being with her, hearing her voice. She told me I was a fine-looking boy. I loved her then. She was a magical creature to me. Dazzling. Like someone from a dream. She seemed to move in a haze of light. So beautiful and so tender. But they argued. He couldn't help asking her to come back when he saw her, but she wouldn't. She told him she was married now and had a new life and we should leave her alone if we wanted her to be happy.'

'What did your father do?'

'What she asked. He was devastated. I think he'd always hoped that one day, perhaps, she would come back. We tried once more, when it was all over.' He turned so he was speaking into Vivian's ear. 'But this lying bitch here told us she had run away and she didn't know where. All my life I believed that, believed my mother had run away and abandoned us for ever. I tried to find her. I'm good at finding people, but I got nowhere. Now I find out she was dead all the time. Murdered and buried right here.'

'Let her go, Frank!' Banks shouted over a peal of thunder. 'She didn't know.'

'What do you mean, she didn't know? She must have known.' Frank tore his attention away from Vivian and glared at Banks. His eyes were wild, his lank hair was plastered to his skull and rain dripped from his eyes like tears. 'I want to hear it all. I want to hear her admit it to you. I want the truth.'

'You've got it all wrong, Frank. Vivian didn't kill Gloria. Listen to me.'

'Even if she didn't do the actual killing, she was involved. She covered for somebody. Who was it?'

'Nobody.'

'What do you take me for?'

'Vivian had nothing to do with your mother's death.' As he spoke, Banks noticed Vivian's eyes fill with curiosity, despite the gun at her neck. Annie stood beside him now, and Frank didn't seem to care about her presence. Banks was aware of the activity in the background, but he didn't think anyone would make a move yet. Thunder rumbled and lightning flashed. His raincoat and trousers stuck to his skin and rain stung his eyes.

'What do you mean, she had nothing to do with it?' Frank said. 'She told my father that my mother had gone away, when all the while she was buried up here. She lied. Why would she do that unless she'd killed her, or knew who had?'

'As far as she was concerned,' Banks said, 'your mother *had* gone away. She had spoken about running away often since Matthew got back from the war. He'd been badly hurt by the Japanese. He wasn't the man she had married. Life was miserable for her. It seemed only natural to everyone who knew her that she'd go, just like she left you and your father in the first place.'

'No!'

Frank's grip tightened on Vivian's throat and she gasped. Banks felt his heart lurch. He held his hands out, palms towards Frank.

'Okay, Frank,' he went on. 'Calm down. Please. Calm down and listen to me.'

They waited a moment, the four of them, all silent but for the pattering of the rain and the storm disappearing into the distance, the occasional crackle of a police radio from the rim.

Then Banks felt things relax, the same way as when you undo a tight button. 'Matthew drove her away,' he went on. 'It was only natural for Gwen to assume that was what happened. Your mother's suitcase was gone. Her things were gone.'

Frank didn't say anything for at least a minute. Banks could see him processing information, trying to shore up his defences. The storm passed into the distance now and the rain eased off, leaving the four of them soaked to the skin.

'If it wasn't her, who was it?' Frank said eventually. 'I'll bet you can't tell me that, can you?'

'I can, Frank.' Annie stepped forward and spoke. Frank turned to her and blinked the rain out of his eyes.

'Who?' Frank asked. 'And don't you lie to me.'

'His name was Edgar Konig,' Annie said. 'He ran the PX at Rowan Woods USAAF base, about a mile from here.'

'PX?' Vivian gasped.

'I don't believe you,' said Frank.

'It's true,' said Banks, picking up the thread. He realized that Annie didn't have the full story yet. 'Konig killed your mother. He also killed at least one other woman over here the same way, down in East Anglia. There were others, too, in Europe and America.'

Frank shook his head slowly.

'Listen to me, Frank. Edgar Konig knew your mother and her friends from the dances they went to. He was attracted to her from the start, but he had serious problems with women. He was always tongue-tied around them. He brought her presents, but even then she didn't offer herself to him, she wouldn't help him overcome his shyness. She went out with other men. He watched and waited. All the time the pressure was building up in him.'

'You say he killed other women?'

'Yes.'

'How do you know it was him?'

'We found a collar button from an American airman's uniform. We think your mother must have torn it off as they struggled. Then we looked into the unsolved murder in Suffolk and found he had been questioned in connection with that, too. Are you listening, Frank?'

'I'm listening.'

Frank's grip around Vivian's throat had loosened a little, and Banks could tell that he had relaxed the hand holding the gun. 'Edgar Konig went to Bridge Cottage that night to collect what he thought your mother owed him while her husband Matthew was at the pub as usual. The bomber group was due to move out in a couple of days and that had pushed him to the brink. He didn't have much time. He'd been torturing himself for over a year. He'd been drinking that night, getting more and more lustful, and he thought he had plucked up the courage, thought he could overcome his inadequacies. Something short-circuited, though. She must have rejected him, maybe laughed at him, and the next thing he knew he'd killed her in a rage. Do you understand what I'm saying, Frank? There was something wrong with him.'

'A psycho?'

'No. Not technically. Not at first, anyway. He became a sex murderer. The two things – sex and murder – became tangled up in his mind. The one demanded the other.'

'If that's how it happened, why did no one know about it?'

Slowly, Banks reached for his cigarettes and offered Frank one. 'Gave them up years back,' he said. 'Thanks for the offer, though.'

Banks lit up. Definite progress. Frank seemed less tightly wound, more willing to listen to reason. And he didn't appear to be drunk or on drugs. Better not cock it up now.

'No one knew about it,' Banks went on, 'because Edgar Konig realized what he'd done. That sobered him up fast. He covered his tracks well.' Banks looked at Vivian Elmsley as he spoke. She averted her eyes. 'He cleaned up the mess and he buried the body in the outbuilding. Then he packed a few of her clothes and belongings in a suitcase to make it look as though she had run off. He even faked a note. It was wartime. People went missing all the time. Everyone in the village knew Gloria wasn't happy with Matthew, what a burden she had to bear. Why should they question that she'd just done a moonlight?'

Frank spoke in Vivian's ear. 'Is that right, what he's saying?'

Banks couldn't hear her, but he saw her mouth form the word 'Yes.'

'Frank,' Banks pressed on, playing his advantage. 'The gun. I know you don't want to hurt anyone, but it's dangerous. It's easy to make a wrong move. Nobody's been hurt yet. No harm's been done.'

Frank looked at the gun as if he were seeing it for the first time.

Banks stepped on to the fairy bridge and moved forward slowly, holding his hand out. He knew there were probably two or three trained marksmen aiming in his direction, and the thought made his stomach churn. 'Give the gun to me, Frank. It's all over. Vivian didn't kill your mother. She had nothing to do with it. She loved Gloria like a sister. It was Edgar Konig.'

Frank let his gun hand drop and released his grip on Vivian Elmsley's throat. She staggered aside and slipped down one of the muddy holes the SOCOs had dug in the Bridge Cottage floor. Annie ran to help her. Frank handed the gun to Banks. It weighed heavy in his hand. 'What happened to him?' Frank asked. 'This Konig. Did he ever get caught?'

'I'll tell you all about that later, Frank,' said Banks, taking Frank by the elbow. 'Just for now, though, we're all a bit tired and wet. Okay? I think we should leave here, go somewhere to dry off and get some clean clothes, don't you?'

Frank hung his head. Banks draped an arm across his shoulder. As he did so, he noticed something on the ground, partially covered by mud. He bent and picked it up. It was a photograph of a sixteen-year-old Gloria Shackleton, her beautiful, determined, defiant face staring out at the camera. It was damaged by the water, but still salvageable.

Several police officers had already come dashing and

sliding down the embankment. Two went to help Annie get Vivian out of the pit, and two of them grabbed Frank roughly and started handcuffing him.

'There's no need to be so rough with him,' said Banks.

'Leave this to us, sir,' said one of the officers.

Bank sighed and handed over the gun, then he held up the photograph of Gloria. 'I'll get this cleaned up for you, if you want, Frank,' he said.

Frank nodded. 'Please,' he said. 'And don't worry about me. I'll be all right. It's not the first time I've had the cuffs on.'

Banks nodded. 'I know.'

They hustled Frank Stringer away, practically dragging him up the muddy slope, and Banks turned to see Annie and the other policemen helping Vivian Elmsley stumble over the fairy bridge.

Vivian stopped in front of him, covered in mud, while the others went on ahead. 'Thank you,' she said. 'You saved my life.'

'I lied for you,' said Banks. 'I also sullied Gloria's loyalty to Matthew.'

She paled and whispered, 'I know. I appreciate what you did. I'm sorry.'

'There was a chance, you know. Maybe just a small chance, but a chance. If you'd come forward after you found Gloria dead, if you hadn't destroyed all the evidence, if you'd gone to the police . . .' Banks held his anger in check; this was neither the time nor the place for it. 'Ah, to hell with it. Too late now.'

Vivian bowed her head. 'Believe me, I know what I've done.'

Banks turned and slogged on alone through the mud. It was difficult, but he made it up the edge without falling down. At the top, he was aware of Annie standing beside him. Before he could say anything, Jimmy Riddle came running over and grabbed his arm. 'I'm glad you've salvaged at least something out of this situation, Banks,' he hissed, 'but you're bloody incompetent. I don't want incompetent officers under my command. I'll be talking to you first thing Monday morning.' Then he turned to Annie. 'As for you, DS Cabbot, you disobeyed a direct order. I don't like insubordinate officers, either. I'll be talking to you, too.'

Banks shook his arm free, turned on his heel and walked back towards his car. All he wanted was a long hot bath, a large Laphroaig and a change of clothes.

And Annie.

She was already leaning against her car, arms folded.

'Are you all right?' Banks asked.

'I'm fine. Fine as anyone can be who's spent the last half-hour standing in the rain wondering if someone was going to get her head blown off.'

'Frank Stringer wasn't going to hurt anyone.'

'Easy for you to say. I respect what you did out there, by the way.'

'What do you mean?'

'You lied to protect Frank Stringer's feelings. I told you, my mother died when I was six. I like to remember her as a beautiful, dazzling creature moving in a haze of light, the same way he remembers Gloria. And I wouldn't want anyone to spoil that illusion for me, no matter what the truth.'

'I lied to get us all out of there alive.'

Annie smiled. 'Whatever. It worked both ways.'

'What next?'

Annie stretched, arching her back and reaching her

arms towards the sky. 'Onward to St Ives. After I've stopped off at home for some dry clothes. I was already on my way when I heard. I couldn't just leave it.'

'Of course not. Thanks for being here.'

'You?'

'Home, I suppose.' Banks remembered dinner with Jenny. Too late now, especially the state his clothes were in, but he could at least borrow a mobile from someone and phone her, apologize.

Annie nodded. 'Look, I'll be gone for two weeks. Right now I'm still a bit mixed up about my feelings. Why don't you phone me when I get back? Maybe we can have that talk?'

'Okay.'

She grinned at him crookedly. 'If there weren't so many policemen about I'd kiss you goodbye.'

'Not a good idea.'

'No. See you, then.'

And with that she opened the car door and got in. Banks ignored his cutting-down programme and lit another cigarette, aware that his hands were shaking. Without looking back, Annie started her car. Banks watched the red tail-lights disappear down the muddy track.

EPILOGUE

After a long, rainy winter and overdue repairs by Yorkshire Water, Thornfield Reservoir filled up again and Hobb's End once more disappeared. On 27 July of the year after the Gloria Shackleton murder had entered and left the public's imagination, Vivian Elmsley lay on a king-size bed in her Florida hotel room, propped up with pillows, and watched the local news channel.

Vivian was in the midst of a national book tour, seventeen cities, and while Gainesville wasn't on the itinerary, she had enough clout with her publishers for this brief diversion. She would have come anyway, tour or no tour. Yesterday she had been in Baltimore, Bethesda and Washington, DC, tomorrow she was going to Dallas, but tonight she was in Gainesville.

For tonight was the night that Edgar Konig had his appointment with Old Sparky, and after everything she had been through, Vivian desperately needed *some* sense of an ending.

It was a sultry, mosquito-ridden night, but that didn't seem to deter the crowds that gathered outside the gates of Starke Prison, about twenty-five miles away. One or two were quietly carrying placards that asked for an end to capital punishment, but by far the majority were chanting, 'Fry Konig! Fry Konig!' Bumper stickers echoed the same sentiments, and the crowd had created what the commentator called a tailgate-party atmosphere. It wasn't big enough to attract any of the national networks – after all, executions in Florida were as common as muggings – but the Konig case had caught a lot of local interest.

Frank Stringer would have come, too – and Vivian would have willingly paid his way – but he was in gaol. English gun laws are far stricter than they are in Florida. Besides, no matter how good his reasons for taking Vivian hostage at Thornfield the past September, he had committed a serious crime and occasioned a hugely expensive and highly publicized police operation. Vivian had visited him several times in gaol and told him she would help him get back on his feet when he came out. It was the least she could do for Gloria's memory.

In his turn, Frank had told her how his father's sister Ivy and her husband John had taken good care of him during the war and how he had thought of them as his parents. When his real father came home on leave, they would spend time together. That was when they had made the first journey north, in 1943, and he had seen his mother.

After the war, his father married and took him away from Ivy and John. Frank's stepmother turned out to be a drunk and a shrew who had no time for her husband's bastard son. Increasingly isolated and neglected, he got involved with crooks and gangs, and one thing led to another. The only constant was that he had always worshipped his true mother's memory.

Frank also told Vivian how the death of his father that spring and the re-emergence of Hobb's End from Thornfield Reservoir had caused his obsession with the past to escalate. His father had been the first to recognize Gwen Shackleton as Vivian Elmsley on television, but Frank had confirmed it; he had memorized her eyes and her voice all

IN A DRY SEASON

those years ago, when he was eight, the same way he had also memorized his mother's face.

He couldn't explain why he had taken the trouble to find out where Vivian lived and why he had followed her and approached her at the bookshop; it was just that she was the only one left, the only one who had known Gloria. He said that he meant no harm at first, that he might even have found the courage to approach her eventually.

Then the skeleton was discovered, and he knew she must have lied all those years ago. He hated her after that; he telephoned to scare her, to make her suffer. He could have taken her anytime, but he enjoyed the anticipation. After all, once he had confronted her, it would be all over. So he followed her, watched her. When she got the taxi outside her hotel, he knew where she was going, and he felt it was fitting that things should end there, where they began.

But tonight, Vivian was alone in Gainesville with her memories, the television, a bottle of gin, ice and tonic water. And an execution.

They had already shown a fairly recent photograph of Edgar Konig. Vivian hadn't been able to recognize the gangly, baby-faced young airman with the shy eyes and the blond brush cut. His hair was gone, his cheeks had sagged and wrinkled, his brow was creased, and his eyes were deep, dark pits in which slimy monsters squirmed.

As she watched the coverage, Vivian imagined the officials carrying out the preliminary steps of state-sanctioned murder with swift and impersonal efficiency, much like dentists or doctors.

First they would settle the patient in the heavy oak chair and buckle thick leather straps round his arms and legs. Then they would place the bit between his teeth and attach electrodes to his body as if they were carrying out an ECG.

She wondered if the leather straps smelled, if they were sour with the sweat and fear of previous victims. How many hands and legs had they strapped down before? Or were they replaced after every execution? What about the chair itself? How many bladders and bowels had emptied there?

Then they would clamp the metal skullcap on.

Vivian shook her head to clear the images. She felt dizzy, and she realized she was already a bit drunk. If anyone deserved this sort of end, she told herself, ambivalent as she was about the idea of capital punishment, it was probably Edgar Konig.

Vivian had been shocked when Banks told her the day after Frank's arrest that Gloria's murderer was not dead, but on death row in a Florida prison.

Did he think of Gloria now, Vivian wondered, now the end was so close? Did he spare a thought for a beautiful young woman all those years ago in a village that no longer existed, in a war long since won? And what about the others? How many had there been? Even Banks hadn't been able to give her a definite number. Did he think about them?

If he was like most such killers she had read about in the course of her research, he probably felt nothing but self-pity and spent his last moments cursing the bad luck that resulted in his capture. What Banks had told her a few days after the scene at Hobb's End did nothing to dispel that idea.

Banks's FBI contact had interviewed Konig last December and sent in a report. Konig said he remembered the first one he did was in England during the war. He

IN A DRY SEASON

couldn't remember her name or the circumstances, but he thought maybe she was a blonde. He *did* remember that he had been giving her stockings and gum and cigarettes and bourbon for more than a year and when he came to collect she didn't show a scrap of gratitude. He'd been drinking. He remembered the way the pressure had been building and building in him all that time until he'd had too much that night and the dam finally burst. She wouldn't have anything to do with *him*, a lowly PX grunt. Oh, no. She was fucking a *pilot*.

It was always the drink, he said. If it hadn't been for the drink he would never have done any of them. But booze made something deep inside him just snap, and the next thing he knew, they were dead at his feet. Then he was angry at them for dying and he used the knife. It was like that with the second one. Berlin, 1946. When he didn't get found out the first time, when he realized there wasn't even going to be an investigation, he thought he must be leading a charmed life.

It was all her fault. If she hadn't stopped to straighten her stockings as he was driving by, hiking her skirt up and showing those long, white legs in his headlights, then he would never have done her. If he hadn't been drunk, too, which he wouldn't normally have been while driving if he hadn't known the lonely road like the back of his hand. *If. If. If.* His life was a tragedy of cruel *ifs*.

She was willing enough to go into the field with him. He hadn't planned to hurt her; he had only seen her flashing her legs for him on the road back there and wanted a piece, like any normal guy would. But she had shown no patience with him and his little problem – it happened sometimes when he'd been drinking – and she had asked him for money. That made him see red.

Literally see red. The knife? Yes, he usually carried a knife with him. A habit from the farm days back in Iowa when he used to whittle pieces of wood.

The third woman, back Stateside in 1949, he didn't really remember at all, and of the second one in England, all he remembered was something red happening in a barn. Again, it was the drink. Konig's daddy had been a vicious alcoholic who regularly beat poor Edgar to within an inch of his life; his mother was a drunken whore who'd do it with anyone for a dime. All his life the drink had caused his problems; it made him do these evil things, and then he had the bad luck to be caught on that highway in California.

So went Edgar Konig's story.

The drink. Vivian looked at her glass, then, with a shaking hand, she poured herself another tumbler of gin and grasped a fistful of ice cubes from the bucket on the bedside table, tossing them in the glass carelessly, so a little gin splashed on the table. An American habit she had picked up, that, ice in her drink.

It was almost time.

Edgar Konig, just turned seventy-six, was finally getting what he deserved. Vivian still felt a twinge of guilt when she realized that Banks was right, that she *might* have helped put an end to his killing all those years ago, after Gloria, the very first victim. She was partly responsible for Konig's feeling that he led a charmed life of murder without consequence.

She had tried to rationalize it to herself so many times since Banks told her what had happened and turned his back in scorn that evening when the storm broke at Hobb's End. Even if she had reported what happened, she told herself, they would have still probably arrested

Matthew. He wasn't well enough to face that sort of treatment. Though Banks was a little easier on her when they spoke the next day, she could still feel his censure, and it stung.

But what could she have told the police that would have pointed them specifically towards Edgar Konig? The whisky and Lucky Strikes on the kitchen counter? They were hardly evidence. Gloria could have got them anywhere, and they could have been lying there on the counter for a couple of days. She and Gloria had known plenty of American air force officers in the area, and she had no reason at the time to suspect any of them of murder. It was all very well for Banks to say in retrospect that *she* was responsible for all those deaths, that *she* could somehow have stopped all this had she acted differently, but it wasn't fair. Twenty-twenty hindsight. And who wouldn't, given the chance, go back and change *something*?

Time.

The first shock would boil his brain and turn all the nerve cells to jelly; the second or third shock would stop his heart. His body would jerk and arch against the straps; his muscles would contract sharply, and a few small bones would probably snap. Most likely the fingers, the fingers he had used to strangle Gloria.

If he didn't have a leather band strapped across his eyes, the heat would cause his eyeballs to explode. The death chamber would be filled with the smell of burning hair and flesh. Steam and smoke would puff out from under the hood. The hood itself might catch fire. When it was over, someone would have to turn on an air vent to get rid of the stench. Then a doctor would come, pronounce him dead, and the public would be informed.

Besides, Vivian told herself as she watched the people chanting outside the prison gates, others could have stopped him, too, if the system had worked properly. It wasn't only her fault. She had acted only from the purest of motives: love of her brother. These past few weeks, she had read all the articles on Edgar Konig and his impending doom. There had been plenty of them.

Konig had finally been caught in California in the late sixties, when he was about forty-five, attacking a young female hitch-hiker by the side of a lonely road. Fortunately for her, another motorist had happened along. Even more fortunate, this man wasn't the kind who scared easily or who didn't want to get involved. He was an ex-serviceman, and he was armed. When he saw a woman in trouble, he stopped and managed to disarm and disable Konig before calling the police. Already the girl was unconscious from strangulation. She had five stab wounds, but she survived.

Konig served nine years of a fourteen-year sentence. He was released early because of good behaviour and prison overcrowding. A lot of people in the know opposed his release, regarding him as extremely dangerous and suspecting – but never being able to prove – his involvement in at least four murders. The prison officials said there wasn't much else they could do at the time but let him go.

After his release in the late seventies, for years Konig was driven from one community to another as people found out what he was, trying to get work as a store clerk, more often than not failing and going on welfare. Just a few years ago he had finally settled in the small Florida town where it all came to a messy and predictable end.

His neighbours had already started protesting, and one local business had even offered him money to up sticks and move elsewhere. But Konig stayed on. Then, one day, a couple of Jehovah's Witnesses came to call and saw, through the screen door, Konig with a knife in his hand standing over the body of a woman, who turned out to be a local prostitute. They called the police on their mobile phone. Konig was drunk; he offered no resistance. After that, of course, came the obligatory years of waiting for trial, for sentencing, the failed appeals, death row.

And it was all over now. A cheer went up from the crowd outside the prison. News had come out. Edgar Konig was dead.

Why was it that Vivian felt no relief, felt nothing but the stirrings of a bad headache? She closed her eyes and pressed her fingers to the lids. *All over. All over.* She was so tired. Konig's statement to the FBI had been bald and unembellished, but with her morbid imagination, Vivian was able to fill in the nuances and the emotions.

She saw Gloria run into the kitchen as she became frightened by PX's erratic behaviour, behaviour she had witnessed in embryo at the VE Day party – saw her frantically pulling tins of tea and cocoa out of the kitchen cupboard, looking for the gun, shocked and scared to find that it wasn't there. Did she realize in the last moments of her life that Gwen must have taken it?

Next, Vivian saw PX grab Gloria, put his hands round her throat, felt the breath going out of her. Then she saw him pick up the kitchen knife from the counter, felt one sharp pain, then another, another, everything starting to slip away from her.

Vivian put her hand to her throat.

The gun.

She was the one who had taken the gun, the one thing

that *might* have saved Gloria's life if she had got to it in time. And Brenda Hamilton's life. And all the others.

Then, for all those terrible years, she had cared for Matthew in his fallen state, believing he was a murderer. Poor, gentle Matthew, who wouldn't harm a soul, who couldn't even kill himself, no more than her husband Ronald could, despite the pain. Vivian had helped them both: Ronald with an extra dose of morphine, and Matthew, all those years ago . . .

Before she started crying, she had a vivid memory of that afternoon in Leeds when she came back from the shops and saw Matthew sitting in the chair with the gun in his mouth, the gun she had taken from Gloria, kept and brought all the way from Hobb's End. He was trying to find the courage, willing himself to pull the trigger.

But he couldn't do it. Just like all the other times he had tried and failed. He had such a forlorn expression on his face, such a hopelessness about him. His eyes pleaded with her, and this time, almost without thinking, she walked over to him, tenderly wrapped her hand around his, kissed his forehead and pressed his finger on the trigger.

Outside Starke Prison the crowd was dancing and chanting, shaking up bottles and spraying beer at each other. In the hotel room, Vivian Elmsley let her tears flow freely for the first time in over fifty years and reached again for her gin.

ACKNOWLEDGMENTS

Many people helped, both directly and indirectly, with this book. On the writing side, I would particularly like to thank my wife Sheila Halladay for her perceptive first reading and my agent Dominick Abel for his encouragement and hard work. Special thanks to my editor at Avon Books, Patricia Lande Grader, for her faith and for pushing me to the limit, and to Cynthia Good at Penguin for keeping me on track, as ever. I would also like to thank Robert Barnard for reading and commenting on the manuscript, and copy-editors Mary Adachi and Erika Schmid for spotting those important details the rest of us overlooked.

Then there are those who helped me reconstruct the past. Thanks to my father, Clifford Robinson, for sharing his wartime memories of Yorkshire; to Jimmy Williamson for informing me about the war in Burma; to Dan Harrington, USAFE History Officer, for patiently answering my e-mail messages; to Jack McFadyen for tracking down the uniforms and buttons, and to Dr Aaron Elkins for his help with the forensic anthropology.

A number of police officers also answered my questions, and if I got any of it wrong, it's not their fault. Thanks to Detective Sergeant Keith Wright, as ever, and to the crowd who drink in The Whale: Sergeant Claire Stevens, Chief Inspector Phil Gormley and Detective Inspector Alan Young. Particular thanks to Alan for the tour of the police station and the pint in the police bar afterwards.

Last but not least, thanks to John Halladay, of the Law Faculty at the University of Buckingham, and to Judith Rhodes, of the Leeds Library Services, for answering a variety of questions.

A DEDICATED MAN

For Jan

1

ONE

When the sun rose high enough to clear the slate roofs on the other side of the street, it crept through a chink in Sally Lumb's curtain and lit on a strand of gold blonde hair that curled over her cheek. She was dreaming. Minotaurs, bank clerks, gazelles and trolls cavorted through the barns, maisonettes and Gothic palaces of her sleep. But when she awoke a few hours later, all she was left with was the disturbing image of a cat picking its way along a high wall topped with broken glass. Dreams. Most of them she ignored. They had nothing to do with the other kind of dreams, the most important ones that she didn't have to fall asleep to find. In these dreams, she passed her exams and was accepted into the Marion Boyars Academy of Theatre Arts. There she studied acting, modelling and cosmetic technique, for Sally was realistic enough to know that if she lacked the dramatic talent of a Kate Winslet or a Gwyneth Paltrow, she could at least belong to the fringes of the world of glamour.

When Sally finally stirred, the bar of sunlight had shifted to the floor beside her bed, striping the untidy pile of clothes she had dropped there the night before. She could hear plates and cutlery in the kitchen downstairs, and the rich smell of roast beef wafted up to her room. She got up. It was good policy, she thought, to get downstairs as soon as possible and help with the vegetables before her mother's call – 'It's on the table!' – came grating up to her. At least by showing a willingness to help, she could probably avoid too probing an investigation into her lateness last night.

Sally stared at herself in the full-length mirror of her old oak wardrobe. Even if there was still a little puppy fat around her hips and thighs, it would soon go away. On the whole, she decided, she had a good body. Her breasts were perfect. Most people, of course, complimented her on her long silky hair, but they hadn't seen her breasts. Kevin had. Just last night he had caressed them and told her they were perfect. Last night they had gone almost all the way, and Sally knew that the next time, soon, they would. She looked forward to it with a mixture of fear and desire that, according to what she had read in magazines and books, would soon fuse into ecstasy in the heat of passion and longing.

Sally touched her nipple with the tip of her forefinger and felt a tingle in her loins. The nipple hardened and she moved away from the mirror to get dressed, her face burning.

Kevin was good. He knew how to excite her; ever since summer began he had played carefully with the boundaries of her desire. He had pushed them back a little further each time, and soon the whole country would be his. He was young, like Sally, but still he seemed to know instinctively how to please her, just as she imagined an experienced older man would know. She even thought she loved Kevin a bit. But if someone else came along – somebody more mature, more wealthy, more sophisticated, someone who was at home in the exciting, fast-paced cities of the world, well, after all, Kevin was only a farm boy at heart.

Dressed in designer jeans and a plain white T-shirt, Sally drew back the curtains. When her eyes had adjusted to the glare, she looked out on a perfect Swainsdale morning. A few fluffy little clouds – one like a teddy bear, another like a crab – scudded across the piercing blue sky on a light breeze. She looked north up the broad slope of the valley side, its rich greens interrupted here and there by dark patches of heather and outcrops of limestone, to the long sheer wall of Crow Scar, and noticed something very odd. At first she couldn't make it out at all. Then she squinted, refocused and saw, spreading out along the slope just above the old road, five or six blue dots which seemed to be moving in some kind of pattern. She put her finger to her lips, thought for a moment, then frowned.

TWO

Fifteen miles away in Eastvale, the dale's largest town, somebody else was anticipating a Sunday dinner of succulent roast beef and Yorkshire pudding. Detective Chief Inspector Alan Banks lay flat on his stomach in Brian's room watching an electric train whizz around bends, over bridges, through signals and under papier mâché mountains. Brian himself was out riding his bike in the local park, but Banks had long since given up the pretence that he only played with the trains for his son's sake and finally admitted that he found the pastime even more relaxing than a hot bath.

He heard the phone ring out in the hall, and a few seconds later his daughter, Tracy, shouted through, 'It's for you, Dad!'

As Banks rushed downstairs, the aroma from the

kitchen made his mouth water. He thanked Tracy and picked up the receiver. It was Sergeant Rowe, desk officer at Eastvale Regional Headquarters.

'Sorry to bother you, sir,' Rowe began, 'but we've just had a call from Constable Weaver over in Helmthorpe. Seems a local farmer's found a body in one of his fields this morning.'

'Go on,' Banks urged, snapping into professional gear.

'Chap said he was looking for a stray sheep, sir, when he found this body buried by a wall. Weaver says he shifted one or two stones and it's a dead 'un all right. Looks like someone bashed 'is 'ead in.'

Banks felt the tightening in his stomach that always accompanied news of murder. He had transferred from London a year ago, sickened by the spiralling of senseless violence there, only to find in the Gallows View case that things could be just as bad, if not worse, up north. The business had left both him and Sandra emotionally exhausted, but since then things had settled down. There'd been nothing but a few burglaries and one case of fraud to occupy his attention, and he had really begun to believe that murders, peeping Toms and vicious teenagers were the exception rather than the rule in Eastvale.

'Tell Constable Weaver to get back up there with as many local men as he can muster and rope off the area. I want them to start a systematic search, but I don't want anyone else closer to the body than ten yards. Got that?' The last thing he needed was half a dozen flatfoots trampling down the few square feet where clues were most likely to be found.

'Tell them to put everything they find into marked envelopes,' he went on. 'They should know the procedure, but it won't do any harm to remind them. And I mean everything. Used rubbers, the lot. Get in touch with Detective Sergeant Hatchley and Dr Glendenning. Tell them to get out there immediately. I'll want the photographer and the forensic team too. Okay?'

'Yes, sir,' Sergeant Rowe replied. He knew that Jim Hatchley would be enjoying his usual Sunday lunchtime pint in the Oak and that it would give Banks a great deal of satisfaction to interrupt his pleasure.

'I suppose the super's been informed?'

'Yes, sir. It was him as said to tell you.'

'It would be,' Banks complained. 'I don't suppose he wanted to miss *his* Sunday dinner.' But he spoke with humour and affection. Superintendent Gristhorpe, of all his new colleagues, was the one who had given him the most support and encouragement during the difficult transition from city to country.

Banks hung up and slipped on his worn brown jacket with the elbow patches. He was a small, dark man, in appearance rather like the old Celtic strain of Welshman, and his physique certainly didn't give away his profession.

Sandra, Banks's wife, emerged from the kitchen as he was preparing to leave. 'What is it?' she asked.

'Looks like a murder.'

She wiped her hands on her blue checked pinafore. 'So you won't be in for dinner?'

'Sorry, love. Doesn't look like it.'

'And I don't suppose there's any point in keeping it warm?'

'Shouldn't think so. I'll grab a sandwich somewhere.' He kissed her quickly on the lips. 'Don't worry. I'll give you a call as soon as I know what's happening.'

Banks drove his white Cortina west along the valley

bottom by the riverside. He was entitled to a police car and driver, but he actually enjoyed driving and preferred his own company when travelling to and from a case. A generous mileage allowance more than compensated for the cost.

With one eye on the road and one hand on the wheel, he flipped through an untidy pile of cassette tapes on the passenger seat, selected one and slipped it into the deck.

Though he swore that his passion for opera had not waned over the winter, he had to admit that he had been sidetracked into the world of English vocal and choral music. It was a change Sandra heartily approved of; she had never liked opera much in the first place, and Wagner had been the last straw for her. After she had finally gone so far as to attack one of his tapes with a magnet – the one with 'Siegfried's Funeral March' on it, Banks remembered sadly – he had got the message. With Ian Partridge singing Dowland's 'I Saw My Lady Weepe', he drove on.

Like the larger and more famous Yorkshire Dales, Swainsdale runs more or less from west to east, with a slight list towards the south, until the humble river loses itself in the Ouse. At its source near Swainshead, high in the Pennine fells, the River Swain is nothing more than a trickle of sparkling clear water, but in carving its way down towards the North Sea it has formed, with the help of glaciers and geological faults, a long and beautiful dale which broadens out as it approaches the Vale of York. The main town, Eastvale, dominated by its Norman castle, sits at the extreme eastern edge of the dale and looks out over the rich, fertile plain. On a clear day, the Hambleton Hills and the North York Moors are visible in the distance.

He saw Lyndgarth on the valley side to the north, near the dark ruins of Devraulx Abbey, and passed through peaceful Fortford, where the remains of a Roman fort were still under excavation on a hillock opposite the village green. Ahead, he could see the bright limestone curve of Crow Scar high up on his right, and, as he drew closer, he noticed the local police searching a field marked off by irregular drystone walls. The limestone shone bright in the sun, and the walls stood out against the grass like pearl necklaces on an emerald velvet cushion.

To get to the scene, Banks had to drive through Helmthorpe, the dale's central market village, turn right at the bridge on to Hill Road, and then turn right again on to a narrow road that meandered north-eastwards about halfway up the valley side. It was a miracle that the track had ever been tarmacked – probably a gesture towards increasing tourism, Banks guessed. No good for tyre tracks, though, he thought gloomily.

Being more used to getting around in the city than in the countryside, he scraped his knee climbing the low wall and stumbled over the lumpy sods of grass in the field. Finally, out of breath, he got to where a uniformed man, presumably Constable Weaver, stood talking to a gnarled old farmer about fifty yards up the slope.

By the side of the north–south wall, loosely covered with earth and stones, lay the body. Enough of its covering had been removed to make it recognizable as a man. The head lay to one side, and, kneeling beside it, Banks could see that the hair at the back was matted with blood. A jolt of nausea shot through his stomach, but he quickly controlled it as he began to make mental notes about the scene. Standing up, he was struck by the contrast between the beautiful, serene day and the corpse at his feet.

'Anything been disturbed?' he asked Weaver, stepping carefully back over the rope.

'Not much, sir,' the young constable replied. His face was white and the sour smell on his breath indicated that he had probably been sick over the wall. Natural enough, Banks thought. Probably the lad's first corpse.

'Mr Tavistock here' – he gestured towards the whiskered farmer – 'says he just moved those stones around the head to see what his dog was scratting at.'

Banks looked at Tavistock, whose grim expression betrayed a man used to death. Ex-army, most likely, and old enough to have seen action in two world wars.

'I were lookin' fer one 'o my sheep,' Tavistock began in a slow, thick Yorkshire accent, 'and I saw that there damage to t' wall. I thought there'd bin a c'lapse.' He paused and rubbed his grizzly chin. 'There shouldn't a bin no c'lapse in a Bessthwaite wall. Bin there sin' eighteen thirty, that 'as. Any road, old Ben started scratting. At first I thought nowt on it, then . . .' He shrugged as if there was nothing more to be said.

'What did you do when you realized what it was?' Banks asked.

Tavistock scratched his turkey neck and spat on the grass. 'Just 'ad a look, that's all. I thought it might a bin a sheep somebody'd killed. That 'appens sometimes. Then I ran 'ome' – he pointed to a farmhouse about half a mile away – 'and I called young Weaver 'ere.'

Banks was dubious about the 'ran' but he was glad that Tavistock had acted quickly. He turned away and gave instructions to the photographer and the forensic team, then took off his jacket and leaned against the warm stone wall while the boffins did their work.

THREE

Sally slammed down her knife and fork and yelled at her father: 'Just because I go for a walk with a boy it doesn't mean I'm a tramp or a trollop or any of those things!'

'Sally!' Mrs Lumb butted in. 'Stop shouting at your father. That wasn't what he meant and you know it.'

Sally continued to glare. 'Well that's what it sounded like to me.'

'He was only trying to warn you,' her mother went on. 'You have to be careful. Boys try to take advantage of you sometimes. Especially a good-looking girl like you.' She said it with a mixture of pride and fear.

'You don't have to treat me like I'm a baby, you know,' Sally said. 'I'm sixteen now.' She gave her mother a pitying glance, cast another baleful look at her father, and went back to her roast beef.

'Aye,' said Mr Lumb, 'and you'll do as you're told till you're eighteen. That's the law.'

To Sally, the man sitting opposite her was at the root of all her problems, and, of course, Charles Lumb fitted easily into the role his daughter had assigned him: that of an old-fashioned, narrow-minded yokel whose chief argument against anything new and interesting was, 'What was good enough for my father and his father before him is good enough for you too, young lady.' There was a strong conservative streak in him, only to be expected of someone whose family had lived in the area for more generations than could be remembered. A traditionalist, Charles Lumb often said that the dale as he had loved it was dying. He knew that the only chance for the young was to get away, and that saddened him. Quite soon, he was certain, even the inhabitants of the dales villages would belong to the National Trust, English Heritage or the Open Spaces Society. Like creatures in a zoo, they would be paid to act out their quaint old ways in a kind of living museum. The grandson of a cabinetmaker, Lumb, who worked at the local dairy factory, found it hard to see things otherwise. The old crafts were dying out because they were uneconomic, and only tourists kept one cooper, one blacksmith and one wheelwright in business.

But because Lumb was a Yorkshireman through and through, he tended to bait and tease in a manner that could easily be taken too seriously by an ambitious young girl like Sally. He delivered the most outrageous statements and opinions about her interests and dreams in such a deliberately deadpan voice that anyone could be excused for not catching the gentle, mocking humour behind them. If he had been less sarcastic and his daughter less self-centred, they might have realized that they loved each other very much.

The thing was, though, Charles Lumb would have liked to see more evidence of common sense in his daughter. She was certainly a bright girl, and it would be easy for her to get into university and become a doctor or a lawyer. A damn sight easier, he reflected, than it was in his day. But no, it had to be this bloody academy, and for all he tried, he could see no value in learning how to paint faces and show off swimsuits. If he had thought she had it in her to become a great actress, then he might have been more supportive. But he didn't. Maybe time would prove him wrong. He hoped so. At least seeing her on the telly would be something.

Sally, after a few minutes' sulking, decided to change the topic of conversation. 'Have you seen those men on the hill?' she asked. 'I wonder what they're doing?'

'Looking for something, I shouldn't wonder,' her father replied dryly, still not recovered from the argument.

Sally ignored him. 'They look like policemen to me. You can see the buttons of their uniforms shining. I'm going up there to have a look after dinner. There's already quite a crowd along the road.'

'Well, make sure you're back before midnight,' her mother said. It cleared the air a bit, and they enjoyed the rest of their meal in peace.

Sally walked up the hill road and turned right past the cottages. As she hurried on she danced and grabbed fistfuls of dry grass, which she flung up high in the air.

Several cars blocked the road by the field, and what had looked from a distance like a large crowd turned out to be nothing more than a dozen or so curious tourists with their cameras, rucksacks and hiking boots. It was open country, almost moorland despite the drystone walls that criss-crossed the landscape and gave it some semblance of order. They were old and only the farmers remembered who had built them.

There was more activity in the field than she could recollect ever seeing in such an isolated place. Uniformed men crawled on all fours in the wild grass, and the area by the wall had been cordoned off with stakes and rope. Inside the charmed circle stood a man with a camera, another with a black bag and, seemingly presiding over the whole affair, a small wiry man with a brown jacket slung over his shoulder. Sally's eyesight was so keen that she could even see the small patches of sweat under his arms.

She asked the middle-aged walker standing next to her what was going on, and the man told her he thought there'd been a murder. Of course. It had to be. She'd seen similar things on the telly.

FOUR

Banks glanced back towards the road. He'd noticed a flashing movement, but it was only a girl's blonde hair catching the sun. Dr Glendenning, the tall, white-haired pathologist, had finished shaking limbs and inserting his thermometer in orifices; now he stood, cigarette dangling from the corner of his mouth, muttering about what a warm night it had been as he made calculations in his little red notebook.

It was just as well, Banks thought as he looked over at the spectators, that two of the forensic team had first examined the roadside. They had found nothing – no skid marks or tyre tracks on the tarmac, no clear footprints on the grassy verge – but it looked as if someone or something had been dragged up the field from the road.

Glendenning confirmed that the victim had been killed elsewhere and merely dumped in this isolated spot. That would cause problems. If they had no idea where the man had been killed, they wouldn't know where to start looking for the killer.

The doctor rambled on, adjusting his column of figures, and Banks sniffed the air, feeling again that it was too fine a day and too beautiful a spot for such unpleasant business. Even the young photographer, Peter Darby, as he snapped the body from every conceivable angle, said that normally on such a day he would be out photographing Rawley Force at a slow shutter speed, or zooming in on petals with his macro lens, praying that a bee or a butterfly would remain still for as long as it took to focus and shoot. He had photographed corpses before, Banks knew, so he was used to the unpleasantness. All the same, it was worlds away from butterflies and waterfalls.

Glendenning looked up from his notebook and screwed up his eyes in the sunlight. A half-inch of ash floated to the ground, and Banks found himself wondering whether the doctor performed surgery with a cigarette in his mouth, letting ash fall around the incision. Smoking was strictly prohibited at the scene of a crime, of course, but nobody dared mention this to Glendenning.

'It was a warm night,' he explained to Banks, with a Scottish lilt to his nicotine-ravaged voice. 'I can't give an accurate estimate of time of death. Most likely, though, it was after dark last night and before sunrise this morning.'

Bloody wonderful! Banks thought. We don't know where he was killed but we know it was sometime during the night.

'Sorry,' Glendenning added, catching Bank's expression.

'Not your fault. Anything else?'

'Blow to the back of the head, if I may translate the cumbersome medical jargon into layman's terms. Pretty powerful, too. Skull cracked like an egg.'

'Any idea what weapon was used?'

'Proverbial blunt instrument. Sharp-edged, like a wrench or a hammer. I can't be more specific at this point but I'd rule out a brick or a rock. It's too neat and I can't find any trace of particles. Full report after the autopsy, of course.'

'Is that all?'

'Yes. You can have him taken to the mortuary now if you've finished with the pictures.'

Banks nodded. He asked a uniformed constable to send

for an ambulance, and Glendenning packed his bag.

'Weaver! Sergeant Hatchley! Come over here a minute,' Banks called, and watched the two men walk over. 'Any idea who the dead man was?' he asked Weaver.

'Yes, sir,' the pale constable answered. 'His name's Harry Steadman. Lives in the village.'

'Married?'

'Yes, sir.'

'Then we'd better get in touch with his wife. Sergeant, would you go over to Mr Tavistock's house and take an official statement?'

Hatchley nodded slowly.

'Is there a decent pub in Helmthorpe?' Banks asked Weaver.

'I usually drink at the Bridge, sir.'

'Food?'

'Not bad.'

'Right.' Banks turned to Hatchley. 'We'll go and see Mrs Steadman while you attend to Tavistock. Let's meet up in the Bridge for a bite to eat when we've done. All right?'

Hatchley agreed and lumbered off with Tavistock.

There was no chance of a roast beef dinner at home now. In fact, there would be few meals at home until the crime was solved. Banks knew from experience that once a murder investigation begins there is no stopping and little slowing down, even for family life. The crime invades meal times, ablutions and sleep; it dominates conversation and puts up an invisible barrier between the investigator and his family.

He looked down at the village spread out crookedly by a bend in the river, its grey slate roofs gleaming in the sun. The clock on the square church tower said twelve thirty.

Sighing, he nodded to Weaver, and the two of them set off towards the car.

They passed through the small crowd, ignoring the local reporter's tentative questions, and got into the Cortina. Banks cleared the cassettes from the passenger seat so that Weaver could sit beside him.

'Tell me what you know about Steadman,' Banks said as he reversed into a gateway and turned around.

'Lived here about eighteen months,' Weaver began. 'Used to come regular for holidays and sort of fell in love with the place. He inherited a fortune from his father and set himself up here. Used to be a university professor in Leeds. Educated chap, but not stuck-up. Early forties, bit over six-foot tall, sandy hair. Still quite young-looking. They live in Gratly.'

'I thought you said they lived in the village.'

'Same thing really, sir,' Weaver explained. 'You see, Gratly's just a little hamlet, a few old houses off the road. Doesn't even have a pub. But now the newer houses have spread up the hill, the two are as near as makes no difference. The locals like to keep the name, though. Sense of independence, I suppose.'

Banks drove down the hill towards the bridge. Weaver pointed ahead over the river and up the opposite valley side: 'That's Gratly, sir.'

Banks saw the row of new houses, some still under construction; then there was a space of about a hundred yards before the crossroads lined with older cottages.

'I see what you mean,' Banks said. At least the builders were doing a tasteful job, following the design of the originals and using the same local stone.

Weaver went on making conversation no doubt intended to help him forget the sight of his first corpse.

'Just about all the new houses in Helmthorpe are at this side of the village. You'll get nothing new on the east side. Some bright sparks say it's because it was settled from the east. Vikings, Saxons, Romans and whatnot. Course, you don't find many traces of them now, but the place stills seems to spread westwards.' He thought about what he'd said for a moment and added with a smile, 'Spreads slowly, that is, sir.'

Much as Banks was interested in snippets of local history, he lost track of Weaver's words as he drove over the low stone bridge and crossed Helmthorpe High Street. He cursed to himself. It was early Sunday afternoon and, from what he could see around him, that meant car-washing time in the village. Men stood in driveways in front of garages with their sleeves rolled up and buckets of soapy water by their sides. Shiny car roofs gleamed and water dripped from doors and bumpers. Polished chrome shone. If Harry Steadman had been dumped from a local car, all traces of that grisly journey would have been obliterated by now in the most natural way: soaped and waxed over, vacuumed and swept out.

Steadman's house, last in a short block running left from the road, was larger than Banks had imagined. It was solidly built and looked weather-beaten enough to pass for a historic building. That meant it would sell for a historic price, too, he noted. A double garage had been built on the eastern side, and the large garden, bordered by a low wall, consisted of a well-kept lawn with a colourful flower bed at its centre and rose bushes against the house front and the neighbour's fence. Leaving Weaver in the car, Banks walked down the crazy paving and rang the doorbell.

The woman who answered, holding a cup of tea in her

hand, looked puzzled to find a stranger standing before her. She was plain-looking, with stringy, lifeless brown hair, and wore a pair of overlarge, unbecoming spectacles. She was dressed in a shapeless beige cardigan and baggy checked slacks. Banks thought she might be the cleaning lady, so he phrased his greeting as a question: 'Mrs Steadman?'

'Yes,' the woman answered hesitantly, peering at him through her glasses. He introduced himself and felt the familiar tightening in his stomach as he was ushered into the living room. It was always like that. No amount of experience purged that gut-wrenching feeling of sympathy that accompanied the soothing, useless words, the empty gestures. For Banks there was always a shadow: it could be *my* wife, it could be someone telling me about *my* daughter. It was the same as that first glimpse of the murder victim. Death and its long aftermath had never become a matter of routine for him but remained always an abomination, a reminder one hardly needed of man's cruelty to his fellow man, his fallen nature.

Although the room was messy – a low table littered with magazines, knitting spread out on a chair, records out of their sleeves by the music centre – it was clean, and sunlight poured over the red and yellow roses through spotless mullioned windows. Above the large stone fireplace hung a romantic painting of what Swainsdale must have looked like over a hundred years ago. It hadn't changed all that much, but somehow the colours seemed brighter and bolder in the picture, the contours more definite.

'What is it?' Mrs Steadman asked, pulling a chair forward for Banks. 'Has there been an accident? Is something wrong?'

As he broke the news, Banks watched Mrs Steadman's

expression change from disbelief to shock. Finally, she began to weep silently. There was no sobbing; the tears simply ran down her pale cheeks and dripped on to the wrinkled cardigan as she stared blankly ahead. They could have been caused by an onion, Banks found himself thinking, disturbed by her absolute silence.

'Mrs Steadman?' he said gently, touching her sleeve. 'I'm afraid there are a few questions I have to ask you right away.'

She looked at him, nodded and dried her eyes with a screwed-up Kleenex. 'Of course.'

'Why didn't you report your husband missing, Mrs Steadman?'

'Missing?' She frowned at him. 'Why should I?'

Banks was taken aback, but he pressed on gently. 'I'm afraid you'll have to tell me that. He can't have come home last night. Weren't you worried? Didn't you wonder where he was?'

'Oh, I see what you mean,' she said, dabbing at her damp, reddened cheeks with the crumpled tissue. 'You weren't to know, were you? You see, I wasn't expecting him home last night. He went out just after seven o'clock. He said he was calling for a pint at the Bridge – he often went there – and then driving on to York. He had work to do there and he wanted to make an early start.'

'Did he often do that?'

'Yes, quite often. Sometimes I went with him, but I was feeling a bit under the weather last night – summer cold, I think – and besides, I know they get much more done without me. Anyway, I watched television with Mrs Stanton next door and let him go. Harry stayed with his publisher. Well, more of a family friend really. Michael Ramsden.'

'What kind of work did they do on a Sunday?'

'Oh, it wasn't what you or I would understand by work. They were writing a book. Harry mostly, but Michael was interested and helped him. A local history book. That was Harry's field. They'd go off exploring ruins – Roman forts, old lead mines, anything.'

'I see. And it was normal for him to go the night before and stay with Mr Ramsden?'

'Yes. As I've said, they were more like friends than anything else. We've known the family for a long time. Harry was terrible at getting up in the morning, so if they wanted a full day, he'd go over the night before and Michael would be sure to get him up on time. They'd spend the evening going over notes and making plans. I'd no reason to report him missing. I thought he was in York.' Her voice faltered and she started to cry again.

Banks waited and let her dry her eyes before asking his next question. 'Wouldn't Mr Ramsden be worried if he didn't arrive? Didn't he call you to find out what had happened?'

'No.' She paused, blew her nose and went on. 'I told you, it wasn't that kind of work. More like a hobby, really. Anyway, Michael doesn't have a telephone. He'd just assume that something had come up and Harry couldn't make it.'

'Just one more thing, Mrs Steadman, then I won't bother you any further today. Could you tell me where your husband might have left his car?'

'In the big car park by the river,' she replied. 'The Bridge hasn't got a car park of its own so the customers use that one. You can't really leave cars in the street here; there's not room enough.'

'Do you have a spare key?'

'I think he kept one around. I don't use it myself. I have an old Fiesta. Just a moment.' Mrs Steadman disappeared into the kitchen and returned a few moments later with the key. She also gave Banks the number of Steadman's beige Sierra.

'Could you tell me where Mr Ramsden lives, too? I'd like to let him know what's happened as soon as possible.'

Mrs Steadman seemed a bit surprised, but she gave the information without questions. 'It's not so hard to find,' she added. 'There are no other houses within half a mile yet. Do you need me to . . . er . . .'

'To identify the body?'

Mrs Steadman nodded.

'Yes, I'm afraid we do. Tomorrow will do, though. Is there anyone you can get to stay with you for a while?'

She stared at him, her features ugly and swollen with crying; her eyes looked fishy behind the harsh magnification of the glasses. 'Mrs Stanton, next door . . . if you would.'

'Of course.'

Banks went next door. Mrs Stanton, a long-nosed, alert-looking little woman, immediately grasped the situation. Banks sympathized with her shock. 'I know,' he said. 'It must seem so abrupt. To think that you saw him only last night.'

She nodded. 'Aye. And to think what was happening while me and Emma were watching that silly old film. Still,' she ended stoically, 'who are we to question the ways of the good Lord?' She told her husband, who sat slouched in an armchair reading his *News of the World*, to keep an eye on the roast, then went over to comfort her neighbour. Sure that he was leaving the widow in capable hands, Banks returned to his car and got in next to Weaver, who had regained his pinkish colour.

'I'm sorry, sir,' he mumbled. 'About being sick. I've—'

'Never seen a corpse before? I know. Never mind, Constable, there's a first time for everyone, more's the pity. Shall we go to the Bridge for a bite to eat?' Weaver nodded. 'I'm starving, myself,' Banks went on, starting the car, 'and you look like you could do with a drop of brandy.'

As he drove the short distance down to the Bridge on Helmthorpe High Street, Banks thought about his inter- view with Mrs Steadman. It had made him feel edgy and uneasy. At times, after the initial shock, her reaction had seemed more like relief than grief. Perhaps the marriage had been shaky, Banks found himself thinking, and Mrs Steadman had suddenly found herself both wealthy and free. Surely that would explain it?

2

ONE

Weaver pulled a face. 'I don't like brandy, sir,' he admitted sheepishly. 'My mum always used to give me a drop for medicinal purposes whenever I got a cold as a lad. Never could stomach the stuff.'

The two of them sat in a corner of the Bridge's quiet lounge. Banks nursed a pint of hand-drawn Theakston's bitter, and Weaver complained about his brandy.

'Did it do you any good?' Banks asked.

'I suppose so, sir. But it always reminds me of medicine, of being poorly, if you follow my drift.'

Banks laughed and went to buy Weaver a pint to chase away the bad taste. They were waiting for Detective Sergeant Hatchley, who was still with Tavistock, no doubt enjoying a good cup of tea or something stronger and, perhaps, a plateful of roast beef.

'Tell me,' Banks asked, 'why is this place so empty? It's Sunday dinner time and the village is crawling with tourists.'

'That's right, sir,' Weaver said. His boyish face had fully regained its natural pink flush. 'But look around you.'

Banks looked. They were in a small lounge with faded wallpaper and a cracked brown ceiling. A few water-colours of local scenes, reminiscent of the ones in old railway carriages, covered the most obvious damp spots on the walls. The tables were worn and scored from years of dominoes and shove-ha'penny, and ringed by generations of overflowing beer glasses; around the edges were charred semicircles where cigarettes had been left to burn out. A rack holding tongs and a bent poker stood by the small tiled fireplace. True, it didn't look much.

'There are three pubs in Helmthorpe, sir,' Weaver began, counting them off on his chubby red fingers. 'That's if you don't count the country club, for the nobs. There's the Dog and Gun, and the Hare and Hounds; they're for the tourists mostly. Real olde worlde country inns, if you get my meaning, sir – horse brasses, copper bedwarmers, antique tables with kneecapper wrought-iron legs, you name it. They have big old fireplaces too, all done up with black lead. Now that every pub in Christendom seems to offer real ale, it's got trendy to advertise a real fire.

'The Dog and Gun's a kind of family place with tables out back by the river and a little enclosed area for the kiddies to play in, and the Hare and Hounds is more for the younger set. They have a disco there every Friday and Saturday in season and you get a lot of the campers going along. That's when we get most of our bother here – the odd fight, that kind of thing. Some nights during the week they have folk music, too. A bit more civilized, if you ask me.'

Weaver sniffed and nodded towards the wall. 'And then there's this place. It's fairly new by village standards – Victorian, I'd say at a pinch. And it's all that's left for the serious drinkers. The only people who drink here are the locals and a few visitors who know about the beer. It's a pretty well-guarded secret. Course, on weekends you do get a few hikers and whatnot in the public bar. They've all read their good beer guides these days, it seems. But they never cause much trouble; they're a quiet lot, really.'

'Why did Steadman drink here, do you think?'

'Steadman?' Weaver seemed surprised to be so quickly jolted back to business. 'Liked the beer, I suppose. And he was pally with a few of the regulars.'

'But he had money, didn't he? A lot of money. He certainly didn't get that house on the cheap.'

'Oh yes, he had money. Rumour has it he inherited over a quarter of a million from his father. His pals have money too, but they're not nobs. Much more down-to-earth.'

Banks was still puzzled why someone so well off would drink in such a dump, good beer or not. By rights, Steadman ought to have been chugging champagne by the magnum to wash down his caviar. Those were London terms, though, he reminded himself: ostentatious display of wealth. Maybe people with over a quarter of a million who lived in Helmthorpe by choice were different. He doubted it. But Steadman certainly sounded unusual.

'Liked his drink, did he?'

'Never known him drink too much, sir. I think he just enjoyed the company here.'

'Glad to get away from the wife?'

Weaver reddened. 'I wouldn't know about that, sir. Never heard anything. But he was a funny sort of chap.'

'In what way?'

'Well, sir, like I said, he used to be a professor at Leeds University. When he inherited the money, he just packed in his job, bought the old Ramsden house and moved up here.'

'Ramsden house?' Banks cut in. 'That wouldn't have

anything to do with Michael Ramsden, would it?'

Weaver raised an eyebrow. 'As a matter of fact, sir, yes,' he answered. 'It was his parents' house. Used to be a bed-and-breakfast place when Steadman and his wife started coming up here for their holidays ten years ago or more. Young Michael went to university and landed a good job with a publishing firm in London. Then, when old Mr Ramsden died, the mother couldn't afford to keep on the house, so she went off to live with her sister in Torquay. It all happened at just the right time for Steadman.'

Banks looked at Weaver in astonished admiration. 'How old are you?' he asked.

'Twenty-one, sir.'

'How do you manage to know so much about things that happened before your time?'

'Family, sir. I was born and raised in the area. And Sergeant Mullins. He runs the show around here usually, but he's on holiday right now. There's not much escapes Sergeant Mullins.'

Banks sat in silence for a moment and enjoyed his beer as he sifted the information.

'What about Steadman's drinking companions?' he asked finally. 'What kind of people are they?'

'He brought them all together, sir,' Weaver answered. 'Oh, they all knew each other well enough before he moved up here, like, but Steadman was a friendly sort, interested in everything and everyone. When he wasn't busying himself with his books or poking around ruins and abandoned mines he was quite a socializer. There's Jack Barker, for one – you might have heard of him?'

Banks shook his head.

'Writer. Mystery stories.' Weaver smiled. 'Quite good

really. Plenty of sex and violence.' He blushed. 'Nothing like the real thing, of course.'

'Oh, I don't know,' Banks said, smiling. 'Go on.'

'Well, sir, he's been here three or four years. Don't know where he started from. Then there's Doc Barnes, born and raised hereabouts, and Teddy Hackett, local entrepreneur. He owns the garage over there, and a couple of gift shops. That's all, really. They're all fortyish. Well, Doc Barnes is a bit older and Barker's in his late thirties. An odd group, when you think about it. I've been in here a few times when they were together and from what I could hear they'd take the mickey out of Steadman a bit, him being an academic and all that. But not nasty like. All in good fun.'

'No animosity? You're certain?'

'No, sir. Not as far as I could tell. I don't get in here as often as I'd like. Wife and kid, you see.' He beamed.

'Work, too.'

'Aye, that keeps me busy as well. But I seem to spend more time giving directions to bloody tourists and telling the time than dealing with local affairs. Whoever said "If you want to know the way, ask a policeman" ought to be shot.'

Banks laughed. 'The locals are a fairly law-abiding lot, then?'

'On the whole, yes. We get a few drunks now and then. Especially at the Hare and Hounds disco, as I said. But that's mostly visitors. Then there's the odd domestic dispute. But most of our troubles come from tourists leaving their cars all over the place and making too much noise. It's a peaceful place, really, though there's some as would say it's boring.'

At this point, Sergeant Hatchley walked in and joined

them. He was a bulky, fair-haired and freckle-faced man in his early thirties, and he and Banks had developed a tolerable working relationship despite some early hostilities – partly due to north–south rivalry and partly to Hatchley's having hoped for the job Banks got.

Hatchley bought a round of drinks and they all ordered steak and kidney pies, which turned out to be very tasty. Not too much kidney, as Weaver remarked. Banks complimented the landlord and was rewarded with an ambiguous 'Aye.'

'Anything new?' Banks asked the sergeant.

Hatchley lit a cigarette, lounged back in his chair, rubbed a hand like a hairy ham across his stubbly cheek, and cleared his throat.

'Nowt much, by the look of things. Old Tavistock went looking for a stray sheep and dug up a fresh corpse. That's about the strength of it.'

'Was it unusual for him to go poking around by that wall? Would other people be likely to go there?'

'If you're thinking that anyone could expect to dump a body there and leave it undiscovered for weeks, then you're barking up the wrong tree. Even if old Tavistock hadn't gone out looking for his bloody sheep, someone would've come along soon enough – hikers, courting couples.'

Banks sipped some more beer. 'So he wasn't dumped there for concealment, then?'

'Shouldn't think so, no. Probably put there just so we'd have to leg it halfway up to Crow bloody Scar.'

Banks laughed. 'More likely so we wouldn't know where he was killed.'

'Aye.'

'Why wasn't Steadman reported missing, sir?' Weaver

cut in. He seemed anxious to restore to the chief inspector the respect that Hatchley appeared to be denying him.

Banks told him. Then he told Hatchley to get back to the Eastvale station, find out as much as he could about Steadman's background and collate any reports that came in.

'What about the press?' Hatchley asked. 'They're all over the place now.'

'You can tell them we've found a body.'

'Shall I tell them who it is?'

Banks sighed and gave Hatchley a long-suffering look. 'Don't be so bloody silly. Not until we've got a formal identification you can't, no.'

'And what will you be doing, sir?'

'My job.' Banks turned to Weaver. 'You'd better get back to the station, lad. Who's in charge?'

Weaver blushed again, his pinkness deepening to crimson. 'I am, sir. At least, I am at the moment. Sergeant Mullins is away for two weeks. Remember I told you about him, sir?'

'Yes, of course. How many men have you got?'

'There's only two of us, sir. It's a quiet place. I called some of the lads in from Lyndgarth and Fortford to help with the search. There's not more than half a dozen of us altogether.'

'All right, then,' Banks said, 'it looks like you're in charge. Get a request for information printed up and distributed – shops, pubs, church notice board. Then start a house-to-house enquiry up Hill Road. That body wasn't carried all the way up there, and somebody might just have seen or heard a car. At least it'll help us narrow down the time of death. All right?'

'Yes, sir.'

'And don't worry. If you need any more men, let Eastvale station know and they'll see what they can do. I'm going to pay Michael Ramsden a visit myself, but if you ask for Sergeant Rowe, I'll make sure he has full instructions.'

He turned to Hatchley again. 'Before you go back, go and tell the men up in the field that they're temporarily transferred to Helmthorpe and they're to take their orders from Constable Weaver here. They'll probably understand the situation already, but make it official. And check the car park for a beige Sierra.' He gave Hatchley the number of the car and handed him the keys. 'It's Steadman's car,' he added, 'and while it doesn't look as if he got to use it last night, you never know. It might tell us something. Get forensic on to it right away.'

'Yes, sir,' Hatchley said through clenched teeth as he left. Banks could almost hear the 'three bags full, sir' that the sergeant probably added when he got outside.

He grinned broadly at the nonplussed young constable and said, 'Don't mind him; he's probably just got a hangover. Now, off you go, Weaver. Time to get to work.'

Alone, he slipped his new pipe from his jacket pocket and stuffed it with shag. Drawing in the harsh tobacco, he coughed and shook his head. He still couldn't get used to the damn thing; maybe mild cigarettes would be better, after all.

TWO

Excited, Sally had watched Banks drive off towards the village and followed in the same direction. She stopped to pick a campion by the hedgerow and casually admired its pinkish-purple colour, the petals like a baby's splayed fingers. Then, thinking about what she had to tell her friends, she let it drop and hurried on her way.

She had actually seen the man, the policeman in charge, close up, and had had to stifle a giggle as he lost his footing climbing the low wall. It was obvious he wasn't used to bounding about the northern countryside; perhaps he'd been sent up by Scotland Yard. She found his gaunt angled face under the short neat black hair attractive, despite a nose that had clearly been broken and imperfectly reset. The sharp restless eyes expressed energy and power, and the little white scar beside his right eye seemed, to Sally, a mark of exotic experience. She imagined he'd got into a fight to the death with a blood-crazed murderer. Even though he seemed too short for a policeman, his wiry body looked nimble and strong.

At the western edge of the village, near the Bridge, was a coffee bar where Sally and her friends hung out. The coffee was weak, the Coke warm and the Greek owner surly, but the place boasted two video games, an up-to-date jukebox and an ancient pinball machine. Of course, Sally would rather have expertly applied a little make-up and passed for eighteen in one of the pubs – especially the Hare and Hounds on disco night – but in such a small community everyone seemed to know a little about everyone else's business, and she was worried in case word got back to her father. She had been in pubs in Eastvale with Kevin, though even that was risky with the school so close by, and in Leeds and York, which were safer, and nobody had ever questioned her about her age.

The door rattled as she pushed it open and entered to the familiar bleeping of massacred aliens. Kathy Chalmers and Hazel Kirk were engrossed in the game, while Anne

Downes looked on coolly. She was a bookish girl, plain and bespectacled, but she wanted to be liked; and if that meant hanging around with video-game players, then so be it. The others teased her a bit, but never maliciously, and she was blessed with a sharp, natural wit that helped her hold her own.

The other two were more like Sally, if not as pretty. They chewed gum, applied make-up (unlike Sally, they did this badly) and generally fussed about their hair and clothes. Kathy had even got away with a henna treatment. Her parents had been furious, but there was nothing much they could do after the fact. It was Hazel, the sultry, black-haired one, who spoke first.

'Look who's here,' she announced. 'And where have you been all weekend?' The glint in her eye implied that she knew very well where Sally had been and who she had been with. Under normal circumstances Sally would have played along, hinting at pleasures she believed Hazel had only read about in books, but this time she ignored the innuendo and got herself a Coke from the unsmiling Greek. The espresso machine was hissing like an old steam engine and the aliens were still bleeping in their death throes. Sally leaned against the column opposite Anne and waited impatiently for a silence into which she could drop her news.

When the game was over, Kathy reached for another coin, a manoeuvre that necessitated arching her back and stretching out her long legs so that she could thrust her hand deep enough into the pocket of her skintight Calvin Kleins. As she did this, Sally noticed the Greek ogling from behind his coffee machine. Choosing her moment for best dramatic effect, she finally spoke: 'Guess what. There's been a murder. Here in the village. They dug up a body under Crow Scar. I've just come from there. I've *seen* it.'

Anne's pale eyes widened behind her thick lenses. 'A murder! Is that what those men are doing up there?'

'They're conducting a search of the scene,' Sally announced, hoping she'd got the phrasing right. 'The scene of the crime. And the forensic team was there too, taking blood samples and tissue. And the police photographer and the Home Office pathologist. All of them.'

Kathy slid back into her seat, forgetting the game. 'A murder? In Helmthorpe?' She gasped in disbelief. 'Who was it?'

Here Sally had to admit lack of information, which she disguised neatly by assuming that Kathy meant 'Who was the murderer?' 'They don't know yet, you fool,' she replied scornfully. 'It's only just happened.' Then she hurried on, keen not to lose their attention to further fleets of aliens. 'I saw the superintendent close up. Quite a dish, actually. Not at all what you'd expect. And I could see the body. Well, some of it. It was buried by the wall up in Tavistock's field. Somebody had scraped away some of the loose soil and then covered it with stones. There was a hand and a leg sticking out.'

Hazel Kirk tossed back a glossy raven's wing of hair. 'Sally Lumb, you're a liar,' she said. 'You couldn't see that far. The police wouldn't have let anyone get that close.'

'I did,' Sally countered. 'I could even see the wet patches under the superintendent's arms.' She realized too late that this outburst clashed with her more romantic image of the 'superintendent' and rushed on, hoping nobody would notice. Only Anne wrinkled her nose. 'And old man Tavistock was there. I think he discovered the body. And all the policemen from miles around. Geoff Weaver was there.'

'That pink-faced pansy,' Kathy cut in.

'It wasn't so pink today, I can tell you. I think he'd been sick.'

'Well, wouldn't you be if you'd just found a dead body?' Anne asked, coming to the defence of young Weaver, on whom she had had a schoolgirl crush for nearly six months. 'It was probably all decomposed and rotten.'

Sally ignored her. 'And there was another inspector, or whatever they call them. He wasn't in uniform anyway. Tall, strawy hair – a bit like your dad, Kathy.'

'That'll be Jim Hatchley,' Anne said. 'Actually, he's only a sergeant. My father knows him. Remember when the social club was broken into last year? Well, they sent him from Eastvale. He even came to our house. My dad's treasurer, you know. Hatchley's a coarse pig. He's even got hairs up his nose and in his ears. And I'll bet that other chap was Chief Inspector Banks. He had his picture in the paper a while back. Don't you ever read the papers?'

Anne's stream of information and opinion silenced everyone for a moment. Then Sally, who read nothing but *Vogue* and *Cosmopolitan*, picked up the thread again. 'They're here now. In the village. They drove down before I came.'

'I'm surprised they didn't give you a lift,' Hazel said, 'seeing as how you're on such good terms.'

'Shut up, Hazel Kirk!' Sally said indignantly. Hazel just smirked. 'They're here. They'll be questioning everybody, you know. They'll probably want to talk to all of us.'

'Why should they want to do that?' Kathy asked. 'We don't know anything about it.'

'It's just what they do, stupid,' Sally retorted. 'They do

house-to-house searches and take statements from everyone. How do they know we don't know anything till they
ask us?'

Sally's logic silenced Kathy and Hazel.

'We don't even know who the victim was yet,' Anne
chimed in. 'Who do you think it was?'

'I'll bet it was that Johnnie Parrish,' Kathy said. 'He
looks like a man with a past to me.'

'Johnnie Parrish!' Sally sneered. 'Why, he's about as
interesting as a . . . a . . .'

'A dose of clap?' Anne suggested. They all laughed.

'Even that would be more interesting than Johnnie
Parrish. I'll bet it was Major Cartwright. He's such a
miserable, bad-tempered old bugger there must be lots of
people want to kill him.'

'His daughter, for one,' Hazel said, and giggled.

'Why?' Sally asked. She didn't like to think she was
excluded from what appeared to be common knowledge.

'Well, you know,' Kathy stalled. 'You know what
people say.'

'About what?'

'About Major Cartwright and his daughter. How he
keeps such a tight rein on her since she came back to the
village. Why she ran off in the first place. It's unnatural.
That's what people say.'

'Oh, is that all,' Sally said, not quite sure she understood. 'But she's got her own place, that cottage by the
church.'

'Maybe it was Alf Pringle,' Hazel suggested. 'Now
there's a nasty piece of work. Be doing us all a favour if
somebody did away with him.'

'Wishful thinking.' Kathy sighed. 'Do you know, he
chased me off his land the other day. I was only picking

wild flowers for that school project. He had his shotgun with him, too.'

'He sounds more like a murderer than a victim,' Anne chipped in. 'Who do you think did it?'

'Well, it might not be anyone from around here,' Kathy answered. 'I mean, we don't know, do we? It could have been a stranger.'

'Of course it was someone from around here,' Sally said, annoyed at the way her discovery seemed to have become common property. 'You don't think somebody would drive a body all the way from Leeds or somewhere like that just to dump it under Crow Scar, do you?'

'They could have done.' Kathy defended herself without much conviction.

'Well, I'm not going out after dark until he's been caught.' Hazel hugged herself and shuddered. 'It might be one of those sex murderers, another Ripper. It could even be Major Cartwright's daughter up there, for all we know. Or that Mrs Caret, the new barmaid at the Dog and Gun.'

'I shouldn't worry,' Kathy said. 'Nobody would want to sex murder you.' She spoke in the usual spirit of friendly banter, but somehow her joke flopped and the girls seemed distracted, each wrapped in her own thoughts. Kathy blushed. 'Still,' she said, 'we'd better be careful.'

'I'll bet it was Jack Barker that did it,' Anne suggested.

'Who? That writer bloke?' Sally said.

'Yes. You know what kind of books he writes.'

'I'll bet you haven't read any,' Kathy taunted her.

'Yes, I have. I've read *The Butcher of Redondo Beach* and *The San Clemente Slasher*. They're lurid.'

'I've read one too,' Hazel said. 'I can't remember what it was called but it was about this man who went to his

beach house somewhere in America and he found two
people he'd never seen before chopped to pieces in his
living room. It was grisly. I only read it because he lives
here.'

'That's *The Butcher of Redondo Beach*,' Anne informed
her patiently. 'That's what it's called.'

Sally was bored by the direction the conversation was
taking, and, besides, she thought Jack Barker looked far
too handsome and debonair to be a murderer. He was a
bit like one of those old film stars her mother was always
going on about – Errol Flynn, Clark Gable or Douglas
Fairbanks – the ones who all looked the same with their
oily, slicked-down hair and little moustaches. He was the
type, she thought, who might shoot his adulterous wife (if
he had one) in a fit of passion, but he certainly wouldn't
carry her body all the way up to Crow Scar afterwards,
that was for sure. He was far too much of a gentleman to
do that, whatever kind of books he wrote.

Sally finished her Coke and turned to leave, but before
she did so she whispered, 'The police will see me. I can
tell you that for sure. I know something. I don't know
who's dead or who the killer is yet, but I know
something.'

And with that she exited quickly, leaving the others to
gape after her and debate whether she was telling the
truth or simply trying to draw attention to herself.

THREE

There are two routes to York from Helmthorpe. The first
winds up through Gratly, continues diagonally across the
dales, more or less as the crow flies, and eventually joins

the main road a couple of miles outside the city; the second, longer but quicker, involves taking the main road back to Eastvale, then driving south-east on the busy York Road. Because it was a beautiful day and he was in no real hurry, Banks took the first route on his visit to Ramsden.

He slipped the cassette back into the player and to the strains of 'O, Sweet Woods' drove up the hill, turned left past the Steadman house and followed the road as it climbed the dale side slowly. He passed through the tiny hamlet of Mortsett and paused with his window down to look at an attractive cottage with a post office sign above its door and a board advertising Wall's Ice Cream propped outside. Insects hovered and hummed in the still, warm air; it seemed unreal, an image of England from before the First World War.

Beyond Relton, at the junction with the Fortford road, he seemed to leave civilization behind. Soon, the greens of the hillsides gave way to the darker hues of the heather-covered moors, which continued for about two miles before dropping slowly into the next dale. It was like a slow roller coaster ride, and the only obstacles were the sheep that sometimes strayed on to the unfenced road, itself only a thin band hardly distinguishable from the landscape around it. Banks saw a few hikers, who stepped on to the rough grass when they heard his car, smiling and waving as he drove by.

The main road, busy with lorries and delivery vans, came as a shock. Following Mrs Steadman's directions, Banks found the turn-off, a narrow track with a lonely red phone box on the corner, about a mile from York's boundary. He turned left and, after a quarter of a mile, came to the converted farmhouse. He pulled into the smooth dirt driveway and stopped outside the new-looking garage.

Ramsden answered the door shortly after the first ring and asked who he was. When Banks showed some identification, he slipped off the chain and invited him in.

'Can't be too careful,' he apologized. 'Especially in such an isolated place as this.'

Ramsden was tall and pale, with the melancholic aspect of a Romantic poet. He had light-brown hair and, Banks soon noticed, a nervous habit of brushing back the stray forelock even when it hadn't slid down over his brow. The jeans and sweatshirt he wore seemed to hang on him as if they were a size too big.

'Please excuse the mess,' he said as he led Banks into a cluttered living room and installed him by the huge empty fireplace. 'As you can see I'm decorating. Just finished the first coat.' A clear polythene sheet covered half the floor, and on it stood a stepladder, a gallon of pale blue paint, brushes, tray and rollers. 'It's not about that woman, is it?' he asked.

'What woman?'

'An old lady not far from here was murdered by thugs a few months ago. I had a policeman around then.'

'No, sir, it's not about the woman. That would have been York Region. I'm from Eastvale CID.'

Ramsden frowned. 'I'm afraid I don't understand then. Pardon me, I don't mean to seem rude, but . . .'

'I'm sorry, sir,' Banks apologized, accepting the whisky and soda Ramsden had poured for him without asking. 'This isn't easy for me. Would you care to sit down?'

Ramsden looked alarmed. 'What is it?' he asked, fitting himself awkwardly into a small armchair.

'You were expecting Mr Steadman to visit you last night?'

'Harry? That's right. We had some notes to go over

before today's field trip. Why? Has something happened?'

'Yes, I'm afraid it has,' Banks said as gently as he could, aware of the muscles in his stomach clenching tightly. 'Mr Steadman is dead.'

Ramsden brushed back the phantom forelock. 'I don't follow. Dead? But he was coming here.'

'I know that, Mr Ramsden. That's why I wanted to tell you myself. Weren't you surprised when he didn't show up? Weren't you worried?'

Ramsden shook his head. 'No, no, of course I wasn't. It wasn't the first time he hadn't come. But are you *sure*? About Harry, I mean. Can't there have been some mistake?'

'I'm afraid not.'

'What on earth happened?'

'We're not certain about that yet, sir, but a farmer found his body this morning in a field under Crow Scar. It looks as if he was murdered.'

'Murdered? Good God! Harry? I can't believe it.'

'You know no one who'd have a reason?'

'Absolutely not. Nobody. Not Harry.' He rubbed his face and stared at Banks. 'I'm sorry, Chief Inspector, I can't really think straight. I'm having trouble taking this all in. I've known Harry for a long time. A long time. This is such a shock.'

'I realize it must be, sir,' Banks persisted, 'but if you could just spare the time to answer a couple of questions, I'll be on my way.'

'Yes, of course.' Ramsden got up and made a drink for himself.

'You said it had happened before, that he hadn't turned up?'

'Yes. It wasn't a formal arrangement. More casual, really.'

'Why didn't he come?'

'Once when Emma wasn't too well he couldn't make it. And one time he had a stomach upset. Things like that. We were very close, Chief Inspector. There was always a bed made up for him, and he had a key in case I had to go out.'

'Didn't it cross your mind to phone and ask what was wrong?'

'Not at all. I've already told you our arrangement was casual. I don't have a phone. I spend enough time on the blasted thing at work. The nearest public call box is on the main road.' He shook his head. 'I just can't believe this is happening. It's like a bad dream. Harry, dead?'

'Did you go out last night?'

Ramsden looked at him blankly.

'You said Mr Steadman had a key in case you were out,' Banks pressed on. 'Were you out last night?'

'No, I wasn't. Actually, when Harry hadn't arrived by eleven o'clock, I was rather – I mean, don't get me wrong – a little relieved. You see, I'm working on a book of my own. A historical novel. And I was glad of the opportunity to get some writing done.' He looked embarrassed about it.

'Didn't you like working with Mr Steadman?'

'Oh, of course I did. But it was his baby, really. I was just the editor, the research assistant.'

'Where were you planning to go today?'

'We were going to visit an old lead mine in Swaledale. Quite a distance really, so we wanted to get an early start. Emma!' he exclaimed suddenly. 'Emma must be in a terrible state.'

'She's upset, of course,' Banks said. 'Mrs Stanton, the neighbour, is looking after her.'

'Should I go?'

'That's up to you, Mr Ramsden, but I'd say best leave her for today at least. She's in good hands.'

Ramsden nodded. 'Of course, of course . . .'

'What about you? Will you be all right?'

'Yes, I'll be fine. It's just the shock. I've known Harry for more than ten years.'

'Would it be possible to talk to you again about this? Just to get some background, that kind of thing?'

'Yes, I suppose so. When?'

'The sooner the better, really. Tuesday morning, perhaps? We might know a bit more by then.'

'I'll be at work. Fisher and Faulkner. We're not terrifically busy at the moment. If you want to drop by . . .'

'Yes, that'll be fine.'

Banks asked directions to the publishers, then left Ramsden and returned to Eastvale by the quickest route. At the station, an invitation to call at Superintendent Gristhorpe's for tea awaited him. He phoned Sandra, who wasn't at all surprised at his absence, checked that no important news had come in while he had been at Ramsden's, and set off for Helmthorpe for the second time that day. It was only three o'clock, and, as he wasn't expected at Gristhorpe's until five, he would have plenty of time to see how the locals were coping.

The Helmthorpe police station was a converted cottage on a narrow cobbled road that forked from the eastern end of the High Street towards the river. There, Weaver, who was running off more copies of the request for information, told him that three constables were still making door-to-door enquiries along Hill Road and another had been dispatched to the campsite.

That was the biggest headache, Banks realized. They

would have to try and find out who had been staying at the campsite on Saturday night. Most of the campers would have moved on by now and it would be damn near impossible to get comprehensive or reliable information.

There was also the press to deal with. Besides Reg Summers of the local weekly, two other reporters were still hanging around outside the station, as Hatchley had warned, thrusting their notebooks at everyone who entered or left. Banks certainly liked to maintain good relations with the press, but at such an early stage in the investigation he could give them little of value. However, to gain and keep their goodwill – because he knew they would be useful eventually – he told them what he could in as pleasant a manner as possible.

At twenty to five, he left Weaver in charge and drove off to see Gristhorpe. On the way, he decided he would visit the Bridge that evening to see what he could get out of Steadman's cronies. More, he hoped, than he'd managed to pick up so far.

3

ONE

Banks pulled into the rutted drive at five to five and walked towards the squat stone house. Gristhorpe lived in an isolated farmhouse on the north dale side above the village of Lyndgarth, about halfway between Eastvale and Helmthorpe. It was no longer a functioning farm, though the superintendent still held on to a couple of acres where he grew vegetables. Since his wife had died five years ago, he had stayed on there alone, and a woman from the village came up to do for him every morning.

The building was too austere for Banks, but he could see it was ideally suited to the environment. In a part of the country windswept and lashed by rain much of the year, any human dwelling had to be built like a fortress to provide even the most basic domestic comforts. Inside, though, Gristhorpe's house was as warm and welcoming as the man himself.

Banks knocked at the heavy oak door, surprised at how the hollow sound echoed in the surrounding silence, but got no answer. On such a fine afternoon, he reasoned, he was more likely to find Gristhorpe in his garden, so he walked around the back.

He found the superintendent crouching by a heap of stones, apparently in the process of extending his wall.

The older man got to his feet, red-faced, at the sound of footsteps and asked, 'Is that the time already?'

'It's almost five,' Banks answered. 'I'm a few minutes early.'

'Mmm . . . I seem to lose all track of time up here. Anyway, sit down.' He gestured towards the rough grass by the stones. The superintendent was in his shirtsleeves, his ubiquitous Harris tweed jacket lying on the grass beside him. A gentle breeze ruffled his thick mop of silver hair. Below it, a red pockmarked face, upper lip all but obscured by a bristly grey moustache, grinned down at Banks. The oddest thing about Gristhorpe's appearance – and it was a facet that disconcerted both colleagues and criminals alike – was his eyes. Deep set under bushy brows, they were those of a child: wide, blue, innocent. At odds with his six-foot-three wrestler's build, they had been known to draw out confessions from even the hardest of villains and had made many an underling, caught out in a manufactured statement or an over-enthusiastic interrogation, blush and hide in shame. When all was well though, and the world seemed as fresh and clear as it did that day, Gristhorpe's eyes shone with a gentle love of life and a sense of compassion that would have given the Buddha himself a good run for his money.

Banks sat for a while and helped Gristhorpe work on the drystone wall. It was a project that the superintendent had started the previous summer, and it had no particular purpose. Banks had made one or two attempts at adding pieces of stone but had at first got them the wrong way around so that the rain would have drained inwards and cracked the wall apart if a sudden frost came. Often, he had chosen pieces that simply would not fit. Lately, however, he had improved, and he found the occasional wall-building afternoons with Gristhorpe almost as relaxing and refreshing as playing with Brian's train set. A silent understanding had developed between them about what stone would do and who would fix it in place.

After about fifteen minutes, Banks broke the silence: 'I suppose you know that somebody dismantled one of these walls last night to cover a body?'

'Aye,' Gristhorpe said, 'I've heard. Come on inside, Alan, and I'll make a pot of tea. If I'm not mistaken there are still a few of Mrs Hawkins's scones left, too.' He rhymed 'scones' with 'on', not, like a southerner, with 'own'.

They settled into the deep worn armchairs, and Banks cast his eyes over the bookcases that covered one entire wall from floor to ceiling. There were books on all kinds of subjects – local lore, geology, criminology, topography, history, botany, travel – and shelves of leather-bound classics ranging from Homer, Cervantes, Rabelais and Dante to Wordsworth, Dickens, James Joyce, W. B. Yeats and D. H. Lawrence. Jane Austen's *Pride and Prejudice* lay on the table; the position of the bookmark indicated that Gristhorpe had almost finished it. As always when he visited the superintendent, Banks mentally reminded himself that he should read more.

Gristhorpe's office in Eastvale was much the same: books everywhere, and not all of them relevant to police work. He came from old dales farming stock, and his decision to join the police after university and army service had caused trouble. Nevertheless, he had persevered, and he had also helped out on the farm in his spare time. When Gristhorpe's father saw that his son's natural aptitude and capacity for hard work was getting him places, he stopped complaining and accepted the situation. Gristhorpe's father had been sad to see the farm dwindle to little more than a large back garden before he died, but his pride in his son's achievement and the status it gave him locally eased him, and his death was without acrimony.

Gristhorpe had told Banks all this during their frequent meetings, usually over a good single malt whisky after a wall-building session. The older man's candour, along with more practical advice, made Banks feel like an apprentice, or protégé. Their relationship had developed this way since the Gallows View affair, Banks's dramatic introduction to northern police work. As he told what he knew about the Steadman murder, he was alert for any tips that might come his way.

'It's not going to be easy,' Gristhorpe pronounced after a short silence. 'And I won't say it is. For one thing, you've all those tourists and campers to consider. If Steadman had an enemy from the past, it would be an ideal way of doing the job. They never keep records at campsites as far as I know. All they care about is collecting the money.' He nibbled at his scone and sipped strong black tea. 'Still, the killer could be a lot closer to home. Doesn't look like you've got much physical evidence, though, does it? Somebody might have heard a car, but I doubt they'd have paid it much mind. I know that road. It swings north-east all the way over to Sattersdale. Still, I don't suppose I need tell you your job, Alan. First thing is to find out as much as you can about Steadman. Friends, enemies, past, the lot. Nose about the village. Talk to people. Leave the donkey work to your men.'

'I'm an outsider, though,' Banks said. 'I always will be as far as people around here are concerned. I look out of place and I sound out of place. Nobody's going to give much away to me.'

'Rubbish, Alan. Look at it this way. You're a stranger in Helmthorpe, right?' Banks nodded. 'People notice you. They'll soon get to know who you are. You don't look like a tourist, and no villager will mistake you for one. You're even a bit of a celebrity – at least for them as reads the papers around here. They'll be curious, interested in the new copper, and they'll want to find out what makes you tick. You'll be surprised what they'll tell you just to see how you react.' He chuckled. 'Before this is all over you'll feel like a bloody priest in his confessional.'

Banks smiled. 'I was brought up C. of E.'

'Ah. We're all Methodists or Baptists hereabouts,' Gristhorpe said. 'But some of us are more lapsed than others, and most of the daftest sects – your Sandemanians, for example – have all but disappeared.'

'I hope I won't have the same obligation to secrecy as a priest.'

'Heavens, no!' Gristhorpe exclaimed. 'I want to know everything you find out. You've no idea what an opportunity this is for me to catch up on Helmthorpe gossip. But seriously, Alan, do you see what I mean? Take Weaver. He's a pleasant enough lad. Trustworthy, competent, thorough. But as far as the villagers are concerned he's a fixture, boring as a rainy day – though I shouldn't make that comparison around these parts. See what I mean, though? Half the womenfolk in Helmthorpe probably changed his nappies when he was a nipper, and most of the menfolk've given him a clip around the ear once or twice. Nobody will tell Weaver anything. They won't confide in him. There's nothing in it for them. But you . . . You're the exotic newcomer, the father confessor.'

'I hope you're right,' Banks said, finishing his tea. 'I was thinking of dropping in at the Bridge tonight; Weaver told me Steadman used to drink there regularly with a few friends.'

Gristhorpe scratched his pitted red chin, and his bushy eyebrows merged in a furrow of concentration. 'Good idea,' he said. 'Imagine it'll be a bit of a wake tonight. Good time to pick up stray words. They'll all know who's been killed, of course, and probably how. Would that chap Barker be one of Steadman's cronies, by the way?'

'Yes. Jack Barker, the writer.'

'Writer be damned!' Gristhorpe almost choked on a mouthful of scone. 'Just because he makes money from the claptrap doesn't mean he's a writer. Anyway, it's a good idea. You'll get something out of them, however useless it might seem at first. What time is it now?'

'Ten to six.'

'Supper?'

'Yes, any time you're ready.' Banks had almost forgotten how hungry he was.

'It won't be owt special, you know,' Gristhorpe called out as he went to the kitchen. 'Just salad and leftover roast beef.'

TWO

Sally and Kevin raced the last few yards and collapsed, panting, by Ross Ghyll. They were high up on Tetchley Fell, on the south side of the dale, having walked to the source of one of the numerous becks that meander their way down to the Swain.

When they had caught their breath, Kevin kissed her,

thrusting his tongue deep into her mouth, and they lay down together on the pale springy grass. He touched her breasts, felt the nipples harden through thin cotton, and slowly let his hand slide down between her legs. She was wearing jeans, and the pressure of the thick seam against her sex made her tingle with excitement. But she broke free and sat up, distracted.

'I'm going to tell the police, Kevin,' she said.

'B-but we—'

She laughed and hit him lightly on the arm. 'Not about this, stupid. About last night.'

'But then they'll know about us,' he protested. 'They'll be sure to tell.'

'No, they won't. Why should they? You can tell them things in confidence, you know, like Catholics and priests. Besides,' she added, twirling a strand of hair between her slim fingers, 'my mum and dad know we were together. I told them we were at your house and we forgot about the time.'

'I just don't think we should get involved, that's all. It could be dangerous, being a witness.'

'Oh, don't be daft. I think it's rather exciting, myself.'

'You would. What if the killer thinks we really saw something?'

'Nobody knew we were up there. Nobody saw us.'

'How do you know?'

'It was dark, and we were too far away.'

'He might see you going to the police station.'

Sally laughed. 'I'll wear a disguise, then. Now you're being really silly. There's nothing to be afraid of.'

Kevin fell silent. Once again he felt he'd been outwitted and outreasoned by a mere girl.

'I won't tell them who you are if it bothers you so

much,' Sally went on, reassuring him. 'I'll just say that I was with a friend I'd rather not name. Talking.'

'Talking!' Kevin laughed and reached for her. 'Is that what we were doing?'

Sally giggled. His hand was on her breast again, but she pushed him away and stood up, brushing the grass from her jeans.

'Come on, Sally,' he pleaded. 'You know you want it as much as I do.'

'Do I now?'

'Yes.' He made a grab for her ankle but she stepped nimbly aside.

'Maybe,' she said. 'But not now. Especially with someone who's ashamed to admit he was with me last night. Besides, I have to be home for tea or my dad'll kill me.' And she was off like the wind. Sighing, Kevin got to his feet and plodded along behind her.

THREE

'When you hit someone over the head, Doc,' Jack Barker asked, 'does the blood gush, pour or just flow?'

'That's a pretty tasteless question at a time like this, isn't it?' Barnes said.

Barker reached for his pint. 'It's for my book.'

'In that case, I shouldn't think accuracy matters, then, does it? Use the most violent word you can think of. Your readers won't know any more than you do.'

'You're wrong there, Doc. You should see some of the letters I get. There's plenty of ghouls among the reading public. Do you know how many of those little old ladies are hooked on gruesome forensic details?'

'No. And I don't want to, either. I see enough blood in my line of work as it is. And I still think you're showing poor taste talking like that before poor Harry's even in the ground.'

It was early, and Barnes and Barker were the only members of the informal group sitting in the snug.

'Death comes to us all in the end, Doc,' Barker replied. 'You ought to know that. You've helped enough people shuffle off their mortal coils.'

Barnes scowled at him. 'How can you be so bloody flippant? For God's sake, have a bit of decency, Jack. Even you've got to admit that his death was an untimely one.'

'It must have been timely enough for the killer.'

'I don't understand you, Jack. Never in a million years . . .' Barnes sighed over his beer. 'Still, I have to keep reminding myself you write about this kind of thing all the time.'

'It's just shock,' Barker said, reaching for a cigarette. 'Believe it or not, I didn't personally witness every murder I've written about. And as you well know, I've never set foot on American soil either.' He ran a hand across his slicked-back hair. 'It's a bloody sad business, all right. I know we used to tease the poor bugger about his rusty nails and pigs of lead, but I'll miss him a lot.'

Barnes acknowledged the eulogy with a curt nod.

'Have the police been talking to you yet?' Barker asked.

The doctor seemed surprised. 'Me? Goodness, no. Why should they?'

'Oh, come off it, Doc. I know you're an eminent GP, pillar of the community and all that crap. But that kind of thing doesn't cut much ice with the CID, old man. And it doesn't alter the fact that you were here last night with the rest of us and you left quite a bit earlier than usual.'

'You surely don't think the police would . . .' he began. Then he relaxed and mumbled almost to himself, 'Of course, they'll have to check every angle. Leave no stone unturned.'

'Cut the clichés,' Barker said. 'They hurt.'

Barnes snorted. 'I can't see why; you write enough of them yourself.'

'It's one thing giving the public what it wants and the publishers what they pay for, but quite another to spout them out in intelligent company. Anyway, you look worried, Doc. What skeletons will they find in your cupboard?'

'Don't be ridiculous,' Barnes said. 'And I don't think you should joke about a matter as important as this. After all, poor Harry *is* dead. And you know damn well where I had to go last night. Mrs Gaskell is already a week overdue with her delivery and, frankly, I'm getting a bit worried.'

'I suppose she can give you an alibi, then?'

'Of course she can, should it ever come to that. Besides, what possible motive could I have for harming Harry?'

'Oh, still waters run murky and deep,' Barker replied, mimicking the doctor's own style of speech.

At that moment, Teddy Hackett arrived, looking every inch the flamboyant entrepreneur. He was a vain dresser, always wearing a shirt with a monogram or an alligator embroidered on its top pocket, gold medallion and expensive designer jeans. He tried to look younger than he was, but his dark hair was receding fast at the temples and a flourishing beer belly hung over his belt, almost obscuring a hand-wrought silver buckle depicting a growling lion's head.

It was well known around the village that when Hackett wasn't making money or drinking with his cronies, he was living it up in nightclubs in Leeds, Darlington or Manchester, turning on the charm for any attractive young woman who came his way. He had certainly done well for himself – the garage, a couple of gift shops – and he kept a keen eye open for anything else that came on the market. He was the kind of businessman who, given free rein, would probably buy up the whole dale and turn it into a gigantic funfair.

'Bloody hell,' he said, easing into his chair with a brimming pint grasped in his fist. 'What a turn-up for the book, hey?'

Barnes nodded and Barker stubbed out his cigarette.

'Got any details?' Hackett asked.

'No more than anyone else, I should think,' Barker replied. 'I bet the doc'll find out a thing or two after the autopsy.'

Barnes reddened with anger. 'That's enough, Jack,' he snarled. 'These things are confidential. It'll be done in Eastvale General by the pathologist, Glendenning. They're bloody lucky to have him up here. One of the best in the country, or so I've heard.' He looked at his watch. 'I wouldn't be surprised if he's at it already. Dead keen, they say.' He faltered, catching the unintentional pun a moment after he'd let it out. 'Anyway, you can be sure it'll go no further.'

'Like young Joanie Lomax's recent dose of clap, eh?'

'You're going too far, Jack. I know you're upset like the rest of us. Why can't you admit it instead of behaving like some bloody actress waiting for opening night reviews?'

Barker shifted uncomfortably in his chair.

'Has anyone been questioned yet?' Hackett asked.

The other two shook their heads.

'It's just that I saw that detective fellow – I'm sure I recognize him from that photo in the local rag last autumn. He's at the bar right now.'

They all looked over and saw Banks leaning against the bar, foot on the rail, apparently enjoying a quiet pint alone.

'That's him,' Barker confirmed. 'I saw him leaving Emma's this morning. What are you so nervous about anyway, Teddy? You've got nothing to hide, have you?'

'Nothing, no. But we were all here last night with him, weren't we? I mean, they're sure to want to question us. Why haven't they done it yet?'

'You left after Harry, as I remember,' Barker said.

'Yes. It was Saturday night, wasn't it? Had to get up to Darly for Freddy's new club opening. Bloody good night it was, too. There were some real corkers around, Jack. Why don't you come along with me sometime? Handsome young bachelor like yourself ought to get around and about a bit more.'

'Ah,' Barker replied, shaking his head. 'Better things to do with my time than chase scrubbers in a disco, mate. A writer's life . . .'

'Writer, my arse!' Hackett said. 'I could turn out that junk in my coffee break.'

Barker raised an eyebrow and grinned. 'Maybe so, Teddy, but you don't, do you? There's the difference. Besides, I hear you've had to hire a secretary with a BA in English to translate your business letters for you.'

'My English would hardly be a handicap if I was in your line of work. Anyway, there's no room for fancy footwork in a business letter. You know that, Jack. Short and to the point.'

'That's what the reviewers said about my last book.'
Barker sighed. 'Well, perhaps not in so many words.'

And even Doc Barnes had to laugh at that.

After that brief and traditional exchange the three of
them fell silent, as if they knew that they had been talking
and joking as usual just to fill the void of Harry's absence,
to pretend for as long as possible that nothing had
changed, that nothing so brutal and final as murder
had touched the cosy little group.

Barker volunteered to buy another round and went to
stand next to Banks at the bar. 'Excuse me,' he said, 'but
aren't you the policeman investigating Harry Steadman's
death?' When Banks nodded, Barker stuck out his hand.
'Jack Barker. I'm a friend of his.'

Banks offered his condolences.

'Look,' Barker went on, 'we were wondering – I mean,
we were all pals of Harry's and we spent a good deal of
yesterday evening with him – would you care to join us in
the snug? It'll be a sight more comfortable and convenient than hauling us all in to the station individually for
questioning.'

Banks laughed and accepted the offer. 'I reserve the
right to haul you in if I want to, though,' he added, only
half in jest.

Banks had been intending to drop in on them all along.
He had been imitating the vampire, who will not enter his
victim's room until invited, and was pleased that his little
trick had worked. Perhaps there was something in
Gristhorpe's advice after all. Curiosity had got the better
of them.

Barker looked happy enough to be bringing him back
in tow, but the other two appeared uneasy. Banks, however, was experienced enough not to read too much into

their reaction. He knew what discomfort the arrival of the police always caused. Even the most innocent of men and women begin to worry about that forgotten parking ticket or the little income tax fiddle as soon as a copper comes in range.

A tense silence followed the introductions, and Banks wondered if they expected him to begin a formal inter-rogation, notebook in hand. Instead, he began to fill his pipe, glancing at them in turn as he did so. Barker looked suave in a forties film star kind of way, and Barnes was a little balding grey man with glasses. He had the shabby look of a backstreet abortionist about him, Banks thought. Finally, Hackett, the flashy one, started to chat nervously.

'We were just talking about Harry,' he said. 'Sad business. Can't think who'd want to do such a thing.'

'Is that what you all think?' Banks asked, keeping his eyes on the pipe.

They all murmured their agreement. Hackett lit an American cigarette and went on: 'It's like this. Harry might have been a bit of a dotty professor type, and I don't deny we teased him a bit, but it was all in good humour. He was a fine man, good-tempered, even-natured. He had a sharp mind – and a tongue to match when it came to it – but he was a good man; he never hurt a soul, and I can't think why anyone would want to kill him.'

'Somebody obviously felt differently,' Banks said. 'I hear he inherited a lot of money.'

'Over a quarter of a million. His father was an inventor. Patented some electronic device and opened a factory. Did very well. I suppose the wife'll get it now?'

'That's how it usually goes. What's your opinion of Mrs Steadman?'

'I can't say I really know her well,' Hackett answered.

'She only came down here occasionally. Seems a good woman. Harry never complained, anyway.'

Barnes agreed.

'I'm afraid I can't add anything,' Barker said. 'I know her slightly better than the others – we were, after all, practically neighbours up in Gratly – but she seems unremarkable enough to me. Not much interested in Harry's work. Stays in the background mostly. But she's not stupid – and she knows how to cook a good dinner.'

Banks noticed Barker look over his shoulder at the bar and turned to see what the attraction was. He was just in time to see a young woman with glossy black hair down to her waist. She wore a blue shawl over a white silky blouse, and a long loose skirt that curved from her slim waist over the graceful swell of her hips. He only glimpsed her face in profile for a moment as she walked out. It looked good: angular, high cheekbones, straight nose, like a North American Indian. Half obscured by her hair, a crescent of silver flashed where her jaw met her long neck.

'Who's that?' he asked Barker.

Barker smiled. 'Oh, you noticed, I see. That's Olicana.' He pronounced the foreign word slowly.

'Olicana?'

'Yes. At least that's what Harry used to call her. Apparently it's what the Romans called Ilkely, the spirit of the place, the *genius loci*. Her real name is Penny Cartwright. Not half as exotic, is it?'

'What happened last night?' Banks asked with an abruptness that startled Barker. 'Was it a normal evening's drinking as far as you were all concerned?'

'Yes,' Barker answered. 'Harry was on his way to York and dropped in for a couple of swift halves.'

'He didn't drink any more than usual?'

'A little less, if anything. He was driving.'

'Did he seem unusually excited or worried about anything?'

'No.' Barker assumed the role of spokesman. 'He was always excited about his work – some rusty nail or broken cartwheel.'

'Rusty nail?'

'Yes. That's how we used to joke about it. It was his field of study. Industrial archaeology. His one great passion, really. That and the Roman occupation.'

'I see. I've been told that Mr Steadman was supposed to visit an old lead mine in Swaledale today. Know anything about that?'

'I think he mentioned it, yes. We tried not to let him get away with too much shop talk, though. I mean, it's not everyone's cup of tea, is it, rusty nails?'

'What time did he leave here last night?'

Barker concentrated for a moment. 'It'd be about a quarter to nine,' he answered finally, and the others nodded in agreement.

'When did you leave?'

Barker glanced at Barnes and Hackett before answering. 'I left about ten fifteen. I was alone by then and it was no fun.'

Banks turned to the other two and they gave him their stories.

'So you see,' Barker concluded, 'any one of us could have done it. Our alibis are all weak.'

'Just a minute!' Barnes cut in.

'Only joking, Doc. Sorry, it was in poor taste. But it is true, isn't it? Are we suspects, Inspector? It *is* Inspector, isn't it?'

'Chief Inspector,' Banks answered. 'And no, there aren't any suspects yet.'

'I know what that means. When there are no suspects, everybody's a suspect.'

'You write detective stories, don't you, Mr Barker?' Banks asked mildly. Barker flushed and the others laughed.

'Defective stories, I always call them,' Hackett chipped in.

'Very droll,' Barker growled. 'There's hope for you yet.'

'Tell me,' Banks went on, pushing the pace now he'd got them going. 'You're all well off. Why do you drink in a dump like this?' He looked around at the peeling wallpaper and the scored, stained tables.

'It's got character,' Barker replied. 'Seriously, Chief Inspector, we're not quite so well off as you think. Teddy here's been living on credit ever since he bought up Hebden's Gift Shop, and the doc's making as much as he can fiddle from the NHS.' Barnes just glared, not even bothering to interrupt. 'And I'm just dying for someone to buy the film rights to one of my books. Harry was loaded, true, but when it came, it came as a bit of a surprise to him, and he didn't know what to do with it. Apart from quitting his job and moving up here to devote himself to his studies, he didn't change his way of life much. He wasn't really interested in money for its own sake.'

'You say it came as a surprise to him,' Banks said. 'I thought he inherited it from his father. Surely he must have known that he was in for a sizeable inheritance?'

'Well, yes he did. But he didn't expect as much as he got. I don't think he really paid much mind to it. Harry was a bit of an absent-minded prof. Took after his father.

It seems that the old man had patents nobody knew about tucked away all over the place.'

'Was Steadman mean, stingy?'

'Good heavens, no. He always paid for his round.'

Hackett smiled tolerantly while Barnes sighed and excused Barker's flippancy. 'What he's trying to say in his charming manner,' the doctor explained, 'is that none of us feel we belong to the country club set. We're comfortable here, and I'm not being facetious when I say it's a damn good pint.'

Banks looked at him for a moment then laughed. 'Yes, it is, isn't it?' he agreed.

This was another thing Banks had picked up during his first year in the north – the passion a Yorkshireman has for his pint. The people in Swainsdale seemed to feel the same way about their beer as a man from, say, Burgundy would feel about wine.

Banks got himself another drink and, by directing the conversation away from the murder, managed to get everyone talking more openly on general matters. They discussed ordinary things, it turned out, just like anyone else: politics, the economy, world affairs, sport, local gossip, books and television. They were three professionals, all more or less the same age, and all – except perhaps Barnes – just a little out of place in a small community that had its roots deep in agriculture and craftsmanship.

FOUR

Penny Cartwright locked and bolted the sturdy door behind her, drew the thick curtains tight and switched on the light. After she had put down her package and dropped her shawl over a chair, she went around the room lighting candles that stood, at various lengths, on saucers, in empty wine bottles and even in candlesticks.

When the room was flickering with tiny bright flames which made the walls look like melting butter, she turned out the electric light, slipped a tape in the cassette player and flopped down on the sofa.

The room was now as private and cosy as a womb. It was the kind of place that looked bright and happy in sunlight, and warm and intimate by candlelight. There were a few things tacked to the walls: a postcard-size reproduction of Henri Matisse's *The Dance*, which a friend had sent her from New York; a framed copy of Sutcliffe's photograph, *Gathering Driftwood*; and a glossy picture showing her singing at a concert she and the band had given years ago. Shadowed by candlelight, the alcoves at both sides of the fireplace overflowed with personal knick-knacks such as shells, pebbles and the kind of silly keepsakes one buys in foreign lands – things that always seem to bring back the whole atmosphere of the place and details of the day on which they were bought: a plastic key ring from Los Angeles, a miniature slide viewer from Niagara Falls, a tiny porcelain jar emblazoned with her zodiac sign, Libra, from Amsterdam. Mixed in with these were earrings, which Penny collected, of all shapes and colours.

Penny took out papers and hash from a battered Old Holborn tin and rolled a small joint; then she unwrapped the half-bottle of Bell's. There seemed no point getting a glass, so she drank straight from the bottle, and the whisky burned her tongue and throat as it sank to stir a warm glow deep inside her.

The tape played unaccompanied traditional folk songs
– a strong clear woman's voice singing about men going
off to war, lifeboat disasters, domestic tragedies and
supernatural lovers of long ago. With part of her mind,
Penny studied the vocal style critically; she admired the
slight vibrato, but winced at the blurring on some of
the high notes. As a professional, or an ex-professional, it
was second nature to her to listen that way. Finally, she
decided that she liked the woman's voice, flaws and all. It
had enough warmth and emotional response to the lyrics
to make up for the occasional lapses in technique.

One song, about a murder in Staffordshire over two
hundred years ago, she knew well. She had sung it herself
many times to appreciative audiences in pubs and concert
halls. It had even been on the first record she had made
with the band, and its modal structure had stood up well
to the addition of electric guitars and percussion. But this
time it sounded fresh. Though the song had nothing to do
with the bad news she had heard that afternoon, murder
was murder, whether it had been committed the previous
night or two hundred years ago. Perhaps she would write
a song herself. Others would sing it or listen to it in warm
secure rooms hundreds of years in the future.

The whisky and hash were doing their work; Penny
was drifting. Suddenly, the memory of that summer so
many years ago sprang clear as yesterday into her mind.
There had been many good years, of course, many good
times before the craziness of fame spoiled it all, but that
summer ten years ago stood out more than the rest. As she
relived it, she could smell the green warmth of the grass
and catch the earth and animal scents on the feather-light
breeze.

Then the general memory crystallized into one

particular day. It was hot, so hot that Emma had refused to move out of the shade for fear of burning her sensitive skin. And Michael, who was sulking for some reason, had stayed at home reading Chatterton's poems. So it was just Penny and Harry. They had walked all the way over to Wensleydale, Harry, tall and strong, leading the way, and Penny keeping up the best she could. That day, they had sat high on the valley side above Bainbridge, below Semerwater, where they ate salmon sandwiches and drank chilled orange juice from a flask as they basked in the heat and looked down on the tiny village with its neat central green and Roman fort. They could see the white-washed front of the fifteenth-century Rose and Crown, and the River Bain danced and sparkled as it tripped down the falls to join the gleaming band of the Ure.

Then the scene dissolved, broke apart and shifted back in time. So vividly had Harry recreated the past in her mind that she felt she had been there. The valley bottom was marshy and filled with impenetrable thickets. Nobody ventured there. The hillmen built circular huts in clearings they made high on the valley sides near the outcrops of limestone and grits, and it was there that they went about the business of hunting, raising oats, and breeding a few sheep and cattle. A Roman patrol marched along the road just below where they sat, strangers in a cold alien landscape but sure of themselves, their helmets shining, heavy cloaks pinned at the chest with enamelled brooches.

The two scenes overlapped: ten years ago and seventeen hundred years ago. It had all been the same to Harry. She could sense the stubborn pride of the Brigantes and the confidence of the Roman conquerors. She could even, in a way, understand why Queen Cartimandua had sided with the invaders, who brought new, civilized ways to that barbaric outpost. The tension spread throughout the dales as Venutius, the Queen's ex-husband, and his rebellious followers prepared for their last stand at Stanwick, north of Richmond. Which they lost.

Harry brought it all alive for her, and if there had been, sometimes, an inexplicable awkwardness and uneasiness between them, it had always disappeared when the past became more alive than the present. How bloody innocent I was then, Penny thought, laughing at herself, and all of sixteen, too. How long it took me to grow up, and what a road it was.

Then she remembered the coins they had gone to see in the York museum – VOLISIOS, DUMNOVEROS and CARTIMANDUA, they were marked – and the pigs of lead stamped IMP, CAES: DOMITIANO: AVG. COS: VII, and, on the other side, BRIG. The Latin words had seemed like magical incantations back then.

And so she drifted. The joint was long finished, the tape had ended, the level in the whisky bottle had gone down and the memories came thick and fast. Then, as suddenly as they had started, they ceased. All Penny was left with was blankness inside; there were vague feelings but no words, no images. She worked at the bottle, lit new cigarettes from the stubs of old ones, and at some point during the evening the tears that at first just trickled down her cheeks turned into deep, heart-racking sobs.

4

ONE

Monday morning dawned on Helmthorpe as clear and warm as the five previous days. While this wasn't exactly unprecedented, it would have been enough to dominate most conversations had there not been a more sensational subject closer at hand.

In the post office, old bent Mrs Heseltine, there to send her monthly letter to her son in Canada ('Doin' right well for 'imself . . . 'E's a full perfesser now!'), was holding forth.

'Strangled by a madman,' she repeated in a whisper. 'And right 'ere in our village. I don't know what the world's coming to, I don't. We're none of us safe anymore, and that's a fact. Best keep yer doors locked and not go out after dark.'

'Rubbish!' Mrs Anstey said. 'It was 'is wife as done it. Fer t' money, like. Stands to reason. Money's t' root of all evil, you mark my words. That's what my Albert used ter say.'

'Aye,' muttered Miss Sampson under her breath. 'That's because 'e never made any, the lazy sod.'

Mrs Dent, having read every lurid novel in Helmthorpe library and some especially imported from Eastvale and York, was more imaginative than the rest. She put forward the theory that it was the beginning of another series of moors murders.

'It's Brady and Hindley all over again,' she said. 'They'll be digging 'em up all over t' place. There was that Billy Maxton, disappeared wi'out a trace, and that there Mary Richards. You'll see. Digging 'em up all over t' place, they'll be.'

'I thought they'd run off to Swansea together, Billy Maxton and Mary Richards,' chipped in Letitia Stanford, the spindly postmistress. 'Anyway, they'll be questioning us all, no doubt about that. That little man from Eastvale, it'll be. I saw 'im poking about 'ere all day yesterday.'

'Aye,' added Mrs Heseltine. 'I saw 'im, too. Looked too short for a copper.'

''E's a southerner,' said Mrs Anstey, as if that settled the matter of height once and for all.

At that moment, the bell jangled as Jack Barker walked in to send off a short story to one of the few magazines that helped him eke out a living. He beamed at the assembled ladies, who all stared back at him like frightened prunes, bid them good morning, conducted his business, then left.

'Well,' sighed Miss Sampson indignantly. 'And 'im a friend of Mr Steadman's too. I'd like to see what the poor man's enemies is doing.'

'He's an odd one, all right,' Letitia Stanford agreed. 'Not the killing type, though.'

'And how would you know?' asked Mrs Dent sharply. 'You should read some of 'is books. Fair make you blush, they would. And full of murder, too.' She shook her head and clucked her tongue slowly at the sprightly figure disappearing down the street.

TWO

Sally Lumb sat in her best underwear before the dressing table mirror. Her long honey-blonde hair was parted in the middle and brushed neatly over her white shoulders. A short, carefully maintained fringe covered just enough of her high forehead. As she studied her milky skin, she decided it was about time she did some sunbathing. Not too much, because she was so fair and it made her red and sore, but just an hour or so each day to give her skin a deep golden hue.

She had a good face, and she knew all her weak points. Her eyes were fine – big, blue and beguiling – and her nose was perfectly in proportion, with just a hint of a bob at its tip. If anything was wrong, it was her cheeks; they were a little too plump and her cheekbones weren't well enough defined. It was only puppy fat, though. Like that around her hips and thighs, it would disappear completely in time. Nevertheless, there were ways to play down its effect right now, so why wait? The same with her mouth. It was too full – voluptuous would be the kindest word – and that wasn't likely to change by itself.

Sally studied the array of tubes, palettes, brushes, sticks and bottles in front of her, then made her skilful choice of the correct shades and tints calculated to highlight the best and obscure the worst of her facial features. After all, Chief Inspector Banks was from London, so she'd heard, and he would naturally expect a woman always to look her best.

As she applied the cosmetics, she ran through the scene in her mind, imagining what she would say, and how he would jump up and dash off to make an arrest.

Her name would be in all the papers; she would be famous. And what better start could an aspiring star wish for? The only thing better than that, she thought, carefully drawing her eyeliner, would be to catch the killer herself.

THREE

Banks sat in his office and gazed out over the market square with its ancient cross and uneven cobbles. The gold hands of the blue-faced clock on the church stood at ten fifteen. A small group of tourists stood in front of the plain sturdy building taking photographs, and shoppers in twos and threes ambled along narrow Market Street. Banks could hear occasional calls of greeting through his open window. He had been at the office for almost two hours, keen to read and digest all the information on the Steadman case as it came in.

After leaving Barker and company at the Bridge the previous evening, he had driven straight home, enjoyed a mug of hot chocolate and gone to bed. Consequently, on Monday morning he felt unnaturally fresh and wide awake, much to the surprise of Sandra and the children, who had been half asleep at the breakfast table as usual.

On his arrival at Eastvale station, he first found a message from Constable Weaver informing him that the house-to-house had produced negligible results. One person reported hearing a motorcycle at about eleven thirty and two cars between midnight and twelve forty-five (he had been eating Indian food in Harrogate and the resulting heartburn kept him awake later than usual). Everybody else was either away on holiday or fast asleep. One woman, who had spotted the request for information in Helmthorpe parish church at evening service, had dropped in early to rant about the Devil, Hell's Angels, skinheads and the price of local produce. When the patient Weaver had tried to pin her down to specifics, so the laughing Sergeant Rowe reported to Banks, it turned out that she had spent all Saturday, including the night, with her married daughter in Pocklington.

Banks fiddled with his pipe and frowned, annoyed at how little there was to go on. Every good policeman knew that the first twenty-four hours of an investigation were the most crucial ones. As time went on, the trail cooled. The press, of course, had been pestering him again on his way in, and he regretted that he had nothing to tell them. As a rule, for every piece of information he passed on to the papers, he had four more up his sleeve.

There was always the chance that visitors at the campsite might have seen something. Banks doubted it, though. Most of the ones questioned on Sunday afternoon and evening had either just arrived that day or had heard nothing at all. Many of Saturday's guests had left before the discovery of the body, according to the site manager, who explained that they had to be out by ten o'clock in the morning or pay an extra day's rent. Unfortunately, he kept no register of names and addresses, and he hadn't noticed anyone running around waving a bloodstained candlestick or hammer.

Banks had asked Sergeant Hatchley to check Dr Barnes's alibi and to issue an appeal for information in the *Yorkshire Post*, but his hopes were slim. One problem was that the campsite was on the northern bank of the River Swain, next to the cricket pitch, and the car park was on the south side, well set back from High Street and practically surrounded by trees and tall hedges. It was an ideal

secluded place for a murder after dark, except between
eleven and half past, when the pubs were emptying. It
was possible, according to Dr Glendenning's unchanged
estimation of the time of death, that Steadman had been
killed between nine and ten o'clock, shortly after he left
the Bridge. At that time it would have been just about
dark enough, and the car park would have been quiet.
Drinking hours being what they were, most people arrived
between eight and nine and stayed until closing time.

So far, a thorough search had failed to find any traces
of blood on the car park's pitted macadam surface. In fact,
forensic had turned up little of interest at all. Glendenning, however, had proved as conscientious as usual. He
had spent half the night on a thorough autopsy, and a
clear, jargon-free report was waiting in Banks's in tray at
eight a.m.

The wound had been made by a metal object with at
least one sharp edge, and was indeed the cause of death.
Stomach contents revealed a low alcohol level, consistent
with the evidence of the Bridge crowd, and the remains of
an earlier dinner. The blow itself could have been inflicted
by either a man or a woman, Glendenning had added, as
the actual strength required to kill with such a weapon
was minimal. Also, the killer was probably right-handed,
so it would do Banks no good to follow the fictional
detective's procedure of watching out for a left-handed
suspect. It did, however, appear to rule out Emma
Steadman, who was left-handed, but she had a solid alibi
anyway.

Hypostasis indicated, as Banks had suspected, that
Steadman had been killed elsewhere and his body driven
to the field. Much of the lividity had formed on his right
side but he had been buried on his back.

There were no traces of blood in the car, but Vic Manson found plenty of prints. The trouble was that the few clear ones proved to be Steadman's. The prints on the steering wheel and the door handle were smudged, as they almost always were. When people drive or open and close doors, their fingerprints slide against the smooth plastic or metal surface of the handle, and the result is a mess.

What fibres remained on the vinyl-covered seats were so common as to implicate half the dale, if taken seriously. They indicated nothing so unique as a personally imported Italian suit or a yak's-wool sweater supplied by an exclusive local outfitter. Nor was there, on the tyres, any trace of mud, soil or clay that could only be found in one specific place. There wasn't even, wedged in the tread, a chip of gravel from an easily identifiable driveway.

Banks had little faith in forensic evidence, anyway. Like most detectives, he had convicted criminals on fingerprints and blood groups, but he had found that if the criminal had any brains at all, forensic evidence, though it might narrow the field of suspects, was useless until he had been caught by other means; then it might help to ensure a guilty verdict. It was surprising how many jury members still seemed to trust the experts, even though a skilled defence lawyer could easily discredit almost any scientist's testimony. Still, Banks supposed, if the public were willing to accept the 'scientifically proven' superiority of certain toothpastes or breakfast cereals that advertisers claimed, then nothing was surprising.

Just after eleven o'clock, Sergeant Hatchley poked his head around the door. Although the station coffee had improved greatly since the introduction of an automatic filter system, the two men had established a tradition of walking across to the Golden Grill for their morning break.

They weaved through the groups of strolling tourists, called hellos to the few locals they recognized, and walked into the café. The only available table was at the back, by the toilets. The petite waitress shrugged apologetically when she saw them take it.

'Usual?' she called out.

'Yes please, Gladys love,' Hatchley boomed back.

The usual was coffee and toasted teacakes for both of them.

Hatchley put his buff folder on the red checked tablecloth and ran his hand through his hair. 'Where the bloody hell's Richmond these days?' he asked, fishing for a cigarette.

'He's on a course. Didn't you know?'

'Course? What bloody course?'

'The super sent a memo round.'

'Never read them.'

'Maybe you should.'

Hatchley scowled. 'Anyway, what course is this?'

'Something to do with computers. It's down in Surrey.'

'Jammy bastard. Probably at the seaside with his bucket and spade.'

'Surrey doesn't have a coast.'

'He'll find one. When's he due back?'

'Two weeks.'

Hatchley cursed, but their order arrived before he could say anything else. He would have, Banks knew, two objections to Richmond's absence: in the first place, the sergeant had often said that he thought education was about as useful as a rubber with a hole in it; and secondly, even more serious, with Detective Constable Richmond away, Hatchley would have to do most of the legwork on the Steadman case himself.

'I checked on Doc Barnes's alibi this morning, like you asked,' Hatchley said, reaching for his teacake.

'And?'

'It's true – he was there with that Mrs Gaskell, all right. Seems she's having a difficult pregnancy.'

'What times?'

'Arrived about nine thirty, according to the husband, and left at ten fifteen.'

'So he could still have easily killed Steadman first and stuffed him in the boot of his car, or done it later.'

'No motive,' Hatchley said.

'Not that we know of yet. What's that?' Banks pointed at the folder.

'Gen on Steadman,' Hatchley mumbled, his mouth half full of toasted teacake.

Banks browsed through the report as he ate. Steadman had been born in Coventry almost forty-three years ago, at a time when his father was busy setting up his electronics business. Educated at a local grammar school, he won a scholarship to Cambridge, where he got a first in history. After that, he did postgraduate work at Birmingham and Edinburgh, then landed a teaching job at Leeds University at the age of twenty-six. There he began to develop and pursue his interest in industrial archaeology, a new field then, and in local history. In his first year of teaching, two important things happened. First, just before Christmas that year his mother died, and second, at the end of the final term he married Emma Hartley, whom he had known for two years. Emma was the only daughter of a Norwich shopkeeper, and she had been working as a librarian in Edinburgh when Steadman was studying there. She was five years younger than her husband. They had no children.

The couple honeymooned in Gratly, staying at the house they now owned. Hatchley had put an asterisk by this piece of information, and when Banks turned to the note at the bottom of the page, it read: 'Check with Ramsden. The house belonged to his parents.' Banks knew this already, but he praised Hatchley's thoroughness; it was so unusual it deserved encouragement.

As Steadman's career continued to flourish – publications, praise, promotion – his father's health steadily declined. When the old man had finally died two years ago, the son inherited a considerable fortune. He first took his wife on a European tour, then, after seeing out the university year, he bought the house in Gratly, left his job and began to concentrate on his own interests.

'What do you make of it?' Banks asked Hatchley, who had finished eating and was now picking his teeth with his fingernails.

'Well, what would you do with all that money?' the sergeant said. 'I'm damned if I'd buy a house around here and spend all my time poking about ruins.'

'You think it was foolish of him?'

'Not much of a life, is it?'

'But it's what he wanted: independence to pursue his own studies.'

Hatchley shrugged as if there were no answer to such a silly statement. 'You asked what I'd do.'

'But you didn't tell me.'

Hatchley slurped down the last of his coffee; it was syrupy at the bottom with undissolved sugar. 'I reckon I'd make a few choice investments first. Just enough so I could live comfortably off the interest, like. Nothing risky.

Then I'd take a few thousand and have a bloody good holiday.'

'Where?'

'Everywhere. Fleshpots of the world.'

Banks smiled. 'And then?'

'Then I'd come back and live off the interest.'

'But what would you do?'

'Do? Nowt much. Bit of this, bit of that. Might even go and live in Spain or the south of France. Or maybe one of those tax havens like Bermuda.'

'You'd leave your job then?'

Hatchley looked at Banks as if he was insane. 'Leave my job? Course I'd leave my job. Wouldn't anyone?'

'I suppose so.' But Banks wasn't sure what he would do himself. A holiday, yes. But afterwards? To him, Steadman had made an admirable choice; he had extricated himself from the pedestrian and stultifying elements of his work and turned to concentrate on its essence. Perhaps I'd set myself up like Sherlock Holmes – a dalesman, himself – Banks thought, if I suddenly found myself with a private income. Take only the most interesting cases . . . wear a deerstalker.

'Come on,' he said, shaking off the fantasy. 'It'll be a cold day in hell before you and I have to worry about problems like that.'

When Banks got back to his office, he found Emma Steadman waiting for him. She had just been to identify her husband's body and was still distraught. There was little expression in her pale face, but the owlish eyes magnified by the lenses of her spectacles showed traces of recent tears. She sat upright on the hard chair, her hands clasped together on her lap.

'I won't keep you long,' Banks said as he took his seat

opposite her and started filling his pipe. 'First, I'd like to know if your husband had any enemies. Is there anyone you can think of who might have wanted to do him harm?'

'No,' she answered quickly. 'Not that I can think of. Harold wasn't the kind of man who made enemies.'

Banks decided not to point out the lack of reason in that statement; the bereaved relatives of murder victims frequently assumed that there could be no possible motive for the crime.

'Was there anybody he argued with, then? Even a slight disagreement? It could be important.'

She shook her head, frowning. 'No, I told you. He wasn't . . . Just a minute. There was something. I don't know how important it was though.'

'Tell me.'

'He had complained a bit about Teddy Hackett recently.'

'Hackett? When was this?'

'About a week ago. They were friends really, I know, but they had some kind of ongoing feud about land. Oh, I suppose it was just silly. Men often are, you know. Just like little boys. Anyway, I'm afraid I don't know all the details. You'll have to ask Mr Hackett.'

'Do you have any idea what it was about?'

Mrs Steadman frowned again, this time in concentration. 'I think it might have been something to do with Crabtree's Field. That's just a bit of overgrown land by the river. Harold was certain he'd located some Roman ruins there – he had some coins and bits of pottery he said were evidence – but Teddy Hackett was trying to buy the land.'

'Why? What did he want with it?'

'Knowing Hackett, it would be some vulgar project for

making money. I don't know exactly what he had in mind – a discotheque perhaps, or a fairground, video arcade, supermarket . . .'

'Let me get this clear.' Banks said, leaning forward. 'What you're saying is that Hackett wanted some land for development and your husband was trying to get it preserved as a historic site? Is that right?'

'Yes. It wasn't the first time, either. Last year, Harold wanted to start a small local museum in a shopfront on High Street, but Hackett bought the place up quickly and turned it into a gift shop. They argued about that, too. Harold was too trusting, too . . . nice. He wasn't aggressive enough.'

'There's no one else you can think of? What about Dr Barnes? Did your husband ever say anything about him?'

'Like what?'

'Anything.'

'No.'

'Jack Barker?'

'No. He thought Jack Barker was a bit of a cynic, a bit too flippant, but that's all.'

'What about visitors to the house? Did you have many?'

'Just friends we entertained.'

'Who?'

'Locals, mostly. We seem to have lost touch with the crowd from Leeds. Barker, Penny Cartwright, Hackett and Dr Barnes occasionally. Sometimes Michael Ramsden came over from York. Some of the teachers and kids from Eastvale Comprehensive – Harold gave guest lectures and took classes on field trips. That's all I can think of.'

'There'll be a lot of money,' Banks said casually.

'Pardon?'

'A lot of money. Your husband's. You'll inherit, I should imagine.'

'Yes, I suppose so,' she said. 'I hadn't really thought . . . I don't know if Harold made a will.'

'What will you do with it all?'

Mrs Steadman looked startled behind her glasses, and more than a little disapproving. 'I've no idea. As I said, I haven't really given the matter much thought.'

'What about your relationship with your husband? Were you on good terms? Was the marriage stable?'

Mrs Steadman froze. 'What?'

'I have to ask.'

'But I don't have to answer.'

'That's true.'

'I don't think I like what you're insinuating, Chief Inspector,' she went on. 'I think it's a very impertinent question. Especially at a time like this.'

'I'm not insinuating anything, Mrs Steadman. Just doing my job, that's all.' Banks held her cold gaze and remained silent.

'If that's all, then . . .' She stood up.

Banks followed her to the door and shut it quietly behind her before breathing a sigh of relief.

FOUR

After shocking the old ladies in the post office, Jack Barker set off down Helmthorpe High Street. It was only about ten thirty, but already clusters of tourists sauntered along the pavements, cardigans draped over their shoulders to keep off the morning chill. They would stop now and then, holding on to impatient children, to glance at displays of local craftware in shop windows. Crow Scar loomed to the north, and the shadow of an occasional wispy cloud drifted across its limestone face.

Barker hesitated for a moment outside the tiny second-hand bookshop run by Mr Thadtwistle – at ninety-eight the village's oldest inhabitant – then hurried on and turned into the narrow street of cottages opposite the church. At number sixteen he paused and knocked. Nothing happened. He knocked again. Then he heard stirrings inside and smoothed back his hair as he waited. The door opened a few inches.

'Oh, it's you,' Penny Cartwright said, squinting at him closely.

'My God, you look awful,' said Barker. 'Old man not around, is he?'

Penny began to shake her head but immediately thought better of it.

'Can I come in?'

Penny stood aside and let him enter. 'If you'll make me a strong cup of coffee.'

'It's a deal. And I didn't mean what I said earlier. You look as lovely and fresh as a white rose in the morning dew.'

Penny pulled a face and flopped down on the couch. Her long jet-coloured hair was uncombed and the whites around her blue eyes looked greyish and bloodshot. She had dark puffy bags under her eyes, and her lips were cracked and dry. She held a bottle-green kimono-style dressing gown closed at her throat. A red dragon reared and breathed fire on the back.

Barker busied himself in the small untidy kitchen and soon came out carrying two steaming mugs of coffee. He sat in the battered armchair at right angles to Penny. As she reached forward to pick up her mug from the low table, he could see her lightly freckled cleavage. The folds of her silky gown also revealed a long delightful curve of thigh as she crossed her legs. She seemed entirely oblivious to the way she was making Jack Barker's pulse race.

'I suppose you've heard about Harry,' he began, lighting a cigarette.

Penny reached out for one too. 'Yes.' She nodded, blowing out a lungful of smoke and coughing. 'I've heard. These things'll ruin my voice.' She glared at the cigarette.

'Have the police been to see you yet?'

'Why should they?'

'That chief inspector – Banks his name is – he was at the Bridge last night,' Barker explained. 'He talked to us for quite a bit. Anyway, he saw you – at least he saw me glancing over at you and asked who you were.'

'And you told him?'

'Yes.'

'You told him I was a friend of Harry's?'

'Had to. He'd have found out sooner or later, wouldn't he? Then he'd have been suspicious about why I didn't tell him in the first place.'

'So what? You've got nothing to hide, have you?'

Barker shrugged.

'Anyway,' Penny went on, 'you know how I feel about the police.'

'He's not a bad sort. Quite friendly, really. But sharp as a knife. Doesn't miss a trick. He's the kind who'll spend a pleasant evening buying you drinks, then ask you hard questions when you're sozzled.'

'Sounds awful.' Penny pulled a face and ground out her half-smoked cigarette in the ashtray. 'Still, they're all much the same.'

'What will you tell him?'

She looked at him and frowned. 'What is there to tell?'

'The old man?'

She shook her head.

'He's sharp,' Barker repeated.

Penny smiled. 'Well, then, he'll be able to find out all he wants to know, won't he?'

Barker leaned forward and took her hand. 'Penny . . .'

She shook him off gently. 'No, Jack, don't. Not now.'

Barker slumped back in his chair.

'Oh come on, Jack,' Penny chided him. 'Don't behave like a sulky boy.'

'I'm sorry.'

Penny gathered her gown around her and stood up. 'Think nothing of it. You'd better go, though; I'm a bit unsteady on my pins today.'

Barker got to his feet. 'Are you singing this week?'

'Friday. If my voice holds out. You'll be there?'

'Wouldn't miss it for the world, love,' Barker answered. Then he left.

FIVE

The police station didn't look at all like Sally expected. For one thing, the old Tudor-fronted building was modern inside, and the walls weren't papered with 'wanted' posters. Instead, it was more like one of those pleasant open-plan offices with potted plants all over the place and nothing but screens separating the desks behind the reception area. It smelled of furniture polish and pine-scented air-freshener.

She told the polite young man at the front desk that she

wanted to see Chief Inspector Banks, the man in charge of the Helmthorpe murder. No, she didn't want to tell the young man about it, she wanted the chief inspector. She had important information. Yes, she would wait.

Finally, her persistence paid off and she was shown upstairs to a network of corridors and office doors with things like 'Interview Room' stencilled on them. There she was given a seat and asked if she would mind waiting a few moments. No. She folded her hands in her lap and stared ahead at a door marked, disappointingly, 'Stationery Supplies'.

The minutes dragged on. She wished she had brought a copy of *Vogue* to flip through like at the dentist's. Suddenly sounds of scuffling and cursing came from the stairwell and three men fell into the corridor only feet from where she was sitting. Two of them were obviously police, and they were struggling with a handcuffed third who wriggled like an eel. Finally, they dragged him to his feet again and hauled him off down the hall. He was squirming and swearing, and at one point he managed to twist free and run back down the hall towards her. Sally was terrified. At least half of her was. The other half was thinking how exciting, how much like *Hill Street Blues* it was. The policemen caught him again before he got too close and hustled him into a room. Sally's heart beat fast. She wanted to go home, but the chief inspector came out of his office and ushered her inside.

'I'm sorry about that,' he apologized. 'It doesn't happen often.'

'Who is he?' Sally asked, wide-eyed and pale.

'A burglar. We think he broke into Merriweather's Stereo Emporium last week.'

Sally found herself sitting before a flimsy metal desk

littered with paper clips, pens and important-looking folders. The air was thick with pipe smoke, which reminded her of her father. She coughed, and Banks, taking the hint, went to open the window. Fragments of conversation drifted up on the warm air from Market Street.

Banks asked Sally what she wanted.

'It's private,' she whispered, looking over her shoulder and leaning forward. She was unsettled by what she had just witnessed and found it much harder to get started than she had imagined. 'I mean,' she went on, 'I want to tell you something but you have to promise not to tell anyone else.'

'Anyone?' The smile disappeared from his lips but still lingered in his lively brown eyes. He reached for his pipe and sat down.

'Well,' Sally said, turning up her nose at the smoke like she always did at home, 'I suppose it's up to you, isn't it? I'll just tell you what I know, shall I?'

Banks nodded.

'It was last Saturday night. I was up below Crow Scar in that little shepherd's shelter – you know, the one that's almost collapsed.' Banks knew it. The derelict hut had been searched after the discovery of Steadman's body. 'Well, I heard a car. It stopped for about ten or fifteen minutes, then drove off.'

'Did you see it?'

'No. I only heard it. I thought it was maybe a courting couple or something at first. But they'd stay longer than that, wouldn't they?'

Banks smiled. It was clear from the girl's desire for secrecy and her knowledge of the temporal requirements of courting exactly what she had been doing in the shepherd's shelter.

'Which direction did the car come from?' he asked.

'The village, I think. At least, it came from the west. I suppose it could have come from over the dale, up north, but there's nothing much on that road for miles except moorland.'

'Where did it go?'

'Up along the road. I didn't hear it turn round and come back.'

'The road that leads to Sattersdale, right?'

'Yes, but there's plenty of other little roads that cross it. You could get almost anywhere from it.'

'What time was this?'

'It was twelve fourteen when it stopped.'

'Twelve fourteen? Not just after twelve, or nearly quarter past twelve? Most people aren't so accurate.'

'It was a digi—' Sally stopped in her tracks. Banks was looking down at her wrist, on which she wore a small black watch with a pink plastic strap. It wasn't digital.

'Better tell the truth,' he said. 'And don't worry, your parents needn't know.'

'I wasn't doing anything wrong,' Sally blurted out, then she blushed and calmed down. 'But thank you. I don't think they'd understand. Yes, I was with somebody. My boyfriend. We were just talking.' This didn't sound convincing, but Banks didn't regard it as any of his business. 'And then this car came,' Sally continued. 'We thought it was getting late anyway, so Kev, my boyfriend, looked at his watch – it's a digital one with a light in it – and it said twelve fourteen. I knew I should have been home hours ago, but I thought I might as well be hung for a sheep as a lamb. We just stayed where we were not paying it much mind really, then when we heard it go Kevin looked at his watch again and it said twelve twenty-nine. I remember because it was funny. Kevin said they hadn't much time to . . .'

Sally stopped and reddened. It had been all too easy, once she got going, to forget who she was talking to. Now, she realized, she had not only told this strange man with the pipe her boyfriend's name but had also given him the impression that she knew all about what men and women did together at night in cars on lonely hillsides.

But Banks didn't pursue her romantic activities. He was far more concerned about the accuracy of the information he was getting than about her love life. Besides, she looked at least nineteen – old enough to take care of herself, whatever her parents thought.

'I imagine Kevin, your boyfriend, could confirm these times?' he asked.

'Well . . . if he had to,' she answered hesitantly. 'I mean, I told him I wouldn't mention his name. We don't want any trouble. My mum and dad wouldn't like it, see. I told them we were at his house watching telly. They'd tell his mum and dad where we really were and they'd stop us seeing each other.'

'How old are you, Sally?'

'Sixteen,' she answered proudly.

'What do you want to do with your life?'

'I want to be an actress. At least, I want to be involved in films and theatre, that kind of thing. I've applied to the Marion Boyars Academy of Theatre Arts.'

'I'm impressed,' Banks told her. 'I hope you get accepted.' He noticed that she was already a dab hand at make-up. He had thought she was nineteen. Most girls of her age never seemed to know when enough was enough, but Sally obviously did. Her clothes sense was good too. She was dressed in white knee-socks and a deep-blue skirt, gathered at the waist, that came to just above her dimpled knees. On top she wore a white cotton blouse and a red ribbon in her gold-blonde hair. She was a beautiful girl, and Banks wouldn't have been at all surprised to see her on stage or on television.

'Is it true you're from London?' Sally asked.

'Yes.'

'Did Scotland Yard send you?'

'No. I moved here.'

'But why on earth would you want to come up here?'

Banks shrugged. 'I can think of plenty of reasons. Fresh air, beautiful countryside. And I had hoped for an easier job.'

'But London,' Sally went on excitedly. 'That's where it all happens. I went there once on a day trip with the school. It was fabulous.' Her wide eyes narrowed and she looked at him suspiciously. 'I can't understand why anyone would want to leave it for this godforsaken dump.'

Banks noted that in about twenty seconds Sally's opinion had undergone a radical reversal. At first she had been coquettish, flirtatious, but now she seemed disdainful, almost sorry for him, and much more brusque and businesslike in her manner. Again, he could hardly keep from smiling.

'Did you know Harold Steadman?'

'Is that who . . . the man?'

'Yes. Did you know him?'

'Yes, a bit. He often came to the school to give lectures on local history or geology. Boring stuff mostly about old ruins. And he took us on field trips sometimes to Fortford, or even as far as Malham or Keld.'

'So the pupils knew him quite well?'

'As well as you can know a teacher.' Sally thought for

a moment. 'But he wasn't really like a teacher. I mean, I know it was boring and all that, but he liked it. He was enthusiastic. And he even took us to his home for hot dogs and pop after some of the trips.'

'Us?'

'Yes, the pupils who lived in Helmthorpe or Gratly. There were about seven of us usually. His wife made us all some food and we just sat and talked about where we'd been and what we'd found. He was a very nice man.'

'What about his wife, did you know her?'

'Not really She didn't stick around with us. She always had something else to do. I think she was just shy. But Mr Steadman wasn't. He'd talk to anybody.'

'Was that the only time you saw him? At school, on trips?'

Sally's eyes narrowed again. 'Well, apart from in the street or in shops, yes. Look, if you mean was he a dirty old man, the answer's no.'

'That's not what I meant,' Banks said. But he was glad that she had reacted as if it was.

He made her go through the story again while he took down all the particulars. She gave the information unwillingly this time, as if all she wanted was to get out of the place. When she finally left, Banks slouched back in his chair and grinned to think that all his appeal, all his glamour, had been lost in his move from London to Eastvale. Outside in the market square the clock chimed four.

5

ONE

On Tuesday morning, having sent Sergeant Hatchley to
Helmthorpe to check on Weaver's progress, search Harold
Steadman's study and bring in Teddy Hackett for questioning, Banks set off for York to visit Michael Ramsden
again.

He drove into the ancient Roman city at about eleven
o'clock through suburbs of red-brick boxes. After getting
lost in the one-way system for half an hour, he found a
parking space by the River Ouse and crossed the bridge to
Fisher & Faulkner Ltd, a squat ugly brick building by the
waterside. The pavements were busy with tourists and
businessmen, and the huge Minster seemed to dominate
the city; its light stone glowed in the morning sun.

A smart male receptionist pointed him in the right
direction, and on the third floor one of Ramsden's
assistants called through to the boss.

Ramsden's office looked out over the river, down
which a small tour boat was wending its way. The top
deck was bright with people in summer holiday clothes,
and camera lenses flashed in the sun. The boat left a long
V of ripples, which rocked the rowing boats in its wake.

The office itself was small and cluttered; beside the
desk and filing cabinets stood untidy piles of manuscripts,
some stacked on the floor, and two bookcases displaying

a set of Fisher & Faulkner's titles. Even in a dark business suit, Ramsden still looked as if his clothes were too big for him; he had the distracted air of a professor of nuclear physics about to explain atomic fission to a layman while simultaneously working out complex formulae in his mind. He brushed back an invisible forelock and asked Banks to sit down.

'You were a close friend of Harold Steadman's,' Banks began. 'Could you tell me a little about him? His background, how you met, that kind of thing.'

Ramsden leaned back in his swivel chair and crossed his long legs. 'You know,' he said, looking sideways towards the window, 'I was always just a little bit in awe of Harry. Not just because he was nearly fifteen years my senior – that never really mattered – but because I don't think we ever really got over the student–professor relationship. When we met, he was a lecturer at Leeds and I was just about to begin my studies in London, so we weren't even at the same university. We weren't in the same field, either. But these ideas get fixed in one's mind nonetheless. I was eighteen and Harry was nearly thirty-three. He was a very intelligent, very dedicated man – an exact role model for someone like me at that time.

'Anyway, although I was, as I said, just about to go to university in London, I always came home at Christmas and in summer. I'd help around the house, do odd jobs, make bacon and eggs for the guests. And I loved being at home, being in the Yorkshire countryside. It was best when Harry and Emma came to stay for their annual holidays. I'd walk for hours, sometimes alone, sometimes with Harold or Penny.'

'Penny?' Banks cut in. 'Would that be Penny Cartwright?'

'Yes, that's right. We were very close until I went off to London.'

'Go on.'

'We used to go out together, in a casual sort of way. It was all very innocent. She was sixteen and we'd known each other nearly all our lives. She'd even stayed with us for a while after her mother died.'

'How old was she then?'

'Oh, about ten or eleven. It was tragic, really. Mrs Cartwright drowned in a spring flood. Terrible. Penny's father had a nervous breakdown, so she stayed with us while he recovered. It seemed only natural. Later, when . . . well, you know, we were a bit older . . . Anyway, Harold was very knowledgeable and enthusiastic about the area. He took to Swainsdale immediately, and pretty soon he was teaching me more than I'd learned living there all my life. He was like that. I was impressed, of course, but as I was about to study English at university I was insufferably literary – always quoting Wordsworth and the like. I suppose you know he bought the house when my mother couldn't afford to keep it on?'

Banks nodded.

'Yes,' Ramsden went on, 'they came every year, Harry and Emma, and when father died they were in a position to help us out a great deal. It was good for Harry, too. His work at the university was too abstract, too theoretical. He published a book called *The Principles of Industrial Archaeology*, but what he really wanted was the opportunity to put those principles into practice. University life didn't give him time enough to do that. He fully intended to teach again, you know. But first he wanted to do some real pioneering work. When he inherited the money, all that became possible.

'When I graduated, I went to work for Fisher and Faulkner in London first. Then they opened the northern branch and offered me this job. I missed the north and I'd always hoped to be able to make a living up here some day. We published Harold's second book and he and I developed a good working relationship. The firm specializes in academic books, as you can see.' He pointed towards the crowded bookshelves, and most of the titles Banks could make out had *principles* or *a study of* in them. 'We do mostly literary criticism and local history,' Ramsden went on. 'Next Harry edited a book of local essays, and since that we've been working on an exhaustive industrial history of the dale from pre-Roman times to the present. Harry published occasional essays in scholarly journals, but this was to be his major work. Everybody was looking forward to it tremendously.'

'What exactly is industrial archaeology?' Banks asked. 'I've heard the term quite often lately, but I've only got a vague idea what it means.'

'Your vague idea is probably as clear as anyone else's,' Ramsden replied. 'As yet, it's still an embryonic discipline. Basically, the term was first used to describe the study of the machinery and methods of the Industrial Revolution, but it's been expanded a great deal to include other periods – Roman lead mines, for example. I suppose you could say it's the study of industrial artefacts and processes, but then you could argue for a month about how to define "industrial". To complicate matters even further, it's very hard to draw the line between the subject as a hobby and as an academic discipline. For instance, if someone happens to be interested in the history of steam trains, he can still make a contribution to the field, even though he actually works nine to five in a bank most days.'

'I see,' Banks said. 'So it's a kind of hybrid area, an open field?'

'That's about it. Nobody's yet come up with a final definition, which is partly why it's so exciting.'

'You don't think Mr Steadman's death could be in any way linked to his work, do you?'

Ramsden shook his head slowly. 'I can't see it, no. Of course, there are feuds and races just like in any other discipline, but I can't see any of it going that far.'

'Did he have rivals?'

'Professionally, yes. The universities are full of them.'

'Could he have uncovered something that someone might wish to keep quiet?'

Ramsden thought for a moment, his sharp chin resting in his bony hand. 'You mean the unsavoury past of a prominent family, that kind of thing?'

'Anything.'

'It's an interesting theory. I can't say for certain one way or the other. If he had discovered something, he didn't tell me. It's possible, I suppose. But we're a long way from the Industrial Revolution. You'd have to dig back a very long way if you want to find a descendant of someone who made his fortune by exploiting child labour, for example, which wasn't entirely uncommon back then. I don't think there are many direct descendants of the Romans around who still have anything to hide.'

Banks smiled. 'Probably not. What about enemies, academic or otherwise?'

'Harry? Good Lord, I shouldn't think so. He wasn't the kind to make enemies.'

Again, Banks refrained from stating the obvious. 'Do you know anything about this business with Teddy Hackett?' he asked.

Ramsden glanced sharply at him. 'You don't miss much, do you?' he said. 'Yes, I know about it, for what it's worth. There's a field in Helmthorpe over the river near the cricket pitch – it's called Crabtree's Field because it used to belong to a farmer named Crabtree. He's long dead now, though. There's a small bridge which connects the field with the campsite on the other side, and Hackett wants to provide more "facilities" for the campers – by which he no doubt means junk food and video games. You must have noticed the increasing Americanization of the English countryside, Chief Inspector. McDonald's seems to be springing up everywhere now, even in places as small as Helmthorpe. Harold had good reason to suppose – and I've heard his evidence – that there was once a Roman camp there. It could be a very important discovery. He was trying to persuade the local authorities to protect it for excavations. Naturally, that caused a bit of friction between Harry and Teddy Hackett. But they remained friends. I don't think it was a serious quarrel.'

'Not serious enough to lead to murder?'

'Not in my opinion, no.' Ramsden turned sideways again and looked out over the river at the shining Minster towers. 'They were quite close friends, though God knows why, seeing as their views on just about everything were always diametrically opposed. Harry enjoyed a good argument for its own sake – that was the academic in him – and Hackett is at least a fairly intelligent, if not a very tasteful, adversary. I'm afraid you'll have to ask Harry's friends in the village how serious the quarrel was. I didn't get over there often enough. I suppose you've met the good doctor and the resident scribbler?'

Banks nodded. 'Do you know them?'

'A little. Not very well, though. As I said, I don't get to

Helmthorpe as often as I'd like. Doc Barnes has been around as long as I can remember, of course. And I've had one or two beery evenings in the Bridge. Naturally there was quite a bit of excitement when Jack Barker moved to Gratly three or four years back, but it soon settled down when he proved to be much like everyone else.'

'Where did he come from? What made him choose Gratly?'

'Haven't a clue, I'm afraid. I have a vague notion he's from somewhere in Cheshire, but I couldn't swear to it. You'll have to ask him.'

'Did he know Mr Steadman before he moved to Gratly?'

'Not as far as I know. Harry never mentioned him.'

'Does your company publish his books?'

'Lord, no.' Ramsden made curious snuffling noises through his nose, and Banks took the sound for laughter. 'I told you what we specialize in. I believe Barker writes paperback originals.'

'Did Mr Steadman ever say anything about Dr Barnes or Jack Barker?'

'He said a number of things, yes. What do you have in mind?'

'Anything odd. Did he ever tell you anything about them that you thought they might not want to be common knowledge?'

'Are you trying to suggest that Harry was a black-mailer?'

'Not at all. But if he did know something, they weren't to know what he'd do with the knowledge, were they? You say he was a decent upright man – fair enough. If he knew of anything illegal or immoral anyone was involved in, what do you think he would have done?'

'I see what you mean.' Ramsden tapped a yellow pencil on his bottom teeth. 'He'd have done the right thing, of course. Gone to the authorities. But I still can't help you. He never indicated to me that either Barker or Barnes had ever been involved in anything untoward.'

'What about Penny Cartwright?'

'What about her? Harry certainly never spoke ill of Penny.'

'What about your relationship with her?'

Ramsden paused. 'I'm not sure it's any of your business.'

'Up to you,' Banks said.

'It was all a long time ago. There was certainly nothing odd about it. I don't see how knowing can possibly help you.'

Banks kept silent.

'Oh, what the hell, then,' Ramsden said. 'Why not? I told you – we were good friends, then we drifted apart. We were both in London at roughly the same time, but we moved in very different circles. She was a singer, so she hung around with musicians. She was always a bit of a rebel, too. You know, had to be different, embraced all the causes. She made a couple of records and even toured in Europe and America, I believe. It was traditional folk music they played – at first, anyway – but they jazzed it up with electronic instruments. Then she got tired of life in the fast lane and came home. Her father forgave her and she settled into her cottage. Apart from the old man getting a bit overprotective now and again, she more or less gets on with her own life. Still sings a bit around the local pubs, too.'

'What's her father like?'

'The major? To do him justice, he never really

recovered from his wife's death. He's a strange old bird. Lives right on High Street with his dog. Has a flat over old Thadtwistle's bookshop. There were rumours, you know, when Penny left. Look, I'm not sure I should be telling you this. It's just silly local gossip.'

'I shouldn't worry about that, Mr Ramsden. I know a hawk from a handsaw.'

Ramsden swallowed. His Adam's apple bobbed up and down. 'People said they were a bit too close, father and daughter, living together after the mother died. They say the old man wanted her to take her mother's place in his bed and that's why she took off so young. Do you know what I'm saying? It's not entirely uncommon around these parts.'

Banks nodded. 'Do you believe it?'

'Not for a moment. You know how vindictive gossip can be.'

'But what did anyone have against the Cartwrights?'

Ramsden picked up his pencil again and started rolling it between his fingers. 'People thought they were a bit stuck-up, that's all. The major's always been stand-offish, and his wife wasn't from around these parts. People in the dale used to be a lot more parochial than they are now so many outsiders have moved in. Even now most of them think of Penny as some kind of scarlet woman.'

'You were close to her. Did she say anything?'

'No, she didn't. And I think she would have done if anything unusual had been going on.'

'Was she friendly with Mr Steadman?'

'Yes, they were very good friends. Penny knows a lot about folk traditions through her music, you see, and Harold was always willing to learn. She even taught him some guitar. Also, she was very disorientated for a while after she came back from her brush with fame and fortune, and I think Harry's support meant a lot. He thought the world of her. They both loved going for long walks, watching birds and wild flowers, talking about the past.'

There was plenty to follow up in that, Banks thought. But he had no more questions to ask. He already had more than enough information to digest and analyze.

He thanked Ramsden, said goodbye and walked back over the sluggish Ouse to his car.

He stopped at the first likely-looking village inn he saw and enjoyed a late, leisurely pub lunch of shepherd's pie and a refreshing pint of shandy made from Sam Smith's Old Brewery bitter. As he drove back to Eastvale listening to Purcell's airs, he began to go over the list of involved characters in his mind, trying to imagine motives and opportunities.

First there was Teddy Hackett. That field business might only be the tip of the iceberg, and if Steadman had been blocking similar projects, Hackett would have a good enough reason for wanting rid of him.

Then there was Jack Barker. No obvious motive there but no alibi either, as Barker himself had admitted on Sunday evening. His glance at Penny Cartwright in the Bridge had spoken volumes, and if there was more to her relationship with Steadman than Ramsden had told him, then jealousy may have provided a very strong motive.

As for Dr Barnes, his alibi hadn't been nearly as solid as he had seemed to think, and though there was no motive apparent yet, Banks wasn't willing to consider him out of the running.

It seemed pointless to include Emma Steadman; for one thing she was left-handed, and for another she had been watching television with Mrs Stanton all evening. But there was the money. She did have a great deal to gain from her husband's death, especially if the two weren't seeing eye to eye anymore. She could, possibly, have hired someone. It was unlikely, but he couldn't rule it out.

Ramsden seemed to have neither the motive nor the opportunity. In a way, Steadman was his bread and butter, an important client as well as an old friend. Perhaps he did envy Steadman, but that was no reason to kill him. Banks couldn't quite work Ramsden out. There was the business of the novel, for a start. He sensed that perhaps great things had been expected of Ramsden artistically but had never really materialized. Why? Indolence? Lack of talent? He seemed to have a rather precious personality, and Banks guessed that he had been pampered as a child, most likely by his mother, and led to believe that he was special and gifted. Now he was in his twenties and the talent hadn't really made itself manifest.

Penny Cartwright remained a grey area. She might have had both motive and means, but they had yet to be discovered. Banks wanted very much to talk to her, and he decided to go to Helmthorpe that evening. He would have to see her father, too, at some point.

One problem was that there was so much time to account for. If Steadman had left the Bridge at about a quarter to nine and his body had been dumped at twelve fourteen, where had he been and what had he been doing during those three and a half hours? Surely someone must have seen him?

Slowly, Banks's thoughts faded as the countertenor sang a mournful 'Retir'd from any Mortal's Sight' and the poplars and privet hedges that lined the road gave way to the first houses in Eastvale.

TWO

'So you told him everything then?'

'I didn't mean to, Kevin, honest – not your name and all. But it just slipped out.'

Kevin leered and Sally's expression darkened. She elbowed him in the ribs. 'You've got a filthy mind, you have. It was the time that did it. Twelve fourteen. He could see I hadn't got a digital watch. Why do you have to wear that silly thing anyway?'

Kevin looked down at his watch as if examining it for faults. 'I don't know,' he said.

'It beeps every hour,' Sally went on, her voice softening. 'No matter what you're doing.'

Kevin leaned forward and kissed her. She squirmed beneath him and he slipped his hand under her blouse to hold her soft warm breast. Her body was pressed down hard against the ground, and the moist sickly smell of grass filled the air. Insects buzzed and whined all around. Finally, she broke away and gasped for breath. Kevin lay back with his hands behind his head and stared at the deep-blue sky.

'What did you think of him, then, this hotshot from London?' he asked.

Sally snorted. 'Some hotshot. Fancy leaving London to come up here. The bloke must be barmy.'

Kevin turned to face her, leaning on one elbow and sticking a long stalk of grass between his teeth. 'What did he say?'

'Didn't seem very interested, really. He just asked me a lot of daft questions. I don't know why I bothered. I won't be so fast to go out of my way and help the police next time, that's for sure.'

'What do you mean, "next time"?'

'I mean if I find out anything else.'

'Why should that happen? It was only by chance we heard the car. We didn't even know what it was.'

'But we do now. Aren't you curious? Don't you want to know who did it?'

Kevin shrugged. 'I wouldn't want to get involved. Leave all that to the police. That's what they get paid for.'

'Well, isn't that a typical small-minded attitude?' Sally said scornfully.

'It's a sensible one, though.'

'So? It's no fun being sensible all the time.'

'What are you getting at?'

'Nothing. I just might do a bit of snooping on my own, that's all. I've lived here all my life. I ought to know what's going on in the village.'

'What can you do that the police can't?'

'I don't know yet, but I bet I can do better than them. Wouldn't it be exciting if I solved the case for them?'

'Don't be an idiot, Sally. We've been through this before. You know what I think. It's dangerous.'

'How?'

'What if the killer knew what you were doing? What if he thought you might be getting too close?'

Sally shivered. 'I'll be careful, don't worry. Besides, you never get anywhere if you're frightened of a bit of danger.'

Kevin gave up. Sally smoothed her skirt and lay on her back again. They were high on the southern slope of the dale, overlooking cross-shaped Gratly and Helmthorpe's chequerboard pattern of slate roofs. Sally plucked a buttercup and held it to her chin. Kevin took the flower from her hand and trailed it over her throat and collarbone. She shuddered. He kissed her again and put his other hand up her skirt to caress the tender flesh of her thighs just below her panties.

Suddenly Sally heard a sound: a snapping twig or a thwacking branch. She sat up quickly, leaving Kevin with his face in the grass.

'Someone's coming,' she whispered.

A few moments later, a figure appeared from the small copse by the beck side. Sally put her hand over her eyes to shield them from the sun and saw who it was.

'Hello, Miss Cartwright,' she called out.

Penny walked towards them, knelt on the grass and tossed back her hair. 'Hello. It's a beautiful day, isn't it?'

'Yes,' answered Sally. 'We're just having a breather. We've been walking most of the afternoon.'

'I used to walk around these parts a lot, too, when I was your age,' Penny said quietly, almost to herself. 'It seems like centuries ago now, but it was only ten years. You'll be surprised how quickly time passes. Enjoy it while you can.'

Sally didn't know what to say; she felt embarrassed. After an uneasy silence, she said, 'I'm sorry about your friend, Mr Steadman, really I am. He was a nice man.'

Penny seemed to return from a great distance to focus on her. At first Sally thought the commiseration had gone unheard, but Penny smiled warmly and said, 'Thank you. Yes, he was.' Then she got to her feet and brushed the scraps of grass from her long skirt. 'I must be off, anyway. Mustn't bore you young people with my memories.'

In silence, Sally and Kevin watched her walk up the hillside with a strong, determined stride. She looked a lonely, wild figure, Sally thought, like Catherine in *Wuthering Heights*: a woman of the moors, spirit of the place. Then she felt Kevin's palm against her warm thigh again.

THREE

Further up the hillside, Penny paused as she stood on a stile and looked back on the dale she loved spread out below her. There was the church by her cottage. High Street and the whitewashed frontage of the Dog and Gun. On the other side of the river, past the cricket pitch and Crabtree's Field, the commons sloped up, rougher and rougher, to Crow Scar, which that day was almost too bright to look at.

But she couldn't gaze long without thinking of Harry, for he was the one who had shown her Swainsdale's secrets, given it depth and life beyond its superficial beauties. And now she fancied she could see the collapsed section of Tavistock's wall. The stones that had been used to cover Harry's body seemed darker than the rest.

Looking back the way she had come, Penny saw the two young lovers fuse in a tight embrace on the grass. She smiled sadly. When she'd first approached them, she had noticed how flustered and embarrassed they had looked.

Again she thought of Harry. Suddenly, the memory of a picnic they'd had ten years ago came into her mind. It must have been on the exact spot where Sally and Kevin were lying. She remembered the view of the village clearly, and they had been near a small copse, as Emma had sat in the shade, knitting. The more she concentrated on it, the more details came back. It was just around the time when she and Michael had started drifting apart. He had been reading Shelley's poetry. Penny could even remember the scuffed brown leather of the book's cover; it was a second-hand edition she'd bought him for his birthday. She and Harry had spread the red checked cloth on the grass and started to unload the hamper. Somehow, their hands had touched by accident. Penny remembered blushing, and Harry had busied himself looking for the corkscrew. It was for the Chablis. Yes, they had drunk Chablis, a good vintage, that day, and now, ten years later, she felt the crisp flinty taste of the cool wine on her tongue again.

The picture faded as quickly as it had come. How innocent it had all been, how bloody innocent! Wiping the tears from her eyes with the back of her hand, she jumped down from the stile and strode sharply on.

FOUR

Hackett had already been waiting an hour when Banks got back from York, and he was not at all amused.

'Look here,' he protested, as Banks led him upstairs to the office. 'You can't do this to me. You can't just drag me in like this without an explanation. I've got a business to run. I told you everything last night.'

'You told me nothing last night.' Banks took off his jacket and hung it on the back of the door. 'Sit down,' he said. 'Make yourself at home.'

The room was stuffy, so Banks reopened the window and the smells of Market Street wafted up: exhaust fumes, fresh-baked bread, something sweet and sickly from the chocolate shop. Hackett sat rigidly in his chair and lapsed into a tense affronted silence.

'There's nothing to get excited about,' Banks told him,

taking out his pipe and fiddling with it over the waste-paper basket.

'Then why did your sergeant kidnap me like that and rush me over here, eh? I want my lawyer.'

'Oh, do relax, Mr Hackett! There's really no need for melodrama. You've been watching far too many American films on television. I've not brought you here to lay charges or anything like that. I'm sorry if Sergeant Hatchley seemed a little brusque – it's just his manner. I've got a few questions to ask you, that's all.' He gave Hackett a sharp glance. 'Just one or two little things we'd like to get cleared up.'

'Why pick on me? What about Jack, or the doc?'

'Do you know of any reason they might have had for killing Mr Steadman?'

'Well, no, I didn't mean to imply that. It's just that . . .'

'Did he ever say anything about them to you, give you any reason to think one of them might want him out of the way?'

'No. That's not what I meant, anyway. I'm not trying to put the blame on someone else. I just want to know why you picked on me to haul in like this.'

'Crabtree's Field.' Banks picked up his pipe and reached for the matches.

Hackett sighed. 'So that's it. Someone's been telling tales. I should have known you'd have found out before long.'

Banks lit his pipe and gazed at the ceiling. Some old juices trickled down the stem and caught in his throat; he coughed and pulled a face.

Hackett looked at him angrily. 'You don't give a damn, do you? Anyway, it's nobody's bloody business—'

'It's police business now, Mr Hackett,' Banks interrupted. He put his pipe aside and drained the cold coffee left in his mug. 'If it's all the same to you, the sooner we get it cleared up, the better.'

Hackett shuffled in his chair and smoothed his droopy moustache. 'It was nothing,' he said. 'Just a minor disagreement over an acre or two of land, that's all.'

'Countries have been invaded for less,' Banks remarked, and went on to give Hackett the details as he had heard them.

'Yes,' Hackett agreed, 'that's more or less it. But I wouldn't kill anyone for that, let alone a close friend like Harry. Even if he did want to wrap up the whole bloody dale and give it to the National Trust, I liked the man. I respected his principles, even though they weren't the same as mine.'

'But you did argue about the field?' Banks persisted.

'We argued about it, yes. But it was half in fun. The others will tell you. Harry liked a good argument as well as the next man. It wasn't that important.'

'Money is always important, Mr Hackett. How much did you expect to make from the land if you got it?'

'That's impossible to say. I wouldn't stand to make anything for ages, of course. I'd be out of pocket, in fact. There's the purchase price, construction, publicity . . . It could have been years before I started showing a profit.'

'So you were only in it for the fun?'

'Not only that, no. I mean, I like business. It's a way of life that suits me. I like doing deals. I like building things up. But of course I wouldn't put out good money if I didn't think the eventual returns would be substantial.'

'Can we agree,' Banks asked, 'that you did hope at some point to make a considerable amount from your investment?'

'Hell, yes. Eventually.'

'And now?'

'What about now? I don't understand.'

'Oh, come on, Mr Hackett. Don't play the innocent. The pitch is clear now, isn't it? The field's yours.'

Hackett laughed and relaxed in his chair. 'That's just where you're wrong, I'm afraid. You see, I think Harry pulled it off. At least there's a freeze on the place right now. I suppose young Ramsden will carry on his master's work and wrap it up. A bloody Roman camp! I ask you! What's there but a few broken pots and stones? No wonder the bloody economy's in the state it's in. No room for initiative anymore.'

'Oh,' said Banks, feigning surprise, 'I thought our government wanted to encourage small businesses.'

Hackett glared at him; whether for the slight about his fiscal proportions or for picking up a throwaway comment, Banks wasn't quite sure. 'You know what I mean, Chief Inspector. We're hamstrung by these historical societies and tourist boards. They're all a load of bloody romantics as far as I can see. It's all a myth. The past wasn't like that; it wasn't neat and tidy like they all seem to think, for Christ's sake. Life was nasty, brutish and short, as the man said. Just because I never went to university, it doesn't make me an ignoramus, you know. I've read books, too. If you ask me, Harry walked around seeing the past through rose-coloured glasses. Penny Cartwright, too. In reality, life must have been bloody misery back then. Imagine them poor Roman sods freezing their balls off up north when they could have been lounging around in the sun on the seven hills drinking vino and rogering the local tarts. And as for the bloody Industrial Revolution, it was nothing but exploitation – hard, harsh work for most people. No,

Chief Inspector, Harry hadn't a bloody clue about the past, for all his degrees.'

'Maybe you should move somewhere else,' Banks suggested. 'I doubt they care much for local history in Wigan, for example, or Huddersfield.'

'You'd be surprised,' Hackett said. 'It's all over the bloody place. They call it civic pride. They're even flogging Bradford as the "gateway to Brontë country" now – and if they can get away with that they can do anything. Besides, I like it here. Don't think just because I'm a businessman I lack a finer appreciation of nature. I'm as much for the environment as the next man.'

'What were you doing on Saturday night?' Banks asked, renewing the attack on his pipe with a cleaner.

Hackett scratched his receding hairline. 'After I left the Bridge I went to a new club in Darlington. I drove up there, had a couple of drinks in a local, then went on to the club. I know the owner, like. We've done a bit of business together.'

'So you left the Bridge at what time?'

'About half nine.'

'And drove straight to Darlington?'

'Well, not exactly. I went home first to get changed.'

'What time did you leave for Darlington?'

'About ten to ten.'

'And arrived?'

'About half past, twenty to eleven.'

'And you went to the club when?'

'Half eleven, quarter to twelve.'

'What's it called?'

'The KitKat Klub. Only been open a few weeks. It's a sort of disco place, but not too loud. Caters for the more mature crowd.'

'I suppose you knew people there, people who can corroborate your story?'

'I talked to a few people, yes. And there's Andy Shaw, the owner.'

Banks took down the details, including the name of the pub, and noticed how anxious Hackett looked throughout the process.

'Anything else you can tell us, Mr Hackett?'

Hackett chewed on his lower lip and frowned. 'No, nothing.'

'Right then, off you go,' Banks said. He stood up and walked over to open the door.

As soon as Hackett was out of the building, Banks called Sergeant Hatchley in and asked if he'd found anything in his search of Steadman's study.

'Nowt much of interest, no,' Hatchley said. 'A few manuscripts, letters to historical preservation societies – they're on my desk if you want to look at them.'

'Later.'

'And he had one of those fancy computers – a word processor. I suppose he had to spend his brass on something. Remember how much wheeling and dealing it took us to get central admin to let us have one downstairs?'

Banks nodded.

'And now they send bloody Richmond off t' seaside to learn how to use the bugger.' Hatchley shook his head slowly and left the office.

FIVE

It was about six thirty, after what passed for rush hour in that part of the country, when Banks pulled into Helmthorpe's main car park. He had attended the brief inquest, given the press a snippet or two of information, and managed a quick dinner at home with Sandra and the kids.

Penny Cartwright was washing up the dinner dishes and enjoying the play of evening sunlight as it reflected from the shiny surfaces and skittered about the walls. When she heard a knock at the front door she quickly wiped her hands on her apron and went to answer it. She knew immediately that the dark-haired wiry man standing there was the policeman Barker had told her about. She hadn't expected him to be so good-looking, though, and immediately felt unattractive in her apron with her hair tied back in a long ponytail.

'You'd better come in,' she said. 'We wouldn't want to give the neighbours too much to talk about.' She pointed him to a worn armchair and slipped into the kitchen, where she quickly divested herself of the stained apron, untied her hair and brushed it swiftly so that it fell around her face and spilled over her shoulders.

If Banks was struck by the abrupt casual manner of his hostess, he was also struck by her beauty. She looked good in close-fitting jeans, and her striking hair framed a proud, high-cheekboned face without a trace of make-up. The combination of jet-black hair and sharp blue eyes added to the stunning effect.

Penny sat in a straight-backed chair by a writing table and asked Banks what she could do for him.

He began casually, trying to establish a friendly tone: 'Maybe nothing, Miss Cartwright. I'm just talking to Mr Steadman's friends, trying to get some idea of what he was like.'

'Do you really need to know?' Penny asked. 'I mean, do you care?'

'Perhaps not in the way that you do,' Banks admitted. 'After all, I didn't know him. But it might help me to find out who killed him. And I care about that. Obviously somebody did, but all I've heard so far is how wonderful he was – the kind of man who didn't have an enemy in the whole wide world.'

'What makes you think you'll get anything different out of me?' Penny asked. Her lips curved slightly in a mocking smile.

'Just fishing.'

'Well, you won't catch anything, Inspector. Not from me. It's all absolutely true. I can't imagine for the life of me who'd want to do a thing like that to him.'

Banks sighed. It was going to be a difficult evening. 'Fortunately, Miss Cartwright,' he said, 'it's not your life we're concerned about, it's Mr Steadman's. And somebody brought that to an abrupt and cruel end. Do you know anything about his business affairs?'

'Do you mean that fuss over Crabtree's Field? Really, Inspector, does Teddy Hackett strike you as the murdering kind? He wouldn't have the guts to kill a worm if his life depended on it. He might be a ruthless businessman – though the competition around here isn't much cop and, if you ask me, he's got by more on good luck than good management – but a killer? Hackett? Never.'

'Stranger things have happened.'

'Oh, I know. "There are more things in heaven and

earth, Horatio, than are dreamt of in your philosophy,"' she quoted.

'It might not be a serious possibility,' Banks went on, 'but it's the only one we've got so far.'

'Typical bloody police, that is,' Penny mocked. 'Crucify the first poor bastard that comes out less than squeaky clean. Still,' she added, 'Hackett's no great loss to society. Not like Harry.'

'How long had you known Mr Steadman?' Banks asked.

'Depends on what you mean by "know".' Penny lit a long filter cigarette and went on. 'I first met him years ago when I was a teenager and he and Emma came up to Gratly for their holidays. They'd been two or three times before I got to know them through Michael. That's Michael Ramsden. They stayed at his parents' bed-and-breakfast place, the house they live in now. I was about sixteen, and Michael and I were sweethearts at that time, so, naturally, I saw them quite often.'

Banks nodded and sucked on his pipe. That archaic word 'sweethearts' sounded wonderfully erotic coming from Penny's lips. It seemed unselfconscious, at odds with her tight and aggressive manner.

'We went on walks together,' she continued. 'Harry knew a lot about the countryside and its history. That was his real love. And then . . . well. It was a beautiful summer, but it passed, as all summers do.'

'Ah, yes. "But where are the snows of yesteryear?"' Banks quoted back at her.

'It was summer; there wasn't much snow.'

Again Banks noticed that tiny twitch of a smile at the corners of her pale lips. 'That would be about ten years ago, wouldn't it?' he asked.

Penny nodded slowly. 'Ten years, almost exactly. Yes. But things changed. Michael went to university. He was eighteen. I went away. Years passed. Harry came into some money and bought the house. I'd been back about eight months then – sort of return of the prodigal daughter. Black sheep. Most people had no time for me, but Harry always did.'

'What do you mean they had no time for you? Where had you been? Why did you come back?'

'That's a long story, Inspector,' Penny said, 'and I'm not sure it comes under the heading of relevant information. Briefly though, I spent about eight or nine years away, in the music business. Mostly I was homesick, despite all the fun and a moderate amount of acclaim. Finally, I got very cynical, and I decided it was time to come home. People weren't friendly because they can't accept anything modern around here and they no longer knew how to behave towards me. I'm sure they made up stories to suit their opinions. They didn't know who or what I was, so they made a lot of assumptions based on what they read in the Sunday papers about the music business – and I don't mean the *Sunday Times*, either. To them I became a degenerate, a scarlet woman. In fact, I always had been – they couldn't admit they'd ever been wrong about me. Does that answer your questions?'

She paused but didn't look at Banks for a response. 'It was very hard for my father, but he took me back. Why don't I live with him? Is that what you were going to ask next? For my sanity, Inspector, my mental health. He's just a bit too solicitous of my welfare, shall we say. And I think I'm a big girl now. It seemed best for both of us if I took this little cottage. Surely you can understand that?'

'Of course. There were rumours, too, weren't there?'

Penny laughed. 'Oh, you know about that as well, do you? See what a nice close little community our village is? Well, don't be embarrassed, Inspector, ask me. Go on, ask me.'

Her bright blue eyes glittered with anger. Banks said nothing. Finally, Penny gave him a scornful look and turned away to pull another cigarette from her packet.

'So only your father and Harold Steadman were kind to you?'

'Yes.' Penny hesitated. 'And Jack Barker, too. He'd been here a year or so by then, but he knew nothing of what had happened. Not that it would have mattered to him. He's a friend, too.'

'And now?'

'Oh, now?' Penny laughed. 'People are beginning to say hello again.'

'Do you still see Michael Ramsden?'

'Not much. Only when he calls in at the Bridge or drops by with Harry. Sometimes when you drift apart you never really drift back together.'

'And you can't think of any reason why anyone would want to harm Mr Steadman?'

'None at all. I've told you.' Penny's smooth brow creased in thought and she shook her head sadly. 'He wasn't greedy or scheming. He never cheated or lied.'

'What did his wife think of your relationship?'

'Emma? Nothing much, I should imagine. Probably glad to get him out of the way.'

'Why do you say that? Were they unhappy together?'

Penny looked at him as if he'd just crawled out from under a stone and blew her smoke out angrily. 'How should I know? Ask her.'

'I'm asking *you*.' Things were taking the kind of turn he had hoped to avoid, but with someone as anti-establishment as Penny Cartwright, he reflected, it was bound to happen. She had been toying with him all along. He pressed on: 'Still no answer?'

'I told you, I don't know,' she said. 'For God's sake, what do you want me to say?'

'Was their marriage normal?'

'Normal! Ha! What the bloody hell does that mean? Yes, I suppose so. I've never been married myself, so I'm hardly the best person to ask.'

'Were they happy?'

'I should think so. As I said, I don't really know. It's not as if I was his confidante or his shoulder to cry on.'

'Did he need one?'

Penny sighed and rested her head in her hands. 'Look,' she protested tiredly, 'this is getting us nowhere. What do you want from me?'

Banks ignored her question and pressed on: 'What were you to Mr Steadman?'

'Harry and I were friends. Just friends; I told you. We had interests in common.'

'And his wife didn't object?'

'She never said anything to me. Why should she? Harry never said anything, either.'

'You do know her, then?'

'Of course I bloody well know her. Harry and I weren't carrying on a clandestine relationship, like you seem to think. I went to their house for dinner plenty of times. She was always very kind and charming. She was a good cook, too.'

'What did you talk about?'

'When Emma was around?'

'Yes.'

'Nothing much. Just the usual stuff. She didn't really share Harry's passions. She likes music – mostly classical, though. Christ, what do you talk about when you go to someone's house for dinner?'

'Were you having an affair with Harold Steadman?'

At last, the inevitable question. And Banks felt a fool the moment it was out. If he had been expecting a burst of pent-up anger or a howl of derisive laughter in reply, he couldn't have been more surprised. His question seemed instead to deflate the interview of all its mounting tension, and Penny gazed at him steadily, a spark of amusement in her sapphire eyes, as if, in fact, she had goaded him into bluntness.

'No, Inspector,' she said, 'I was not having an affair with Harry Steadman, or with anyone else, for that matter. In fact, I'm not having an affair with Emma Steadman, or with my father, either. Everything is exactly as I've told you. I just didn't feel that way about Harry, nor he about me, as far as I could tell.' Banks thought Steadman must have been mad. 'He didn't excite me physically,' she went on, lighting another cigarette and walking around the small room as she smoked it. 'Only my mind, my imagination. And I liked him very much. I think he was a good man, a bright, sweet person. Perhaps I even loved him in a platonic sort of way, but that's as far as it went.' She tossed her hair back and sat down facing him, chin held high. Bright tears shone in her eyes but they never began to flow. 'There you are, Inspector,' she said with dignity. 'I've bared my soul for you. Aren't you pleased?'

Banks was moved by the obvious intensity of her feeling, but he didn't want to let his disadvantage show.

'When did you last see him?' he asked.

Her eyes reflected a chain of options running through her mind. It was a phenomenon Banks had often observed in people who were trying to decide quickly whether to lie or tell the truth.

Penny opened her mouth, then closed it. She took a final drag on her cigarette, ground it out half smoked and whispered, 'Saturday. Saturday evening.'

'What time?'

'About nine.'

'After he'd left the Bridge?'

'Yes. He dropped by here.'

'Then why the hell didn't you tell me before? You knew damn well you were holding back important information.'

Penny shrugged. 'You didn't ask me. I didn't want to get involved.'

'Didn't want to get involved?' Banks echoed scornfully. 'You say you liked the man, that he helped you, and you couldn't be bothered to help us try and find his killer?'

Penny sighed and began to wind a strand of hair around her index finger. 'Look, Inspector,' she said, 'I know it sounds shabby, but it's true. I don't see how his visit to me could help you in any way. And, dammit,' she flashed, 'I don't think I owe the police any bloody favours.'

'That's not the point. I don't care about your personal feelings towards the police. What was important was the time. If nothing else, your information could help us pinpoint the time of the murder. When did he leave?'

'About ten.'

'Did he say where he was going?'

'I assumed he was going to York. He'd mentioned it.'

'But he didn't mention any other calls he wanted to make first, any errands to run?'

'No.'

It was another hour accounted for, anyway. Banks had nothing more to say; his session with Penny had exhausted him. She seemed irritated and the tension grew between them again, as tangible as a tightening hacksaw blade. Finally, Penny broke it.

'Look,' she began, 'I'm sorry, I really am. I do care about Harry. The thing is that in my life involvement with the police has always meant trouble. I've never been involved in a murder investigation before, so I don't know what matters and what doesn't. When you're a musician, young, in with a certain crowd, you get a very warped view of authority – police, customs men, immigration officials, security guards – they all seem against you; they're all such a royal pain in the arse.'

Banks couldn't help but grin. 'Drugs?' he asked.

Penny nodded. 'Not me. I was never into it. Not in a heavy way. But you know how it is in London. There's drugs all around you, whether you take them or not. Sure, I smoked a joint or two, maybe took some amphetamines to keep me awake on tour, but never the heavy stuff. Try and tell the drug squad that.'

Banks wanted to argue, to defend the police, but he was too tired and he knew there would be no point anyway. Besides, he also knew that the police were just like everyone else; a lot were bastards and a few weren't. He had known a high-ranking officer in the drug squad who routinely planted illegal substances on people he wanted out of the way, and that was by no means rare or unusual behaviour. Also, he smelled something familiar in the air of Penny's cottage. He knew what it was, but he didn't care to pursue the matter any more than he wanted to tell her that his full title was Chief Inspector. People often got it wrong.

He stood up, and Penny walked to the door with him. He felt that she was seeking some kind words of reassurance from him, some forgiveness for acting in a way contrary to her feelings for Steadman. But he didn't know how to give it. At the door he said, 'I hear you sing, Miss Cartwright?'

'Actually, it's Ms,' Penny corrected him, a playful smile lighting her eyes. 'Yes, I sing.'

'Locally?'

'Sometimes. I'm at the Dog and Gun this Friday and Saturday. Competing with the disco in the Hare and Hounds.'

'I'll see if I can drop by, then,' Banks said. 'If nothing turns up.'

'Feel free.' There was a trace of doubt in Penny's voice, as if she couldn't quite believe that a policeman would be interested in traditional folk music, or in any kind of music for that matter.

Banks walked down the narrow cobbled street by the church wall, and as soon as he got to the corner he heard a hissing sound behind him and turned. An old woman stood at the door of the cottage next to Penny's and beckoned him over. When he got close enough she whispered, 'You'll be that there policeman they're all talking about.'

'Detective Chief Inspector Banks,' he said, reaching for his card. 'At your service.'

'Nay, nay lad, there's no need for that. I believe thee,' she said, waving it aside. 'Been talking to 'er ladyship next door, I see.' She jerked a shrivelled thumb in the direction of Penny's cottage. Puzzled, Banks nodded.

'Did she tell 'ee about Sat'day night?'

'What about Saturday night?'

'I thought she wouldn't,' the old woman said triumphantly, crossing her arms with great satisfaction. 'A proper ruckus there were. T' old major near flung 'im down t' garden path.'

'Flung who?'

'Why, 'im as got 'isself murdered,' she announced with obvious relish. 'I don't 'old wi' married men sniffing around young lasses. And she's a flighty one, yon missy is, you mark my words. There again, though,' she laughed, 't' major's mad as an 'atter 'isself.'

'What are you talking about, Mrs . . . ?'

'Miss,' she said proudly. 'Lived seventy-one years and never saw t' need for a 'usband yet. Miss Bamford it is, young man, and I'm talking about Sat'day night when Major Cartwright popped in on 'is daughter and caught 'er wi' that murdered chappie. 'Bout ten o'clock, it were. Now, don't ask me what they was doing, cos I couldn't say, but 'e flew off t' handle, t' old man did. Told 'im not to come around no more.'

'You mean the major physically threw Mr Steadman out of Penny Cartwright's house?' Banks asked, trying to get things straight. He was sure that something was bound to have got lost in translation.

'Well, not in so many words.' Miss Bamford backed down; her chin retracted deep into the folds of her neck. 'I couldn't see proper, like. Pushed 'im, though – and that chap so pale and weakly from shutting 'imsen up wi' books all day and night. I'll bet she didn't tell you about that, did she, yon Lady Muck?'

Banks had to admit that Penny had not told him about that. In fact, he had backed away from the whole issue of her father after she had challenged him to be direct.

'Did she go out afterwards?' he asked.

''Er Royal 'ighness? No. T' door banged about eleven, but that were t' major.'

'Surely there's a back door, too?'

'Oh, aye,' Miss Bamford answered. She hadn't missed his meaning.

Banks thanked her. With a smug smile on her wrinkled face, the old woman shut her door. After a quick and puzzled glance back at Penny's cottage, Banks walked towards his car and drove home.

6

ONE

'So according to your mate in Darlington—'

'Sergeant Balfour, sir. A good man.'

'According to your Sergeant Balfour,' Banks went on, 'Hackett didn't arrive at the KitKat Klub until after one o'clock in the morning, and nobody in the pub he mentioned remembered seeing him?'

'That's right. The landlord said he often dropped by, but last week it was on Friday, not Saturday.'

'So the bastard's been lying.' Banks sighed. He was becoming more and more irritated with the inhabitants of Helmthorpe, and as many London villains would testify, the more annoyed he got the harder it was all round. 'I suppose we'd better have him in again. No, wait . . .' He glanced at his watch and stood up. 'Better still, let's have a drive into Helmthorpe. There's a couple of things I want to do there.'

Sandra was using the Cortina, so they signed out a car from the pool and Banks let Hatchley drive. The hedge-rows by the river were dotted with clumps of white, yellow and purple wild flowers, none of which Banks could name. A few dark clouds skulked about the sky, but the sun pierced through here and there in bright lances of light that picked out green patches on the shadowed dalesides. The effect reminded Banks of some paintings he'd seen in a London gallery Sandra had dragged him to, but he couldn't remember the artist's name: Turner, Gainsborough, Constable? Sandra would know. He made a mental note to look into landscape painting a bit more closely.

'What do you think, then?' Hatchley asked. He drove with one hand and lit a cigarette from the glowing red circle of the dashboard lighter. 'About Hackett, I mean.'

'Could be our man. He's certainly hiding something.'

'What about the others who were with Steadman that night?'

'We just don't know, do we? Any one of them could have done it. They've no real alibis, not even Barnes.'

'But what motive could he have for killing Steadman? He's got a good reputation locally, always has had.'

Banks fiddled with his pipe. 'Could be blackmail. Maybe Barnes had something on Steadman, or vice versa. Maybe Steadman learned something that would ruin the doctor's reputation.'

'It's possible, I suppose,' Hatchley said. 'But Steadman was rich; he didn't need to blackmail anyone, surely? And if he was paying Barnes it'd be daft to kill the goose that laid the golden egg, wouldn't it?'

'Agreed. But it needn't have been money. Perhaps Steadman felt morally bound to tell what he knew. From all accounts, he was just the kind of person who would. I know it's all speculation at this point, but I still think we should look into the doctor's finances and background, and find out if Steadman made any large bank withdrawals recently.'

'Won't do any harm, I suppose. Bloody hell!' Hatchley swerved to avoid a wobbling cyclist and yelled out of the window, 'Watch where you're going, bloody road hog!'

Banks tightened his seat belt; he remembered one of the reasons why he preferred driving his own car on the job.

They arrived safely and parked by the river, where Steadman had left his car, and walked up the alley to High Street. It was about midday; tourists thronged the small ice-cream shop, and the locals were out shopping or gossiping by cottage gates up the narrow cobbled side streets. The two policemen were now well known in the village, and voices lowered as they passed. Banks smiled to himself; he enjoyed the effect his presence had on people. In London, nobody but the criminals he'd put away more than once knew who he was.

They paused by a newsagent's, where racks of coloured postcards, maps and local guidebooks outside on the pavement flapped in the light breeze.

'Let's take Hackett together after lunch,' Banks suggested.

'All right.' Hatchley looked at his watch. 'Want to eat now?'

'Not yet. Why don't you drop in on Weaver and see if anything's turned up? I want a word with Major Cartwright. Then we'll have a pie and a pint at the Bridge and work out how to tackle Hackett.'

Hatchley agreed and walked off to the small local police station.

Nobody, Banks thought, could look more like a retired major than the man who opened the door next to Thadtwistle's bookshop. He was elderly but trim-looking, with silver hair, a brick-red complexion and a grey handlebar moustache. After Banks had identified himself, the major grunted and led him up a narrow staircase. The flat turned out to be directly above the bookshop.

Banks followed him into a sitting room dominated by a huge framed reproduction of a bare-breasted woman carrying a flag over a battlefield of dead and wounded soldiers; she was accompanied by a small boy with a gun in each hand.

'*Liberty Leading the People*,' the major said, catching him staring at it. 'Delacroix. That's what we were fighting for, isn't it?'

Luckily, Banks could recognize a rhetorical question when he heard one. He turned his attention to the terrier sniffing around his ankles and tried subtly shifting his feet to make it go away. Banks didn't like dogs – if anything, he was a cat man – but he liked it even less when their proud owners expected him to fuss over the damned animals as if they were newborn babies. Kicking out a bit harder, Banks finally persuaded the pooch to slink off to its basket, from where it gazed at him with an expression of resentment mingled with arrogance. The major was pouring drinks, so fortunately his back was turned.

Stale smoke made the warm room stuffy. Banks spotted an antique pipe rack on the wall above the fireplace and, hoping to establish a rapport, he sat in a straight-backed chair and coaxed his own briar alight.

The major handed him a small whisky and soda, took a larger one for himself, and sat down in the scuffed leather armchair that had obviously been his since time immemorial.

Some military types, Banks found, regarded the police as fellow professionals, colleagues-in-arms almost, but others looked upon them as upstarts, petty dabblers who had not quite made the grade. Major Cartwright seemed to be of the latter type. He looked at Banks with open hostility, the purple veins around his nose showing a clear predilection for early morning snifters.

'What is it, then?' he asked, as if he had been interrupted in the midst of planning a new assault on the Boers.

Banks explained about the murder, drawing only grunts and sharp nods, and tried as delicately as he could to mention that the major had probably been the last person, apart from the killer, to see Steadman alive.

'When would that be?' Cartwright asked.

'Saturday night, about ten o'clock.'

The major stared at him with icy blue eyes and sipped his whisky. 'Who told you that?'

'It doesn't matter who told me, Major. Is it true?'

'I suppose it was that busybody of a neighbour, eh? Silly old biddy.'

'Did you see him and did you have an argument?'

'You can't be suggesting—'

'I'm not suggesting anything. I'm just asking you a simple question.'

The major swirled the whisky in his glass for a moment, then answered, 'All right, what if I did?'

'You tell me.'

'Nothing to tell, really. Found him hanging about my daughter again and told him to sling his hook.'

'Why did you react so violently?'

'It's not right.' Cartwright leaned forward in his chair. 'A married man, older than her. What would you do? It's not healthy.' He slumped back again.

'Did you assume they were having an affair?'

'Now hold on a minute, young man. Hold your horses. I never said anything like that.'

'Look,' Banks pressed on, 'I'm not making any

accusations or charges. I'm asking you what you thought. If you didn't think your daughter was likely to be involved in anything unsavoury, then why did you practically kick Steadman down the street?'

'She's exaggerating, the old bag.' Cartwright sniffed. He tossed back the rest of his drink, then got up and picked an old briar from the rack and filled it with twist from a pouch. 'We had words, yes, but I never laid a finger – or a toe – on him. Anyway, it's a matter of principle, isn't it? A married man. People talk.'

Banks found it hard to see the link between principle and the fear of gossip, but he ignored the issue. 'Is that why you objected to a harmless relationship that both parties seemed to enjoy?' he asked instead. 'Did you behave the same way over all your daughter's friendships?'

'Dammit, the man was married,' the major repeated.

'He was married ten years ago when they first met, but you didn't object then, did you?'

'That was all in the open. Always someone else around – young Michael. She was just a girl. Look, if they want to meet, they can do it openly, can't they? In a pub with other people there, for example. No reason to shut themselves up in private like that. They're a sharp-tongued lot in this village, lad. You don't know the half of it.'

'Were you worried that they'd talk like they did about you and your daughter? Is that what you wanted to protect her from?'

The major whitened and sagged in his chair. All of a sudden his belligerence seemed to desert him and he looked his age. He got up slowly and mixed himself another drink. 'Heard about that, did you?'

Banks nodded.

'You weren't there,' he said in a sad, bitter tone. 'You can't know what it was like for the two of us after my wife died. I couldn't look after myself, had to go into hospital for a while, had to send Penny away to the Ramsdens. But she came back and cared for me. Selflessly, God bless her. She's an only child, you know. And then the vicious gossip started. It only takes one to start the rumour – just one rotten bastard – then it spreads like the plague until everyone's had enough of it and something better comes along. And it's just a game to them. They don't even care whether it's true or not; it just titillates their imaginations, that's all. I blame them for driving her away. They said it wasn't natural, the two of us together. After she left, I sold the house and moved here.'

'I thought she left to start a career in music?'

'Oh, she'd have gone eventually. But she was too young. She shouldn't have gone so soon; then things wouldn't have turned out the way they did for her.'

'She seems well enough adjusted to me. Maybe a little sharp at the edges.'

'You didn't know her before. Lost a lot of her spirit, her joy. Too young to be a cynic. Anyway, she couldn't stand it here with people staring at her that way. Took a lot of courage for her to come back.'

'So you forgave her?'

'Nothing to forgive, really. She thought she'd let me down, leaving me like that. There'd been rows, fights, yes. But I never stopped loving her. Steadman wasn't a bad sort, I know that. A bit wet, I always thought, but not a bad sort. I just wanted to spare her it all again. She's bitter enough already. But it's not the first time I've had words with him. Ask anyone. My argument with Steadman wasn't new.'

'What happened on Saturday night?'

'Nothing, really. I told him not to call on her alone after dark again. I'd told him before. I suppose I just made things worse, drawing attention to it.'

'What did you do afterwards?'

'When he'd gone?'

'Yes.'

'I stayed and talked to Penny for an hour or so. She was a bit upset with me but we settled things amicably enough.'

'Can you remember what time you left?'

'I can remember the church bells ringing eleven. It wasn't long after that.'

'And Steadman left at ten?'

'That was when I arrived, yes.'

'Did you notice anyone hanging around the area?'

'No. It was quiet. Always is up there. There were a few people on High Street, but nothing unusual.'

'Did Steadman say where he was going? Did he give you any idea at all what he intended to do next?'

Major Cartwright shook his head. 'No, he just left. Sorry I can't be of more help to you, Inspector.'

'Never mind. Thanks for your time, anyway, Major.'

Cartwright turned and walked over to the drinks cabinet, leaving Banks to make his own way back downstairs.

TWO

With her head propped up on cushions, Sally lay in the back garden, sunbathing in her pale blue bikini. It was a luxury she felt entitled to as she had made temporary peace with her parents by breaking a date with Kevin the previous evening in order to visit boring Aunt Madge in Skipton. There, she had sipped tea from tiny fragile china cups with gilded rims and red roses painted on their sides, and had answered politely all the dull and predictable questions about her schoolwork. At least the television had been on – Aunt Madge never turned it off – so she had been able to half-watch an old Elizabeth Taylor film while pretending to pay attention to the conversation, which ranged from the shocking state of the neighbour's garden to news of a distant cousin's hysterectomy. The odd thing was that her parents hadn't seemed to enjoy the evening much either; her father hardly said a word. They all seemed relieved when the goodbyes had been said and they could troop out to the car.

With a sigh, Sally put down *Wuthering Heights* and rolled over on to her stomach. Her skin was already glowing pleasantly, and even with the lotion she would have to be careful how long she spent outside.

She was puzzled and frustrated by the book. In the film – even the old black and white version with Laurence Olivier – Heathcliff had seemed so sexy and tragic. She remembered sharing tissues with her mother while they watched it on television and her father had laughed at them. But the book was different; not the story – that was basically the same – but the character of Heathcliff. True, he loved Catherine passionately, but in the book he was so much more cruel and violent. He seemed to want to destroy everyone around him. And worse, he was even more interested in getting his hands on the house and property. That was the real reason he married Isabella – though he did appear to be taking revenge for Edgar marrying Catherine – and an obsession with acquiring property was hardly romantic. He acted more like a demented (and much more handsome) Teddy Hackett than a true heroic figure.

She reached for her glass of Perrier. It was warm; the ice had all melted and the sparkle had vanished. Pulling a face, she rolled on to her back again and started thinking rather despondently about her sleuthing. There wasn't much to think about. She had no idea who the police suspected, what clues they had, what they knew about motives and opportunities. All she had to go on was what anyone in the village would know about Steadman: that he seemed fond of Penny Cartwright, much to her father's chagrin; that he worked a lot with Michael Ramsden; that he had been able to help the Ramsden family by buying the house when the father died; that he was generally well liked; that he drank in the Bridge with Jack Barker, Teddy Hackett and Dr Barnes. He just didn't seem the type to go around inflaming people's passions, like Heathcliff. But he must have done; somebody had killed him.

It had to be a man. Of that, Sally was sure. Steadman had been quite tall and must have weighed a bit; no woman could have manoeuvred his body over the wall and all that way up the field. But that still left too many suspects. If only she had had the foresight to watch from the shelter that night. Sally began to apply her imagination to the facts. Everyone knew that Michael Ramsden had once courted Penny Cartwright. What if he was still carrying a torch for her, like Heathcliff for Catherine, and was jealous of Steadman's attentions? But she remembered seeing Ramsden – and avoiding him – that evening she went drinking in Leeds with Kevin. He had been with a good-looking woman, and though Sally had only got a fleeting glance while pulling Kevin quickly back out through the door before they were seen, she knew it wasn't Penny. And he'd hardly be going out with someone else if he was still in love with her.

There was Jack Barker. At first she hadn't suspected him, but now she could see him acting in the heat of passion. She'd noticed how often he'd been out walking with Penny around the village lately and wondered if Barker might have seen Steadman as an obstacle. He wrote detective stories, after all, so he must know all about murder. Even though he was a gentleman, he would hardly stand there with the gun smoking in his hand and wait for the police to come. Surely he would try and get rid of the body so he could remain free and win Penny's love. She wondered if he had an alibi and if there was any way of finding out.

And then there was Hackett. No love interest there, of course, but she'd heard rumours of arguments over property. People certainly seemed to get all steamed up about such things in *Wuthering Heights*.

She reached out for her suntan lotion. One more coat, another hour or so, then she'd go in. As far as catching the murderer was concerned, all she could do was try to remember all she'd seen and heard in the village since the Steadmans came to Gratly eighteen months ago. Maybe there was something she'd overlooked: a word or gesture that had meant nothing or made no sense at the time but took on more significance in the light of the murder. She had a good visual memory – it probably came from watching so many films – so she could review facial expressions and body language. Maybe something would click if she worked at it.

The oil felt good as she massaged it slowly into her stomach and thighs, and she wished Kevin's hands were rubbing it on her flushed skin. A bee droned around the neck of the open bottle, then floated away. Sally picked up her book again, leaving oily fingerprints on the pages.

THREE

The two men walked slowly along Helmthorpe High Street deep in conversation. Banks had one hand in his trouser pocket, and the other held a light sports jacket slung casually over his shoulder. The sleeves of his white shirt were rolled up above the elbows and he had loosened his tie enough to allow him to open his top button. Banks hated ties, and wearing them loosely was his way of compromising. He walked with his head bowed, listening to Hatchley, who towered beside him. The sergeant had both hands clasped behind his back and his head was tilted back on his thick neck as if he were examining the rooftops; a well cultivated beer belly hung over his tight belt. The weather was still undecided, and the sun popped in and out between quick-moving clouds that raced over on the wind and cast their shadows across the bright face of Crow Scar.

'Said he was in a bit of a state,' Hatchley went on. 'Shook up, like. Downed a quick double Scotch and went on his way.'

The scrap of information Constable Weaver had been so eager to impart was that the barman of the Dog and Gun had told him Steadman had dropped in just after ten o'clock on Saturday night. He hadn't come forward earlier because he had been away fishing in Scotland and hadn't even heard about the murder.

'I can tell you the reason for that,' Banks said, and

proceeded to tell Hatchley about his interview with Major Cartwright. This took some of the wind out of the sergeant's sails, and he muttered a surly 'No' when Banks asked him if there had been any other developments.

Hatchley began to smile again, however, as soon as he sniffed the beer fumes and tobacco smoke in the Bridge. They sat at the same scarred table as they had on their previous visit, and soon had two pints of Theakston's bitter before them and two steak and mushroom pies on order.

'Steadman could have gone back to the cottage though, couldn't he?' Hatchley said. 'Maybe he came to the boil when he thought about how he'd let the major walk all over him, so he went back to settle things. We can't rule him out yet, or the girl.'

'No, we can't. Steadman could have waited for the coast to clear and gone back to finish what he and Penny had started before they were interrupted. The major's certainly very protective towards her.'

'From what I hear,' Hatchley said with relish, 'she always was a bit of a wild 'un. Running off to London, hanging about with those freaks and musicians. There were probably drugs involved, too, and I doubt she was very careful about who she hopped in and out of bed with. I think if she were a daughter of mine I'd keep her on a short leash after that.'

'But the woman's twenty-six years old. Besides, Steadman was a safe enough companion, wasn't he?'

Hatchley shrugged. 'As far as we know he was. But there could be more to it.'

'Oh, there's more to it all right. There's always more to things like this. As far as Penny Cartwright's concerned, there are two points in her favour. First, the old woman didn't hear anyone else call at the cottage later, and she says Penny didn't go out either; and second, I doubt that she was strong enough to drag the body to its hiding place.' Banks was about to add that he had also been convinced by Penny's genuine display of affection for Steadman, but he knew it wasn't the kind of evidence Sergeant Hatchley would appreciate. Besides, the spell of her presence had worn off, and he was beginning to wonder if she was not just a consummate actress. 'Still,' he went on, 'she could have had help with the body; and there is a back door, so the old woman might not have heard if she was in the front room.'

'Do you think the Cartwright girl really was having it off with Steadman, then?' Hatchley asked.

'I don't know. You can never tell about things like that. Sometimes couples can be having affairs for years and nobody knows.'

'Why else would he be hanging around her?'

'There is such a thing as friendship, you know.'

'In a pig's eye,' Hatchley muttered.

The pies came and the two men ate silently until their plates were empty.

'Steadman had a lot of money,' Banks said, reaching for his second pint. 'And his wife stands to inherit. I'd say that was a pretty good motive, wouldn't you?'

'But we know she couldn't have done it,' Hatchley objected. 'I mean, why complicate something that's difficult enough already?'

'She could have hired someone.'

'But Helmthorpe isn't New York or London.'

'Doesn't matter. I once knew of a chap in Blackpool who had a price list – arms fifty quid, legs seventy-five and so on. Mind you, his rates have probably gone up a bit with inflation now. It's naïve to think that kind of thing is restricted to the south, and you should bloody well know that as well as anyone. Are you telling me there's no one in Eastvale would take a job like that? What about Eddie Cockley, for one? Or Jimmy Spinks? He'd slit his own mother's throat for the price of a pint.'

'Aye,' said Hatchley, 'but how would a woman like Mrs Steadman get mixed up with the likes of Cockley and Spinks?'

'I admit it's unlikely, but hardly more than anything else in this bloody business. Put it this way: we don't know much about the Steadmans' marriage. It seemed ordinary enough on the surface, but what did she think about him and Penny Cartwright, for example? Maybe she was mad with jealousy. We just don't know. And even if we ask them, they'll lie. For some reason, they're all protecting one another.'

'Perhaps they suspect each other.'

'I wouldn't be surprised.'

Hatchley guzzled his pint.

'You know what the trouble with this case is, Sergeant?' Banks went on. 'Everyone except Major Cartwright seems to think the sun shone out of Steadman's arse.'

Hatchley grinned. They drained their glasses and set off to see Hackett.

FOUR

Teddy Hackett sat in his office, part of an old mill that looked out on the River Swain behind the garage. The window was open and scents of flowers floated in with the sound of water rushing over pebbles. Occasionally a bee strayed from the clematis that clung to the stone wall, buzzed into the room and, finding nothing of interest in human affairs, meandered out again.

Hackett was nervous and sweaty right from the start. He sat behind the defence of his cluttered desk, back to the window, and toyed with a letter opener as Banks faced him from a chair. Hatchley leaned against the wall by the window. Banks filled his pipe, got it going, then brought up the subject of Hackett's false alibi.

'From what we've been able to discover, you arrived at the KitKat Klub alone and after one o'clock, a little later than you said.'

Hackett squirmed. 'I'm not very good at times. Always late for appointments, that's me.'

Banks smiled. 'That's not a very good habit for a businessman, is it? Still, that's no concern of mine. What I want to know is what you were doing before then.'

'I told you,' Hackett said, slapping his palm with the letter opener. 'I went to a pub and had a couple of drinks.'

'But closing time on Saturday is eleven o'clock, Mr Hackett. Even on the most liberal of premises you'd be out in the street by eleven thirty. What did you do between eleven thirty and one o'clock?'

Hackett shifted his weight from cheek to cheek and rubbed his chin. 'Look, I don't want to get anyone into trouble. Know what I mean? But when you get pally with the bar staff you can sometimes get in an extra drink or two. Especially when the local copper's there, too.' He winked. 'I mean, if young Weaver ever wanted to—'

'I don't want to hear about Constable Weaver,' Banks cut in. 'I want to hear about you, and I'm getting impatient. What you're saying is that the publican broke the licensing laws by serving you after hours, as late as one o'clock. Is that what happened?'

'I wouldn't put it quite like that. It was more in the nature of a drink or two together. Privacy of his own home, like. There's no law says a man can't have a mate in for a drink whenever he wants, is there?'

'No, not at all,' Banks answered. 'Let's say you weren't breaking any laws, then. If you were so pally with the manager you'll remember the name of the pub, won't you?'

'I thought I told you already. Didn't I?'

Banks shook his head.

'I thought I did. I meant to. It was the Cock and Bull on Arthur Street, near the club.' Hackett put down his letter opener and lit a cigarette, taking deep noisy drags.

'No, it wasn't,' said Banks. 'It wasn't the Cock and Bull on Arthur Street. The manager says he knows you, right enough, and that you'd been in on Friday, but not Saturday. Where were you, Mr Hackett?'

Hackett looked crestfallen. 'He must have been mistaken. Got a bad memory, old Joey. I'm sure if you ask him again, jog his memory a bit, he'll remember. He'll tell you it's true. I was there.'

'Come off it, man, tell us where you were!' Hatchley's loud voice boomed out from behind Hackett, unnerving him completely. During the preliminary part of the interrogation, the sergeant had remained so quiet that Hackett must have forgotten he was in the room. Now he half-turned and looked terrified to find a new, more aggressive adversary towering over him. He got to his feet but Hackett still had the advantage of height.

'I don't know what you're getting at—'

'We're not getting at anything,' Hatchley said. 'We're

telling you loud and clear. You never went to the Cock and Bull, did you? That was just a cock and bull story, wasn't it? You never went to any pub in Darlington. You waited for Steadman outside the Bridge, followed him to Penny Cartwright's, waited there, then followed him to the Dog and Gun and back to the car park. There, where it was dark and quiet, you hit him on the head and hid him in the boot of your car. Later, when the whole village was asleep, you dumped him in the field on your way over the dale to Darlington, didn't you? The timing's just right, Hackett, we've checked. What with all the lies you've told us and the traces we'll find in the boot of your car, we've got you by the short and curlies, mate.'

Hackett turned to Banks for sympathy and support. 'You can't let him bully me, accuse me like this,' he spluttered. 'It's not . . .'

'Not cricket?' said Banks. 'But you must admit, Mr Hackett, it is a possibility, isn't it? A very strong possibility.'

Hackett flopped back down into the chair behind his desk and Hatchley walked over to stand in front of him. 'Look, sir,' the sergeant began softly, 'we know you didn't arrive at the club until after one o'clock, and that gives you plenty of time to dump Steadman's body and get there. Don't you think it would be easier all round if you told us what happened? Perhaps it was manslaughter? Perhaps you had an argument and came to blows; you didn't mean to kill him. Is that how it happened?'

Hackett stared at him, wary of his apparent friend-liness. Banks got up and walked over to the window, through which he appeared to be gazing at the river.

'I walked around,' Hackett said. 'That's all. I set off for Darlington as soon as I'd left the Bridge and got changed, then I stopped on the way. It was a lovely evening. I didn't feel like a drink just then, so I went for a walk. I wanted to be alone.'

'You and bloody Greta Garbo,' Banks snarled from behind him, turning quickly from the window and knocking his pipe out in the thick glass ashtray. 'I'm fast losing patience with you,' he rushed on, raising his voice and glaring. It was a measure of Hackett's terror and confusion that he now looked to the huge Hatchley as a benign presence.

'But I—'

'Shut up,' Banks ordered him. 'I don't want to hear any more lies from you, Hackett. Get it? If I'm not satisfied your next story's true I'll have you in Eastvale nick before your feet touch the ground. Understand?'

Hatchley, enjoying himself tremendously, played the role of kindly uncle. 'Best do as the chief inspector asks, sir,' he advised the pale Hackett. 'I'm sure it can't do any harm if you've nothing to hide.'

Hackett stared at Hatchley for a good half-minute, then came that visible relaxation of tension, the moment that signalled the truth. Banks could feel it in his veins; he recognized it well from years of experience. Hackett was still so mixed up that he glowered at Hatchley and directed his statement toward Banks, who smiled and nodded at various points with benevolent understanding.

All in all, it was a great disappointment, but it did get one red herring out of the way. After leaving the Bridge, Hackett had gone home to shower and change, then he had driven to Darlington, where he first spent about two hours of uninhibited carnal bliss with a young married woman whose husband worked the night shift at the local colliery. After that, he had gone on to the KitKat Klub alone because he didn't want to be seen with her locally. People would talk. Banks finally extracted her name and address from him, along with pleas and warnings about not letting her muscle-bound husband find out.

'Please,' he begged, 'if you must talk to Betty, do it after ten at night. I'll get her to come in. That'll be even better, won't it?'

'If you don't mind, Mr Hackett,' Banks replied, 'we'll do it our way.'

'Have a heart, Chief Inspector. Haven't you ever had a bit on the side?'

The muscles in Banks's jaw tightened. 'No,' he answered sharply. 'And even if I had it wouldn't make a jot of difference to your situation.' He put his hands on the desk and leaned forward so that his face was only inches from Hackett's. 'What you don't seem to realize is that this is a murder investigation. A friend of yours has been murdered, or don't you remember, and all you're concerned with is some bloody tart you've been poking in Darlington.'

'She's not a tart. And there's no reason to ruin a perfectly good marriage, is there? That's what you'll be doing, you know.'

'No. That's what you've done. It's what she's done too. If I thought for a moment that you cared more about the marriage than about your own skin, I might just consider doing things differently.'

Banks nodded to Hatchley and the two of them left Hackett biting his fingernails and cursing the day he met nubile little Betty Fields in the Cock and Bull.

'Fancy a trip to Darlington, Sergeant?' Banks asked when they reached High Street. 'Best if you check it out yourself.'

'Yes, sir,' Hatchley replied, grinning.

'Right then. After ten o'clock tonight, if you can make it.'

'What? But . . .'

'If you don't mind.'

'It's not that I mind. I've got a couple of mates up there I've not seen in a while. But what about Hackett?'

'Simple really. Hackett's right; I don't see any point putting unnecessary strain on a marriage, even one as flimsy as Betty Fields's. But he doesn't know that, does he? By the next time he hears from his young lady he'll be a gibbering wreck. Some of these miners are big chaps, so I've heard.' He smiled as comprehension dawned on Hatchley. 'You have to balance your cruelty with compassion, Sergeant. Come on, just one more visit to make then home. And by the way . . .'

'Yes, sir?'

'That was a terrible pun back there. Cock and bull story.'

'Oh, I thought it was quite good myself.'

Taking advantage of the fine weather, Banks and Hatchley walked to Gratly. They took the short cut through the cemetery and along a narrow path through a field. Lynchets led down to the beck like a broad flight of green velvet stairs. Sheep grazed under a clump of ash trees in the lush green grass by the water.

This time, Banks was struck by the tranquillity and individuality of Gratly. At the centre of the hamlet was a low stone bridge under which a broad stream ran over several abrupt terraces and descended in a series of small waterfalls past a disused mill and down the valley side to the all-consuming Swain.

Gratly itself radiated like a cross from this central point, and ginnels and snickets here and there led to twisting backstreets and hidden outhouses. The houses were all old, built of local stone, but their designs varied. Some, originally weavers' cottages, had many windows in their upper stories, while others looked like old farmhouses or labourers' quarters. The sun on the light stone and the steady music of water as it trickled relaxed Banks, and he found himself thinking that this was no day and no place for his kind of business. The hamlet was silent and still; there were no signs of life at all.

Emma Steadman, wearing a brown apron over her shirt and slacks, answered the door at the second ring and invited them inside, apologizing for the mess. She stopped at the entrance to the front room and ushered the two men in, running a grimy hand over her moist brow. Banks saw immediately what she meant. All Steadman's books had been taken down from the shelves and stood in untidy, precariously balanced piles on the floor.

The widow moved forlornly into the middle of the room and gestured around. 'They're all his. I can't stand it, having them all over the place. I don't know what to do with them.' She seemed less frosty than when they had parted on Monday afternoon, vulnerable among the detritus of a shared life.

'There's a book dealer in Eastvale,' Banks advised her. 'I'm sure he'll come out and appraise them if you give him a call. He'll give you a fair price. Or what about Thadtwistle in Helmthorpe?'

'Yes, that's an idea. Thank you.' Mrs Steadman sat down. 'It'll have to wait though, I'm afraid. I can't face that kind of thing yet. I don't know what I'll do with all his things. I never realized he'd collected so much junk. I wish I could just get up and leave Gratly, go somewhere else.'

'You'll not be staying here?' asked Hatchley.

She shook her head. 'No, Sergeant, I don't think so. There's nothing for me here. It was Harold's work, really. His place.'

'Where will you go?'

'I haven't really thought. A city, I suppose. Maybe London.' She looked at Banks.

'I shouldn't worry about it yet,' he said. 'You need a bit of time. It'll all get taken care of.'

Silence followed. Mrs Steadman offered to make a cup of tea, but Banks, much to Hatchley's distress, refused for them both. 'No thanks. It's just a flying visit. We were in the area.'

She raised her eyebrows, hinting that he should get to the point.

'It's about Penny Cartwright,' Banks began, noting that her expression didn't alter a jot at the mention of the name. 'I gather that she and your husband were rather close. Didn't that bother you at all?'

'What do you mean, "bother me"?'

'Well,' Banks went on cautiously, 'she's an attractive woman. People talk. People have talked about her before. Weren't you worried that your husband might have been having an affair with her?'

It was immediately clear that the suggestion surprised rather than annoyed Emma Steadman, as if it were something she had never even thought of. 'But they'd been friends for years,' she answered. 'Ever since she was a teenager, when we first came up here for our holidays. I don't— I mean, I never really thought of her as anything else, really. A teenager. More like a daughter than a rival.'

Banks felt that it was short-sighted in the extreme to look upon a woman only twelve or thirteen years one's junior as a child, especially if that woman was over the age of sixteen. 'It didn't bother you at all, then?' he went on. 'It never caused any trouble, any jealousy?'

'Not on my part it didn't, no. As I said, Chief Inspector, she's been a friend of the family for years. I suppose you know that she and Michael Ramsden used to go out together ages ago? He brought her up here quite often – after all, it was his home then; we were only summer visitors. I think she had a lot in common with Harry. She looked up to him as a teacher, a man of knowledge. So did Michael, for that matter. I'm sorry, I'm afraid I can't really see what you're getting at.'

'I simply wondered whether you suspected your husband of having an affair with Penny Cartwright.'

'No, I didn't. First you cast doubts on my marriage, now you accuse my husband of adultery. What's going on? What is all this about?'

Banks held up his hand. 'Wait a minute. I'm not making any accusations; I'm asking questions. It's my job.'

'That's what you said last time,' she said. 'It didn't make me feel any better then, either. Don't you realize they're burying my husband tomorrow?'

'Yes I do, and I'm sorry. But if you want us to carry out a thorough investigation into his death, you've got to be prepared for some awkward questions. We don't find the truth by skating over the surface or by skirting difficult patches.'

Mrs Steadman sighed. 'I understand that. It's just . . . so soon.'

'Did you see much of Penny after she left Helmthorpe?' Banks asked.

'Not much, no. Sometimes, if we were in the same

place – London, say – we'd have dinner together. But you could count the times on the fingers of one hand.'

'What did she seem like during that period?'

'Like herself.'

'She never seemed depressed, on drugs, strung out?'

'Not when we saw her.'

'How well did your husband know Jack Barker?'

'Jack? I'd say they were fairly close. As close as Harry could be to someone who didn't share his enthusiasms.'

'How long had Barker been living in Gratly?'

'I don't really know. Before us. Three or four years.'

'How long had your husband known him?'

'They got to know each other over the past eighteen months. We'd met before, on our visits here, but it wasn't till we moved in that Harold really spent much time with the locals.'

'Where did Barker come from?'

'He's from Cheadle, in Cheshire. But I think he lived in London for a while.'

'And neither your nor your husband knew him when you first visited Gratly?'

'No. I don't think anyone in Helmthorpe or Gratly did. Why this fascination with the past, Chief Inspector?'

Banks frowned. 'I'm not really sure, Mrs Steadman. I'm just trying to get a sense of the pattern of relationships: exits and entrances.'

'And that's why you were asking me about Harry and Penny?'

'Partly, yes. Major Cartwright didn't seem too pleased about their friendship.'

Mrs Steadman made a sound halfway between a sneeze and a guffaw. 'The major! Everybody knows he's a crackpot. Mad as a March hare. She's all he's got, you know, and she did desert him for a long time.'

'You know about the rumours?'

'Who doesn't? But I don't think you'll find anyone who takes them seriously these days.'

'Forgiven and forgotten?'

'Something like that. People tire easily. Surely you don't think . . . the major?'

Banks didn't answer.

'You policemen have such wild imaginations,' Emma Steadman went on. 'What do you think happened? Do you think the major found out about this mythical affair and killed Harry to protect his daughter's virtue? Or do you think I did it in a jealous rage?'

'You couldn't have done it, could you? You were watching television with your neighbour at the time. We don't rely entirely on imagination, Mrs Steadman. I know it's a difficult period for you right now, and I apologize if I seem to be pestering you, but I'm simply trying to build up as complete a picture as I can of your husband and his circle. This is a difficult and vital time for us, too. Memories fade and stories change with every hour that goes by. As yet, I don't know what's important and what isn't.'

'I'm sorry for mocking you,' Mrs Steadman apologized. 'I know you have your job to do, but it is upsetting, you coming around talking about Harold having affairs and suggesting our marriage was in trouble. You must try and see it from my point of view. It's almost as if you're accusing me.' She paused and smiled weakly. 'He just wasn't that kind of man, and if you'd known him you'd see what I mean. If there's anything Harry was having an affair with, it was his work. In fact, sometimes I thought he was married to his work and having an affair with me.'

She said this with good humour, not in bitterness, and Banks laughed politely. 'I'm sure my wife thinks the same,' he said, then called to Hatchley, who had turned to browse through the decimated bookshelves.

'I won't trouble you any further,' Banks said at the door, 'but there is one small piece of information you might be able to help me with.'

'Yes?'

'Your husband taught at Leeds in the history department, am I right?'

She nodded. 'Yes. That was his field.'

'Who were his colleagues? Who did he spend most time with during your years there?'

She thought for a moment before replying. 'We didn't socialize a great deal. Harry was too intent on his career. But let me see . . . there was Tom Darnley, he was a fairly close friend, and Godfrey Talbot. I think he knew Harry at Cambridge, too. That's about all, except for Geoffrey Baynes, but he went off to teach in Winnipeg, in Canada, before Harry left. That's all I can think of.'

'Thank you, Mrs Steadman,' Banks said as the door closed slowly. 'That'll do fine for a start. See you tomorrow.'

They walked back the same way to the car, which was hot from standing in the sun most of the day, and drove back to Eastvale. Banks regretted not having the Cortina; the landscape inspired him to listen to music. Instead, Hatchley drove too fast and droned on about never having seen so many bloody books outside Gristhorpe's office. 'Funny woman, that Mrs Steadman, don't you think?' he asked finally.

'Yes,' Banks answered, staring at a pattern of six trees on a distant drumlin, all bent in the same direction. 'She makes me uncomfortable, I've got to admit. I can't quite make her out.'

7

ONE

Had an adventurous fell-walker found himself on top of
Crow Scar at eleven o'clock that Thursday morning, he
would have seen, to the south, what looked like two shiny
black beetles followed by green and red aphids make their
way slowly down Gratly Hill and turn right at the bottom
into Helmthorpe village.

Pedestrians on High Street – locals and tourists alike –
stopped as the funeral cortège crawled by. Some averted
their gaze; others doffed their caps; and one or two,
clearly visitors from afar, even crossed themselves.

Harold Steadman had been a believer because belief
was, for him, inextricable from the men and the actions
that had helped shape and mould the area he loved;
therefore, the funeral was a traditional, if nowadays rare,
graveside ceremony conducted by a visiting minister from
Lyndgarth.

On the hottest day of the year thus far, the motley
group stood uneasily around the grave as the Reverend
Sidney Caxton recited the traditional words: 'In the midst
of life we are in death; of whom may we seek succour but
Thee, O Lord . . . Thou knowest, Lord, the secrets of our
hearts; shut not Thy merciful ears to our prayer; but spare
us, Lord most holy.' He followed this, at Mrs Steadman's
request, with the twenty-third Psalm: 'The Lord is my

shepherd; I shall not want. He maketh me to lie down in green pastures: he leadeth me beside still waters . . . Yea, though I walk through the valley of the shadow of death, I will fear no evil: for Thou art with me; Thy rod and Thy staff they comfort me . . . Surely goodness and mercy shall follow me all the days of my life: and I will dwell in the house of the Lord forever.' It was a sombre and eerily appropriate farewell for a man like Harold Steadman.

To Sally Lumb, representing Eastvale Comprehensive School along with Hazel, Kathy, Anne and Mr Buxton, the headmaster, it was a gloomy and uncomfortable affair indeed. For one thing, in the tasteful navy-blue outfit her mother had made her wear, she was far too hot; her blouse was absolutely stuck to her back, and the beads of sweat that occasionally ran down her spine tickled like spiders.

Reverend Caxton took a handful of earth and cast it down on the coffin. 'For as much as it hath pleased Almighty God of His great mercy to receive unto Himself the soul of our dear brother here departed; we therefore commit his body to the ground . . .'

To pass the time, Sally studied the others covertly. Penny Cartwright was the most striking. Dressed in black from head to foot, her pale face in stark contrast, she wore just enough make-up to hide the bags under her eyes from all but the most discerning of onlookers, and to highlight her tragic, romantic cheekbones. She really did look extraordinarily beautiful, Sally thought, but in an intense, frightening and overwhelming way. On the other hand, Emma Steadman, in a conservative, unfashionable, charcoal-grey suit, didn't look much. She could have done herself up a bit, at least for the funeral, Sally thought, mentally adding a touch of blusher, eyeliner and a slash of lipstick. Immediately, though, she felt ashamed of herself for thinking such worldly thoughts at a time like this; after all, Mrs Steadman had always been nice to her.

'Earth to earth, ashes to ashes, dust to dust; in sure and certain hope of the Resurrection to eternal life, through our Lord Jesus Christ, who shall change our mortal body . . .'

Between the two grieving women stood Michael Ramsden, who looked, to Sally, rather like one of those doomed tubercular young men in the black and white gothic films her mother liked to watch on Channel Four. At Penny's other side was Jack Barker in a dark suit with a black armband. He really did look dashing and dangerous – that Errol Flynn moustache, the glint in his eyes – and Sally lost herself for a few moments in a swashbuckling fantasy.

The policeman, Banks, didn't detain her for long. True, he was handsome in a lean and bony kind of way and the scar was mysterious, but she had seen his true colours and found them lacking. He was soft; he had lived in London, had adventure all around him, countless opportunities for heroism, and he had given it all up to retire to this godforsaken part of the country. Old before his time, obviously. Dr Barnes looked as grey and insignificant as ever, and Teddy Hackett wore an ostentatious gold medallion which glinted in the sun against the background of his black shirt whenever he shifted from foot to foot.

'. . . that it may be like unto His glorious body, according to the mighty working whereby He is able to subdue all things to Himself.'

When Sally turned her attention back to the ceremony, it was all over. Slowly, as if reluctant to leave the deceased once and for all, the mourners edged away. Penny and Emma had their handkerchiefs out, and each hung on to the arm of the nearest man. In Penny's case that was Jack Barker, and Sally noticed what an attractive couple they made. The others left in groups of two or three, and the policeman sidled away alone. Harold Steadman, lowered to rest, had become a part, in death, of the dale he had loved so much in life.

TWO

At one o'clock, after having spent an hour discussing their lack of progress with Constable Weaver in the Helmthorpe station, Banks sat alone at a white table in the back garden of the Dog and Gun sipping a pint of shandy. The tables around him were all full. Tourists chatted about their holidays, the weather, their jobs (or lack of them), and children buzzed around unhindered like the wasps that flitted from glass rims to the remains of gateaux and sticky buns left on paper plates.

Banks didn't mind the squealing and the chatter; he was always able to shut out distracting background noise when he wanted to. He sat in his shirtsleeves and fiddled with his pipe, dark suit jacket slung over the back of a chair. The pipe was a blasted nuisance. It kept going out or getting clogged up, and the bitter juices trickled down the stem on to his tongue. It suited him, though; it was a gesture towards establishing the kind of identity and image he wanted to develop and project.

A wasp droned on to his sleeve. He brushed it away. Across the dazzling river with its overgrown banks the local club was playing cricket on a field of freshly mown grass. The slow pace of the game made it look like a Renaissance pavane. The harmony of white against green, the sharp crack of willow against leather, and the occasional smatterings of applause seemed to blend with the scent of the grass and enhance the sensation of peace. He rarely went to matches these days – and if he did, got bored after a few overs – but he remembered the famous England cricketers of his school days: Ted Dexter, 'Fiery' Fred Trueman, Ken Barrington, Colin Cowdrey; and the classroom games he had played with dice and paper, running his own county championship and Test Match series. The clichés about cricket were true, he reflected; there was something about the game that was essentially English – it made one feel that God was in his heaven and all was well with the Empire.

Far from it, though, he realized with a jolt. Beyond the pitch, the valley side sloped up gently at first, veined with drystone walls, then steepened and peaked into the long sheer curve of limestone, Crow Scar, above which Banks actually fancied he could see crows wheeling. And about halfway between the pitch and the scar, as far as the eye's imperfect perspective could make out, was the spot where Steadman's body had been found.

Banks didn't like funerals, and in a way it seemed a pointless convention to attend the funerals of people he had never known. Not once had he caught a murderer that way: no graveside confessions, no mysterious stranger lurking behind the yew trees. Still, he did it, and when he probed his motives he found that it was because of a strange and unique bond he felt with the dead man, perhaps more intimate even than if he had known him. In a sense, Banks saw himself as the victim's appointed avenger, and, in an odd way, he worked together with the

dead man to redress the balance of nature; they were co-
workers of light against darkness. In this case, Steadman
was his guide from the spirit-world: a silent and shapeless
guide perhaps, but present nonetheless.

Banks looked back at the game just in time to see
the batsman swipe a badly paced off-spinner towards the
boundary. The bowler found his length in the next two
deliveries though, and play slowed down as the batsman
was forced to switch to defensive tactics. Banks, aided by
the warm air, drifted back into a reverie about his first
year and a half in Yorkshire.

The landscape, it went without saying, he found
beautiful. It was wild and rough, unlike the southern
downs, but its scale inspired awe. And the people. Whatever he had heard about the stubborn intractability of the
Yorkshire character, the gruffness, the slowness in taking
to strangers, was all true to some extent, but like all
generalizations didn't do justice to the full reality. He had
grown to appreciate the stoic humour, the quick wit and
instinctive good sense, the friendliness beneath the crusty
surface.

Banks also liked the feeling of being an outsider. Not a
stranger, as he had been among the anonymous inter-
national crowds of London, but an outsider. He knew he
always would be, no matter how deep he put his roots.

Knocking out his pipe, he tried to bring his mind to
bear on the case again. It had the same sordid elements as
any murder, but in such an environment it seemed even
more of a blasphemy. The whole way of life in the small
dale – the people, their priorities, beliefs and concerns –
was different from that in London, or even in Eastvale.
Gristhorpe had said that being an outsider would give him
an advantage, a fresh perspective, but Banks wasn't too

sure; he seemed to be getting nowhere fast.

He turned as a long shadow brushed across the white table and saw Michael Ramsden disappearing into the pub.

'Mr Ramsden!' he called after him. 'A word, if you've got a moment to spare.'

Ramsden turned. 'Chief Inspector Banks. I didn't see you there.'

Banks thought he was lying, but it meant nothing. As a policeman, he was used to being avoided. Ramsden perched on the very edge of a chair, indicating through his body language that he had no intention of staying for more than a minute or two.

'I thought you'd be at the funeral lunch,' Banks said.

'I was. You know what those things are like: all that false humour and bonhomie to cover up what's really happened. And someone inevitably drinks too much and get silly.' He shrugged. 'I left. Was there something you wanted to ask me?'

'Yes. Are you certain you didn't go out on Saturday night?'

'Of course I'm certain. I've already told you.'

'I know, but I want to make absolutely sure. Not even for half an hour or so?'

'You've seen where I live. Where would I go?'

Banks smiled. 'A walk? A run? I've heard that writers get blocked sometimes.'

Ramsden laughed. 'That's true enough. But no, not me, not on Saturday anyway. I was in all evening. Besides, Harry had a key; he would have let himself in and waited.'

'Had he done that before?'

'Once, yes, when I had to work late at the office.'

'He wouldn't, say, visit another friend in the area and come back later?'

'I don't think Harry really knew anyone else in the York area. Not well enough to drop in on, at least. Why do you want to know all this, if you don't mind me asking?'

'We need to know where Mr Steadman was between ten fifteen and the time of death. But there's something else,' Banks went on quickly, sensing Ramsden's restlessness. 'I'd like to talk to you a bit more about the past – your relationship with Penny Cartwright.'

Ramsden sighed and made himself more comfortable. A white-coated waiter passed by. 'Drink?' Banks asked.

'Might as well, if you intend to keep me here a while. But it's all so long ago – I don't see how you expect me to remember. And I can't imagine what any of it has to do with Harry's death.'

Banks ordered two pints of lager. 'Just bear with me, that's all. Ten years ago,' he went on, 'was a very important time in your life. It was summer, and you were eighteen, all set for university, courting the prettiest girl in Swainsdale. Harold and Emma Steadman came to stay at your parents' guest house for a month, as usual. By all accounts that was a memorable summer – long walks, expeditions to local sites of interest. Surely you remember?'

Ramsden smiled. 'Yes, of course I do, now you put it like that. I just hadn't realized it was so long ago,' he said wistfully.

'Time does seem to pass quickly,' Banks agreed. 'Especially when you lose your sense of continuity, then look back. Anyway, it came to an end. Things changed. What happened between you and Penny?'

Ramsden sipped his lager and brushed away a trouble-some wasp. 'I've told you before. Like most teenage lovers, we just drifted apart.'

'Did you ever regret it?'

'What?'

'The turn of events. Perhaps you could have been happily married to Penny now, and none of this would ever have happened.'

'None of what? I fail to see the connection.'

'Everything: Penny's adventures in the music business, your bachelorhood.'

Ramsden laughed. 'You make it sound like a disease, Chief Inspector. I may be a bachelor, but that doesn't mean I live a celibate life. I have lovers, a social life. I enjoy myself. As for Penny . . . well, it's her life. Who's to say things haven't turned out for the best for her, too?'

Banks tried to coax his pipe alight. A baby in a high chair two tables away started to cry. Its cheeks were smeared with strawberry jam. 'Perhaps if Steadman hadn't come along, though, and spirited her away . . . ?'

'What are you suggesting? That Harry and Penny were involved?'

'Well, he was older, more mature. You have to admit it's a possibility. She certainly spent a lot of time with him. Isn't that why you split up? Didn't you argue about Steadman?'

Ramsden was on the edge of his seat again. 'No, we didn't,' he said angrily. 'Look, I don't know who's been telling you all this, but it's lies.'

'Did you split up because Penny wouldn't give you what you wanted? Maybe she was giving it to Steadman?'

This time Ramsden seemed on the point of getting up and hitting Banks, but he took a deep breath, scratched the back of his ear and smiled. 'You know, you really are irritating,' he said. 'I should imagine people tell you things just to make you go away.'

'Sometimes,' Banks admitted. 'Go on.'

'Maybe there's some truth in the first part of your question. A man can only wait so long, as you probably know yourself. I was definitely ready, and Penny was a very beautiful girl. It's only natural, isn't it? We were both a bit naïve, scared of sex, but it didn't help that she kept saying no.'

Banks laughed. 'It certainly wouldn't,' he said knowingly. 'I dare say I'd have been climbing the walls myself. But why do you think she kept saying no? Was it something to do with Steadman? Or did she have another boyfriend?'

Ramsden thought, frowning, before he answered. 'No, there wasn't another boyfriend, I'm sure of that. I think it was just a matter of morality. Penny was brought up to be a nice girl, and nice girls don't. As for Harry, I don't think he did what you're suggesting. I'm sure I'd have known, somehow. I suppose at times I was a bit peeved about how close they were. Not that I thought there was anything going on, mind, but they did spend a lot of time together, time she could have spent with me. Harry was so much more sure of himself than I was. I was shy and clumsy. So yes, I might have been a bit envious, but I didn't feel the kind of jealousy you have in mind.'

'Oh? What kind of jealousy do I have in mind?'

'You know. The kind that eats away at you and ends in murder,' he answered, deepening his voice for dramatic effect.

Banks laughed. Ramsden had nearly finished his drink and looked anxious to leave, but there were a couple more areas Banks wanted to probe. 'What about her father, the major? Do you think he had anything to do with you two drifting apart?'

'I don't think so, no. As far as I know, he approved of me. He's a bit cracked, but he never really gave us any trouble.'

'Did you ever get together with Penny again later? You were both in London at times, weren't you?'

'I suppose so. But I never saw her. Once it was over, that was it.'

'What did you do while she was off with Steadman?'

'It wasn't the way you make it sound, Chief Inspector. Often we all went together; sometimes I just didn't want to go with them. I read a lot. I'd just discovered the pleasures of literature. My sixth-form English teacher, Mr Nixon, was a brilliant inspiring man, and he managed to undo, in one year, all the damage that the others had done. For the first time, I could enjoy Shakespeare, Eliot, Lawrence, Keats, and the rest with a joy I'd not known before. What I'm saying is that I was a very romantic and introspective young man; I was happy enough to sit by a "babbling brook" and read Wordsworth.'

'When you weren't trying to get Penny into bed,' said Banks, who had once, on Gristhorpe's recommendation, tried Wordsworth and found him an insufferable bore.

Ramsden blushed. 'Yes, well . . . I was a normal adolescent; I don't deny that.' He looked at his watch. 'Look, I don't mean to seem rude, but I do have to get back to the office. Tell me, before I go, why this fascination with past events?'

'I'm not really sure,' Banks said, reaching for his glass. 'I'm just following my instincts.'

'And what do your instincts tell you?'

'That Harold Steadman's death wasn't a spur-of-the-moment affair; it was premeditated and it probably had its roots in the past. You see, you were all together ten years ago – you, Penny Cartwright, her father, the Steadmans – and now you're all back in more or less the same place. Eighteen months after Steadman comes to live in Gratly, he's dead. Doesn't that strike you as odd?'

Ramsden brushed back his forelock, which this time actually had slipped over his eyes, then he drained his glass and stood up. 'Put that way, I suppose it does,' he said. 'But I think your instinct is wrong. Things aren't the same as they were before. For one thing, there are other people around now, too. If you think Harry's death had anything to do with Penny, I suggest you follow your instinct to Jack Barker. He's been hanging around with her a lot lately, so I hear. Now good day, Chief Inspector, and thanks for the drink.'

Banks watched Ramsden thread his way between the tables and turned his attention back to the cricket match just in time to see a wicket fall dramatically. The bails flew high in the air and the bowler threw up his arms and yelled, 'Owzat!'

Banks thought about his talk with Ramsden and wondered if there was anything in what he'd said about Barker. 'Men have died from time to time, and worms have eaten them, but not for love.' So his daughter Tracy, playing the fair Rosalind, had said in *As You Like It*, which had been Eastvale Comprehensive's school play that term. But it wasn't true; many had killed and many had died for love. And Penny Cartwright was certainly the kind of woman to stir up such strong feelings.

Suddenly, the air roared and screamed as two F-111s from a nearby US airbase shot overhead. They flew so low that Banks could almost see the pilots' faces. It was a common enough occurrence in the dales; jet bombers frequently ripped through the peaceful landscape and shattered the idyll as they broke the sound barrier. On the hillside below Crow Scar, scared sheep huddled together and ran for the cover of a drystone wall. People at the tables put their hands over their ears and screwed up their faces.

The planes broke the spell for Banks. There was paperwork to be done that afternoon. Grabbing his jacket, he drained his glass and left the cricketers to finish their game.

THREE

Dinner in the Banks household that evening was a lively affair. It seemed like ages since the family had all sat down together and enjoyed one of Sandra's delicious concoctions: chicken in tarragon and white-wine sauce. She had a wonderful knack of making the most inexpensive cuts of meat taste like gourmet creations. This skill, Banks thought, was characteristic of someone with inborn good taste and a poor working-class background. All it took, said Sandra, clearly delighted with the compliments, was the right cooking method and a little care with the sauce.

Most of the conversation was taken up by the children's accounts of their day trip to York.

'The Minster was smashing,' enthused Tracy, the bright fourteen-year-old with a passion for history. 'Do you know, Daddy, there's more stained glass in there than in any other cathedral in Europe?'

Banks expressed interest and surprise. Architecture had not, so far, been one of his interests, but it was becoming more and more appealing. At the moment he was still reading up on the geology of the dales.

'And the Five Sisters are simply stunning,' Tracy went on.

'Five Sisters?' Banks asked. 'In a minster?'

'Oh, Daddy,' Tracy laughed, 'you don't know anything, do you? The Five Sisters are lancet windows in the north transept. They're made of grisaille glass. Thirteenth century, I think. And the Rose Window—'

'It was boring,' cut in Brian, who all the while had been feeling left out. 'Just a lot of old statues of dead kings and stuff. Junk, it was. Boring.'

'You're just a philistine,' Tracy retorted, pronouncing the word with both difficulty and authority. 'I'll bet you didn't even notice that monument to Archbishop Scrope.'

'Scrope? Who's he?' Banks asked. While sympathizing with Brian, he didn't feel justified in cheating Tracy out of her excitement. She was at an age now when one of her great thrills was to educate her parents, whom she thought dreadfully ignorant of the past that surrounded them. Very soon, Banks mused sadly, all that would be forgotten, at least for a few years, and life would be all clothes, pop music, make-up, hairstyles and boys.

'He was a rebel,' Tracy informed him. 'Henry the Fourth had him executed in 1405.'

'Oh shut up with all them dates, clever clogs,' Brian burst out. 'You think you know it all.' And before Tracy could respond, he turned to his father and launched into his own account.

'We went on a boat down the river, Dad, and she felt seasick.' He cast a look of pitying contempt at his sister. 'And we passed this big chocolate factory. Me and some of the boys wanted to go on a tour but the teacher wouldn't let us. She just wanted to show us history and stuff and all those silly old narrow streets.'

'The Shambles,' Tracy interrupted. 'And Stonegate and Petergate. Anyway, the chocolates would only have made you sick.'

'It didn't need chocolates to make *you* sick, did it?' Brian taunted her.

'That's enough, Brian!' Sandra cut in. 'Stop it, both of you!'

And so it went on; Brian sulked and Tracy scowled at him until they both went upstairs to watch television while Sandra cleared the table and Banks helped her with the dishes. Finally, still arguing, they were packed off to bed, and Banks suggested a nightcap.

'I've got a new job,' Sandra said, pouring the Scotch. 'Well, not really new, just different.'

Banks asked what it was. Sandra worked as a dentist's receptionist three mornings a week in Eastvale.

'Mr Maxwell's going on holiday, shutting up shop for three weeks, and Peggy Matthews – that's Mr Smedley's receptionist – is off at the same time, too.'

'Not together, I hope?'

Sandra laughed. 'No. Fine bedfellows they'd make, I'm sure. Maxwell's going to the Greek Islands and Peggy's off to Weymouth. Anyway, apparently Smedley asked if he could borrow me while the boss was away. Maxwell asked me and I said yes. It's all right, isn't it? I didn't think we had any plans.'

'Yes, it's fine if you want to. I can't really plan anything until this Steadman business is settled.'

'Good. Smedley's a real perfectionist, so I hear. Especially when it comes to fitting caps and crowns, matching the colours and all that. They say he's one of the best in Yorkshire.'

'You might get to meet the local gentry, then. Who knows?'

Sandra laughed. 'Well, Peggy did say that Mrs Steadman goes there. She's having some root canal work done. She's a bit of a local celebrity now.'

'It's amazing, isn't it?' Banks said. 'The husband gets murdered and people suddenly line up to look at the wife as if she were bloody royalty.'

'It's only natural, though. We all have some morbid curiosity.'

'Not me. Look,' Banks said, 'we haven't been out for a long time, and there's supposed to be a good folk singer on in Helmthorpe tomorrow. Do you fancy going?'

'Changing the subject, eh? Helmthorpe? Isn't that where the Steadmans live?'

'Yes.'

'This isn't work, is it, Alan? It's not connected to the case?'

'Cross my heart. We'll just go and listen to some good folk music like we've done plenty of times before. Ask Harriet and David along, too.'

'If they can get a sitter. It's such short notice. What about Jenny Fuller? Think she might like to come?'

'She's in France,' Banks said. 'Don't you remember? That wine-tasting tour. Took off as soon as term ended.'

'Lucky her. All right, then, I'll call Harriet. As long as you promise it's nothing to do with work! I don't much fancy sitting there like a spare part while you grill some suspect.'

'Scout's honour. And I'm not sure I like what you're implying. I don't grill people.'

Sandra smiled. Banks moved closer and put his arm around her. 'You know—' he began.

'Ssshhh . . .' Sandra put her finger to his lips. 'Let's go to bed.'

'What's wrong with the sofa?' Banks asked, and pulled her gently towards him.

FOUR

Sally Lumb was finding it difficult to get to sleep. She had put aside *Wuthering Heights* because her eyes were getting tired, but sleep just would not come.

First she thought of Kevin. She would have to give in soon or he'd be off after someone more experienced. He was right on the edge and she couldn't tease him for much longer. She didn't want to, anyway. The last time they'd been together, the day they saw Penny Cartwright, she had let him put himself close to her sex; she had felt his heat and hardness right at her very entrance and it made her tremble and go all wet, just like it said in the books. It had been cruel to stop him then, she knew, but they had no protection; she didn't want to get pregnant. There were ways around that, though. Next time . . .

Turning over and praying for sleep to come, she started thinking about the implications of what she had remembered that afternoon. Not the car on Saturday night – that was nothing – but something she hadn't fully perceived at the time that now had more sinister far-reaching possibilities. It was her first real clue, and she had to decide what to do about it. She wouldn't go to the police, that was for certain – a proper fool she'd make of herself if she was wrong! Besides, she was already determined to solve the affair herself. Perhaps she might even become a heroine.

And the police were fools anyway; she could easily one-up them. That man from London had treated her like a silly child. And what had he done that was so wonderful? Given up an exciting metropolitan life for the boredom of Swainsdale, that's what he'd done. Lord, the man could have been working for Scotland Yard!

And so, as her mind tossed and turned towards sleep, the first step became clear. If she was right, then someone was in danger; a warning had to be given. She would arrange a secret meeting, and maybe after that, if her suspicions were proved correct, she could go about setting a trap. That thought worried her, as she really would be making herself vulnerable. But she could always rope Kevin in; he was a big strong lad, and he'd do anything for her.

As Sally finally drifted into the dream world that usually puzzled and irritated her, she could see the lights of London strung out before her like a diamond necklace. Why stop there? the dream insisted. And the images progressed, built up from magazine photographs and television programmes: *Vogue* models sashayed down the Champs Elysées, famous actresses stepped out of limousines under the neons of Sunset Strip, and all the well-known television personalities she had ever seen chatted over cocktails at a party in Manhattan . . . But soon it all faded, and what she remembered in the morning was a rather absurd image of being in Leeds, a place she had visited several times on shopping expeditions with her mother. In the dream it felt like a foreign city. There were uniformed policemen all over the place, and Sally had to push her bicycle because she didn't have a licence – at least, not one that was valid in Leeds. She was there, she vaguely remembered, because she was searching for a bird, a white one that had flown from her garden, a vast dark expanse like a tilled field after rain. She didn't know if the bird had been her pet, her responsibility, or just a wild creature she had taken a fancy to, but it was important, and she was there in an alien familiar city pushing her bicycle among the policemen looking for it . . .

FIVE

Banks slipped Finzi's choral setting of 'Intimations of Immortality' into the car stereo as he turned off the A1 at the Wetherby roundabout and took the A58 to Leeds. It was eleven thirty on Friday morning, just five days after the discovery of Steadman's body. Hatchley, under the weather on Thursday morning after his visit to Darlington, had checked Hackett's alibi thoroughly and found that it held. Barnes, too, was out of the running; though he was unmarried and had no one to confirm that he went straight home after visiting Mrs Gaskell, his finances were in order and there had never been even the slightest hint of malpractice or wrongdoing of any kind during his twenty years as a doctor in Helmthorpe.

In his office earlier that morning, Banks had completed the mass of paperwork he had started the day before: transcripts of interviews, maps and timetables of people's movements, lists of unasked or unanswered questions. He had gone over the forensic evidence again, but found nothing new. Constable Weaver and his reinforcements were still asking questions around the village, the campsite and outlying farms, but the likelihood of their turning up new evidence after so long was fast diminishing.

The hushed choir entered, repeating the opening theme, 'There was a time when meadow, grove, and stream . . .' over the baritone's solo line, and Banks forgot his frequently distasteful job for a few moments. Finzi's music made Wordsworth's poem bearable.

The drive, which he took slowly, turned out to be quite pleasant once he'd left the Great North Road and its never-ending stream of lorries. It was the quickest way, the same route as he had taken on his last trip to Leeds, to interview a pawnbroker in connection with a series of robberies. But that had been a grey, rainy day in late October. Now it was summer and he drove through the kind of peaceful green countryside one so often finds close to large English cities.

Banks puffed at his pipe as Finzi played on, not bothering to relight it after the second time it went out, and soon found himself in the Seacroft area. He had to concentrate hard on directions; the tower blocks all looked much the same and there were few landmarks to go by. He came out finally through an underpass near the city centre and parked close to the Town Hall. From there, he could see the high white tower of the library building, something Gristhorpe had told him about that morning in his potted history of the city and its architecture.

Banks had no fixed ideas about how to approach the academics; he intended to play it by ear. He had called earlier and arranged to have lunch with Darnley and Talbot in a pub near the university. Though term was officially over, they still travelled to their offices almost every day to carry on with their research or simply to get out from under their wives' feet. Darnley, to whom Banks had spoken, seemed quite excited by the prospect of a chat with the police, or so he had said in a rather detached way, as if he were discussing the mating habits of lemurs.

Banks still had an hour to kill, so he decided to take Gristhorpe's advice and take a look at the Town Hall. It was an impressive Victorian edifice, complete with fluted columns, huge domed roof, clock and a pair of lions guarding the entrance by the broad flight of stone steps. The stone, sandstone by the look of it, seemed light and clean. Gristhorpe had told him it had been sandblasted a few years ago, as few such structures had withstood a hundred years or more of industry without turning black.

Banks admired the bulk of the place and the bold classical lines of its design. He felt he could grasp, just by looking, some of the civic pride that had gone into its construction. Queen Victoria herself had attended the grand opening. She must have spent a lot of time opening buildings, Banks reflected.

He ventured inside past the statues of Victoria and Albert in the foyer and into the main hall, which appeared to have been recently restored. Enormous pillars of what looked like marble streaked with pink, green and blue were spaced along the walls, and the ceiling was divided into brightly coloured square panels, gilded around their edges. Mottoes and proverbs beloved of the pious Victorians adorned the high places: EXCEPT THE LORD BUILD THE HOUSE, THEY LABOUR IN VAIN THAT BUILT IT; EXCEPT THE LORD KEEP THE CITY, THE WATCHMAN WATCHETH BUT IN VAIN; WEAVE THE TRUTH WITH TRUST; and LABOUR OMNIA VINCIT. At the end stood a majestic pipe organ.

Banks glanced at his watch and walked out slowly; his footsteps echoed in the silence. Yes, it was impressive, and he could begin to see what Steadman found so fascinating about northern history.

But he also remembered Hackett's outburst about false romanticized views of the past. The wealthy city officials and merchants had gone to great trouble to make sure that Queen Victoria's route avoided the more squalid areas of the city: row upon row of overcrowded back-to-backs with leaky roofs and damp walls where the nameless masses lived. It was from their labours and in their name, the name of civic pride, that such glories as the Town Hall were built, yet they were condemned to live in squalor and then accused of becoming animals. There had even been one man, a chemist according to Gristhorpe, who had perfumed the air outside his shop as the royal progress passed. It all depended on what side you were on, Banks thought, as to what your perspective was.

He consulted his pocket map and walked up between the Town Hall and the library, carried on along Caverley Street past the Civic Hall, a white building with twin pointed towers and colourful gardens, then past the General Infirmary and Leeds Polytechnic and into the outer reaches of the university campus. Finally, he came to a quadrangle surrounded by modern office-style buildings. It was a long way from the dreaming spires of Oxford and Cambridge, but Leeds was supposed to be a red-brick university, even if there were no red bricks in sight.

He found Darnley's office in the History Department with the help of an angular bespectacled secretary. After a quick firm handshake, Darnley was ready for a pub lunch.

'Talbot's going to meet us there,' he explained. 'He's got a session with one of his doctoral students right now.'

He led Banks across a dirt path behind the building and on to a narrow cobbled street. The pub was actually part of a hotel, and it stood back from the road at the end of a short driveway. As it was such a warm sunny day, they sat at one of the outside tables.

Darnley was a tall man about forty, well built and fit. He had a trace of a northern accent and did not seem at all the absent-minded professor type that Banks had expected. His short brown hair was neatly combed and although his suit seemed half a size too big, it was of good quality. It had probably been a perfect fit when he bought it, Banks guessed, but like many men of his age, fearing heart attacks and other plagues of the sedentary life, he had begun to exercise.

The two men sipped draught Guinness, squinting in the bright sun, and Banks laid his pipe, tobacco and lighter on the table.

'Aha, a pipe-smoker, I see,' Darnley noted. 'Touch of the Maigret, eh? Thought of taking it up myself but it's too much trouble. Wasted years trying to stop smoking, cutting down, switching to milder brands, and in the end I found the only way to bloody well stop was cold turkey.'

'It can't have been as easy as you make it sound,' Banks said, stuffing his pipe with rubbed flake and tamping it gently.

'No, no, it wasn't.' Darnley laughed. 'I had a few relapses. But I've been playing a lot of squash and tennis lately and running a few miles each day. You'd be surprised how that kind of thing puts you off smoking. You'd never believe it, but a year or so ago I was overweight, drinking too much – ugh!'

'Doctor's orders?'

'Told me point-blank. "Go on like you are doing, and I'll give you another ten years at most." It was a toss-up which would go first – heart, liver or lungs. Anyway, he said if I shaped up the sky's the limit. Well, not in so many words, but I got the point.' He watched Banks light his pipe. 'Still,' he said, 'I suppose you need props in your business. False sense of security and all that.'

Banks smiled and admitted it helped. He liked the look of curiosity and intelligence in Darnley's eyes.

'I hope you don't think you need it with me? I mean, I'm not a suspect, am I?' He was smiling, but the tension showed in the tight set of his lips.

'Not yet,' Banks replied, returning his gaze.

'Touché. You mean if I start to put myself forward as one, all offers are welcome?'

'I shouldn't worry about it,' Banks assured him. He was still trying to work out the best approach to this edgy intelligent man whose quick playful exterior no doubt masked a mind like a steel trap and covered up a complex, perhaps even devious, personality.

He decided to play along a little longer, certain that the arrival of Talbot would alter the light-hearted mood. 'You might as well tell me where you were last Saturday night, though,' he asked.

Darnley looked at him, bright eyes twinkling but hard. 'Do you know, Chief Inspector, I have no alibi at all for last weekend. I had a lot of work to do so I stayed in all Saturday evening marking examination papers and reading a new account of the Peterloo massacre. Of course, my wife was at home too, but I don't suppose she counts, does she?'

Banks laughed. 'I wouldn't know till I asked her, would I?'

'You're a canny man, as the Scots say. No, I don't suppose you would.'

'Why weren't you at the funeral yesterday?'

'Wasn't invited, was I? Neither of us. Actually, I didn't even know about it. I only knew about Harry because I read it in the *Yorkshire Evening Post*.'

'You'd lost touch?'

'Sort of, yes.'

After a little more banter and a good draught of stout, Darnley seemed to relax more. Trying to establish the conversation as one between professionals, Banks asked the professor about his job: 'I suppose you need props, too? It can't be easy standing up there alone in front of a hundred or so students and just talking for an hour.'

'Put like that, it does sound rather awful,' Darnley conceded. 'You get used to it, of course, but you're right, there's always a bit of stage fright till you get going. I've always got my notes to fall back on, though. No teacher worth his salt dries up in front of a class. You can always waffle and students would never know the difference. Sometimes I think I could tell them that Adolf Hitler was one of the heroes of twentieth-century politics and they'd just write it down without question. But props . . . yes . . . One tends to find a position one is comfortable in. Funny thing, that. Some people pace back and forth, some hunch over the lectern, and others sit on the edge of a desk and fold their arms. One chap I knew always used to play with his keys while he was lecturing. Trouble was, they were in his trouser pocket and the students all thought he was playing with himself.'

They both laughed. 'What about Harry Steadman?' Banks asked casually.

Darnley squinted. 'Harry was good,' he answered. 'It's true we've been out of touch and I've not seen much of him since he left, but we were quite close at one time, and I was sorry to hear about his death. I'd say we were colleagues rather than friends, if there's a difference. He was exceptionally bright – but I suppose you know that already. Ambitious, yes, but only in his field. He genuinely believed in what he was doing: teaching, research, breaking new ground. He thought it all had some real value for society. And, believe me, that's rare these days. There's so much cynicism around in education, especially as the government doesn't seem to set much store by us any more.'

Banks nodded. 'It's the same with crime. You're fighting a losing battle, or so it seems most of the time, and that's no good for anyone's professional pride.'

'But at least the government believes in your value: pay rises, recruitment, modern equipment.'

'True,' Banks agreed. 'But it's all long overdue.' He didn't want to get sidetracked into an argument, especially as he had many objections to the way the government seemed to look upon the police as a private army of paid bully boys to pit against people with genuine grievances and a constitutional right to air them. A copper with humanist socialist leanings would be a bit hard for Darnley to take, he thought. Besides, he was a detective – CID, a paid thinker – and he didn't have to go on crowd control, bashing the bonces of the proletariat.

'I'm envious,' Darnley said. 'That's all. I just wish we could get a larger slice of the cake, too. Academics are very big on pride as well, believe me. Harry was a good lecturer and he always managed to stimulate enthusiasm among his students. That's hard to do these days when you're in competition with television, video games and God knows what. Stop me if I'm beginning to sound too much like a good reference for him, but it's true. Most of all, he loved research, real field work, and that's why he left. When he found himself with enough money to do as he pleased, that's exactly what he did. Some chaps might have packed it all in and buggered off to the south of France for a life of idleness, sin and luxury, but not Harry. He was a dedicated man.'

At this point they were joined by a smaller, pudgy man, bald except for a few wisps of grey hair above his ears. He had a deeply ingrained frown in his broad brow and a tiny pursed mouth that gave him, overall, a surly and miserly look. His cultured voice was surprisingly soft, and Banks wondered how he managed with a large room full of students. He proved rather taciturn, and after they had ordered roast beef sandwiches and another round of stout, he simply sat and listened as Banks and Darnley went on talking.

'I think I've got a fairly clear picture of Mr Steadman's professional life now,' Banks said. 'It's something everyone seems to agree on – bright, dedicated, obsessed even.'

At this Talbot tut-tutted, and when he spoke his voice was redolent of Cambridge quadrangles, effete dons and afternoon glasses of amontillado. 'Surely, er, Chief Inspector, an obsession is something we might define as intrinsically unhealthy, wouldn't you say? I don't mean to nit-pick over semantics, of course, but one must admit that the term has definite connotations of mental imbalance. Harold Steadman was most certainly not unbalanced; therefore, he was not obsessed.' And all the time he talked he frowned, as if the usage really upset him.

Banks apologized. 'I didn't mean to imply anything as drastic as that. No, I realize that there's a difference between dedication and obsession. What I'd like to know is whether he found time for other pursuits. Social life, for example. Did he mix, go to parties, drink?'

Talbot returned in moody silence to his drink, perhaps

to contemplate the exact *OED* definition of 'obsessed', as if such eccentricities as 'social life' were best left to the lower classes.

'Do you know, Godfrey,' Darnley said cheerfully, oblivious to his colleague's disdain, 'the chief inspector might not be far wrong.' He turned to Banks and winked. 'Yes, Harry liked a few drinks now and then, and he went to the occasional faculty party. But he was never really at ease socially – especially when he was out of his element, so to speak, when there was nobody to talk to about his field. He didn't care much for sports, never watched television, and he certainly wasn't a woman chaser.'

'Do you mean he was uncomfortable in the presence of non-academics?'

'Oh no, not that at all. I didn't mean to give you that impression. Harry certainly wasn't an academic snob. As a matter of fact he invited me up to Gratly once, shortly after he'd moved, and we spent a very pleasant evening in a dingy local with a thriller writer and some other chaps. No, Harry would talk to anybody. That was one of his beefs against academic life, the rampant intellectual snobbery. What I mean is that his heart was in his work and his work was basically to do with people, so he enjoyed their company. There's a strong human element in his field, you know. It's not all abstract. He was interested in ordinary people, their background and ways of life. I suppose you know that his main fields were industrial archaeology and the Roman occupation? But he also loved folk music, local lore, things like that. He was fascinated by the history of trade unions, the early working class radicals. So you could say that Harry was quite at home with the common man, he'd just no time for petty chit-chat like you so often get at parties. He always tended to edge conversations in the direction of his interests.'

Talbot nodded in grudging agreement and lit a cigarette. 'Let me put it this way, Chief Inspector Banks,' he said in a tone of professor to lowly student. 'If you were to – if you were able to – sit down now and talk to Harold Steadman, he would probably begin by asking you about your job, how you feel about it, just to get things going. He would discover where you come from and find out about your family background. Then, depending on how interesting he found all that, he would either question you further – say, if your father had been a union man or a farm labourer in the dales – or he would proceed to tell you about the history of your area, how it fits in with the rest of the country, what the Romans did there, and so on. People usually enjoyed his company. He could sense when he was becoming a bore and would usually stop and listen politely for a while. Of course,' Talbot added, with a deft flick of ash, 'if he found you boring, then you wouldn't get much out of him. Am I right, Darnley?'

Darnley nodded.

'What about Mrs Steadman?' Banks asked. 'Did you see much of her when she was in Leeds?' He addressed the question to Talbot, who seemed to have become quite garrulous, but it was Darnley who answered.

'At first we did, yes. Quite a pretty little thing, really. Naturally, they were in a new environment and wanted to meet people and settle in. But like many faculty wives, she soon withdrew. It's common enough, believe me. My wife, for example, wouldn't be seen dead at an academic gathering these days. It bores them, you see. And they let themselves go over the years. You know, not bothering much about their appearance any more.'

Banks couldn't be sure whether Darnley was talking about his own wife or about Emma Steadman.

The conversation moved on to generalities again, with Darnley doing most of the entertaining, and Banks soon realized he wasn't going to learn anything more of value.

When he left, he carried away with him the image of a young couple – perhaps not unlike Sandra and himself in the old days – newly married, the husband beginning what was likely to be a distinguished academic career. There were long summer holidays in Gratly at the Ramsden house; there was the young ambitious Michael courting Penny, the flower of the dale; it was pure peace and innocence with nothing but a bright future ahead for them all.

For Steadman, things seemed to get better and better; for Emma, there was withdrawal from the dull academic life into domestic boredom; for Penny, a wild exciting fling in the fast lane which left her isolated and cynical, cut off from her roots; and for Ramsden, a steady advance up the publishing ladder and a return to his beloved north. It all sounded so idyllic, but one of them was dead. What had gone wrong and why?

An hour later he was no closer to the solution, but his spirits felt lighter, despite the clouds, as he drove into the dales countryside and sang along with Britten's versions of old English folk songs.

SIX

They were sipping Coke and talking about boys under the scornful lascivious eyes of the old Greek. Hazel Kirk had had her first date with Terry Preston, son of the local grocer, the previous night, and she was titillating her friends with an account of her attempt to keep his wandering hands from her most private parts. Once in a while she would blush while describing the indefinable feelings she had had when she failed in her task.

But Sally Lumb, usually so interested – not to mention condescending – during such discussions, seemed preoccupied. The others noticed, but Hazel, for one, was not going to be done out of her moment of glory simply because madam was sulking.

Anne Downes, perhaps more sensitive to mood and certainly less interested in boys and their inexplicable desires, waited patiently until Kathy Chalmers had stopped giggling and tried to change the subject.

'They haven't caught him yet, you know,' she announced, adjusting her glasses on the bridge of her nose.

'Who?' Hazel asked abruptly, annoyed at being dragged away from other, more important thoughts.

'The killer, of course. Who else? The man who killed Mr Steadman.'

'How do you know it was a man?' Hazel asked. It was a question she'd heard on countless television programmes.

'Stands to reason, doesn't it,' Anne snorted. 'It'd have to be a pretty strong woman to slug him and carry him all the way up that field below Crow Scar.'

'Mrs Butterworth could have done it,' Kathy chipped

in. They all giggled. Mrs Butterworth was the butcher's wife, an enormous red-faced woman who towered above her meek hunched husband.

'Don't be silly,' Anne said, allowing herself a smile. 'Why should she do it? Besides, the effort would probably give her a heart attack.'

'Jimmy Collins told me the police have been talking to Penny Cartwright and the major,' Kathy said. 'He said the old man didn't give them much time.'

'How would Jimmy Collins know?' Anne asked.

'He was in the shop downstairs. "Where there's a will, there's a way," my mother always says. I think Penny did it. I think her and Mr Steadman were having a torrid love affair and when she wanted him to leave his wife and marry her he wouldn't do it so she killed him.'

'Don't be so stupid,' Anne said. 'If it was really like that she'd have killed Mrs Steadman, not him.'

That silenced Kathy, but Hazel picked up the thread. 'Well if that wasn't why,' she said, 'there could have been plenty of other reasons. Everybody knows she went away for ages and took drugs and was pro . . . prom . . .'

'Promiscuous?' suggested Anne.

'Yes, promiscuous, clever clogs – that's what I said. Maybe she had his baby or he knew something about her past. They've known each other a long time, you know.'

The others were silent, taking it all in. 'You might be right about the last bit,' Anne allowed, 'but she wouldn't kill him just because she had his baby, would she? I think it was Jack Barker.'

'Why would he do it?' Kathy asked.

'Maybe he was just doing research for his next book,' Hazel joked.

'And maybe he's in love with Penny Cartwright and

wanted to get Mr Steadman out of the way so he could have her all to himself,' Anne said. 'And there's another thing: I heard the police gave Teddy Hackett a nasty time the other day.'

'He certainly looked a little pale when I saw him,' Hazel added.

'My dad heard them arguing a couple of weeks ago – Hackett and Mr Steadman,' Anne said.

'But they can't think he did it,' Hazel reasoned, 'or they'd have arrested him in custody by now. I bet he's got a skintight alibi.'

'It's "watertight", you fool.' Anne laughed. 'And he can't be "arrested in custody", only "in custody".'

'All right, Miss Know-it-all. So what?'

'I wonder who she was,' Kathy said. 'Teddy Hackett's alibi.'

And they all laughed. To them, Hackett, with his droopy moustache, receding hairline, gold medallions and beer belly hanging over his fancy belt buckle, was a figure of ridicule, the male equivalent of mutton dressed as lamb.

'What do you think, Sally?' Anne asked. 'You're very quiet today.'

'I've got a few ideas of my own,' Sally replied slowly and quietly. 'But I've got to check them out.'

And with that she walked out, leaving them all gaping again, not knowing whether to believe her or not.

8

ONE

By seven thirty, the lounge bar of the Dog and Gun was almost full. It was a long narrow room with only one vaguely demarcated aisle down the centre. The audience was clustered around small tables, and a white-jacketed waiter had been employed so that people wouldn't have to move about to get drinks. He moved awkwardly among the crowd, a tray of black and amber drinks tottering menacingly at shoulder height. The jukebox had been unplugged for the evening, and piped folk music played softly enough to make conversation easy. Dim wall lights gave the room a dark orange glow, and at the bar the brass rail, polished hand pumps and coloured bottles by the mirrors gleamed. At the far end of the room was a low wooden platform, too makeshift to be dignified with the name of a stage, and on it stood a couple of microphones on stands, two large speakers, three stools and an amplifier with its red light on.

Banks and Sandra sat with Harriet and David about halfway down the room on the right-hand side. Harriet, pixieish in looks, animated and intelligent in character, drove a mobile library around the more remote dales villages. Her husband David was an assistant bank manager in Eastvale and, if truth be told, Banks found him a bit of a bore.

David had clearly said something that required more than a mere nod in response, but Banks had been watching a fresh-faced young camper, probably under eighteen, who was already displaying the effects of too much alcohol in his desire to show off to his girlfriend.

'Pardon?' Banks said, cupping his hand to his ear.

'I said, I suppose you know all about computers yourself, being on the force,' David repeated. 'I'm afraid I've been boring you.'

'Not at all,' lied Banks. He tamped down the tobacco in his pipe and lit it in defiance of Sandra's sharply aimed frown. 'No, not at all. But yes, I know a little bit about computer languages.' That old-fashioned phrase, 'on the force', made him smile. It was an odd way of looking at his job, he thought. On what force? The forces of law and order, no doubt. 'May the force be with you.' The force of good against evil? It was a stiff dry phrase that hardly did the job justice.

While telling David what little he did know about the subject, Banks noticed Penny Cartwright come in with Jack Barker. The two of them made their way to the front, where chairs had been saved for them. Shortly afterwards, a nervous spotty young man took the stage, tapped the microphones, said 'testing' in each one three or four times, then welcomed everyone to folk night at the Dog and Gun. One by one, conversations died down until all that could be heard was the barman ringing up sales and the steady humming of the amplifier. The microphone shrieked when the young man got too close, and he backed off quickly, pulling a face. Banks couldn't catch the names of all the scheduled performers, but he gathered that Penny was set to sing two forty-minute sets, the first starting at eight thirty and the second at about ten fifteen.

After more notices and introductions, a duo clambered on to the stage. The boy had only a guitar, but the girl spread several ancient and obscure stringed instruments on the floor around her. First they launched into a Bob Dylan song, and what they lacked in talent, Banks thought, they made up for in enthusiasm. After the applause, the young man made jokes about the notes he had missed and apologized for the rawness of his technique. It worked: after that the audience wanted him to succeed and most people were willing to overlook the rough edges.

The girl said nothing but concentrated on tuning what looked to Banks like a mandolin. She played extremely well on the next number, a medley of old English dances. On the whole, the audience was respectful and attentive, but there were occasional, unavoidable interruptions as the waiter passed by and more drinks were ordered. Someone told the inebriated young camper to shut up, too.

Banks and David seemed to have settled into buying rounds, the two men drinking pints of bitter and the women lager and lime. Banks had to watch his intake because he didn't want to appear even slightly intoxicated in the village where he was conducting a murder investigation. Two pints in an hour and a half wasn't at all bad, he told himself, but it was only just after eight o'clock. He was aware that he tended to speed up towards closing time.

The first intermission came and people started making their ways to the toilets and the bar. As he walked down the narrow aisle, Jack Barker noticed Banks's party and came over.

'Good evening,' he said, extending his hand. 'What a

surprise to find you here. I'd no idea you were a folkie.'
There was just enough of a twinkle in his eye to make
the irony apparent. 'Mind if I join you for a moment?'
He grabbed a nearby chair and pulled it up before Banks
could object. 'Is it just Miss Cartwright you've come to
hear?'

'Actually, it's Ms Cartwright,' Banks corrected him.
'And yes, I've heard she's very good.' His tone was
brusque; he wished Barker would go away.

'You're in for a real treat, Chief Inspector, a real treat.
People come from miles away to hear Penny Cartwright,
you know. She's got a solid reputation in these parts,
especially since she gave up fame and fortune to return to
her roots. People appreciate that.'

From what Banks had heard, appreciation wasn't quite
the word for the gossip that had surrounded Penny's
return to her roots, but he kept quiet. Barker obviously
wanted to show off, and, short of being rude, there was
no way to stop him. Sandra returned from the Ladies and
looked at Barker curiously. There was no escape, Banks
realized, cursing himself; he would have to introduce
them.

Barker favoured the women with what Banks suspected was a well-practised Clark Gable smile.

'Delighted,' he said theatrically, taking Sandra's hand.
'I never imagined a policeman's wife could be so charming and so beautiful.' Banks was irritated; David simply
looked on, a vacant grin on his face.

It was not only Barker's charm and social finesse that
annoyed Banks. It was all very well socializing in the
community, but to be seen with his wife openly frater-
nizing with a suspect jarred against his deepest instincts
as a detective. It made him feel conspicuous, for one

thing, and that was a feeling he disliked. Gristhorpe's advice – get in there and let them talk to you – was all very well, but a line had to be drawn. He was off duty, and the whole thing was just too pally for his taste. He was sucking on his dead pipe, glowering and contributing monosyllables only when necessary.

'How do you manage to fit in here?' Sandra asked after Barker had told her his occupation. 'Aren't writers usually regarded with a good deal of suspicion?'

Barker nodded. 'True. They didn't like me being here at first,' he replied. 'Not one bit. You're right – people don't trust writers in small communities, and they've good reason not to. Some communities have had bad experiences with chaps who live among them, fit in, then go and write devastating critiques, hardly even bothering to disguise names and identities. It's like the way some Indians see photographers – people who steal their souls. Quite right too, in my opinion. The kind of writers they have in mind are unscrupulous. They give us all a bad name.'

'But don't you think writers have to be a little ruthless?' Harriet asked. 'Especially if they're to tell the truth.'

'Perhaps. But the ones I'm talking about accept your hospitality, then strip you naked on the page. Some writers even worm their way into people's confidence and set up situations, manipulate events just to see how their "characters" will react. I knew one chap, for example, who used to throw regular parties. This was in London. Real lavish dos they were, no expense spared – champers, single malt Scotch, beluga caviar, quail – more than anyone could hope to devour in an evening. When everyone got sozzled and started arguing, crying or pawing other people's partners, there he was, sober as a judge, sitting in a corner making mental notes. It took people a long time to figure out what was going on – after all, they were having a good time – but sure enough, they'd appear, thinly disguised, in stories published in magazines, and their friends and colleagues would recognize them. A couple of marriages broke up, reputations were destroyed. All in the name of "art". After a while, attendance dropped dramatically.'

'What happened to him?' Harriet asked, sitting on the edge of her chair.

Barker shrugged. 'Moved on, I suppose. I've no idea where he is now. Pastures new. He still publishes regularly.'

'And is that what you do, Mr Barker?' Sandra asked. 'Move in on people and steal their souls.'

Barker laughed. 'Please, call me Jack,' he said, and Banks felt his upper lip begin to curl. 'No, that's not what I do at all. At first everyone was suspicious of me, but then they always are like that with incomers, as they call us. After a while, out of curiosity I suppose, someone read a couple of my books, then someone else, and their comments got around. As soon as everyone realized I wrote hard-boiled private-eye stories set in southern California in the thirties, they decided I wasn't a threat. Believe it or not, I even have a few fans here.'

'I know,' Harriet said. 'I've carried enough of your books around in the mobile library.'

Barker honoured her with a smile. 'As soon as they get to know you're harmless,' he went on, 'you're as close to being accepted as you'll ever be. It was the same with Harry.'

'What about Harry?' Banks asked, trying to sound casual but failing miserably. Sandra frowned at him for being a killjoy.

'All I meant,' Barker explained, 'was that Harry was a writer too, in his way, but nobody ever worried about him because he wrote about the Romans and old lead mines. I mean, only people like Penny and Michael Ramsden were interested. That stuff's as dry as dust to most people.' He looked back at the ladies and smiled again, clearly hoping to get off on another track.

'Do you know Ramsden well?' Banks asked, unmoved by Barker's discomfort and Sandra's piercing glances. Harriet and Sandra began to chat between themselves, and David looked on, lost.

'I've met him,' Barker replied curtly.

'What do you think of him?'

'Pleasant enough fellow,' he said, looking to the women for support in his levity. 'But you can hardly expect a writer to say nice things about an editor, can you? I spend two days working on a fine descriptive paragraph, and my editor wants it cut out because it slows the action.'

'Ramsden's not your publisher, though, is he?' Banks persisted.

'Good Lord, no. He only deals with academic stuff.'

'Did you know about Ramsden and Penny Cartwright?'

'That was years ago. What on earth are you getting at?'

'Just trying to sort out the tangle of relationships,' Banks answered, smiling. 'That's all.'

'Look, they're starting again,' Barker said, rising. 'Please excuse me.' He gave a brief bow to Harriet and Sandra, then made his way back to the front. It was almost eight thirty. As the lights dimmed, Banks saw him talking to Penny and glancing back over his shoulder. The last thing he noticed before it got too dim was Barker whispering in Penny's ear and Penny looking behind her and laughing.

As the master of ceremonies began his rambling and incoherent introduction, Sandra leaned over to Banks. 'You were a bit sharp with him, weren't you?' she said. 'Was it really necessary? You did promise we were having a social evening.'

Banks muttered a sullen apology and busied himself with his pipe. It wasn't a new situation, the job interfering with his personal life, but it never ceased to cause friction. Perhaps Sandra had expected the move to change all that. A new life. What rubbish, Banks thought. Different landscapes, same old people with the same old failings. He gestured to the waiter to bring another round. Bugger it, let someone else drive home. It was a social occasion, after all, he reminded himself ironically.

Penny Cartwright took the stage to much applause and several loud whistles from the back of the room. Banks was still furious with Barker for being so damn charming and witty, and with Sandra for encouraging him and with himself for spoiling it. He attacked the fresh pint of bitter with angry gusto and glared at his pipe as if it were at the root of all his troubles. It had gone out yet again and he was sick to death of tamping, emptying, cleaning, scraping and relighting it.

Penny began with an unaccompanied ballad called 'Still Growing'. It was a sad tale about an arranged marriage between a woman and a boy on the edge of manhood. The husband died young and the widow lamented, 'O once I had a sweetheart, but now I have none. / Death has put an end to his growing.' The story was simply and economically told, and Banks found himself entering into the music as he did with opera, his recent irritation wrapped up and put away in a dim corner of his mind. Her voice had both passion and control – it was that of a survivor singing about the lost and the less fortunate with honest sympathy. She was an alto, pitched lower than Banks had expected, husky on the low notes but pure and clear in the higher range.

Banks clapped loudly when she finished, and Sandra turned to him with raised eyebrows and a smile of appreciation. Other songs in the same traditional folk vein followed, and sometimes Penny accompanied herself on guitar while another young woman playing the flute or the fiddle joined her. Mixed in with the stories of demon lovers and forbidden affairs were light-hearted jigs and reels and sensational broadside ballads, like 'The Murder of Maria Marten'.

Despite his enjoyment of the music, Banks found his mind wandering back to Barker's reaction to the mention of Michael Ramsden. There had seemed to be a dislike beyond the general lack of love between writers and publishers. Ramsden had been a close friend of Steadman's and had known Penny Cartwright since childhood. Did they still see each other, despite what they said? Was Barker simply jealous? And if he was jealous of Ramsden, wasn't he also likely to have felt the same way about Steadman?

Banks looked at Penny and noticed Barker's finely chiselled handsome profile in silhouette. He was in love with her, of course. Ramsden had been right to suggest that possibility. And who could blame him? Her beauty was radiant; her talent was moving. But she and Ramsden had parted. Of course, it had happened years ago, before she had fully blossomed, and it could only have been puppy love. Still, such events endure in small communities. Perhaps to some of the more shrewish local gossips Penny would always be known as a wayward lass who lost that nice Michael Ramsden who had gone on and done so well for himself. And what did Ramsden really feel about their parting?

Banks laid his pipe to rest in the ashtray and Penny announced 'Like Musgrave and Lady Barnard', the last song of the set.

TWO

At about nine o'clock, Sally Lumb left the house on Hill Road. Because it was Friday, her mother was at bingo in Eastvale with Mrs Crawford, and her father was down in the public bar of the Bridge playing in a local darts match. They wouldn't be back till about eleven o'clock, which gave her plenty of time. There would be no awkward questions to answer.

Despite the gathering clouds, it was a warm evening: a bit too hot and sticky, if anything. Sally knew from experience that such signs meant a storm was on its way. She walked down the hill and turned left, by the Bridge, on to High Street. It was a quiet time in Helmthorpe; most people were either in the pubs or sat glued to the idiot box in their living rooms. There'd be nothing much stirring until closing time unless a party of campers got too rowdy at the Hare and Hounds disco and Big Cyril had to chuck them out.

She walked on down the street and paused outside the Dog and Gun. The front door was open and she could hear singing from inside. Penny Cartwright, by the sound of it. Sally had heard her before but hadn't known she was singing in the village that evening. She looked at her watch. Plenty of time. The words of the song drifted out on the humid air:

'A grave, a grave,' Lord Barnard cried,
  'To put these lovers in;
 But bury my lady on the top
  For she was of noble kin.'

With the familiar tune in her mind, Sally walked on, pausing for a moment to listen to the broad beck flowing under the bridge at the eastern end of High Street. She quickened her pace and, leaving the road, struck out up the long wild southern slope of the dale, past where she and Kevin had seen Penny the other day. She had an appointment to keep, a warning to give. Everything would be sorted out soon.

THREE

During the intermission, Penny Cartwright walked by Banks on her way out of the pub and flashed him a cool smile of acknowledgment. Barker, following closely behind her, nodded and bowed to Harriet and Sandra.

'She's so talented and beautiful,' Sandra said after they'd gone. 'Surely she can't be one of your suspects?'

Banks just told her that Penny had been a friend of the victim, and Sandra left it at that. The four chatted about the music, which they had all enjoyed, ordered more drinks, suffered through a mercifully short set of contemporary 'protest' folk music, and awaited Penny's second set. She came back at ten fifteen and walked straight to the stage.

This time there was a new, slightly distant quality in her performance. She was still involved in what she did, but it didn't have the same emotional cutting edge. Banks listened to the ballads and was struck by the parallel that he was dealing with exactly the same kinds of feelings and events that the old songs were forged from. And he wondered how the ballad of Harry Steadman would end. Nobody would be 'hung high', of course, not these days. But who would the killer turn out to be? What was his motive, and what would be Banks's own part in the song? All of a sudden, it seemed as if he was in another century, and that this beautiful young woman in the spotlight, life's disappointments and cruelties showing just enough in her voice to intensify her beauty, was singing a tragic ballad about the murder of Harry Steadman.

The sharp change to a brisk singalong tune snapped him out of his reverie, and he finished off his drink, noting that he immediately felt impatient for another. He was drunk, or at least tipsy, and it wasn't far off closing time. If Barker was in love with the girl, and if there had been anything between her and Steadman . . . If Ramsden still . . . If Mrs Steadman knew . . . If Steadman and his wife hadn't been quite as close as everyone made out . . . The random thoughts curled like pipe smoke and evaporated in the air.

When the set ended to loud and prolonged applause, Banks caught the passing waiter and ordered another pint for himself and a half for David. Sandra looked at him with a hint of reprimand in her eyes, but he just shrugged and grinned foolishly. He had never had a problem with alcohol, but he knew he could sometimes be quite adolescent in his consumption of numerous pints. He could tell that Sandra was worried he might make an idiot of himself, but he knew he could handle his drink. He hadn't had all that much, anyway. There might even be room for another one if he had time.

FOUR

There was going to be a storm, Sally was sure of it. She sat on the low packhorse bridge dangling her legs over the warm stone as she watched the sun go down. When it had disappeared behind the hills, leaving a halo of dark red-gold, it seemed to shine upwards from the depths of the earth and pick out the relief of the heavy grey clouds that massed high above. Insects buzzed on the still, humid air.

It was an isolated spot, ideal for such business, barely even suitable for cars. During her walk, Sally had enjoyed the peace and the strange tremors of excitement that the anticipation of a storm seemed to lay on the landscape. The colours were richer, the wild flowers and rough grass more vibrant, and the clouds' shadows seemed palpable masses on the distant valley side.

But now she was nervous, and she didn't know why. It was the coming storm, she told herself, the electricity in the air, the isolation, the gathering darkness. Soon the wind would shake the rough moorland grass and rain would lash the dale. It was the perfect place for a secret meeting; she understood that. If they were seen together, word might get back to the chief inspector and awkward questions would be asked. She wanted to handle this herself, perhaps save a life and catch a killer. Nonetheless, she knew deep down that her shivers were not entirely due to the weather.

Idly, she cast a loose stone from the bridge into the shallow slow-moving beck. After the rain, she thought, it would be swift, sparkling and ringing with fresh water cascading down the valley side and right under Helmthorpe High Street.

She looked at her watch. Twenty to ten. Tired of waiting, she wished it was all over. The aftermath of sunset was quickly vanishing as the clouds thickened overhead. A curlew called plaintively in the distance. The place began to feel like a wilderness in a gothic romance. It was creepy, even though she'd been there often enough. A flock of rooks spun across the sky like oily rags. Sally became aware of a new sound throbbing through the silence. A car. She pricked up her ears, cast another stone in the beck and stood to face the track. Yes, she could see the headlights as they dipped and flashed on the winding road. It wouldn't be long now.

FIVE

The storm finally broke at about five a.m. Sharp cracks of thunder woke Banks from a vaguely unpleasant dream. He had a dry mouth and a thick head. So much for control. But at least he hadn't made a fool of himself; that he remembered.

Careful not to disturb Sandra, he walked over to the window and looked out on the back garden just in time to see a jagged bolt of lightning streak from north to south across the sky. The first few drops of rain, fat and heavy, came slowly. They burst at intervals on the windowpane and smacked against the slates of the sloping tool shed roof; then they came more quickly and slapped against the leaves of the trees that lined the back alley beyond the garden gate. Soon the rain was coursing down the window and over the slates into the gutter before it gurgled down the drainpipe.

Banks made his way to the bathroom, took two Panadol

tablets and went back to bed. Sandra hadn't woken and the children remained silent. He remembered when Tracy had been afraid of storms and had always run to her parents' bed, where she nestled between them and felt safe. But now she knew what caused the electrical activity – knew more about it than Banks did – and the fear had gone. Brian had never really cared either way, except that an evening thunderstorm meant the television had to be unplugged sometimes in the middle of his favourite programme. It was something Banks's father had always done, and Banks followed suit without really knowing why.

The steady rhythm of the rain and the sudden release from tension that the start of a storm brings helped Banks to drift uneasily off to sleep again. Only seconds later, it seemed, the alarm clock rang and it was time to get ready for work.

When Banks arrived at the station, he was surprised to find an unusual flurry of activity. Superintendent Gristhorpe was waiting for him.

'What's going on?' Banks asked, hanging his wet mackintosh in the cupboard.

'A young girl's been reported missing,' Gristhorpe told him, bushy eyebrows knitted together in a frown.

'From Eastvale?'

'Get yourself some coffee, lad. Then we'll talk about it.'

Banks took his mug to the small lunch room and poured himself a cup of fresh black coffee. Back in the office, he sat behind his desk and sipped the hot drink, waiting for Gristhorpe to begin. He knew there was never any point in hurrying the superintendent.

'Helmthorpe,' Gristhorpe said finally. 'Local bobby down there, Constable Weaver, got woken up by worried parents just after the storm broke. Seems their young lass hadn't come home, and they were worried. The mother said she sometimes stayed out late – she was at that age, sixteen or so – so they hadn't worried too much earlier. But when the storm woke them and she still wasn't back . . . Apparently she's not done anything like that before.'

'What's the girl's name?'

'Sally Lumb.' The words sounded flat and final in Gristhorpe's Yorkshire accent.

Banks rubbed his face and drank some more coffee. 'I was talking to her just the other day,' he said at last. 'In here. She came to see me.'

Gristhorpe nodded. 'I know. I saw the report. That's why I wanted to talk to you.'

'Attractive young girl,' Banks said, almost to himself. 'Looked older than she was. Sixteen. Interested in acting. She wanted to get away to the big city.' And all of a sudden he thought of Penny Cartwright, who had been to so many big cities only to return to Helmthorpe.

'We're covering that angle, Alan. You know as well as I do how most of these cases turn out. In all likelihood she's run off to Manchester or London. Her mother told Weaver there'd been a few rows at home lately. Seems the lass didn't get on too well with her father. She probably just took off somewhere.'

Banks nodded. 'Most likely.'

'But you don't believe it?'

'I didn't say that, sir.'

'No, but you sounded like it.'

'Shock, I suppose. There could have been an accident. She goes off with her boyfriend. You know, they find isolated places where they can kiss and cuddle. That area's full of old lead mines and gullies.'

'Aye, it's possible. For the moment we'll just have to

assume it's either that or she's run off. We've wired her description to all the big cities. I just hope to God we've not got a sex killer on our hands.' He paused and looked through the window, where the steady downpour had almost emptied Market Street and the square. Only a few shoppers soldiered on under umbrellas. 'Trouble is,' he went on, 'we can't organize search parties in this kind of weather. Too bloody dangerous by far up on the moors and valley sides.'

'What do *you* think's happened?' Banks asked.

'Me?' Gristhorpe shook his head. 'I don't know, Alan. Like I told you, I've been reading through that interview report again and I can't really see as she gave us any valuable information. She just helped us pinpoint the time the body was dumped, that's all. She didn't actually see anything.'

'You mean she wasn't a danger to anyone – to our killer?'

'Aye. Naturally you make connections when something like this happens. You'd be a poor copper if you didn't. But you can't let it get in the way. As it stands now, we've still got a murder to solve and we've got a missing girl to cope with, too.'

'But you do think there might be a connection?'

'I hope not. I bloody hope not. It's bad enough knowing there's someone who killed once out there, but a hell of a lot worse thinking they'd go as far as to kill a kid too.'

'We can't be sure she's dead yet, sir.'

Gristhorpe looked at Banks steadily for a few moments then turned back to the window. 'No,' he said. 'Was there anything else? Anything else to link her to the Steadman case?'

'Not that I know of. The only time I saw her was when

she came to tell me about hearing the car. I got the impression that she went away distinctly dischuffed with me for giving up the bright lights. We had Willy Fisher in at the time, too. He put up a bit of a struggle with two uniformed lads, and I think that unnerved her a bit.'

'What are you getting at, Alan?'

'I don't know, really. But maybe if she did figure anything out, she might not have come to me with it.'

'You can't blame yourself for that,' Gristhorpe said, rising wearily to leave. 'Let's hope she's run off somewhere. The link's got to be pursued, though. Were you thinking of going to Helmthorpe today?'

'No. It's so bloody miserable outside I thought I'd go over the paperwork again. Why?'

'The paperwork can wait. I'd feel easier if you did go.'

'Of course. What do you want me to do?'

'Have a word with the boyfriend, for a start. Find out if he saw her last night, or if not, why not. And Weaver tells me she hung around the coffee bar with three other girls. You might have a chat with them. Weaver will give you the names and details. Be as casual as you can. If she knew anything, or had any theories, she's far more likely to have told her friends than her parents. No need to trouble them.' Banks was relieved. Twice before he had had to spend time with the parents of missing children and he could think of no worse task.

'I'll take care of the rest,' Gristhorpe added. 'We'll be getting search parties organized as soon as this rain slackens off a bit.'

'Should I leave now?' Banks asked.

'No hurry. In fact, it might be better if you held off till mid-morning. I don't know a lot about teenage lasses, but I shouldn't imagine they'll be up and about right now. It might be best if you can find them in the coffee bar. It'll be a more comfortable environment for the kind of chat you want, and you'll get them all together.'

Banks nodded. 'You'll keep me up to date, sir?'

'Yes, of course. Just check in with Weaver. I'll send Sergeant Hatchley on later, too. He's busy getting the girl's description around the country right now.'

'Just a small point,' Banks said, 'but it might be a good idea if you had someone get in touch with theatre companies, drama schools, that kind of place. If she has run off, the odds are she's headed for the stage.'

'Aye,' Gristhorpe said, 'I'll do that.' Then, looking tired and worried, he left the office.

Outside, it was still pouring bucketfuls on to Market Street and looked as if it would never stop. Banks stared down at the shifting pattern of umbrellas as pedestrians dodged one another crossing the square on the way to work. He scratched his chin and found a rough patch the electric razor had missed. Gristhorpe was right; they had to think in terms of a connection with the Steadman business. It had to be pursued quickly, as well, and the irony was that they had to hope they were wrong.

Banks looked over Sally Lumb's interview transcript and tried to visualize her as she had sat before him. Was there something she hadn't told him? As he read the printed words he had written up from his notes, he tried to picture her face, remembering pauses, changes in expression. No. If there was anything else, it must have occurred to her after the interview, and she might then have gone to the wrong person with her information or ideas. Banks tried to stop himself imagining her battered body stuffed down a disused mineshaft, but the images were hard to dismiss. Sally may have been eager to move away to the big city but she had struck him as a sensible girl, even calculating – the kind who would make a clean and open move when the right time came. According to her mother, nothing dramatic had happened at home to make her run away. Rows were common enough surely, and, if anything, the parents seemed too liberal. Banks remembered the curfews (broken, many of them) of his own adolescence as he tried to coax his pipe alight. The blasted thing remained as reluctant as ever. In a sudden flash of anger and frustration, he threw it across the room and the stem snapped in two.

SIX

As Banks approached Helmthorpe later that Saturday morning, the coloured tents across the river strained at their ropes in the wind and rain like the sails of hidden boats, and the dark water danced wildly with ripples. In such weather, the houses themselves looked like dull out-crops of the stone they were built from, and the valley sides were shrouded in haze. A few locals and unfortunate holidaymakers tramped the streets.

Banks pulled into the small parking space next to the police station, and the first person he saw inside was PC Weaver. The constable looked pale, and there were dark smudges under his eyes.

'We can't even organize a search,' he said, pointing out of the window. 'Our men would get bogged down on the moors, and the visibility's hopeless.'

'I know,' Banks said. 'Any luck?'

Weaver shook his head. 'Her parents last saw her just before they went out for the evening at about seven thirty.

Before that, her friends saw her in the coffee bar earlier in the afternoon. We've not had time to ask much yet, sir. I've still got some lads out there. There'll likely be more information coming in before long.'

Banks nodded. 'And she didn't say to anyone where she was going?'

'No, sir. Her mother thought she might have met her boyfriend somewhere.'

'Did she?'

'He says not, sir,' Weaver pointed toward a bedraggled young man in a clinging wet T-shirt and soggy jeans, hair plastered down by the rain. 'That's him there, sir. He's pretty upset, and I see no reason not to believe him.'

'Have you questioned him?'

'Just talked to him, really, sir. Not questioned him proper. I mean, I thought I'd leave that . . .'

'That's fine, Constable,' Banks said, smiling his approval. 'You did right.'

He walked over to Kevin, who was staring fixedly at a 'Crime Doesn't Pay' poster and chewing his fingernails. Banks introduced himself and sat down on the bench.

'How long have you known Sally?' he asked.

Kevin rubbed his eyes. 'Years, I suppose. We only started going out together this summer.'

'How do you feel about Swainsdale?'

'What?'

'How do you feel about living in the dales, your home? Sally doesn't like it much, does she? Wasn't she always talking about going away?'

'Oh aye, she talked,' Kevin said scornfully. 'She's full of big talk is Sally. Got a lot of grand ideas.'

'Don't you think she might have run off to London or somewhere, then?'

Kevin shook his head. 'No. I can't see her leaving like that. That's why I'm worried. She'd've told me.'

'Perhaps she's running from you, too.'

'Don't be daft. We've just started going together. We're in love.' He bent forward and put his head in his hands. 'I love her. We're going to get married, start a little farm . . . I know Sally, and she just wouldn't run off without telling me. She wouldn't.'

Banks held himself back from agreeing. Whatever Kevin believed, there was still hope. He couldn't picture Sally Lumb settling down to domestic rural life in the dales, though. Kevin had a lot to learn about women and about dreams, but he seemed a decent and honest enough boy on the surface. Banks was inclined to agree with Weaver and see no harm in him, but he had to press on with the questioning.

'Did you talk to Sally yesterday?' he asked.

Kevin shook his head.

'You didn't see her at all yesterday evening?'

'No. I was playing cricket with some mates over in Aykbridge.'

'Did Sally know about that? Didn't she expect to see you?'

'Aye, she knew. You can't see each other every night, can you?' he burst out. 'You'd soon get sick of each other, then, wouldn't you? You've got to do other things sometimes, don't you?'

He was blaming himself, and Banks helped him fight back the guilt. He wanted to ask him about the night he and Sally had heard the car; he wanted to know if she had said anything more about it, or if either of them had noticed something they hadn't mentioned. But if he did that, he realized, he would be putting ideas into Kevin's mind, making him think that Sally's disappearance was somehow related to Steadman's murder. He would have to do that eventually, but it could wait. If there was anything, Kevin would probably blurt it out himself in his attempt to help find Sally.

It was almost noon. If the girls were going to meet up as usual in the coffee bar, they'd probably be there by now, Weaver told him. Banks dashed out to the car. In good weather, he would have walked the short distance, but after only a moment's exposure to the heavy rain, droplets were running down his neck from his sodden collar.

The three girls sat in silence, toying with straws angled in their Coke cans. Banks told them who he was and pulled up a chair to the stained and cracked Formica table. The video games and pinball machine were silent.

'Do you think Sally's the kind of girl to run away without telling anyone?' he asked first.

They all shook their heads slowly. The plain-looking girl with thick glasses, who had introduced herself as Anne Downes, answered, 'She's full of ideas, is Sally. But that's all they are. She's nowhere to run to. She doesn't know anyone outside Swainsdale.'

'Was she doing well at school?'

'Well enough,' replied Kathy Chalmers, the one with the henna hair. 'She's clever. Not a swot, like. She could always get away without studying much and get good marks. She's bound to pass all her exams.'

'A sensible girl, you'd say?'

'As sensible as any of us teenagers,' Anne Downes answered, and the irony wasn't lost on Banks. 'It depends on your point of view.'

Kathy gave a short giggle and blushed. 'I'm sorry,' she

apologized, putting her hand over her mouth. 'But her parents might not have thought she was sensible. You know parents.'

Being one himself, Banks did. 'But she's not the kind of girl to . . .' He paused, searching for words to avoid the phrase 'get into trouble', with all its connotations. 'She doesn't cause trouble, make a nuisance of herself?'

Kathy shook her head. 'No. Not at all. She's well behaved enough. Gets on well with most of the teachers. She's just full of ideas, like Anne said. A big dreamer. She wouldn't do anything to hurt anybody.'

Banks wondered if the girls connected Sally's disappearance with the Steadman business; her visit to the Eastvale station was exactly the kind of thing she'd tell them about, and he wanted to know if she had made any remarks. Again, the problem was to avoid alerting and alarming them.

'I suppose you know she came to see me a few days ago?' he began casually. 'And I agree, she struck me as being exactly like you all say – bright, full of plans, well behaved. I didn't really get to hear much about any of her ideas, though.'

Kathy Chalmers blushed again. The other girl, Hazel Kirk, who had so far sat silently throughout the conversation, began to seem ill at ease. Again it was Anne Downes who answered with a forthrightness completely in harmony with her precocious intelligence.

'Take this murder business,' she began. 'I suppose that's what she went to see you about?'

Banks nodded.

'Well, she found it all rather glamorous, exciting, as if it was something she was watching on telly. I don't mean to say she wasn't sorry about poor Mr Steadman, we all were, it's just that she didn't see it from that point of view. To Sally it was an adventure. Do you know what I mean? It was all a bit of a game with her as the heroine.'

This was exactly what Banks wanted. He nodded in appreciation of Anne's observation. 'Did she talk about it much?' he asked.

'Only in a mysterious kind of way,' Anne answered.

'As if she knew something nobody else did?'

'Yes. Exactly like that. I think it made her feel important, that she'd noticed something and been to see you. She thought you were rather dishy at first.' Anne said this with a perfectly straight face, as if she didn't quite know what the word meant. 'Then she seemed disappointed with your response. I don't know what it was, she didn't say, but she got even more mysterious as the week went on.'

'Did she say anything specific?'

'Oh, she tried to convince us that she was hot on the trail,' Anne said, adjusting her glasses. 'That she had an idea who dunnit. But that's all. Just hints. She didn't do anything about it, as far as I know.'

Banks was dreading the moment, which surely couldn't be far off, when Anne would realize the significance of his line of questioning. But luckily it didn't come. He thanked the girls for their time and, as he left, noted again how distracted Hazel Kirk seemed to be. Instead of questioning her there and then, he decided to leave it for a while and see what developed.

9

ONE

It was time to concentrate on the Steadman case again. However disturbing her disappearance was, Banks thought, Sally Lumb might turn up in Birmingham or Bristol any moment. But Steadman was dead and his killer was still free.

He told Weaver where he was going and drove up the hill to Gratly, turning right after the small low bridge in the centre of the hamlet and pulling up outside Jack Barker's converted farmhouse by the side of the broad beck. The water was already running faster and louder over the series of terraced falls. In a day or two, when the rain percolated down from the moorlands and higher slopes, the stream would turn into a deafening torrent.

Banks realized as he rang the doorbell that he had not visited Barker at home before, and he wondered what the house would reveal of the man.

'Oh, it's you, Chief Inspector,' a puzzled-looking Barker said, after keeping Banks waiting at the door for an unusually long time. 'Come in. Excuse my surprise but I don't get very many visitors.'

Banks took off his wet mac and shoes in the hall and followed Barker inside. Although it wasn't cold, the rain had certainly put a damp chill in the stone, and Banks decided to keep his jacket on.

'Do you mind if we talk in the study?' Barker asked. 'It's warmer up there. I've just been working, and that's where the coffee pot is. You look as if you could do with some.'

'Good idea,' Banks replied, following his host through a sparsely furnished living room and up a very narrow flight of stone stairs into a cosy room that looked out on the fell sides at the back of the house. Two walls were lined with books, and by a third, where the door was, stood a filing cabinet and a small desk stacked with papers. Barker's work table, on which an electric typewriter hummed, stood directly by the window. Through the streaming rain, the sharply rising slope outside had the look of an Impressionist painting. At the centre of the room was a low coffee table. The red light of the automatic drip-filter machine was on, and the Pyrex pot was half full of rich dark coffee. By the table, there were two small but comfortable armchairs. The two men sat down with their coffee; both took black, no sugar.

'I'm sorry to disturb you at work,' Banks said, sipping the refreshing liquid.

'Think nothing of it. It's an occupational hazard.'

Banks raised an eyebrow.

'What I mean is,' Barker explained, 'that if you work at home, you're at home, aren't you? Fair game for any salesman and bill collector. Somehow, the old Protestant work ethic won't allow most people to accept that writing books in the comfort of one's own home is really work, if you see what I mean. I can't think why, mind you. It was common enough for weavers and loom operators to work at home before the Industrial Revolution. These days, work has to be something we hate, something we do in a noisy dirty factory or an antiseptic fluorescent office. No offence.'

But Banks could tell by the sparkle in his eyes that Barker was baiting him gently. 'None taken,' he replied. 'As a matter of fact, I'd be happier to spend a bit more time in my office and less of it tramping about the dales in this weather.'

Barker smiled and reached for a cigarette from the packet on the table. 'Anyway,' he said, 'I don't seem to get many visitors, except salesmen. I take the phone off the hook, too. Work was going well. I'd just got to a good part, and it's always been my practice to stop for a while when things get good. That way I feel excited about going back to work later.'

'That's an interesting work habit,' Banks remarked, trying to ignore the craving he felt when Barker lit his cigarette and inhaled deeply.

'Sorry,' Barker said, offering him a cigarette as if he had read his mind.

Banks shook his head. 'Trying to stop.'

'Of course. You're a pipe man, aren't you? Please feel free. Pipe smoke doesn't bother me at all.'

'It broke.'

After the two of them had laughed at the absurdity of the broken pipe, Banks gave in. 'Perhaps I will have a cigarette,' he said. As he reached for one, he noticed Barker tense up to face the inevitable questions. The cigarette tasted good. Every bit as good as he remembered. He didn't cough or feel dizzy. In fact, he felt no indication that he had ever given up cigarettes in the first place; it was like a reunion with a long lost friend.

'So, what can I do for you this time?' Barker asked, putting unnecessary emphasis on the last two words.

'I suppose you've heard about the girl from the village, Sally Lumb?' he asked.

'No. What about her?'

'You mean you don't know? I'd have thought in a community this size the news would spread fast. People certainly knew about Harold Steadman soon enough.'

'I haven't been out since I walked Penny home after the folk club last night.'

'The girl's missing,' Banks told him. 'She didn't go home last night.'

'Good Lord!' Barker said, looking towards the window. 'If she's wandered off and got lost in this weather . . . What do you think?'

'It's too early to know yet. She could have got lost, yes. But she grew up around here and she seemed like a sensible girl.'

'Run away?'

'Another possibility. We're checking on it.'

'But you don't think so?'

'We just don't know.'

'Have you got search parties out?'

'We can't in this weather.'

'But still . . . Something's got to be done.'

'We're doing all we can,' Banks assured him. 'Did you know her?'

Barker narrowed his eyes. 'I wouldn't say I really knew her, no. I've seen her around, of course, to say hello to. And she once came to me about a school project. Pretty girl.'

'Very,' Banks agreed.

'I don't suppose that's what you came to talk to me about though, is it?'

'No.' Banks stubbed out his cigarette. 'I wanted to ask you about Penny Cartwright.'

'What about her?'

'Are you in love with her?'

Barker laughed, but Banks could see the strain in his eyes. 'What a question. I don't know whether to tell you it's none of your business or applaud your insight.'

'You are, then?'

'I'll admit I'm rather smitten with Penny, yes. What red-blooded young bachelor wouldn't be? But I don't see what my feelings for her have to do with anything else.'

'Was she having an affair with Harold Steadman, do you think?'

Barker gazed at Banks for a few moments. 'Not that I know,' he answered slowly. 'But how would I know?'

'You knew the two of them quite well.'

'True. But a man's private life . . . and a woman's? If they wanted to conceal something like that from the world, it wouldn't have been very difficult, would it? Even here, it could be done. Look, if you want my answer to your question, you'll have to understand that it's just an opinion, like yours. Certainly neither of them confided in me, or anything like that. And I'd say no, they weren't having an affair. As you guessed, I am very fond of Penny and, given that, I'd naturally be interested in her relationships. As far as I can make out though, their friendship was based on mutual respect and admiration, not sexual desire.'

This was almost exactly what Banks had heard from Penny herself and from Emma Steadman. Indeed, the only person who seemed to think differently about Penny and Harold Steadman was the major, and he was very much a victim of his own obsessions. But what if he was right?

'You seemed rather sharp last night when I mentioned Michael Ramsden,' Banks said, changing tack. 'Do you have any particular reason to dislike him?'

'I don't dislike him. I hardly even knew him. He's been in the Bridge a few times with Harry, and he always seemed pleasant enough. I will admit that I found something a little sly about him, a bit off-putting, but that's a minor personal reaction; it's neither here nor there.'

'I suppose you knew about his relationship with Penny?'

'Yes, and I'm quite willing to confess to a touch of instinctive lover's jealousy. Come to that, I may have been envious of her relationship with Harry, too; it seemed so close and easy. But I've no claim on Penny's emotions, sad to say. And as far as Ramsden was concerned, that was years ago. They can't have been more than kids.'

'Where were you then?'

'What? On the night of the twelfth of February, nineteen sixty-three, between the hours of—'

'You know what I mean.'

'Ten years ago?'

'Yes.'

'I lived in London then, in a poky little bedsit in Notting Hill writing real novels that nobody wanted to buy. Penny wasn't around when I first came to Gratly – we didn't meet till she came back – but I did see her play once down south.'

'Why do you think Ramsden and Penny split up?'

'How should I know? It's not a question I've concerned myself with. Why does any young couple split up? I suppose they felt themselves moving in different directions. Christ, they were only kids.'

'That was when Michael lived at home with his parents, wasn't it? In the same house Steadman and his wife used to visit on holidays?'

'Yes,' Barker answered. 'Ten years ago. It was just before Ramsden went off to university. Penny was just discovering her talent then. Harry told me he used to teach her folk songs he'd collected.'

'And the kids just drifted apart?'

'Well, Michael went to university, and Penny went all over the place with the group. That kind of folk music was still popular then. It still is, actually. I mean, there's always a sizeable audience for it.'

'How was Penny discovered?'

'The usual way, as far as I know. An agent for a record company was scouting the provinces for new folk talent. He offered her a chance to make a demo and off she went. The rest is history, as they say.'

'Has she talked to you about the past much, the time she spent away?'

'Not a great deal, no.' Barker seemed interested in the conversation now, despite himself. He poured more coffee and Banks cadged another cigarette. 'I'm sure you know, Chief Inspector,' he went on, 'that we all have phases of our lives we're not particularly proud of. Often circumstances give us the opportunity to behave in a careless irresponsible way, and most of us take it. It pains me to admit that I was once a very young Teddy boy and I even ripped a few seats in the local fleapit.' He grinned. 'You won't arrest me, will you?'

'I think the statute of limitation has run out on seat-ripping,' Banks answered, smiling. 'It would be rather difficult to prove, too.'

'You make me feel old.' Banks sighed. 'But do you see what I mean? Penny was not only young and inexperienced, she was also, for the first time in her life, fairly well off, popular, in with the "in crowd". I don't doubt that she tried drugs and that sex was a fairly casual matter. "Make love, not war," as they used to say. But the important thing is that she grew up, left all that behind and pulled her life together. Plenty of people don't survive the modern music world, you know; Penny did. What I'd like to know is why on earth you seem so obsessed with the events of ten years ago.'

'I don't know,' Banks answered, scratching the scar at the side of his eye. 'Everybody speaks so highly of Steadman. He didn't seem to have an enemy in the world. Yet somebody murdered him. Don't you find that strange? He wasn't robbed, and his body was taken up to the hillside below Crow Scar. We don't know where he was killed. I suppose what I'm saying, Mr Barker, is that if the answer isn't in the present, which it doesn't seem to be, then it must be in the past, however unlikely that may seem to you.'

'And has this background information given you any clues?'

'None at all. Not yet. But there's one more thing that's been on my mind. Could Harold Steadman have been a homosexual?'

Barker almost choked on his coffee. 'That takes the biscuit,' he spluttered, wiping at the spilled liquid on his lap. 'Where on earth did you get a wild idea like that?'

Banks saw no reason to tell him that he had got the idea from Sergeant Hatchley, who had said in the Queen's Arms, in his usual manner, 'About this Steadman business, those weekend trips to Ramsden's place; do you think he was queer?'

Banks had admitted that it was an angle he had not considered; he had taken Steadman's dedication to work at face value and presumed that the overnight visits took place for the reasons Ramsden and Mrs Steadman had given him.

'Even assuming you're right,' Banks had said, 'it doesn't really help us much, does it? His wife can't have killed him out of disgust – she has an alibi. And Ramsden would hardly have killed his lover, even if he could have.'

'There's blackmail, though,' Hatchley had suggested. 'Steadman was a rich man.'

'Yes. It's a possibility. Who do you think was black-mailing him?'

'Could have been anyone he knew: Barker, the girl, Barnes, one of his old mates from Leeds.'

'We'll check it out, then,' Banks had said. 'Ask around about Ramsden, and I'll ask some more questions in Helmthorpe. I wouldn't hold out too much hope though. It doesn't feel right to me.'

How did you ask someone if a friend was homosexual, he wondered. Just come right out with it? How would they know? Penny would certainly assume Ramsden was straight if he had been ten years ago, and there was still a chance that she knew more about Steadman's sexual habits than she let on.

So now he sat in Barker's study waiting for him to get over the shock and attempt an answer. When it came, it was disappointing. Barker simply denied the possibility and would only admit, when pushed, that anything however outlandish was possible, but that didn't mean it was true.

'Look,' Barker said, leaning forward. 'I realize that I must be a suspect in this business. I've no alibi and I seem unable to convince you that I really had nothing against Harry – I'm not gay either, just for the record – but I assure you that I did not kill him, and I'm perfectly willing to help in any way I can. I just don't know how I can help, and, if you don't mind my saying so, some of the directions you're pursuing seem to me to be quite silly.'

'I can understand that,' Banks said, 'but it's for me to decide what's relevant and what isn't.'

'You pick up bits and pieces from everyone and put them together. Yes, I suppose that's true. None of us gets to touch any more than a small area of the elephant, do we? But you get to see the whole beast.'

Banks smiled at the analogy. 'Eventually, yes,' he said. 'I hope so. What are you working on, or don't you like to discuss work in progress?'

'I don't mind. As a matter of fact, you've just given me an idea. All that about putting the pieces together. I think I can use it. It's another in the Kenny Gibson series. Have you read any?'

Banks shook his head.

'Of course not,' Barker said. 'I ought to know by now that few real policemen read detective novels. Anyway, Kenny Gibson is a private eye in the Los Angeles area. Period stuff, the thirties. I get most of my background information from Raymond Chandler and the old *Black Mask* magazines, but don't tell anyone! This time he's working for a rich society woman whose husband has disappeared. The plot's taken care of; it's the characters and atmosphere that are really hard to do.'

'Sex and violence?'

'Enough to sell a few thousand copies.'

'Just out of interest,' Banks asked as he got up to leave, 'do you have it all planned out in advance – the plot, the solution?'

'Good Lord, no,' Barker answered, following him down the stairs. 'The plot takes care of itself as I go along. At least I hope it does. If it's going well, there are fewer and fewer options at each turn until it's perfectly clear who the criminal is. I'm never really sure where I'm going from one day to the next. It'd be boring any other way, don't you think?'

'Perhaps,' Banks answered, putting on his shoes and mac. 'In writing, yes. In fiction. But in real life, I'm not so sure. It'd be a damn sight easier if I knew who the criminal was without having to write the whole book and make all the mistakes along the way. Anyway, goodbye, and thanks for your time.'

'My pleasure,' said Barker.

And Banks ducked quickly through the rain to his car.

TWO

On High Street, Banks glimpsed Penny Cartwright nipping into the Bridge. Consulting his watch and his stomach, he decided it was well past lunch time, and he could do with a pie and a pint if the landlord had any food left.

Penny was at the bar shaking her umbrella when she glanced over her shoulder and saw Banks enter.

'Can't a lady indulge her alcoholic cravings without the police turning up?' she asked sharply.

'Of course,' Banks replied. 'As a matter of fact, I'd be honoured if you'd join me for a late lunch.'

Penny looked at him through narrowed eyes. 'Business or pleasure, Inspector?'

'Just a chat.'

'For "chat" read "interrogation", I'll bet. Go on then. I must be a fool. You're buying.'

They were lucky enough to get two steak and

mushroom pies and Penny asked for a double Scotch. Carrying the drinks, Banks followed her into the lounge.

'Why don't they do something with this place?' he asked, looking around and turning his nose up.

'Why should they? I wouldn't have taken you for one of these horse-brass and bedpan types.' Penny stood her umbrella by the fireplace and sat down, shaking her hair.

Banks laughed. 'I always thought they were bed-warmers. And no, I'm not, not at all. Give me spittoons and sawdust any day. I was simply thinking that the owner might see renovations as a way to do more business in the long run.'

'Oh, Inspector Banks! I can see you're not a true Yorkshireman yet. We don't care about a speck or two of dirt in these parts. It's the company and the ale that count, and this is one place the locals can count on for both.'

Banks grinned and accepted the criticism with a humble sigh.

'So what is it you want to know this time?' Penny asked, lighting a cigarette and leaning back in her chair.

'I enjoyed your performance last night. I liked the songs, and you've got a beautiful voice.'

Did she blush just a little? Banks couldn't be sure, the lighting in the room was so dim. But she faltered over accepting the compliment and was clearly embarrassed.

The pies arrived and they each took a few bites in silence before Banks opened the conversation again.

'I'm stuck. I'm not getting anywhere. And now there's a girl gone missing.'

Penny frowned. 'Yes. I've heard.'

'Do you know her? What do you think might have happened?'

'I know Sally a little, yes. She always wanted to know

about the big wide world out there. I think she was secretly a bit disappointed with me for leaving it behind and coming home. But she struck me as a sensible girl. I can't really picture her running off like that. And she was born and raised in these parts, like me. She knows the countryside around here like the back of her hand, so she wasn't likely to get lost either.'

'Which leaves?'

'I don't like to think about it. You hear of young girls going missing so often in the cities. But here . . .' Penny shuddered. 'I suppose it could mean we've got a maniac in our midst. What are the police doing, apart from buying me lunch?'

It was the second time Banks had been asked that, and he found it just as depressing to have so little to say in reply again. But Penny understood about the weather; she knew how dangerous it made Swainsdale, and she showed a surprising amount of sympathy for Banks's obvious frustration.

They sat in silence again and returned to their food. When they had finished, Banks put his knife and fork down and faced Penny.

'Tell me about your father,' he said.

'You sound like a bloody psychiatrist. What about him?'

'You must know better than anyone else what a hothead he is?'

'I probably gave him reason enough.'

'You mean the city, the wild life?'

She nodded. 'But honestly, you make it sound much worse than it was. What would you do in that position? Everything was new. I had money, people I thought were my friends. It was exciting then, people were trying new things just for the hell of it. My father didn't speak to me for a long time after I left. I couldn't explain; it was just too claustrophobic at home. But when I came back he was kind to me and helped me to get set up in the cottage. He takes it upon himself to act as my protector, I know. And yes, he has a temper. But he's harmless. You can't seriously suspect him of harming Harry, can you?'

Banks shook his head. 'Not any more, no. I think it was too well planned to be his kind of crime. I just wanted to know how you saw things. Tell me more about Michael Ramsden.'

Flustered, Penny reached for another cigarette. 'What about him?'

'You used to go out with him, didn't you? Can I have one of those?'

'Sure.' Penny gave him a Silk Cut. 'You know I used to go out with him. So what? It was years ago. Another lifetime.'

'Were you in love?'

'In love? Inspector, it's easy to be in love when you're sixteen, especially when everybody wants you to be. Michael was the bright boy of the village, and I was the talented lass. It was one match my father didn't oppose, and he's always held it against me that we didn't marry.'

'Did you think of marrying?'

'We were talking about getting engaged, like kids do. That's as far as it went. Look, I was young and innocent. Michael was just a boy. That's all there is to it.' Penny shifted in her seat and pushed her hair back over her shoulders.

'Was it a sexual relationship?'

'None of your bloody business.'

'Did he ditch you?'

'We just drifted apart.'

'Is that all?'

'It's all you're getting.' Penny stood up to leave, but Banks reached out and grabbed her arm. She stared at him angrily, and he let go as if he had received an electric shock. She rubbed the muscle.

'I'm sorry,' he said. 'Please sit down again. I haven't finished yet. Look, you might think I'm just prying into your personal life for the fun of it, but I'm not. I don't give a damn who you've slept with and who you haven't slept with, what drugs you've taken and what you haven't taken, unless it relates to Harold Steadman's murder. Is that clear? I don't even care how much hash you smoke now.'

Penny eyed Banks shrewdly. Finally she nodded.

'So why did you split up?' Banks asked.

'Buy me another drink and I'll tell you.'

'Same again?' Banks got up to go to the bar.

Penny nodded. 'I can't promise it'll be interesting, though,' she called after him.

'There was nothing mature about our relationship,' she said as Banks sat down with a pint and a double Scotch. 'Neither of us really knew anything different until something else came along.'

'Another man?'

'No. Not until later. Much later.'

'You mean university for Michael and a singing career for you?'

'Yes, partly. But it wasn't as simple as that.'

'What do you mean?'

Penny frowned as if she had just thought of something, or tried to grasp the shadow of a memory. 'I don't know. We just drifted apart, that's all there is to it. It was summer, ten years ago. Every bit as hot as this one. I told you it wasn't exciting.'

'But there must have been a reason.'

'Why do you want to know?'

'Because I think the answer to Steadman's death lies in the past, and I want to know as much about it as possible.'

'Why do you think that?'

'I'm asking the questions. Did he dump you because you wouldn't have sex with him?'

Penny blew out a stream of smoke. 'All right, so I wouldn't let him fuck me. Is that what you want to hear?' The word was clearly meant to shock Banks.

'You tell me.'

'Oh, this is bloody insufferable. Here.' She tossed him another cigarette. 'Maybe sex was part of it. He was certainly getting persistent. Perhaps I should have let him. I don't know . . . I'm sure I was ready. But then he seemed different. He got more withdrawn and distant. Things just felt strange. I was changing, too. I was singing in the village pubs and Michael was studying to go to university. Harry and Emma were up for quite a while and it was hot, very hot. Emma would hardly go outside because her skin burned so easily. Harry and I spent quite a bit of time at the Roman site near Fortford. It was just being excavated then. We went for walks as well, long walks in the sun.'

'Did Michael go with you?'

'Sometimes. But he wasn't very interested in that kind of thing then. He'd just discovered the joys of English Literature. It was all Shelley, Keats, Wordsworth and D. H. Lawrence for him. He spent most of the time with his nose stuck in a book of poems, whether he was with us or not. That's when he wasn't trying to stick his hands up my skirt.'

'Must have been Lawrence's influence.'

Penny's lips twitched in a brief smile. She put her hand to her forehead and swept back her hair. 'Maybe.'

'And Mrs Steadman?'

'As I said, she didn't like the sun. Sometimes she'd come if we went in the car and sit under a makeshift parasol by the side of the road while we had a picnic like characters from a Jane Austen novel. But she wasn't really interested in the Romans or folk traditions, either. Maybe it wasn't the best of marriages, I don't know. Lord knows, they didn't have much in common. But they put up with it, and I don't think they treated each other unkindly. Harry shouldn't have married, really. He was far too dedicated to his work. Mostly I just remember him and me tramping over the moors and naming wild flowers.'

Steadman must have been in his early thirties then, Banks calculated, and Penny was sixteen. That wasn't such an age difference to make attraction impossible. Quite the contrary: he was exactly the age a girl of sixteen might be attracted to, and Steadman had certainly been handsome, in a scholarly kind of way, right up to the end.

'Didn't you have a crush on Harry?' he asked. 'Surely it would have been perfectly natural?'

'Perhaps. But the main thing – the thing you don't seem able to understand – is that Harry really wasn't like that. He wasn't sexy, I suppose. More like an uncle. I know it must be hard for you to believe, but it's true.'

If I don't believe it, Banks thought, it's not for want of people trying to convince me. 'Don't you think Michael might have seen the relationship differently?' he suggested. 'A threat, perhaps. An older, more experienced man. Might that not have been why he seemed strange?'

'I can't say I ever thought of it that way,' Penny answered.

Banks wasn't sure whether he believed her or not; she lied and evaded issues so often he was becoming more and more convinced that she was an actress as well as a singer.

'It's possible though, isn't it?'

She nodded. 'I guess so. But he never said anything to me. You'd think he would have, wouldn't you?'

'You didn't argue? Michael never said anything about you going off with Harry? He didn't always insist on accompanying you?'

Penny shook her head at each question.

'He was very shy and awkward,' she said. 'It was very difficult for him to express himself emotionally. If he did think anything, he kept it to himself and suffered in silence.'

Banks sipped his pint of Theakston's, brooding on how best to put his next question. Penny offered him another Silk Cut.

'If I read you right, Inspector,' she said, 'you seem to be implying that Michael Ramsden might have killed Harry.'

'Am I?'

'Come on! Why all the questions about him being jealous?'

Banks said nothing.

'They became great friends, you know,' Penny went on. 'When Michael graduated and got interested in local history, he helped Harry a lot. He even persuaded his firm to publish Harry's books. It was more than just a publisher–author relationship.'

'That's what I was wondering,' Banks cut in, seizing

his opportunity. 'Is there any possibility of a homosexual relationship between them? I know it sounds odd, but think about it.'

Unlike Barker, Penny took the question seriously before concluding that she doubted it very much. 'This had better not be a trick,' she said. 'I hope you're not trying to trap me into admitting intimate knowledge of Harry's sexual preferences.'

Banks laughed. 'I'm not half as devious as you make out.'

Her eyes narrowed sharply 'I'll bet. Anyway,' she went on, 'I really can't help you. You'd think you'd know all about a friend you've known for years, but it's just not so. Harry could have been gay, for all I know. Michael, on the other hand, seemed very much like a normal adolescent, but there's no reason why he couldn't have been bi. Who can tell these days?'

And she was right. Banks had known a sergeant on the Metropolitan force for six years – a married man with two children – before finding out at the inquest into his suicide that he had been homosexual.

'You still seem to be saying Michael did it,' she said. 'In fact, you're hounding all of us – his friends. Why? Why pick on us? What about his enemies? Couldn't it have been somebody just passing through who killed Harry?'

Banks shook his head. 'Contrary to popular belief,' he said, 'very few murders happen that way. I think the myth of the wandering vagrant killer was invented by the aristocracy to keep suspicion away from their own doorsteps. Most often people are killed by family or friends, and motives are usually money, sex, revenge or the need to cover up damaging facts. In Harold Steadman's case, we found no evidence of robbery and we've had no luck so far in digging up an enemy from his past. Believe me, Ms Cartwright, we dig deep. We've been checking the alibis of anyone outside his immediate circle who might have had even the remotest reason for killing him. Really, not many people walk around the country bashing others on the head for no reason. So far, statistics and evidence point to someone closer to home. According to his friends, though, he was too damn perfect to have an enemy, so where am I supposed to look? Obviously Mr Steadman was a far more complicated man than most people have admitted, and his network of relationships wasn't a simple one either. His murder wasn't a spur of the moment job, or at least the killer was frightened or cold-blooded enough to throw us off the scent by moving the body.'

'And you're not going to stop pestering us until you know who it is?'

'No.'

'Are you close?'

'I can't see it if I am, but detection doesn't work like that, anyway. It's not a matter of getting closer like a zoom lens, but of getting enough bits and pieces to transform chaos into a recognizable pattern.'

'And you never know when you have enough?'

'Yes. But you can't predict when that moment will come. It could be in the next ten seconds or the next ten years. You don't know what the pattern will look like when it's there, so you might not even recognize it at first. But, soon enough, you'll know you've got a design and not just a filing cabinet full of odds and sods.'

'What about money as a motive?' Penny asked. 'Harry was very well off.'

'He didn't leave a will, which was foolish of him.

Naturally, it all goes to Mrs Steadman. It would have been more convenient for us if he'd left it all to the National Trust and we could have pulled in the first nutty conservationist we could find, but life isn't as easy as fiction. Motive and opportunity just don't seem to go together in this case.'

'Well, that's your problem, isn't it?'

'Yes. Have I explained why I'm pestering you so much now?'

'Very clearly, thank you,' Penny said, giving him a mock bow.

'You don't see Michael much these days?'

'No, not often. Occasionally in the Bridge. He was always especially awkward with me after we split up, though. You're not suggesting that Michael is still in love with me, are you? Let me get this right. He thought Harry and I were having an affair all those years ago and backed off. But all the time he's been holding a grudge. He worked his way into Harry's confidence over the years just looking for an opportunity to do away with him, and finally took his revenge. Am I right?'

Banks laughed, but it sounded hollow. Perhaps Ramsden did have sufficient motive, but he would have been hard-pushed to make an opportunity. First of all, he could hardly come to Helmthorpe and hang around in the car park all evening waiting, even if he was certain Steadman would be going there. And if Steadman had gone to York, how did his car get back to Helmthorpe? Ramsden could hardly have driven two cars, and he would have needed his own to get home. There were certainly no buses at that time of night, and he would not have risked arranging for a taxi.

'It's ludicrous,' Penny said, as if she had been listening

in on Banks's thoughts. 'I see what you mean when you say you're stuck.' She finished her drink, put down the glass, and stood up to leave.

Banks stayed on, drinking rather gloomily and craving another cigarette. Then Hatchley walked in. The sergeant brought two pints over and wedged himself into the chair Penny had just left.

'Any developments?' Banks asked.

'Weaver's men have talked to someone who saw Sally Lumb in the public call box on Hill Road at four o'clock Friday afternoon,' Hatchley reported. 'And someone else thinks he saw her walking along Helmthorpe High Street at about nine o'clock.'

'What direction?'

'East.'

'She could have been going anywhere.'

'Except west,' Hatchley said. 'By the way, I've been in touch with a mate of mine in York. Keeps tabs on all the queers and perverts down there, and there's nothing on Ramsden at all. Not a dicky bird.'

'I didn't think there would be,' Banks said glumly. 'We're barking up the wrong tree, Sergeant.'

'That's as maybe, but who's going to lead us to the right 'un?'

Banks watched the rain stream down the dirty window-pane and sighed. 'Do you think the two are linked?' he asked. 'Steadman and the Lumb girl?'

Hatchley wiped his lips with the back of his hand and burped. 'Bit of a coincidence, isn't it? The girl has the only piece of real information we get about the dumping of Steadman's body, and she goes missing.'

'But she'd already told us what she knew.'

'Did the killer know that?' Hatchley asked.

'It doesn't matter, does it? He didn't even know anybody had heard him burying Steadman below Crow Scar, unless . . .'

'Unless the girl let him know.'

'Right. Either intentionally or otherwise. But that still assumes she knew more than she told us, that she knew who it was.'

'Not if it was unintentional,' Hatchley pointed out. 'A girl like that tells all her friends, maybe hints that she knows more than she does. This is a small place, remember. It's not like London. It's easy to be overheard here, and word travels quickly.'

'The coffee bar,' Banks muttered.

'Come again?'

'The coffee bar. The place she hung around with her friends. Come on, we'd better question those girls again. If they know what Sally knew, they could be in danger as well. I didn't want them to think that Sally had been killed, or that her disappearance had anything to do with Steadman, but there's no time for softly-softly any more.'

Hatchley gulped down the rest of his pint, then dragged himself to his feet and plodded along behind.

10

ONE

Anne Downes was both nervous and excited to find herself in the police station. Not that it was much of a place, but it was alive with important activity: people coming and going, phones ringing, the ancient telex machine clattering. The two other girls paid less attention to their surroundings and seemed more preoccupied with their internal sense of unease. Hazel was the worst, biting her nails and shifting position as if she had St Vitus's dance; Kathy pretended to lounge coolly, casually uninterested in the whole affair, but she was biting her lower lip so hard it turned red.

The policewoman had been friendly enough when she'd picked them up at the coffee bar and driven them the short distance to the station, and the small attractive chief inspector had smiled and said he wouldn't keep them long. But they all knew there was something going on.

Anne was the first to be called into the tiny interview room. Its walls were bare and the mere two chairs and a table made the place seem over-furnished. It was the kind of room that made you claustrophobic.

Banks sat opposite Anne, and a policewoman with a notebook in her hand stood in the corner by a narrow barred window.

'I'd just like to ask you a few questions, Anne,' Banks began.

She looked at him quizzically from behind the thick lenses and nodded.

'First of all, I suppose you know why I want to see you again?'

'Yes,' Anne replied. 'You think Sally's been murdered because of something she knew.'

Banks, taken aback by her directness, asked what her opinion was.

'I'd say it's possible, yes,' Anne answered, her young brow furrowed in thought 'I've already told you that I don't believe she's run away or got lost, and that doesn't leave much more to choose from, does it, especially with this other business going on?'

She'd make a good detective, Banks thought – quick, perceptive, logical. 'Have you got any other ideas?' he asked.

'Maybe I was wrong,' Anne said, her voice beginning to shake.

'Wrong about what?'

'When I said Sally was all talk, all big ideas. Maybe she really did know something. Maybe she thought she'd make a name for herself by following it up.'

'Why should she do that?'

Anne adjusted her glasses and shook her head. The thick lenses magnified the tears forming in her eyes. 'I don't know,' she answered.

'Did she tell you anything at all that indicated she knew who the person was? Think about it. Anything.'

Anne thought, and the tears held off. 'No,' she said finally. 'She just hinted that she knew things, that she'd solved some kind of mystery. I mean, yes, she did sort of say that she knew who it was, but she didn't give us any names or anything. She said she had to make sure; she didn't want to cause any trouble.'

'Do Sally's parents have a telephone?'

'Yes. They've had one for ages. Why?'

'Can you think of any reason why Sally would use a public phone box on Friday afternoon?'

'No.'

'Not even if she wanted to call Kevin or some other boyfriend? I know that parents aren't always understanding.'

'There was only Kevin, and Sally's mum and dad knew about him. They weren't a hundred per cent keen, but he's a nice enough boy, so they didn't make a fuss about it.'

'Did Sally say where she was going on Friday evening?'

'No. I'd no idea she was going anywhere.'

'Thank you very much, Anne,' Banks said.

The policewoman showed her out and brought Kathy Chalmers in next. Kathy was upset by then, but there were no tears, and although she seemed to realize dimly what it was all about, she had nothing to add.

The last girl, Hazel Kirk, was another matter. She knew as well as the others what was going on, but she pretended ignorance. She said she couldn't even remember whether Sally had said anything about knowing who the killer was. The more Banks questioned her, the more fidgety and edgy she became. Finally she burst into tears and told Banks to leave her alone. He nodded to the policewoman, who moved forward to speak to her, and left the room.

Sergeant Hatchley was sitting on the edge of Weaver's desk looking over reports from provincial police and railway authorities. He glanced up as Banks approached. 'Any luck?'

Banks shook his head. 'The first one's the most intelligent, but even she couldn't tell us much. What she did say confirms our suspicions though. If Sally thought she knew who the killer was and arranged for a meeting, then we can be pretty sure what's happened to her. It must have been someone she knew, someone she wasn't afraid of. There's got to be a motive, dammit, and it's got to be right before our eyes.' He banged his fist on the desk, surprising Hatchley with the sudden violence. It reminded the sergeant that his boss came from a tough patch. He wasn't a plodder; he was used to action.

'Got a cigarette?' Banks asked.

'Thought you'd stopped and taken up pipe puffing,' Hatchley said, handing over his packet of Senior Service.

'Not any more. I never could stand the blasted thing.'

Hatchley smiled and gave him a light. 'Then I suggest, sir,' he said, 'that you start buying your own.'

The door of the interview room opened and a pacified Hazel Kirk came out to rejoin her waiting friends, who had all been whispering, wondering what was going on. The policewoman, looking concerned, stood in the doorway and beckoned Banks over.

'What is it?' he asked, closing the door behind him.

'The girl, sir,' the PC began. 'Why she was upset. It might mean something.'

'Well? Go on.'

'Sorry, sir. She got upset because Sally had told her she thought she knew who the killer was, and when she got home, Hazel told her parents.' She paused, and Banks drew on his cigarette waiting for her to continue. 'They just laughed and said Sally Lumb always did have an overactive imagination, but the girl's father had had a bit of a run-in with Steadman a few weeks ago, and Hazel thought . . .'

'Yes, I can imagine what she thought,' Banks said. For all his virtues, Steadman had certainly been a thorn in the side of some locals. 'What was it this time?' he asked. 'Arguments over land or charges of moral laxity?'

'Sir?'

'Sorry, it doesn't matter,' Banks said. 'Go on. What's the background?'

'She didn't say, sir. Wouldn't. I'm brought in from Wensleydale. Constable Weaver might know something.'

'Yes, of course. Thank you very much, Constable . . . ?'

'Smithies, sir.'

'Thank you very much, Constable Smithies. You did a good job calming her down and getting her to open up like that,' Banks said, then left her blushing in the interview room.

Weaver was on the phone when Banks reached the desk, but he cut the conversation short.

'The weather people from Reckston Moor, sir,' he explained. 'They say it'd be madness to send out search parties on the moors for at least twenty-four hours.'

'Bloody northern weather,' Banks cursed. Hatchley, eavesdropping, grinned and winked at Weaver, who ignored him.

'They don't expect the rain to let up for a while, and the land's boggy. Visibility is as bad as you can get up the valley sides. It's all moorland above there, sir, both ways, miles of it.'

'Yes, I know,' Banks said. 'And there's nothing we can do about it, is there? Just make sure everything's set to go the minute the situation improves. Have you arranged for helicopters?'

'Yes, sir. Superintendent Gristhorpe's handling it. But they can't go out in this weather.'

'No, of course not. Look, you know that girl who was in here a few minutes ago?'

Weaver nodded. 'Hazel Kirk. Yes.'

'Know anything about her father?'

'Robert Kirk. Family's been here for generations. Came from Scotland originally.'

'What does he do?'

'He works at Noble's in Eastvale. You know, the big shoe shop in that new shopping centre near the bus station.'

'I know it. Anything else.'

'He's very active in the local church, sir,' Weaver went on. 'One or two people think he's a bit of a religious nutter, if you know what I mean. Touch of the fire and brimstone. Strong Presbyterian streak – his ancestors brought it with them from Scotland, if you ask me. Anyway, he's always writing letters to the papers about too much sex on television. His latest fad is a campaign to ban rock videos and bring censorship into the music business. There's not much support for that round here though, sir. Nobody really cares one way or another.'

'What's your opinion of him?'

'Nutty but harmless.'

'Certain?'

Weaver nodded. 'Never been in trouble with us, sir. And he is very religious, like. Wouldn't harm a fly.'

'Religious people are often the most violent. Aren't the Iranians religious? Anyway, have a chat with him, would you, and ask him what he argued with Harold Steadman about.'

'There wasn't any argument, sir,' Weaver replied. 'Kirk complained to the headmaster of Eastvale Comprehensive about letting someone with such lax moral standards as Harold Steadman mix with teenage girls.'

'What?'

'It's true, sir,' Weaver went on, grinning. 'He'd seen Steadman with Penny Cartwright now and then, and to Kirk she was nothing less than the whore of Babylon. Remember, he was around when Penny left Helmthorpe in the first place; all those rumours of incest, then the Sodom and Gomorrah of the music business. Steadman would sometimes give Hazel and the other girls a ride home from school, and he'd take them on field trips and invite them to his house. Kirk complained. Nobody took him seriously, of course. I even overheard Steadman and his mates having a good chuckle over the business in the Bridge one night.'

'Why didn't you tell me this before?' Banks asked. There was something in the icy quietness of his tone that sent danger signals to Weaver.

'I— It didn't seem important, sir.'

'Didn't seem important?' Banks repeated. 'We're investigating a murder, laddie. Do you realize that? Everything's important. Even if it's not important it's important if it has anything to do with the victim and his circle. Do you understand?'

'Yes, sir,' Weaver said shakily. 'Will that be all, sir?'

'Is that all?'

'Sir?'

'Is there anything else you ought to tell me?'

'No, sir. I don't think so, sir.'

'Then that's all. Come on, Sergeant Hatchley, let's get back to civilization.'

'Bit rough on him, weren't you, sir?' said Hatchley as they turned up their collars and walked to their cars.

'It won't kill him.'

'Think there's owt in it, this Kirk business?'

'No. No more than there was in the major. Unless Kirk's a serious nutter, and Weaver assures me he isn't. Like nearly everything else in this case, there's just too much damn gossip. That's why it's hard to tell the lies from the truth. Kirk, Major Cartwright – nothing but gossip. Better run a check on his background though, just to make sure. I suppose he thinks Steadman was trying to corrupt his angelic young Hazel.'

'I wouldn't blame him,' Hatchley said. 'The jeans these kids wear nowadays . . . You'd need a bloody shoehorn to get into them.'

Banks laughed. 'Enough lewd thoughts about teenagers, Sergeant.'

'Aye,' Hatchley said. 'It's a bloody good job we can't be arrested for what we think. Look, sir, there's a tobacconist's. And it's open.'

TWO

It was late Sunday afternoon before the rain stopped completely, but the first search parties set out at midmorning. By then it was only drizzling; the clouds had thinned, promising a fine day, and visibility was good. Plenty of locals had been willing to go out on Saturday, despite the weather conditions, but they had been warned against doing so.

The Sunday search was coordinated by Superintendent Gristhorpe, who had marked out areas on Ordnance

Survey maps and assigned these to each small party. He directed operations from the communications room in Eastvale Regional Headquarters, and as the reports came in, he shaded the ground that had been covered.

Meanwhile, enquiries continued in the major cities. In addition to their regular duties, police on car and foot patrols in Newcastle, Leeds, London, Liverpool, Manchester, Birmingham and other large cities were also keeping an eye out for the young blonde girl. Theatres, drama companies and acting schools were all checked carefully, and though numerous sightings were called in and followed up, they all proved to be false. Closer to home, Robert Kirk was investigated, questioned and let go. For one thing, he couldn't drive, and certainly nobody had carried Harold Steadman all the way from Helmthorpe to Crow Scar.

Sally's father, enraged with grief after receiving a letter from the Marion Boyars Academy of Theatre Arts saying they would be pleased to accept Sally as a student, had begun his search alone on Saturday in the rain. The weather so affected his rheumatism and his spirits that he was confined to bed by Dr Barnes the following day. Charles Lumb knew that Sally hadn't run away, despite their differences; anxiety and anger gave way to resignation. Even if the searchers did find her, what state would she be in after three or more nights out in the wilds?

On Sunday, the first area searched was the wide stretch of moorland to the north of Helmthorpe above Crow Scar. Gristhorpe, in making his decision, realized he might have been influenced by the fact that Steadman's body had been found on the northern slopes, but he reasoned that the area was, after all, the wildest spread of countryside – seven miles of rough high moors before the next dale – and had the greatest number of hiding places: old mines, steep quarries, potholes.

The only result of Sunday's effort was an accident in which a police constable drafted in from Askrigg fell down a twenty-foot bell pit. Fortunately, his fall was broken by accumulated water and mud, but it took over two hours of valuable time to rig up ropes and pull him out. Up on the moorland, two small parties got so bogged down in mud that they were unable to continue, and progress everywhere was slow.

By Monday, the sun was out to stay and conditions had improved. Gristhorpe, who had been up since five in the morning, sat red-eyed in the communications room logging check-in calls from search parties, and the map before him soon began to look like a chessboard. This was one task he refused to delegate.

At about three o'clock, the superintendent took Sergeant Rowe's advice and dropped by Banks's office to suggest a walk.

They walked into Market Street, which was crowded with tourists from the nearby cities who, seeing an end to the rain, had decided on an afternoon out. It was also market day, and the cobbled square in front of the church was thronged with colourful stalls selling everything from Marks and Spencer rejects to dinner sets and toilet-bowl brushes. There were stalls of second-hand paperbacks, yards of plain and patterned material – cotton, linen, muslin, rayon, denim, cheesecloth – spilling over almost to the ground, and stalls piled with crockery and cutlery. Skilled vendors drew crowds by shouting out the virtues of their wares as they juggled plates and saucers. The people milled around to listen, take photographs and, occasionally, to buy things. In the narrow twisting side

streets around the central market square – old alleys
where the sun never penetrated and you could shake
hands across second-storey bay windows – the small
souvenir and local delicacy shops with magnifying-glass
windows did good business. Everything, from toffee and
tea to spoons and fluffy toys, was labelled 'Yorkshire', no
matter where it had actually been made.

Gristhorpe directed Banks to a small tea shop and the
two of them settled down to tea and buns.

Gristhorpe ran his hand through his thick messy mop
of grey hair and smiled weakly. 'Had to get out for a bit,'
he said, spooning sugar into his mug. 'It gets so damn
stuffy in that little room.'

'You look all-in,' Banks said, lighting a Benson and
Hedges Special Mild. 'Perhaps you should go home
and get some sleep.'

Gristhorpe grunted and waved away the smoke.
'Thought you'd given that filthy habit up,' he grumbled.
'Anyway, I suppose I am tired. I'm not as young as I used
to be. But it's not just tiredness, Alan. Have you ever
taken part in an operation like this before?'

'Not a search in open country, no. I've looked for
missing teens in Soho, but nothing like this, in these
conditions. Do you think there's any hope?'

Gristhorpe shook his head slowly. 'No. I think the girl's
been killed. Stupid bloody kid. Why couldn't she have
come to us?'

Banks had no answer. 'Have you been involved in this
kind of search before?' he asked.

'More than twenty years ago now,' Gristhorpe said,
adding an extra spoonful of sugar to his tea. 'And this
makes it feel like only yesterday.'

'Who was it?'

'Young girl called Lesley Ann Downey. Only ten. And a lad called John Kilbride, twelve. You'll have heard about all that, though: Brady and Hindley, the Moors Murders?'

'You were in on that?'

'Manchester brought some of us in for the search. It's not that far away, you know. Still, that was different.'

'Sir?'

'Brady and Hindley were involved in Nazism, torture, fetishism – you name it. This time it's more calculated, if we're right. I don't know which is worse.'

'The result's the same.'

'Aye.' Gristhorpe gulped some tea and nibbled at his bun. 'Getting anywhere?'

Banks shook his head. 'Nothing new. Hackett's in the clear now. Barnes, too, by the looks of it. We're stuck.'

'It's always like that when the trail goes cold. You know that as well as I do, Alan. If the answer isn't staring you in the face within twenty-four hours, the whole thing goes stale. When you get stuck you just have to push a bit harder, that's all. Sometimes you get lucky.'

'I've been thinking about the time of Sally Lumb's disappearance,' Banks said, trying to waft his smoke away from Gristhorpe. 'She was last seen on Helmthorpe High Street walking east around nine o'clock on Friday evening.'

'Well?'

'I was in Helmthorpe at that time, in the Dog and Gun with Sandra and a couple of friends. We went to listen to Penny Cartwright sing. Jack Barker was there too.'

'So that lets them off the hook.'

'No, sir. That's just it. She finished her first set just after nine, then she and Barker disappeared from the pub for about an hour.'

'Right after Sally had been seen in the village?'

'Yes.'

'Better follow it up, then. What do you think?'

'I've talked to them both a couple of times. They're difficult, sharp. If I were easily swayed by sentiment, I'd say no, not a chance. Penny Cartwright seems sincere, and Barker's a clever bugger but likeable enough when you take the time to chat to him. He swears blind he'd nothing to do with Steadman's death. But I've met some damn good liars in my time. He's got no alibi and he might have been jealous about Steadman and the Cartwright woman.'

Gristhorpe ate the final few crumbs of his bun and suggested they carry on walking. They headed east and looped down by the river near the terraced gardens.

'The Swain's filling up,' Gristhorpe said. 'I hope we don't have a bloody flood to contend with, too.'

'Does that happen often?'

'Often enough. Usually at spring thaw after a particularly snowy winter. But if you get enough water channelled down from the dales, it might break the banks here.'

They turned up a dank waterside alley, where moss and lichen grew on the rough stone, skirted the base of Castle Hill and arrived back at the market square. Gristhorpe headed straight for the communications room and Banks accompanied him. There was nothing new.

THREE

Even Purcell's 'Hail Bright Cecilia' failed to cheer Banks up as he drove into Helmthorpe that evening. When he walked along High Street past the gift shop with its revolving racks of postcards and the small newsagent's with the evening papers outside fluttering in the light breeze, he could sense the mood of the village. Nothing was obvious; people went about their business as usual, shutting up shop for the day and coming home from work, but it felt like a place that had drawn in on itself. Even the air, despite the wind, seemed tight and grim. The small noises – footsteps, doors opening, distant telephones ringing – sounded eerie and isolated against the backdrop of the silent green valley sides and massive brow of Crow Scar, bright in the evening sun.

Push, Gristhorpe had said, so push he would. Push hard enough, in the right places, and something would give. Push those closest to Steadman – Penny, Ramsden, Emma, Barker – for if none of them had actually done it, Banks was sure that one of them knew who had. He would probably have to revisit Darnley and Talbot too. There was something one of them had said – a chance remark, a throwaway line – that Banks felt was important, but he couldn't remember what it was. It would return to him in time, he knew, but he couldn't afford to sit and wait; he had to push.

Would Sally Lumb have confronted any of them with her evidence? he asked himself as he took the short cut through the cemetery and turned right along the pathway to Gratly. It didn't seem likely; she wasn't a fool. But she had phoned someone, and had used a public call box for privacy. It must, then, have been someone she knew, someone she had no reason to fear.

The sheep on his right fled and stood facing the drystone wall, their backs to him; the ones on his left scampered down the grassy terraces to the stream and stood bleating under the willows. Funny creatures, Banks thought. If they're frightened, they simply run a short distance and turn their backs. It might be effective against people who wish them no harm, but he doubted if it would deter a hungry wolf.

Emma Steadman was watching television but turned the sound down after Banks followed her into the living room. The place was much barer now that most of the books and records were gone; it was more of an empty shell than a home.

Banks waited until Emma had made some tea, then sat opposite her at the low table.

'I've been meaning to ask you a few things for a while now,' he said. 'Mostly to do with the past.'

'The past?'

'Yes. Those wonderful summers you used to have up here when the Ramsden family ran the guest house.'

'What about them? You don't mind, do you?' she asked, picking up some knitting. 'It helps me relax, takes my mind off things. Sorry, go ahead.'

'Not at all. It's just that the impression I got was of your husband running around the dales with Penny Cartwright while Michael Ramsden buried his head in his books.'

Emma smiled but said nothing.

'And you never thought anything of it.'

'Perhaps if you'd known my husband, Chief Inspector, you wouldn't think anything of it, either.'

'But something's missing.'

'What?'

'You. What were you doing?'

Emma sighed and put her knitting down on her lap. 'Contrary to what you seem to believe, I'm not simply a passive housewife. I did have, and still do have, interests of my own. Back in Leeds I was involved in amateur dramatics for a while. On holidays in Gratly I used to knit and read. I even tried my hand at writing a few short stories – unsuccessfully, I'm afraid – but I can't prove it; I threw them away. I also went for walks.'

'Alone?'

'Yes, alone. Is that so strange?'

Banks shrugged.

'What you seem to forget is that we were only up here for a month or so at a time. During that period I spent a lot more time with my husband than you think. I did accompany them sometimes, especially if they went by car. But I'm very susceptible to the sun, so I never ventured far on sunny days unless I could find some shade. I still fail to see why you find all this so fascinating.'

'Sometimes present events have their roots in the past. Did you enjoy your visits?'

'They made a nice break. Leeds isn't the cleanest city in the world, I enjoyed the fresh air, the landscape.'

'One more thing. I've been given to believe that your husband was universally liked. Even Teddy Hackett, who had good reason to disagree with him, thought of him as a friend. Since I've been looking into his death though, I've found at least two people who didn't feel the same way – Major Cartwright and Robert Kirk. We might regard them as cranks, but I'm beginning to wonder if there's anyone else. Someone I don't know about. You were a close group all those years ago, and your husband was still close to Michael Ramsden and Penny Cartwright when he died. Was there anybody else around? Anybody who might have held a grudge?'

Emma Steadman pursed her lips and shook her head slowly.

'Think about it.'

'I am. Of course there were other people around, but I can't imagine any of them had a reason to harm Harold.'

'The point is, Mrs Steadman, that somebody did. And if none of you can help me find out who it was, I don't know who can. Is there any reason why he was killed at this particular time rather than, say, a year ago, or five years ago?'

'I've no idea.'

'You must know something about his affairs. Was he planning to do anything with his money? Write a will, leave it to the National Trust or something? Was there any other land he was after, anyone else's toes he was treading on?'

'No. No to all those questions. And I think I would have known, yes.'

'Well, that doesn't leave much, does it?'

'You think one of us did it, don't you?'

Banks kept silent.

'Do you think I did it? For his money?'

'You couldn't have, could you?'

'Maybe you think Mrs Stanton was lying to give me an alibi?'

'No.'

'Then why keep bothering me? I only buried my husband a few days ago.'

As Banks could think of no answer to that question, he sighed and got up to leave. Before Emma closed the door on him, he turned and spoke again: 'Just consider what I said, will you? Try to remember any enemies your husband might have made, however insignificant they might have seemed at the time. Think about it. I'll be back.'

Penny Cartwright was listening to music, and when

she grudgingly let Banks in, flashing him a 'you again' look, she didn't bother to turn it down.

'I won't keep you,' Banks said, sitting on a hard-backed chair by the window and lighting a cigarette. 'It's just about the other night.'

'What night? There's been a lot lately,' Penny said, pouring herself a drink.

'Friday night.'

'What about it?'

'You were singing at the Dog and Gun, remember?'

Penny scowled at him. 'Of course I remember. You were there too. What is this?'

'Just refreshing your memory. Between sets you went off with Jack Barker. You were gone for about an hour. Where were you?'

'What's that got to do with anything?'

'Look, it's about time you got this right. I ask the questions; you answer. Understand?'

'Oh, poor Inspector Banks,' Penny cooed, 'have I been undermining your authority?' Her eyes challenged him. 'What was the question again?'

'Friday night, between sets. Where were you?'

'We went for a walk.'

'Where?'

'Oh, hither and thither.'

'Can you be more specific?'

'Not really. I go for a lot of walks. There's a lot of places to walk around Helmthorpe. That's why so many tourists come here in summer.'

'Stop the games and tell me where you went.'

'Or else?'

After a thirty-second staring match, Penny looked away and reached for a cigarette.

'All right,' she said. 'We came here.'

'What for?'

'What do you think?'

'Sex?'

'That's not the kind of question a lady answers. And it's nothing to do with your investigation.'

Banks leaned forward and spoke quietly. 'Would it interest you to know that I've got a damned good idea why you came here? And I've got some colleagues back in Eastvale who'd be more than happy to come out here and prove it for me. Help me and you help yourself.'

'I'm not admitting anything.'

'Where were you at four o'clock on Friday afternoon?'

'I was here practising. Why?'

'Anybody with you?'

'No. There usually isn't when I practise.'

'Did you receive any telephone calls?'

Penny looked confused. 'Telephone calls? No. What are you getting at?'

'And you refuse to tell me what you did during the interval on Friday evening?'

'Wait a minute. Sally. Sally Lumb. She disappeared on Friday, didn't she? Christ, you bastard!' She glared at Banks. Angry tears made her eyes glitter. 'Are you implying that I had something to do with that?'

'What did you do?'

'If you already know, why do you want me to tell you?'

'I need to hear it from you.'

Penny sagged in her chair and looked away. 'All right. So we came back here and smoked a couple of joints. Big deal. Is that what you wanted to hear? What are you going to do now, bring in the dogs and tear the place apart?'

Banks stood up to leave. 'I'm not going to do anything.

I remember the difference between the last set and the first, how you seemed more remote, detached. If it's any consolation to you,' he said, opening the door, 'I believe you, and I'm glad I was right.'

But Penny didn't move or say anything to make his exit easier.

FOUR

Later, as Penny lay in bed that night unable to sleep, the images came again, just as they had been coming ever since Harold Steadman's death: those summers so long ago – innocent, idyllic. Or so they had seemed.

It was a time she had had neither reason nor inclination to think about over the past ten years – the kind of period, like an idealized childhood, that one looks back on when one gets older and life loses its edge. Life had been too busy, too exciting, and when she finally had crashed, she had been as far in her mind from idyllic summers as ever a person could be. It had seemed, then, that her earlier life had been lived by somebody else. Next she had come back to Helmthorpe, where they were all together again. Now Harold was dead and that wretched detective was probing, asking questions, churning up memories, like tides stir sand.

So she re-examined it. She reran the walks to Wensleydale along the Pennine Way and the drives to Richmond or the Lake District in Harold's old Morris 1100 like old movies, and she spotted things she had never noticed at the time – little things, vague and unclear, but certainly disturbing. And the more she thought about old times, the less she liked what she was thinking.

She turned over again and tried to cast the images from her mind. They were like dreams, she told herself. She had taken the truth, in all its purity, and warped it in her imagination. That must be what had happened. The problem was that now these dreams seemed so real. She couldn't shake them, and she wouldn't rest until she knew what was fantasy and what was reality. How could the past, something that had really happened, become so altered, so unclear? And as she finally drifted towards sleep, she began to wonder what she should do about it.

11

ONE

The numerous becks that ran down the slopes of Swainsdale to the river were flowing copiously, bringing rainwater from the higher land. A fine mist, like baby's hair, rose from the valley sides as the sun warmed the waterlogged earth. The colours were newly rinsed, too; fresh vibrant greens sloped up from the road, and bright skullcaps of purple heather, softened by the thin veil of mist, fringed the peaks.

Penny, walking with Jack Barker along High Street, was the first to notice a small crowd gathered on the bridge, under which a combination of becks, grown almost to the strength of a river themselves, cascaded from the southern heights down to the Swain.

A woman in a sleeveless yellow dress was pointing up the valley side, and the others followed her gaze, leaning over the low stone parapet. Penny and Barker soon reached the spot and stopped to see what the excitement was. They had an uninterrupted view up the dale side along the beck's course, on to which backed several gardens full of bright flowers. Some distance away they could see what looked like a child's rag doll tumbling recklessly down the swollen stream. It was hypnotic, Penny thought, to watch the thing turn cartwheels and flail, snag on the rocks and break free as the water pushed and dragged it.

Then the woman in the yellow dress put her hand over her mouth and gasped. The others, including Penny, whose long-distance eyesight had never been good, leaned further over and screwed up their eyes to peer more closely. It was only after the shock wave had rippled through the crowd that Penny realized what was happening. It was not a rag doll that came head over heels down the stream, but a body. Tufts of clothing still clung to the torn flesh. It looked raw, like a side of beef in a butcher's window; patches of skin had been ripped clean off, hair torn away from the scalp, and splintered bones stuck through at elbows and shins.

There was no face to recognize, but Penny knew, as did all the other locals on the bridge, that it was the body of Sally Lumb come back to the village where she was born.

Penny wrenched her eyes away while Barker and the others still stared in disbelief. Somebody mentioned an ambulance, somebody else the police, and the group split up in chaos.

Penny and Barker walked in a daze until they got to the Hare and Hounds, then they went inside and ordered double Scotches.

'Seen a ghost?' the barman asked.

'Something like that,' Barker said, and gave a garbled version of what had happened. Soon, customers went streaming out to look, leaving drinks on tables, cardigans and handbags on chairs.

The barman gave them each another double Scotch on the house and rushed off to see himself. The pub was empty; anybody could have walked in and robbed the place blind, but nobody did. Penny downed the fiery whisky; she was aware of her hand gripping Barker's so tight that the nails must have dug into his flesh.

TWO

'It's a bugger, Alan,' Gristhorpe said, rubbing his eyes, which had lost much of their childlike innocence through lack of sleep. He looked tired, pale and hurt, as if the whole affair, done right on his doorstep, was a personal affront. 'A bugger . . .'

They were in the Queen's Arms opposite the station, and it was almost afternoon closing time. Only a few dedicated drinkers and tourists in need of a late sandwich and shandy sat scattered around the lounge.

'We've got nothing so far,' the superintendent went on, sniffing as Banks lit a cigarette. 'The body was so bloody waterlogged and badly battered Glendenning couldn't give us any idea of what killed her. For all he can say, she might have fallen in and hit her head, or just drowned. A full autopsy's going to take time, and even then they can't promise owt.'

'What's Glendenning doing now?'

'You know him, Alan – couldn't wait to get at it. Stomach contents, organs, tissue samples. God knows, they've got to keep looking. It could even be poison.'

'What do you think?' Banks asked, sipping his pint of Theakston's bitter.

Gristhorpe shook his head. 'I don't know. They've got their jobs to do. Does it matter what killed her at this point? If we're right, and it's what we think it is, there was probably just a blow to the head, like Steadman. Glendenning might not even be able to verify that.'

'I just wish we knew a bit more about why it happened,' Banks said. 'Certainly I think there's a connection to the Steadman case – has to be – I just don't know what it is. The girl knew something and instead of coming to me she confronted the killer. I suppose she wasn't sure and simply wanted to find out for herself. Add it all up and we've still got nothing. So she knew something. What? She phoned someone. Who? Why? They met. Where?'

'We might be able to answer that last one soon,' Gristhorpe said. 'I've got men following the becks all the way up the hillside looking for physical evidence. There'll be some kind of grisly map of her progress.'

THREE

'That's scotched work for today,' Jack Barker punned weakly as he accepted his third refill from Penny. It was over two hours since they had seen the wreckage of Sally Lumb tumble down the valley side. Penny had stopped after her second drink, but Barker was still at it.

'Maybe you shouldn't,' Penny warned him.

'It's already too late. Thanks for your concern, though.'

When Penny looked down at Barker, she felt the stirring of something like love. Whatever it was, the feeling disoriented her and she was angry with herself for not knowing what to do. Though it had felt good at first when they had come back to the cottage and he had held her, she hated the feelings of weakness that came with it. She knew that her feelings for him were not platonic, but instead of reaching out, she drew in and strengthened her shell.

Barker seemed to sense something of her chaotic emotions, she thought, when he reached out again for her hand, which she allowed him to hold lightly.

'I suppose I always did have a weak stomach,' he said.

'Pathetic really, isn't it? Here I am writing about blood and guts for a living and as soon as I see . . .' His words trailed off and he started to shake. He put his glass on the table, spilling some Scotch as he did so. Then Penny sat beside him and held him. It seemed ages to her before either of them moved, and each would have said the other broke away first.

'You should get some sleep, Jack,' Penny said softly.

'What the hell's going on, Penny?' he asked. 'What's happening to this place?'

'I don't know,' Penny answered, stroking his hair. 'At least, I . . .'

'What?'

'Nothing,' she said. 'Or maybe nothing. I don't know. But it's got to stop.'

FOUR

'Under a packhorse bridge,' Banks said. 'That's what the super told me. On the south slope.'

'What does that mean?' Sandra asked. They were having an early evening drink in the Queen's Arms. Sandra had just finished shopping, and Banks had suggested that, as they had seen so little of one another the past few days, they meet for a chat. Brian and Tracy were old enough to manage on their own for an hour or two.

'It means he was wrong about where to look first, and he's kicking himself for that.'

'But he couldn't have known,' Sandra said. 'It made perfect sense to look on the north side first.'

'That's what everyone says, but you know what he's like.'

'Yes. Just like you. Stubborn. Takes it all on himself.'

'He'll get over it,' Banks said. 'Anyway, they found clothes fibres on the stones under this bridge. She must have been hidden there and covered with stones. Then when the heavy rains came, some of the stones were washed aside and she was carried down the valley. They've not found any traces above the bridge, and it looked like an ideal place – isolated but accessible by car, just.'

'Does it help, finding the body?'

'Not really. Not the state it's in. And too much time has gone by. We'll ask around of course – anybody heading that way, or back – but we can't expect too much. Whoever we're dealing with is smart, and he's not likely to make silly mistakes.'

'This probably had to be done in a hurry, though,' Sandra reminded him. 'There wouldn't have been much time for planning.'

'Still, it's not going to be easy.'

'Is it ever?'

Banks shrugged and lit a cigarette.

'By the way,' Sandra said. 'I haven't had a chance to say so before now, but I'm glad you got rid of that bloody pipe.'

'It didn't suit me.'

'No.'

'Too *Country Life*?'

Sandra laughed. 'Yes, I'd say so. You'd not fool many, though. Least of all yourself.'

'There's not many would say they're glad to see a person smoke, either,' Banks said, holding out the pack while Sandra, an occasional smoker, helped herself. 'But I do intend to cut down and stick to these mild things.'

'Promises!'

'The girl, you know,' Banks said after a brief pause, 'was a virgin as far as forensic could make out. Hadn't been shot, stabbed, poisoned or sexually assaulted. Virgin.'

'I wonder if that's a good thing,' Sandra asked.

'What? That she hadn't been assaulted?'

'No. That she died a virgin.'

'It won't make any difference to her now, poor beggar,' said Banks. 'And I doubt it's the kind of thing they inscribe on tombstones. But at least we can be sure she wasn't tormented or tortured. She probably died very quickly, without even knowing what was happening.'

'Are you going to get the killer soon, Alan?' Sandra asked, swirling the smooth fragments of ice in the bottom of her glass. 'And don't treat me like a reporter. Be honest.'

'I'd like to say yes, but we've got so damn little to go on. We can trace the girl's movements until about nine o'clock Friday evening, and that's it.'

'While we were at the folk club?'

'Yes.'

Sandra shivered. 'We were so close.'

'Does that make a difference?'

'It's just a funny feeling, that's all. What about the writer and the singer?'

'She could be protecting him, or they could be working together. It's hard to know what to believe when things are clouded by so much gossip. The others all go back so far, too. Lord knows what complex webs of feelings they've set up between one another over the years. It seems to me that in a place like Helmthorpe emotions go deeper and last longer than in a big city.'

'Nonsense. Think about all those feuds and gang rivalries in London.'

'That's business, in a way. I mean the ordinary things between people.'

'Who had the best motive?' Sandra asked.

'The one with the least opportunity.' Banks smiled at the irony. 'That's if you call a lot of money a good motive. There could also be all kinds of jealousies involved. That's why I can't leave Barker and Penny Cartwright out of it altogether.'

'The wife inherits?'

'Yes.'

'She came in for some bridge work yesterday.'

'What did you think of her?'

'I didn't see much of her, really. Only when she came to the window to confirm her appointment. She seemed quite an attractive woman.'

'She didn't look much to me.'

'That's typical of a man,' Sandra said. 'All you can see is the surface.'

'But you must admit she's let herself go.'

'It looks like it, yes,' Sandra said slowly. 'But I don't think so. It's all there. She's fine under all those awful clothes. Her bone structure's good, too. Of course, if you'd known her before or not seen her for a long time, she'd definitely look as if she'd gone downhill, I suppose.'

'A pretty young thing.'

'Pardon?'

'Oh, nothing,' Banks said. 'Just remembering something. Go on.'

'All I'm saying is the potential's there for her to be an attractive woman. She can't be much older than me.'

'Late thirties.'

'Well, then. She must only look plain because she wants to, because it doesn't matter to her. Not all women are obsessed with their looks, you know. Perhaps there are other things more important to her.'

'Perhaps. What you're saying,' Banks went on slowly, 'is that with the right hairstyle, good clothes and a little make-up . . .'

'She could be quite a stunner, yes.'

FIVE

Penny was at the stove roasting spices for a curry when Barker made his way down the narrow stairs.

'So, the sleeper awakes,' she greeted him.

'What time is it?'

'Seven o'clock.'

'At night?'

'Yes. It's still the same day. Hungry? I shouldn't think so, with a hangover like you must have. Anyway, I'm making a curry. Take it or leave it.'

'Your generosity and grace overwhelm me,' Barker said. 'As a matter of fact, I don't feel too bad. I've just got a hell of a headache.'

'Aspirin's in the bathroom cabinet.'

'What happened?' Barker asked.

'You mean you don't remember?'

'Not after the third drink. Or was it the fourth?' He rubbed his eyes with his knuckles.

'You really don't remember?' Penny repeated, sounding shocked. 'Well, that's a fine compliment, isn't it?'

'You mean . . . ?'

Penny laughed. 'Don't be a fool, Jack. I'm only kidding. You got tired and I helped you upstairs to sleep it off. That's all.'

'All?'

'Yes. You don't think I'd fall into bed with you the way you were earlier, do you?'

'I'll get some aspirin,' Jack said, and made his painful way back upstairs to the bathroom.

'We'll let that simmer for a while,' Penny said when he came back, 'and have a sit-down. Drink?'

'My God, no!' Barker groaned. 'But on the other hand, hair of the dog and all that. Not whisky, though.'

'Beer do?'

'Yes.'

'Sam Smith's?'

'Fine.'

'Good. It's all I've got. Chilled too.'

Penny got the beer and Barker sat on the sofa drinking out of the bottle.

'What you said, Penny,' he began, 'about not, you know, sleeping with me in a state like that . . .'

'I doubt you'd have been able to get it up, would you?' she mocked, a mischievous smile crinkling the corners of her mouth.

'I might be a bit slow,' Barker replied, 'but are you implying that if I'd been sober . . . I mean, you might actually . . . you know?'

Penny put her finger to his lips and stopped him. 'That's for me to know and you to find out,' she said.

'Dammit, Penny,' he said, 'you can't just ignore me half the time and then tease me the rest. It's not fair. I'm upset enough as it is about the girl floating down and all that.'

'I'm sorry, Jack. It just doesn't come out right. I stop one game and start another, don't I?'

'That's how it seems. Why don't you give me a straight answer?'

'What's the question?'

'I've already asked you.'

'Oh, that. I'm glad you were drunk, Jack, because no, I don't think I would have. Is that straight enough?'

'It seems to be,' Barker said, disappointment clear in his tone.

Penny went on quickly, 'It's not as simple as you think. What I mean is, I'm glad I wasn't forced into making a decision there and then. I'm weak, I might have said yes and regretted it. It would have been so easy then, so natural to make love after being confronted with death. But I wouldn't have been able to get Sally out of my mind, that awful torn body . . .'

'I understand that. But why would you regret it?'

Penny shrugged. 'Lots of reasons. So much has happened. It's too quick, too soon. It would be easy to jump into bed with you. You're an attractive man. But I want more than that, Jack. I don't just want to be like one of the bimbos you sleep with when you're down in London publicizing your books.'

'I don't, and you never could be.'

'Whatever. I've had enough disappointments in my life. I want some stability. I know it sounds conventional and corny, but I want to settle down, and I think I might be better off doing it by myself. I'm not one of these women who depends on a man.'

'It's just as well; I'm hardly dependable.' Barker lit a cigarette and coughed. 'Look,' he said. 'I don't care whether this is the right place and time or what it is, but

I love you, Penny. That's what I'm trying to get at. Not whether you'll sleep with me or not. There, I've said it. Maybe I've made a fool of myself.'

Penny looked at him carefully for a long time, then she said, 'I don't know if I can handle being in love.'

'Try it,' Barker said, leaning forward and stroking her hair. 'You never know, you might like it.'

Penny looked away. Barker moved closer and took her in his arms. She tensed, but didn't break the embrace.

Finally, she disengaged herself and looked at him seriously. 'Don't expect too much of me,' she said. 'I'm used to fending for myself and I like it.'

'You and I,' Jack said, 'we've been living alone so long it's frightening to think about change. So let's just take it easy, slowly.'

A bell rang in the kitchen.

'That's telling me the curry's ready.' Penny got up.

Barker followed her into the kitchen and leaned in the narrow doorway as she stirred the pungent sauce. 'Do you know,' he said, 'it took that bloody policeman, as you call him, to make me realize that I was jealous of you and Harry. I wondered, why the hell should you give so much of yourself to him and so little to me?'

'That's not fair, Jack.' Penny's face darkened as she turned to him. 'Don't talk like that. You sound just like Banks.'

'I'm sorry,' Barker apologized. 'I didn't mean anything by it.'

'Forget it.'

'The past won't go away, Penny,' Barker said. 'There's a lot of things need explaining.'

'Like what?' Penny asked suspiciously, taking the pot off the ring.

'You know more about it than I do.'

'More about what?'

'Everything that's happened. Come on, Penny, don't tell me you haven't got any ideas. You know more about this business than you're letting on.'

'Why should you think that?'

'I don't really know,' Barker answered. 'It's just that you've been awfully mysterious and touchy about it these past few days.'

Penny turned back to the curry in silence.

'Well?' Barker asked.

'Well what?'

'Do you?'

'Do I what?'

'Oh come on. You know what I mean. Do you know something I don't?'

'How do I know what you know?'

'I don't know anything. Do you?'

'Of course not,' Penny said, putting the curry into dishes. 'It's your imagination, Jack. You writers! Don't you think if I knew something I'd tell you?'

'As a matter of fact, I don't. Sally Lumb didn't tell anyone either. Or she told the wrong person.'

'And you think it was me?'

'Don't be ridiculous.'

'Go on, you might as well say it,' Penny shouted, brandishing the spoon like a club. 'Just like Banks. Go on!'

'I don't know what you're talking about.'

'Friday evening, when she disappeared.'

'But we were in the Dog and Gun.'

'Not all the time.'

'So? You came home for a rest and I went for a walk. So what?'

'You don't know?'

'Know what?'

'Banks hasn't been to pester you?'

'About what?'

'That's when Sally was last seen. While we were away. Somebody saw her in High Street about nine o'clock.'

'So Banks thinks . . . ?'

Penny shrugged. 'He asked me. You?'

'No. I've not seen him for a few days.'

'You will. He's getting very pushy.'

'I suppose he must be desperate. Surely you don't think I was implying you had anything to do with it?'

'Well, weren't you?'

'I'd hardly declare my undying love to someone I thought was a murderess, would I?'

Penny smiled.

'And what about you?' he went on. 'Do you believe me?'

'About what?'

'That I just went for a walk.'

'Well, yes. Of course I do. I don't even remember how all this started.'

'I was simply asking you if you knew anything you hadn't told me. That's all.'

'And I thought I'd answered that,' Penny said, her dark eyes narrowing. 'I've been no more mysterious about it than you have.'

'Oh come off it, Penny. You can't get out of it that easily. You've been around here much longer than I have. You're bound to know more about what goes on than I do.'

'You seem to be treating me like a criminal, Jack. Is this your idea of love? If this is what it comes down to, just how bloody jealous were you?'

'Forget it.' Barker sighed. 'Just forget I opened my mouth.'

'I'd like to, Jack. I really would.'

They eyed each other warily, then Penny broke off to carry the bowls through to the dining table. She pushed one towards Barker, who sat down to eat.

'You've put me in a right mood for a romantic candle-light dinner, you have,' she complained. 'I'm not even hungry now.'

'Try some,' Barker said, offering her a spoonful. 'It's very good.'

'I've lost my appetite.' Penny reached for a cigarette, then changed her mind and picked up her jacket. 'I'm going out.'

'But you can't,' Barker protested. 'We've got a lot to talk about. What about the candles? You've made dinner.'

'Eat it yourself,' Penny told him, opening the door. 'Eat the bloody candles too, for all I care.'

Barker half rose from the table. 'But where are you going?'

'To see a man about a dog,' she said, and slammed the door behind her.

SIX

Though the sun still lingered low on the horizon, it was dark on Market Street in the shadow of the buildings on the western side, and the cobbled square was deserted. Banks hadn't even bothered to turn on his office light after returning to go over his notes. Sandra had gone home to assure Brian and Tracy that they weren't becoming latchkey children. The door was closed and the dark room was full of smoke. Occasionally he heard footsteps in the corridor outside, but nobody seemed to know he was there.

As was his habit when a case felt near to its end, he sat by the window smoking and rearranged the details in his mind four or five times. After about an hour things still looked the same. The pattern, the picture, was complete, and however unbelievable it was, it had to be right. Eliminate the impossible and whatever is left, however improbable, must be the truth. Or so Sherlock Holmes had said.

It was time for action.

Banks played no music as he drove towards the purplish-red sunset west along Swainsdale; his mind was far too active to take in anything more. Finally he swung up the hill to Gratly, turned sharp left after the bridge and pulled up outside the Steadman house. There were no lights on. Banks cursed and walked down the path to Mrs Stanton's.

'Oh, hello Inspector,' she greeted him. 'I didn't expect to see you again. Please come in.'

'Thank you very much,' Banks said, 'but I don't think I will. I'm a bit pushed for time. If you could just answer a couple of quick questions?'

Mrs Stanton frowned and nodded.

'First of all, have you any idea where Mrs Steadman is?'

'No, I haven't. I think I heard her car about an hour or so ago, but I've no idea where she was going.'

'Did you see her?'

'No, I wasn't looking. Even if I was it wouldn't matter, though. They've got a door from the kitchen goes straight into the garage. Money,' she said. 'They've even got those automatic doors. Just press a button.'

'Which direction did she drive off in?'

'Well, she didn't come past here.'

'So she went east?'

'Aye.'

'Do you remember that Saturday you spent watching television with her?' Mrs Stanton nodded slowly. 'Do you know if she went out again after she got home?'

Mrs Stanton shook her head. 'I certainly didn't hear her, and I was up for more than an hour pottering around.'

'Last Friday night, did she go out at all?'

'Couldn't tell you, Inspector. That was my bingo night.'

'Your husband?'

'Pub. As usual.'

'This was a regular Friday night arrangement?'

'Ha! For him it's a reg'lar every night arrangement.'

'And you?'

'Aye, I go to bingo every Friday. So does half of Swainsdale.'

'Mrs Steadman?'

'Never. Not her. Not that she's a snob, mind. What pleases some folks leaves others cold. Each to his own is what I say.'

'Thank you very much, Mrs Stanton,' Banks said, leaving her mystified as he got back into the Cortina and set off toward Helmthorpe.

He parked illegally in High Street by the church, right at the bottom of Penny's street. There was a light on in her front room. Banks walked quickly up the path and knocked.

He was surprised when Jack Barker answered the door.

'Come in, Chief Inspector,' Barker said. 'Penny's not

here, I'm afraid. Or have you come to ask me where I was on Friday evening?'

Banks ignored the taunt; he had no time for games. 'Has she said anything odd lately about the Steadman business?' he asked.

Puzzled, Barker shook his head. 'No. Why?'

'Because I got the impression she was holding something back. Something she might not have been sure about herself. I was hoping I could persuade her to tell me what it was.'

Barker lit a cigarette. 'As a matter of fact,' he said, 'Penny has been a bit strange the few times I've seen her lately. Secretive and touchy. She hasn't said anything, though.'

Banks sat down and began tapping the frayed arm of the chair. 'You two,' he said, looking around the room. 'Are you . . . er . . . ?'

'Playing house? Not really. No such luck. I was here for dinner. We just had a bit of a row about the very thing you just mentioned, actually. She left and I'm waiting for her to come back.'

'Oh?'

'I suggested she knew more than she was letting on, and she accused me of treating her like a criminal, just like you did.'

'That's what she thinks?'

'Well, you have been giving her a rough time; you can't deny it.'

Banks looked at his watch. 'Is she coming back soon?'

'I've no idea.'

'No idea? Where is she?'

'I told you,' Barker said. 'We had a row and she stormed out.'

'Where to?'

'I don't know.'

'Did she say anything?'

'She said she was going to see a man about a dog.'

'A lot of help that is.'

'Just what I thought.'

'And you'd been on at her about knowing something?'

'Yes.'

'Did she take the car?'

'Yes.'

'Right.' Banks got to his feet. 'Come on.'

Without thinking, Barker jumped up and obeyed the command. Banks only gave him time to blow out the candles and lock the door.

'Look, what's going on?' Barker asked as they shot into the darkening dale. 'You're driving like a bloody lunatic. Is something wrong? Is Penny in danger?'

'Why should she be?'

'For Christ's sake, I don't know. But you're behaving damned oddly, if you ask me. What the hell's happening?'

Banks didn't reply. He focused all his concentration on driving, and the silence intensified as darkness grew. On the northern outskirts of Eastvale, he turned on to the York Road.

'Where are we going?' Barker asked a few minutes later.

'Almost there,' Banks replied. 'And I want you to do exactly as I say. Remember that. I've only brought you with me because I know you're fond of Penny and you happened to be in her house. I'd no time to waste, and you might be some use, but do as I say.' He broke off to overtake a lorry.

Barker gripped the dashboard. 'So you've not brought me along for the pleasure of my company?'

'Give me a break.'

'Seriously, Chief Inspector, is she in danger?'

'I don't know. I don't know what we're going to find. Don't worry, though, it won't be long now,' he said, and the tyres squealed as he turned sharp left. About a quarter of a mile along the bumpy minor road, Banks pulled into a driveway and Barker pointed and said, 'That's her car. That's Penny's car.'

A face peered through a chink in the curtains as they jumped out of the Cortina and hurried towards the door.

'No time for pleasantries,' Banks said after trying the handle to no avail. He stood back and gave a hard kick, which splintered the wood around the lock and sent the door flying open. With Barker close behind, he rushed into the living room and quickly took in the strange tableau.

There were three people. Michael Ramsden stood facing Banks, white-faced and slack-jawed. Penny lay inert on the couch. And a woman stood with her back to them all.

In a split second, it came to life. Barker gasped and ran over to Penny, and Ramsden started to shake.

'My God,' he groaned, 'I knew this would happen. I knew it.'

'Shut up!' the woman said, and turned to face Banks.

She wore a clinging red dress that accentuated her curves; her hair was drawn back into a tight V on her forehead and carefully applied blusher highlighted the cheekbones of her heart-shaped face. But the most striking thing about her was her eyes. Before, Banks had only seen them watery and distorted through thick lenses, but now she was wearing contacts they were the chilly green of moss on stones, and the power that shone through them was hard and piercing. It was Emma Steadman, transformed almost beyond recognition.

Ramsden collapsed into an armchair, head in hands, whimpering, while Emma continued to glare at Banks.

'You bastard,' she said, and spat at him. 'You ruined it all.' Then she lapsed into a silence he never heard her break.

12

ONE

But Ramsden talked as willingly as a sinner in the confessional, and what he said over the first two hours following his arrest gave the police enough evidence to charge both of them. Banks was astonished at Ramsden's compulsion to unburden himself, and realized only then what terrible pressure the man must have been under, what inner control he must have exerted.

As for Penny, she said she had been doing a great deal of thinking over the last few days. Steadman's death, Banks's questions and Sally's disappearance had all forced her to look more deeply into a past she had ignored for so long, and especially into the events of a summer ten years ago.

At first she remembered nothing. She hadn't lied; everything had seemed innocent to her. But then, she said, the more she found herself dwelling on the memory, the more little things seemed to take on greater significance than they had done at the time. Glances exchanged between Emma Steadman and Michael Ramsden – had they really happened or were they just her imagination? Ramsden's insistent overtures, then his increasing lack of interest – again, had it really happened that way? Was there, perhaps, a simple explanation? All these things had inflamed her curiosity.

Finally, after the argument with Jack Barker, she knew it wouldn't all just go away. She had to do something or her doubts about the past would poison any chance of a future. So she went to visit Ramsden to find out if there was any truth in her suspicions.

Yes, she knew what had happened to Sally Lumb and she also knew the police linked the girl's death to Steadman's, but she honestly didn't believe she had anything to fear from Michael Ramsden. After all, they'd known each other off and on since childhood.

She questioned Ramsden and, finding his responses nervous and evasive, pushed even harder. They drank tea and ate biscuits, and Ramsden tried to convince her that there was nothing in her fears. Eventually she found difficulty focusing; the room darkened and she felt as if she were looking at it through the wrong end of a telescope. Then Penny fell asleep. When she awoke she was in Barker's arms and it was all over.

Banks told her that Ramsden had sworn he wouldn't have hurt her. True, he had drugged her with some prescription Nembutal and driven to the public telephone on the main road to send for Emma, but only because he was confused and didn't know what to do. When Emma had insisted that they would have to kill Penny because she knew too much, Ramsden claimed that he had tried to stand up to her. She had called him weak and said she would do what was necessary if he wasn't man enough. She said it would be easy to arrange an accident. According to Ramsden, they were still arguing when Banks and Barker arrived.

Penny listened to all this at about one o'clock in the morning over a pot of fresh coffee in Banks's smoky office. All she could say when he had finished was, 'I was right, wasn't I? He wouldn't have hurt me.'

Banks shook his head. 'He would,' he insisted, 'if Emma Steadman told him to.'

TWO

It was a couple of days before all the loose ends were tied up. Hatchley made notes and wrote up the statements, complaining all the while about DC Richmond sunning himself in Surrey, and Gristhorpe went over the details. Emma Steadman said nothing; she didn't even bother to deny Ramsden's accusations. To Banks, she was a woman who had risked everything and lost. There was no room for regret or recrimination now it was all over.

Later in the week, Banks took Sandra over to Helm-thorpe, where they heard Penny sing at a special memorial concert for Sally Lumb. Afterwards, as it was a warm night and the show ended early, they went with Penny and Jack Barker for a drink in the beer garden of the Dog and Gun. Crow Scar gathered the failing light and gleamed as the hills around it fell into shadow. It looked like a pale curtain hanging in the sky.

Sandra and the others pressed Banks for an explan-ation of the Steadman business, and though he felt very uncomfortable in the role they forced on him, he did feel he owed Barker and Penny something; nor had he had much time to talk to Sandra since the arrests, and she had helped him arrive at the correct pattern.

'When did it start?' Sandra asked first.

'About ten years back,' Banks told her. 'That makes Penny here sixteen, Michael Ramsden eighteen, Steadman about thirty-three and his wife just twenty-eight. Harold Steadman had a promising career as a university lecturer.

If he wasn't exactly rich, he was certainly comfortably off, and he did have the inheritance to look forward to. Emma too, must have been quite pleased with life in those days, but I imagine she quickly got bored. She was beginning to fade into the background like so many faculty wives.

'When I talked to Talbot and Darnley, two of Steadman's colleagues at Leeds University, one of them remembered Emma as a "pretty young thing" at first, then she just seemed to disappear into the woodwork. I dare say she'd have liked to go abroad for her holidays more often, but no, Steadman had discovered Helmthorpe – Gratly rather – and that satisfied all his requirements for a busman's holiday, so that was that. For Emma, life seemed to be passing by too quickly and too dully, and she felt too young to give it all up.'

'That summer was beautiful, just like this one.' Banks paused to look around at the other drinkers with their jackets and cardigans hung on the backs of chairs. 'How often can you do this in England?' he asked, sipping chilled lager. 'Especially in Yorkshire. Anyway, Penny and Michael were the pride of the village – two bright kids with their whole lives ahead of them. Michael was a lean serious romantic young fellow, and if he imagined he was losing Penny to an older wiser man, then he still had a steady diet of Keats and Shelley to keep him nicely melancholy. Penny here simply enjoyed Steadman's company, as she's told me often enough. They had a lot in common, and there were no amorous inclinations on either side. Or if there were, they were well repressed.'

He glanced at Penny, who looked down into her beer.

'So,' Banks went on after a deep breath, 'one sunny day Penny's out with Steadman looking at the Roman excavations in Fortford say, and Michael's languishing in the garden reading "Ode to a Nightingale" or something. His parents are out shopping in Leeds or York and won't be back till it's time to prepare the evening meal. Emma Steadman is moping around the place staying out of the sun, and probably feeling bored and neglected. I'm making this up, by the way. Ramsden didn't give me a blow by blow account. Anyway, Emma seduces young Michael. Not so difficult when you consider his age and his obsession with sex. Surely it's every schoolboy's fantasy – the experienced older woman. To Emma, he must have seemed like a younger more vital version of her husband. Perhaps he wrote poetry for her. He was certainly gawky and shy, and she gave him his first sexual experience.

'Most people probably thought of Emma Steadman as a married woman going quickly to seed, but Michael made her feel wanted, and then she began to see definite advantages in not being thought particularly attractive. That way, nobody would think of her as the type to be having an affair.'

Banks stopped to drink some more lager, pleased to see that he hadn't lost his audience. 'The affair went on over the years,' he continued. 'There were gaps and breaks, of course, but Ramsden told us they often got together in London when Emma went down for a weekend's "shopping", or when she went to "Norwich" to "visit her family". I don't think her husband paid her a great deal of attention, he was far too busy poring over ruins.

'Anyway, Emma developed a powerful hold over Michael. As his first lover, she had a natural advantage. She taught him all he knew. And he was still shy in company and found it hard to meet girls his own age. But why bother? Emma was there and she gave him all he needed, far more than the inexperienced girls of his own age group could have given him. And, in turn, he made her feel young, sexy and powerful. They fed off each other, I suppose.

'Over the years, Emma developed two distinct personalities. Now I'm not suggesting for a moment that she's mentally ill – there's nothing at all clinically wrong with her – all her actions were deliberate, willed, calculated. But she had one face for the world and another for Ramsden. If you think about it, it wasn't that difficult for her to change her appearance. She only had to do it to please Ramsden, and he was strongly under her influence anyway. Visiting him in London would have been no problem, of course. But even after she moved to Gratly and he moved to York, it was simple enough. She could easily do herself up a bit in the car on the way to see him – a little make-up, a hairbrush. She could even change her clothes after she arrived, if she wanted. With Harold gone, it was even easier. Her neighbour told me there's a door from the kitchen right into the garage, and it's a lonely road over the moors to Ramsden's place. But it wasn't just looks, it was attitude, too. With Ramsden she felt her sexual power, something that was more or less turned off the rest of the time.

'As time went by, everything she expected to happen, happened. Steadman threw himself more and more into his work, and she found herself, except for Ramsden, increasingly isolated. Why did she stay with her husband? I'm only guessing here, but I can think of two good reasons. First of all security, and secondly the promise of the inheritance, the possibility that things might improve when they became rich. And what happens? The money comes through all right, but nothing changes. In fact, things get worse. And here I can sympathize with her, to some extent. She's a woman with dreams – travel, excitement, wealth, a social life – but all that happens is her husband buys the Ramsden house and she ends up even more bored and cut off while he spends the money on historical research. A dedicated man. Even though I can't condone what she did to him, I can understand why she was driven to it. Steadman wasn't exactly sensitive to her needs, emotional or material. He was selfish and mean. There they were, rich as bloody Croesus, and he spends his time drinking in the Bridge and his money on his work. I'm sure Emma Steadman would have preferred the country club. In fact she was little more than a prisoner, and the only person her husband was really close to was Penny again.'

'That's not quite true,' Penny said. 'He was close to Michael. He liked him.'

'Yes,' Banks agreed. 'But that was much more of a working relationship. Michael was of use to him. I think they were colleagues, or partners, rather than friends. Don't forget, Michael killed him.'

'She made him.'

'Yes, but he did it.'

A waiter came out and they ordered another round.

'Go on,' Penny urged him after the drinks arrived.

'Michael Ramsden is ambitious but he's weak. He's not good with people. He shared Steadman's interests, yes, but he wasn't obsessed – a word that offended one of Steadman's colleagues, but apt, I think. Also, Ramsden resented Harold Steadman, and this really had nothing to do with you, Penny, even if he did feel jealous all those years ago. No, he resented Steadman in the way many of us come to detest people we first set up as examples, models, call them what you will. He hated always playing second fiddle – the publisher, the assistant – never the creative one, the leader, although he was busy working on a novel himself. Emma must have played on this, I think, dwelling on her husband's bad points when she was with Ramsden, playing on Michael's growing resentment towards his mentor. Soon he began to recognize Steadman's meanness and his lack of consideration for anybody with interests other than his own. I think too that he was always, deep down, irritated at the way Harold could communicate so easily with Penny, how fond they were of one another. Anyway, this animosity grew and grew over the years, fuelled by sexual desire for Emma, and finally there came a chance to get rich, to take it all.

'Emma Steadman used Ramsden, manipulated him without a doubt. But that doesn't absolve him from blame. Slowly, she introduced the idea of murder to him, helped him over his initial resistance and nervousness. She did this partly by playing on his existing feelings about her husband, and partly through sex. Denial, satisfaction. More denial, greater satisfaction than he'd ever had before. That's what he told me, anyway. He's not a fool; he knew what was happening and he went along with it. Together, they killed Harold Steadman.

'Naturally, as Emma stood to inherit, she'd be the first suspect so she had to be sure of an airtight alibi, which she had. Also, Ramsden seemed to have neither motive nor opportunity, no matter how I went at him, until the connection with Emma finally came into focus. There were also a number of other possibilities I had to pursue.'

Both Barker and Penny looked at him reprovingly as he said this.

'Yes,' he went on, acknowledging them. 'You two.

Hackett, for a while. Barnes. Even the major and Robert Kirk, fleetingly. Believe me, I blame myself for not arriving at the answer before Sally Lumb had to die, too, but I couldn't see the truth for the gossip, or the past for the present.'

'Why did Sally have to die?' Barker asked. 'Surely she couldn't have been a threat? What could she have known?'

'Sally was older than her years in many ways,' Banks replied. 'She misread the situation. But I'll get back to her a bit later. On the Saturday that Steadman was killed, Ramsden drove close to Gratly. He parked his car in one of those derelict old barns on the minor road just east of the Steadman house, the one Emma always used to get to York. Remember, Ramsden had been brought up in Gratly; he knew every twist and dip in the dale.'

'But how did he get back?' Penny asked. 'It's an impossibly long walk, and the only bus to Eastvale goes early in the morning.'

'Easy,' Banks answered. 'He wouldn't have taken the bus anyway; too many people might have noticed him. Emma Steadman drove him back. She picked him up on the road at a prearranged time – a fairly isolated spot so there'd be no chance of their being seen. Then she dropped him off at the end of his lane and went shopping in York. We've checked on that now, and her neighbour remembers it because Emma brought back some material she'd asked for. There was nothing unusual in all that. Emma Steadman often spent afternoons shopping in York. After all, she was a lady of leisure. They just had to be careful not to be seen. And even if they had been, Ramsden looked enough like Steadman from a distance through a car window, so nobody would have thought twice about seeing them.'

'What about that night?' Penny asked. 'After Harry had the row with my father?'

'That's another thing hindsight tells me I should have known,' Banks answered. 'There was only one place Steadman would have gone after the argument, and that's exactly where he intended to go in the first place, to Ramsden's. Remember he was a dedicated man, and you, Penny, were the only person he allowed to make emotional inroads into his valuable time. So he did exactly what he intended; he drove to York. And Ramsden killed him.

'It was all planned in advance, perhaps even rehearsed. Ramsden already had plastic sheeting on the floor because he was painting his living room. He hit Steadman from behind with a hammer, wrapped his body in the sheet, bundled it in the boot of Steadman's own car, drove it up near Crow Scar and buried it. He couldn't bury him in the plastic because that might have given too much away, but he told us where he buried it and we've dug it up.'

Penny put her head in her hands and Barker put his arms around her.

'I'm sorry, Penny,' Banks said. 'I know it sounds brutal, but it was.'

Penny nodded and took a sip of her drink, then reached for a cigarette. 'I know,' she said. 'It's not your fault. I'm sorry to be such a crybaby. It's just the shock. Please go on.'

'It was well after midnight and the village was deserted. He put Steadman's car back in the car park, cut through the graveyard and over the beck, then drove his own car home to York. All he had to worry about was getting stopped on the way, but the road he chose made

that most unlikely. As I said, the whole thing was carefully planned to throw all suspicion away from Ramsden
and Emma Steadman, who had the best motive. It even
helped them that Steadman's car was a beige Sierra.
They're quite common around here. I looked in the car
park myself yesterday and saw three of them. And there
are others that look much the same, especially in dim light
– Allegros, for example. Of course there were minor risks,
but there was a hell of a lot at stake. It was worth it.'

'What about Sally then?' Sandra asked. 'How does she
fit into it?'

'She wasn't part of the plan at all,' Banks said. 'She
was just one of the innocent bystanders whose memory
got jogged too much for her own good. Like Penny here.'

'There but for the grace of God,' Penny muttered.

'Too true,' Banks agreed. 'Whatever you believe,
Emma would have convinced Ramsden it was necessary
to get rid of you. She'd probably have had to do it herself,
but he wouldn't have stopped her. He was too far gone.'

'You said he seemed almost glad when you arrived,'
Penny said.

'Yes, in a way. It was the end; he was free. I really
think he was relieved. Anyway, according to Ramsden,
Sally said she saw him and Emma together in Leeds. They
were very careful; they'd never think of going out in York
or Eastvale, but Leeds seemed safe enough. None of
Steadman's old colleagues would have recognized Emma,
and she knew the kind of places they went to, the places
to avoid. Sally was there with her boyfriend. I've talked to
him again and he said they did go to Leeds once when he
borrowed a friend's car, and Sally pulled him out of a pub,
Whitelock's, pretty sharpish when she spotted someone
she knew. But she didn't realize who it was at the time.

She was more concerned with Ramsden not seeing her than about who he was with. I suspect she and Kevin went to quite a few pubs. Sally certainly looked old enough to pass for eighteen, but she was under age, so she couldn't afford to get caught.

'Now, most people would have just thought that Michael Ramsden had got himself a good-looking girl-friend, and I'm sure that's what Sally believed until events in Helmthorpe made her start re-examining little things like that. She was perceptive and imaginative. But it wasn't until I'd managed to link Emma and Ramsden that I knew how Sally fitted in at all. One thing I noticed when I saw her was that she seemed very skilled with make-up for a girl of her age, and she was interested in acting, the theatre. She had seen Ramsden in Leeds with an attractive woman, forgotten about it, then seen the image again when her mind was on the Steadman business – maybe at the funeral, when she had plenty of time to examine what everyone was wearing and how they looked. I was there too, and I noticed how she seemed to be scrutinizing us all, though it didn't mean anything to me at the time. However it happened, she remembered, and she became convinced it was Emma, carefully made up, she had seen with Ramsden. So Sally phoned her.

'That was where she went wrong. Emma Steadman told Ramsden later that Sally had gone on about *Wuthering Heights* on the phone, and about how she thought Ramsden had killed Harold Steadman so he could marry Emma just to get his hands on the house and money. Sally was convinced that Ramsden would murder Emma too, after he had married her. She seemed to think the Ramsdens had gone down in the world and that Michael must resent Steadman tremendously for buying the house from his family and taking over. She suggested a secret meeting to discuss things and see if they could find a way to deal with the situation. She thought that, together, they could solve the case and make the police look silly. Emma was terrified of anything that could link her with Ramsden, so she killed the girl.'

'Emma killed Sally Lumb?' Penny repeated numbly.

'Yes. Up by the packhorse bridge on Friday night. She hid the body under the bridge – the water was low then – and piled stones on it.'

'But why on earth did Sally meet her like that?' Barker asked. 'She must have known it might be dangerous.'

'Not at all. As far as Sally was concerned, she was simply warning Emma, saving her life. Besides, even if she did have second thoughts, ask Penny. She was about to do much the same thing, and she never seriously considered that Ramsden would harm her.'

'But that was different,' Penny argued. 'I'd known Michael all my life. I knew he wouldn't hurt me, even if what I thought was true.'

'Somebody would have hurt you,' Banks replied. 'You wouldn't find much comfort in being right about Ramsden while Emma was killing you. It wouldn't matter then, would it?'

'Only to the police, I suppose.'

'You're wrong about that,' Banks said, leaning forward and looking straight into her eyes. 'It matters to everyone except the corpse. Murder is the one crime that can't be put right. It upsets the balance. The dead can't be restored like stolen property; death doesn't heal like physical or emotional scars left by assault or rape. It's final. The end. Sally Lumb made a mistake and she died for it.'

'She was reading the wrong book,' Barker said. 'And

misreading it, at that. She should have been reading *Madame Bovary*. That's about a woman who considers murdering her husband.'

Banks hadn't read *Madame Bovary* but made a mental note to do so as soon as possible. When the waiter reappeared, Banks and Penny were the only ones to order more drinks.

Banks lit another cigarette. 'Ramsden got really scared after Emma killed Sally,' he said. 'But life went on and no thunderbolts from heaven struck him down. Then Penny started to figure things out. You know the rest.'

Penny shivered and draped her shawl over her shoulders.

'Emma Steadman was far more powerful than any of us had imagined,' Banks said. 'She also had a solid alibi for her husband's murder. There was no way she could have done that, and though I flirted with the idea that she might have paid someone, it didn't seem likely. Sergeant Hatchley was right – she wouldn't have known how to contact a hired killer. Besides, if she had, it would have meant someone else to fear, someone who knew about her and what she'd done. Ramsden was ideal; Emma could control him, and he stood to gain too. Sally knew that Mrs Steadman couldn't have carried the body up Tavistock's field – another reason not to fear her – but she didn't know that Ramsden seemed to have a perfect alibi. I certainly didn't tell her, and I don't think anyone else did.

'I was thinking about all the wrong combinations,' he said to Penny. 'You and Steadman, you and Ramsden, you and Barker here. For a while I even wondered whether Ramsden and Steadman were homosexually involved. Like everyone else, I was taken in by Emma

Steadman's outer drabness. I just couldn't picture her as a woman of passion and power. I didn't even try. But she had the most dangerous combination of all, a passionate and calculating nature.'

'What did make you think of her?' asked Barker. 'I'd never have got it in a million years.'

'That's because you only write books,' Banks joked, 'while I do the real work.'

'Touché. But really? I'm curious.'

'Tell me, didn't you ever notice anything odd about Emma Steadman?'

Barker thought for a while. 'No,' he answered. 'I can't say I did. I didn't really see a lot of her. When I did I always felt a bit uneasy.'

'Why?'

'I don't know. There are some women just make you feel like that.'

'You didn't tell me that when I asked you about her.'

'Never really thought of it till you mentioned it just now,' Barker said. 'Besides, what difference would it have made?'

'None, I suppose,' Banks admitted. 'It's just that I felt uneasy with her too. Claustrophobic even. It was a kind of gut reaction, and I ought to know better than that.'

'But what did it mean?' Barker asked.

'This is all hindsight,' Banks said, 'so it did me no good until it was too late, but I think I was responding to her sexual power unconsciously and I was put off by her appearance. I couldn't accept being attracted to her so I felt dislike, revulsion. It might sound silly, but I couldn't see beneath the surface. Still, that was the last thing I realized. First of all there was something Darnley had said in Leeds that I couldn't for the life of me remember. It was just the kind of casual, throwaway remark anyone might overlook.'

'What was it?' Penny asked.

'He said that Emma had been a pretty little thing at first in Leeds. Of course, that meant nothing at the time. Then Sally disappeared. I thought she must be connected in some way to the Steadman business but I couldn't figure out how. I knew about her theatrical interests, but there was no way of getting from that to seeing Michael Ramsden as Steadman's killer. Besides, I was still too busy looking in every direction but the right one. I was blinded by Emma's alibi, too.

'Finally, Sandra said she'd seen Emma and noticed that she still looked pretty good. That was when the bits and pieces seemed to fit together: a pretty young thing, Sally's skill at make-up – which is just altering appearances when you get right down to it – and Emma Steadman as the outline, still, of an attractive woman. And she did tell me she'd been involved in amateur dramatics. When I thought about what others had told me about Emma, I realized that nobody had ever mentioned her being attractive. Penny wouldn't of course – like her husband, I don't think you ever really noticed Emma – and Jack here hadn't known her that far back. Ramsden never said that she was attractive either, and that, finally, seemed odd. Then I got to thinking about Ramsden alone with her at the house that summer, about how he suddenly seemed to drift away from Penny. I'd always seen him as a kind of pale loiterer, but it took me a long time to see Emma Steadman as a *belle dame*. My view of the past was wrong, just like Teddy Hackett said Steadman's was, and everyone else seemed to look back on that summer through rose-tinted glasses. If truth be told, it was a period of desire, greed, deception, adultery – hardly an idyll at all. Even Sally got it wrong.

'When I asked my questions, I never had Ramsden and Emma in mind, but it was easy enough to review what I'd learned in the light of a new perspective. Once I'd got that far, it seemed possible. Two people working together could have handled the Steadman killing, while both seeming to have solid alibis. Sally could have posed a threat to Emma if she had seen her transformed from the drab housewife into the sexy siren with Michael Ramsden. All I had to do then was go and push even harder. At least I knew I was going in the right direction. But events turned out differently.'

'You were certainly fixed in your ideas about me and Harry,' Penny said.

'Yes,' Banks agreed. 'Maybe Ramsden and Emma was a combination I shouldn't have overlooked. But it's easy to say that now it's over. Whenever I thought of that summer I knew there was something missing, so I assumed that people had been lying to me, hiding something. They hadn't. As far as you knew, it had all happened the way you told me. Almost all, anyway.'

'Don't blame yourself,' Sandra said to him, winking at Penny. 'After all, you're only a man.'

'I'll drink to that,' Penny said, raising her glass and nudging Jack Barker.

While Banks joined in the toast and the chit-chat that followed, he thought deep guilty thoughts about Sally Lumb, who had seen beneath the surface only to find yet another romantic illusion. Above them, as all traces of the sun disappeared, Crow Scar began to gleam like bone in the light of the rising moon.

1881 / peter -